9/02
D0031117

A
Sorcerer's
Treason

Tor Books by Sarah Zettel

Isavalta
A Sorcerer's Treason

FORTHCOMING:

The Usurper's Crown
The Firebird's Vengeance

A TOM DOHERTY ASSOCIATES BOOK
NEW YORK

This is a work of fiction. All the characters and events portrayed in this novel are either fictitious or are used fictitiously.

A SORCERER'S TREASON

Design by Heidi Eriksen

This book is printed on acid-free paper.

Edited by James Frenkel

A Tor Book
Published by Tom Doherty Associates, LLC
175 Fifth Avenue
New York, NY 10010

www.tor.com

Tor® is a registered trademark of Tom Doherty Associates, LLC.

Library of Congress Cataloging-in-Publication Data

Zettel, Sarah.
A sorcerer's treason / Sarah Zettel.—1st ed.
p. cm.—(Isavalta ; 1)
"A Tom Doherty Associates book."
ISBN 0-312-87441-3 (acid-free paper)
I. Title.

PS3576.E77 S67 2002
813'.54—dc21

2001058466

First Edition: April 2002

Printed in the United States of America

0 9 8 7 6 5 4 3 2 1

This book is dedicated to the memory of Ida Lewis,
who kept the light at Lime Rock,
Rhode Island, 1879–1911.

Acknowledgments

As ever, the author gratefully acknowledges the Untitled Writers Group for their help and patience. She would also like to thank the Bayfield Historical Society and the rangers at the Sand Island light for their help with her research, as well as the folks at Groenke's First Street Inn, who were there when she needed them.

Additional thanks to Mary Louise Clifford and J. Candace Clifford, authors of *Women Who Kept the Lights,* which was partly responsible for starting this book, and Lee Murdock, whose rendition of "Keeper of the Light" also had a lot to do with it.

A
Sorcerer's
Treason

I have gone into the open land . . .
I have drawn a transparent line around me,
and I have cried out in a great voice.

(*From* A RUSSIAN PROTECTIVE CHARM)

Chapter One

Lighthouse Point, Sand Island, Wisconsin

At midnight between November first and November second of the year 1899, Bridget Lederle's eyes snapped open of their own accord, bringing her instantly awake. For a moment, she lay and listened to the gale outside her window shaking the shutters and rattling the frame in the sash. The faintest breath of the November wind crept through the cracks, brushing past her cheek. The fixed beam from the lighthouse shined steadily, warning anyone unlucky enough to be out on Lake Superior that they sailed near Sand Island's rocky shore.

There was a boat out there. That warning had not been sufficient for some poor soul. Bridget's inner eye saw it clearly. It was a klinker-built vessel with a single mast. The storm drove it toward the rocky shelf that protruded into the lake under the lighthouse beam. The single sailor aboard struggled helplessly with a sail in tatters and a broken tiller. He seemed to be trying to reach her tiny jetty and boathouse, but he wasn't going to make it.

Bridget saw it all, and her heart pounded hard at the sight.

She did not waste any time on panic or think to question the vision. Her visions had been coming to her ever since she was a child, and she was years past wondering whether they were true. Without hesitation, she swung herself out from under the quilts, planting bare feet against the frigid floorboards.

Outside, the wind whistled under the eaves. Vicious drafts curled around Bridget's ankles as she minced her way across the floor to the clothes pegs.

She had to hurry. There was a boat out there.

As was her custom, she'd left her thickest skirt and sweater hanging on the pegs. Her woolen stockings lay on the dresser. Her oilskin and boots waited downstairs by the front door, along with the covered lantern and kitchen matches.

She moved with assurance, even though the room was lit only by the reflection of the golden beam of the lighthouse lamp. From its tower overhead, it cut through the gale, warning the ships from the rocks and shoals that surrounded the island, and helping to keep sailors safe from Lake Superior and its grasping, grey waters.

But, soon, Lake Superior would throw a small, painted boat up onto the rocks, smashing its hull and swamping its single sailor.

I will save him. Determination pressed Bridget's mouth into a thin line and she threw open the white painted fire door that led to the tower's spiral staircase, the only stairs the house possessed. She ran down to the first floor, each footfall clanging against the filigreed iron steps. *The lake does not get anyone tonight.*

Bridget did not even take the time to rouse her housekeeper, Mrs. Hansen, or Mrs. Hansen's big son Samuel. She just shrugged into her father's old oilskins and stuffed her feet into cracked Wellington boots.

Wrapped against the weather as well as one could be, Bridget lit her lantern. With the tiny light clutched in one hand, she unlatched the door and stepped out into the gale.

The wind slammed against her as if it meant to lay her flat. It grabbed at her skirts, pulling them tight around her legs. Despite the ferocious wind, the night remained clear, and Bridget could see the light from Devil's Island beaming as brightly as any of the stars overhead. But the wind carried the smell of ice, and Bridget shivered involuntarily against its onslaught. This was not the worst Lake Superior could do, but it was bad enough.

As quickly as she could, Bridget made her way down the steep wooden stairs to the boathouse at the lake's edge. The lake boiled black beneath the night sky and the steady light from the house shined on the steep curl of white-capped waves. Icy spray lashed her from head to toe, blurring her vision and making it hard to breathe. It stung her cheeks with cold and dribbled down her collar, making her skin twitch into goose pimples.

Bridget suppressed another shiver, as if she did not want the lake to see how she feared its moods. She pulled the hood of her thick mens' coat further down and lifted her lantern high. Spray hissed against the tin housing and Bridget strained to separate the shadows from each other.

There. The thin, guttering beam of her lantern touched the painted, battered prow jutting out of the water at the ugly angle where it had been smashed on the edge of the sandstone shelf. The single mast still stood, but the tattered sail flapped wet and useless in the wind.

Bridget planted her boots carefully on slick, uneven stone and made her way forward with a cautious, rocking gait. Waves surged around her ankles, soaking her hems and tugging at each step. All around, the late-autumn wind howled high and sharp, angry at its failure to drive her back indoors. Each wave of the lake roared back its response that it would have her yet.

In front of her, the broken boat swayed, half in, half out of the water. The lake pulled at it, trying to suck the traveler down to where it could swaddle him in its cold. Bridget gripped her drenched skirt in one hand and slogged ahead, until at last she stood grasping the soaking gunwale. A jagged outcropping had impaled the boat. Ropes, casks, nets, all the paraphernalia of a small fishing craft floated in a tangle at the stern.

The man lay facedown in the bilge. Bridget hung the lantern carefully on the end of a splintered spar and heaved the man onto his back. She could see just enough to gain the impression of dark skin, black hair and a black coat. Without hesitation, she pried his mouth open and swept her finger around inside, to make sure he had inhaled nothing but water. Even as she did so, he began to cough. She turned him onto his side, letting him vomit up gouts of fresh water into the bilge. The boat rocked unsteadily with each motion, rattling the flotsam, and it seemed to Bridget that the lake chuckled as it pulled at the broken stern.

The man's chest heaved against her hand, and Bridget shoved him into a sitting position. He gasped, dragging great breaths of air and spray into his tortured lungs.

"Can you stand?" shouted Bridget in his ear to be heard over the wind and the lake. "We must get you inside!"

He lifted his head and Bridget saw that his eyes were as dark as the night-blackened lake, but behind them, there was light. That light seeped through her skin even as the cold did, and touched her blood and heart.

She started then, and would have let him go had he not clamped one death-cold hand on her wrist. He strained to lift himself out of the sloshing, rattling stew that filled his ruined boat. Bridget got her arm under his shoulders and helped him balance on the wreckage. It was then she realized he did not wear normal fisherman's clothes. His coat was a heavy, woolen thing with many buttons and a high collar. The lantern light glinted on a metal clasp at the throat.

Bridget shoved this oddity aside. The lake threw all kinds onto shore. What was important right now was to get this man into the warmth.

She reclaimed the lantern and they forced their way back through the relentless waves to the boathouse and dry land, with Bridget at times half-dragging the stranger. But she was no petite miss, and he was determined. He always found his footing again, no matter how badly he slipped. At last, they came to the foot of the boathouse stairs and he staggered, catching himself against the railing, just in time to keep Bridget from completely dropping him. His wide black eyes traced the length of the stairs, and Bridget thought for a moment he was going to tell her he could not make it. But then, he caught sight of the lighthouse beam. He gazed up at the light, and then at her, and he smiled a smile so sweet that Bridget felt her throat tighten.

From somewhere, he found the strength to help haul himself up the stairs and to stand on his own as Bridget opened the door to the summer kitchen. They staggered inside together. Buckets' worth of water sluiced off them both, making rivers and lakes on the flagstones.

As soon as the man crossed the threshold, he sank to his knees in the middle of the frigid water. He would have fallen onto his face, had Bridget not dropped to her own knees and grasped his shoulders. He smelled of lake water, cold and wet wool. There was nowhere about him the trace of any human warmth.

"Mrs. Hansen!" Bridget called. "Mrs. Hansen! Samuel!"

The Norwegian widow and her son were used to being roused at all hours by Bridget's shout, and both appeared within moments—Mrs. Hansen wrapping her shawl around her nightdress, and Samuel just standing there like a great bullock with his nightshirt over his red flannels.

"Get him to the spare bedroom, Samuel," Bridget ordered as she shucked her coat and boots. "Mrs. Hansen . . ."

"Hot-water bottles," finished Mrs. Hansen. "I'll get the stove going." Mrs. Hansen knew what was needed as well as Bridget did, having kept the house for Bridget's father as well as for Bridget. She gathered up the hem of her nightdress and hurried up the three steps into the winter kitchen, where a fire waited banked in the stove. Samuel lumbered forward and, without so much as a grunt of effort, lifted the stranger in both arms to carry him up the stairs to the small bedroom that waited down the short hallway from Bridget's own.

Bridget followed him, stopping at the closet for an armload of quilts. They were all old, patched and water-stained, but, nonetheless, warm enough. She also pocketed a cup and the square bottle of strong brandy that she kept there.

When Bridget reached the spare room, Samuel had the stranger laid out on the metal-framed bed and had already stripped off his boots and stockings. The strange, wide-skirted coat hung on one of the clothes pegs, dripping its allotment of Lake Superior onto the floorboards. Bridget deposited the quilts at the foot of the bed and the brandy on the dresser beside the wash jug and basin. The gale still rattled the window and the shutters, but it was losing force. It seemed to consider that it had already done enough for one night and all that remained was to remind Bridget that it would be back, and next time it would bring the snow.

Bridget lit the hurricane lantern as Samuel fumbled to remove the man's trousers. She moved to help him without a blush or second thought. After eight years of pulling sailors out of Lake Superior, the sight of a naked man held no terror for her.

She at once saw the source of Samuel's difficulty. The man wore a worked leather belt. Samuel's big fingers struggled with its ornate buckle, which seemed to be woven of bands of pure gold. Bridget's smaller hands found the trick of it and snapped the buckle open. She laid the belt and its ornament on the sill, where the stranger would be sure to see it when he woke.

The pants were not the canvas trousers she expected. They were leather pantaloons of some kind, with laces where she would have expected buttons. Underneath them he wore woolen hose, with linen hose underneath those. He also wore a woolen tunic over a linen shirt with tails almost as long as Samuel's nightshirt. They stripped him of those too. His well-muscled chest was an expanse of rich tan skin marred, Bridget saw, by two old scars—one long slash on his belly and one short, puckered scoring far too near his heart.

A lumpy cloth bag hung on a leather thong around his neck. Bridget left that where it was.

Bridget and Samuel layered the quilts over him just as Mrs. Hansen came through the door carrying the chipped basin filled with a half-dozen hot-water bottles. Bridget laid four of them at the man's icy feet and two on his chest.

The man did not move. Fear and disappointment touched Bridget's mind.

"Hold his head, Mrs. Hansen. I'll try to get some brandy into him."

Mrs. Hansen lifted the man's dark head while Bridget unstoppered the bottle. She tipped a measure of the sharp-smelling liquid into the cup and held it to his lips. He did not respond. Mrs. Hansen gently opened his mouth so Bridget could dribble a little brandy down his throat. He coughed once, then swallowed. Bridget gave him the rest of the dose, and he drank it easily.

His eyes opened again. They remained dark, almost black, even in the lamplight, and nothing of that light she had seen in them before waited there. His whole face registered deep confusion. Bridget laid her hand on his brow, pushing back the damp curls that had plastered themselves to his forehead. To her relief, she felt his skin warming, but not to the point of fever.

"You are quite safe," Bridget told him as she straightened up. "You are in the lighthouse on Sand Island. I am Bridget Lederle, keeper of the light."

He spoke, his voice still rattling from the water he had breathed, but Bridget understood nothing of the language he used. Its lilt made it sound a bit like Norwegian, although its hard consonants sounded like German, but it was not either.

Russian? she wondered to herself. It was possible. There had been a Russian man down in the village once, a sailor, and he was dark like this, but his clothes and his eyes . . .

She shook herself. Those were thoughts for the morning, not for a storm-tossed night.

The man did not seem to see her in comprehension. He fumbled for his bag on its thong, still muttering.

"Rest," she told him, hoping he understood her tone, if not her words. "You will feel better in the morning."

She patted his shoulder, and all at once, he caught her hand in a strong grip. Mrs. Hansen gave a little shriek. Bridget, startled, froze for a bare instant. In that instant, the stranger wrapped a braid of cloth around her wrist and pinned her eyes with his own gaze, all that strange light shining inside him. She felt it burn through her then, and it forced open her mind's eye and she saw . . .

She saw a girl dressed in the golden robes of a queen and knew the girl was afraid.

She saw a dark man looking out over sea cliffs, his face set in a frown of worry and suspicion. He hunted the man who lay in her bed.

She saw herself, standing in front of a golden cage that held a bird made entirely of flame. The cage was weakening and the bird inside would soon be free.

The next thing she knew, Samuel had grabbed the man's hand

and pulled it away from her. The braid around her wrist loosened and the light blinked out of the stranger, and out of her. A tremor ran through Bridget. She lifted her water-roughened hand and slammed it hard against the stranger's ear.

"Never again, sir!" she ordered. "Or I swear by God I'll give you back to the lake!"

"Forgive me," he whispered, but Bridget did not miss the smile that played around his lips. "I wished only to speak with you."

"Then from now on you will use your tongue." She squared her shoulders and tried to pull her ragged composure back together.

"I will." He nodded, his craggy face as solemn as could be now. "Forgive me."

"Mrs. Hansen, Samuel, let's go." Bridget turned on her heel and left the room. Outside the door, her knees trembled so that she had to stop and lean against the wall.

"Miss Bridget?" Mrs. Hansen hurried to her side. "Are you all right? What did he do? Should Samuel stay to watch him?"

"I'm fine, Mrs. Hansen," Bridget said. It was only partly a lie. Bridget pushed herself away from the wall. "And I think you and Samuel may return to bed." She frowned and reached inside herself, searching for some hint of immediate danger. She almost wished she'd find something, so she would have an excuse to remove the stranger from her house. But there was no warning, only a nameless sensation of change that felt neither distinctly good, nor distinctly bad.

"He is just a foreigner. He will not trouble us further." *At least, not tonight.* "I was only startled."

"If you're certain," said Mrs. Hansen uneasily. Bridget nodded, and Mrs. Hansen accepted her affirmation in silence, but Bridget also knew the housekeeper would be tying an amulet against the evil eye around Samuel's neck before she went to sleep. For once, Bridget could not chide the old woman for this precaution.

"Good night, Mrs. Hansen," was all Bridget said.

"Good night, Miss Bridget."

Bridget did not watch them descend the stairs. She just returned to her own room and shut the door behind her. Her wet dress dragged heavily at her tired body, sending shivers up and down her clammy skin. She wanted badly to retreat to the warmth of her bed, but duty had its own call, especially on nights like this. It was vital that she be certain of the light. So, clenching her teeth to keep them from chattering, she changed out of her wet things into her nightdress and, wrapping her knitted shawl around herself, returned to the hallway.

Whitewashed fire doors separated the lighthouse from the keeper's quarters, one for each story of the house, and one for the cellar. Bridget kept small tables beside these doors laid out with candles and matches. The tiny flame felt blessedly warm against her skin as she carried the candle up the tight, rust-stained iron spiral of the stairway to the very top and the metal hatch that led to the lamp room.

The lamp room was a cramped, circular chamber. The brass and glass workings of the light took up most of the space, leaving only a thin circular aisle between itself and the windows. The light's clockwork ticked as steadily as any timepiece, keeping the oil pumping from the reservoir to feed the lamp wicks to send the beam across the lake's restive waters. Bridget stooped and opened the small brass door under the main lamp to expose the reservoir and check the level of the mineral oil. It was already half-empty, so she topped the level off from one of the oil cans placed there for that purpose. Satisfied there was enough to last the night, she closed the door up and gave the works a few extra cranks to ensure that the pumps continued their function.

Outside, the wind had died down. The lake had ceased to rage and had fallen back on its usual quiet muttering. The light beside her burned evenly, shining its clear beam across the water, warning the ships, warning the world, "Here is the shore, here are the rocks, here are the dangers. Stay back, stay away. Do not come near to trouble yourselves."

Or to trouble me. Bridget shivered and wrapped her arms tightly around her.

"What have you brought me?" she asked the fading gale. "What is this man?"

But Lake Superior was not prepared to give her any answers.

Eventually, cold and simple weariness overtook her. Bridget climbed back down to her room to seek what warmth there was left in her bed.

When daylight returned, there would be time enough for answers.

Deeply ingrained habit woke Bridget with the dawn the next morning. She was used to long nights and interrupted sleep, and so was not particularly weary when she rose to wash her face and dress her hair and body. Outside, the morning's first light showed a clear day, but a grey sky and an uneasy lake. She checked the barometer that hung on her wall. The glass was holding steady, for now, at least.

She could hear Mrs. Hansen in the kitchen, making the usual domestic bumpings and singing to herself in Norwegian. The very thought of breakfast and coffee left Bridget weak with hunger, but, as always, the light came first.

Again she climbed to the top of the tower. This time she extinguished all four of the lamp's wicks and halted the works. She checked the reservoir and the oil on hand. She'd need to bring up several cans from the oil house in the cellar before dark. She shone the lens with chamois leather, although it didn't really need it. Her father had told her tales of how older lights burned whale oil, which formed a crust of black soot every night. Memory of his stern warnings made her diligent.

"I want you to be able to take over the light when I'm gone, Bridget," he would say to her, as he was showing her how the pumps worked, or making her help carry the oil cans up the iron stairs. "The job is all I have to leave you."

He said it more frequently after his bout of pneumonia robbed him of the wind needed to climb the lighthouse stairs. No matter how many times he said the words, though, he never once added, "since you spoiled what good our name had left," but Bridget was sure he thought it. She certainly did.

When the lamp cooled, Bridget trimmed the wicks carefully so they would be ready for lighting at dusk. Finally, she drew the curtains that hid the light from the sun. Sunlight, focused by the lens, could ignite the oil within the reservoir and set the tower aflame.

Routine made Bridget feel solid and whole. She could deal with anything now. She had faced out storm and tempest, insult and attack. What was left to frighten her?

So, well in command of herself, Bridget descended the tower stairs to the top floor of the quarters. When she reached the stranger's door, she knocked softly. No sound rose from within.

Bridget pushed the door open. The stranger lay on his back in the bed, one hand hanging out in the cold, one thrown across his chest. Despite its natural clear brown color, his skin seemed pale against the white sheets. Bridget crossed to his side, relieved to see that his chest still rose and fell. She might have her doubts about this person, but they were not strong enough for her to wish him dead. She laid a hand on his brow. He felt neither too hot, nor too cold. It was probably simple exhaustion that kept him sleeping now.

His hair, she noted, had dried into a curling black mane in severe need of a trimming. Black stubble obscured his strong jawline and square chin. She would have to hunt out Poppa's old razor and strop as soon as the man was well enough to attend to himself.

She tucked his hand back under the quilts. He did not shift at all.

Bridget went down to the winter kitchen and the smell of biscuits, bacon, coffee and frying eggs. Mrs. Hansen tended the stove on which breakfast sizzled so deliciously. Bridget reached around the housekeeper for the coffeepot and poured herself a mug of steaming, black brew.

"Did our visitor stir last night, Mrs. Hansen?" she asked, sipping the hot coffee.

"I heard nothing, nor did Samuel," Mrs. Hansen answered, her square, sun-browned face stern. "But I'll tell you this, I'm not easy with him in the house."

"Well, when he wakes, we will have an accounting from him." Bridget set the mug down on the kitchen table.

"If you're determined to wait then, you'd best make good use of your time and see to the chickens." Mrs. Hansen fastened her gaze severely on her cookery, as if worried about what she would say to Bridget if she looked up.

It was going to be one of those days. Bridget suppressed a sigh. Nominally, Bridget was in charge of the house, but neither of them could forget that Mrs. Hansen had helped care for Bridget since she was a little girl. When the widow was worried for Bridget, or uncertain for her future, she seemed to forget Bridget had ever grown up and took to ordering her about as if Bridget were still ten years old.

"Yes, Mrs. Hansen," answered Bridget obediently as she stood. Her answer was a wave of the hand, shooing Bridget out the door. Bridget made her way to the back door with a small smile that faded rapidly. Mrs. Hansen was right to be concerned about the stranger. Bridget knew what her housekeeper was thinking. If the man upstairs could not give good account of himself and his strangeness, there was going to be talk and, no matter what he said, if Bridget didn't move him into Eastbay or Bayfield as soon as could be, that talk would spread. Her gruffness this morning was only worry, for Mrs. Hansen knew how badly Bridget had been harmed by rumors before.

There was, however, nothing either of them could do about it now, and no reason to disturb the morning's routine. Bridget wrapped her shawl around her head and shoulders against the sharp November cold and picked up the egg basket from its place by the kitchen door. Outside, she crossed the frostbitten, scrubby yard. The wind blew briskly off the lake, stinging her nose and finger ends, but promising nothing more dire this dim day than a deepening of the late-autumn cold. Below the blunt cliff, she could see the wreck of the stranger's boat rocking gently with motion of the waves. That would have to be salvaged soon, or the lake would have it all.

Bridget fed the chickens scratching in their patch of gravel and then filched their eggs from the laying boxes in the coop. As she passed the barn, she praised Samuel, who was busy working on the woodpile with saw and ax. She brought the eggs into the kitchen, just in time to sit down and consume the hens' work of the previous day, with plenty of bacon and hot biscuits spread thickly with honey. Mrs. Hansen and Samuel ate their portions with gusto, and all seemed to agree that conversation should be held to remarks about the weather and the small gossips from Eastbay.

At last, Bridget drained her coffee mug. "I am going to take the boat around to Eastbay and the tug to the mainland, if it's going," she told Mrs. Hansen. "Is there anything we need from Mr. Gage?"

"Some salt would be useful, if you please," replied Mrs. Hansen. "And some coffee."

"A keg of tenpenny nails, if you please, miss," added Samuel. "And a bucket of whitewash."

"Thank you." Bridget noted the requests down on the back of a used envelope with a stub of grease pencil. "I'll be back before nightfall." She reached across the table and touched Samuel's arm to make sure she had his attention. "Samuel, if you can do it safely, I want you to go down to the stranger's boat and see what you can salvage. All right?"

Samuel, his mouth full of bacon, swallowed hastily. "Yes, miss."

"Thank you." Bridget patted Samuel's hand and turned back to his mother. "I'll just go look in on our guest before I go."

"Do you want me with you?" asked Mrs. Hansen gamely.

"I believe I can take care of myself," said Bridget. "If not, you can be sure you'll hear my shout."

Rising from the table, she climbed back up to the stranger's room. Her knock brought no response, so she pushed the door open. He lay still as death in the narrow bed, and did not stretch or shift when her footsteps caused the floorboards to creak. Bridget lifted his belt from the sill where she'd laid it the night before. The gold buckle glinted in the grey light filtering through the curtains. Bridget peered more closely at the artifact. Fine threads of gold had been twisted together to make thicker strands, and those strands had then been braided and coiled to make a solid oval. Bridget hefted it in her hand. It must have weighed at least a pound. She hesitated. She did not want to take so valuable an object without permission, but she also did not want to wake the exhausted stranger. The workmanship of the buckle was so curious it might give some clue to his origin if it could be recognized. Someone might even know the owner, and so might know if friends or family could be telegraphed.

Momentarily undecided, Bridget ran her thumb across the buckle.

And she saw a woman, well past middle age, in a gown of burgundy velvet embroidered all over with gold. The woman handed the buckle to the stranger.

She saw the stranger in a forest clearing, offering a wine flask to a fox.

She saw the dark man she had seen before standing in front of a patch of ice, and on the ice stood a monster with red skin and horns on its head and a terrible mouthful of fangs.

Bridget staggered against the window, barely getting her hand out in time to catch herself against the low sill. *What is happening to me?*

The visions had never come so fast or clear before, not even during the worst of storms, and those had always been comprehensible. She had always seen plain, honest men and women, in some form of trouble—stormwreck, or broken band saw, or perhaps a fall of rocks in the quarry, something of the kind. Very occasionally she'd been able to see the future happiness or heartache of a woman being married, or if a baby would be male or female.

But the things this man caused her to see . . . these were scenes from fairy tales. They were not possible. She pressed her hand against her forehead, as if she thought the gesture could somehow hold back her confusion. The single consolation of her visions had always been that she had known what to do about them. She had to speak out. Even years ago, when people had not yet believed her, she had to tell them about the ships that were in trouble, or the bridge that had been washed away. She had been certain since childhood that God, if no one else, wanted her to speak aloud about what appeared to her mind's eye.

But these new visions were not the familiar kind. These brought no compulsion, no certainty of purpose. They brought only fear.

This cannot continue. Bridget straightened up, leaving the belt on the windowsill. She could not keep this man here, pressing on her mind and distracting her thoughts. *I have work to do.*

"What did you see?"

Bridget whirled around. The stranger regarded her calmly from his bed. Only his head protruded from under the quilts, and for a disconcerting moment, he appeared to be disembodied.

"What did you see?" he asked again. His voice was soft, but harsh, as one might expect from a throat that had no lungs connected to it.

"I am glad you're awake." Bridget shoved aside her ignorant fancies. She walked briskly to his bedside and poured water from the wash jug into the cup she'd brought in last night, holding it out to the stranger. His hand stayed steady as he accepted the cup, and he drank the water off in three swallows.

"Thank you." He gave her the cup and she set it back on the nightstand.

"How do you feel?" Bridget asked, smoothing down her apron. "Are you dizzy at all? Does your head ache? Is there fever, or a pain in any of your limbs?"

"None of these, thank you, mistress." With a small grunt, he pushed himself up on the pillows, proving that he did indeed still have a whole body. "But that I am a bit weak and extraordinarily hungry, I am well."

"Very good." Bridget nodded. This again was familiar territory. However foreign or exceptional, this was a half-drowned man who needed care, nothing more, and nothing less. "I will speak to my housekeeper directly about a meal for you. Plain porridge with a little milk would be best at present, I think. If that agrees with you, a more solid meal can be provided later."

He inclined his head. "Whatever you consider best, mistress."

Bridget blinked. Not one fisherman in a thousand would calmly accept porridge when the scent of bacon still lingered in the house. *Still, I should be grateful for small favors.* She folded her hands in front of her. "May I ask your name, sir?"

He paused for a moment, his wide mouth frowning; then he seemed to reach a decision. "My name is Valin Kalami. I am lord sorcerer and advisor to Her Grand Majesty the Dowager Empress

Medeoan Edemskoidoch Nacheradavosh of Isavalta. I sailed through the Land of Death and Spirit at her behest in order to find you."

Bridget blinked again. "I see." *What knot on your head did I miss, sir?*

Kalami, or whoever he was, shook his head. "Forgive me, mistress, but at present you do not."

"That is neither here nor there." Bridget drew herself up and tried to sound businesslike. "I will have your food sent up. I would advise you to rest quietly—"

In response to this advice, the man raised one fine, brown hand. "Will you not condescend to answer my question, mistress."

"What question, sir?" she asked, already turning away from him and starting for the door.

"When you touched my buckle, what did you see?"

Now it was Bridget's turn to hesitate, but it was only for a bare instant, after which she faced him fully to show that his question did not disturb her in the least. "I saw a piece of fine metalwork." She cocked her head. "What should I have seen?"

Kalami dropped his gaze to the quilt and shook his head once. "That is something best known to yourself, mistress. I will not presume."

In this, at any rate. Bridget felt herself frown. *Who are you? What have you heard of me? Who has been talking? Did you believe me to be as mad as yourself? Was that why you came here?*

All at once, Bridget felt she did not want to be near this person anymore. She wanted to be anywhere else in the world, anywhere she could be all alone and think, and recover herself. She did not want to be near someone who could see her visions, who could burn her with the light from his black eyes, who spoke to her as if she were a lady worthy of his respect.

"I suggest you rest, sir." Bridget rounded the bed and headed for the door, hoping against hope that he would not see she was retreating from him. "Wherever you may be from, you have had a rough time of it and need to recover your strength."

"Yes, mistress," he said, sounding disturbingly like Mrs. Hansen when she was humoring Bridget.

I am surrounded. Suddenly more annoyed than concerned, Bridget left the room, closing the door firmly behind herself.

Down in the kitchen, Mrs. Hansen was up to her elbows in a basin full of breakfast dishes.

"Mrs. Hansen." Bridget rested her fingertips on the edge of the freshly scrubbed kitchen table, inhaling the comforting scents of warm water and strong soap. "I believe our guest suffers from some delirium."

"A madman?" Water drops flew from Mrs. Hansen's hand as she grasped the cross she wore at her throat.

Somehow, the sight of the older woman's panic made Bridget feel more at ease. "Possibly he is merely confused, from some blow to the head, or an excess of water in his lungs. Dr. Hannum will be able to say more." She touched Mrs. Hansen's arm. "I will return directly with the doctor and news of a safer house where the stranger may be lodged." She smiled reassuringly at her housekeeper, and reluctantly Mrs. Hansen's water-reddened hand released the cross. "He is weak still and will most likely sleep. Try to be easy. Send Samuel up with some porridge. There is nothing to fear."

"If you're certain." Mrs. Hansen met her gaze searchingly.

"I am," she said firmly. "I would know if there were danger under my own roof." Most of the time, the fact of Bridget's second sight went unspoken between them, but by now, Mrs. Hansen trusted Bridget's visions almost as much as Bridget herself did.

But not, it seemed, this time. "Have a care, Bridget Lederle," she said. "I don't like this one."

Bridget grasped Mrs. Hansen's wet hand and squeezed it briefly. "We'll see it through, Mrs. Hansen. Whatever comes." She straightened up. The day was short, and she did not want to be caught on the mainland when darkness fell and the time to light the lamp came. "I will be back as soon as I may."

Mrs. Hansen nodded once, satisfied, at least for the moment. "I'll watch for you."

Bridget paused by the door to collect her shawl and bonnet. She tucked her few pieces of correspondence, which included her quarterly report to the Lighthouse Board, into her apron pocket along with the shopping list and walked out into the morning, taking the creaking stairs down to the jetty where her small boat waited.

From the window of his small, spare room, Kalami watched his hostess leave. It was plain that she believed him so lost and exhausted that he posed no real danger to her household. It was also plain, however, that she believed him quite mad.

But then, she also believed this was the first time they had met.

In truth, he was exhausted. The freshwater sea that lay at Bridget Lederle's door had almost swallowed him whole in its wrath. During the passage of the last eight years, he had forgotten the lake was so vast, and his previous two visits had been made in calm weather. A mighty world this was. Kalami shook his head. He would have liked to spend a year or so here, exploring its lands.

Perhaps one day, he thought as he shuffled back to the hard bed. *At present, I have other concerns.*

Believing him mad, Bridget had most likely gone to fetch some sort of physic to pronounce a diagnosis. This meant he was in danger of being removed from her household before she heard his tale. Who would voluntarily keep a madman under their roof?

As understandable as it was, it did him no good. Kalami lifted and bent his stiff body to sit on the edge of the bed. It was she he needed to speak to, she he needed to make understand.

There was a soft knock at the door. Kalami dropped onto the pillows and threw the bedclothes back over his naked body.

"You may enter."

The door opened and through it came the big, slow boy, carrying a tray with a bowl full of something that steamed. As the boy walked toward him with exaggerated caution, Kalami smelled the deeply homey scent of oaten porridge and smiled.

During his first visit, Kalami had only needed to understand

Bridget, not the world around her. During his second, he had needed only darkness and a soundly sleeping house. Consequently, his knowledge of this world remained sketchy at best. If he was to reassure some learned person of his sanity, he would need to be able to bring the proper words to his tongue.

"Thank you," he said as the boy, who'd probably been warned not to spill the tray, handed across his breakfast. *Now then, my boy, might you have what I need to keep me here?*

"You're welcome," said the boy, backing away. His pale blue eyes grew wide as he looked Kalami up and down.

Obviously, you have never seen a madman before, and so you stare. Kalami set the tray aside. "Might I please have some water?"

The boy must have been used to doing as he was told. Without question or hesitation, he filled the cup from the jug. While his back was turned, Kalami pulled his reading braid from the bag that hung about his neck.

The boy handed Kalami the water. As he did, Kalami captured his wrist in the braid.

The boy froze. "Uhhh . . ." he grunted feebly as he tried to struggle, sloshing water onto the floor, but the spell held him fast.

"Shhh . . ." Kalami touched the boy's lips with his fingertips, silencing him. He took the cup gently from the boy's paralyzed hand and set it on the night table. "Fear not, there's a good boy. I just need a few memories from you, that is all." This was not the same working he had used on Bridget. There it had been a simple understanding he had sought. Peering at her mind had been enough. Here, he needed something deeper. "You are to remember for me a man, a sound man, a good man. Someone you have seen at work among the boats perhaps. Let me see him . . . Samuel." He smiled as the boy's name reached him through the braid.

Unable to help itself, Samuel's mind did as it was bidden. Kalami relaxed as the memories drained from the boy into himself. The memories were lost to Samuel now. But the boy had little use for them, and he was so simple that no one else would remark that they were gone.

When he had enough, Kalami unwrapped the braid from Samuel's wrist and took the cup of water.

"Thank you, Samuel. You may go now."

Samuel swayed on his feet and stared hard at his wrist, as if trying to remember something important.

"You may go now," repeated Kalami firmly. "You have told me that your mistress has asked you to salvage my boat. You are to take particular care that you save the sails, and the length of rope you will find tied with the red ribbon. They are most important. Do you understand?"

"Yes, sir." Still staring at his wrist, Samuel turned and shuffled toward the door. As he moved away from Kalami, however, he began to straighten up, and soon he walked away as if nothing had ever happened.

Kalami smiled as he picked up his spoon and attacked the hot, thick porridge. He could wait now, rest and gather his strength. He had all he needed.

At least, until Bridget returned.

Chapter Two

Bayfield, Wisconsin, was large, muddy and noisy. The harbor sprawled under the watchful gaze of the rich stone houses on the bluff. Grey steamers and worn fishing boats lined the docks, where the air stank of fish and oil, sawdust and pitch, despite the continual breezes off the lake. Shouts, swearing and banging filled the air from the men and boys loading stone, fish and timber into the steamers and unloading finished goods. The constant noise pressed in on Bridget, who was used to the silence of Lighthouse Point. She set her jaw and picked her way up the dusty boardwalk, past the cooperage and the transfer depot, to join the traffic, both foot and cart, on Washington Avenue. The day had cleared a bit and the sun shone warm on Bridget's shoulders. The crowds of workers and errand runners flowed past her without recognition, allowing her the freedom of anonymity that usually enabled her to relax, if only for a moment. But today, she had no choice except to go where she was known and face all that meant. However, she first had an errand of her own to run.

Bayfield possessed two cemeteries, which faced each other across a dirt and gravel track just over the crest of the long hill. Bridget had never set foot in the ground reserved for the Catholic dead, but she knew the other graveyard well. She made her way across the frost-burned grass, between the slablike granite markers and the more fanciful marble memorials, to the far side, where the yard ended and the woods began. Here, the noises of the docks and the town were faint. The roots of an ancient oak made a hollow in the grass. Beside it waited two modest, plain grey stones. The first was Momma's, bearing the words INGRID LOFTFIELD LEDERLE, BELOVED WIFE AND MOTHER,

MARCH 12, 1848–OCTOBER 15, 1872. The second, of equal size, was Poppa's. EVERETT LEDERLE, BELOVED HUSBAND AND FATHER, JULY 19, 1845–FEBRUARY 27, 1892. Bridget passed both these by, brushing her fingers against the tops of the cool stone to signal her silent regret. The third stone in the hollow was smaller than the other two, a piece of white marble graven with the words ANNA LEDERLE KYOSTI, AUGUST 2, 1891–AUGUST 28, 1891. BELOVED DAUGHTER.

Two brown oak leaves had fallen onto the stone. Bridget brushed them away.

"Good morning, dear heart," she murmured to the stone that marked her daughter's grave. "I'm sorry I've nothing for you today. It's autumn again and the flowers have all gone to sleep. I have some business at the church, but I wanted to stop by to say hello." She bent down and pressed her lips against the cold marble. Tears pricked her eyes. Eight years had passed and gone, but the fact of her infant daughter's death could still strike her like a blow to her heart. "Mama loves you, Anna," she whispered. "I'll come again soon."

Bridget stood there for a time, blotting at her tears with the back of her hand. When she was sure her eyes would stay dry, she made her way back between the more prestigious graves, gathering her composure with difficulty as she walked. So much lay under that white stone, she thought some days it would all drag her straight into the ground. Anna had been the result of a single night. Bridget had been nineteen then. She could still remember all too well, some nights, the passion she and Asa had shared in the darkness by the lake. Asa had met her without a word, and left her just as silently. She had thought he would return. She had believed he loved her. Before that moonless night, he had said that he did, and she had believed. Then, when he did not return, she had thought Anna would be her consolation, but Anna had died before her first month was up. Even now, Bridget could see the harsh, unforgiving eyes of the women who crowded the gallery at the coroner's inquest, eager to see if "that Lederle woman" would be found to have caused the death of her newborn, illegitimate, child. She remembered their murmurs weaving through the unrelieved heat of the courtroom, passing back and forth the old stories—

how she was possessed of the second sight, and was wicked enough to use it, how Everett Lederle was not her real father, how her mother had disappeared when she was young, only to return a year later, probably already pregnant and most certainly grieving for some vanished lover.

Bridget had heard most of those whispers since the day she was old enough to hear anything. They made a constant background for her life, fencing her in the way the lake fenced in her island home.

Lost in her thoughts, Bridget failed to note she was not alone, until she heard the gruff sound of a throat being cleared.

Bridget started, glancing reflexively toward the sound. Another woman occupied the track. She was round and pale, with a powdered face and washed-out gold hair that had been brutalized by a poorly done marcel wave. Golden loops hung with coins jangled from her ears. They matched the necklace spread out across her freckled bosom. More gold, or, at least, the semblance of gold, glittered on her hands. Her shawl was a fringed square of black lace, its several holes carefully mended, as were the tears in her green-and-cream-paneled skirt.

Bridget felt her spine draw itself up as straight as it would go. "Aunt Grace," she said in as neutral a voice as she could manage. "What brings you out here today?" *Surely you can't have come to visit your sister's grave?* Bridget managed to keep herself from speaking that last thought aloud.

Grace Loftfield's face soured, as if she heard Bridget's thought, but she pulled her shoulders back, indicating plainly that she was magnanimous enough to forgive it. "I need to speak with you, Bridget," she declared.

Bridget sighed. "Then do so," she said, folding her hands over her apron. Her toe tapped the gravel impatiently, but she stilled it.

If Grace noticed the gesture, however, she gave no sign. Her eyes had shifted toward the graveyard. Bridget could not tell what she thought she saw there, but it made her uneasy. "Not here. Come to my flat."

This time Bridget's sigh was one of exasperation. *I'm in no mood for humoring you, Aunt.* "I have business I must take care of and I have to get back to the light before dark." Bridget brushed past Grace, her shoes crunching on the gravel underfoot. "If you have something to say, you can walk with me."

Aunt Grace let her walk a few steps, just far enough for Bridget to hope she had decided her niece was not worth the trouble. But the sounds of rustling cloth and jingling coins caught up behind her. Bridget kept her eyes straight ahead, letting the sides of her bonnet shelter her from Grace's peering eyes.

"Bridget!" Aunt Grace announced finally, obviously at the end of her own patience. "I've come to help you!"

"Help me!" Bridget stopped, turning on her heel to stare at her aunt in complete astonishment. "You've never offered to help me in my entire life. Why would you do so now?"

Aunt Grace squared her shoulders, lifting her little chin with affected dignity and again showing her nobility and propriety by letting this further slight pass by.

"Bridget, you're in danger," she announced. "I've seen it."

Bridget stared at her a moment longer while those last three words sank into her mind. Then, she let out a laugh, a disbelieving bark of a noise. "You've seen it? Oh, honestly, Aunt Grace."

Aunt Grace had moved off Sand Island into Bayfield while still a young woman. Shortly afterward, she set herself up as a spiritual medium and palm reader. The same ladies who drew their skirts aside when Bridget walked up the street crept trembling into Grace Loftfield's dim parlor so she could gaze into her blue glass ball and tell them what she saw.

Although Poppa had forbidden it, Bridget had managed to sneak into one of Aunt Grace's séances when she was sixteen. She'd thought that if Aunt Grace really did have the second sight, she'd have an ally. There'd be someone who understood what it was to have reality fade away and be replaced by visions. Maybe Aunt Grace would even take her in so she could live in town, where there were people, instead of out all alone at Lighthouse Point. Maybe she would even talk to Bridget about Momma.

So, Bridget had sat in the dim parlor, the sunbonnet she almost never wore drawn up tight around her cheeks so none of the ladies would be able to see her face, and her hands fidgeting nervously with her apron. Grace had whisked in from behind a lace curtain and circled the parlor, stopping before each one of the half-dozen ladies who sat there.

"Your question shall be answered today," she said to the first lady. To the second she'd just shook her head. "I'm sorry, but the news you are waiting for will bring a sad reversal."

Then, she whisked up to Bridget and Bridget lifted her eyes to meet her aunt's. She knew in a heartbeat that Aunt Grace recognized her.

But all Grace said was "I'm sorry, I have nothing for you." And she moved on.

Bridget sat cold as stone through the rest of the event, with its invisible tambourine banging, and its restlessly moving table, and Grace rolling her eyes and moaning and gabbling in outlandish voices. As soon as Grace let her head drop forward in feigned exhaustion, Bridget broke the circle and left. Grace Loftfield was a fake. Worse, she did not care one bit for her own flesh and blood.

"I know you believe you are the only one gifted with sight," said Grace. "But let me tell you, you're not the first our family who—"

Which was simply beyond the pale. "Please, Aunt Grace," Bridget held up her hand to stop whatever else might be forthcoming. "You can peddle your wares to the ladies of this town, but you cannot expect me to buy them. I've seen what you do and I don't think much of it."

The flesh under Grace's chin quivered. "I do not have to explain myself to you, young woman," she snapped.

"No, you don't. In fact, nothing requires you to say a single word to me." Bridget snatched up her hems and strode down the lane, eyes determinedly pointed forward.

Behind her, Aunt Grace's voice cried, "There's a man at the lighthouse. He means to take you away with him."

Despite herself, Bridget stopped in her tracks. For a moment, all she could hear was the sound of her own breathing and the rush of the wind through the trees.

I will not be tricked. I will not *be overawed.* She made herself turn around. "What could you know about what happens at the lighthouse?"

Grace walked up to her, one slow step at a time, as if she were a cat who meant to pounce as soon as she reached her prey. "You get him away from you, Bridget." Grace's voice was fierce, and Bridget could not help noticing that her face had gone pale. "He'll take you away, like . . ."

Too much, Aunt Grace. This is far too much. "Like what?"

But Grace had shut her mouth and pulled herself up primly. "Like a sack of sugar in that little red boat of his."

It was not possible. Aunt Grace was a fraud. But how did she know about the oddly painted boat? Rumor moved quickly from Sand Island to Bayfield, but no one except Mrs. Hanson and Samuel had seen the stranger yet.

Her aunt's face softened with what might have been real concern. "I just don't want to see you in trouble, Bridget," she said softly.

Bridget found her hands had knotted themselves into the ends of her shawl, twisting the fabric together as if she meant to tear it. "Why are you doing this now?" she asked, ashamed at how shaky and hoarse her voice sounded. "I have been in all manner of trouble, and you've never cared before."

But Grace did not even have the decency to look apologetic. "I make my living off the ladies of this town," she said steadily. "They expect eccentricity from me, but there are things they will not tolerate."

With those words, the moment broke. All the distant sounds of Bayfield blew back on the wind and Bridget knew again with absolute certainty what her place among them was. "Such as your being seen with a bastard and murderer?" she inquired.

This time, Grace did look away, an angry sideways slip of her eyes, while her arms crossed over her corseted bosom. "I've never said you are either of those things, Bridget."

"But you've never denied it either, have you?" Grace had not come to the lighthouse when Bridget was sick after her labor. She had not come to the inquest when Bridget stood accused of killing her child. Yet she came here, of all places, to tell Bridget what to do.

"You aren't the only one who has had to live as best she can, Bridget." As if that were explanation enough for years of silence. "Perhaps I have made a mistake in waiting until now to speak with you. But here I am." She spread her fat, beringed hands. "And I am doing my best. You are in danger from this man."

Bridget resisted the urge to snort. She would sacrifice no more of her dignity to Aunt Grace. "And what am I to do about this danger, then?" she asked, disentangling her fingers from her shawl. "Did your vision tell you that?"

Grace hesitated. It was a split second only, but there was no mistaking it. "Get him away from you. Live your life. Make do as you have done."

"As I have done." Bridget let the words go with a sigh. "Well." She adjusted her shawl and looked up to see how far the sun had climbed over the trees. "I suppose I should thank you for your advice, Aunt. Now if you don't mind, I really do have business to attend to."

But Aunt Grace had one shot left. "Your mother would want you to listen to me."

That was the final straw. Bridget rounded on her. "How dare you suggest you know what my mother would want?" she said, her voice low, and her words even and distinct. "According to Poppa, you did not even come to her funeral. Good-bye, Aunt Grace."

This time, Aunt Grace did not try to stop her from walking away. Bridget's chest swelled to bursting with all the things she had not said. But for all her anger, she could not help the feeling that Aunt Grace had left at least as much unsaid. She could not, however, make herself turn around to find out what any of those unsaid words might be. All she had the strength to do was keep walking down the hill and back into town.

A thriving community, Bayfield provided its residents a selection of six churches where they might worship. Bridget aimed her steps down Third Street toward Christ Episcopal with its sloping roof and delicate gingerbread trim. Like the church, the priest's house next door was white and neat. Its flower beds had all been turned in preparation for winter and its lawn had been raked clear of leaves.

Bridget mounted the steps of the brownstone porch and rang the bell that had been imported by the town shortly after the house was built as a gift for the first priest, the current Mr. Simons's father.

Unfortunately, it was Mrs. Simons, the priest's upright wife, who answered the door. Mrs. Simons recognized Bridget immediately, but still looked her up and down, taking in the state of her dress, her bonnet with her hair somewhat disordered underneath it, her mended shawl, and her creased and muddied shoes.

"Good morning, Mrs. Simons," said Bridget, as if she had not seen the disapproval on the other woman's face. "Is Mr. Simons at home?"

"No he is not," replied Mrs. Simons in a tone that suggested Bridget was ignorant for even posing the question. "Mr. Simons is a very busy man and is not generally to be found wasting time at home."

"Of course," said Bridget calmly. "Would it be possible for me to leave a message for him? A matter has arisen at the lighthouse which—"

"Surely any such matter would be the concern of your employers at the Lighthouse Board."

Bridget pressed her lips together. She should have known better than even to try. Mrs. Simons would not let Bridget cross her threshold if she could help it, lest her very presence soil the sanctity of this respectable, Christian home. Old frustration roiled inside Bridget, and the encounter with Aunt Grace had worn her patience paper thin, but she knew from long experience that any expression of it would only make the situation worse, and give the good women of the town something more to talk about.

"I apologize for having disturbed you, Mrs. Simons. Good morning."

"Good morning." At least Mrs. Simons had the decency to wait until Bridget had turned away before shutting the door.

Anger and embarrassment burning in her cheeks, Bridget descended the steps. She was halfway down the block when a voice hailed her.

"Good morning, Miss Lederle."

The Reverend Zachariah Simons proceeded up the cobbled walk with several parcels of brown paper in his arms. Bridget allowed herself a small smile.

"Good morning, Mr. Simons. I was just at your house and disappointed to find you not at home."

"Well, I shall be at home momentarily." He nodded toward his porch. "Will you walk with me?"

"Thank you very much, Mr. Simons." Bridget fell into step beside him.

Reverend Simons was a tall, grave man with a long, brown face and a prodigious Roman nose. His lack of ambition and pretense had not recommended him for a brilliant career of any kind and left him somewhat marooned in northern Wisconsin. Mrs. Simons had never managed to forgive him this failing.

Mr. Simons asked after Bridget's health, and that of Mrs. Hansen and Samuel. He inquired how she had weathered the recent gale. Bridget replied quite well, thank you, omitting the rescue of the stranger. She wanted to go into that in detail, somewhere other than the public street.

Mr. Simons climbed the porch and held open his door for her. Bridget stepped into the foyer and had the satisfaction of seeing Mrs. Simons come out of the sitting room and blanch.

"Your shopping, Mrs. Simons," said Mr. Simons, handing off the parcels. "And if we might have some coffee in my study? Miss Lederle has a matter on which she wishes to consult."

The internal struggle was so plain on Mrs. Simons's face, Bridget thought she might explode. But the priest's wife kept her manners, if not her countenance.

"I will have Margaret see to it." Mrs. Simons retreated toward the kitchen.

"Miss Lederle?" Mr. Simons gestured for Bridget to follow him. They both walked along the narrow corridor, pretending the previous scene of domestic tenderness had not occurred.

Bridget truly did not wish to bring discord to the priest's house.

While in his wife's eyes she was irrevocably a fallen woman, Mr. Simons himself had been as understanding of her circumstances as it was possible for him to be. He had made several offers, meant to be nothing but kind, for the provision of her daughter. At the time, Bridget had been confident that Anna's father would return and had not taken Mr. Simons up on any of them. Still, she appreciated his attempts. Even more, she appreciated the fact that when the time came, he had been the only one willing to give Anna a Christian burial.

Mr. Simons's study was a small, book-lined room with two deep chairs and a lovely inlaid writing desk he had inherited from his father. Mr. Simons drew back the drapes to let in the watery sunshine and settled into one of the chairs.

"Please, sit down, Miss Lederle, and tell me how I might be of assistance."

Bridget did as she was bidden. She described the rescue of the stranger, leaving out her vision. Her second sight was a touchy subject with the priest. She described the stranger's odd clothing and boat, and then his startling declaration.

"It was my intent to return with Dr. Hannum to ascertain whether this is a temporary disorder in his wits, or a more permanent condition. In either case, I do not believe it safe or appropriate to lodge him in a house with only two women and an overgrown boy. I was hoping to apply to you to find him more secure quarters." Mr. Simons she could trust to hold his tongue about where the man had come from. He would help keep any additional rumors at bay.

Mr. Simons nodded soberly. "I quite understand. Unfortunately, you will not find Dr. Hannum in his office. He was called away to the lumber camp, where there has been an accident involving a band saw, I believe. He is not expected back for at least another day."

"Oh." Bridget's face fell. She smoothed her sleeve down. "Well then, I . . ."

"If I may offer a suggestion?"

"If you please, Mr. Simons," said Bridget.

"Permit me to accompany you back to the lighthouse and interview the gentleman. I have some acquaintance with medicine." He dropped his gaze as he spoke, a modesty that looked almost girlish. "I may be able to form at least a provisional diagnosis, and thus determine the most appropriate place to lodge him for everyone's comfort." He lifted his eyes and went on with greater confidence. "If he is too weak to move, I shall stay the night at the light station and we shall make a further determination in the morning." A slightly pleading look came over his long, horsy face.

Now it was Bridget's turn to look down at her hands. The offer was a sound one, made with good intentions. But Mr. Simons's relations with Mrs. Simons were not peaceful; even she knew that. An excuse to get out of the house and into more . . . agreeable female company was probably extremely welcome to him. Not that he meant anything harmful by it. Oh, no, of course not. Mr. Simons's conscience was too well honed an instrument to permit even the thought. But it opened the door to accusation. Mrs. Simons, if she took it into her head, could blacken Bridget's name so thoroughly and so widely that when the next inspector came from the Lighthouse Board, Bridget might find herself in truly desperate circumstances. Her savings were not such that she could live in comfort. She needed her income.

On the other hand, there was a madman on Sand Island, which was more than she was willing to handle on her own, and, whether she liked it or not, Aunt Grace's warning nagged at the back of her mind.

"Thank you, Mr. Simons," she said at last. "I appreciate your offer. If it will not inconvenience Mrs. Simons, of course . . ."

Mr. Simons's face fell, just a little, but he rallied. "Mrs. Simons will certainly understand the requirements of the situation." *I am glad you are able to think so well of her, sir,* thought Bridget, as the priest went on. "I shall ask Johann Ludwig to accompany us, if his father can spare him." Johann was the eldest son of Tod Ludwig, the blacksmith back in Eastbay on Sand Island. He was a big, cheerful young man who was patiently courting Vale Johnson's daughter, and was unconcerned about anything that did not involve her or ironmongery.

Involving him, however, would mean that news of the stranger at the lighthouse would spread rapidly throughout the town, for Johann would tell his mother and his mother would tell the entire world.

Well. Bridget steeled herself. *It cannot be helped. It would look much worse if no one else came with you.*

"Thank you, Mr. Simons. That is an excellent suggestion."

Mr. Simons beamed kindly, and Bridget tried not to see the relief in his eyes. "Then it is settled." He stood. "If you will wait here, I will explain matters to Mrs. Simons and see to a small bag of necessaries."

Mr. Simons left her there. Bridget was quite content not to have to venture forth into the household. She sipped the good coffee Margaret brought and looked at the titles of the books. Mostly there were books of philosophy and theology, but interspersed among them were a few novels, Twain and Dickens and the like, a book on the moral education of children and a few treatises on medicine. She picked up *The Pickwick Papers* and did her best to peruse it, ignoring the shrill voice of Mrs. Simons, which penetrated the walls with its rise and fall, and the occasional comprehensible phrase, such as "that woman," or "how could you."

At length, however, the furor died away. Bridget finished her coffee and skimmed the book until Mr. Simons returned with a carpetbag in his hand.

"If you are quite ready, Miss Lederle." His voice was strained. Bridget had half a mind to dismiss the matter, but she merely stood up.

"Thank you, Mr. Simons. Let us go."

Mr. Simons was a good sailor, and quite comfortable aboard Francis Bluchard's noisy, smoky tugboat. She knew he spent much time going back and forth among the Apostle Islands, seeing to his various charges, whether or not they were parishioners. He stood beside her in the bow, content to watch the blue-grey water, the gulls and the passing islands of red stone, their green crowns of trees tattered and torn from the attentions of the lumber companies.

Unlike Bayfield, with its straight streets and fine, stone houses, Eastbay was a haphazard settlement. Clapboard houses with fieldstone chimneys were scattered along dirt tracks and rutted paths. Its inhabitants mostly divided their time between fishing and farming, but there was a general store, a post office and the smithy to serve them.

While Mr. Simons sought out the Ludwigs' forge, Bridget stopped in at Mr. Gage's store, where she had left her list to be filled and where she could now supervise the loading of her little dory. The amount for the supplies went onto her account, which would be paid with her next check from the Lighthouse Board. She answered Mrs. Gage's righteous glower with her own cool stare, until the bone-thin woman dropped her attention back to her cans and bales.

Upon joining Mr. Simons at the forge, Bridget found Johann and his father amenable to the plan, and his mother eager to hear the details of the stranger's arrival. Bridget gave as good an account as she felt able, knowing it would be embellished and improved on, no matter what she said.

The two men and the household purchases were almost too much for Bridget's little boat. It sailed low enough in the water that the occasional wave lapped over the side, but Bridget was an expert hand at sail and tiller and they rounded Sand Island safely, reaching Lighthouse Point a little after four in the afternoon.

The house was quiet as they came up the path from the jetty. Bridget noted that the broken boat had been shifted from the rocks to the boathouse. Samuel, back to sawing at the woodpile, seemed unperturbed by anything, to Bridget's relief. She was not such an expert liar that she could tell herself she had not been in the least concerned.

Johann volunteered to help Samuel shift the stores from the dory to the cellar. Bridget thanked him, and let herself and Mr. Simons into the house, which smelled deliciously of Mrs. Hansen's smoked meat and bean soup. The sound of their entry brought the housekeeper to the kitchen threshold.

"Good afternoon, Mrs. Hansen, is all well?" asked Bridget.

"Yes, Miss Bridget," she answered without hesitation, and, despite all, Bridget found herself much relieved. If anything had happened to Mrs. Hansen or Samuel, she would be unable to forgive herself. "Good afternoon, Reverend." Mrs. Hansen went on to make a small curtsy to the priest, and vanished back into the kitchen to tend her soup.

"Can I offer you some supper, Mr. Simons?" Bridget asked as she removed her shawl, coat and bonnet and hung them on their pegs.

"Thank you, but I think I would like to see the patient first." He handed her his own coat and hat as she held her hands out for them.

"Very well." Bridget hung Mr. Simons's outer clothes next to her own. "This way, if you please."

She took Mr. Simons upstairs. The guest-room door was closed. Bridget knocked.

"Come in."

Bridget hesitated for a bare instant. Something had changed in the stranger's voice. She could hear it even through the door. It held a rough, nasal quality that had not been there before.

Wondering what fresh oddity was occurring, Bridget walked into the room. The stranger sat up in bed, wearing an old shirt of Poppa's that Mrs. Hansen must have given him. The remains of a bowl of porridge and a mug of coffee sat next to the bed on the nightstand.

" 'Evenin', Miss," the stranger said brightly. " 'Evenin', Reverend," he added, seeing her companion's collar.

Mr. Simons looked at Bridget with raised brows and turned back to the stranger. "Good morning, sir. I am Reverend Zachariah Simons."

"Pleased to know you." The stranger held out his hand. "Dan Forsythe. I'm from over Marquette way. Come to see if I could swap the fish trade for lumberjacking for the winter."

"Pleased to make your acquaintance, Mr. Forsythe." Mr. Simons shook the man's hand. "How do we find you today?"

"A little battered, but I'm still breathing, thanks to Miss Lederle, here." The stranger nodded toward Bridget. "Hauled me straight out of the water after my boat smashed up. Don't know what I would've done else. I was out cold."

"You are not the first to have cause to thank God for Miss Lederle and her diligence," said Mr. Simons soberly.

"I'm sure I'm not." The stranger beamed at her, all sincere friendliness and attention.

Bridget frowned, but what could she say? *What about the things you told me earlier? What about the visions you made me see?*

Mr. Simons pulled up the bedside chair. "Mr. Forsythe, Miss Lederle brought me here because she was concerned that some of your earlier statements might indicate a more serious condition than just the aftereffects of a severe ducking."

"Statements?" The stranger's smile faded and his gaze shifted from Mr. Simons to Bridget. "I said something? Improper, I mean? 'Cause I swear, Reverend—"

"No, no, Mr. Forsythe, not improper," Mr. Simons reassured him. "Peculiar, perhaps." He proceeded to give a decent repetition of Bridget's story.

As Mr. Simons spoke, the stranger, Mr. Forsythe?, grew grave. "I said that?" He ran a hand through his hair. "God Almighty . . .'scuse me, Reverend. I must've been under way too long, or maybe it was sailing all alone in that d . . . darned Finn's boat, put me out of my head for a while."

"Finn's boat?" inquired Mr. Simons.

"Yes, sir. Seen it? Outlandish-looking thing, but had it for a song. A Finn sailed it up the Soo. Said he was staying in Marquette and needed a stake. Swore it'd get me across Superior, or wherever else I wanted to go. He was mostly right." The stranger shook his head ruefully. "All I can say, miss, is that I'm sorry if I alarmed you at all. I don't even remember saying any of . . . what you say I said."

Bridget stared hard at him. She saw nothing in his eyes but confused innocence. Yet something was not right. She knew it. "That's quite all right, Mr. Forsythe," she said at last, because she could think of nothing else to say. "I'm sure you did nothing deliberately."

"Still, it is best to err on the side of caution in these cases," said Mr. Simons heartily. "I am sure we are both pleased to see your health of mind restored." He stood. "I shall let you rest now. Perhaps, Miss Lederle, we might have that luncheon you suggested?"

"Of course, Mr. Simons." She backed into the hallway, not taking her eyes off the stranger. "If you'll come with me, please."

Halfway down the stairs, Bridget stopped. "Please go ahead to the kitchen, Mr. Simons. I've forgotten something in my room." She turned and hurried back up the stairs.

She paused to make sure the priest did not take it into his head to follow her, and opened the stranger's door without knocking.

He was sunk back against the pillows, breathing heavily. He blinked when he saw her, but did not sit up.

"Forgive me, mistress," he said. The nasal tone was completely absent from his voice.

"An excellent ruse." Bridget planted her hands on her hips. "What lie do you next intend to tell?" *He is dangerous. He means to take you away with him.*

"I knew you did not believe my assertions," he said, his voice was harsh, whispery. "I could not let you send me away before I had a chance to prove them."

"You can prove this fantastic tale of dowagers and sorcerers?"

He nodded. "Come to me again. Bring a mirror and some cording or thongs such as might be fashioned into a net or braid. I will prove all I say then." He closed his eyes. "I am sorry. I am most profoundly wearied."

Bridget simply stared at him, uncertain what to think. His breathing grew deep and regular as he drifted once more into deep sleep.

What am I to do? When his madness comes and goes with such control? Can that truly be madness? Or is it something else? Cold disquiet formed inside her. What else could it be? Surely the laws of God and nature did not permit such things as sorcerers.

No, Bridget Lederle? Why would those laws permit your second sight and yet forbid other such miracles?

At last, Bridget closed the door behind her. Whatever the name of the man in the bed, he had promised her proof positive of his assertions.

She would give him his chance to display that proof.

Chapter Three

That evening, as the sun sank behind the island's trees and the light faded, Bridget installed Mr. Simons in the parlor with a book and a pot of coffee and told him she would be a while attending to her duties. Johann had elected to stay in the winter kitchen with Mrs. Hansen and Samuel, so to catch them up on all the latest doings in Eastbay and on the mainland. As she passed by on her way to the tower, he was giving them an enthusiastically detailed account of the accident that called Dr. Hannum away to the lumber camp.

Bridget filled the reservoir with oil she had carried up earlier, wound the works and lit the wicks. She stayed there for several minutes to make sure the beam was strong and steady, noting that she could see the light from Devil's Island burning brightly—a sign that caused her to hope for another clear night. Then she went back down the long spiral stairs, to the second floor and the stranger's room.

He seemed much more alert this time, sitting up straight with a small smile on his face. The hurricane lamp at his bedside created reflections in his rich, black eyes.

"What you requested." From the deep pockets in her apron, Bridget drew a handful of colored cloth strips that she had been saving to braid into a rag rug. Then she brought out the silver-handled mirror that was the only thing she had of her mother's.

"Thank you, mistress," said the stranger solemnly as he received them. "You may perhaps wish to sit down. This will take some few moments."

Bridget sat in the bedside chair, back straight, hands folded. She had left the door open a crack, just in case a prompt retreat should be required. She also kept an ear open for footsteps on the stairs, for she did not wish to be seen encouraging a lunatic. But none came. The household with all its additions remained oblivious of whatever he was about to do.

The stranger spread out the cloth scraps on the quilt in front of him. With a smoothness of motion that indicated long practice, he began to weave the scraps in and out of each other, knotting their ends tightly together.

After a moment, Bridget realized he was fashioning a small net. It seemed to be ordered not just by the pattern of knots, but by the colors of cloth, with the more reddish strips occupying one half and the more bluish occupying another.

As the stranger worked, sweat beaded his brow. His lips moved constantly, as if he recited some litany or prayer. Not once did he stop, not even when the drops of perspiration trickled down his cheeks and splashed onto the bedcovers.

Bridget didn't move. The faint remains of the daylight faded away, leaving them alone with only the candle and the lamp to see by. It seemed to her that the room grew steadily colder and more stale. The air became thin and chill to breathe, as if some vital element had been sucked from it. Goose pimples prickled her flesh, and the the nape of her neck itched. The stranger's breathing grew labored. He blinked fiercely to clear the perspiration from his eyes, but his fingers did not stop moving. Bridget forced herself to hold still.

At last, the stranger fell back against the pillows. The net held loosely in his fingers was roughly two handspans across and as delicate and complex as any spider's web.

"So hard," he murmured between gasps for air. "Never so hard . . ." He wiped at his face.

Bridget did not move. Her own heart labored in her chest, although she could make no guess as to what distressed her. At least it was again easy to breathe.

When he had collected himself, the stranger spread his net on the quilt and laid Momma's hand mirror faceup in its center.

For a moment, Bridget saw the faint, candlelit reflection of the plastered ceiling, a fold of the quilt and the stranger's hand drawing away. Then all became blank and silver, as if the mirror saw nothing but a dense fog.

"What is this?" Bridget leaned forward.

"My proof," said the stranger, pushing himself up a little straighter.

While Bridget watched, amazed, a swirl of color shone through the silver mist. The color strengthened and gradually separated until it became a great, sprawling edifice of grey stone with pillars and towers. The whole of the construction seemed to be covered in fantastic scrollwork and gargoyles. She was certain she heard the tolling of iron bells rising from the mirror, the distant shouts of men, and even the barking of dogs.

Her hands clutched each other, but she forced herself to sit calmly.

"This is the palace Vyshtavos, the winter home of my mistress, Her Grand Majesty, the Dowager Empress Medeoan of Isavalta." The stranger ran his finger along the edge of the mirror and the mist swallowed the image whole. In another moment, it cleared to reveal an aging woman, her hair quite grey under its veil of gold tissue, but her back still straight. She wore robes of silver fur and rich purple velvet, embroidered all over with silver thread. She paced down a corridor of polished stone hung with embroidered tapestries that depicted feasts, hunts and dancers in bright costumes. Bridget's mind tipped. She recognized this woman. This was the woman Bridget had seen in her private vision, giving the stranger his belt buckle.

As Bridget watched the old woman, she saw that all the while her thin hands clasped and unclasped, as if seeking to capture something elusive.

"What grieves her?" asked Bridget, startled by the sound of her own voice.

"Her son, the Emperor Mikkel Medeoansyn Edemskoivin." Again his finger traced the mirror's rim and again the vision changed. In place of the old woman, it showed a well-formed young man in a long coat of fur-trimmed red velvet. A jeweled cap was perched on his thick, dark blond hair. He stood beside a chessboard whose pieces were carved of coral and ivory. He picked up one of the pawns and stared at it, without intelligence, or even recognition, showing in his otherwise handsome face. Then, he dropped the piece carelessly down upon the board and wandered away, his hands tucked up into his velvet sleeves. His whole attitude made Bridget think of a little boy, slouching away with his hands in his pockets.

"This is an emperor?" she said incredulously.

The stranger nodded. "I knew him well, once. He was a most excellent and able prince. Full of sound judgment and discretion, even as a boy." His voice caught in his throat. "Beloved by the people, and even more so by his illustrious mother, who saw that he was trained and educated in every good science and art. She required him to attend council meetings as soon as he was old enough to talk, so that he might be raised wise in the ways of good governance." His eyes grew distant, seeing something other than the vision he displayed for Bridget.

"What happened to him?" she asked.

"Ananda." The stranger spoke the word as if it were poisonous, and changed the vision once more.

This time it showed a chamber hung with tapestries as the corridor had been. These were mostly country scenes—trees and hills and a variety of animals. The room was full of women, some in dress similar to the dowager's, but less rich, and others in gowns of draped silk. They were engaged in a variety of activities—writing with silver pens, needlework, spinning, reading. One played a small flute, another a drum. The soft tune became faster and more insistent, until a lady in drapings of royal blue silk with a thread of gold braided through her dark hair rose to her feet. She began to dance, turning and laughing, swaying her hips and shoulders in complete abandon. Bridget had never seen anything like it. In that moment she didn't know whether to be shocked or envious at the sight of such shamelessness.

The sour look on the stranger's face told her plainly which emotion he suffered. He glanced up to see Bridget's gaze on him, and looked quickly away, staring out the window at the night and the steady glow of the lighthouse beam.

"The Princess, the Empress, Ananda was brought from the country of Hastinapura to be Emperor Mikkel's bride." Kalami's voice was low and harsh, as if he fought to hold his anger back. "Their marriage was to conclude a peace between Hastinapura and the Empire of Isavalta. There is need for peace, as both are threatened by the Empire of Hung-Tse, which lies between our lands." He dropped his gaze to the quilt on the bed, where his hands lay, clenched into fists. "It was also to be a guarantee against a repetition of those wrongs that Hastinapura had visited upon Isavalta when Medeoan first came to the throne." He shook his head. "I should have seen," he whispered. "I should have known they would only see our search for peace as weakness.

"We welcomed Ananda and the peace her presence promised." The stranger struggled with the words as a combination of anger and exhaustion shook him. "But we were misled. She has no thought but the advancement of Hastinapura and her father's cause in all things. His cause, it seems, is our conquest."

The stranger lifted his gaze from the quilts and met Bridget's eyes. "Ananda is a sorceress of such power that all the dowager's skills cannot counter her. She has enchanted our emperor with a spell of love and bemusement so deep, he will do only what she tells him. And we can do nothing, nothing! without we jeopardize his life."

Bridget looked again at the mirror. Ananda spun on her slippered toes, and paused suddenly, her head thrown back. In that moment, Bridget recognized her as well. Ananda was the frightened girl Bridget had seen in golden robes. Bridget's throat tightened and she was forced to swallow before she could speak another word.

"This is a fascinating narration," she allowed. "And what you show me . . ." She waved at the mirror. "Is beyond comprehension. But why are you here instead of back in . . . your own country?"

The stranger—Valin Kalami was his real name after all, Bridget supposed—picked up his net with trembling hands. He began plucking at the knots, unweaving the net he had made with such care.

"I told you, Ananda is so deep, so strong and calculated that my mistress can do nothing against her. She has insinuated herself into the hearts of the nobility and the common people, through flattery, and, no doubt, a liberal distribution of her charms, both physical and magical." He jerked two strings apart. "So, my mistress was forced to seek elsewhere for help. She wove herself a vision that would allow her to see the one who could save her son, indeed, save all of Isavalta." The net parted under his fingers. He dropped the colorful scraps into a heap in his lap.

"My mistress saw a woman, beyond the Land of Death and Spirit, who kept a great light at the edge of a sea of fresh water. She saw that if this woman came to Isavalta, Ananda would be laid low, and Isavalta and Mikkel would be returned to the dowager's keeping."

Bridget laughed, unable to help herself. "You are playing a game with me, sir." She waved her hand as if to clear his words from the air before her. "What on Earth, or any other world, for that matter, could I do?"

Kalami lay back against his pillows and contemplated her for a moment. His eyes were empty of any but reflected light. Still, Bridget found herself growing warm under their careful consideration. "To begin with, I suspect once you are in Isavalta you will prove to be a sorceress of such power that even Ananda will tremble."

Bridget shook her head, incredulously. "Now I know you are playing with me."

"No." He held up a hand to stop her protests. "You have visions of the mind, do you not?"

Bridget felt herself pale. "How can you know that?"

"I saw you when you touched my belt buckle." Bridget's gaze strayed to the windowsill, where the golden oval gleamed in the lamplight. "Despite your unwillingness to speak of it, your eyes at that moment looked on something other than the contents of this room."

"Be that as it may," said Bridget, unwilling to let the conversation dwell on her, "the occasional insight is paltry compared to what I saw you do here." She gestured at the mirror.

"Not so," replied Kalami. "Visions, unasked for and with no spell woven to call them, are among the deepest gifts granted to a soul cradling magic." For a fleeting instant, something hardened behind his words, and Bridget found herself wondering if it might, of all things, be jealousy. "Properly taught in a world where natural law is amenable, you would be among the greatest sorcerers who ever lived."

Bridget felt the corner of her mouth turn up into a half-smile. "You came here to flatter me, sir?"

"If it brings you to Isavalta, mistress, yes I did." His face was nothing but earnest. "I will reason, flatter, entreat, bribe, if necessary, whatever I must do to convince you to return with me."

Bridget shifted her gaze to the hurricane lamp, the window curtains, the darkness outside, the bare floor, all the everyday things that surrounded her. All the everyday things that reminded her where she was, and who she was. The rest was air, fantasies, nonsense. The beam shone, lighting the world, and showing nothing had changed, or would change. What Valin Kalami said could not be true, none of it. She was Bridget Lederle, Everett Lederle's daughter, no matter what the wagging tongues in Eastbay and Bayfield said. She was the keeper of the light on Sand Island, a folly-ridden woman, and, occasionally, she was a seer. Nothing else was true or possible.

Except, it seemed that something else was, and he was looking steadily at her.

He means to take you away with him. Aunt Grace's voice rose unbidden in her mind. *He's a danger to you.* Could it be true?

Bridget's fingers twisted in her lap. "I am to return with you to do what, exactly?"

"That I do not know," he admitted. "To meet the dowager first. To be trained in the ways of magic. After that . . ." He shrugged. "It must be as events unfold." He met her eyes again, and reached out his fingertips to touch her wrist. "I can tell you this much, it is a noble life I take you to. I see the way of it here for you. Your work is hard, your house small and lonely."

His remarks stiffened Bridget's spine. She moved her hand away. "I am quite content, thank you."

"I doubt it not, but you could be more than that." He smiled, drawing his own hand back onto the quilts where it belonged. "The patronage of the dowager, and your own gifts and beauty, will earn you many friends. You will be feasted, your opinion sought, gifts bestowed, entertainments provided. It will be a rich life and full, mistress, I promise you that."

Of all that fine speech, one word stuck in Bridget's mind, somewhat to her embarrassment. "Beauty?"

"Your wondrous beauty." His dark eyes sparkled. "Has no one spoken to you of that?"

Bridget's cheeks heated and she knew they were turning pink. "Not in many years."

"Then the men of this land are fools." His hand slashed through the air, dismissing them entirely. "In Isavalta, the poets will compose great themes upon your graces."

"Now you do flatter me," said Bridget, uncomfortable that those shallow words had touched her at all. Vanity. After all these years, it still squirmed in her bosom. Asa's praise of her beauty had led her to open her door and her bed to him, and where had that left her?

Bridget stood. "I must think about what you have said."

Valin Kalami picked up Momma's mirror and held it out to her. "Promise me in truth you will do that," he begged softly.

Bridget grasped the mirror's handle, her suntanned fingers brushing his brown ones. "I give you my word." She clenched her hand around the mirror, as if she was afraid of what it might do next.

"Then with that I must be content." Kalami sank down into the bed and his eyes closed. "I swear, I have not slept so much since I was a babe as I have upon arrival in your world. It is very hard to live here."

"I will let you rest." Bridget turned to leave, but she paused, her free hand resting against the window frame. "I have only one more question. If you truly are from some other world, as you say, where did that performance you gave Mr. Simons come from?"

"Ah." Kalami's eyes drifted open. "That was someone your Samuel overheard."

Anger, sharp and sudden, rose in Bridget. She turned on the stranger, the silver mirror held out in front of her as if she meant to swing it down. "If you touched Samuel—"

"No, no, I did him no harm, I swear it," said Kalami hurriedly.

"I only looked at his memory. I knew I would need a tale. I could not permit you to send me away thinking me merely mad. I had to be able to put on a show of familiarity for whomever you brought to examine me."

"Well." Bridget took a deep breath and lowered the mirror slowly. "You made an excellent job of it."

"Thank you, mistress." His head inclined in what Bridget suspected to be the suggestion of a bow.

Still clutching the mirror tightly, Bridget left the room.

Down in the parlor, Mr. Simons had fallen asleep, his book dangling from his fingertips. Bridget removed the book and returned it to the library cabinet. She laid a knitted coverlet over the priest. Given his domestic situation, this was probably not the tenth, or the thousandth, time he'd fallen asleep in a chair rather than making his way to bed. There was a candle and matches on the table beside him. He knew where his room was. He could shift for himself if he cared to, for from the silence emanating from the kitchen, Bridget guessed Mrs. Hansen had already gone to bed.

Is it that late? Bridget glanced at the clock on the wall. The moonlight glinted off the hands and showed her it was coming on half past eleven. It didn't seem like it should be anything near so late. Had Kalami's . . . magic, bent time as well as vision? The idea disturbed her. She shook herself. More likely she had been so caught up in what was happening that she failed to notice the passing of time.

Despite her broken night and long day, Bridget did not feel in the least tired. Almost without thinking, she made her way to the tower door and lit the waiting candle. By its flickering illumination she climbed up the iron stairs to the great light.

In the lamp room, all was well. The clockwork clicked and clacked, pumping the oil smoothly and allowing the beams to strike out across the black waters. The lake was fairly calm tonight. Faint ripples showed up as flashes of silver under moonbeam and lighthouse beam. The mineral oil burned with a clean, penetrating smell that reminded her of all the thousand other nights she had spent up here, tending her light and watching the water.

And now, this man had come and he offered her . . . what? Madness? She could not believe any longer it was that simple. Magic then? A kind of magic that even she with her second sight had never dreamed of.

But it was more than that. Bridget pulled her shawl more tightly around her shoulders. He offered her a new life. A life away from Mrs. Simons and her black looks, and Mrs. Ludwig and her gossip, and even old Mrs. Hansen and her "Yes, Miss Bridget." A life where no one knew who she was and what she'd done. A life where no one had ever seen her belly big with a bastard child, had never seen her weeping beside a tiny grave and yet still believed it was more than the hand of God that had laid the body in the coffin.

What kind of life would it be, though? In a world strange beyond imagining, she had only his word that she would be welcomed. The patronage of a dowager? It sounded very grand, but she had read enough history to know that princes were fickle creatures and could easily change their minds about who their favorites were.

And could she really leave Anna cold and alone in the ground with no one to tend her stone and pray for her infant soul?

Then there was the light, of course. The light had to be kept. It had to shine, each and every night the shipping lanes were open.

But that wouldn't be for much longer. She could already smell snow on the wind. Soon the lake would freeze and all the ships would be laid up for the winter. She would be required to close down the light and move back to town for another long winter of gossip and sideways glances and the cruel emptiness that being alone amid a crowd of people could bring. Another winter of nothing to do but brush the snow from her daughter's grave, and wait for spring and the resumption of her duties.

Duty, responsibility, fault, guilt. These made up her life. They bounded it on every side and made her choices for her, or removed her choices from her.

But now this stranger waited downstairs, and his promises offered to topple those boundaries. Bridget snorted and knotted her shawl between her fingers. She'd had that thought before with another man.

That, however, had been in this world. But could she really believe this new world, this Isavalta, would be any better?

Did she really have to believe it could be any worse?

But what of Aunt Grace's warning? Could she truly put any credence in that? There was still the fact of her hesitation when Bridget asked how this predicted danger might be avoided. She had not told the truth when she said Bridget must simply get rid of the man and go on about her life. Bridget had seen the lie in her face and felt it in that tiny pause. But what about the rest of the warning? What if Aunt Grace really did have the second sight, and hid it under her shams? Heaven knew Bridget had wished often enough she could hide hers.

She would not waste her time believing it was affection for her that drove her aunt to make those extraordinary statements, but maybe, just maybe, Grace still loved her sister who lay in the graveyard. Maybe, she had just enough honesty in her to truly wish to help her niece, if only this once. Maybe she did see something and Bridget should send this man, this Valin Kalami, into Eastbay or Bayfield as soon as daylight returned.

But, if she did that, would she ever forgive herself for closing this extraordinary door that had opened and locking it behind herself?

The light shone across the water. The candle burned low in its holder. The moon rose, outlining the pines, the wavelets and the boulders on the shore. Bridget stood, hugging herself against the cold and letting the too solid past and the too often imagined future wash over her. She felt keenly aware of every sensation—the draft that touched her skin, the press of her toes against the rough wool of her stockings and the leather of her shoes, the weight of mother's hand mirror in her pocket.

Bridget pulled the mirror out and stared at her own reflection, lit up by the lamp from behind. Turned this way, and she had clear eyes, nose, skin, all features in good order. But turn that, she was a ghost of shadows floating over yet more shadows. Turn, she was herself again. Turn, she was gone.

"Momma," she whispered as she turned this way and that, trying to find some meaning, reach some decision from the movements of her reflection. "Momma, of all the things I've wanted to see, why haven't I ever been able to see what I really need to know?"

Turn, she appeared, bright, tired, whole, true. Turn, shadows only flitted and twisted across the glass so recently enchanted.

Turn, turn, a child's fortune-telling game, which showed more, the lit reflections or the shadows? Turn, and Bridget saw the shadows and the shadows saw Bridget, and they reached out to her in the turning, and she felt herself fall forward giddy and unafraid. Turn, turn, turn, turn . . .

And she walked in a snowy forest with Momma by her side. Momma wore a white shirtwaist dress, as she did in the one photograph Bridget owned of her, but her hair was not swept up into the severe bun the photograph showed. Instead, a long braid swung down her back.

Bridget felt no cold. The snow made no sound under her feet. It came to her that she did not belong here. Not as herself, not in this shape. She could not witness what had happened here as she was. She had to change before anything important could happen to her here.

"Where are we going?" she asked softly, reluctant to break the silence that surrounded them.

"To see something you should know about," replied Momma. She also spoke softly, and her voice felt deeply familiar.

"Where's Poppa?"

"He's waiting for you to decide who you should be." Momma reached out, and without touching the branches, pushed the bracken screen aside. In the clearing waited Valin Kalami in his long black coat. Bridget watched him as he set a heavy pack down in the snow. She was not the only one who stared at him, fascinated by his presence in this place where he had no more right to be than she. A fox watched him as well, staring at him from between a screen of twigs that would be ferns in summertime.

"Get along now, dearest."

Bridget walked through the bracken up to Kalami's side. She knew the change needed now, to understand what was so important that Momma had come all this way to show it to her. She settled down inside Kalami, and she was Bridget watching Kalami, and she was Kalami watching the fox, and the fox was all that he had hoped for. As she felt that hope, the world rushed in to swallow Bridget, and she felt the cold, and heard the trees and saw the fading daylight, and she was Kalami and Kalami spoke.

"Good evening, Master Fox."

The red-brown animal stood out sharply against the fresh snow. Frost glinted on its whiskers and the cold light of intelligence shone in its green eyes. Wary but curious, it looked up at Kalami, taking his measure in the day's thin, fading light. Behind it, the winter-bare underbrush rattled, but whether the sound meant amusement or warning, Kalami could not tell.

Kalami had entered the thicket alone and on foot. His horse was tethered some yards back. The animal had caught wind of this particular fox long before Kalami had seen it. Despite Kalami's skills as a rider and a sorcerer, he could not persuade the horse to come any closer to the fox.

"Will you have a drink with me, sir?" The glittering snow creaked under him as Kalami knelt and pulled a round-bottomed flask from under his cloak. A plait of reeds had been woven all around the precious green glass. It made the flask easier to hold and harder to break. Kalami, who had worked on weaving the plait for hours, sincerely hoped it would add a few other properties as well.

Kalami took a swig of the wine, forcing himself to swallow despite the tightness in his throat. The fox stalked forward, its tail bristling. Kalami held the flask out for it, and its pink tongue lapped at the flask's mouth for a moment. The fox regarded Kalami again.

"And for my brothers?" the fox asked.

"I would be honored if they would join us," Kalami replied, gesturing to the clearing with its fence of skeletal trees as he would to a spare chair in his own house.

The fox cocked its head. Its breath, Kalami noted distractedly, did not steam in the cold. Perhaps it did not have any. "Would you indeed be so honored, sorcerer?"

"Sir, I would." Kalami bowed his head. His heart hammered hard against his ribs, and he knew the fox heard every beat.

The fox sat back on its haunches. In the next moment, a curtain of red and gold light obscured the animal. When the fey glow cleared, a lean, naked man covered in wiry, reddish-brown hair crouched in the fox's place. The man's chin was as pointed as his nose. His eyes glittered green as forest leaves in springtime. The intelligence behind those eyes was lively, but it was far from kind.

"My older brother will be along by and by." The fox-man sat back on the snow, seemingly unconcerned about the cold or the wet. "He will expect the same as I have had." As he spoke, it seemed that the black branches overhead pulled themselves closer, waiting for a misspoken word as an excuse to snatch Kalami up.

"I promise, there will be enough for all who want it." Kalami suppressed a shiver. The cold seeped through his coat and hoes. That his every nerve was stretched tight did not help his comfort any.

The fox-man seized the flask in his fine-fingered hand and tipped his head back. He poured the wine down his throat as if it were water and he were dying of thirst. The moments passed, and he kept right on drinking.

I wove that spell taut and true, but can it hold up under this draining? It must, just for a little while longer. There are limits to the capacity of even such as he. That thought did little to comfort Kalami as the fox-man continued to drink.

After what seemed an age, the fox-man lowered the flask and licked his lips with a red-stained tongue.

"An excellent wine, Sorcerer." He tossed the flask back to Kalami. "I commend you."

Kalami caught the bottle and inclined his head. The contents sloshed, and he found he could breathe again. Not yet drained after all. "Merely something to lighten the heart of a weary traveler," he said with a deprecating shrug. "Had I known I would meet such an illustrious person when I set out, I would have brought better."

"You are too modest, I am sure," replied the fox-man easily, reclining back on one hand. Kalami's own cold hands tightened reflexively. The fox-man saw, and he smiled a thin, sharp smile. Then, one of his ears twitched. "Ah, here comes one of my brothers," he said, keeping his green eyes turned toward Kalami. "We will see what his opinion may be."

The bracken rustled beside Kalami's right shoulder. A shadow of movement glided between the snow-laden twigs that were the winter remains of fern and silver seal, and then a second fox paced into the clearing. This one carried a wide-eyed rabbit clutched tight in its jaws, its eyes bright with the success of its hunt.

"Come brother," said the fox-man. "What fare is that? Here we have a sorcerer with an excellent bottle of wine. I have already drunk my fill, and he swears that you may do the same."

The fox brother's eyes gleamed. He tossed the rabbit carelessly to the ground. The rabbit lay there, stupefied, its biscuit-brown sides heaving, steam rising from both its nose and its bloody wounds. In the next moment, the rabbit turned into a white dove and flew away, leaving behind only a scattering of scarlet droplets and one white feather on the scuffled snow.

Neither fox-man nor brother seemed to notice, and Kalami did his best to keep his attention where it needed to be. The brother also took the shape of a man, as tawny, naked and sharp-faced as the first. He showed blood-reddened teeth as he grinned.

"Let us taste this wine, then." Brother held out his hand.

Kalami handed Brother the flask. His heart thudded in his chest, and the gleam in Fox-Man's eye told Kalami plainly that he knew Kalami was afraid. Brother sniffed the wine, and squinted at the flask. Then, with one swift motion, he tore the plaited reeds that bound the glass.

Kalami froze. No human hand could have slashed that plait, the plait holding the spell that filled the flask. With the reeds torn, the spell was broken, and the enchanted wine was gone.

Brother raised the flask and shook it. Not a single drop swirled within. "Your bottle is empty, Sorcerer."

"What will our eldest brother say to that when he comes?" Fox-Man cocked his head toward Kalami. "You promised there would be enough for all, Sorcerer." His green eyes gleamed so brightly with hunger and mischief that Kalami imagined he could feel their heat against his icy skin. "You have broken your word."

"And what," said Brother, leaning forward so that his hands rested in the snow, "may we not do to one who has broken their word with us? By my mother's heart, I am most insulted by this behavior." His lip curled up and the growl from his throat was nothing human.

"Perhaps he could be our next rabbit," suggested Fox-Man, shifting himself so that he crouched on his feet. "To replace the one that flew away."

"Or a badger kit mewling for its mother as it stumbles along," mused Brother, letting his jaw hang open in a silent laugh, so that Kalami could again see his bloodstained teeth.

"A grouse."

"A pheasant."

Fox-Man licked his mouth with his wet, red tongue. "A sweet, sweet farmyard hen."

"Wait." Kalami held up both hands, which, he was ashamed to see, had begun to shake. "Masters, I am humbled before you. Yet, give me the chance to make good my promise." *Speak well, man, or you end this day with body dead and spirit devoured.* "There is, close at hand, the sweetest drink in the wide world."

"Sweeter than you, little sorcerer?" inquired Brother, leaning forward. Kalami could smell him now, the sharp scent of animal musk and human sweat. "With enough for all? Even for our eldest brother, who will be here so soon?"

Kalami tried to calm his beating heart, but it was too late. The scent of his fear already filled the air, and the noses of the foxes twitched as it reached them. Fox-Man smiled and showed teeth as yellow as parchment, but sharp and sound. He stretched himself forward, planting hands and knees on the snow, the organ between his legs growing hard and red.

"Let him be a rabbit," Fox-Man breathed. "I want to run."

"But while you are hunting me"—Kalami spread his hands, fighting to keep himself from cringing—"will you let the woman slip by?"

"Woman?" Fox-Man repeated. "What woman is this?"

"The one that passes through your wood even now, hurrying to return home from her tryst." Kalami's words tumbled over themselves, before he regained control and slowed his speech. "Little more than a girl she is, but already fair as mortal woman may be. She rides scornful of your domain and rights, believing herself safe in her spells and trickery."

"Safe is she?" Brother's bloody smile grew sly. "Safe from us?"

"Not from us, Brother." Fox-Man stroked Brother's shoulder. "Nor yet from our eldest. A girl is a sweet thing, a sweet thing indeed." His body even more clearly than his words showed his eagerness for such treat.

"But the sorcerer has broken his word before." Brother nodded at the flask where it lay. A few drops of wine had spattered from it, staining the white snow like the blood of the vanished dove. "Can we trust him now?"

"That is a thought, Brother." The Fox-Man tapped his sharp chin. "And if this lady stays on the road, how may such simple, honest folk as we come to converse with her in all her pomp and state?"

Now it was Kalami's turn to cock his head and make his voice ingenuous. "Do you say that anything can slip past you in this forest?"

Brother held up one long finger. "Ah, but you see, Sorcerer, the road is not part of the forest. The agreements that free the road are very old. Our mother would not be pleased if we broke them."

I feared this. Then Kalami stiffened. He felt eyes at his back, and they poured fear into him, as the gaze of a dog would frighten a cat, or, indeed, the gaze of a fox would frighten a barnyard hen.

But I am neither of these things. I have begun this game, I will see it through. These creatures will not have me. There is too much to be done yet.

Kalami steeled himself to make his last bid. "If I could persuade her to abandon the road," said Kalami, "would you then consider my debt discharged?"

The presence behind him grew stronger. He felt it loom close to his shoulders. He smelled its carrion-laden odor. His heart thumped so hard in his chest that its beat shook his entire frame, but Kalami did not allow himself to turn around. There was no telling what apparition waited there, calculated to freeze his very soul.

"Our eldest brother likes this notion." Fox-Man stroked the snow with one fine hand. "It suits my thinking as well."

"And mine." Brother's grin grew even wider.

Relief rushed through Kalami and slowed the frantic pace of his heart. *It will work yet,* he thought, but he still did not dare to move.

"There is an ash tree felled by lightning that lies across the road," said Kalami, his gaze darting from one fox brother to the other, trying futilely to guess their thoughts. "Meet me there at dusk, and I will fulfill my promise."

"We know that place." Fox-Man inclined his head without taking his gaze from Kalami. "We will be there, Sorcerer. See that you are also."

Before Kalami could blink, three foxes, two red and one grey, trotted silently through the underbrush, leaving him alone.

Kalami retrieved his flask, stowed it again in the pouch he carried over his shoulder and forced his cramped and frozen legs to stand. He needed to hurry. If the empress and her train had already passed the fallen tree, he was undone.

He waded through the heavy snow and frozen bracken back to his horse. The poor animal, held still and obedient only by the spells woven into its bridle, sweated and trembled as Kalami approached. It smelled the foxes on him, something he could not help.

"There now, my friend, there now." Kalami patted its neck. The animal only whickered and rolled its eyes.

Kalami took the bridle and led the horse into the trees. Its head drooped as its hooves moved, for its own fear exhausted it. Kalami felt for the creature, but he could not let it go, not yet.

"You must endure. It will not be much longer."

He walked his horse through rustling thickets and grey clearings, choosing the deer paths that would make for the easiest going. Sometimes he thought he felt the fox brothers' sharp gaze on him. But he could not be sure without stopping to look, and he could not stop.

Twilight was already gathering, turning the white and crystal world to shades of grey and black. A knife-edged wind blew, rattling the tree branches and frozen bracken, and this time Kalami was sure the sound meant laughter.

It might already be too late. What then? The thought chilled him worse than the wind.

The ash had been a venerable tree before the lightning strike shattered its trunk and toppled it across the road. Kalami paused in the shadows beside the scorched and splintered stump, straining his ears. He heard the wind in the dead leaves, the sigh and creak of branches, the thousand rustlings of the small creatures that scurried from their burrows and hidey-holes with the fading light, and the soft thump of snow falling from branches to the ground. Beneath all of these, though, he heard another sound, and his heart warmed inside him. He heard hoofbeats on frozen mud, accompanied by the sounds of human voices.

Not too late, then. Almost, but not quite.

Kalami retreated a little more deeply into the shadows, his spells more than his skills requiring his trembling horse to back up.

"Now then, my friend. It is but another moment." He uncinched the saddlebags and set them on the ground. He opened one and drew out a thick cord of braided silk. It was a gaudy thing—red, blue, green, lavender and yellow had all been twined together with threads of gold and silver binding it tight at either end.

On the road, the hoofbeats and voices grew stronger. The golden gleam of lanterns showed between the trees, bobbing like will-o'-the-wisps from the motion of the horses that carried them.

Kalami tied the bright cord to his horse's saddle girth. He tugged the knot tight, and, in an instant, the horse was gone. Instead, a horned deer stood beside him. His gloved hands still felt horse hair and horse tack, but his eyes saw only a sleek, wild animal. Kalami's searching fingers found the invisible bridle and curled around it. Stroking the horse's neck to soothe it, and himself, Kalami waited. Every moment drove the cold deeper into his bones, but Kalami scarcely noticed. Every scrap of his attention was turned outward, toward the road.

At long last, Empress Ananda and all her company emerged from the forest's thickening shadows. Eight soldiers rode before her and eight more rode behind, each wearing the green and silver livery of the emperor of Hastinapura, who was Ananda's father. Around them rode pages on ponies carrying lighted lanterns swinging on the ends of long poles.

The empress herself rode at the center of a crowd of ladies, some who had come with her from Hastinapura, some who had been assigned to her by the dowager empress. Furs swaddled them all in brown, black and grey, with hoods pulled up and obscuring their faces.

Despite that, Kalami could make the empress out clearly. Her cloak was a white so pure it gleamed in the lantern light. She was tall for a woman of her country, rounded and full, a flower in bloom. But all one needed was a chance to look into her eyes, to see the line of her brow and the set of her chin, to know that beneath the flower lay a will and a mind that were anything but fragile.

It is that will, Empress, which is going to cost you all you might have had.

Beside the empress rode a man in a heavy woolen cloak trimmed with silver fur. He gestured to her with gloved hands, making some point in their conversation, which Kalami couldn't hear.

"Sakra," murmured Kalami to himself. Kalami had gambled heavily that Ananda's sorcerous advisor and chief conspirator would insist on accompanying her through the Foxwood. Gambled heavily, and won.

Kalami drew his knife and held it beside his horse's neck.

The horse in its illusion of deer form danced and nickered. The foxes must be closing. The memory of the gaze from the unseen fox brother pressing against his shoulders drained the blood from Kalami's heart to the soles of his feet.

Ananda's lead soldiers approached the burned and shattered tree.

"Halt," called one, reining in his horse. He was a heavy man, round in the shoulders. He heaved himself gracelessly to the ground and stalked forward to examine the fallen ash. The company's horses neighed and champed at their bits as strange scents drifted out of the forest.

On the road, Sakra sat up even straighter in his saddle. Ananda said something, and a moment later some of the ladies tittered nervously. The empress urged her mount gently through her retinue, so she could deliver some order to her lead guard without even having to touch the dirt of Foxwood with her pretty boots.

Kalami sliced through his horse's bridle, severing the braid and breaking the spell that bound the animal's obedience. The horse bolted at once, heading for the road it knew led to home. It leapt over the tree right in front of Empress Ananda. Already skittish, her horse shied and bolted off the protected road and into the forest, scattering snow and rotting leaves under its hooves.

Kalami's dark-adapted eyes saw three small bodies flow out of the shadows and follow hard behind her, before the lead guard, before Sakra, could gather their wits and give chase.

Kalami felt himself smile. He picked up his bags and strode deeper into the forest. He had a walk of three miles to reach the sea cliffs and the little harbor where his boat waited. He had to set sail before his distraction had run its course and Sakra was back on the road to receive report from his spies that Kalami had sailed.

But by that time, Kalami would not even be in the world anymore. He would be in a world where he did not belong, far across the Land of Death and Spirit, and across a freshwater sea, where the one he sought waited in her tower beside her great lamp, holding a silver mirror that belonged to a woman long dead, and staring at her own face as she turned to play the lamp's beam across it, light, dark, light, dark . . .

The mirror fell from Bridget's hand and clattered to the floor.

God Almighty! She staggered against the outer rail, gasping for air. *What is happening?*

For a moment all she could do was stand there and breathe. She felt as if she had run a hundred miles. Every part of her trembled, and she swallowed to try to clear the sand that seemed to have clogged her throat.

"What is happening?" she croaked to the light, the lake and the night. None of them answered. She stared at the back of Momma's mirror, with its tracery of roses and lilies, as if she thought it might rear up and bite her.

But it did not move. Gradually, as the iron railing warmed under her hands, her trembling eased and she was able to breathe calmly and stand on her own.

"Well," she said, brushing a few loose hairs back from her face. "You might have warned me, Mr. Valin Kalami."

Valin Kalami and the wine, and the foxes in the snow, and the empress on her horse. Why hadn't he told her about any of that?

What else hadn't he told her?

Bridget gritted her teeth and reached down for the mirror. She grasped the handle. Nothing happened. She picked it up without looking at the glass, and stuffed it into her apron pocket.

Why had Momma shown her that?

"That was not Momma, that was your fevered imagination," Bridget told herself. Except she knew that she lied. It was Momma's mirror, and, Heaven help her, it was Momma's ghost. Her hand tightened around the mirror handle. So many impossibilities breeding so many questions.

None of which would be answered by her staying here. Of that she was also unshakably certain.

So, there remained only two choices. Live with those questions and make her way in the world as Aunt Grace advised, or go away into this place where foxes spoke, and Momma's ghost could walk with her in the winter woods.

Finally, she picked the candle back up and went down the stairs. She paused in front of Kalami's door, took a deep breath and opened it.

The candle light touched his sleeping face and his eyes opened.

"I will come with you," she said softly.

"Thank you, mistress." Even in his whisper, she heard gratitude. "You will have no regret."

Bridget closed the door. "No," she whispered to the chipped, wooden surface. "I don't know what will happen next, but it will not be that. Not this time."

After Bridget closed his door, Kalami lay still, listening. First he heard her soft footsteps moving down the corridor, and then he heard a second door open and close. After that, there was only silence underneath the continual rushing of the wind under the eaves.

When he was certain no one stirred outside his door, Kalami threw back his covers and sat up. Outside, the light beamed across the waters, steadfast in its ceaseless labor. It was not the only one who had a task to perform.

Kalami picked his belt up off the windowsill. Laying it on the bed, he lifted the window sash and pushed back the shutters. The late-autumn wind blew straight through his borrowed nightshirt to his skin, raising a host of goose pimples.

He unclasped the buckle from the leather strap. The gold lay cool and heavy in his hand. He was tired down to his bones, and this was going to exhaust what strength was left to him, but it was necessary.

Kalami lifted the oval of woven gold to his mouth and kissed its rough surface. He breathed across it. Then, he bit down hard on the inside of his cheek and spat, so blood and spittle now marred the gold.

"This is my word," he breathed, rubbing the blood into the braided gold. "And my word is strong. The wind hears my word and carries it forth. The wind is strong. The word is clear. Let the wind carry the word to the one I will. Let the wind carry the word to Medeoan Edemskoidoch Nacheradavosh."

The magic rose to his call, but only slowly. Kalami felt his spirit strain to find its touch, to wrap around its shaping and make the spell whole.

"Hear me," he croaked, his voice shaking with effort. "Hear me, my mistress imperial. Our salvation is achieved. She will come. She will come, and all will be well."

The world swam in front of Kalami's eyes. He could not hear the wind for the ringing in his ears. Too much gone. He should have waited. Darkness more profound than night nibbled at the edge of his vision. He could not hold his mind steady. The hand holding the buckle trembled violently.

But then the wind blew again, and inside his wavering mind, Kalami heard. "Well done, my lord sorcerer, my faithful one. Come swift home."

The buckle slid from his fingers then, and Kalami did not even hear it hit the floor. He fell sideways, curling up on the sheets like a child.

Done. Done. Much more left to do, other messages, more questions, more tales to be told, his own plans to be carried out to their separate ends, but that could wait. Everything could wait now.

With the very last of his strength, Kalami drew the covers over himself. A heartbeat later, his private darkness laid its claim over the whole of his spirit.

Chapter Four

Ananda's gaze swept the court as she walked down the central aisle with its thick, red carpet for her weekly presentation to her mother-in-law. It did not take her long to see that Lord Sorcerer Valin Kalami was absent once again.

Dowager Empress Medeoan Edemskoidoch Nacheradavosh of the Eternal Empire of Isavalta kept a court about her that glittered, flattered and displayed great wit, but did little else. Everyone here was beautiful, after the Isavaltan fashion. They were universally tall, fair-skinned, dressed in velvets and furs, and adorned with more jewels than Ananda had worn in her entire life before coming here. They were all young as well. The dowager, it was well known, did not like to have age about her.

Ananda did not mind all the outward display so much. Rather, it was what they did, or did not do, that knotted her stomach. The ladies spent their time gossiping behind their fans or shawls. Their highest pursuits seemed to be needlework and reading out insipid ballads to each other. The men were equally bad. Their talk consisted of horses and rents, and mighty deeds on the fields of display. Most of these tales, she was sure, were woven of air and fancy. In truth, their favorite pursuit seemed to be trying to insinuate themselves into the bosoms, and under the skirts, of the attendant ladies.

Every week, the walk to the dais and the dowager seemed to get a little longer. Every week, she missed her father's court a little bit more. Now, that was a truly resplendent court. Real artists, philosophers and deep sorcerers congregated there. Ladies schooled in the arts poetic and mathematical as well as domestic were housed in their own rooms and their discourses read with great attention. The debates carried on were of weighty matters, not airy vanities.

While Mikkel was still himself, she'd told him about the court she'd been raised in. He'd been fascinated and vowed to model his own court on the ideals of wisdom and real learning.

He never had the chance.

The courtiers all reverenced as Ananda passed with her ladies and officers in train behind her. Men and women alike bent from the waist and held their folded hands to their breasts, but only a few dropped their eyes in proper respect, unless she looked right at them. Why should they? Everyone knew she had enchanted their emperor, her husband. Just as everyone knew she wove spells every night on the great loom she kept locked in her apartments.

At last, she reached the stone dais that held the dowager's throne. Her attendants remained standing at the foot of the broad steps while Ananda climbed up to kneel at the dowager's feet. At least, she assumed there were feet under the layers of deep green velvet with its trimmings of mink and overlay of gold and silver tissue. She realized absurdly as she knelt there that she'd never actually seen the dowager's feet. The cumbersome, stylized Isavaltan skirts hid all suggestion of leg, ankle or toe.

As if anyone would still want to see the dowager's.

Ananda was quite aware it was fear that made her so snippish. Kalami, the dowager's chief spy and sorcerer, had been absent from court for three weeks now. Where had he gone? What mischief was he working in the dowager's name? How could those two possibly make things worse than they were?

"I give you pleasant greeting, my daughter." The dry back of the dowager's hand touched Ananda's right cheek, then her left.

"Thank you, my Mother Imperial." *Mother. You are not fit to repair my mother's sandals.* "I trust that I find you in excellent health this day."

"I am well, thank you, my daughter. You may stand."

Ananda rose gracefully. She'd spent hours learning to manage court dress before she'd even come to live here. Her mother, her real mother, had insisted that the then Empress Medeoan should not be able to fault her deportment or conduct.

How could either of them have known that Medeoan would find fault with the fact that Mikkel had fallen in love?

"Your secretary informs us you ride out to Lord Master Hraban's today," the dowager went on.

"Yes, Mother Imperial," replied Ananda, keeping her eyes modestly turned downward. She sometimes felt she had done nothing since she came but study various carpets. "He has invited me and some of my ladies to his hall to dine and watch a troop of masquers this evening."

"You show him great favor, my daughter. This is, I believe, the third time in as many months you have ridden to Sparavatan." The fluttering and whispering around her increased as the courtiers passed this tidbit to and fro.

"Yes, Mother Imperial. He has invested heavily in ships. His captains dine with him and they frequently have news of Hastinapura, which, as a natural daughter of that land, I am always interested to hear."

"To the exclusion of much else, I venture. Such as the comfort your presence at my table brings to me." Medeoan pitched the words to carry, as she always did when she had opportunity to complain.

Ananda, however, had been ready for this.

"Have I offended my mother imperial?" she asked innocently. "It has always been my understanding that I was to foster closer relations between the empires of Isavalta and Hastinapura. I can only perform this task if I have word of the doings in that land." *Your turn, Mother Imperial.*

"And what news do you hope to hear today?"

Ananda shifted her weight. "I could not hope to say, Mother Imperial."

"Oh"—she heard the smile in the dowager's voice—"I think you could."

"No, in truth, Mother Imperial . . ."

"Come now, my daughter." There was a great shuffling of cloth as the dowager leaned forward. Ananda imagined she could feel the entire court doing the same. "You must tell me."

Tell us all, you mean, Dowager. Ananda's gaze flickered to the dowager's lean face and saw the challenge written there. She sighed, as one who knew herself to be outmaneuvered.

"I had hoped the twelve dozen gilded oranges packed in snow I had sent for as a gift for my mother imperial had arrived on Lord Master Hraban's ship *Swiftheart*." She dropped a reverence. "If that pleases my mother imperial."

"Ah!" A sigh of approval rippled through the court, with a scattering of applause to accompany it. Ananda suppressed a smile. How could anyone disapprove of a gift of the rare fruits, especially the dowager in front of her court? Even if it did come from her sorcerous daughter-in-law.

"I had hoped to be able to present this gift to my mother imperial with my own hands," Ananda went on, folding the hands in question in front of her. "But if she prefers to receive it from my attendants, then gladly I will wait at her table this evening."

A pause followed, longer than was appropriate. "Nothing would please me more than to receive such a gift from my daughter's hands," said the dowager at last, as Ananda had known she would. For even the dowager to say she preferred servant hands to imperial hands would have been unthinkable. "I give you good leave to go about your errand."

"I render you thanks, Mother Imperial." Ananda dropped another reverence. "If it pleases you, I shall set out at once."

"It does please me, my daughter. You may depart to make your preparations."

"My thanks, Mother Imperial." One more reverence, and a careful retreat backward down the dais steps, trusting Sruta and Kiriti to get her train out of the way before she trod on it. When she reached the bottom of the dais, her entire retinue reverenced and held the pose for a full thirty breaths. Etiquette then permitted them to rise, turn around and leave by the route they had come.

Back in Ananda's apartments, Sruta and Nala hurried to get her travelling clothes. Behule and Kiriti accompanied the empress behind the changing screens to start unlacing and unbuttoning the complex layers of court clothing with Izmaragd standing by to receive the jewels as they were removed. Ananda, now used to the ritual, stood stock-still with her arms held straight out to her sides. Squirming only prolonged the process.

"So, Kiriti my friend," said Ananda in the court language of her home. "Were you able to learn anything new?"

Kiriti removed Ananda's ruby and sapphire necklace and passed it to Izmaragd while Behule successfully disengaged the golden collar.

"Only more rumor, Princess." Kiriti started on the ties for the blue and gold girdle. "Kalami is hunting your servant, Sakra. He is spying on the Nine Elders of Hung-Tse."

Behule undid the hooks on the indigo velvet outer skirt and lowered it to the floor so Ananda could step out. "I had heard he was out in the Foxwood, courting a river nymph so he could steal her jewels for the dowager."

"Had my father such storytellers, I should have never lacked for amusement all my years at home," muttered Ananda. In perfect synchronization, her ladies drew off her trailing velvet outer sleeves.

Sruta stepped around the screens and covered her eyes briefly in salute to her princess. "Secretary Mathura is here, Princess."

"Your arrival is welcome, Secretary," called Ananda as her maids began untying the scarlet laces of her cloth of silver gown. "Have you news?"

"My reports are all insufficient, Princess," he replied. When speaking in the language of Hastinapura, her people used the title she had been born to.

The final lace came undone and Ananda let out a mighty, undignified, sigh of relief as the dress loosened around her waist.

"I have for you only three letters. These were written by my lords Gantes, Tok and Avra," Mathura went on, tactfully ignoring her noise. "The last concerns the disposition of your estates."

Ananda gave another clearly audible sigh and stepped out of her first layer of petticoats. "Thank you, Secretary," she called. "You may leave the letters with Lady Taisiia."

"With a good will, Princess."

The second layer of petticoats came off. "Now, leave, man, before the sight of so many beauties in one place strikes you blind."

"As my princess commands."

Kiriti and Behule peeled off the third and fourth layers of petticoats, leaving Ananda in a linen shift with silken hose and drawers underneath.

Lady Taisiia came around the screens with three folded and sealed letters in her hands. She reverenced to the princess and handed them across. Ananda thanked her briefly without meeting her gaze. Ananda had known for weeks that Lady Taisiia spied for the dowager. After she had become certain, Ananda had Kiriti acquire one of Lady Taisiia's handkerchiefs so that Sakra could determine whether she was carrying anything other than messages for the dowager. One of the letters might contain useful information about that question.

Ananda hated the scheming, calculating creature she had become with a bitterness that rivaled her hatred for the dowager's person. But she wished to live, and that with mind and will intact. She had thought a thousand times about running away, but she could not quit this place without endangering the land of her birth and all who depended on her, including Mikkel. Sometimes at night she would lie awake and invent new curses to speak against her cousin Kacha, who had once been emperor of Isavalta. His treacheries had poisoned the dowager against Hastinapura, when his mission was supposed to have been to unite the realms. Oh, the dowager was her enemy, but Ananda could not ignore the fact that this canker that was her life had been formed by a worm from the heart of her own family.

Ananda broke the seal on the letter with Lord Avra's crest on it. Around her, her ladies dressed her in a woolen riding habit with a slashed green velvet overdress and sleeves that were almost manageable.

The letter did a creditable job of appearing to report on her estate at Kanjit. Inventories, slaughtering records, rents, the price on the crops of almonds and lemons.

She let Kiriti sit her in a chair, so her boots could be laced on.

The letter also contained the words "I will be there," no less than three times.

This time, Ananda suppressed her sigh of relief. The letter, in truth, was from Sakra. Lord Avra was a name they had made up to pass information back and forth under the dowager's nose, and Kanjit was the estate they spoke of when they meant to refer to the holdings of Sparavatan. By Sakra's repetition of the phrase "I will be there," he meant to tell her he would be able to meet her when she rode out today.

Regarding the question you put to me about the lady's gold sleeve trimmings, the letter went on, *I believe there is more to be had from the same workman as we used previously, and several garments may be obtained with that particular adornment.*

So, there it was. Lady Taisiia did carry some spell from the dowager. Woven into the gold braid adorning her sleeves there was some new magical poison or influence the dowager hoped to use against Ananda.

Ananda tried to feel fury or sorrow; instead, she felt only weariness.

"Well, the price of lemons this season is good." She handed the letters back to Lady Taisiia. Let her read them, for all the good it would do her now. As the gentlewoman took them, Ananda saw that the sleeves of Lady Taisiia's burgundy gown had great loops of gold braid loosely attached to their hems, giving the impression that she wore chains of actual gold.

Clever. Functional, yet most decorative. That thought gave Ananda an idea of how to proceed. "Am I attired yet, Kiriti?"

"Almost, Princess." Kiriti tied the final knot in her bootlace just as Behule pinned the white silk veil with its rose embroidery over her hair. "Now you are attired, with only this small addition." Kiriti handed the princess a pair of silken undergloves that had been embroidered with roses to match her veil. Her ladies graciously allowed her to put those on herself.

"I am grateful." Ananda took the gloves and emerged from behind her screens.

Kiriti, Behule, Sruta, Nala, Taisiia and Izmaragd, as her chief ladies, fell in behind her as she pulled the gloves on. Two of the little page girls in white, fur-trimmed satin and green sashes hurried on ahead to tell the grooms their empress and her party were departing. But before she quite reached the door, however, Ananda pulled herself up short and turned.

"Lady Taisiia?" she said, smoothing her embroidered glove over her hand.

"Mistress?" Lady Taisiia stepped forward from the neat line of gentlewomen and reverenced.

"Like you this glove?" Ananda inquired, tracing its scarlet roses with her fingertip.

"It is a lovely creation, mistress," replied Lady Taisiia with practiced politeness.

Ananda met her gaze. "What would you say if I told you it could speak?"

"I . . ." stammered Lady Taisiia. Kiriti drew back, and Behule with her. The other ladies followed their example, leaving Lady Taisiia and Ananda standing face-to-face.

"What would you say"—Ananda took a step closer to the startled gentlewoman—"if I told you the thorns in the roses prick my hands when there is danger, and the leaves rustle to tell me what that danger may be?" She held her gloved palm in front of the lady's face. "The thorns touch me, Lady Taisiia. Is there danger?"

Lady Taisiia reverenced, clutching her hands tightly together over her bosom. "Surely, my mistress does not believe . . ."

Ananda let her hand weave through the air before the lady's face. "The leaves rustle, Lady Taisiia. They are quite clear. There is danger near me." Her hand drifted up. "It is less here . . ." Her hand brushed the lady's arm. "It is greater here. It grows greater as my hand falls. Is that not strange?"

"Mistress . . ." Lady Taisiia's voice trembled ever so slightly.

Ananda seized the lady's arm, twisting roughly so she fell to her knees with a sharp cry. "Bring me a knife, Kiriti."

"No, no, mistress, please," begged Lady Taisiia from what had to be a most uncomfortable position. Her arm trembled in Ananda's grip. "There is nothing. You are wrong. I swear, I have done nothing, nothing!" The lady squirmed, but Ananda held her fast.

Kiriti reverenced and handed Ananda a little jeweled dagger that was meant to be worn as an ornament during hunts but that was, nonetheless, quite sharp. Ananda took it in her free hand, and touched its tip to the lady's frightened face. "Nothing, Lady Taisiia?"

Lady Taisiia froze. "No, no, please, I was ordered, I had to . . ."

Ananda brought the knife down sharply, severing the golden lacework on the lady's sleeve. Lady Taisiia gave a little shriek as the braid parted, letting Ananda know she'd gotten the correct sleeve, but to be sure, she slashed the other ornaments as well.

"There. The danger is gone." Ananda pushed Lady Taisiia away. Taisiia fell back against the floor, an untidy heap of silk and tears.

"Tell she whom you truly serve that I will not have those who deal double among my ladies." Ananda swept out. "Tell her to keep you from my sight."

Ananda did not look back. Taisiia would creep away to her mistress with the story of the magic gloves. Yet one more weaving possessed by the sorceress Ananda. Yet one more enchantment for the dowager to try to find her way around. Never mind that it was a complete lie. As long as the dowager believed Ananda was a sorceress, she would attack her as a sorceress. Weavings that worked on a sorcerer would pass over more ordinary souls.

The lie of her sorcerous nature had kept Ananda alive and in possession of herself. Every day she prayed that the lie would hold. If it unraveled, so too would her life.

Ananda proceeded along the sharply angled corridors that skirted the octagonal courtyard lost in thought. She walked down the Rotunda stairs with their pillars of white-veined pink marble and the painted dome overhead portraying the ascension of Edemsko, Medeoan's father. The sunlight from the small windows set high in the outer wall made her blink and, for a moment, look up.

She saw Mikkel, and she froze.

He lounged against one of the stair's polished blackwood rails. His fingers picked restlessly at the golden embroidery that bordered the sash of his deep purple kaftan. His dull eyes flickered back and forth, unable to rest on any one thing. Ananda's throat closed.

"Go on ahead," she said to Kiriti as soon as she could speak. "I will meet you outside."

"As you wish, Princess."

Her retinue moved on with many a sideways look. Mikkel watched them go, as if he could see only what moved and was too blind to see his bride standing still in front of him.

Ananda reverenced toward him. "Good morning, my husband."

His mouth worked for a moment before words came out. "Good. Good morning."

"Have you been out today?" she asked, ashamed at how small her voice sounded. "Is it fine?"

His gaze flicked up to the windows. "I suppose. I don't know."

"Would you like to see?" She stepped forward, faint hope rising in her. "I am going out. Come with me."

He shrugged. "I suppose."

Ananda held out her hand. Mikkel stared at it for a moment, as if trying to remember what to do with such an object, but then he reached for her.

"My son."

Ananda's gaze jerked up to the top of the stairs. There stood the dowager, magnificent in her emerald velvet and drapings of diamonds and pearls.

"Come with me, my son," she said.

Mikkel hesitated just a bare instant. "No," breathed Ananda. "Mikkel, come with me."

But Mikkel just shrugged and turned. He mounted the stairs carefully, putting both feet on one before climbing to the next, like a child uncertain of its footing. Anger and helplessness burned in Ananda as Mikkel took his mother's hand. The dowager's face showed nothing but pure triumph. But even as the dowager led her son away, Mikkel turned his face to look back down the length of the stairs, and Ananda thought she saw his mouth shape her name. Her heart contracted.

I will free you, my love, she thought after him. *I swear, somehow, I will find out what she has done to you.*

But at the moment, there was nothing to do but leave him with the dowager.

Because the dowager did not permit any to be unpunctual in her household, particularly if they were servants, the horses and all other necessary trappings for Ananda's journey were waiting at the foot of the stairs by the time she emerged into the daylight from the cloaking rooms wrapped in her furs and thick outer gloves.

She mounted Isha, the delicate little grey mare who had come with her from Hastinapura. Her ladies mounted their own horses and raised a green silk canopy over their princess. The usual escort of guards and pages, dogs and trumpeters took their places all around them.

When all had formed up, the great iron gates were cranked open by their keepers and the procession was allowed to venture forth.

In spring and summer they would have proceeded along the canal in barges. In winter, however, the waterway was nothing but black ice frosted with snow.

For all that the cold still bit to her bones, Ananda could see beauty in the winter that lay so heavily over her new home. The stark grey trees of the park surrounding the palace still reached for the sun, despite their nakedness. The towering pines screened the worst of the wind with their thick needles to protect their disrobed comrades. The pure white snow created new landscapes by filling in hollows and building up hills. All sparkled in the faint sunlight and the thin wind picked up whorls and snakes of diamond powder and scattered them all around.

Ananda remembered when she first saw snow fall from the sky. She was just fifteen and had been sent from her father's court to the court of Isavalta that she might learn the language, customs and all proper observances before she became empress. Her arrival had been greeted with a week of processions, pageants and receptions, all in languages she barely understood. In that time, she saw her intended husband a total of three times and spoke to him not at all.

That evening, it was another presentation of dance and masquerade. In truth, the display was lovely, but she was tired and missing her home, and the stranger she was to marry sat on the other side of his formidable mother, making any communication impossible. She had known all her life that she would be married to someone she had never met. That fact did not bother her, but she had always entertained the hope that there would at least be letters between them. The art of the courtly letter was much talked of in Isavalta, but it seemed little practiced, at least between imperials and their intendeds. She had not had one line from Mikkel during their courtship negotiations.

Sunken in her own thoughts, she didn't notice that Mikkel had left his place until he reverenced in front of her.

"With respect, the Moon's Daughter seems dull," he said, speaking in her own language. Slowly, to be sure, but he was trying, and he had even gotten her familial title right.

Ananda roused herself, aware that she was being extremely rude with her inattention. "No, no, I assure my cousin imperial," she replied in her High Isavaltan, which was about as good as his Court Hastinapuran. "The entertainment is excellent." She felt the weight of the empress's eyes on her. "I am quite enchanted."

"I am glad to hear of it," he said with a gravity that was so obviously affected, it bordered on teasing. Ananda felt a little warmth spark inside her. "But perhaps she will permit me to show her something truly wonderful?" It had been he who had extended his hand then, following the courtesies of his own court.

"I would be delighted to see whatever my cousin imperial wishes me to see." She took his hand, and noted that it was warm, and that the light from the lamps and tapers sparkled in his eyes, which were the color of sapphires.

He walked her at arm's length down the hall, holding on to just her fingertips with his free arm folded behind his back. Around them, the court parted in a rustle of heavy cloth, and bending heads and backs.

At the far end of the hall, velvet curtains screened the doors to the balcony, keeping out the drafts. Mikkel pushed the curtain back. In the next second, some servant took it from him. Mikkel opened the carved doors and let the frigid air in. Ananda shivered.

"There," said Mikkel.

The clouds had blossomed. They shed fat white petals that filled the black night and landed on rails and tile floor. Cold made a sharp perfume, like fresh mint, for these broken flowers. Ananda felt a smile of delight spread on her face, not only because of this sudden, small beauty, but because Mikkel had thought she might like to see it.

She cupped her hand to catch a petal. Her palm tingled as it touched her. For a bare instant, she saw the snowflake's lacy perfection, and then it vanished away, leaving nothing but a few drops of water.

"It is beautiful," she murmured.

"I am glad you like it," he whispered back, dropping into Isavaltan. "I am sorry if things have been tedious. Appearances have to be kept up, you know."

"Of course," she breathed.

"It'll all be over in a little while, and then maybe we'll be able to find another few moments to talk. Would that be all right?" A note of anxiousness crept into his voice.

"I'd like that," said Ananda. "Truly, I would."

He smiled then, and it was a bright smile. "Then, O Moon's Daughter and my cousin imperial, we will see what can be accomplished. I think we must return now, before my mother is displeased and my court begins to talk."

Ananda let another flake of snow touch her fingertips. "As my cousin imperial thinks is best."

He took her hand again, and led her back inside, and now Ananda noticed she was not cold at all.

For three years after that, she had truly believed she and Mikkel might be happy.

Ananda shook herself out of her memories before they could raise a sigh. That would not suit the person the dowager's spies believed her to be, and there were doubtlessly spies among the guard. She must be rock and ice, all attention and calculation. If word got back to the dowager that she had displayed any weakness at all, the campaign against her would only be stepped up.

Fortunately, they were almost to Lord Master Hraban's house. They passed the road marker—a stone pillar with its carving of an ermine obscured by snow—indicating they had passed onto the lord master's estate. Ananda allowed herself to be cheered. For today, at least, she would not be so alone. Sakra would be there.

Snow turned the ancient earthworks around Sparavatan into sweeping drifts. The wall that the current lord master's grandfather had erected around his ancestral home stretched behind the drifts, strong, grey and defiant. Its gates, however, were raised in welcome and green-and-white pennants festooned its turrets.

The world outside the wall was stark and slumbering, but inside it teemed with life. Women with baskets on their heads or backs strode between the stone houses. Girls in groups of twos and threes carried yoked buckets on their shoulders, or herded geese or sheep to and fro. Men leaned in the doorways and bartered with each other for this service, and that bundle of goods. They worked at carpenter's benches, small, metallic-smelling forges, or with mallet and chisel on stone. Soldiers marched past in their ordered columns. Carters led their oxen out the gates and into the wide world. Children, some half-naked despite the cold, darted here and there between their elders. The air felt crowded with the sounds of voices, footsteps, hammers on metal and stone and all the other varied noises of living.

But where Ananda and her retinue passed, activity stopped while hoods and caps were doffed and heads bowed in respect. Ananda gestured to Kiriti, and Kiriti handed her the purse she carried for these occasions. Ananda loosened the knot and reached in for a handful of silver pennies, which she scattered liberally throughout the crowds. As the money cascaded onto the snow, a riot of cheers added itself to the general cacophony of living. Once again, Ananda silently blessed her father for being generous with her income. Largesse contributed to popularity, and her popularity helped prevent the dowager from quietly doing away with her.

Sparavatan itself was a combination of ancient stone and newer brick existing in an uneasy truce with each other. Lord Master Hraban had made noises about trying to smooth over the disagreements of time and style between the central house and the eastern wing, which his father built. It seemed, however, that his political concerns did not leave him leisure or time for mere improvements to his home.

Ananda and her retinue rode into the courtyard of snow-sprinkled gravel. Lord Master Hraban Rasinisyn Sparavin caught her gaze from his place on the steps and reverenced deeply. Ananda returned a half-bow and waited for her ladies and pages to dismount, so there would be a step placed near her horse, someone to give her a hand down and someone to take her train immediately, as was proper and necessary according to Isavaltan ceremony.

A glance told her Behule had the train and Kiriti had the box containing the offering for Sparavatan's house god. Ananda proceeded up the steps and gave a shallow reverence to her host, who returned a deep, almost obsequious one to her.

Lord Master Hraban was approaching middle age. His black hair thinned under his velvet cap, but his body under its silks and velvets remained trim and strong. He looked down on Ananda from a height of almost six feet and always seemed to want to apologize for being taller than a member of the imperial family.

"Empress Ananda *tya* Achin Divyaela." He had practiced long and hard to keep his tongue from tripping over her full name. "Please accept the humble welcome of my home, Mistress Imperial." From a tray held by a servant, he took a silver cup that steamed and smelled invitingly of cinnamon and cloves and held it out to her.

"Lord Master Hraban Rasinisyn Sparavin, I thank you most heartily for the open gate and the open door." She took the cup to sip the hot wine. "And for a delicious welcome as well, Lord Master," she said as the warmth flowed through her veins.

Lord Master Hraban reverenced, this time with a broad smile on his round, lined face. "Allow me to conduct you to your apartments, where you may rest from your journey. Afterward, may I invite you to take some light refreshment with myself and some select gentlemen?"

"That would be most welcome, sir. I thank you."

Lord Hraban took his place at her left side. At his signal, the doors opened, and he walked with Ananda into the hall. The reception hall of Sparavatan was all stonework hung with tapestries, some of them of great antiquity, and, it was said, enchantment.

As was required, they went first to the deep, gilded alcove that was Sparavatan's god house. The god of Sparavatan and its family was an ancestor named Salminen. Salminen had risen to divinity in Sparavatan's defense when he had saved the land from invasion by calling down a storm of snow and lightning with nothing but the sweep of his sword. The icon on its pillar showed a fiercely handsome man with his sword held high. An ermine on his shoulder whispered wisdom, and wolves crouched at his feet gave strength and insight.

Behule opened the gift box and handed Ananda a scarf of silver, embroidered with small sapphires. Ananda laid the offering at the god's feet and kissed the hem of his robe.

That ceremony completed, Lord Master Hraban took Ananda and her ladies through the house. He had set aside her usual rooms, which were among the newest in the eastern wing. They possessed an actual fireplace and chimney rather than just a firepit. Three leaded-glass windows let in what there was of the winter sun, along with a view of the snow-covered gardens. Seeing her pleased with her quarters, Lord Master Hraban reverenced and closed the doors behind himself.

Then it was off with the furs and outer woolens, straighten and arrange the indoor clothes, primp the hair, make sure everyone had time to drink the spiced wine that had been left for them and properly thaw, and try not to hope too hard that Sakra would be among Hraban's "select gentlemen." Since the dowager had banished him from court, Sakra had to make shift to see her when he could. The dowager could not get rid of Sakra completely without inflicting a substantial insult on Ananda's father. She could, however, make the country hostile enough for him that he had to be circumspect in his comings and goings.

"Is all in hand, Kiriti?" asked Ananda at last, rising from her chair. "I believe we cannot delay meeting with our host any longer."

Kiriti rose smoothly, as did the rest of the ladies. "We are all ready to accompany the princess."

"Excellent." *I just wish the princess were more ready to accompany you.*

Kiriti picked up Ananda's train and the others formed up behind, except the two who went to open the doors. The gentlemen waiting outside escorted Ananda and her party to Lord Master Hraban's parlor rooms.

Hraban was waiting for her with three other gentlemen, all of whom reverenced deeply as she entered with her escort. None of them was Sakra. Ananda's mood sank a little, but she kept her disappointment far away from her features.

Ananda did recognize one of the men as Captain Nisula of Chultak, who had carried letters and other necessaries back and forth between Ananda and her father for several years now. The captain's dress was noble, velvets adorned with goldwork and a golden chain with a single great sapphire on it hanging from his neck. None of this could hide the fact that he was a man meant for rough work. His face was so windburned as to be leathery. His hands were knobby, stiff and callused. But Ananda knew his measure and she stepped up to him at once.

"Good Captain Nisula, let me give you my best greeting." She brushed his fingertips with hers, which was the closest familiarity their ranks allowed. "I trust that you are well and your voyages have been prosperous?"

"It is my good fortune to be able to answer yes to both, Majesty Imperial." Nisula always gave the impression of having to hold his voice back, lest he inadvertently let loose a shout. "My latest trip to your father's domain promises to bring great good to myself and my associates. I am pleased to report, also, that I have with me your gilded oranges, which but await your approval."

"I am in your debt, Captain." Ananda bowed her head. "I have promised them to the dowager today. She will be most disappointed in me if they do not appear."

"A thing to be most scrupulously avoided," said Lord Master Hraban dryly. "My Mistress Imperial, let me make known to you Lord Master Oulo Obanisyn Oksandrivin of Kasatan."

Lord Master Oulo was a corpulent man, and if his lands were half as well tended and improved as his clothes, he was twice again as rich as Lord Master Hraban. Gold embroidery lay so thick on his kaftan that it almost obscured the velvet, and the band of his cap was studded with diamonds. His face, though, was florid and thickly veined, which told her he enjoyed displays at the cask and flagon as much as displays at the tailor.

He reverenced as deeply as his thick waist and knees would allow. "My Empress Ananda, it is a thing surpassing wonderful to meet your gracious self."

Ananda kept her countenance and waited for the man to straighten himself up. "I do thank you, Lord Master Oulo, for your good words. You do me much honor."

Lord Master Hraban smiled at his friend as if to say "Is she not all I promised?" before he turned to the other man. "And let me also make known to you Lord Master Peshek Pachalkasyn Ursulvin of Seliinat."

Unlike Oulo, Lord Master Peshek appeared to be a sober and serious man. He did not look delighted to see her. Conscience pricked him, Ananda guessed, and she couldn't blame him, considering the turn the conversation would soon be taking. Whatever might or might not be happening at the palace Vyshtavos, Mikkel was the emperor ordained and the dowager was not only the duly chosen regent, but a woman who had led her lands to peace and unity. During her time on the throne, she wrung a great victory out of the Nine Elders of

Hung-Tse with very little loss of life. None of her later follies could completely erase that greatness.

"Please accept my good greeting, Majesty Imperial." Peshek gave her a reverence that was polite, but nothing more.

"Your greeting honors me, Lord Master." Ananda bowed her head once.

Lord Hraban did not cough exactly, but he did shuffle a bit. "If the empress would care to be seated . . . ?"

There was a little fuss while Ananda sat and Kiriti discreetly adjusted Ananda's skirts and train before retiring with Behule and the others to the servants' alcove. Several of Hraban's men moved forward with flagons of thick, black beer and dainties of smoked fish, herbs and dried apples. Ananda kept the conversation firmly on Hastinapura and what Captain Nisula had seen when he was there. He was willing to oblige with stories about the health of various families Ananda knew, as well as some of the usual talk sailors were so known for—wonders seen in port and storms endured at sea.

But she could not stall Lord Hraban forever. Eventually there came a pause in the conversation when Ananda had her mouth full of beer and could not conveniently put forth another question to Nisula. Instead, Lord Master Hraban turned to Lord Master Oulo.

"It does not go so well for you in the south lands, you were telling me, Lord Master Oulo."

Lord Master Oulo shook his head until his beard waggled. "It does not, it does not. Again this year, Hung-Tse permitted its raiders to menace us. Grain, pigs, market fees, all gone. Tracts of land burnt out to cover their retreat. Good men dead on the ground, their widows weeping in the mud over their bodies."

"Those are grievous fates, indeed," murmured Ananda, more toward her beer than Lord Master Oulo.

"Six letters I sent to the imperial dowager for succor." Oulo gestured broadly with his fat hand. "Six, followed by a deputation which fell on their knees before her. I did not even ask for fresh troops, I just asked that my levies be lightened so there would be men left to defend their homes." He dropped his gaze and twiddled with his finger rings. "I fear my wording was not as diplomatic as it might have been. Her Grand Majesty mistook my request for a criticism as to how the empire was to be ruled during her son's . . . illness of spirit."

Ananda remembered that delegation. She'd heard the dowager's voice rise high and shrill out of the council room. A few moments later, four of the imperial house guard marched a group of stunned-looking men out of the door and, she found out later, all the way to the cells below the palace. As far as she knew, they were still there.

"Her Grand Majesty's motives can be obscure," said Ananda. "Perhaps, if you'll permit, I can share with you some thoughts as to how she might be persuaded there is another interpretation to the message." *Especially if you are willing to part with a few of your diamonds and distribute them to a few of her councillors.*

Light from the fire twinkled on Lord Master Oulo's rings. Ananda counted them. Two bands of braided gold, two of knotted silver, a ruby, an emerald with small sapphires, and a great golden topaz on one thick thumb.

"That would be most welcome, Majesty Imperial," he said. "Especially for the sake of those poor men in the cells. But I fear"—he twisted the ruby all the way around—"I fear it will bring only temporary relief."

"A temporary relief in some ways perhaps, but surely a permanent one for those men's families," said Ananda sincerely. "Who minds their estates while they are imprisoned for poor command of courtly language?"

"My Mistress Imperial," began Lord Master Hraban, in his best diplomatic tone. "I ask you frankly, how does our emperor in his illness of spirit?"

The sudden memory of Mikkel's mouth shaping her name made Ananda bite her lip, and then it was too late to lie. "He seems steady under his affliction."

Lord Master Hraban leaned forward, as if afraid the walls would overhear his words. "Have you any hope of even temporary relief for him?"

"I cannot say, Lord Master," answered Ananda primly. "The dowager consults the deepest sorcerers and learned doctors from all the imperial lands." That was the tale given out to the public, and probably all these men realized that. The dowager had expelled all sorcerers save her lord sorcerer from the court years ago, and everyone knew it. It was that fact that made Ananda's deception possible. "She knows much more of her son's illness than I ever shall." She looked at Hraban sideways. *And you and I both know that to be true in so many ways, Lord Master.*

"There is great concern in many of the duchies about the health of the emperor and the judgment of the dowager," said Peshek. His voice was grave, matching his face. "Some are even growing restive concerning the question."

"Lands growing restive is the perpetual condition of Isavalta," replied Ananda with a small smile. "Or so it seems."

Lord Master Hraban chuckled. "That cannot be denied, Imperial Majesty. Yet, that restiveness can be checked by, say, changes in policy, or councillary opinion."

"This is not Hastinapura," muttered Peshek. "Here, the rulers must be seen to rule."

Ananda stiffened. "Are we now to discuss varieties of custom, Lord Master Peshek?" *Is it the dowager that discountenances you so, sir? Or is it the fact that your friend is urging you to appeal to a foreigner?*

Peshek dropped his gaze. "I did not mean any disrespect, my Mistress Imperial. I meant . . ." His voice sank low, but its intensity was plain to hear. "If you will do as Lord Master Hraban and his friends have urged, if you will take the throne beside the emperor in the dowager's place, then may we have a return to reason. Then may we keep the peace that Medeoan herself won for us a generation ago." He shot a look, venomous and bold, at Lord Master Hraban. "There, I have spoken it, for all of us. Does that please you?"

And what tale would these walls tell of your talk before my arrival?

Here came the delicate portion of the conversation. Ananda had been rehearsing it to herself for months, ever since Lord Hraban had begun hinting at this subject and parading his landed friends for her approval. "My lords master, my good captain, I have been duly married to your emperor. I have been handed the scepter and sacred regalia of empress, but"—she held up one finger—"the emperor has been judged, due to his illness of spirit, to not be of legal majority. Until that judgment is reversed by the Council of Lords and the keeper of the emperor's god house, or until they appoint another regent, the Dowager Empress Medeoan rules Isavalta. Another vote may change this, but as you know, in Isavalta such things do not happen without consultation or support." She let her gaze rest for a moment on each one of them. "Without the authority of the Council of Lords, and the intercession of the Keeper of the Emperor's God House, nothing, nothing at all, could be done on such a matter."

Gazes shifted, as the men looked from one to the other.

"But, were that authority engaged . . ." prompted Lord Master Hraban.

"Were that authority engaged, it would be an entirely different matter." Ananda folded her hands. "That is all I have to say upon this subject, Lord Master Hraban. I ask you to be content."

Lord Master Hraban bowed his head. "I am most content, believe that, my Mistress Imperial."

For which I thank the Seven Mothers. Ananda took a swallow of beer. *You mean to do it, don't you? You mean to overthrow the imperial family and set me on the throne. The worst part of this tale is that I may have to let you.* Her hands suddenly lost the strength to hold her flagon and she set it down with a clumsy thud.

"Is something the matter, Mistress Imperial?" asked Lord Master Hraban earnestly.

Ananda let her head droop a little. "I find I am unwell, Lord Master Hraban. A headache. I will retire a little and surely it will right itself." She rose, and Kiriti and Behule were at once beside her. "I do not wish to miss the entertainments you have planned this evening."

The men all rose at once, but Ananda waved them back to their chairs. She did not want to have to face them one instant longer. "My ladies will accompany me. I shall see you at dinner, my lords master, Captain." She reverenced briefly while Kiriti caught up her train. Lord

Master Hraban himself hurried forward to open the door for Ananda and her ladies, reverencing deeply as they passed.

Yes, let me out of here. I want nothing to do with your plans and ambitions. I want Mikkel's freedom. I want my freedom. I want . . . Mothers help me, I want to go home.

They reached the door to her rooms and Behule opened it. As she did, a flash of color fell from the latch. Ananda bent down to retrieve a slender thread of scarlet that had been woven into a small circle.

Ananda smiled broadly and stepped into the rooms. "Behule, send the others to their dinners. I only need you and Kiriti."

The ladies took their orders with only a brief murmur. They filed back out through the door, bobbing their reverences as they passed. She acknowledged them impatiently until Behule closed the doors behind them all. Then, Ananda's gaze swept the room and, as she expected, she saw faint movement behind one of the tapestries.

"My father would be shocked, sir, shocked, to know you were creeping surreptitiously into a lady's chamber."

The tapestry lifted aside and a masquer, one of the many brought in for the evening's entertainments, stepped out. He wore silks of red and green. A creation of ivory and feathers made to resemble a parrot's head concealed his face. The masquer knelt and removed his headdress to reveal a dark-skinned man well past his youth, but not yet at middle age. His black hair was bound in elaborate braids and eyes that drank deeply of everything they saw.

"Your father would be even more shocked to find his eldest daughter had sent her ladies away when she knew an unescorted man waited for her."

"*Agnidh* Sakra." Ananda crossed the room swiftly and raised him to his feet. She kissed both his eyes in greeting. "How is it with you?" She sat on the edge of the nearest chair and motioned for him to sit as well.

Sakra set his mask on the chair and himself on the footstool so his head would not be higher than hers. "My body is well, Princess, but my mind is far from easy."

Ananda nodded. "Kalami has not been seen in court for three weeks at least."

"Kalami has not been seen anywhere for three weeks at least. I have worked every weaving I know and I still have no sign." Impatience creased his brow. "I thought I had eyes in this frozen waste, but I am as blind as a kitten."

"What does it mean?" Ananda threw out her hands. "It is not possible that he should abandon his mistress. Has she killed him for some offense?"

Sakra shook his head. "No. If the dowager Medeoan were to take that course, she would take it openly. He would have been publicly arrested and disgraced. No, he has gone somewhere on some errand for her." His gaze strayed across the tapestries, as if he could see the answer in their threads. Recollecting himself, he brought his attention back to Ananda. "I have made a bargain with the crow's stepchildren. They have sworn to find him for me."

Ananda felt the blood drain from her cheeks. "Oh, Sakra, no, the powers of this place, they are not as those of home . . ."

"I know it well, Princess." His voice was firm and his eye clear, but for once, his confidence failed to lend her strength. "But we must know where he has gone. Half-measures will not serve us."

She closed her fist around his words and kissed her hand to indicate her faith in what he said. "If he can be found, you will find him, Sakra." She paused before her next question could tumble out. She felt almost selfish that her mind skipped so swiftly from Sakra's danger to her own trouble.

"Is there any news to help Mikkel?"

Sakra straightened his shoulders. A smile lit his deep eyes. "There I hope we may be close."

Sudden hope warmed Ananda's heart. "Tell me," she said, leaning forward eagerly.

"I spent the week in the far hills with an old woman they call Mother Robber. She's half-blind, and half-mad, but I've seldom met so much raw power and old cunning." The smile spread down to his mouth, as he remembered savoring the presence of a true and unexpected power. "She heard the symptoms of Mikkel's distress. This is an ancient weaving, she says, not one new. It cannot have been worked from afar. It must be on the emperor's person. He's wearing his chain, Princess." Sakra pressed his palms together, pointing his fingertips toward her. "Think. Is there any weaving you have never seen him without? A cap, or a brooch, anything that has threads of some substance intertwined?"

Ananda shook her head. "Unless it be his rings of state, there is nothing else he wears daily." She drew back. "Surely not. Such a spell in the symbols of imperial rule?"

"Where better?" Sakra spread his hands. "Spells in metal are hard to work, but they will last the centuries through. Mother Robber told me a tale of one of the child emperors from their Wars of Consolidation. It was said his father stole his heart and kept it bound in a silver girdle, which might truly be . . ."

"A ring." Ananda leapt to her feet. "Kiriti, send my regrets to Lord Master Hraban. I am most unwell and must return home. Summon our train and have all make haste."

Sakra rose swiftly. "Ananda, Princess, this may not be the right guess."

She waved his words away. "It is the best we've had in an age, Sakra, and better than any other you've brought me since Mikkel became lost to himself."

"All I say is take care when and how you test this latest theory. You have waited this long, Princess." He reached for her, his hand touching the air just over her shoulder. "A day or two more for care will do no harm."

"No harm?" repeated Ananda, aghast. "No harm when I'm surrounded by spies searching for any weakness? No harm when I must shut myself up with a loom each night so that the dowager continues to think I'm a sorceress and not just a mere mortal who can be dispatched with slow poison or fast horse?" The force of her words caused her body to tremble. Her hands felt suddenly ice cold, although her cheeks burned like fire. "You wish to condemn me to a day or two more of scheming, and watching, and fearing for my life and

Mikkel's, when it all may be because his vile, vile mother put a ring on his finger!" Tears, long suppressed, ran down her cheeks.

"Forgive me, Princess." Sakra dropped to his knees before her. "I meant only—"

"No, no!" Ananda fell beside him, gripping his shoulders. "Forgive me, Sakra, it is only that I am so tired."

He held her then, as he had when she first saw Mikkel's mind gone from behind his eyes and he let her weep herself dry on his shoulder while her ladies turned away and pretended not to see.

"All will be well, child," he murmured. "All will be well."

At last, Ananda composed herself enough to blot her face with her kerchief and draw back from Sakra's shoulder. "One day I will find a way to repay you for all you have done for me."

"Your long life and happiness are all I ask." From anyone else that might have been a platitude, but from Sakra it was the plainest truth. "Now, before you leave, tell me, did you deal with the Lady Taisiia?"

Ananda sat back on her heels. "I sent her away with a shocked face and the fear of my foreign wrath." She smiled tiredly. "Once again we prove what a mighty force is Ananda *tya* Achin Divyaela, Empress of Isavalta, the Moon's Daughter Who Is First Princess of Hastinapura." She raised her clenched fist.

Sakra covered her fist with his great, callused hand. "Once again we prove how wise is Ananda *tya* Achin Divyaela of Isavalta and Hastinapura," he said gently. "And how brave is she."

Ananda's smile grew wan. "May the Seven Mothers grant me soon a day when I can be a coward again."

"May it be so." Sakra dipped his eyes reverently.

Ananda got to her feet. "But I will go, Sakra. I cannot stay here. Lord Master Hraban again importunes me to take the throne and I do not feel up to sparring with him any more today."

Sakra bowed until his forehead touched the floor. "As the princess wishes."

No, as the princess, as the empress, must do. Ananda suppressed her sigh. *Or she will surely run mad.*

Two of the pages rode on ahead, so that when Ananda and her train returned to Palace Vyshtavos, there were lighted lanterns and warm drinks to greet them, as well as a meal to replace the one they missed at Lord Master Hraban's. Ananda ate in her rooms with her ladies by the light of fire and candle. The short winter day had long since faded into night and all the household was preparing for bed.

When the meal had been finished and the last of the dishes cleared away, Behule and Kiriti rose, ready to accompany Ananda behind her screens to start changing her out of her day clothes, as was usual.

Instead of rising immediately, however, Ananda touched Behule's hand. "Run now and see if you can find out whether the emperor has retired or not. If he has not, bring me news of where he is."

Behule reverenced and hurried away. Sruta took Behule's place with Ananda behind the screens, and she and Kiriti got Ananda out of her visiting clothes and into a nightgown lined in fur and trimmed in silver with a pair of matching slippers.

By that time, Behule had returned. Reverencing before Ananda, she said. "The emperor has not been put to bed yet. He is in the Portrait Hall with only three of his men."

Ananda touched Behule's shoulder gratefully. "A robe, Kiriti, and a light."

Kiriti threw a thick robe of dark green velvet over Ananda's shoulders and tied the woven belt around her waist while Behule fetched a candle. But when they tried to accompany her out the door, Ananda waved them back.

"This is my errand," she said before they could protest.

There were times when the palace Vyshtavos felt as if it went on for miles. Holding her candle low and to the side, so it left her face in shadow, Ananda padded through the galleries, the reception chambers, past the rooms for music, for sunning, for reading, for sewing, for taking counsel, for drinking wine before meals and for nibbling dainties after meals. Servants whose masters had not yet permitted them to seek their beds passed her once or twice, but none stopped to bow. They assumed that the lone figure was another like themselves, up late and running for a cup of tea or another blanket, or whatever it was the noble ones wanted.

The Portrait Hall was just that—a hall that angled itself to make the northwest wall of the courtyard—and instead of tapestries had been hung with portraits of great ancestors and famous battleplaces. Ananda had spent hours diligently learning the history of each of the paintings in their gilded frames, back when she thought she might still be able to please the dowager.

Mikkel stood in front of the central fireplace, staring into the flames as if they held the whole world for him. Three of his servants sprawled behind him in overstuffed chairs. One took a swig from a clay crock and passed it on to his fellows. Engaged in their drinking, they did not see the small gleam of her candle, which she quickly snuffed out.

"Perhaps the emperor should take a step closer to the fire," said one servant.

"Perhaps he should, he looks cold." The man lifted his voice. "Emperor, take a step closer to the fire."

Mikkel, unhesitating, did.

"Nah, nah," said the one who currently held the crock. "He'll get a spark on his fine velvets, and then where would we be? Waiting on imperial toast is where. Emperor, take a step back."

Mikkel did as he was told.

"I want to see—" began one.

"How dare you!" thundered Ananda.

All three of them shot to their feet. One dropped the crock, spilling clear liquor all across the stone floor. Ananda strode down the gallery as fast as she could without breaking into a run. "Is this how you treat your master imperial? Is this how you serve the dowager and your realm?" she demanded, anger nearly choking her by the time she reached them.

"Mistress Imperial." They all reverenced shakily. The boldest of the trio spoke up. "How come you here alone, mistress? You should be—"

"You dare to tell me where I should be?" shouted Ananda. "You should be hanging over a fire with weights around your ankles for what I have seen! Get out of my sight! Go!"

That sent them off in a mad scramble for the nearest door. Trembling with fury, Ananda turned to Mikkel. Despite all the commotion, he had not turned once from his contemplation of the flames. Ananda laid her trembling hands on his shoulders and turned him gently around. His sapphire eyes blinked at her, unknowing and unconcerned.

"They will not return, my love," she whispered. "I'll find some way to tell the dowager. They . . ."

"Ananda?" whispered Mikkel.

Ananda seized his hand. "Yes, yes. Ananda. Mikkel, do you know me?"

His eyes searched her face for a moment, but then they wandered away, looking at the portraits, at the fire, at the reflections on the polished wooden panels. "I thought I . . . It might be." His hand did not move in hers.

"I am here to help you, my love. Bear with me just this little while." She spread his fingers out against her palm. He did not resist.

Mikkel wore three rings on his fingers. Two had bands of braided silver; one was surmounted with a ruby and one with an emerald. The stones had each been etched with soaring eagles. These were the rings of the emperors. The third ring was gold and pearl. That was her gift. Her promise to him of her faithfulness and her love.

Ananda tugged the first ring free from Mikkel's limp hand. She searched his face anxiously, but saw no change. She removed the second ring, and the third.

A door slammed open. Lantern light spilled across Ananda, dazzling her eyes and making her cringe.

"What are you doing!" cried the dowager.

Ananda drew herself up tall and met Mikkel's eyes. But those eyes had not changed. They remained restless and dull. All Ananda's hope fell away and confusion swept through her. How could the dowager be here already? There had been no time for the drunkards to have summoned her. She must have been waiting. She must have known what Ananda meant to do. That meant she had been told. That meant, as she had suspected, there was a spy among her servants that Ananda had not yet caught. Ananda felt no joy at being once again proved right.

That also meant the dowager had stood there and let those three drunken wastrels make a puppet of her son.

The realization sent Ananda reeling against a stone column. *Every day, I believe I have seen the worst. Every day I believe she can do no more than she has done. Ah, Mothers! How often will you prove your too proud daughter wrong?*

The dowager stayed where she was, trembling, though from what emotion Ananda could not guess. "It is not enough," the old woman's voice cracked, "that you steal his soul from him, you must rob his body as well." Candlelight sparkled against tears streaming down the dowager's cheeks.

Ananda glanced down at the rings in her palms. The dowager's ladies stood behind their mistress, there faces stony as they stared at Ananda. They were there as witnesses, Ananda was certain, and they would speak of what they saw. So, now there would be a new tale of her iniquity to circulate. Another battle in their little war of words. She looked despairingly at Mikkel. Mikkel stood in his place, bored, indifferent.

Ananda bit down hard on her lip to keep back her own tears. She pressed the rings into Mikkel's hands. He took them without comment and looked at them without interest.

Then she turned, her anger pounding against her temples, and walked up to the dowager. She leaned close to the false, weeping, foul old woman and spoke straight into her ear.

"I will find it, you demon. I will free him."

"You will fail, little girl," murmured the dowager in return. "Your cousin could not win my realm from me, and neither shall you win it from my son!"

Ananda drew away and met the dowager's gaze. The woman's

eyes were black holes in her face, reflecting no light, no thought. They simply watched, and waited.

Ananda could do nothing but retrieve her candle and walk the long, slow way back to her rooms. Kiriti and Behule rose as she entered, but took one look at her face, and sensibly remained silent. They simply removed her robe and led her to her bed. There, behind the carved screens, the sheets and coverlets were turned down, the candle was taken away, and her hair was unbound, except for the three spell-braids. Ananda accepted their ministrations without comment. She laid herself on the bed, and her ladies smoothed the blankets over her and let the bed-curtains down.

Alone in the darkness, Ananda let her tears stream down her cheeks until, worn out from shock, sorrow and anger, she fell asleep.

Ananda dreamed, then, that she was back in the Foxwood with her grey horse running panicked beneath her while she fought to control the animal. Three small, sleek foxes streaked along beside her. Isha, obedience utterly lost to panic, reared high. Ananda fell crashing to the ground, all breath knocked out of her. Dizzy, she pushed herself to a sitting position.

Three men surrounded her. They had thin, pointed faces and shining green eyes. Two had red hair, one had grey. They were dressed in tunics and hose of fur that exactly matched the colors of their hair.

"Pretty princess," whispered the first. "Come with us."

"Come with us," repeated the second. "Let us show you our forest."

"Come with us," said the third, the grey one. "There is a green glen near here, where it is summer still. Let us show you the wonders there."

Compulsion filled her, taking hold of soul and sense. Their words caressed her skin, her heart. She climbed to her feet. She wanted to go with them. She needed to go with them. Their eyes lit fires of promise within her and pulled her forward.

A confusion of noise tumbled over her. Men and horses burst out from between the trees. Moonlight flashed on swords, men shouted, animals squealed in high-pitched terror and dark blood splashed onto snow. Ananda stood in the middle of it all, utterly stupefied, until the commotion died away and Sakra came to take her hand. She looked up at him with tears in her eyes, like a child who had lost a pretty toy.

Then the dream changed. Sakra vanished. In his place stood a fox with a long, sleek tail and eyes like beads of jade.

"They are weaker today," said the fox. "If they grow much weaker, they will die, and what will their mother do then, poor thing?"

The fox vanished, taking the dream with it. When Ananda finally awoke the next morning, she only knew that she was afraid.

Chapter Five

It had taken several hours of argument before Bridget would see the sense in letting him sail to this town called Bayfield.

Kalami faced her in the front room of the house she simply called "the keeper's quarters," and had forced himself to be patient. As she had risked herself to pull him from the water once, it was easy to see how she would have no desire to perform such feat again. "If my boat cannot journey safely as far as your mainland, it will not be able to carry us all the way to Isavalta. I must be sure of my repairs."

"You do not know the lake," she had countered. "Superior is not like an ocean. The waves can come at you from any direction. There are squalls that give no warning sign, and all of a sudden you can find yourself swamped by waves that are thirty feet high."

She had opened her mouth and stabbed her finger at him to make some other point, but Kalami had held up a hand to interrupt. "Bridget, you may be sure I shall take all the care there is. I am used to a storm-tossed sea."

She threw up her hands, astounded at his deficiencies. "What I am trying to tell you is that this is not a sea, it's a lake. There is a difference."

Kalami had smiled at her then. "As I learned the night I first came here."

"Well if you go down between here and Bayfield, I'm not going to be able to pull you out, am I?"

At first he had thought it was just concern for him that weighted her words down with all that bitterness. But, as he finally set sail between the red and green islands that Bridget named "the Apostles," he realized there was something more there.

Bridget's life had been punctuated by emergencies that had dragged her from her bed at night. More than once, it had been to stand helplessly by to witness this lake claim yet more lives. She had told him of one of these accidents, one night when he had accompanied her into the cramped room at the top of her house's tower to watch with fascination while she lit the great lamp. She spoke of watching a ship founder, run aground on the shoals and battered by the random swell of the waves, and her horror as she realized that not even her father could do anything but stand in the rain and pray. She had not looked at Kalami at all as she told her tale, or for a long time afterward. She had just watched the beam of her light playing over the waters.

But despite all Bridget's warnings, and her insistence on going over the chart with him five separate times, the lake of which she was so wary remained calm. The danger came as he neared Bayfield and its busy quay. His borrowed memories told him something of steamships, but he was not prepared for the size and number of them, or for the sight of the metal sides rising so high over his tiny craft. He felt like a minnow trying to work its way through a school of whales.

But in the end he did find a slip at the pier to which he could tie up and he was able to make his way down the dock to the harbormaster's office to pay his fee with the money Bridget had counted out for him. It was there he saw that his world and Bridget's were not so different after all. He recognized the kind of men who lounged about the wooden building—men in thick coats and mended trousers with caps of cloth or knitted wool on their heads. The style of their clothing was strange, but their weather-roughened faces and their thick hands were infinitely familiar, as was the rise and fall of their voices, arguing about events of local import, the business of ships, and the likely turns of the weather as predicted by the frigid wind that blew across the lake. Also familiar was the powerful smell of fish and human sweat that rose from the gathering.

Kalami had lived his boyhood among such men as these on the

island of Tuukos. That was, before his father had signed himself and Kalami into service with the Isavaltan lord master. To be sure, there they ate better, but what little freedom they had possessed was forever given away.

"Mornin', boys," said Kalami genially in Dan Forsythe's voice as he passed. "Fine day."

"Fer now," allowed one elder fisherman as he turned his head to spit in the dirt.

A few of the younger men rolled their eyes and poked each other with their elbows. Evidently, this was the anticipated response.

They went back to their own conversation immediately as Kalami stepped up to the harbormaster's window and laid down the coins Bridget had given him on a small ledge. They were then collected by a young man in a white shirt adorned with black bands to gather up the sleeves. The young man made a few notations on a piece of paper and handed that back to Kalami, who tucked it into his pocket.

"Thanks." He gave the young man a wave as he turned away.

"Where you in from?" asked one of the younger of the loungers. He had an enormously long neck. A good three inches of it protruded above the high collar of his deep blue coat. His ears stuck out on either side of his head as if to balance it on its precarious perch.

"Run in from Sand Island." Kalami stuck his hands in his coat pockets, which seemed to be the thing to do here if you were not whittling, or tossing a knife into the dirt, or fiddling with a clay pipe or a bit of fishing line.

The men considered this for a bit. Then one stout follow with a face as brown as the frozen dirt under their boots removed his grimy pipe from his mouth, took a clasp knife from his pocket and began to gouge the one into the other. "Don't know you from Eastbay."

"Ain't been there." Kalami leaned one shoulder against the harbormaster's building, to assume an appropriate posture of leisure. "I'm stopping up at the lighthouse for a piece."

"The lighthouse?" Long Neck popped his pale brown eyes out. "You mean you actually got something out of that frigid old biddy?"

"Not that he'd be the first," added the hatchet-faced man with the black cap pulled down over his sandy red hair. In case no one got the jest, he dug an elbow into Long Neck's ribs.

"Jealous?" asked the Elder with the Pipe as he replaced his knife into his pocket and his pipe into his mouth.

"Nah," said Hatchet Face. "He's just mad because she didn't believe him when he said his prick was as long as his neck." He chortled. "Offered to prove it too, from what I hear."

There was general laughter at this, but a shrill voice cut them all short.

"That's enough out of you, Jack Chappel." A fishwife with her heavy skirts tucked up into the band of her apron stood on the dock with one fist planted on her stout hip and the other clutching her broom. "And the rest of you. I won't be hearin' any more of it."

"Now then, Mrs. Tucker," said Elder Pipe Smoker sagely. "It's just the young lads."

"It's just the young lads who need a clout on the ear so they know to mind their manners." She shook the broom at them, as if to put this observation into practice. "And you!" She marched up to Kalami so that she could poke him in the chest with one dirty finger. "What do you have to say about it?"

Kalami pushed himself away from the wall and met her furious gaze steadily. "Ma'am, I say Miss Bridget is a fine lady. She pulled me out of the drink when I might have drowned and give me someplace to stay while I fix my boat."

"Good. Good." The fishwife nodded with satisfaction and stepped back as if he now rated the respect of some room to stand. "Maybe you can teach something to these young skunks." For good measure, she spat at the feet of Jack Chappel and Long Neck before she shouldered her broom and stalked off.

It was only when she was out of earshot that the rueful chuckles and the shaking of heads started.

"Pay her no mind," said Elder Pipe Smoker. "I suppose she's got a right. Bridget Lederle saved her boy."

"Plenty others in town could say the same," remarked a little man with bright black eyes who had not spoken before. "The lake's the very devil, and the islands only make it worse. Could maybe use a few more like her out there."

There were thoughtful nods all around this, except from Jack Chappel, who looked like he wanted to make another salacious remark, but his friend, Long Neck, helpfully kicked him in the ankle and he seemed to decide it was time to keep quiet.

When the oldest man shifted his pipe from one side of his mouth to the other and sucked contemplatively and noisily on the stem, Kalami judged the silence had run its course.

"As it happens"—Kalami scratched the back of his head—"I'm on an errand for Miss Bridget." He tucked his hand back in his pocket and jerked his chin inland. "Any of you can tell me where I can find Grace Loftfield?"

"Gypsy Grace?" Elder Pipe Smoker lifted his eyebrows in surprise. "Those two ain't spoken in . . ." He removed his pipe from his mouth and squinted into the bowl. "Them two just ain't spoken."

"I wouldn't know about that." Kalami shrugged. "I just know I've got a message to deliver."

The keen look Elder Pipe Smoker gave him said that the man was eager to know what that message might be, but apparently there were limits to the rudeness he himself would commit.

He pointed his pipe stem up the broad street that ran straight inland rather than heading off up the looming bluff.

"That's Rittenhouse. You take that to Second Street. You're looking for the pharmacy. She's up above that. Can't miss the sign."

"Maybe he figures to have better luck there," suggested Long Neck, and the group laughed again. Flashing them a grin to let them know he appreciated their wit, Kalami left them to their guesses and their gossip.

Except for the fact that Second Street was the third turning along the way, Kalami had little trouble finding the place that was meant. The pharmacy was familiar to both Samuel Hansen and Dan Forsythe. Kalami could not read the letters on the remarkably clear glass window, but through their eyes he recognized the two bottles, one of red liquid, and one of green, that stood on display amid an amazing array of jars and bottles of colored, clear and cut glass. Despite himself, Kalami took a moment to marvel. Never had he seen so much glass in his life, except for the decorations of the holy days at the imperial palace, and those were the work of a hundred years.

More windows looked out of the stone building's second story. Kalami squinted up at them and saw in one a white card dominated by a complex drawing of a human hand. That, surely, was the sign Elder Pipe Smoker told him he could not miss.

He marked the window and found a narrow door with yet another window in it, which showed a battered wooden staircase leading up. Twisting the knob let him in and he climbed the dark stairway into a paneled hall with a single strip of worn carpet running down the center of it.

As he observed was the polite custom, Kalami took off the cap Bridget had loaned him and knocked on the first scarred and pitted door on the left.

"You may enter," said a woman's voice from the other side.

Hat in hand, Kalami did as he was instructed.

The room on the other side of the door was as different a place from Bridget's house as he could have imagined. Bridget lived in a sparse comfort, with plain painted walls around her. This place was crammed with pillows, carpets and heavy furniture. Equally heavy shelves had been stuffed with a dizzying array of figurines and oddments, some of which he could not identify even with the aid of his borrowed memories. The walls were covered with elaborate charts delineating features of hands, heads and eyes. Between these hung images of stiff, staring people rendered in grey and white, all of whom looked grim and surprised. The artist who was responsible for these evidently had not had much sense of cheer about his life.

Grace Loftfield seemed an afterthought in her own room. It was easy to see her relationship to Bridget. He had no idea of her height. She was seated behind a tapestry-covered table dominated by some great round thing draped with a length of fringed red lace. She did, however, own Bridget's sturdy bones, wide eyes and blunt nose. Her hair was more fair than Bridget's, but even in the dim light that filtered through the heavy curtains, he could see they shared the same pale skin.

"Good mornin', ma'am," he said in Dan Forsythe's best manner. "I'm—"

But Grace Loftfield did not let him finish. "I know who you are." The words were thick with anger.

"You do?" Kalami made himself twist his cap in his hands. " 'Cause . . ."

The woman rose slowly and Kalami saw that she was even smaller than Bridget, more round and less strong, but as she stalked around her table, Kalami also saw a long wooden club clutched in her hand.

"Get out of here," she grated.

"But Miss Bridget told me—"

"Pah!" She did not actually spit, but the sound was the same. "You're a skilled liar, sir, but I've seen you." Her finger shook as she pointed at him. "You're one of them. One of the ones who took my sister away."

"Perhaps you do know me," said Kalami in his own voice. "But the one who took your sister is long dead."

This statement did nothing to drain the livid anger from Grace Loftfield's face. "As is my sister. You go, back to wherever you came from." Now the accusing finger pointed toward the window as if she expected him to jump, or fly away. "You leave me and my niece alone."

Slowly, without taking his eyes off her, Kalami shook his head. "I cannot."

He noted how her fist tightened around the handle of her club. "You will not."

"I cannot," he repeated, firmly. "She is needed."

"I told you to go!" she screeched, her whole face twisting with the strength of her anger and fear.

"I cannot do that either, for I need you as well."

Which was too much for her. She swung the club for his skull and Kalami ducked, falling onto her overstuffed sofa. She brought the club down again, but he rolled sideways. She'd swung too hard and overbalanced, toppling forward and catching herself with one hand on the sofa cushions. Before she could recover, Kalami grabbed the club, wrenching her around and trying to rip it away from her. She stomped hard on his foot, but her shoes were light and his boots were strong. He yanked the club out of her hands and they stood facing each other, both panting for breath.

"Will you sit?" inquired Kalami, gesturing toward her chair with his empty hand. "We have much to say to each other."

Her eyes flickered to the door, and then to the window. Her face clearly said she was contemplating that perilous exit and Kalami tensed in preparation. But she read his movement as clearly as he had read hers, and instead returned to her own chair and sat.

"Thank you." Without looking away, Kalami cleared some of the pillows from the sofa and sat himself on its edge, laying the club across his knees. "Now, mistress, your niece tells me you are what is here called a medium."

"What is that to you, sir?" She smoothed back the several locks of hair that had become disordered in the struggle.

"I have need of such skill."

One corner of her mouth turned up in a thin smile of triumph. "Well, you are to be disappointed. I am a professional medium only. My séances are a sham. I am rather surprised my niece neglected to point that out to you, but I can display their works for you, if you like."

"This also your niece tells me." He paused to make sure she was fully attentive. "I believe she's wrong."

Grace struggled with herself for a moment, her strong rounded jaw working back and forth, as if her mouth were trying to decide what to say. She wanted, Kalami saw, to acknowledge the reality of her abilities, but she did not wish to acknowledge her lie.

"I would be most willing to pay for your services," said Kalami softly.

Her eyes narrowed. He had read it right then. The luxuries around her were threadbare, and the dimness of the place was due not only to what Bridget described as a "theatrical air of mystery," but to the fact that this woman could not afford much in the way of lamps or candles.

Her face twitched again, betraying yet another internal struggle. "How much?" The words came out reluctantly, but they came.

As a sign of good faith, Kalami laid the club aside, although admittedly it was on the side away from Grace and still within his reach. "I would pay in kind," he told her. "I have skills of my own. Surely, there is something you want that you lack the ordinary means to obtain."

She looked away at that, biting down on her lower lip. Kalami let her think about it. As in all things, a willing participant was so much more to be trusted than someone who had to be coerced.

Kalami watched Grace rub one hand back and forth on the arm of her chair. There was too much flesh on that hand, and it was beginning to sag into the wrinkles of old age. He leaned forward. "You know I can do as I say. You've seen it, haven't you?"

She still said nothing, but her hand rubbed the chair arm even harder, as if she were attempting to scrape something off her palm.

Slowly, Kalami stood. He circled the tiny table and crouched beside her chair. "You are worried about your niece because you have a good heart." He touched her hand, stilling its restless motion. "You know she is an outcast here, without friends, and, through no fault of her own, without family. I am trying to help her. I mean to take her to someplace where she will be honored for who she is, not despised."

He lifted her hand, pressing it between both his own. "But I need your help before I can give my help to Bridget."

His words almost reached her. Her face softened, and she made no move to pull her hand away. But she had one final defense to be breached. "The last one of you to come here took my sister from me."

"No, Grace," said Kalami gently. "Childbirth took your sister from you. It could have happened on any shore, in any world. It is not a charge you can lay against us."

She gazed down at him with hard eyes, and he held himself still, his head tilted up to meet her gaze. He could see clearly that she was balancing her spirit's scales with all the care and precision of someone who had made many a hard choice in her life. For a moment, she looked very like the dowager empress.

Then, she did pull her hand away, laying it on her lap and covering it with the other. "Very well. What do you need from me?"

Kalami stood. He hoped that she would take the light in his eyes and the smile on his face as gratitude rather than relief. He was fairly certain that he could have compelled her if need be, but he was not certain that afterward he would have the strength to reach through her conduit to his own world.

Kalami pulled his leather bag from out of his shirt and from it he took a jade ring carved in the shape of a dragon lying across its own tail. "I need for you to find me the one who owns this."

She took the ring and held it up to see how the light slipped across the jade's polished surfaces. She turned it over, examining the carving as if she meant to appraise the thing for its worth.

"I will need quiet," she said, closing her fist around the ring.

Kalami nodded and pulled up one of the slick horsehair chairs so that he might sit across the table from her.

Grace pulled the red lace covering from the object occupying the center of her table, revealing a sphere of translucent blue glass. "You also have eyes that see," she said as she rolled the lace into a bundle and set it aside. "There may be something shown here to you."

Again, Kalami nodded, becoming fascinated almost against his will. What would the woman do? This place was so different from all that he knew. Bridget's visions came to her unbidden and unaided. How would Grace ensure her will was worked?

"Give me your hand," she said, extending her own.

Kalami held out his hand for her to clasp. Her palm was soft and dry, but there were calluses on her fingertips indicating that she had indeed done some work in her life. For a while, all she did was stare at her glass, holding Kalami's hand to one side of the sphere, and the hand that clutched the ring to the other. Nothing happened. Kalami resisted the urge to shift his weight or to ask any questions. She had power and she knew how to make use of it, of this there was no question. He needed to be patient.

Even as he thought this, he felt the air grow cold around them. A draft curled around his ankles and fluttered the lace curtain behind Grace. Then, Grace leaned forward, her eyes widening. Kalami peered into the depths of the blue glass, but he saw nothing beyond the distorted reflection of the room.

"See . . ." Grace lifted his hand and pressed it flat against the sphere's smooth surface. "See there is a man. He walks along a corridor made of all colors of wood fitted close. His clothes are silk and shimmer with so many colors I cannot name them all. It took someone years to make that robe. It is his, but it is not his. Many have worn it before him, and will wear it after, and yet it makes him what he is. See!" Her own hand pressed against the sphere, and the other gripped the ring so tightly that her knuckles grew white. Kalami felt unexpected wonder take hold of him. With no weaving, with no chant or seeming work, this woman herself could see across the worlds. In this place where power was so hard for a stranger to grasp, it bestowed itself lavishly upon its children. What had touched this family that left such gifts behind?

Eagerness brightened Grace's eyes and face as she stared at the distant scene playing itself out before her eyes. "His skin is covered in tattoos, in as many colors as his robe. All the winds of the world are drawn on his face and his arms are covered in the images of dragons. These to make him what he is and mask who he used to be. He is old, old, but there are those he goes to meet who are older yet, but the oldest of them is missing. He is in a cage far away. No, not him, what he has become." Confusion furrowed her brow as she struggled with that idea.

Kalami swallowed. He could not allow her to become distracted, nor could he let this conduit be broken. "He is the Minister of the Air. Can you speak to him?"

Grace did not seem to hear him. All her attention remained fastened on her sphere. "He turns. He lifts his head. He knows he is observed. He raises his hand. So many colors on that hand. The dragons and the wind twirl together as he moves his hand. They swirl and pull. They call, they call . . ."

Grace slumped forward, her jaw hanging slack and her eyes closed. Then, all at once, she jerked upright as if someone had pulled her hard by the hair. Her whole body went rigid, and her eyes were wild and her mouth pulled back tight against her teeth.

"Who are you?" Grace's mouth opened and closed like a puppet's. Her lips shaped no words but remained drawn back in their death head's grimace, and yet a familiar voice issued from her. Not her own, but the deep, mild voice of Taun Chi-Thanh, the Minister of the Air and one of the Nine Elders of Hung-Tse.

Kalami forced himself to remain relaxed. He did not wish Chi-Thanh to know that anything remarkable occurred here. "I am Valin Kalami, Eternal Chi-Thanh."

"You have not the touch of Valin Kalami." Chi-Thanh did not sound upset, merely curious.

"I am aided by an intermediary for I must speak to you from further away than is usual."

Grace's head flicked sideways in a mockery of the way Chi-Thanh cocked his head when he was considering something. "Interesting. You will then forgive me if I ask for proof of your assertion."

Which was Kalami's proof that Grace had in truth reached the Minister of Air. "Eternal Chi-Thanh, I would be most disappointed in you if you did not. You have found the voice of my intermediary. Can you find her eyes?"

Grace's head jerked upright again and her teeth clacked a few times as her jaw was opened and closed by Chi-Thanh's distant will. Her green eyes seemed to flash with awareness for a moment; then, slowly, as if she were about to faint, they rolled upward until the irises disappeared and all Kalami could see were the whites.

"I see you, Valin Kalami." Grace's chin tipped up and he saw her tongue lolling between her teeth. "You are very far from your home."

It took Kalami a minute to be certain that his voice would remain under his control. Grace's complete abandonment of herself turned his stomach uncomfortably. "I am on an errand for the dowager empress."

Grace's jaw dropped to let out Chi-Thanh's long sigh. "Ah. Your last missive indicated that this errand would not be long in coming."

"Nor long in completion," Kalami told him. "I have found what the dowager seeks."

"And have you determined how much of a danger it is to our plans?"

Kalami nodded. "It is powerful, but it is untrained, and has been left without knowledge of its true lineage. I can control for several months what it hears and understands as it will not speak the language, or understand Isavaltan ways for some time. By then, it will have been guided to the proper understanding of what is happening."

Grace's body leaned forward, the whites of her eyes glittering in the faint flight. "As beneficial as that would surely be, surely it would be better if it never arrived in Isavalta."

"Eternal Chi-Thanh," said Kalami, putting all the humility he could manage into the title. "You must see that without its power, I will not be able to keep the Heart of the World safe while your emperor redresses his grievances with Isavalta."

"You forget that what the dowager holds is a protector to Hung-Tse." Grace's head swung back and forth, signaling Chi-Thanh's negation. "We are in no danger from it."

"Are you certain?" Kalami drew the question out, giving Chi-Thanh time to consider it carefully. "She found a way to cage it. Are you certain she did not in the meantime find a way to distort it?"

For the first time, anger touched Chi-Thanh's voice. "You speak of one of the great powers of the world. Do you suggest that so tiny a figure as your dowager could alter its nature?"

It occurred Kalami than that Chi-Thanh must be tired. Almost thirty years ago, the Nine Elders, the most powerful sorcerers in the world, had worked a mighty spell only to see it fail utterly. If that was not humiliation enough, they then found their ancient empire held hostage to the word of one who was then little more than a girl. How many hours had he spent in study, seeking a way to reverse what had happened? How many hours had the Nine spent in debate, trying to convince themselves that the very worst could not possibly have happened?

Kalami chose his words with care. "I ask are you so sure of what it is? It is one of the great powers, yes, but it is also a bird in a cage, and it also may be a frightened old man. You yourself are many things, surely you understand this."

That had always been the threat. The dowager was ruthless in pursuit of the security of her domain. It was very possible that she would ignore her own safety and all mortal levels of prudence to guard her borders.

Grace's head swiveled abruptly left, then right. "When?" The snap of her teeth clipped off the word.

Inside himself, Kalami smiled. "Before spring. When the snow melts and the bays thaw, you and your emperor will be well placed to begin the redress of which we spoke."

"I shall inform those who need to know."

"And I shall send fresh news as I may."

Grace's head jerked up and down, a gesture Kalami took as Chi-Thanh's nod of assent. He wondered briefly if Grace also was tired, and if this contortion hurt her. Even so, he could not let her go quite yet. There remained a few last questions. "Eternal Chi-Thanh, may I ask after the health of my daughter?"

Grace's grimace tightened, which might have been a smile of approval from Chi-Thanh. It was very hard to tell. "She thrives and excels at her studies. Her abilities with the stars and planets and all manner of omens are astonishing for such a small child."

And she will excel at much more before she is grown. "Will you, of your courtesy, tell her that you and I have spoken? That I tender her my affection and remind her to remain a good child and obedient to her teachers and protectors?"

"It will be my honor to deliver such a message." Grace's whole body tipped forward, stiff-spined. "I shall await your next communication."

Kalami had no time to catch Grace before she slammed against the table, all her puppet strings cut. The sudden, sour stink of urine told Kalami she had lost control of more than one function.

Swallowing a mild disgust, Kalami scooped Grace up in his arms and carried her past the lace curtain. As he suspected, back here waited the more mundane furnishings of everyday living. He laid her on the battered brass-framed bed and spread a knitted coverlet over her. Gently, he pried open her mouth to make sure that she had not bitten her tongue and plumped the pillows behind her head so that she would not swallow it.

The shelf above the porcelain washbasin was crammed with bottles and boxes of various shapes. One square vessel of clear glass looked familiar to his Dan Forsythe memories. He pulled out the stopper, sniffed the amber liquid and smelled strong spirits. Returning to Grace, he trickled a thin stream of the stuff down her throat until she coughed, swallowed, and opened her eyes.

"Thank you." Kalami stepped back to give her room to push herself into a sitting position. From the grimace and the coloring of her face, she felt the dampness of her own garments and probably wished him swiftly gone. But, he would not, even here, leave a promise unfulfilled to a power. That way lay too many dangers.

Grace was rubbing first her temple, then her throat. "I remember nothing," she said, talking at the coverlet over her lap. "I trust you achieved the results you wished for?"

"I did. I also promised you payment for your services. You may name your price now."

Grace watched her blunt fingers picking at the striped coverlet, pulling tiny bits of fluff from first a pink stripe, then a red, then the pink again.

"Just . . . take care of Bridget. Promise me that you will keep her safe." She lifted her eyes and Kalami saw the first glimmerings of tears. "She has had no one to keep her safe since her father died."

And you feel all the guilt of that, but it was never enough to make you aid your own flesh and blood. "I will give her all the protection I can and keep her as safe as she permits me to do. I swear it on the bones and the names of my family."

"I suppose that'll have to do, as stubborn as Bridget is." Grace turned her face toward the wall and her fingers knotted themselves into the coverlet. "You had better go now."

Kalami left her there and went to retrieve Chi-Thanh's ring from where it lay on the table. As he closed the door to the hallway behind him, he cut off the sound of the woman weeping for her own weakness. It did not matter. All the messages were delivered, and all the promises were given. The game was in play and would soon be finished. All that remained was to place Bridget as the final piece on the board.

He strode down the street, heading for the quay to take his boat and sail back to Sand Island. He did not look up to see the crow watching him from the branches of the naked oak tree.

Chapter Six

The hay barn at Sparavatan was not the most dignified place in which to bed down, but it had been stoutly built, which meant that it was dry, and it was warm. All the members of the Temir masquing troupe, even the newcomer, who had paid handsomely to be allowed to join, had at one time or another slept in much rougher, colder beds, and that in homes as ancient and as noble as this. So, none of them had complained when Lord Master Hraban's steward showed them where to stow their packs, their mules, their sledges and themselves until the morning.

The scents of hay, warm animals and warm humans made the night air heavy. The mice crept about their business, undisturbed by the visitors who had made their nests in the fodder and were now all of them sound asleep. One cunning old rat peered at the scene from the corner, as of yet unaware of the grey cat that watched it from the shelter of the rooftree.

The only witness to the small drama was an old black crow perched on the barn's stout center beam. It ruffled its feathers slightly as one of the masquers rolled over in his bed of hay. He was darker than the others, his hair bound into a hundred different braids. The crow knew Sakra well, by the look of him and the rhythms of his breath and heart. It had followed that rhythm across the world, for it had news for him.

Below, the rat had evidently decided the better of crossing the barn floor and retreated through its hole. The cat twitched its whiskers and padded after it. One of the masquers snorted, slurped and dug down further into the hay.

The crow spread its wings, and dropped softly from the beam to land on the canvas satchel Sakra used as a pillow. It looked at him, first from one eye, then the other, as if making sure he was truly asleep.

Satisfied, the bird reached its shiny black beak into his ear. When it drew its head back, the crow held a grey piece of fluff in its beak, like a wisp of cloud or uncombed bit of wool. Gripping this piece of Sakra carefully, the crow flew away, minding neither roof nor wall, until it vanished into the winter darkness.

"I will be closing the light on the ninth. After that date, I ask that you draw a check on the balance of my remaining funds payable to Mrs. Iduna Hansen and have it sent to her at this address." Bridget pushed the paper across Mr. Shwartz's desk. Outside the little office, the bank's daily business went on with muted efficiency, and with only the occasional curious glance from a passing clerk directed toward them through the open door.

"I am sorry you are closing your account with us, Miss Lederle." Mr. Shwartz was a thin man whom time had left completely bald. As if to make up for this, he had cultivated an enormous walrus mustache that completely covered his mouth. "We were always pleased to take care of business for you, as we did for your father." He met her eyes briefly before directing his attention to his desk pad in order to note down her instructions.

"Thank you," Bridget replied. "But I have decided to take a new position down in Madison. As soon as I am settled, I will be writing with a forwarding address, in case there are any details remaining." She had rehearsed the lie all the way out from the island, but she was still startled at how naturally it flowed from her lips.

Perhaps that's because it is so much more believable than the truth.

"I believe that will be all, Mr. Shwartz." Bridget stood, gathering up the notes and coins that would keep her financed.

"I shall look out for your letter, then." Mr. Shwartz also stood and held out his hand. "I wish you the very best of luck in Madison, Miss Lederle."

"Thank you." Bridget took his hand and released it quickly without looking at his eyes. She had not wanted kindness today, not when she had come to town to lie to as many people as necessary so that she could set her affairs in order and take her final leave of them all.

Outside, the frigid air was punctuated by unkind blasts of wind from off the lake. Winter had decidedly moved in for the year, even though, as of yet, there had not been much snow. Only the lightest dusting of powder lay on the cobbles, and the sky overhead was a frozen blue quite clear of clouds.

She had been of two minds about making a close to her affairs in Bayfield. The façade would, after all, last only until Francis Bluchard arrived at Lighthouse Point with his tug on the ninth to find the light shut down and Bridget gone. Then there would be talk. Oh, heavens, there would be talk for nine and ninety days.

The money was in part for the inconvenience that talk would cause Mrs. Hansen. Bridget sincerely hoped the bank would not make trouble about getting it to her. Mr. Shwartz was a good man, and had never shown the least reluctance to deal with Bridget. Surely he would see this request was honored.

Which meant there were only two errands left that Bridget needed to see to.

Rittenhouse Avenue was as crowded as usual. Pedestrians and drivers alike had muffled themselves against the cold. Despite her woolen stockings, worsted mittens and two shawls, Bridget had to walk briskly to keep even a little bit warm. She told herself that was what made her hurry past Second Street and the pharmacy. It was not because she was afraid to meet Aunt Grace and hear of her "prediction" again. It was also most surely not because she had second thoughts about what she was about to do.

Bridget found herself wishing she had asked Kalami, Valin, to come with her. She reminded herself that they were now on a first-name basis, a situation Bridget was still not entirely comfortable with.

It was, however, the only way she could get him to stop calling her "mistress." He had confessed himself equally uncomfortable with the designation "mister," and Bridget was not going to call him by his professed title of "Lord Sorcerer" when Mrs. Hansen and Samuel might hear. So, this was the compromise.

When he was with her, describing the place from which he came and telling her its legends and history, the proposed journey seemed as natural as taking the train to Madison or Chicago. But alone on the streets of Bayfield with the ordinary bustle and clatter of life around her punctuated by the church bells tolling the hour, it was ridiculous. Even the vision she had seen in Momma's mirror seemed more likely to be a waking dream brought on by exhaustion. Surely the whole notion was nothing more than the airy fantasies of a frustrated, embittered old maid whose own regrets had finally turned her head.

Bridget set her jaw and kept walking.

As she passed Christ Episcopal, Bridget paused. The walk had been freshly swept of the sprinkling of snow. She decided to take this as a sign that Mr. Simons might be inside, which, if true, would spare her the trial of meeting Mrs. Simons.

Bridget turned up the walk and tugged on the handle of the sanctuary door. The door came open at once, letting out the sound of two soft voices, one of which belonged to Mr. Simons.

Bridget pulled back immediately, but it was too late. Mr. Simons had already turned his head and seen her. He instantly rose from the pew where he'd been sitting in close conversation with a sturdy, pale-haired woman. Bridget started, afraid she was seeing Aunt Grace. Then the woman also turned, and Bridget saw the broad nose and triple chin of Mrs. Neilsen, the widow who ran the boardinghouse where Bridget stayed each winter.

"I'm sorry," said Bridget, beginning to back up and pull the door closed.

"No, no, Miss Lederle," said Mr. Simons hastily. "This is most fortuitous. Won't you please join us?" He gestured to the next pew.

Bridget could not help frowning, but she did as she was bidden, and entered the tidy blue-painted sanctuary, pulling off her gloves and unwrapping one of her shawls as she did. The rows of wooden pews and the carved choir screen, she noted, were kept as carefully clean and polished as the gilded altar under its three little stained-glass windows. But for the cold, it remained the welcoming place it always had been.

"Bridget, my dear." Mrs. Neilsen got to her feet with a soft "oof," and moved forward to take both Bridget's hands. "I'm so glad you're here. I've been having a little talk with Mr. Simons about you."

"You have?" Any sense of welcome Bridget might have felt melted away at those words. She perched on the edge of the pew, ready to rise at a moment's notice. Mrs. Neilsen let go of only one of her hands, and sat next to her.

"Mrs. Neilsen has been expressing a grave concern, and was not sure how to best approach the matter . . ." said Mr. Simons, reseating himself.

Bridget felt her lips press themselves together in a thin line. She pulled her hand away from Mrs. Neilsen's. "What matter might that be?"

"Now, then, Bridget, it's no good you getting your back up," Mrs. Neilsen said flatly, folding her arms. "You are planning on leaving town with that man up at the lighthouse, and you cannot blame me for being concerned."

Bridget, however, had no patience for a lecture. "If you are concerned about things which are none of your business—"

"Fiddlesticks." Mrs. Neilsen cut her off. "You've stayed with me for seven winters running. I knew your mother. I've seen how it is for you and I am worried." She tapped a finger against Bridget's knee. "You're a good girl and there's many in town who are beholden to you for the work you've done, even if some of them don't care to admit it." She dismissed the entire town with a wave. "I cannot sit by and watch you"—this time the poke at Bridget's knee was severe enough to jar, even through her flannel petticoat—"make a dreadful mistake because you're too stiff-necked to forgive those who have wronged you."

Bridget felt her cheeks burn. Was that truly what she was doing? No. It could not be.

"I am going to Madison, Mrs. Neilsen," she said. "I have a new post. That is all."

"Then you are not going with Mr. Forsythe?" asked Mr. Simons, quietly.

"Whether I am or not is my own concern." Bridget lifted her chin and directed her hard gaze toward the priest to let him know she did not welcome any further questions.

Mr. Simons, however, was not to be deterred. He clasped his hands together in his lap. "Miss Lederle, please. We have been friends, you and I, and you know I only wish to help." His face took on its familiar, honest earnestness and Bridget felt her throat tighten. She did not want to stay here. She did not want to hear this. She most especially did not want to have to lie anymore to this man who had been so consistently kind to her. "I agree, Mr. Forsythe seems a good sort of man, but to travel all the way to Madison, unattended . . ."

Mrs. Neilsen evidently had no time for the priest's circuitous language. "It's not worth breaking your heart again, my girl," she announced. "And, right or wrong, it's not worth the disgrace."

Bridget stood. She could not sit and listen to this. Let them believe what they liked. The truth was impossible to tell. She should have been prepared for this. She should have realized it would happen.

Bridget dug into her pocketbook and brought out a tiny roll of notes.

"Mr. Simons, this is my donation to the church." She held it out. "It's not much, but I wanted to thank you for your many kindnesses, and I was hoping you might see to it that my parents and my . . . that my family's graves are kept clean."

Mr. Simons regarded her, his eyes sad in his kind, horsy face. "Please, Miss Lederle, listen to Mrs. Neilsen. All your future happiness may be at stake."

"Think carefully, Bridget," urged Mrs. Neilsen.

"I have heard every word you both have said," she answered. "Mr. Simons, will you do as I ask?"

"Yes, of course, if that's what you wish." His fingers closed around the bills. "May God go with you, Bridget."

"Thank you." The words came out in a whisper. Bridget swallowed and did not dare turn to see what expression Mrs. Neilsen wore. Instead, she all but ran from the sanctuary.

Once more in the bright winter daylight, she drew in great lungfuls of the freezing air, trying to regain her composure. *What is happening to me?* She fumbled with mittens and shawl, drawing them both back on to shut out the harshest edge of the cold.

She had been so resolved, so certain of what she was doing. Now she was shaking at the thought of returning to Sand Island where Kalam . . . where Valin waited in the keeper's quarters, finishing his painstaking repairs to his sails.

It's only nerves, she told herself, striding down the walk. She did not want to be caught by Mr. Simons or Mrs. Neilsen running from the church to try again to talk sense into her. *This is no small thing I am doing. It is perfectly natural to have second thoughts. Even if I were only going as far as Madison, such feelings would be not be at all unusual.*

None of which changed the fact that it was more than cold causing her chin to shake.

I will see this through. She clutched her shawl tightly around her shoulders. *I will.*

But the hardest task still had to be done. Bridget turned up Washington and began climbing the hill. The very last thing to do was to take leave of her dead.

If I can do this, it will be over. What I do will be my own business. There is just this one, last thing.

The earth of the cemetery had frozen until it was as hard as the granite stones. Snow made mantles for the monuments. It lay in patches at the bottom of hollows and heaped itself into miniature drifts in the lee of the headstones. Bridget tromped past all those silent stones, trying not to see them, trying not to feel the constriction in her chest.

At the edge of the yard waited her own graves under the bare trees. Frost-killed grass poked through the thin layer of snow that covered them. Bridget clamped her jaw tightly closed as she leaned forward to brush away the snow that had collected in the hollows made by the words carved on the unchanging stones. Everett Lederle. Ingrid Lederle. Anna Kyosti.

Anna. Momma. Poppa.

Understand, please understand. He's offering me life, life! And answers. There are so many questions now, I can't refuse to find the answers.

The stones made no reply.

"You will be in my heart always," she told them. "But it's time for me to make a new decision. I can't stay here another winter. I won't survive it."

Silence, except for the rattling of the twigs overhead. Tension filled Bridget, sourceless, unreasonable and inescapable.

"Momma, you came to me. You want me to go. You showed me those things. You must want me to go."

But even that declaration did not bring any relief. There was only cold and silence, the smell of winter, and the patient, sorrowful stones.

Bridget couldn't breathe. The winter cold had paralyzed her lungs, and she could only take in air in choking gasps. Her boots felt rooted to the frozen ground. She could not move, could not think, could not leave. How could she leave? What was she doing? This was her place, here with the dead. Tears spilled from her eyes and she could not even move to dry them. How could she leave?

"Stop," she whispered, to the stones and the winter wind freezing her tears on her cheeks. "Why are you doing this to me?"

"Because it is the bones that bind us most tightly."

The words made Bridget blink. That tiny movement freed her lungs to breathe and her hands to fly to her cheeks, warming the tears and the flesh beneath them.

"Who's there?" She spun, scanning the graveyard for movement, or fresh shadows.

"I am."

The voice was behind her. Bridget spun again to face the copse of trees that fenced the cemetery. A man stood there among the grey and brown winter woods. He had dark skin, and a fantastic costume of red and green silks adorned him. A huge black crow hunched on his shoulder watching Bridget with one glistening eye.

Bridget raked the stranger from head to toe with her gaze, trying to put as much iron as she could into the look. Who was this character, this clown? How dare he spy on her? How dare he . . .

Then she saw that although the winter sun shone brightly, the stranger cast no shadow across the snow. Her eyes jerked back to the man's face, and she saw he had no eyes, only dark hollows above his high cheeks.

Bridget's hand rose involuntarily to her throat. "Are you a ghost?"

The stranger considered this for a moment. "Not yet."

She frowned, suddenly more annoyed than afraid. "Then, what are you?"

That took even more consideration. The apparition's broad brow wrinkled up as he tried to find the words. "A dream," he said at last.

Bridget felt her eyebrows lift. "But I'm awake."

"But I am not."

It came to Bridget that she should still be afraid. Even by the standards of her life lately, this was a very strange thing. Fear, though, refused to return. Perhaps it was because this man, this waking dream in front of her, seemed so confused. The crow preening its pinfeathers on his shoulder seemed much more calm. Perhaps also, it was because he seemed familiar. His craggy face touched some chord of memory in her mind of something she had seen, and recently too.

Bridget shook her head. "Well, Mr. Dream, what do you want?"

"To see you," he replied simply, as if it was thc most obvious thing in the world.

"And now that you have?"

"I don't know." His brow furrowed yet more deeply. The wind blew hard then, rattling the twigs and the underbrush, yet none of his light silk clothing so much as rippled.

"I think . . ." The dream man peered closely at her, as if trying to see her through a fog, but he still had no eyes. "I think I want to ask you to stay away."

"From where?" Bridget wrapped her arms around herself. The

cold bit down on her ears and fingertips, at the same time restlessness crept over her. She suddenly wanted very much to be gone from here. "From whom?"

"From my mistress. From Isavalta."

Comprehension flared brightly inside Bridget's mind. She now knew perfectly where she had seen this face, this man. He had been shown to her in Momma's silver mirror. "Sakra. You're Sakra."

But Sakra did not seem to hear her. His mouth kept moving soundlessly and his face screwed up tight in concentration. "He uses you," she heard at last. "He will use you to death, if you let him."

Bridget shifted her weight, stamping each foot in turn to try to force some feeling back into them. It was so cold. Too cold even for this day. "If you are trying to scare me, I call this a feeble attempt." *There's more to fear from the cold than from you.* Bridget felt herself frown again. What made her so sure of that?

"No. I wish you warned, not frightened. I think . . ." Sakra's fingers grappled with nothing but air, as if seeking to pluck the right words from the ether. "I think there is good you may yet do me, but you must be warned. I am not the only one who does not want you here. I am indeed the weakest of them all."

Bridget could not think what to say. This apparition was Kalami's enemy. He was a dangerous magic worker. Yet, here he stood, as confused as a child and vague as a lost memory.

"I do not want to hear any more of this," she told him, pulling her shawls as tightly around her as she could.

"She brings the cold, she holds the bones," said the dream man, and the shadows deepened in the hollows where his eyes should have been. "She holds you too, by obligations of the blood, and wishes you to stay away so her grip on the land will not loosen."

Cold and confusion seized Bridget's mind, too painful to stand any longer. "Stop it!" she screamed. "Get away from me! Get away!" Her arm swept through the air in front of her, trying to knock the apparition sideways, but she could not touch him. All that happened was that the crow cocked its head toward her, and for one instant, Bridget felt the wild intelligence behind its black eyes. Then, it gave a harsh croaking that sound like deep laughter and spread its wings. The crow launched itself into the air, and the man was gone.

Bridget shook herself, unable to take in the suddenness of the change. Her limbs began to tremble, from cold, from shock, from too many feelings to be named.

Ludicrous. This was ludicrous. Worse, it was insane. She needed to stop this. Now. She must have been insane to agree to Valin's plan. All that had happened since . . . No. She could not go through with this. She'd go back to the bank and give Mr. Shwartz new instructions, she'd talk to Mr. Simons, she'd . . .

New movement in the trees caught her eye and Bridget scrambled backward, her heart hammering hard in her chest.

But it was only a fox, bright red against winter's grey and white. Its green eyes twinkled and its jaw dropped open, as if it laughed at her fear.

Only a fox, with bright green eyes. Summer waited in those eyes, and all the warm secrets of the woods and the wild places. Those eyes saw so much and they drank it all in. They drank so many sights and held so many memories. So many memories all drunk up like wine. Drunk, drained, gone away into the green summer woods with all the other secrets.

Then the fox sneezed.

Bridget blinked and pressed her mittened hand against her eyes. What was she doing standing here freezing herself to death? It must be getting late and she had to get back down to the quay. The tug would not wait forever to take her back.

"Good-bye," said Bridget to the stones where her family slept. "I'll keep you in my heart always."

By the time she reached the quay, Bridget did not even remember having seen the fox.

Sakra dropped hard and suddenly into wakefulness, his eyes wide open and staring about him, trying to understand where he was. There should be woods, and markers for the dead. There should be a woman with auburn hair and rough clothing. Instead, there were men yawning and scratching, splashing their faces in a water barrel, slapping themselves to restore their circulation in the chill, or pulling off their woolen shirts and shaking the hay out of them before putting them back on.

Gradually, dream separated itself from present reality. The dim, grey light of morning filled the hay barn. He had lain down here last night to continue in his role as one of the masquers, and he had dreamed . . . and he had dreamed . . .

Sakra's gaze lifted to the shadows that still clustered around the roof beam. He dreamed a crow had come to show him where Valin Kalami had gone, and that the crow had carried him across the Land of Death and Spirit to the far shore. There, it had shown him a woman with bright eyes looking on the shade of his dream-self without fear, yet without understanding.

Sakra rubbed his eyes. There was no question in his mind that the dream had been a true one, but why had the crow's stepchild chosen to show him a stranger instead of Valin Kalami?

Unless the stranger was the reason for Kalami's voyage. After all, had not help come to Medeoan from across the Silent Lands before? Had she sent her servant to find such help again?

Was it possible Kalami had found the Avanasidoch?

Before Sakra could pursue that thought any further the barn door opened a crack, letting in a blast of the icy morning air. The men cursed and shouted on all sides, and even the mules brayed in protest.

"Come you slugabeds!" roared Misha Sumilosyn Mishavin as he kicked the door shut with his heel and rubbed his hands together. "It's a beautiful morning! You should be up and about, not burrowing in the hay like pigs!"

Groans and a few choice curses rose from the troupe. Inando, first among the acrobats, splashed a handful of water from the barrel in Misha's direction. "Master Misha, if you do not tell us that the reason for your good cheer is that we get to stay here the winter, I'll throw you back to your own mother!" The popular tale among the troupe was that Misha's massive frame came from the fact that his mother was not a woman, but the dancing bear his father had led across Isavalta for a score of years.

"Then, alas, my mother must go hungry." A broad grin split Misha's beard. "Our lord master and his chief steward are most pleased with us. Beds for the winter, my lads! Beds, and three meals to fill those rapacious bellies of yours every day!"

A general cheer went up with men slapping each other on the backs and handfuls of hay tossed into the air. Sakra smiled, but to himself he wondered what Lord Master Hraban really had in mind for this troupe. Considering that the lord master was planning a rebellion, it might be that he needed messengers who were both unknown and innocuous. He wondered if Misha had already agreed to perform such services from time to time, driven by his love of money and hunger for patronage.

Not that Sakra could complain of either trait. Both had already served him well.

While the rest of the troupe were busy congratulating each other, Sakra took his turn at the water barrel, dipping his hands into the frigid water and scrubbing them across his face.

A hearty hand clapped itself across his back. "You should be especially pleased, master," announced Misha as Sakra straightened up and pasted a cheery grin across his face. "So recently begging for work, and now so snugly set up." Then his voice dropped. "Your sea captain has agreed to meet you in the stablemaster's quarters, but only if you hurry."

"My thanks, master." Sakra clasped the man's massive forearm as was the custom among the troupe. Despite the admonition to hurry, he strolled back to his bundle and casually pulled on his wide-skirted outer kaftan and fleece mittens.

"And where you off to?" asked tiny Fiviash, who played most of the mischievous spirit parts that the troupe's mummings called for.

"There's a dairymaid winked at me yesterday," replied Sakra with a wink of his own. "It might please her to know she'll have a chance to do a little more."

That brought him a sly chuckle and freedom from further explanation. Before anyone else had a chance to engage him in idle conversation, Sakra slipped out the door.

The morning outside was as cold and hard as glass. Its brightness dazzled his eyes. Serfs and servants tromped or scurried across the courtyard, hurrying in and out of the buildings' knife-edged shadows about their own business. Sakra joined the bustle, becoming just one more person wrapped against the cold trying to get back indoors as quickly as possible.

The stables were warmer than the barn and much better kept. They smelled sweet with fresh hay and straw, with only the rich odor of clean animals as an accompaniment. Sakra caught a glimpse of the stablemaster, a stout man with a frame to rival Misha's, among the polished horse boxes, directing his boys in the arts of brushing coats, cleaning stalls and arranging blankets on the precious animals. Sakra's passage caught the man's eye, but he only nodded at the sorcerer, and Sakra strode past without pause.

The stablemaster lived in constant sight of his charges. His corner of the stables boasted carpets, a good fire in a tile stove and furniture built bravely enough to accommodate such a man in comfort. Captain Nisula stood in front of the stove, contemplating something Sakra could not see, while the plump, young maid swept the floors around him, humming cheerfully, perhaps because she hoped the handsome captain would notice her, perhaps merely because it was, by the standards of this cold land, a fine morning.

Sakra moved into the shadow of a support beam and rapped his knuckles against it. Nisula lifted his head and turned toward the noise, seeing that someone was there, but not who.

"You may see to your other duties now," he said to the maid, who bobbed a reverence and swept out, her broom held like a talisman in front of her.

Sakra stepped out of the shadows and watched delighted recognition flood Nisula's face.

"*Agnidh* Sakra." The captain pressed his palm to his eyes in the salute of trust as Sakra came to stand with him in front of the stove. "I hoped it was you I would meet here."

"Good Captain Nisula." Sakra returned the salute. "You will forgive me for not being more plain. The less definite the rumors can be here, the better off we are." He pulled his mittens off and held his hands out to the warmth of the stove, luxuriating in the heat that bathed him. Five years he had lived in Isavalta and still he had learned only to tolerate the cold as one must tolerate what one could not overcome. He had never learned to ignore it as the natives seemed to.

Nisula frowned, watching the flicker of the flames behind the stove's narrow grating. "So, you do not believe Hraban is truly an ally of the empress's?"

"We do not know what he is." Sakra shook his head. "We know he prefers the idea of her on the throne rather than the dowager, but we don't yet know why. It may be because he believes that a frightened young woman will be more amenable to his advancement than a shrewd old witch such as Medeoan."

Nisula nodded. "It may indeed be. The man wears a sycophant's mask, but there's too much going on behind his eyes for me to speak with him in comfort." Nisula knocked on the edge of the stove, an old gesture to call forth luck and ward off evil.

"I've had word that you have come here after carrying the new ambassador from the Pearl Throne to the Heart of the World in Hung-Tse." Sakra sat in the chair nearest the stove, and tossed his mittens on the hearth to warm.

"A stormy crossing if ever there was." Nisula seated himself down across from Sakra, with one leg stretched forward onto the hearth and one arm resting on the back of the chair.

"And what news have you from there?"

Nisula shook his head, his face grim. "I was not permitted into the council chamber, of course, but the ambassador had much to say about what went on there." Nisula stopped, and Sakra waited for him to find his words. Nisula first regarded the stove, and then glanced away to the horse stalls, perhaps to see if the master was returning, or perhaps he only wanted to put off having to speak a moment longer.

"Delay, obsfucation and some fairly blatant lies," he said at last. "We came with gifts, and a written offer from the Pearl Throne to enter into treaty negotiations. There was even a hint that the Throne might be willing to cede some of the Eastern Isles back to the Heart, but, I am told, the emperor and the elders sat like sated men after a feast and could not be tempted by even this choicest dainty."

Despite the warmth bathing his skin from the stove, Sakra felt a fresh chill steal over him. "Who was sent as ambassador?"

"Taksaka. His mother was from Hung-Tse and he speaks the language fluently. Do you know him?"

It was Sakra's turn to nod. "A statesman of great skill. I have heard him speak." Memory showed him a slender young man in the red and blue draperies of a scholar, standing before the Pearl Throne, his voice full of passion, and yet his arguments full of reason. "He could not move them?"

"Apparently not." Nisula's palm tapped against the chair arm. "He has remained there, as ambassador." Nisula paused. "And as hostage."

"Hostage?" The word made Sakra sit up straighter.

"To help ensure that the Pearl Throne is sincere in its offer," said Nisula dryly. "Not that those were the words they used. I'd repeat what they actually said, but it would take half an hour to get through the whole speech." Sakra waved the idea away. "The Nine Elders seem to be collecting hostage guests," Nisula went on. "The ambassador said there's a party there from the Peninsula, and another from the Western Islands."

"The Heart is so afraid?"

"If they were afraid, they would have entered into treaty negotiations at once." Nisula got to his feet as if he could not bear to sit still anymore and paced across the master's corner from the stove to the much-scrubbed dining table. "A treaty with the Pearl Throne would eliminate at least the southern half of Hung-Tse's fears, would it not?" Sakra nodded in agreement with this statement. Nisula did not turn around to see him, but went on, "Something hidden stirs in the Heart, of that the ambassador is certain, and they are trying to fix as many games in their favor as possible." He picked up the brass cup that had been left on the table, inspected its bottom to see that it was empty and then tilted it so that he could see the engraving on the side, eyeing it as a man who knew very well what such things were worth. "There is a thing I am hesitant to tell you, *Agnidh*, because I neither saw nor heard anything definite myself."

Another thing, you mean, good captain. Sakra spread his hands. "Tell me and perhaps together we may judge its value."

"Perhaps." Nisula turned the cup around so he could see its opposite side. "Or perhaps I will only raise your hopes."

"Now then, Captain," said Sakra, chiding him. "You must tell me after that."

"I suppose I must. Very well." He set the cup down with a click against the wooden table, as if that was an audible sign of his decision. "The day before I was to leave the Heart of the World, the ambassador came to me and said that he had heard word that there was a hostage guest in the palace from Isavalta."

The words startled Sakra into silence. The soft, random noises of the horses and their keepers seemed suddenly very loud. "From Isavalta?" Sakra repeated. "Why would the dowager send Hung-Tse a hostage guest? She has the strongest of all holds over them."

Nisula faced him again, his eyebrows cocked as if to say, "Doesn't she, though?" "What was even stranger was that he had heard that this hostage was housed in the women's palace."

"A woman?" said Sakra before he could stop himself. This made no sense at all.

"That was what the ambassador had heard." Nisula shrugged. "It was servants' gossip, the chatter of some body slaves who had not yet learned how well their new master could understand them."

"Was there nothing more?" There had to be more. Neither Taksaka nor Nisula would attach such importance to gossip.

Nisula looked away again, and Sakra thought he saw a spot of color on the man's windburned cheek. "The ambassador asked if I could find out more from a lady whose acquaintance I had made."

Sakra felt one corner of his mouth lift into a smile. "You are favored with access to one of the Heart's ladies?"

"I have friends in the outer court. It is one of the reasons my ship was chosen to take the ambassador." For a moment, Sakra thought the captain was actually going to shuffle his feet, and had to suppress a smile. Nisula was an old friend, yet Sakra had never before realized the man had a side to himself that was bashful. It was not a trait for which sailors were much noted.

"And what did your lady say?" asked Sakra soberly.

His gravity seemed to restore the captain's comfort and the color faded from Nisula's face. "She said it was true and that if I wished she would show me."

"How?"

"She was one of those ladies who did not find much time for improvement of her mind, and she longed for a bit of adventure." As a man who had seen perhaps too much adventure, Nisula rolled his eyes at this folly. "She dressed me in the armor of one of their female bodyguards and took me into the women's palace."

Sakra said nothing. On the face of it, it sounded amusing, a piece of mummers' farce, but they both knew that had Nisula been discovered there he would have been killed before he could have spoken a word in his own defense.

"We walked along a wall overlooking one of the gardens," Nisula continued, pacing back to the stove and rapping it again. "She showed me a little girl, perhaps seven, perhaps eight years old, being given lessons by an ancient scholar."

Sakra felt his jaw fall open. He looked right, then left, as if he thought to see the world around him overturned. His thoughts raced ahead without clear direction. "I do not believe it," was all he could manage to say. "The dowager has no child to send."

"That child was not of High Isavalta. Her hair was as black as yours, and her skin almost as brown."

"Then who?"

Nisula licked his lips. "She might have been Tuukosov."

In a land of rebellious provinces, Tuukos was a legend. Its people, they said, had never been conquered in their hearts. According to those who knew such things, there had been a great outcry when Valin Kalami had been elevated to lord sorcerer for that very reason. The Tuukosov had strong traditions of magic of their own, and the evil and blackness of it were a byword in the legends of High Isavalta. Despite all that, the island had produced many a famous artisan, and a single lord sorcerer.

"Captain, you do not suggest that the child is Kalami's?"

"I do not know."

Now it was Sakra who could not bear to sit still. He heaved himself to his feet and walked to the edge of the master's quarters, his mind juggling all the pieces of court intrigue he had collected over the years, trying to make them fit into the new picture Nisula had given him.

"It makes no sense," he said, pounding his fist once against the beam that had hidden him moments before. "Any such hostage would have to be sent as part of an imperial treaty and there has been none, not even in secret. The princess or her ladies would have found it out."

Nisula cleared his throat, glancing down the line of horses. Sakra felt his face flush. This was not the palace of his homeland. There were no bindings of silence here and he could not forget that again. He returned to the stove and made himself sit back down, but the warmth brought him no comfort.

"It may be," said Nisula, folding his hands behind himself, "that this secret was fathered out of wedlock."

Sakra felt the slow sensation of change settle over his thoughts. "Kalami deals with a double agent from Hung-Tse. We knew that. But what messages we have been able to hear . . ." Sakra stared at the captain. "Kalami works against his mistress imperial?"

Nisula shrugged irritably, but Sakra knew his agitation was with his own inability to give clear answers to Sakra's questions. "I do not know. I saw a foreign child in the Heart of the World. I have the word of one of the less auspicious concubines that the child is a hostage guest of Isavalta, but her coloring says she is from farther north than any who willingly call themselves Isavaltan. That is all."

"And now, Kalami has gone to fetch a woman from beyond the ends of the world." Sakra's hands grappled with the empty air. "How am I to hold all these threads?"

"I wish I could tell you, *Agnidh*."

Sakra ran one hand across his braided hair, touching the ends as if he were suddenly afraid one had come loose.

Could it be? Could Kalami be plotting against the dowager? Why? It was through her that he gained all his power. If she fell, so would he. If she fell before the Emperor Mikkel regained his mind and thus Ananda gained her legitimacy, the empire itself would crumble.

Unless that was what he wanted.

Did Kalami bargain with Hung-Tse for the freedom of Tuukos? Was he truly on a mission for the dowager, or did he seek help for his own schemes beyond the Silent Lands?

Sakra stood. "Friend Nisula, can you arrange to take your leave today? I would be grateful if you could help me speed through the Foxwood. Your news tells me plainly there is much that I must soon discover."

"Of course, *Agnidh*," said Nisula at once. "I will say I have had word from my ship. I was to leave tomorrow in any case."

"Thank you." Sakra once more gave Nisula the salute of trust. He had to find the answers to all these new questions, and swiftly. For if he could lay in Ananda's hands the proof that Kalami played the dowager false, she would have an ax that could finally cleave her own danger in two. Her position would then be secure enough that they would be able to bend all their attention and all their skill to freeing her husband and assuring her throne.

Sakra suddenly found himself wishing with every fiber of his spirit that Ananda had guessed correctly when she spoke of Mikkel's binding being in his ring. Perhaps last night Ananda reached Mikkel's side and pulled the chain of his confinement from his hand. Perhaps a messenger already rode like the wind from Vyshtavos to Sparavatan to tell him he was to return and witness the emperor's reinvestiture. For then all would already be done, and he would not have to fear failure anymore.

In the time since Sakra had been banished from Medeoan's court, he had lived in many places: the halls of the lord masters who harbored worries over what their dowager had become, a reaper's hut out in the fields with Grandfather and Grandmother sleeping on the stove, a river barge, a god house, a library, wherever he thought he could gain information or advantage for Ananda.

But the place that had become home waited on the outskirts of the gloom and mystery of the Foxwood. A house of stone with a single tower attached to it. When he first saw it, Sakra thought it was some garrison outpost that had fallen into disuse. Inquiry among the foresters told him, though, that it was haunted. A widow who had lost her husband in some long-ago skirmish had gone mad with grief, and after she had died, the tower had appeared so that her ghost might stand on its ramparts and look out for her husband to come home.

No one sane, they said, would go near the place. The village had paid a sorcerer to go in and exorcise the spirit, but the man had been found the next day sprawled on the road in a stupor, his red hair turned stark white.

Which told Sakra plainly that the "sorcerer" had been one of the many charlatans who made their living off the credulous in Isavalta, although he said nothing of that to his hosts. He just went quietly to the house and opened the way to the Land of Death and Spirit for the unhappy ghost so that her gods and her husband could come for her. Then, he'd moved what belongings he had into the empty dwelling, coming and going at night. It was a rude home, with only two rooms beside the tower and a peasant's furnishings, but it was secure and that was what he required.

Now he squatted before his hearth, striking sparks from his flint and steel and trying not to shiver. Outside, the sound of Captain Nisula's departing escort faded into the twilight. Nisula had left him with the promise that he would be in port for another week should Sakra have need of him. Sakra had thanked him, and at the same time hoped there would be no such need.

At last the tinder of wood shavings and pine needles caught and Sakra sat back on his heels, feeding twigs to the red-gold flames and watching them grow to reflect off the pots and kettles stacked beside the hearth. The familiar sight soothed him, clearing his mind for calm thought, for which he was grateful. He had a long night's work ahead of him.

Sakra laid a split log on the fire and watched the flames curl around it. Satisfied that he had not smothered his infant fire, he set his back to it, his gaze sweeping his home. Bundles of herbs hung from the rafters, and some of Nisula's men had gifted him with small game so he would not go hungry in case the mice had gotten into his flour and corn in his absence. Several shelves adorned the walls to hold his tools and what few dishes he owned, and two small, carved wooden chests. Underneath them waited three more chests, each the size of a man's torso, locked with iron and banded with silver.

The question had become how best to find out what he needed to know. The crow's stepchildren were unreliable in this matter, preferring to show off their cleverness to adhering strictly to their bargains. Besides, Sakra did not wish to turn to them too often. The powers of this land did not deal gently with weakness, or with debt too great and too slowly paid.

Which meant he had to make use of older and, in some ways, more dangerous servants. Which meant he could hesitate in his preparations no longer.

There was that which could not be permitted entry to the home. A spell that used the self could be performed when the self was protected. But for a spell that called on the binding of others, the self had to go into danger. That was the way of things. Without that balance and that discipline, the act of binding could become too easy, the pleasures of the power too corrupting. Such a binding would turn to curse the one who made the bond. This was not a rule anyone seemed to have told to Kalami, or indeed the dowager.

Patience did not rest long with Sakra. He paced the tiny hovel what felt like a thousand times while kettle after kettle of water came to a boil over his fire. The copper bath lifted down from its pegs over the mantelpiece filled only slowly, but it did fill.

When he had emptied the last kettle into the bath, Sakra turned to his smallest chest. Standing close so that his breath would touch its lock, he unbound the thong that held his hair back and let the braids fall loose about his shoulders. He found the three he needed by touch and untied them, combing his fingers through the locks to loosen them. In answer, the lock on the chest came open with a dull click.

Sakra reached inside and brought out the single, grisly talisman the chest contained. A severed foot wound around with a black cord spun from Sakra's own hair squatted on his palm. It was old, dried and shrunken, but one could still see that its tough skin was smooth and a muddy red, and that its stunted toes had black claws curving from them.

Sakra set the unsavory thing down on the table. Composing his mind to the necessity of his actions, Sakra stripped off his coat and his shirt. He folded them carefully and laid them both on the bench. He removed boots and trousers and leggings, until he stood in nothing but his breechclouts. He took up the withered foot and unwound just enough of its binding cord to tie it to his right wrist. With the talisman cradled in one hand, Sakra opened the door.

The winter cold engulfed him immediately and his feet recoiled from being placed in the snow to walk from the hovel to a place in the lee of a drift of snow where he had poured boiling water and permitted it to freeze into an oval of ice black with the night it reflected. A mirror would have been infinitely preferable for this task, but he had none. Kalami had seen to it that his precious glasses had been smashed when he was removed from the court.

The winter scoured his body with its harsh cold. His feet were already numb. His clumsy fingers brushed away the latest coat of snow from the ice patch and set the talisman on its smooth surface. Unwinding more of the cord so that he could stand up straight, Sakra positioned himself at the edge of the ice patch, lifting up one foot and pressing it flat against the joint of his right knee so that he stood balanced. A fresh blast of the winter's wind shook his skin and gripped his bones. Sakra forced his mind clear. He lifted his hands and pressed his palms together directly in front of his eyes.

This was what these northern sorcerers had never learned, the power that came of suffering, of discipline. They reveled in their magics that came at no cost, so it seemed, to themselves. This was why in the end so many of them succumbed to the vanities and fears that were inherent in their own natures.

And before you suffer from too much pride, he told himself, *remember why you have come to be here in this wilderness.*

The cold rocked him again and Sakra swayed on his one leg, coming close to falling, but he righted himself. He pushed his thoughts aside. Now was not the time for reproach or wounded pride. Now was the time to do his work.

Sakra took in a deep breath that nearly paralyzed his lungs, but he forced them into motion. Raising his unbound hand straight in front of him as if lifting a knife to point at the sky, Sakra began to sing.

He sang loud, long and high, his fierce well-trained voice absorbed quickly by the clouds and the snow, and yet the wind shivered at its sound. His breath was a white cloud of steam in the darkness and his free hand moved through it, brushing it from one side to the other, shaping the patterns in breath, wind and song.

"Twelve leagues you walk from me.
Eleven leagues you hear my voice.
Ten leagues you feel my touch.
Nine leagues you know my bond.
Eight leagues you rebel from me.
Seven leagues you hide from me.
Six leagues you deny me.
Five leagues you remember me.
Four leagues you hear me.
Three leagues you turn to me.
Two leagues you run to me.
One league you obey me."

Over and over, his voice forced the song into the world. Over and over his hand wove the pattern through his steaming breath. A crow settled on a branch overhead, sending a shower of snow down onto the nearest drift. Sakra ignored it and began the song again. The cold was gone, the pain and even the numbness was gone. There was only the song and the pattern, again, and yet again.

Around his still wrist, the hair cord thickened and changed until it became an iron chain. Sakra began the song once more, his fingers weaving through the steam in front of his eyes. The ice also to all appearances began to steam, but the vapor thickened and reddened, taking on a weight and opacity that belonged to no such element. Gradually, the form became the color of old blood. It grew heavy and brutish arms. Claws curved from its stubby fingers as well as from its toes. Fangs and a tongue protruded from a gaping mouth beneath eyes yellow and round like golden saucers. Real gold dangled in the shape of rings in its pendulous earlobes. It wore armor of leather and scales and its right hand clutched a spear. The iron chain tethered its ankle to Sakra's wrist.

Sakra lowered his foot so that he might stand more firmly. The warmth of his magic flowed through his blood to sustain him, but that would not last. The cold would have its way before too much longer.

"I require that you see a thing for me," he told his demon.

The demon ran its long, black tongue around its lips. "Then adhere to your promise."

Sakra fingered the chain. It was a thing wholly of his creation and it could not refuse him. With a swift jerk, he pulled free one of the links. The chain was still whole, but it was a handspan shorter now. The freed link vanished in the next puff of wind. When the chain was down to its last link, the demon would be freed from Sakra's service. It would also attempt to kill him. Sakra had known that when he bound it.

The demon licked its lips again.

"See for me who it is Valin Kalami has found."

The demon turned to face the north and squinted its great eyes at the night.

"I see him." The demon pointed to a place where Kalami saw

only darkness and the shadows of trees in starlight. "He boards a boat of his own making and casts off. He raises its sail and starts off across the waters. He seeks the far shores, beyond the Home Lands."

The Home Lands. The demon meant the Land of Death and Spirit.

The demon's eyes narrowed down to yellow slits. "He seeks blood. Blood and an enemy. No. An ally. Innocence and ignorance. A woman. A daughter. A mother. Love and hatred, vision and blindness. He has found all these things."

Here Sakra commanded the demon as he could never command the crows. "Speak clearly, or I shall strengthen your chain."

The demon snarled, and saliva, or perhaps it was blood, fell from his lip and hissed against the snow. "You cannot require me to see so far. There is no place for my kind in that world where he has gone."

"Has it a single name, what he seeks?"

The demon's ears waggled. "Avanasidoch."

Even though he had thought the name himself, it still hit Sakra hard enough to stun his will, and cold slammed back against his body like an iron weight. It could not be. The Avanasidoch was legend. Wishful thinking on the part of troubled Isavaltans.

The demon leered at him. "What else shall I see for you? What other glad tidings can I bring you so that I might see your face so full of fear again?"

Anger rallied Sakra's will and lent him a little, feeble warmth. "Watch your tongue, slave. You are still mine, and if you continue in your insolence, I shall put a ring through that tongue of yours as well."

In answer, the demon stuck its tongue out straight and waggled it at him. "So many years in this wasteland and you still believe it is your home. You still believe that all things are written in the books and you do not heed the words and tales that gather on the wind. They are the wisdom here." It grinned in satisfaction. "But there, you will not listen to me either. Send me away. I grow cold."

It was a taunt that Sakra could not ignore. Pain burned in every limb now and a dull heavy ache spread from behind his eyes and around his skull. His trembling would not stop. But he did not release the demon. Instead he reached out and snapped another link free from the chain.

"If the time is good, show me to Xiau-Li Taun."

The demon snarled and tugged hard on its chain, but the iron was still too strong for it and Sakra remained unmoved. Gnashing its teeth, it faced the south and squinted hard.

"The time is good."

It gathered up two loops of its chain gently around its arm and plunged back into the ice from which it had formed.

The chain played itself out, and further out, until it stretched straight and rigid from Sakra's shaking wrist into the blank, black ice. Sakra forced his frozen feet to shuffle forward and made his aching knees bend until he could see into his ice. His eyes glimpsed dim reflections, and in another heartbeat all became as real and clear as if he stood in that faraway house in Camaracost.

Camaracost waited on Isavalta's southernmost coast. There, they filled their warehouses with goods from every part of Isavalta and Hastinapura, and more than occasionally with smuggled luxuries from Hung-Tse.

And, also more than occasionally, with information from Hung-Tse. It was an open secret in Medeoan's court that her lord sorcerer journeyed to Camaracost to speak with one of those merchants willing to sell his information along with his silks. Patient bribery and application had told Sakra that the merchant's name was Havosh, and that he in turn had a scribe in his employ named Xiau-Li Taun whom he dared not fire, even though Xiau-Li had developed a dangerous habit. Every few days, Xiau-Li would lock himself in the smallest storeroom of the warehouse and drink Isavalta's famous peppery liquor until he grew insensible.

But before he lost consciousness, he frequently saw the ghost of his uncle come to berate him.

Broken barrels and torn bundles filled the tiny, dusty room. A mouse wandered across the dirt floor, nosing at a bale of spoiled cloth. It stood on its hind legs and nibbled delicately at the bale, a connoisseur testing its vintage. Xiau-Li, already collapsed into the corner behind the door, raised his tiny cup to the creature and gulped down its contents. He had dressed carefully for his debauch and it was as well, for the gray cotton robe was smudged with dust and cobwebs, and splashed with liquor. He must have been running his hands through his hair, because more dust and cobwebs smeared his face and head and his hair stuck out wildly in all directions.

"What a fine figure of a nephew I have."

Slowly, Xiau-Li lifted his watery eyes from their contemplation of the mouse, which, having decided the cloth was to its liking, had begun to burrow its nose into the mealy brown folds.

"My uncle." Xiau-Li set his cup down delicately, and with the slow deliberation of one who is very drunk began to bend his legs in an attempt to gather them under him so that he might kneel properly before the ghost of a respected family member.

The ghost waved its hand. "Stay as you are, nephew. I would not have you injure yourself."

"You are most excellent and kind, Uncle." Xiau-Li collapsed back against the wall, his face flushed with his exertions.

Sakra had never known whether the "ghost" truly resembled Xiau-Li's uncle. It did resemble the tomb carving—a bald, withered old man with his hands folded across a gnarled walking stick. That seemed to be enough. Xiau-Li's expectations completed the illusion. "At least you thought to save your good clothes, and thus the expense."

Xiau-Li batted at the wrinkles in his old, cotton robe. "It was you who taught me to think of details, Uncle."

"And no doubt, you are able to buy yourself a better quality of debauchery with that savings." The ghost sniffed his disapproval at this possibility.

Xiau-Li lifted one finger and tapped it against his temple. "Details, Uncle. Just as you taught me. I have always tried to do as you taught me."

In response to this declaration of filial obedience, the ghost only sighed. "I wish I had taught you sobriety instead."

At these words, Xiau-Li's happy face plunged into misery. Tears began to spill from the corners of his eyes. "I have failed you. I have failed my family. I have failed myself. I am unfit." He reached for the leather bottle and tipped it over his cup. "I am unfit." A silver stream of liquor poured down, and Sakra imagined the sharp scent of it burning his nose and palate.

And if he downs much more of that, he will be beyond me.

"Would you redeem yourself, Nephew?"

Xiau-Li lifted his eyes, his mouth open in speechless wonder, as if he had just been told he would be assumed into the home of the gods. He laid the bottle gently down, and gathered his legs under himself so that he bowed on knees and elbows to his uncle's ghost. This time, Sakra let him make the gesture. "Tell me how."

"Your master takes letters from the sorcerer Kalami, does he not?"

"He does, Uncle." Xiau-Li nodded eagerly, believing he had finally found a way to please his stern relative.

"And you read these letters to him, for your master, while he has many skills, cannot read them himself."

"No, Uncle. That is, yes, I read them, for he cannot." Xiau-Li's eyes lifted just far enough so that he could see the liquor bottle lying in front of him, and then slipped sideways to see the little cup brimming with its precious silver fluid.

"Very good, nephew," said the ghost in a more gentle voice than he had used yet. "Have you ever read any that speak of a hostage in the Heart of the World?"

"No, Uncle." Xiau-Li's hand inched along the floor toward the cup, as if he were a child who thought that if he moved slowly enough the grown-up would fail to see what he was doing.

"Do you speak the truth, Nephew?" said Sakra sternly. "I shall be most displeased if you lie to me."

"No hostages." Xiau-Li walked his fingers up the side of the cup, until the tip of his index finger touched the liquor. "He speaks of the movement of cows, the price of wheat, and he urges his daughter to be a good girl."

"Daughter? He speaks of a daughter?"

Xiau-Li lifted his finger out of the liquor and stuck out his tongue so that a drop could fall onto it. He retracted his tongue and closed his eyes in blissful reverence. "His daughter learns well from her tutors. His daughter is an obedient and sober child." Xiau-Li's head dropped forward until his forehead rested on the floor. "Not me. Not me."

"His daughter does this in the Heart of the World?"

Xiau-Li nodded. More liquorish tears spilled down his cheeks, making dark, damp patches on the dusty floor. "Not me. Not me."

"Go to sleep, Xiau-Li." Sakra gripped the demon's chain. "Take me home."

The warehouse, mouse and drunken Xiau-Li all faded into darkness and Sakra became aware of a great heat in his body and a leaden lethargy of all his limbs. Sleep. He had worked so hard and done so much today. He needed sleep and this warm and comfortable darkness was exactly right for that. Perhaps the demon had indeed taken him home. It was that hot. Perhaps he even now lay in his chamber, and on the other side of the carved screen Ananda slept on her silken pillows safe from the world and free from harm. He would open his eyes and he would see the moonlight shining from the window of her sleeping alcove into his. All he had to do was open his eyes and it would be true.

So simple an action seemed an exhausting task, but Sakra wanted so much for it to be true that he struggled against his weariness and his eyes fluttered open. But he did not see moonlight reflected on the warm grain of teak that was the floor of the palace. He saw instead starlight turning snow to silver and his own hand silhouetted black against that snow as it reached for the demon's talisman lying on the ice. He blinked his crusted eyelids a few times, trying to understand.

Slowly, his sluggish brain remembered where he was and what had happened.

I am freezing to death, he thought calmly.

But he was ready for this. He had known it was a possibility and he had prepared. All he had to do was return to his hovel. All he had to do was stand and walk. Yet, all he could do was lie as he was, as sprawled and undignified as Xiau-Li in his dirty corner, and die.

Forgive me, Ananda. I am failing you again.

He stared at his arm and the black cord that tied him to the demon's severed foot. He had spun that thread after a fast of three days. His stomach had ceased to hurt, the hunger becoming only a dizzy awareness of absence. He only felt pain in his scalp from where he had pulled the hairs. This dying was like that. Only a small pain, this one in his heart instead of his scalp. A small pain from the knowledge that Ananda would be alone.

Perhaps it would be all right. Perhaps she had reached Mikkel by now and freed him.

But perhaps she had not. And she was not truly alone. The dowager and Kalami were with her, and she did not know how they might be turned against each other. Only he knew that, and if he died here, naked in the snow, his ghost would watch them tear her apart.

With a will honed by years of instruction and trial, Sakra forced his legs to draw up underneath him. He cried out as if he had been burned, but he stood. Gray blurred the edges of his vision, but he could still see the open door of the hovel, and the low orange light of the coals that must be what was left of his fire. He shoved one leaden foot forward, plowing a path through the snow. His left leg would not move, no matter how hard he urged it, so he dragged it behind him, limping and lurching toward the doorway like a wounded deer. Every movement plunged him deeper into a fog of pain but he stumbled ahead, held upright only by the knowledge that if he fell he would not be able to stand again.

Something slammed hard against his left foot, shooting a bolt of pain up his leg. His knee collapsed, pitching him forward. He measured his length across the threshold of the hovel, his arms splayed out on the stone floor, his legs trailing in the snow. Ahead of him rose the curved copper sides of the bath he had prepared.

Ananda alone, he made himself think. *Ananda alone with the dowager and Kalami. My failure. My fault.*

It was enough, barely, but it was enough. His arms pushed him up far enough that he could get his knees under him and he could crawl. With the last of his strength, he forced his hands to grab the edge of the bath and heave him over the side, so that he splashed like a stone into the water.

Had it not cooled enough, the shock would have killed him. As it was, waves of pain racked his body and sent pins and needles stabbing through every fiber of him. But slowly, the water cooled and his body warmed and he was able to pull all himself into a whole again; body, mind and spirit, so that he could lift himself from the bath, cross to the hovel's second room, cast off his soaking breechclouts and crawl under the pile of fur rugs heaped on his bed.

At long last, warmth without pain came over him, bringing comfort and peace. Now he could sleep. In the morning he would find a way to intercept Kalami as he returned to Isavalta, and discover what he meant to do with the Avanasidoch.

Sakra's fingers knotted around the cord that bound him to the demon's foot. In the morning, all would be put right.

Asleep, he did not see the fox steal through the open door to stare at him, saliva dripping from its hungry jaws. But as it slunk forward, the foot twitched on the end of its tether, and the fox froze, one paw raised. The foot twitched again, and the fox seemed to think the better of what it did, and it slipped back out into the night.

Chapter Seven

Bridget closed the door to the keeper's quarters behind her, twisted the key in the lock, and then tucked the key under the mat. The other key had already gone to Bayfield with Mrs. Hansen and Samuel. She had told the Lighthouse Board as much in the letter she had sent with the Hansens, which had also announced her resignation and advised them of the need to look out for a new keeper. The Board would have until May to find a replacement for her. Surely, that would be enough time. Bridget tilted her chin to stare up at the curtained windows at the top of the light tower. The light would be lit when the ice cleared. No ship, no sailor, would be left without its guidance.

"Bridget?"

Bridget turned to face Kalami, Valin. A slight heat rose in her cheeks at having been caught woolgathering. "This has been my home for a very long time," she said by way of explanation. "It is difficult to think of handing it over to a stranger."

Valin regarded the brownstone house with its octagonal tower through half-lidded eyes for a moment.

"This is your past." Valin turned away from the lighthouse, and with those four words dismissed Bridget's entire life. "I am come to take you to your future."

He wore the same clothes that he had worn the day she pulled him out of the lake—leather hose, linen shirt, a woolen overtunic, and the black, wide-skirted coat with the high collar and embroidered cuffs. The belt with its gleaming golden buckle was wrapped around his waist underneath the coat.

This was the first time Bridget had seen him so got up since the night she had pulled him from the lake. Since then, he had worn old, ill-fitting clothes that had belonged either to her father, or to Samuel. The nights they had sat in the parlor while she read or sewed, and he labored over his torn canvas, she had felt the scene was almost normal. Anyone walking in would think they were husband and wife, enjoying domestic tranquillity.

Anyone who hadn't seen what she had seen, and who didn't know what she was about to do.

Valin smiled, as if he had heard her thoughts and they amused him. He gestured toward the jetty stairs and bowed, waiting for her to precede him.

Bridget managed a smile and squared her shoulders. She tucked her rope-handled board chest under one arm and started down the stairs. She said she would do this thing, and do this thing she would. During the past six weeks she had wavered so many times between anticipation and apprehension that vacillation seemed a permanent part of her being. Even now, as she descended the stairs to Valin's repaired boat, both feelings surged within her. But she did not look back. The decision was made.

The boat that floated beside the jetty was indeed a gaudy thing. Valin had spent at least as much time on remaking the designs of green, blue and black paint that covered its red sides as he had on a patching the hole in its hull.

"They should have protected me from the rocks," he told her one day in November when she had come down to watch him work. He was short of breath, as if he had been running, or digging ditches, rather than just wielding a paintbrush. "I did not make them strong enough. I do not want to make the same mistake while you are in my charge."

Then he saw how Bridget's eyes flickered from him to the swirling lines of paint. "Magic," he said, "is a thing woven. The design traps the magic, channels it, gives it shape and form, and allows it to be directed into the living world."

"But where does the magic come from?"

Valin had given her one of his gentle smiles. "Ah, Bridget, you ask one of the deep questions. Some say it comes from the soul of the sorcerer himself. Some say it waits around us to be drawn in by the gifted. The honest, of which I try to be one, say that they do not know." He mopped his brow and looked at his handiwork. "Philosophy and the deeper mysteries are not my special study. I try only to serve my mistress imperial by the strength of my art."

The boat had a single mast and a lanteen rig, from which Valin could hoist the triangular sail he had labored over repairing. "This will catch the wind to sail us beyond the edge of the world," he had said as he stitched the new seams in the torn canvas.

That too had been hard work, mostly performed by the light of the open woodstove in the parlor. After ten minutes plying the large, curved needle, Valin's hands would begin to shake and then he would have to lean back in the chair and catch his breath.

"Is the . . ." Bridget had hesitated to use the word "magic." She still could not bring herself to fully believe what was happening in front of her, although all her actions were performed as if she believed without question. ". . . your work so difficult?"

Valin had shaken his head. "This should be a relatively simple matter. It is this world that makes it hard. You will see the difference when we reach Isavalta."

The boat rocked as Bridget stepped aboard. It had a sharp prow and narrow stern, telling Bridget at once it was for ocean waters rather than lake waters. Its keel was too sharp for the lake, and its hull too narrow. It was made for slicing through waves that came in swells, not wallowing on top of the waves that could come from any direction. Despite that, it seemed to have done well enough so far, and would only have to last a little longer on Superior.

She stowed her small box of possessions in the cramped hold among the water casks and chest of various tools, materials, ropes and provisions while Valin made certain of his ropes and knots. He was muttering to himself about the nature of his splicing when she emerged. The smile he turned to her now was rueful.

"It is a good thing my old master is not here to see this work. I would be given a clout on the ear for my sloppiness."

"As long as it holds for our journey," said Bridget, stepping over the sternmost bench. "I am certainly not going to complain of its looks."

A look flickered across Valin's face then, and for a minute Bridget thought she saw anger in his dark eyes, but it quickly faded. "Oh, we will reach Isavalta safely, Bridget. I swear that to you." He moved to cast off from the jetty then and she heard him mutter, "I have not come this far to fail in that."

Bridget helped catch up and coil the mooring ropes. Valin used one of the steering oars to push the boat off and start them drifting toward open water. Bridget climbed into the bow and watched while Valin raised the sail to catch the frigid wind. Because of its depth and breadth, Superior took a long time to freeze. The ice had not come here yet, as it had on the smaller lakes farther south, but it would close in soon.

The sail flapped and billowed, filling out until it blocked blue lake and grey sky. Still, Bridget could see past it to where Sand Island sprawled green and rust red, filling the horizon. Was that a glint of pale sunlight on the light tower? Or was it a tear in her eye?

Valin's voice lifted above the wind and cut across her thoughts. "Do you remember what I told you of the Land of Death and Spirit?"

"Yes," said Bridget, wiping a hand in front of her eyes and hoping Valin would think it was only the spray that bothered them. "I am to ignore whatever I may see."

"Much of what you will see is false." Valin's voice was strained, stretched tight like the ropes holding the sail, from which he would not take his gaze. "All of it will be confusing. Trust me, Bridget. Trust in the boat that carries you, but place no trust in anything beyond that. Only we sorcerers may steer through the Outer Land. Ungifted mortals must wander lost in its confines, so too must the unlearned." He bared his teeth to the wind. "If nothing else, hold fast to that thought. I cannot lose you."

Bridget opened her mouth to make some reply, but, around her, the world changed.

In front of her eyes, Lake Superior melted into a bank of white mist. In the next moment, the mist stretched and settled, spreading low across the water until all the waves were obscured by a strange, cold fog.

There was no sound. The world around them lay as profoundly silent as night and death.

New islands rose on either side of the boat, mounds of green so vivid it hurt Bridget's eyes to look at them. A single craggy tree crowned each island and each tree grew golden fruit that shimmered underneath a sky suddenly gone black as pitch. Smells of warmth and honey reached Bridget as a gentle breeze wafted off the strange islands, and her mouth began to water.

What would fruit of gold taste like? she wondered, and her mouth longed to find out. But Valin's words rang in her mind and she clutched the boat's rail.

The mist around them parted and the water became so smooth and green that Bridget was no longer certain that they did sail across water. Was it now a lawn that they glided over? Men and women strolled about that lawn, many wearing fantastical garb of vivid silk, or flowing robes of gold or blinding whiteness. Some could not be bothered with clothing at all. Some wore crowns on their shining hair, some went bareheaded, while others covered their faces with glittering masks, and yet others had great gossamer wings drooping from their shoulders.

As Bridget and Valin passed, the people turned to look at the boat sailing between them. Nothing but contempt showed in their cold eyes. Shame washed through Bridget and she ducked her head. She was not fit to be seen among these noble creatures. She was fit for nothing but to throw herself into the water. The water that would cleanse her, and allow her to rise again, worthy at last to join them and receive their approval. Only the deep green water could wash her clean.

"Hold fast, Bridget!" called Valin, his voice as harsh as any crow's in the profound silence. But it was enough. Bridget closed her eyes and knotted her hand around the railing. A splinter dug into her palm and she welcomed the brief pain. What she saw was illusion, temptation. It was nothing. Nothing at all.

Then, the warm wind blew cold again, and stiffened to whip strands of Bridget's hair across her face. The boat rocked sharply, and she thought she felt the low grating under her heels and hands of the keel scraping stone.

Her eyes flew open. Now they sailed on a brown river through a dense pine forest. Nothing but moss grew between the black trunks. Eyes peered between the trees—glowing animal eyes, curious human eyes, eyes large and eyes small, eyes curious, and eyes hostile. All of them silent, so silent she felt she could not bear it anymore. Something moved in the deep shadows, and for a moment, Bridget thought she saw a house on chicken legs stalk by. But that could not be. None of this could be. Bridget hid her face in her hands. She was not here. She was not doing this. This was not happening. She was home, in bed, in the lighthouse, waiting for the tugboat from the mainland to come take her away to Mrs. Neilsen's boardinghouse for the winter.

Bridget woke. She opened her eyes to the infinitely familiar contents of her darkened room. The comfortable weight of the quilts warmed her, and the lumps of her old mattress shifted underneath her. Rain pounded insistently against the windows.

What a strange dream. Bridget sat up and rubbed her temple, as if she could rub away the fear and ache inside her head. Finally, the enormity of what she was about to do had begun to drive her out of her mind. But it could not turn her from her duties. She and Kalami were to leave for this place, Isavalta, tomorrow, but tonight she was still the keeper of the light. All was darkness outside her window. She did not see the light shining. She must get up and go to the light to make sure that it still burned. That was her responsibility. If the light went out, there would be disaster. Lives would be lost. She could not permit that, even if this was her last night as keeper.

Bridget threw back the covers and got to her feet.

"No! Bridget, no!"

But she had to get to the light. It had gone out. Disaster waited.

She had to climb the tower. It waited for her, behind the iron fire door, tall on its chicken legs there on the bank. The light had gone out and it was for her to light it, only her, without her there would be death, more death, too much death . . .

No, Bridget!

Bridget froze. It was a woman's voice that commanded her. She blinked and saw again the river and the pine forest. A woman in a severe dress of black taffeta with a cameo brooch pinned to its high collar waited on the mossy bank. Her hair had been brushed back into a tidy bun, a style too severe for her kind face. She clutched her hands together and her pale face looked pained. Bridget felt her heart grow sad at the sight of that pain. She wanted to tell the woman she was all right, she would be well, that she loved her.

Bridget reeled backward, the bench catching her hard against the back of her knees. She fell onto it, pressing one hand against her chest.

What's happening? What is this?

Her gaze sought out the woman again, and now Bridget saw a man standing next to her. He was tall and darkly golden, and had one arm wrapped about the woman's shoulders. He wore a black coat of a style that matched Valin's. At his feet sat a golden cage and inside, a bird of flame battered its wings against the bars. Bridget smelled smoke and ash. She shook her head, clasping her hands together as if trying to hold on to herself. The man and the woman watched her with solemn eyes as she sailed away, and their sadness somehow removed all her desire to leave the boat.

"What is this place?" breathed Bridget as she raised her hands to her cheeks, surprised to find them wet.

"This is where the souls of the living are called when their bodies die," said Valin, his voice tight with some emotion Bridget could not name. He sounded hollow, as if this place robbed his voice of its vibrancy. "This is where the immortal and the intangible dwell."

"And that woman?" The banks with their somber trees blurred, as if she saw them through a curtain of tears. Bridget blinked and wiped at her eyes, but the world around her did not clear. "I've seen her before. Who was that woman?"

Valin shook his head. "Each person sees what is around them differently. I saw no woman."

Although Bridget felt no shift in the spectral wind, the sail swung around and the boat heeled hard over. The sail went slack for a moment, then seemed to catch a fresh breeze and bellied full. Valin's head went up as if he suddenly caught some new scent.

"There," he murmured, staring straight ahead and gripping the tiller. "There."

Bridget tried to follow his gaze, but she saw nothing except a blur of gold, grey and brown, with black above and blue below. The silence strained, but beyond it, she could now hear voices whispering. They called to her, trying to tell her things, important things that she needed to hear. She wanted to get closer so she could hear them better, but through it all, her mind's eye showed her the sad woman in black who would be hurt if Bridget disembarked from the boat. Bridget did not wish to cause that woman any more pain, and so she kept her seat.

The voices grew more insistent, and Bridget fought to keep from covering her ears. She concentrated on keeping herself rigid and her eyes straight ahead. She knew how to ignore voices. She had ignored them all her life. All she had to do was not listen. They could tell her nothing she did not know. They were gossips. Liars. They knew nothing.

Then, the blurred colors parted like a torn curtain and fell away on either side. The prow slapped hard against an honest wave. Bridget lurched and grasped the gunwale to keep from being pitched into the bottom of the boat. Spray drenched her shoulder, and she almost laughed out loud over the sudden roar of the wind, the roll of the waves, and the creak of the ropes. They had made it. Wherever they were, this place was real and comprehensible.

She righted herself and saw a sky bulging with clouds making a lid for a rough grey sea. Wind smelling of salt, snow and ice smacked her cheeks and made her shiver.

Ahead, she made out cliffs of stark grey stone dotted here and there with crystalline ice and patches of driven snow. Black trees stretched to the sky as if they sought to catch the low clouds on their crooked branches. It did not look welcoming, but it did look real and Bridget's heart lifted to see it.

"Isavalta!" Valin shouted to be heard over wave and wind.

It happened. I am in another world. Equal parts of excitement and fear squeezed her chest.

"What are these?" called Bridget, pointing toward the cliffs.

"The Teeth of Yvanka." Valin laughed when he saw Bridget's expression at that fierce name. "Do not worry, Bridget, they have not bitten anyone in years. A warm welcome waits beyond them."

Those were the last words Valin spoke for some time. Now back in a living world, he was busy with tiller, boom, line and sail. Bridget offered to help, but Valin waved at her to keep her place. Bridget, upon consideration, realized it was probably for the best. She knew boats well, but she knew nothing of these waters. The shore that curved around to starboard had a rocky look, and who knew what shoals lay beneath the waves?

A new world. A whole new world. A world with magic, empresses and palaces. Bridget covered her mouth to stifle a girlish giggle. What would Everett Lederle think of his daughter if he knew she was to be presented to royalty?

But as even as she thought of her father, Bridget abruptly remembered the woman in black, and the dark-gold man who stood beside her, with the fiery bird in the golden cage at his feet. What did that vision mean? Was it that a true vision, another like the one she had seen in Momma's mirror? Bridget bit her lip and tasted salt. She would have to ask Valin later.

Gradually, the coastline gentled. The cliffs turned into snowy hills and the rocky shore spread out wide and low. Dark silhouettes rose from the snow, and Bridget realized they were heading for a town.

She turned to Valin, pointing toward the shadowy buildings, but before she could speak her question, he called, "Biradost!"

Biradost slowly resolved itself into a cluster of steeply sloping roofs and bulbous spires, all with thick caps of snow. Long jetties ran out into the bay, but Bridget saw no other boats. Obviously, not many people chose to trust the conditions for sailing in this frigid winter.

Nonetheless, their sail had been spotted. Several burly figures clomped down the jetty waving hands as if to say, "Over here!" Valin waved back and turned their course toward the jetty where the men waited.

While Valin worked the tiller and brought in the sail, Bridget found the mooring ropes. When they had sailed close enough to the three figures she tossed the ropes to their ready hands. They were all big bears of men, with shaggy golden brown beards flecked with ice. They dressed alike in thick coats and brightly knitted caps. They pulled the boat snug and close to the jetty. One extended a shovel-like hand to Bridget, and she accepted his help, climbing out of the rocking sloop and onto the pier.

Valin climbed out on his own and said something to one of them that Bridget did not understand. The man answered in a similarly incomprehensible stream, all sharp consonants sprinkled with a few round vowels. That one hopped down into the hold and wrested out Bridget's box, handing it to the shorter of his companions. All three of them were enough alike that Bridget wondered if they might be brothers.

The shortest of the Bear Brothers received the box and balanced it on his shoulder, bowing and gesturing for Bridget and Valin to proceed him.

God above, it is cold. Bridget wrapped her shawl more tightly around her head. A boisterous, merciless wind blew across the bay, snatching at her skirts and worming its way through her woolen stockings. It bit into the skin of her face, and to Bridget's embarrassment, her teeth began to chatter. To make things worse, at that same moment, her stomach let out a mighty growl and she became aware of a raging thirst.

"You're cold, Bridget?" said Valin, solicitously, coming to stand on the windward side of her. "And hungry too, I'll wager. That is a frequent concern of making this crossing. Come, we are not going far, and there is an escort waiting for us."

The single pathway of the jetty soon turned into a whole series of docks and walkways. Obviously, when the season was good, Biradost saw much traffic from ships of all sizes. Its docks appeared even more extensive than Bayfield's.

Beyond the docks and the fieldstone storm wall, Biradost was a wooden town. Its thick-beamed houses sported clapboard sides, and doors painted as fancifully as Valin had painted the sides of his boat. They crowded together along streets that seemed, at the moment, to be a combination of snow and frozen mud. The people who passed by were mere bundles of wool and patterned scarves, with a lucky few in furs and leather boots. Bridget, whose feet had begun to tingle painfully despite her workboots and thick socks, found herself envying them.

Next to the gatehouses flanking the opening in the storm wall, a troop of mounted soldiers waited beside a horse-drawn sleigh. Valin raised his hand and hailed their leader in the local tongue.

"Our guard, sent from the dowager empress," he said, leading her forward.

A guard? Bridget's throat tightened. *Yes,* she told herself. *Don't forget. This is not a peaceful world.*

The lead soldier dismounted and bowed in front of them, placing his hand over his heart. He was a hardened, square man, with skin browned by the sun and by harsh weather. His hair was golden-brown, like that of the Bear Brothers from the harbor, rather than black like Valin's. Where Valin's cheeks and chin were high and sharp, this man's face was square and solid. A puckered white scar running down the right side of his face said that he had once come close to losing an ear. Rather than a coat, like Kalami, he wore a cloak of royal blue that covered a silver breastplate and a leather jerkin and hose sewn with steel scales. A helmet hung from his horse's saddle, Bridget saw, and the sword at his side hung in a leather scabbard as stained and worn as the boots on his feet.

Bridget's gaze wandered to the other eight men, all of whom were similarly dressed. They all wore their helmets. The visors covered their faces, leaving only their eyes visible. Four of them had deeply curved bows slung on their backs, and the other four rested the butts of long-handled, spear-tipped axes against their stirrups. One of them also carried a splendid pennant displaying a golden bird on a field of blue. Despite that, Bridget could see that nothing here was simply for show. These were serious soldiers, ready to deal with serious trouble. She did not know whether to be reassured or unnerved.

The leader straightened up. He spoke in a voice that was as rough and competent as his face. Valin smiled, clapping the man on the shoulder as an old friend, and replied.

Valin turned back to Bridget and said in English, "Mistress Bridget, this is Chadek Chastasyn Khabravin—Captain Chadek, you would call him—of Her Grand Majesty the Dowager Empress's household guard."

Bridget, uncertain of what to do, bobbed a curtsy to the man, who responded with another crisp bow.

Valin smiled, and Bridget hoped it was with satisfaction rather than amusement. "Her Grand Majesty sends you her personal greetings and bids us come to her as quickly as we may. Unfortunately," he added with a sigh, "this means that I will not have the time to weave for you a spell of understanding until after we reach the palace. I must ask you to rely on me as your translator."

The notion made Bridget frown, although she could not quite have said the reason for her unease. "We will have time on this journey, you cannot work it as we travel?"

"Time yes, but not peace," answered Valin. "Even here, I must concentrate to work my will, and I must have the proper materials. Forgive me. I should have completed this before we left Sand Island, but working magic there was so difficult, and I was anxious to be away."

Bridget made herself smile. "Well, we shall manage as best we can, just as we have been doing."

Valin gave her a half-bow in acknowledgment. "Then, let us be on our way." He led Bridget to the sleigh, which was painted bright blue and trimmed with gilded curlicues. Another soldier sat on the driver's box, holding reins decked out with blue ribbons.

At an order from Captain Chadek, Shortest Bear from the harbor set Bridget's box onto a rack at the rear of the sleigh and lashed it down. Valin helped Bridget into the sleigh beside a pile of thick furs. Bridget settled onto the padded seat and resisted the urge to burrow into the rugs Valin heaped onto her lap. Under the rugs lay a fur hood and cape for her head and shoulders, and a rabbit-skin muff for her freezing hands. Even better, under those waited a basket that contained fat wedges of soft white cheese, two loaves of black bread and a crock filled with what smelled like apple cider.

Bathed in warmth, Bridget felt herself smile. She would be traveling in imperial style indeed.

Valin helped himself to one of the loaves and half the cheese and climbed up beside the driver, saying something to the party at large. The captain barked another order, and the soldiers formed up. Captain Chadek took the lead with three others, a single soldier stationed himself on each side of the sleigh, and the last three fell behind.

Captain Chadek said a word and the soldiers urged their horses forward. The sleigh driver cracked the whip over the heads of his team, and the sleigh lurched forward into the snow-covered street.

Flanked by the soldiers and the sleigh's high, curving sides, Bridget could see only snatches of Biradost. Nonetheless, as she ate the food provided, she craned her neck eagerly for whatever glimpses she could catch—a set of carved shutters on a second-story opening so a woman could shake out a dusty rug, a huge but empty bird's nest on a peaked roof next to the chimney, the glint of gilding on a distant spire. Noise filled the air. Bridget was surrounded by a jumble made up of the thudding of hooves, the roll and murmur of voices, the creak of wood, the distant ring of metal against metal, a dog's bark, a man's shout. Now that her nose was no longer stopped by cold and salt spray, she smelled cooking, wood smoke, garbage and manure.

Only a few people stopped to look at them. Evidently, Bridget's party was not grand enough, or unusual enough, to incite comments, other than what were obviously complaints about having to get out of the way in the narrow streets. The faces Bridget saw were weather-roughened and strong, with eyes of amber or bright blue. Most of them seemed to have blond or brown hair, but here and there she saw a lock of red hair sticking out from under cap or hood.

All at once, the sleigh lurched to a halt. Bridget heard a donkey bray and men shouting up ahead, and a sound like a muffled smack. Valin stood up on the box. Whatever he saw, he gave a roar, jumped to the street and ran past soldiers. Bridget leapt to her own feet, shedding rugs and straining to see between the heads and shoulders of the men on horseback.

She saw a cart piled with snow-dusted garbage. It listed to the right, because one of its wooden wheels had stuck in a frozen rut. A man sprawled facedown in the snow, with his hands covering his head. His leather cap lay nearby. One of the soldiers stood over him, rigidly, as if at attention. In front of him, Valin stood with one arm raised. His hand held a riding crop and he seemed frozen in the act of bringing it down against the soldier's face.

Suddenly, Bridget felt herself to be six years old. She stood in the dirt yard of the cooperage in Bayfield. A Negro man in patched clothing huddled on the ground. A spindly white man wearing heavy farm boots drew back his foot to let loose another kick. In front of him stood Everett Lederle, Bridget's father, his chapped, red hands clenched until the knuckles glowed white. Poppa was strong from carrying heavy oil cans up the iron stairs to the light, and from the fury in his face, Bridget knew he was ready to use all that strength against the skinny man with the big, dusty boots. The skinny man saw it too, and he lowered his foot, spat and walked away.

In front of her now, Captain Chadek dismounted and stepped between the two men. He said something to Valin, and Valin lowered his arm, but he did not release his grip on the riding crop. Chadek turned and said something much harsher to the soldier, who scowled, but bowed and pointed at two of the other soldiers in the troop, and then pointed to the cart. The soldiers both dismounted and all three of them put their shoulders to the cart wheel, calling out what was probably the local equivalent of "One, two, three, heave!"

While the soldiers freed the cart, Valin gestured to the man in the snow, who scrambled to his feet, clutching his cap. His hair was coal black, and he had a long, straight nose like Valin's. He stood with shoulders hunched, head ducked, and eyes wide, like a man who was used to hard knocks, and expected the next one to come at any moment.

The captain spoke, and then Valin, and the man's head bobbed nervously. Fortunately, he was spared any further conversation, because at that moment the cart rolled free of the rut and the soldiers stood back, their heavy breath making clouds of steam that even Bridget could see.

Bridget interpreted Captain Chadek's next string of commands as "What are you standing around for? Get back on your horses!" The soldiers certainly acted as if that was what he said, hurrying to swing themselves back into their saddles. Valin said something final to the carter, who gave a hunched bow, and then scrambled to take his donkey's halter and urge the animal and cart out of the soldiers' way.

When Valin climbed back up on the sleigh box, he was breathing as hard as if he had been the one who freed the cart. Bridget, as she sat back down, couldn't help noticing that he still carried the riding crop. He laid it across his knees, and Bridget watched his shoulders shifting under his coat as if he were struggling to relax them as the sleigh started forward again.

"Valin?"

Valin turned to look at her with one black eye.

"You are not from this country, are you? I seem to recall you saying something of the sort."

She saw half of Valin's mouth smile. "Ah, Bridget, you are observant." The mockery in his tone was too gentle for Bridget to bridle at.

"Where is your home?"

Sadness shone in Valin's eye, and for a moment Bridget thought he might answer that he had none. "I was born on the island of Tuukos, which is to the north of here."

"And your people, and . . ." Bridget looked down at her muffled hands for a moment, searching for words. "The other Isavaltans, do not, perhaps, get along?"

The smile grew sharper. "Tuukos did not to join the empire voluntarily, that is true. But, it was all many years ago. My grandfather's father did not even see that battle."

Before Bridget could say another word, Valin turned away. Bridget decided it was best to let the subject lie, for now, anyway.

Eventually, the streets ended at a high wooden wall. Bridget and her escort passed under an iron portcullis out to onto snow-covered fields. The noise and variety of the town was replaced by an undisturbed landscape of snow gently undulating toward the black line of a distant forest. Bridget, satisfied for now by the bread and cheese, warmed by her furs and tired from her long, unspeakably strange day, drifted off into sleep.

Lack of motion and rising voices lifted Bridget from her slumber. She blinked, tried to rub her eyes, got a face full of rabbit-skin muff, disentangled her hands and wiped her eyes clear of sleep and cold-induced tears.

The sleigh had halted in a copse of dark green pines that rattled and whispered in the wind as if telling each other secrets. The captain and several of the guard clustered together, conferring. Valin stood beside them. The remaining men faced outward, scanning the sides of the road, and the way from which they had come. Whatever was going on, their grim, impatient faces told Bridget they did not like it. Neither, it seemed, did their horses, which pawed the ground and whickered to each other.

Bridget twisted in her seat, but all she saw was her escort, the frozen road and the dark trees with their whispering needles and their shrouds of snow.

Seeing her awake, Valin returned to the side of the sleigh.

"What's happened?" Bridget asked, keeping her voice calm against the nervousness she felt building inside.

"The man Captain Chadek sent to scout ahead reports that the bridge we must cross has been blocked." He drummed his gloved fingers on the edge of the sleigh. He looked straight ahead, seeing the possibilities in both the road and future. "We could, of course, cross on the ice, but he does not like the development and neither do I."

Bridget felt the hairs on the back of her neck prickle. Although she chided herself for being foolish, she could not escape the feeling that the black trunks of the trees had moved in a little closer.

The captain trotted his horse back to the sleigh and spoke to Valin. Valin replied with a single syllable and nod. "We're going to try the ice. The area around the bridge is fairly open, and we will be able to see what comes. Bridget, you must listen to me," he said seriously, laying his hand over her hers. "Should there be an ambush, you must get away, no matter what you see happening to us." A thousand questions and protests rose in Bridget, and she bit them all back. Now was not the time to begin second-guessing the man who had brought her this far.

"Follow the road. It will take you to the palace. You must not . . ." His eyes grew hard and he clutched her hand tightly. If it had not been for the layer of rabbit fur, his grip would have hurt. "You must not, under any circumstances, leave the road. The forests are vast, and if you wander into the wrong valley, you could be in serious danger. Do you understand?"

Bridget nodded. Valin held her with his hard hand and harder eyes, as if he thought he could squeeze his words into her, or burn them in with his gaze.

"I promise," said Bridget, pulling her hands away. "I will not leave the road."

Valin flexed his hand a couple of times, and opened his mouth to say something more, but instead he just climbed back up next to the sleigh's driver.

The soldiers touched up their horses, moving the procession forward again, but all seemed changed. The men rode close around the sleigh at a brisk trot. Their eyes scanned the trees, the hindmost checking the road behind them constantly. Bridget found herself straining to hear any unusual noises, but all she heard was the clopping of hooves, the jingle of the harness, the creak and rattle of the tree branches in the wind, and the soft hiss and thump as bundles of snow fell from the branches to the ground.

Bridget shivered and pulled her furs more tightly around herself.

Up ahead, the trees parted to make room for a river of black ice dusted with sparkling snow. A double-arched stone bridge spanned its length, and even from the sleigh, Bridget could see the huge mound of snow and tree branches that blocked the way.

The captain raised his hand, and the procession halted. The archers ringed the sleigh, unslung their bows and nocked arrows into their strings. The men with axes spaced themselves between archers, sitting tall in their saddles. Tension hummed between them, and they muttered to one another in their guttural tongue. Bridget found herself wishing in vain she could understand what worried them.

Valin stood on the sleigh box, shading his eyes with his hand, but Bridget could not tell what he was looking at. Captain Chadek, evidently satisfied with how his men had arrayed themselves, took one of the axes, and led his horse down to the icy bank. He stretched the ax out in front of him to test the ice and make sure it was safe for horse and man.

All at once, Valin shouted. Chadek looked up, startled, but as he did, the ax point touched the ice. Bridget felt a wave of cold like a silent wind rush past her. In the next instant, Chadek shouted. He struggled to pull the point of his ax away from the ice, and for a moment she wondered why he did not drop it. Then she saw that he could not, for his hand was stuck to the shaft. His horse reared and bucked, shaking its head from side to side. Chadek fell on the snow, his boots grappling for purchase and failing to find it while his panicked horse dragged him back and forth like a dead branch. The horse reared again, its hooves flailing dangerously near Chadek's head, and Bridget saw that he could not release the horse's reins either.

One of the soldiers shouted and jumped to the ground, running toward the captain and pulling out a knife as he did. Valin screamed after the man, who veered off, but skidded in the snow and tumbled down the bank, landing sprawled on his back on the ice. He called out and Bridget saw him struggle, but he did not rise.

"Remember what I told you," said Valin to Bridget as he scrambled off the sleigh box.

Valin cautiously approached the madly plunging horse, one hand in front of him, and one hand reaching inside his coat. Chadek cried out, in pain this time, as the horse wrenched his arm yet again. Bridget bit her lip. In the woods, a crow cawed, and then another. Next to her, one of the axmen jerked his head up. He called out something to his fellows and raised his weapon.

They poured out of the woods on all sides, and for a moment Bridget thought they really were crows. Capes made entirely of black feathers flapped like wings, and dark, bony hands scrabbled and clutched like claws. The horses reared up under the sudden attack, and the soldiers all shouted. One man, then another, was pulled to the ground before they had a chance to defend themselves. But the others turned and wheeled, plunging into the flock of cloaked dwarves, stabbing down with sword and ax.

One of the creatures scrabbled over the side of the sleigh, and Bridget caught a glimpse of its wrinkled face and round black eyes, more like a crow's than any human eye should be. It reached for her, and she threw her rug over it. Her driver grabbed the living bundle and threw it back down onto the road. Another crow-dwarf clambered up the side of the sleigh. Bridget snatched up the riding crop that lay on the sleigh box and lashed out, knocking the creature screaming backward. Cries rose on every side, making as much noise as a murder of true crows. The world around her filled with heat, sweat and blood, the frantic calls of men and horses, a hurricane of black feathers, blue cloaks, brown horse hair, and the glint of light on scarlet-splotched metal. The driver had the reins in his fist and was shouting at the team. The horses struggled to back and turn the sleigh. Bridget lurched, grabbing the sleigh's gilded edge to keep her balance. Another of the creatures leapt to reach her and she swung her fist out, shoving it away, trying not to see when the soldier's ax came down to finish it off.

A shadow moved overhead, jerking Bridget's eyes upward in time to see a net drop down from the trees. Voices shouted, crows cawed, and Bridget's hand flew up to knock the net away, but she was too late. It draped heavily across her and all at once she could not move. She froze there, one hand raised, her mouth open, with no limb, no sense, under her control. She could not blink, she could scarcely even breathe. Of all her muscles, only her heart still labored.

Bridget fell, toppling over the side of the sleigh like a log of wood. Panic surged through her, and her mind strained to reach her frozen body. Clawed hands grasped the net that held her, lifting her up onto feather-covered shoulders. Soldiers cried out—she thought she heard Valin's voice mixed in with them—but all around her the crows cawed and would not be silenced. Their calls battered her ears, even as her mind battered at the inside of her skull seeking release that it could not find. Tears of fear and frustration spilled out of the corners of her paralyzed eyes, which stared up at the black branches speeding over her, making bars for the grey sky, which was all she could see. The human shouts faded away, leaving her only with the snickering and chuckling of crows.

Bridget hoped she would faint, but it seemed that respite was denied her. The world became nothing but cold, the clutch of claw-hands, and the blur of black branches and grey sky. Fear turned to anger, then to weariness, and then back to fear. There was a time when she was laid down on the snow and branches and leaves laid over her. Her heart hammered against her ribs, and her mind could only wonder if she had been left there for dead.

But no, the crows pulled away the debris and snatched her up again. The sky was deeper grey now, and the light dwindled with each passing heartbeat, until at last she saw stars sprinkled across the black sky between branches that had become jagged slivers of shadow.

After an unknowable time, when cold and fear had finally numbed her mind, the branches pulled back from the sky. The dwarf-crows cawed perhaps eagerly, perhaps anxiously, and Bridget, who had thought herself past further shock, heard a human voice answer.

Golden light flickered at the corner of her right eye, and wooden beams slid over the sky. She was inside somewhere, somewhere with stone walls to block at least some of the cold, and a stone floor for her to be laid on. The dwarf-crows cawed, the human voice spoke again, followed by the shuffling of feet and rattling of feathers. A door opened, the wind swirled around Bridget, capes—or was it wings?—flapped and the door closed. Bridget lay on the floor, arm raised, mouth open, and eyes staring at the twisted ropes that held her, because she could do nothing else.

After a moment, she heard footsteps again. A man's face with brown eyes and a full mouth bent low over her. He lifted his hand, and she saw a knife flash in the flickering light. Inwardly, Bridget screamed as the knife came down, but it only slit the ropes around her. The severed ends fell away. Bridget felt her mind open and her will rush back down to her limbs.

Her lungs hauled in a great gasp of air. Her lids squeezed shut over her burning eyes. Then, she remembered she was not alone and her eyes flew open and she shoved herself upright, scuttling backward, forgetting all appearance, until her back slammed against the wall.

The man straightened up, regarding her coolly. He still had his knife in his hand, she saw. But she could not help seeing other things now. He stood with his back to a fireplace that held a cheerful blaze. The stone room around them had two doors, one with a little snow melting before it, and another, which might lead to an inner room. Plants hung in bundles from the roof beams, along with a pair of rabbits, and a trio of fat brown birds. Cooking pots were piled in one corner of the hearth, next to some casks and bags. Chests and shelves waited against the walls. That, a table, a bench and the two of them seemed to be the extent of the place.

The man had not moved, not sheathed the knife or done any other thing. Bridget's breathing began to even out. She swallowed, although her throat and mouth were painfully dry. Slowly, keeping her eyes on the man and his knife, she climbed to her feet and stood trembling with cold and strain.

Now she could see that he was a man of medium height. Slowly, carefully, she circled around him so that she was no longer looking straight into the fire and could see him better. He turned to keep his face toward her, but made no other move. His glossy black hair had been swept back from his broad forehead and divided into many braids that were looped and coiled around his head, threaded through beads and woven with scarlet ribbons until they were finally bundled into a ponytail at his neck. His eyes, which watched her, half-lidded under heavy black brows, were the brown of oak leaves in autumn. He had a strong, proud nose and a fine chin. His skin was a clear brown that shimmered almost golden where the firelight touched it.

Like most of the men she had seen since her arrival, he wore thick hose tucked into leather boots and a long, wide-skirted coat with fur at the cuffs and collar. But he did not wear it well. He held himself hunched in and awkward, as if his skin did not want to touch the wool, or perhaps it was just from the cold. This man did not belong in winter, she knew that instinctively.

In fact—Bridget's own shoulders straightened—she knew *him*. This was Sakra, Princess Ananda's chief advisor, and helper. She had seen him in Momma's mirror when Valin had enchanted it for her, and then again afterward when she was alone in the lamp room.

Bridget's throat closed. She had the outside door beside her, could she run? But to where? Out into the frigid night? How far would she get with each step betraying her trail? What if the dwarf-crows waited out there for her? And how would she find the road? The road Valin had warned her not to leave? She would not scream her head off like some silly girl in a melodrama. If this man had been worried about anyone hearing her, he surely would have gagged her before he released her body from the net.

Sakra spoke then, the same hard, consonant-heavy sounds that Valin used when speaking to the soldiers, but his voice had a lilt and a hesitation to it that was not in theirs. This was not his native tongue, probably, and he had learned it but lately.

When Bridget did not respond, he spoke again, loudly, and more slowly. Bridget set her jaw and shook her head. Sakra took three rapid steps toward her, and spoke again, a low harsh, whisper.

Bridget met his eyes without flinching. "It's no good you threatening me, sir," she said. "I cannot understand a word you say. Whatever you are going to do to me, you had best just get on with it."

The man pulled back, searching her face for a moment with his autumn brown eyes. Then, much to Bridget's surprise, he laughed. It was a rueful sound, and Bridget thought it might be directed more at himself than at her.

He stepped back, motioning toward the inner door with the blade of the knife. Bridget understood that gesture plainly enough. She thought again of the outer door at her side, and then of the deathly cold, and the possible dwarf-crows that waited for her outside it. Neck and back straight, she walked through the inner door.

The room inside was a comfortless bedchamber. It held only a thin pallet in a wooden frame covered with furs, a table, a crude stool and a clay jar of fairly obvious purpose. The man motioned with his knife again, and Bridget backed up against the far wall. He vanished from her sight for an instant, and then reappeared, setting a pierced tin lantern on the floor. He pushed the door shut, and Bridget heard the sound of a key turning in a lock, and then a bolt being lowered.

Bridget let her head fall forward. *Marvelous. Marvelous. A new start to a new life in a world filled with magic and wonders. What kind of madwoman have I become that I believed this was a good idea?*

Because there was nothing else to do, she picked up the lantern and set it on the table. She felt absurdly thankful that her captor had thought to give her a light, because otherwise she would have been shut in complete darkness. The room had no window, only the bolted door. As far as she could see in the flickering light, the wooden roof had been snugly made and looked quite sturdy. Even if there had been a way for her to climb up onto the thick roof beam, there did not seem to be any way out through that. Perhaps if she could reach it, she could use the flame from the lantern to burn a hole through which she could creep.

Which still left her lost, with inadequate clothing, in a winter colder than any she had ever known, and the only human being around remained Sakra, who still carried his knife.

She found water in the jug on the table and drank. There wasn't enough, but she still felt somewhat better when she finished. That done, Bridget paced the room restlessly, her thoughts swinging from impossible escape plans to cursing herself for the greatest fool on Earth, or on any other world. A chimney took up part of the wall and provided a little warmth, but Bridget could not stand still to take advantage of it. Perhaps some part of her feared that if she stood still the paralysis that had gripped her before would return.

After a time that might have been an hour, or might have been ten, for all she could tell, Bridget threw herself onto the rickety bed and buried her face in her hands. Then, a familiar smell reached her—the odor of baking bread. Bridget's mouth instantly began to water and her stomach growled painfully. When had she last eaten? At the moment, it felt like a lifetime ago. It must have been the bread and cheese in the sleigh, and before that it was the breakfast she shared with Valin in the lighthouse. The thought of the corn cakes and molasses, the very end of the bacon and the coffee, cramped Bridget's stomach up again. Would her captor remember to feed her? Or was this some new torture? What would its purpose be? It wasn't as if she could tell him anything, as if she would, even if she could speak to him.

But after a few minutes longer of smelling the bread, Bridget realized, to her shame, that if she could tell Sakra anything she might, just for a taste of that wonderful-smelling bread. Could she stand beside the door, wait for it to open, hit him with the stool, possibly even kill him with the knife, eat the bread and wait for morning when she could at least make her escape in daylight?

The plan filling her weary mind, Bridget stood. But, the plan had come too late. The door opened and Sakra walked in. In his hand, he carried a flat, braided loaf of bread. It smelled of warmth and herbs and it took all of Bridget's strength not to lunge for it.

Sakra held out the loaf. Bridget swallowed but did not move. She might not be the only one with plans. Who knew what besides herbs and flour went into that bread?

Sakra nodded, perhaps with approval. He broke off the end of the bread, releasing a cloud of fragrant steam. He popped the bread into his mouth, chewed and swallowed. Bridget stared as if she had been stupefied. How long had it been since she had eaten?

Sakra held the bread out to Bridget again. Bridget realized, or hoped she realized, that he was showing her it was safe to eat. Holding herself in rigid control, she accepted the loaf from his hand, sat down on the bed, broke off a small bite and ate it, chewing thoroughly.

Whatever else he was, her captor was a good baker. The herbed bread was heavy, stout and crusty.

When she swallowed the last bite, Sakra nodded. "Now we may talk."

Bridget stared, she couldn't help it. "You speak English." Her hand flew to her mouth. The sounds issuing forth had no place in the English language. She thought of the bread she had just eaten, the braided bread, and Valin's words about how magic was "a thing woven." Could there have been a spell in the bread? Her stomach cramped again, this time in rebellion against what she had just eaten.

Sakra shook his head, disgusted, or perhaps just disappointed at her ignorance. "Who are you?"

"Bridget Lederle," she answered primly. "Who are you?" No point in letting him know how much she knew.

The question seemed to take him aback for a moment, but then he shrugged. "Sakra *dra* Dhiren Phanidraela. Who is your master? What are his plans?"

Indignation straightened Bridget's spine. "I have no master. What do you take me for?"

That made Sakra frown. "Then what are the plans of the one who brought you here?"

You're very free, said Bridget's mind. *Why would I answer any question of yours? You kidnap me, you terrify me and then you lock me in a cell. You are the one who should explain yourself.*

But her mouth said, "He means to take me to the dowager empress so that together we may break Ananda's hold on the emperor."

It took her a moment to realize she had even spoken aloud. But then her hand clutched her own throat. "What have you done to me?"

The corner of Sakra's mouth turned up. "You are a poor sorcerer indeed if you could not smell the truth weaving in that bread."

Again Bridget's stomach roiled. Idiot! She should have realized. She knew who this man was, she should have known not to take what she was given.

"How does Valin Kalami intend to proceed?"

Bridget's mind tried to clamp her jaw shut, but she said, "He has not told me. He only says that it has been prophesied that my presence will return the rule of Isavalta to the dowager."

Sakra leaned closer. Bridget, unable to endure any more, lashed out, striking him hard against his ear with her open hand. She jumped to her feet and ran to the door, only to find it locked. She had been so intent on the bread she had not heard him turn the key. She pounded her fist against the door and turned to face her captor, who was looking at her with of face full of startled amusement.

"Stop this! Kill me, or whatever it is you intend. I know nothing. I have had no time to learn."

"Who is your mother?" asked Sakra.

Bridget did not even try to struggle against answering. "Ingrid Loftfield Lederle," she said, pushing herself away from the door and crossing back to the bed.

"Hear that, my father-god," breathed Sakra, and there was no mistaking the tone of wonder in his voice. "Who would have believed the Avanasidoch would have so little learning in her?"

Now it was Bridget's turn to frown. "What do you mean?" she demanded, turning to face him fully. "Why would you care about my mother?"

"You do not know?" Sakra rose to his feet. "You truly do not know?"

Bridget's hand clamped around the bedpost. "Would I have asked if I did?" she answered heatedly. But through the rising anger, she felt some small relief. Apparently, she had at least a little control over the form of her answers.

But Sakra did not seem to be listening. His eyes stared off into the distance, and Bridget could not help wondering what he saw. "Where is your mother?"

"She is dead." She paused, and then of her own will she ventured, "She died giving birth to me." Perhaps if she appeared cooperative she could get answers to a few questions of her own.

That brought his attention back to her and the present. "I'm sorry," he said unexpectedly.

Bridget lifted her chin and said nothing. Statements, it seemed, did not compel a response.

Sakra moved closer. Then a smile lit his eyes, perhaps as he remembered a clout on his ear. He stepped back to a more respectable distance. "How do you intend to help Kalami?"

Bridget's mouth opened, but this time she was ready. "I intend to learn what he can teach me." She folded her hands in front of her. "What were those things that kidnapped me?"

Sakra frowned again, but it looked as if he were frowning to keep from smiling. "You mean to question me now? Answer for answer?"

"If I can," said Bridget. She had it now. There was a split second between question and the moment of compulsion. She had that long to formulate her reply.

Sakra snorted, and sat down on the stool. He looked up at her, his forehead wrinkled and his whole manner saying that he was puzzled. "No, I think I will not play that game." He rubbed his chin. "But I think I will ask you what you truly know of Valin Kalami."

Bridget had her answer ready before the last syllable left his mouth. "I know what I've seen."

"Pay attention, for these are the limits of magic," muttered Sakra under his breath, and Bridget felt herself smile a little with satisfaction at his frustration. "What have you seen?"

Anticipating the question, Bridget picked out what she hoped would be the most baffling answer. Perhaps she could distract him with trivialities. "I have seen him giving wine to foxes."

Sakra's head snapped up. "When?" he asked sharply.

Startled, Bridget had no time to form her own answer and one fell from her mouth. "When I had my vision."

Sakra rose slowly to his feet, his face flushed. "You have visions of the mind?"

There was something eager in his eyes that made Bridget's breath catch in her throat. Again, her tongue answered without her. "Yes. I see the future, and sometimes the past."

"Have you seen my mistress?"

Bridget swallowed, struggling to regain her composure. "I have seen her afraid."

"And myself, at a time other than when we met in the graveyard in dream?"

Bridget shook her head. "Only in the reflection of a mirror Kalami showed me." Her tongue her own again, she added, "What do you mean when we met in the graveyard?"

Sakra stepped forward until he was a bare inch from her. Bridget smelled the warmth of him, the scents of baking and smoke from the fire. She swallowed, and tried not to shrink from his closeness or from the way his autumn eyes stared into hers.

"It has been taken from you," he said to her. "I see traces of that in your eyes. Who took it from you? Was it Kalami?"

"No," Bridget herself said. "It was the fox." *What fox?* She struggled to find some memory, some clue, but nothing came to her. New fear made her hands tremble and she shoved them into her apron pockets before Sakra could see.

To her relief, Sakra moved away a few paces. Uneasiness filled his face and he fingered the end of one of his braids. "And when you saw Kalami giving the wine to foxes, was that vision of the past, or future?"

"The past."

That made him pause. Understanding came into his eyes, and turned his whole face grim. Whatever sympathy or amusement he had momentarily felt vanished completely. He thumped his fist once against the wall, and his other hand strayed to his waist, seeking the knife, Bridget was sure. Her hands went suddenly cold and closed around the fabric of her apron.

"Can you compel these visions?" Sakra asked, too quickly for Bridget to shape her answer.

"No." It was all she could do to keep the nervousness out of her voice. "They come when they will."

"Have you had any visions since you came to Isavalta?"

"No."

Sakra stood silent for a moment, measuring Bridget with his eyes and judging what he saw. Bridget met his gaze unflinchingly, daring him to make a move or utter an insult, although inside her resolve wavered and she tried to think what the room contained that could turn a knife's edge. At the same time, she wanted desperately to question him. What was the fox her mouth had spoken of without her consent? Was it related to the foxes she had seen dealing with Valin and chasing Ananda? How could such a creature be in Bayfield? Had it followed Valin?

What else in this land of crow-dwarves and sorcerers did she have to fear?

"I will have to think on what you have told me." Being careful not to turn his back on her, Sakra returned to the door. He produced both key and knife, and let himself out.

Bridget stayed where she was until she heard the bolt slide home. Her hands rubbed restlessly together and she didn't know what to think. Almost automatically, she began pacing again—from the bed, to the door, to the stool, to the night-soil jar and back to the bed again, over and over, as if she were chasing her thoughts around the room.

What did he mean that they had met in dream? Why could she not escape from images of foxes? How could this man have ever heard of Ingrid Loftfield? Momma had once disappeared, yes, but that was to Madison, or maybe Chicago, some big city like that.

But what if it wasn't? Bridget's hands clutched at each other. *What if Momma went someplace much farther afield?*

Bridget carried no images of her mother as a living woman. She had one faded, tintype photograph that Poppa kept framed by his bedside. Ingrid Loftfield had a sweep of dark hair and pale skin, a wide mouth and widely spaced eyes. At some point, she had owned a white shirtwaist dress, for she had been photographed in it.

From the bed, to the door, to the stool, to the night-soil jar and back again.

Had Momma been here? Could it be possible? Was that why she had come back in her own mirror and shown Bridget Valin and the foxes? Had she somehow come to this place of winter and dwarf-crows? Bridget felt herself beginning to warm and her pacing grew more rapid. What had she done here? Where had she wandered? Had she seen those huge forests, the distant mountains? Had she been free? Would Bridget be free again, as Momma might have been, to explore this place, to do what she had set out to do? What had Momma set out to do here? Where had she gone and who had she met? A strange eagerness took hold of Bridget, moving her feet ever faster. She too wanted to be free, to do and to see, to soar through this land.

All at once, Bridget laughed. She practically was dancing her pacing steps, weaving around the room as if she were drunk.

Weaving. Valin said magic was a thing woven. Could one weave a spell just by walking a pattern on the floor?

Why not?

Giddy as she was, Bridget would have believed she could flap her arms and fly to the moon. She began to run, tracing her steps on the floor over and over again, trying to keep from laughing. She thought about freedom. She thought about the places her mother might have been, the magic she might have seen, the royalty she might have met. Her mother had been free here. Momma had been free, Bridget would be free.

Momma was free. I will be free. I will be free.

The air shimmered as if with heat and wrapped around her like a blanket. She could feel it brush her skin. In a moment, it would bind her, lift her up and bear her away. She would be free.

I am *free!*

"No!"

The door slammed open and Sakra lunged forward, his knife in front of him, trying to cut through the air as he had cut through the net that held her. Bridget just laughed at him, raising her arms to the air's embrace.

The world vanished.

Chapter Eight

The Vixen trotted easily through the piney woods, leaping over fallen logs, and picking her way delicately across fresh-running streams. Only the softest green light worked its way through the tightly clenched branches overhead, and the wind that ruffled her fur was cold and stale. The Vixen paid it no mind. She had her business to attend to, and would not be discomfited by such trappings.

The pines gave way grudgingly to other trees—oak, yew and maple. The wind brought the scent of old bones, long picked clean. The Vixen turned toward it. She passed a decrepit birch tree, its tattered bark peeling from its trunk. The tree raised its branches to whip them into her eyes. She regarded it with a steady green gaze, and the tree branches lowered to sway dissolutely in the stale wind.

A great crashing and barking sounded up ahead. The Vixen paused, her right forepaw raised. Two huge, black mastiffs broke through the trees, plunging straight for her, foam dripping from their red jaws. The Vixen, who appeared to be no more than any ordinary fox, looked at them. They snarled and howled, and the Vixen merely watched. At last, the snarls changed to whines and the dogs slunk back the way they came.

The Vixen bristled her tail with impatience and followed them.

Through a screen of thorny bracken, the Vixen came to a wooden fence that had broken and cracked in any number of places, only to be mended with twine and bone. A black cat with a blaze of white on its breast sat on the fence beside the sagging gate, washing its face.

"And what will you do to try to stop me?" asked the Vixen of the cat.

"Nothing," replied the cat, licking its paw and combing its whiskers.

The Vixen laid her front paws against the gate and pushed. It swung slowly open with a long, painful shriek from its rusted hinges. The Vixen, ears alert and whiskers twitching, stalked into the yard.

The yard was a mass of gouged dirt, broken twigs and tufts of dead grass. It smelled of fresh soil and old graves. In its center, a cottage dark with age and secrecy turned slowly on a monstrous pair of scarred and scaled legs, their curling talons gouging up the dirt with every step.

"Ishbushka!" The Vixen called out the house's name. "Stand and face me! Kneel you down, for I have business with your mistress."

Ishbushka halted with the door toward the Vixen and, like an awful parody of an ancient woman, it knelt cautiously until its steps touched the ground. The pitted and worm-scarred door fell open.

The Vixen mounted the stairs, feeling them quiver with each touch of her paws. She paused in the doorway, tail erect, to see how she might be greeted.

Beyond the door, Baba Yaga the Bony-Legged Witch, the Witch with the Iron Teeth, sat wrapped in a tattered black robe working at her loom inside a room built of bones. Bones braced the filthy walls. Ribs curved overhead to make the roof beams. Skulls built the hearth and held up its mantel shelf. Bundles of bones and skulls hung from the white roof beams the way herbs might hang in a midwife's cottage. Among the human bones were the skulls and bones of all manner of animals—birds, badgers, deer, wolf and, the Vixen noted with a twitch of her tail, foxes.

Even the loom where Baba Yaga muttered and mumbled to herself had been built of bones. Giant leg bones made its upright beams, arm bones made the more delicate cross bracing. Instead of thread, the loom had been strung with sinew. The Vixen sniffed delicately at the faded carrion scent and dismissed it.

Baba Yaga bent close over her work under the light of a candle of white fat. Her gnarled fingers shot a shuttle made from an ancient jawbone back and forth, creating a weft made of sinews and hair.

Under her feet, the pedals clacked like great teeth. The air around her trembled as she drew down the magic and trapped it in her grisly weaving.

The Vixen sat back on her haunches, curling her tail around her feet, and, with some little difficulty, composed herself to patience.

The candle burned. The shuttle whispered as the witch whisked it back and forth. The pedals clattered and clacked. The cat sauntered past the Vixen without giving her a glance, curled up in a corner and, to all appearances, went to sleep.

After a time, Baba Yaga said, "The daughter is mine."

"The mother is yours," said the Vixen. "Your claim extends no further."

"Blood makes my claim for me." Baba Yaga stilled her shuttle, but did not raise her milky eyes from her work. "Who owns the mother, owns all the daughters."

The Vixen turned one ear toward the yard, as if what she heard out there interested her more than what she heard inside the cottage. "What if I disputed your claim?"

Now the witch lifted her head and spoke straight to the Vixen. The candlelight glinted dully on the black iron of her teeth. "Who brought the mother here? Set all in motion? Who drew the daughter from the living world into the Silent Lands?"

The Vixen shrugged. "Fate? Chance? Perhaps it was the flight of birds in autumn? How can even we know all that guides the path of the living and the mortal?" The Vixen's green eyes gleamed. "I say you have no claim here. What say you?"

Baba Yaga stood on legs so skinny they might well have been a pair of bones taken from Ishbushka's walls. "I say that if Ishbushka closes her door, you will be trapped in here with me until the world's end. What good will you be to your wounded sons then?"

The Vixen yawned, displaying all her sharp, white teeth. "As delightful as I find your company, and as pleasant as is your invitation, I fear I must decline." She combed one ear with paw. "Perhaps you would be willing to game for her."

The witch threw back her head and laughed. Ishbushka shuddered at the harsh, throaty sound. "What could you possibly have to bet in such a game?"

The Vixen paced back and forth in the threshold, her head cocked, apparently considering this problem. "Perhaps I could bet you my skull for your collection." She lifted her nose toward the bundles of bones hanging from the rib roof beams.

"Oh, no." Baba Yaga narrowed her pale eyes. "I know that trick. How would I lay claim to your skull if I could not touch your skin, or neck, or blood, none of which you will wager to me?" She grinned then, as if at a sudden, entertaining thought. "If you lose, you will deliver to me the skull of your oldest son."

The Vixen's ears flattened against her scalp and she curled her lip up to snarl at the witch. In the corner, the cat lifted its head and the Vixen saw the wary gleam in its golden eyes.

With an effort, she lifted her ears. "Done," she said softly.

"Done," replied Baba Yaga.

The witch stretched up one arm to the nearest bundle of bones and brought down a leather bag. From it, she shook out a handful of bleached knucklebones.

The Vixen changed. Now facing the witch stood a sleek woman with red hair and white skin wearing a long, scarlet shift bound with a girdle of braided hair, rust, black and white. Only her eyes remained her own.

Baba Yaga hefted the bones in her hand. "One, two, three!"

She tossed the bones into the air. Witch and Vixen each snatched at them, grabbing a cluster as they fell. The remaining bones changed at once into small grey moths and flew out the door. The cat leapt up and bounded after them.

"Four," said Baba Yaga, making her guess as to how many bones the Vixen had caught.

"Six," said the Vixen, as her guess of Baba Yaga's catch.

Both opened their hands. Only three bones lay on the Vixen's smooth palm, while Baba Yaga did in fact cradle six bones in her horny hand.

"Mine," said the Vixen, closing her fist around the bones.

Baba Yaga gazed at her shrewdly with one rheumy eye. "There will be those who did not think so."

The Vixen bared her teeth in a fierce, wild smile. "I am counting on that."

Bridget Lederle vanished in a rush of winter air and magic. For a moment, all Sakra could do was stand there gaping like a child with his dagger hanging useless from his fingertips. There was nothing, *nothing* in the tiny chamber she could have woven into a spell, not even the flames of the lantern provided enough fire to work with, and yet she vanished anyway.

Vanished. Escaped. To return to Kalami and tell all she had seen, and then to become his pawn or his pupil, or perhaps both. To become yet one more threat to Ananda.

That thought pulled Sakra upright, closed his mouth, and clenched his hand around his dagger's hilt. He sheathed the knife inside his sash and his eyes scanned the stone floor. As he hoped, Bridget Lederle's boots had left prints on the flagstones, faint traces of dirt and water, but it would be enough.

He retrieved a square of white silk from his cache in the other room. He had no time to carefully choose color, cut and weave. With each heartbeat the ethereal threads that reached from the prints to the woman who made them weakened. He knelt carefully, pressing the silk against the mud and meltwater. Again, his gaze swept the floor and, oh thank the Seven Mothers, found a long, auburn hair that had drifted down while Bridget Lederle worked her escape. Unbidden, the sight of how she had been at that moment filled his mind—tall and magnificent, rejoicing in her own power. How could such a one allow herself to be used by Kalami? Shaking his head, he plucked up the hair and rolled it into the stained silk.

Sakra returned to the cottage's main chamber and knelt in front of the fire. He closed his eyes and willed himself to stillness, drawing up the magic from Earth and soul. He did not open his eyes. Working by touch, he swiftly tied three knots in the roll of silk.

"Where is she?" he breathed, tying the question into each knot. "Where is she?" With a fourth knot, he tied the ends the cloth together and, still without opening his eyes, he pitched it into the fire. Ashes puffed, sparks crackled and he felt the spell open. He opened his eyes and stared without blinking into the flames. The flames fell apart to show him a hubless wheel with many spokes turning slowly in midair. The wheel melted and changed, becoming the sharp face of a fox. In the next heartbeat, the flames snapped shut around the visions and became a normal kitchen fire again.

Sakra sat back on his heels. The wheel was the symbol for the Silent Lands, and the fox . . . the fox could only mean the *lokai* and perhaps even their queen, the Vixen, walked close by her.

Sakra pounded his thigh with his fist. There were too many threads, too many mysteries and shadows. Bridget Lederle said she had seen Kalami giving wine to foxes. Were those the same foxes that had sought to bespell Ananda in the wood? They must have been, for another fox had taken memories from Bridget while she was still on the far shore of the world. Had she gone to them, or been taken by them? Had Kalami made some deal with the *lokai*, the fox spirits? Was he that foolish? The Vixen played no games but her own. It was not possible she had truly allied herself to Kalami's cause.

Whatever the answer to that particular riddle, Sakra had no time to pursue it now. Especially now that he had seen but the beginning of her powers, he could not permit Bridget Lederle to reach Kalami or his allies. He had to stop her. And if he failed in that aim, he had to be sure Ananda was warned.

Sakra got swiftly to his feet and flung open the door, letting in a blast of frigid air and a swirl of crystal snow. He raised his hand to his mouth and gave out the three rough calls he had been taught.

A shadow separated from the greater darkness and stepped onto the tiny patch of snow that Sakra's firelight turned golden. A cunning brown face peered up at him from under a hood of black feathers.

"We told you," the dwarf grinned at him. "We said that you would need more than stone and night to hold her."

Sakra bowed low in the fashion of his own people, with his palms pressed over his face. "And I have paid for my failure to heed your wise words," he said. "I crave your pardon."

The dwarf laughed harshly. "At least your courtesy cannot be faulted, sorcerer." The wind ruffled the feathers of his cloak, but if the dwarf felt the cold, he gave no sign. His breath did not even steam in the firelight. "Nonetheless, we held to our promises, and you have given payment. Why have you summoned me again?"

Sakra remained as he was, bowed and subservient. Among its own kind, this creature was a king, and Sakra would not make the mistake of showing too little respect. "For my carelessness, I must beg another favor."

"There is always another favor." The dwarf shook his head. "Once you have begun, your kind does not know when to stop."

Sakra said nothing, accepting the rebuke. The crows' king would either help or he would not. He would name a price, or he would not. No amount of beseeching from Sakra would change that.

"What is this favor?"

Sakra straightened and lowered his hands. "My mistress must be swiftly warned of this new danger. I ask that you send one of your people with a message to her."

The crow king's face creased. "You ask me to send one of my people to Medeoan's home? Her hatred of other powers is so great that it might well snatch them out of the sky."

"It is Ananda who will bring about the end of Medeoan's reign," countered Sakra. "She and Mikkel will not forget the powers that helped them in their time of need."

The crow king's black eyes glinted. "That is your promise, sorcerer?"

Sakra's heart sank within him. Few things were more dangerous than making a promise to one of the spirit powers in this land. He had so far managed to keep his dealings to solid exchange; for each task honestly performed was given a ring, a song, a day's memory. A promise, though, was only words, and words could be twisted and bent in so many ways, according to the skill of the workman. The crow king was extremely skilled.

Yet one more mistake I have made this day. "It is my sincere belief," Sakra said. "I can only promise that I will not forget."

The crow king smiled, an expression both sly and thoughtful. "No, you will not." He raised his arms, his cloak spreading out like wings. "Make your message. You have my promise that it will reach your mistress's hand, and her hand alone."

And he was gone.

Sakra shut the door against the cold that threatened to sink into his bones and returned to the table by the fire. Never, not in a thousand lifetimes, would he become used to the wildness of this land. In Hastinapura, the spirit powers had all either been bound, or been consulted and parleyed with centuries ago. Their histories filled the scrolls of study and were known by heart by any true sorcerer. Here, they surrounded all things earth and flesh, and earth and flesh lived in an ignorance that was either cheerful or cocky. People, common people, could still lose their lives and their souls in bad bargains with the wild night and its children. It was terrifying. It was wondrous. It made life a continual dance on the edge of a precipice.

And just as tiring. Sakra allowed himself a moment of self-pity as he pulled ink and paper out of one of the large chests and set himself to write a warning to the Princess Ananda, yet again.

In truth, he longed to write to tell her to flee. But she never would. Her loyalty and her heart had been given, and she would not break that trust.

Nor would he.

The message was brief, and there was some measure of relief in being able to write openly. He closed the letter, tied it in silk ribbon and sealed it with his false seal, for there had been no promise that no careless eye would light upon the missive. Then he left it under a stone on the tabletop.

That done, Sakra knelt down in front of the largest of carved chests he had carried from Hastinapura. Inside waited scrolls copied in his own hand, books given to him by his mentors, lengths of silk, knotted and unknotted, threads, tools for cutting and weaving, pots of paints and dyes. The arsenal of a sorcerer. Sakra set all the histories and tomes aside and pulled out instead a blanket of silk and two white feathers.

Sakra had been ten when the ministers from the palace came into his father's courtyard. He had watched from behind carved screens beside his mother and aunts as the ministers showed Father the horoscopes and detailed omens that said that he, Sakra, was not merely gifted, but destined to be one of the great sorcerers of his generation. They came with letters from the Pearl Throne commanding and requiring that Sakra be taken to the palace to be trained in all the arts of spirits and magic that he might become an advisor to the council, or possibly even the personal guardian of one of the imperial family.

Of course Father had said yes, and Sakra, torn between sorrow, fear and pride, had gone with the ministers. He had only been studying a year when they came for him again, this time to escort him deep within the women's quarters. He had walked between the two old men, half-afraid that he would be struck blind if he looked too closely at the lovely and curious faces he passed. At last, they came to a chamber of carved ivory that was hung with red silks and glass mirrors. On a great bed in the center lay the empress. Confused, Sakra fell back on reflex and bowed. His hands were taken gently from his face and a bundle was placed in his arms. He stared, realizing he had been given an infant. He held it carefully, as his mother had taught him to do with his baby brothers.

"This is my daughter Ananda," said the empress from her bed. "My first princess, my precious daughter. We give her into your protection, Sakra."

The first princess, wrinkled and red, waved her tiny fists and blew a bubble at him, and Sakra could only smile.

From that time onward, Sakra spent part of every day with the princess. He helped care for her when she was sick, he helped teach her to read and sing and to watch the stars. He watched her grow from a spindly, boisterous girl to a quiet but sharp young woman, and he loved her as he would love a sister or a daughter, which was the proper way of things.

It was a good life, and it suited him. Because of his position, his family was esteemed and his brothers and sisters would have good marriages and prestige of their own. He liked the purpose of his life. Power without purpose too often turned in on itself and could eat out its own heart with restlessness and envy of what it could not touch. This was what had happened to Kalami there on his subjugated island when he was still a boy. Sakra was quite certain.

Despite the bone-numbing cold and the painful memories of how it had almost taken his life, Sakra opened the door. This spell would not work in a confined space. He spread the white silk blanket in front of the hearth and knelt on it. Laying the feathers aside, he selected several sticks of wood from the pile beside the fire. On the first, he carved the name of the Land of Death and Spirit so that the words twined into a circle. On the second, he carved his full name and the names of his father, his grandfather and the god whose son he had been made. The third was a stick of sandalwood brought from Hastinapura. He ran his hands over the smooth, fragrant bark, checking for flaws and finding none. From the second pile of wood, he pulled several green branches and laid them on the flames. After a moment, they caught and the smoke thickened. He then laid his three prepared sticks on the fire and sat back so that he was in the center of the blanket with the two feathers pressed between his palms.

It was risky, what he did, for the Vixen was wild, capricious and cruel. If she played some game with Kalami and Bridget Lederle, she would not care for it to be interrupted. He might bargain with her for possession of Bridget, but she would demand a price a thousand times greater than any the crow king could imagine. Still, he had to try. He could not leave Bridget Lederle free for Kalami to take for even a moment longer, lest the lord sorcerer secret her beyond his reach.

White smoke, thick and fragrant, billowed out of the fire, defying the chimney's efforts to draw it upward. It wreathed around Sakra, sitting motionless on the silken blanket. He concentrated, drawing deeply on his magic, forcing the smoke to surround him so that he might shape it and at the same time allow it to carry his soul away. He closed his eyes and laced his fingers around the feathers.

When his eyes opened again, Sakra was in the Land of Death and Spirit, and he was a swan, with a long neck and white, graceful wings. He soared on the winds over the dark pine forests that stretched on forever. The scent of water reached him and he turned his flight toward it, dipping his wings and stretching out his neck. A wide, brown river cut through the trees. The river would be a more reliable route than the winds. Sakra dove and cupped his wings until he settled with the cool current against his belly.

In his mind, he concentrated on the Vixen, on all the tales he had heard of her and on the illustrations he had seen of her manifestations in the books of the Isavaltan imperial library when he had still had the freedom of the court. The current under him strengthened, carrying him forward, his wings neatly folded, his head erect and alert.

Movement on the bank caught his eye. A shadow stepped out of the trees. It was a fox the size of a cart horse and grey as a ghost. It held a swan in its jaws. Blood streamed from the fox's mouth and stained the bird's white feathers scarlet. The fox tossed its head and threw the dead swan into the river to drift in the current and leave scarlet rivers in the clear, green water.

Sakra spread his wings. He had expected some challenge, but the oldest laws sided with him. *I only defended my mistress,* said his heart's voice to the fox. *She was in peril. Would you not risk all for your queen?*

The fox drew back its lips in a silent snarl. *You carried a blade of cold iron. You led the men who spilled my brothers' blood.*

They attacked my mistress. I had right and cause.

You spilled my brothers' blood, snarled the fox, *so I too have rights.*

The fox sprang, and Sakra launched himself into the air, but not fast enough. The fox's jaws closed on his wing and his throat trumpeted in pain. His mind reached back for his body, willing himself back into the mortal world, but the pain distracted his concentration.

Be bound, growled the fox. *By your soul's blood and my spirit's teeth, be bound. Be prey, and be afraid. See how well you serve your mistress as a voiceless bird.*

Sakra trumpeted again, calling toward the world and his own body. This time, the call was heard and he dissolved from out of the fox's jaws like the smoke that had brought him here.

Sakra woke before the fire, his mind whirling with panic and pain. The fox had bitten deep, leaving behind both blood and confusion. He knew only one thing. His mistress walked alone in danger, and he must reach her. She could not be alone. He could not fail her again, not now when so much more than just the mortal powers arrayed themselves against her.

Unaware of what was truly wrong, Sakra spread his mighty wings and launched himself through the open door.

The palace Vyshtavos never rested easily, thought Kalami as he stood in the dim antechamber contemplating the muraled alcove that held one of the palace's many gilded house gods. Even through the painted, plastered and tapestried walls he fancied he could feel the gossip and schemes passing back and forth like drafts beneath the doors.

The chief game of Vyshtavos's inhabitants was to try to guess what Her Grand Majesty, the Dowager Empress Medeoan would do next, and how they could make use of that action to advance their position within her court. But none of them would ever win that game, because none of them knew the whole truth about the palace, or about its mistress.

Behind him, a staff thumped once on the polished floor. Kalami wheeled around.

"Her Grand Majesty will see you," announced the footman.

As the servant stood aside to let Kalami pass, Kalami noted that despite the late hour the man's livery was crisp and his golden buttons were all polished. It was not often that Kalami had cause to envy a servant. Now, however, as he strode forward, pushing his hair back and smoothing down the wrinkles in his salt-stained coat sleeves, he wished he had allowed himself time to change from his traveling clothes. Appearances were important to the dowager, but so was strict adherence to her instructions. She had ordered him to report immediately to her upon his return, no matter what the hour. As the dowager seldom slept the night through, Kalami had decided not to risk delay. It would be far better to face the coming storm now.

The dowager's private study was primarily a place of desks and books. On any given day, she could be surrounded by as many as six secretaries copying down her official letters and documents. At the moment, however, there was only one man in a high-necked green coat, drowsing at the corner desk near a low fire in a brass brazier. Another fire, little more than coals, smoldered in the central firepit. It was not anything like enough to heat the room and the cold brushed against Kalami's skin. What little light there was came from six candles in two branched holders the height of a tall man, each of which was made to hold a dozen or more tapers. Liveried servants stood by to tend the meager lights and two ladies-in-waiting sat by the door, ready to tend upon their mistress should she give the word.

Medeoan Edemskoidoch Nacheradavosh, the Dowager Empress of Eternal Isavalta, sat behind a writing desk of dark wood inlaid with ivory representations of the seals of each of the twenty oblasts that made up the Empire of Isavalta. Age had yellowed that ivory, and the wood was ink-stained and chipped. Like the dowager herself, it had grown old before its time, and might soon be cast aside.

Dowager Empress Medeoan was in truth only just beginning her middle years, but she looked much older. This was strange in a noblewoman, and unheard of in a sorceress. That blessing of soul that granted them magic also granted sorcerers a life that could last across an entire century or more. Its price was to render the getting of children by a sorcerous parent difficult at best, but Kalami had found his own solution to that problem, once for himself, and once for Medeoan.

Inside the court it was said that Medeoan's premature aging was caused by a deal she had made with the ancient witch Baba Yaga, swapping years of life for an heir to the throne. It was a serviceable enough rumor, all the better for not having started with him or the dowager.

The truth was, however, that what aged the dowager was a bargain far older and far more dangerous.

Kalami dropped to his knees in front of the dowager, bowing until he pressed his head against the worn pattern of the carpet. As he had supposed, she said nothing immediately, just letting him remain in this uncomfortable and degrading posture. But he had been prepared for that, and was ready to wait.

"Get up."

Kalami rose, keeping his gaze humbly cast down. He had failed. He was in disgrace. For the moment, at least, he needed to act the part.

"What happened?"

"Yvanka's children attacked us and carried Bridget Lederle away."

Cloth and paper rustled. "And why would the crow's stepchildren care what we do on the road through the Foxwood?"

"It is possible that they have made an alliance with Sakra."

"Yes." More rustling, and a gentle rush of wood against carpet as the chair was pushed back. He heard Medeoan rise, rattling the great bundle of keys she wore at her waist. Her faint shadow fell across the carpet in front of him. "And why did we not know of this bargain?"

Because you banished him from court, allowing him to freely roam the countryside where we could not keep any sort of efficient watch on him. "Because my eyes failed Your Grand Majesty."

"Yes." Silence filled the air between them, cold and profound. "Look at me, Lord Sorcerer."

Kalami lifted his eyes. Medeoan had been a tall woman once, golden-haired and fair-complected, or so the imperial artists had rendered her. But she had shrunken in on herself. The gold of her hair had turned to silver streaked with white. Her fair skin had shriveled, and where it had not spotted, it had turned the color of the old ivory on her writing desk. Only her eyes remained as bright as they were shown in those portraits. But where the renderings of her as a girl all showed mild, intelligent eyes, the eyes that looked at him now were hard and calculating, taking in every single detail so it could be judged, or used. In the dim light, those eyes appeared sunken in their own shadows.

"I have not many years left to me, Kalami. Do you see that?"

Kalami said nothing. To speak of an imperial death was tantamount to treason. Instead, he reverenced, showing that he believed whatever his sovereign chose to tell him.

"I need allies around me, my realm needs allies, and that before the day my responsibilities take more from me than I can give them." She took a step closer to Kalami and he could smell her breath, sour from encroaching illness.

"Grand Majesty," he said evenly. "I stand before you. I am ready to serve you however I may. I lay all my skills before you, as I always have."

The dowager turned his unflinching declaration over in her mind and accepted it. "Yes, yes." She touched his hand and he felt how her skin was as dry as paper. "You have always been loyal to Isavalta, and your sacrifice unstinting. But it is not for you to save us." Her gaze turned inward, the hardness of her eyes softening. "The wardship of kingdoms is the duty of bloodlines. She was born for this burden. That was why Avanasy sent her mother away, so that she might be born. I know that. It can be no other way, and now those foul Southerners have taken her, as they tried to take my son, as they mean to take Isavalta from my dead hands." Those hands curled into fists around nothing but air.

"Your enemies are Bridget Lederle's enemies," said Kalami. "She will not betray you any more than I will."

The dowager began to pace. "Today, today perhaps. But the Southerners have their ways. They would have turned my son against me if I had not taken action. They tried to turn me against my own realm once, and in my foolishness I almost let them succeed."

Kalami folded his hands behind himself. The litany was beginning, the recitation of failure, guilt and treachery that every person in the inner court had listened to and would deny to the death that they had heard. It was Medeoan's inability to forgive herself for the failures of her girlhood, as much as the burdens of her rule, that racked her mind and heart. Much of Isavalta saw her as their savior, but she saw herself only as a penitent, somehow hoping for forgiveness from the soul of her realm.

"She plots," said the dowager, one hand clutching her ring of keys.

"I feel her, twisting her threads and knotting her secrets. She thinks she may succeed where her cousin failed. But she shall not. She shall not. I have saved my son. I will save my realm. My need, my weakness brought her here when I should have known better. I, of all people, should have known."

Yes, you should have. Kalami dropped his gaze once again, because he did not trust his face to remain impassive as he watched the dowager and thought these thoughts. *I tried to tell you that it would be so, but you would not listen. Your lord sorcerer, your faithful dog from Tuukos, is only good enough to risk his life so you can share your secrets with an untried girl. He may not presume to advise the great empress of Isavalta.*

"All the more reason we must find Bridget quickly, Grand Majesty," said Kalami, when his control returned. "Before Sakra has the chance to use his persuasions on her."

The dowager paused in her pacing and regarded Kalami as if he had spoken some foreign tongue. "Yes," she said after long moment. "You are quite correct, Lord Sorcerer. I thank you."

With her gaze once more turned outward, Medeoan strode across the room, reminding all who saw that there was strength in her yet. "My lord sorcerer shall attend me," she announced for the benefit of her ladies, who had both jumped to their feet.

At the far end of the study waited a small, unpretentious door that Medeoan opened with a brass key. The room on the other side was cold and dark. She stood aside and let the servant who followed them place a candelabrum within. Medeoan waved her hand. The servant reverenced and left, closing the door behind him.

A soft ticking filled the chamber, worming its way into Kalami's blood as if it sought to control the rhythm of his heart and breath. The contents of this room were a tribute to the artisans of Isavalta. Mirrors with cunningly worked frames of bronze or gold hung on the walls, carefully covered by lengths of linen. Clocks, all of them stopped at different times, stood on shelves between caskets of silver or precious tropical hardwoods.

The prize of the room waited at its very center and was the source of the low, constant ticking noise. On a plain, polished table stood the Portrait of Worlds. The portrait was in actuality a model, the product of a hundred years of study by the lord sorcerer Rachek. He had served Medeoan's grandmother, Nacherada, the last Isavaltan ruler to take for herself so humble a title as queen. Made of bronze and copper and etched with silver, the Portrait rose four feet high from the tabletop, a collection of spheres within spheres, bound together in the cages of their orbits. Each sphere moved independently of its neighbor in a slow dance, which now brought worlds together, now swung them apart with all the steady, punctuated grace that clockwork could provide.

None of the infinitely precious objects that filled this room were of themselves magical, but great magic could be worked with such tools. The fibers of Kalami's being thrummed as he thought of what could be done here, if only, if just for once, Medeoan would entrust him with the keys.

Patience, he reminded himself. *You will soon have a key of your own.*

Isavalta's own world waited at the center of the Portrait. It turned at a stately pace on a spindle of bronze. Blue and green enamels picked out its continents and its oceans. Its sun, a ball of gold, and its moon, a bead of silver, sketched their own orbits around it. Hollow spheres woven of bronze and copper thread represented the realms that composed the Land of Death and Spirit. Each of these was held in its own position by its own carefully formed set of gears.

"When did they take her?" asked Medeoan.

"At dusk."

Medeoan selected a small amber clock and set the hands for half past the hour of four, the time when the sun began to set. She wound the works and the clock's gentle tick joined the chorus from the Portrait of Worlds.

"Have you anything she has touched?"

Kalami reached into the breast pocket of his coat and brought out several of the scraps of cloth that Bridget had given him when he needed to prove to her that he was not a madman. He had kept them against such an eventuality, although he had thought to be using them himself.

Medeoan took the cloth he offered and pulled a length of lace from her own pocket. She closed her eyes and let out a long exhalation, her shrunken mouth beginning to move, forming words Kalami could not hear. Her long fingers swiftly knotted the cloth into the lace. Medeoan opened her eyes, spat on the lace, breathed on it and knotted that place tightly. Kalami felt the air grow cold and every hair on his arms rose with the awareness of a spell being formed from lace and cloth, breath, spittle and even the pattern of ticks and tocks that filled the chilling air.

"Show me," the dowager murmured to her creation. "Show me."

The room was closed and locked, and inside a stone palace, but a wind, wild and frigid, blew through it anyway. The wind a swept the knotted lace off Medeoan's palm, carrying it swiftly toward the Portrait, and tangling it around one of the spheres of bronze and copper wire, one that had a ruby mounted at its center.

"So." Medeoan pressed her mouth into a thin line. "Sakra does not have her, or, at least, not anymore. She is with the *lokai*."

The *lokai*. The fox spirits. Kalami felt his blood run chill. Had the Vixen guessed the extent of the game Kalami had played with her sons? Had she taken Bridget in payment?

No, no, Kalami reassured himself. *The Vixen would do nothing so straightforward. Some other current runs here.*

As if reading his thoughts, the dowager said, "We will understand the why of it later. What is important now is that Bridget Lederle come to us." Her gaze swept the room and paused on one of the silver caskets. She reached the box down and unlocked it with a matching silver key. From inside, she drew a ring of gold set with bright emeralds.

"Go to the Vixen. Give her this my gift." The dowager held the ring out to Kalami. "If that is not enough to secure Bridget Lederle's safe passage to us, hear her terms."

Kalami took the ring, placing it in his coat pocket, and reverenced deeply. "She will be with us to wait upon Your Grand Majesty before another day is over."

"I know this is true." The dowager laid her hand briefly on his head in blessing. "Leave me now. Take rest and food, but do not stay too long. If we found her, it is possible that Sakra, by his tricks, may do so also."

"Grand Majesty." Kalami reverenced briefly one more time and left the room.

Once in the corridor, he strode its length swiftly, looking neither left nor right at the carved pillars, the tapestries, the murals, portraits and mosaics, which he had seen a thousand times before. He used the one palace key that was in his keeping and opened the door to his own apartments, sweeping through them as swiftly as he had walked the corridor. When he reached the outer wall, he hauled aside the curtain that covered the door to his balcony. Cold air blasted against him as he flung that door open and walked into the night. A swirl of snow brushed his cheek. Kalami inhaled deeply, savoring the cold that knifed through his lungs. Pain would clear his head, cold would damp down the hot eagerness running through his veins.

Is this my chance? Is this how I may finally be free of the shadow of Ingrid and Avanasy's bastard daughter?

"My lord Kalami?"

Kalami slung around, for one searing instant afraid his thoughts had been overheard.

"Who's there?"

From inside his chamber a gravelly voice replied, "Finon, my lord. With your meal, as requested."

Kalami knew he had requested no meal, and of course Finon did too. It would make no difference. Finon would have heard the moment he had returned and, as ever, had made shift to reach him.

Kalami took one last breath of the clean, cold air. "And welcome as ever." He pushed the heavy curtain aside, closing the balcony door behind himself.

Finon was a slight man with only a few wisps of white hair still clinging to his age-spotted scalp. His frame appeared overwhelmed by the gold and braid of the imperial livery. This harmless appearance had served them both in good stead. Most dismissed him as nothing more than an aging servant without bothering to see how clear his black eyes remained or how strong and steady his hands were as they went about their tasks—as they did now, pouring hot wine from a silver ewer, laying out bread and cold beef spread thick with paté and rolls of thin pastry stuffed full of honey and nuts.

"Honored Father," said Kalami to Finon in the language they both shared, giving him the title of respect due to an elder man from a younger. "There is no need. There is none to see. Let me serve you."

It was Finon who had seen the possibilities of Kalami's power when Kalami was still a boy and learning his own history in dark barns, behind sheds and in cellars, all of it whispered to him by the servants of the lord master of Tuukos, to whom his father had indentured him. It was Finon who said he should try to come to the imperial court, to insinuate himself into the seat of power. Then, Finon had said, then we may find our way again to freedom.

It had taken years, but as a sorcerer, Kalami had them. Finon, however did not. He was an old man now, however well preserved, and it grieved Kalami to see him so. His victory would be much lessened if Finon, who had begun the journey with him, was not there to see its end.

"It is good to see you still have your manners." Finon did not pause. He laid out a linen napkin beside the food and then turned away to kindle a taper at the firepit and light the room's candles. "But you know and I know that we are always watched."

"A fact I shall not dispute, Honored Father." In truth, the scent of the food was making his mouth water and Kalami set himself down readily and began to eat. He savored the wine especially. It was a luxury of which he had grown particularly fond, and he felt more than a little guilty for so doing. Wine was an Isavaltan affectation.

"Did you find what you sought?" asked Finon, blowing out the taper.

"Found it, and lost it." Kalami stabbed the tip of the silver knife into a slice of beef. "The dowager is not the only power interested in the Avanasidoch."

Finon stood silent for a moment, twirling the taper between his strong, blunt fingers. "Perhaps it is as well. Perhaps it could stay lost."

"Believe me, Honored Father, I have thought of that." More than thought. He had yearned for it in the depths of his heart. *What if,* his mind whispered to him, *what if you fail in your mission? What if the Vixen will not be placated, no matter what you try? What if she keeps Bridget with her to be one of her foxes? Then where will Medeoan turn? There will be no one left but you with whom she could share the secrets she keeps so close to her heart.*

It was a plan that would not work had Bridget merely been captured by Sakra. Kalami was supposed to be Sakra's match, or at least he must appear to be so. But the Vixen was one of the great powers of the world. If she had set her will against him, what could he do?

Kalami looked down at his plate and realized he had shredded the beef, slicing it into strips without even feeling his fingers work the knife. Finon deftly took the plate away, replacing it with the arrangement of pastry rolls.

"You wish to tell me why this is not a wise course," Finon prompted him.

"Because we need the power the Avanasidoch carries. If I try to maintain the empress's cage myself, it will devour me as it has devoured Medeoan. No." He shook his head and took another swallow of the rich, spiced wine. "In order for Tuukos to rule the three empires, we must have the Firebird."

Finon crossed to his side, topping off his wine cup. "But does Tuukos need to rule? If Isavalta falls, we are free, as we were. Surely, that is all we need."

Kalami stared into the depths of his cup. The wine was dark, almost black and so sweet it needed the spices in order to be palatable. "No, that is not all we need. We need to be safe in order to keep our freedom. We need power, and the bones of our dead need their revenge."

The bones of the dead. His great-uncle, a sorcerer trained in the old ways who should have been there to train Kalami. But Great-uncle had been hanged by the overlord for using the blood and the drums to find out a newborn child's true name for its parents. Kalami dreamed of him often, swaying at the end of the rope in the courtyard tree, his eyes wide open, demanding of his great-nephew why those who did this were not yet punished.

Kalami set the cup down. "Do not worry, Honored Father. Bridget Lederle has served me before all unwitting. She will serve me again. And now"—Kalami pushed his chair back from the table and stood—"I must make ready. My mistress imperial has given me my orders and I must obey."

Without another word, Finon cleared away the dishes and left Kalami to himself. Kalami shook his head. Finon was old man and a wise man. He would understand when Tuukos held the cage and all the power it contained. Then he would know what it was to rule, and he would understand why it had to be this way.

When Kalami left her, Medeoan stayed where she was for a moment, swaying on her feet and fighting down exhaustion by sheer willpower. The voice, the thin susurrating voice that filled the palace, was so loud here that she could almost make out its words. It took so much strength to work her magic with that voice whispering to her that sometimes she felt the simplest spell or most basic decision had finally become beyond her capacity.

But that was not possible. She ruled Isavalta, and she must rule until Bridget Lederle came to take her burdens, as Bridget's father had, and until she could rid herself of Ananda, so that she could pass her throne to her son, and her son alone.

The whisper flickered louder.

"Cannot hold me," said the voice. "You grow old, mortal woman, and you cannot hold me."

Slowly, carefully, Medeoan got down on her knees so that she could roll back the edge of the carpet. Her aching fingers traced the edges of the stones underneath, until she found the notch that identified the one that could be heaved loose. Under that stone waited an iron door. Medeoan unlocked it with one of the keys on her ring. Underneath the door waited a ladder, its wood polished smooth from years of use. The ladder led to a stone staircase that descended into the dark and cold between the cellars of the palace.

Medeoan's hands found the lantern that waited at the top of the stairs, and the tinderbox beside it. Her clumsy fingers dropped the steel several times, which caused her to have to search for it on her knees, but at last, she struck a light.

All the world kneels to me, she thought toward the whispering voice at the bottom of the stairs. *But I kneel only to you.*

"Let me go," said the voice. "Let me go!"

Medeoan lifted the lantern in one palsied hand and picked her way down the steep, curving stairs. Her free hand brushed the stone and earth wall, helping to keep her steady. A dozen men—builders, planners, smiths, and stonemasons—had labored to make and secure this stair and the chamber below. All of them had vanished from Isavalta's shores years since, pressed variously by privateers and pirates, all of whom had been paid well for their pains.

At first, the wall was winter cold, making her fingertips ache. But with each step downward, the stones grew a little warmer. Her breath ceased to steam in front of her eyes and Medeoan began to wish she had laid aside her heavy night robe.

At the bottom of the stairs waited another iron door. The metal was warm to the touch, and light flickered through a crack near the floor.

Medeoan set the lantern down and brought out yet another key. This one had wires of tarnished silver woven around its shaft and would burn any hand but hers that tried to touch it.

Medeoan had to press hard against the door to convince its weary hinges to move. It finally gave way with a high-pitched scream of dry, tortured metal.

Light and heat poured over Medeoan, making her squint and blink, and bringing out perspiration instantly on her forehead and upper lip. Her knees, old and tired years before their time, tried to make her shrink backward, but Medeoan held her ground, even if she could not immediately step forward. The thing that waited in the golden cage already knew too much of her weakness. She would not give it any other sign with which to torment her.

The cage hung from the stone ceiling by a stout iron chain and was about the size of a large man's torso. Its charred bars had once been pure gold twisted and bent into the needful shapes. Medeoan's hands still remembered the pain of that work. That cage had cost her, in pain and blood, years of life, and the life of the one man she could trust absolutely. But it had been necessary. Nothing else could hold the Firebird.

The Firebird, the Phoenix, blazed at the center of the cage, a bird made of living flame. Its wings and tail glowed a shifting pattern of gold, red and orange. Its sharp beak shone pure white. The blue from the very heart of the fire glowed in its round eyes.

When it saw Medeoan, it let out a screech that shot a bolt of pain through her ears. Its curved wings battered at the cage bars, raising clouds of smoke and the stench of metal and blood burning together.

"Let me out!" it screamed. "Medeoan! Let me out!"

Medeoan summoned all her strength and walked past that cage. The chamber beyond was made of earth and stone just like the staircase. It might have been a workroom. A crucible stood beside a workbench covered with nuggets of ore and scraps of metal, along with hammers and various tools for shaping that metal. Crouching down, Medeoan tended the fire underneath the crucible, clearing the ashes from the coals and feeding it bits of wood. All the while, she felt the Firebird's burning eyes focused upon the back of her neck.

"Avanasy is here, Medeoan."

Medeoan did not look back. Ordinarily, it would take a crucible hours to become hot enough for the task she required. She did not have hours. Medeoan stared unblinking at the flames, summoning the deepest part of her soul to the surface, willing it to course through her veins, to fill her hands and reach out through her fingertips.

"He stands beside the cage his life created, Medeoan. He says you must release me, or it will take your life as it did his. It will take your life and realm to keep me bound."

Medeoan tightened her jaw. The creature lied, as it always lied. She pushed her sleeves up around her elbows and with bare arms reached into the fire. The flames crawled around her hands, but did not burn her. They felt soft under her fingertips, like clay ready to be shaped. Her fingers willed by her inmost soul could draw heat from the flames, could spread it into the stone of the crucible, could make that crucible blaze with white heat, to melt the metal, to renew the cage, to keep her empire safe. Her hands, her soul, her will, only hers.

"Your heart skips a beat, Medeoan. Your chest grows tight, grows tired."

But the Firebird had waited too long. The flames were hers. Her hands stroked the crucible, spreading the heat, judging the temperature by instinct. True, her heart did labor, but it was from effort and concentration, not from age. Not yet. That was another lie the Firebird told. She could ignore that.

She drew her hands from the flames, stood and turned to the workbench. Lumps of gold ore waited for her and she cast them into the crucible. A knife also waited on the bench. Medeoan picked it up, steadied her arm, and drove the point into her fingertip. She turned her palm up, letting the blood run over her fingers so that she might breathe upon it. The blood fell hissing into the crucible, and its steam mixed with her breath.

"Let me go, Medeoan. Your Avanasy urges you. I will promise not to harm you or yours."

"Liar," said Medeoan through clenched teeth. She plunged her hands into the crucible, cupping the fragments of ore. The magic in her hands felt the gold melting from the stone and drew it forth, her fingers twisting and rolling it the way a weaver might twist thread and then bind those threads into a braid. But this braid was of gold, blood and magic. This braid would be woven into the cage, and help hold back the Firebird for another few days.

Medeoan lifted the soft plait of white-hot metal from the crucible.

"I called to your son, Medeoan."

For an instant, Medeoan's will faltered and unbearable pain lanced through her hands. She smelled the stench of her own flesh burning and she screamed, but she did not drop the braid. She clamped all her will, all her remaining life, down around the pain and raised the magic once again. This magic was hers, Isavalta was hers, hers alone to protect and defend. If she failed now, if she failed again, it would die, all of it would die. Her son would die at the hand of his cursed wife and all her family, as her parents had died at Kacha's hands. Kacha, who had driven her from her own palace. Kacha, who had tried to invade Hung-Tse with her soldiers, so terrifying the Nine Elders that they transformed one of their own into the Firebird and unleashed it against Isavalta.

"He almost heard me, Medeoan. He is so susceptible to suggestion, how will he fail to listen to me?"

Medeoan pressed the braid against the bars of the cage. The Firebird flew at her, beating its wings against the cage and thrusting its beak at her. It sought to burn her alive, but the cage held yet again, and all she felt were minute pinpricks of heat that raised tiny blisters, adding new scars and spots to her face and arms. Nothings. She twisted the braid into place and the scent of burning lessened. Medeoan lifted her hands away, and the braid cooled even as she looked at it, becoming a new layer to the cage and encasing the old, charred metal.

Medeoan staggered and would have fallen if the workbench had not caught her under her elbow. She leaned there for a moment, panting, unable to think of anything but the pain throbbing in her hands. Black lines seared her flesh and that sight accompanied by the intensity of the pain raised a whimper from her throat and wrung tears from her burning eyes.

"Set me free, Medeoan, or he will do it for you." The Firebird turned one burning blue eye toward her. "You are a sorcerer, but he is not. Do you think he will survive the flames when I soar free?"

Medeoan raised her streaming eyes. "He cannot reach you here." She pushed herself away from the bench, forcing her back to straighten. She lowered her arms to let her sleeves fall over her wounded hands. "No one can reach you here. You are mine." Medeoan stalked up to the cage, her voice shaking with rage and pain. "I will keep you here as long as I have need of you. You will not go free until Isavalta is safe, if that takes a thousand years. You will stay here and the threat of you will serve wherever I require."

"Be sure," hissed the bird. "For you do grow old, Medeoan. Grandfather Death measures the candle of your life and sees it will soon go out. Then what of Isavalta? Then what will keep me from taking my revenge?"

Lies. Old lies. Medeoan turned away. She did not look back as she heard the Firebird beating its wings against the renewed cage. She wrapped her hands in her sleeves, and even so had to bite her lip to keep from screaming as she closed and locked the iron door. Unable to face the idea of picking up the lantern, she mounted the stairs in the dark, almost fainting when she had to touch the ladder rungs and pull herself back into the upper chamber.

Necessity and will sustained her as she locked the trapdoor, kicked the stone and the rug back into place and unlocked the chamber door.

"Seydas, Prathad."

Her ladies, strong, capable and bound these many years by promises, threats and spells, supported her back to her private apartments. They laid her fainting on her couch and brought snow, salve and bandages for her hands. This was not the first time they had tended her burns, or even the hundredth. There would be some talk, of course. There was not enough magic in all the world to keep servants from talking. But that was not important. What was important was that the Firebird, and Isavalta, were safe again.

"Bridget will take up this burden," she murmured, lacking the strength to keep her thoughts from her tongue. "Bridget will not betray me."

"No one betrays you, Grand Majesty," murmured Prathad soothingly.

"No." Medeoan closed her eyes. "No one living."

Sleep washed over her then in a great black wave, swamping all conscious thought. After a time, she dreamed. In the dream, she walked in a cave filled with candles, some tall, some melting into mere puddles of wax, all of them burning with a steady white light. A stately figure in black robes walked beside her until they came to one candle among the thousands of others nestled in the sand of the floor. It was barely one inch high, and wax rolled down its sides the way the blood had rolled down Medeoan's fingers into the crucible.

"This is all there is, Granddaughter," said the figure beside her. "I cannot change that."

And Medeoan knew with her whole heart that the Firebird listened, and the Firebird heard.

Chapter Nine

At first, Bridget knew no body. She floated in a warm darkness, without thought or feeling. The darkness simply was, as she was. Gradually, a green light diffused around her, and she remembered she had eyes. With the memory of eyes came the memory of limbs and senses, and that memory opened the world.

Bridget fell coughing to her hands and knees in a pile of loam and pine needles. The thin air around her tingled with cold, and something she couldn't name. Her lungs could not seem to get enough of it. She knelt there gasping and retching, until it seemed as if she would never stop. Gradually, however, her breathing eased and she was able to raise her head and look around her.

Pine trees rose on every side of her with black trunks and great green branches that locked together high overhead. She could not see the sun. Only a dim, green gloom surrounded her. Nothing grew on the ground; just an unbroken carpet of brown needles undulated here and there to show that the something of the forest had been buried. The sent of resin filled in the air so densely that Bridget could taste it in the back of her mouth. There was no sound. Her breathing rasped far too loudly in her ears.

I did it, thought Bridget, sitting back on her heels. Her next thought was, however, *What have I done?*

Bridget listened for a moment, and heard nothing. No voice, not even a bird. She might as well have gone deaf, the silence was so thick around her. There was not even any wind to stir the branches overhead.

Bridget tried to let out a long sigh, but it came out as a series of little coughs, as if her lungs did not want to let go of this hard-won air. She stroked her throat, trying to loosen it, and climbed to her feet. There seemed little point in shouting. In fact, the thought of breaking the silence so rudely tightened her stomach. She saw no shadow under her own feet, or beneath any of the trees, which made all directions the same, because she had no way to tell from which direction the sun shone. It was this detail that finally made Bridget afraid.

Nothing for it then. Bridget dusted off her hands and her apron, primarily to keep herself from trembling. *I either stay here, or I start walking.*

She could not bear the thought of just sitting still and waiting for whatever might find her. She fixed her gaze firmly on one of the trees straight in front of her and walked toward it. When she reached it, she laid a hand on its scaly, black trunk and picked another tree, also straight in front of her, and walked toward it. If she had no idea where she was going, at least she would not walk in circles.

The needles did not crackle under her feet. The branches did not whisper of her passage. Bridget walked from tree to tree wrapped in a blanket of unnatural silence until she felt her mind slipping into a slow dream where she had always been alone in the pine forest walking from tree to tree and trying to move in straight line. Her goal lay at the end of that line, and it was her task to follow it. Hunger did not trouble her, neither did thirst, only a strange light emptiness and a vague sense that something she could not understand was going wrong inside her.

Then, gradually, in keeping with the feeling of the dream into which she had fallen, the forest around her began to change. A flower pushed its white head through the pine needles. A birch tree stood stark and white between the black pines. Then there was a maple, and another. Leaves in all shades of tan and brown covered over the pine needles. Fern and bracken replaced the featureless brown carpet. Wind moved the leaves, although it left behind no rustling sound.

But the air grew no lighter; in fact, it grew dimmer. The green light cast by no sun was nonetheless fading into some sort of night she could not begin to imagine. Her ears rang, as if her body could not stand the silence any longer and was resolved to provide some kind of sound, any kind of sound.

A flash of gold caught Bridget's eye, and she turned her head, thinking to see a firefly. Instead, a pair of golden eyes winked at her from the gathering shadows.

Of course there are animals. Bridget snapped her gaze straight ahead again and held her pace steady. Running would only lead to a chase. She must not run. She must concentrate on picking her trees, on moving in a straight line. She must think about how to find shelter now that it was growing dark.

A pair of green eyes opened right in front of her. Despite her resolve, Bridget jerked backward. The leaves shifted underfoot, almost toppling her. Bridget clenched her jaw, knotted her right fist around a bunch of her apron and skirt to lift her hems, found the tree she had been sighting on and started forward again.

Another pair of green eyes opened, this time on her right, glowing like a cat's in the fading light. Bridget did not allow herself to break stride. A cooling breeze touched her skin, bringing with it a rank animal smell. Another pair of eyes opened ahead and to the left. These were red. Bridget's stomach tightened, but she kept her attention on her chosen tree. Soon, she would pass it, and have to pick another.

Keep walking. Just keep walking.

The tree, a maple with a huge round bole on its side, passed by her right shoulder. She fastened her attention on a pair of beeches several yards ahead. Two sets of green eyes, no, three, opened between her and the new trees. She walked, the rasp of her breath seeming unbearably loud and every inch of skin itching with the knowledge that she was being watched.

When she was ten, Bridget had conceived a fear of bears. She didn't know what brought it on, but she was convinced that somehow a bear would creep up in the night, get into the keeper's quarters and devour her and her father in their beds.

When explanations that there were no bears on Sand Island failed to calm her, Poppa had taken her for a long walk in the woods, showing her squirrels in their nests, and foxes in their dens. As they walked, he had explained slowly and carefully, just as he explained the workings of the gears in the light, that animals rarely attacked human beings. Mother animals with their babies were to be left alone, but other than that, all animals would rather live and let live when it came to humans. Bridget had never forgotten that day. Fear of bears, and other terrors of the woods, had fallen away from her. Even now, she kept his words firmly in her mind. All she had to do was keep walking, and the animals, whatever they were, would fall back.

So, he was kind to you. I'm glad.

Bridget stopped dead in her tracks. She whirled around in a tight circle, clouds of leaves whisking around her hems. But on every side, all she saw were animal eyes. Not one human pair shone in the darkness.

Anger exploded inside Bridget's mind. No more. She would not be terrorized. She would not be laughed at, and whispered about by things she could not see. If whatever waited in the woods wanted to snatch her away like the dwarf-crows, they would have a fight.

Her right toe nudged a dead branch. Slowly, keeping her gaze on the eyes glowing from the darkness, Bridget bent down to pick it up. Chuckling filled the wind, shattering the silence and raising a scream in Bridget's throat.

"All right, then," Bridget said through clenched teeth, more to keep the scream back than to challenge whatever surrounded her. "Come out!" She lifted the branch in both hands, holding it over her shoulder, ready to swing down. "Whoever you are, come out!"

"As you wish, mistress."

They flowed out of the shadows, a river of fur-covered bodies—red, brown, grey and white. Bridget saw pointy ears, bushy tails, sharp noses and bright eyes, but her overwhelmed mind could not resolve what she saw. They ringed her, tongues lolling from their laughing mouths, and Bridget saw that they were foxes. Dozens of foxes. Red foxes the size of small dogs crouched at the feet of white foxes the size of wolves. Brown and grey foxes peered around their shoulders, looking for all the world like they found her amusing.

Bridget turned in a tight circle, keeping her club raised. They surrounded her. Kits peered at her from under a rotten log, adults crouched on their haunches or sat attentive with their ears turned forward, as if they were waiting to hear something interesting. Their stench filled the air, and Bridget had to swallow to keep from gagging. On the edge of the shadows, something grey and far too big, yet still shaped like a fox, paced back and forth, and Bridget could see the faint glow of its huge eyes. A soft warm wind that might have been its breath touched Bridget, and she smelled carrion.

"Well?" she asked. "What do you want?"

The foxes laughed, high-pitched, yipping laughs. The noise rolled over Bridget and she nearly staggered under its assault.

One of the red foxes pointed its muzzle at her. "Be careful, little woman," it said, and Bridget could muster no surprise on hearing it speak. "Ask no questions to which you do not want to know the answer."

"Most excellent advice," said one of the white foxes, closing its mouth with an audible click of sharp teeth. "For instance, what if we should want to taste the dainty in front of us?"

"It has come from a long way away." The red fox whisked its tail back and forth. "I would wager none of us have ever tasted its like." The kits under the logs squealed delightedly at this idea.

I'm going to die. The phrase formed itself clearly and succinctly in Bridget's mind. She shifted her grip on her club. Her heart should have been beating fast. She should have been breathing hard but the action seemed beyond her somehow. All she could do it was stand there, ridiculous with her dead branch, and wait for the foxes to make up their minds.

"If you threaten me," said Bridget, "then I may do whatever I can to save myself, may I not?"

That earned her another chorus of yipping, squealing laughter. "An excellent point," said the red fox. "And which of us will choose to feel the sting of her skills?"

The white fox tossed its head contemptuously. "What could she do? She does not know what she may do, or even what she can do."

"She does not know who she is," said one of the grey foxes, rubbing its whiskers with its paw.

"She knows who she is," replied the white fox. "She does not know where her blood has been."

"Let's find out!" shrieked one of the kits.

"Take her blood," said the grey fox, pausing in its grooming. "Relieve her of her worry."

"Or give her new blood?" suggested the white fox. "Show her how much she has yet to learn."

"I am Bridget Lederle, keeper of the light for Sand Island," said Bridget through clenched teeth. "That is all I need to know."

"She's very sure," said the red fox.

"She's very proud," answered the white fox. "Very like her father."

A wave of dizziness passed over Bridget. Her knees tried to buckle. What was happening? What did they know of her father? What did they know of Everett Lederle?

Or did they mean someone other than Everett Lederle?

Do not be afraid to know. It changes nothing of your love for Everett Lederle, and it can only help you.

"Enough!" shouted Bridget to drown out her own thoughts. "If you mean me harm, get on with it. If not, then let me pass!"

"She should not shout," said one of the kits, poking its nose out from under the log. Bridget saw how very green its eyes were. "She should not be rude."

A second wave of dizziness made Bridget teeter on her feet, but it passed, leaving behind an odd certainty as to what she should say next. "You should not delay me. Your mother will not be pleased."

The hackles rose on the nearest red fox. "Our mother? What do you know about our mother?"

The foxes swam in front of Bridget's vision. *Stop this!* She pressed her hand to her forehead. *Leave me be!*

Do not be afraid . . .

"The Vixen sent for me," said Bridget. "And here I am."

"So you are."

A ripple of sound ran through the foxes, a combination of whispers, snuffling and the gentle whine that comes with an animal's fear. A lane opened through them and a fresh shadow stepped out of the forest. A fox so huge that she dwarfed even the grey one on guard in the shadows picked a delicate path up to Bridget. Her coat was the color of the red stone cliffs on Devil's Island. The tip of her tail and the blaze on her breast shined so white they burned Bridget's eyes. The tips of her alert ears were level with Bridget's shoulder. Her sea green eyes met Bridget's without hesitation, and Bridget had to drop her gaze. She did not want to see what secrets lay in this creature's eyes. At the same time, her branch fell from fingers gone suddenly numb. It landed on the bracken without making a sound.

"Do you know me, Bridget Lederle?" the great fox asked mildly.

Bridget saw the black, clawed paws standing toe to toe with her worn boots, but, she realized with a thrill of fear, she felt no breath from the creature against her skin.

"You are, I assume, the Vixen."

"An excellent guess." The Vixen sounded amused. "But do you know me?"

"No, ma'am," said Bridget, folding her hands across her apron. "I do not."

"I thought not." The Vixen's whiskers twitched. "And yet I know so much about you."

Slowly, Bridget lifted her eyes. "What do you know about me?"

The Vixen opened her mouth in a grin, and paced a tight circle around Bridget. "I know that you are alone, that you are lost, and that you have no idea of the dangers of the place you are in."

Fear rose in Bridget. It wrapped around her like the cold thin air, smothering her ability to think. She clenched the fabric of her apron, as if its familiar roughness could anchor her somehow. "Thank you, ma'am," she said politely. "But I also know that."

"I thought you might. You are a clever girl." The Vixen stopped in front of Bridget and her green eyes gleamed. "As clever as your mother, I think."

Bridget's hands tightened. Another person who would talk about her mother. She would not, could not, rise to this. "Thank you, ma'am."

The Vixen took a step backward, and considered Bridget with her head cocked. "Clever girl," she repeated. "Would you like my help?"

The question lifted the hairs on the back of Bridget's neck. "Forgive me, ma'am, but why would such an important person choose to help me?"

"Because I believe you could help me." The Vixen straightened up her head and both ears turned toward Bridget. "You know something of the healing arts. I smell it on you."

Bridget forced her hands to relax and smoothed out her apron. "I have cared for the sick and injured, yes."

"My three sons have been injured and I cannot save them. If you can, I will see you returned to the living world."

A light shone again in the back of the Vixen's green eyes. It reminded Bridget of the light in Kalami's eyes when he touched her mind, only one thousand times more intense.

"Safely returned?" she asked. "With nothing new taken from me?" Her mind showed her the fox, the fox at the edge of the graveyard, and it had stared at her with green eyes and taken away her fears and the memory of her fears. The fox had wanted her here. Anger roared into Bridget's blood, but she held it back, forced it down. Anger would not serve her, not here, not now. Not in the place of the Vixen's power. How she knew that Bridget could not say, but she knew it all the same.

The Vixen nodded, as if satisfied. "Safely returned." The light gleamed even brighter. "And I will see that you learn what is hidden from you."

Part of Bridget's mind wondered if that was not more of a bargain than she really wanted to make. But the rest of her again felt the thinness of the air, and felt the lack of some vital thing. But even more than that, she felt how very alone she was here, surrounded by these mocking creatures and face-to-face with their gigantic queen.

She could refuse, she knew it. She could choose to walk away from this. The Vixen had done her a wrong, and that left her the right to walk away. She had resources here, knowledge untapped. She shivered at the certainty that filled her. She felt as if her very soul hung in the balance, as if all the world would be changed by her decision. She could leave the Vixen to repent meddling with her. She could save the Vixen's sons and accept the consequences.

Can I leave even a wild creature to die when there is anything I can do?

"Very well," said Bridget. "I will do what I can."

"Yes." The Vixen thrust her muzzle forward until her black nose brushed Bridget's cheek like a damp kiss and Bridget heard her sharp sniff as she took in Bridget's scent. "You will."

The Vixen fell back and turned away from Bridget. "Follow us."

Bridget, realizing that all her choices had for the moment been made, gripped her skirts, and followed.

The foxes fell in step all around Bridget. They pressed against her on either side, snuffling at her heels. She had to walk carefully to avoid stepping on the paws of those in front of her. The outliers gamboled, chasing each other, and tumbling over each other in mock fights. Every now and then one of them would skip off into the forest, and once, one of those returned with a bird hanging limp and bloody in its jaws. Always, always, she could see the largest of the foxes slipping through the trees, shadows among shadows. Not once did the Vixen look back to see if Bridget followed.

After what might have been an hour or a day, the trees up ahead drew their branches back like skirts to let the Vixen pass. Ahead, Bridget saw a round green hill rising from the ground like a bubble from a pot of boiling water. The Vixen slipped through a black crack in its side and her foxes flowed after her.

It's only a cave. Bridget swallowed against the tightness in her throat and stepped into the crevice.

The world went black as suddenly as if the sun itself had been snuffed out. Bridget halted in her tracks. All she could see around her was the gleam of eyes and teeth. Her heart slammed against her rib cage.

Safely returned, Bridget reminded herself even as the cold of the place seeped under her skin. *She promised safely returned.*

Ahead, a green light flickered. It showed Bridget a rough floor of raw stone, and dank walls leaning in less than an arm's length away on either side. Biting her lip, Bridget laid her palms against the chilly stone and picked her way forward as carefully as she would on the rocks beside the shores of Lake Superior.

Gradually, the walls opened up to form a chamber of soil, roots and stone. The green light grew brighter. Now she could see that it came from a fire of emerald and sapphire flames dancing on the chamber floor. It gave off no heat and burned no fuel that Bridget could see. The foxes flowed forward, ringing the den like sentries. Those who could not fit clogged the passage behind her, making any thought of retreat impossible. Their eyes filled the whole world and their gaze touched her like a thousand fingers, making her skin crawl.

Striving to maintain her calm, Bridget stepped into the Vixen's den. A dimple carved by water had been lined with twigs, leaves and tufts of fur so red they could have come only from the Vixen herself. Stretched out on the strange bed lay three men, two of them with red hair and one with grey. All of them were naked, and all of them had been wounded. The first of the redheads had a long gash down his thigh; the second bled from his side. The gray-haired man had been stabbed through the gut and curled around the wound as if to protect it. The wounds were bad, not only because of their size and location but because all had become infected and oozed with blood and pus. Bridget's hand went involuntarily to her nose to block out the smell of putrefaction.

The Vixen trod gently around the edges of the nest, circling behind the three men. One of her foxes whimpered. Another yipped, and for the first time, the Vixen's demeanor grew gentle.

"My sons," she said, nuzzling at the red hair of the closest. In response the man groaned and turned his head away. "Help them."

Bridget closed her mouth, and strode forward briskly. The foxes parted soundlessly to let her crouch beside the nest. Whatever else was going on here, these three obviously suffered. Fever blotched their skin red and white. She could feel the heat of it against her hands as she went from man to man, gently moving aside their hands so she could touch their wounds.

Bridget frowned deeply. Now that she looked closely, what she had taken for great gouges were in reality little more than scrapes. Even the puncture wound Grey Hair suffered was less than a half an inch deep.

"I don't understand," she said, wiping her hands on her apron. "These are not severe, or they should not be. How did they come to cause much distress?"

"Cold iron," said the Vixen, as if that were all the explanation that could possibly be needed. "Can you help them?"

Bridget sat back on her heels, encouraged as much as she was confused. Had the wounds been what they first appeared, she was not certain she could have brought any relief. However, all that these men required was bathing and stitches, two services well within her abilities. She felt in her apron's breast pocket, relieved to find that through all her trials, her sewing kit remained with her. "I will need clean cloths," she said. "Warm water, and alcohol—"

"What is that?" interrupted the Vixen.

How to explain? "Whiskey will do, if that's all there is."

The Vixen trotted over to the fire and stared into it for a moment. Four of the kits came and pressed their noses against her flanks. She ignored them. Bridget could not help but notice how the green of the flames was the same green of her eyes. Bridget felt the air of the cave shift, and for a moment it grew even colder.

Then, a shadow fell across Bridget's hand and next to her she saw a pile of white cloths, a bowl of steaming, clear water, and a crockery jug that had been tightly corked and sealed with wax. Bridget broke the seal and pulled out the cork, taking a cautious sniff. The strength of the fumes made her eyes water. Bridget realized she was intolerably thirsty. For a moment, she considered taking a sip of the liquor, just to see what could possibly smell so strong, but she dismissed the idea. If anything, she needed her head as clear as possible.

Using the cloths, Bridget washed each of the wounds, first with the water, then with the whiskey, and then with the water again. The men moaned and tossed under her ministrations, but their struggles were weak and she did not have to call for them to be held down. With every motion, she felt the weight of the foxes' gaze on her. She did not look up as she stepped around the men, deciding it was better to concentrate on the torn flesh and the clotting blood. Despite that, she always she knew exactly where the Vixen stood to watch her. The fox queen's presence dominated the cave and Bridget could feel it pressing against her like a hand laid on her shoulder.

"Can you bring me silk thread?" asked Bridget, wringing out her last cloth and dabbing it against Gray Hair's side. The man's face screwed up tight from his private pain and he batted at her. Bridget held his hand back and applied her cloth firmly. A fox yapped, another snarled, but none interfered.

"I can," said the Vixen, and within three heartbeats, a spindle wound round with thread waited at Bridget's right hand.

When Bridget was satisfied that the wounds were as clean as she could make them, she drew out her sewing kit, selected a needle and threaded it with the Vixen's silk. Silk would work much better for the task at hand than the cotton stuff she had with her, as it was stronger and smoother. Setting her jaw in concentration, Bridget bent over the leanest of the two red-haired men and began to stitch his thigh closed.

As she worked, a warm calm spread through her. Her thirst forgotten, she was able to concentrate on her work with an astonishing clarity. Calm turned to confidence, and then to delight at her craft as she moved from the first man to the second. She formed her stitches hastily, eagerly, but her mind was buoyed by the knowledge that she worked well, that the stitches would hold, that these men would be healed by her hands, and her skill. She barely realized that she had begun to work on the third wound. The world was red blood, white silk and living warmth under her hand, all bound together and knotted tight, until the red was gone and all that remained was the fresh white and warmth, and fire running through her veins where her blood should have been. Until the world spun, and her vision clouded, and she could no longer feel her hands to clutch the needle.

Bridget felt the flash of pain as she fell upon the stone floor, and then the world went black.

Kalami would have preferred to pass through the Land of Death and Spirit as a shade rather than as flesh and blood. It was always perilous to enter the Silent Lands, but walking physically within them offered special dangers for temptation, confusion and entrapment, especially if one attempted it too often. Not a full day had passed since he had taken Bridget on this route, and like the living world, this world had rumors and struggles and powers that worked to their own ends. But if he had sent only his spirit forth, he could not have carried the empress's ring, nor could he have touched Bridget, should she need help to return to the mortal world.

So, Kalami walked the trackless forests of the Land of Death and Spirit with a stout ash pole in his hand as his anchor to the world, and in addition to the dowager's ring he kept a small twist of red fox fur in his pocket. All mortal foxes carried something of the Vixen inside them. The connection this talisman gave him was tenuous, but it would be enough. If he was patient, and if he could keep his mind clear, the proper path would open before him. He would find the Vixen, and he would find Bridget.

Bridget. Kalami felt his jaw tighten. How had she come to be here? Had Sakra given her to the Vixen? Or had the Vixen taken her? There was no way to know until he found her, and perhaps not even then. Bridget herself might not know what had happened, and there was no guarantee the Vixen would tell them the truth. Whatever had happened, it could not but be dangerous to his careful plans. If Sakra had actually entered into some bargain with *lokai* . . . Kalami ground his teeth together. It could be disastrous, and it would be small comfort when he stood in the ruins of his ambitions to know that bargains with the great powers usually cut down the bargainer.

Kalami stepped through a screen of birch trees into one of the rare clearings of these deep woods. The sky spread green and sunless over him and the waist-high grass bent silently under a wind he could not hear or feel.

Testing each step with his ash pole, Kalami waded into the grass as a man might ford an uncertain river. As he neared the center of the silent meadow, the light dimmed and shifted, growing deep and red as the twilight at day's end. Kalami hesitated a bare instant, but then made himself keep walking. Paying too much attention to the unknown in this place could cause that same unknown to pay attention to you.

Ahead of him, the ferns and low tree branches swayed and parted. A man dressed entirely in red rode into the clearing on a horse the color of old blood. His breastplate shone bright scarlet, as did the helmet that obscured his eyes and the ribbons that streamed from the javelin he rested on the stirrup of his red saddle.

Kalami's hand tightened involuntarily around his walking stick, but he focused his gaze past the strange red knight toward the trees that were his goal.

Despite that, the Red Knight pulled his great horse to a halt in Kalami's path.

"I bring you a message from my mistress, servant of Isavalta."

Kalami, left with no choice, halted. Keeping one hand wrapped firmly around his ash pole, he folded the other over his breast and reverenced. "I am honored to receive it," he said. In this place, courtesy could mean the difference between life and death. "Would it please you, sir, to let me know who your mistress may be?" It was good sign that this knight had not used Kalami's name. Names could have power, even in the mortal world. Here, they were weapons.

"My mistress is the mistress of Ishbushka," said the knight. "She's the Old Witch, Bony Legs, the One with the Iron Teeth."

The Red Knight's words made Kalami's blood go cold. This creature came from Baba Yaga.

"My mistress says," the Red Knight went on, "she requires your attendance and your attention."

Again, Kalami made his reverence. "Sir, with all due respect to your mistress, I am on an urgent commission and cannot tarry." There were many ways to become lost in the Land of Death and Spirit, and letting one's attention stray too long from one's errand was only one of them. Baba Yaga was powerful enough that he could not safely refuse her, yet he could not safely accept.

The knight extended his javelin, butt first. "Take this as a token of your acceptance, and you will cross her path without you leave yours."

I have no time for this! Kalami wanted to shout. Every moment Bridget, untrained and unprotected, stayed in this place she was in more danger of becoming irrevocably lost to it. He had no time for games no matter how great the players might be. But he held his tongue and grasped the javelin the knight offered him.

As soon as Kalami touched the smooth, wooden shaft, the Red Knight wheeled his horse around and galloped noiselessly back into the trees, vanishing like a thought. As he did, the light around Kalami brightened, becoming the same pale green it had been when he started his journey.

Kalami settled the javelin on his shoulder and strode forward, thumping his staff with each step in an impatient punctuation for the delay. Eventually, he did again broach the tree line and was plunged into the shadow of the forest, his footsteps turning a little toward his left shoulder. Would this take him to the Vixen or to Baba Yaga? He no longer knew and his anger was causing his resolution to falter. Kalami planted his ash pole firmly on the leaf-covered ground and stared at its base for a moment, drawing deep breaths of the thin air around him and focusing his will. He had a task at hand. Only by fixing his mind upon it would it ever be completed.

Calmer, Kalami lifted his gaze and had to stifle a shout. Baba Yaga squatted in front of him in an ancient mortar that was chipped and grey with filth. She clutched the pestle in both bony hands, and Kalami could not help but see that its dingy sides were stained with what looked very much like blood.

"You go to the Vixen, Valin Kalami," said Baba Yaga. With each word he could see the black iron of her teeth. "You go to fetch Ingrid Loftfield's daughter for your dowager."

Kalami reverenced as best as he was able with his hands full. Evidently, he was not of such a kind that Baba Yaga would waste her time with courtesies for him. "Nothing may be hidden from you, Great Mother."

Baba Yaga did not even blink at this flattery. "The Vixen will give the woman to you. You will give her to me."

Kalami hesitated. What if he did? It was nothing he had not thought of. With Bridget lost, the empress with no one left to turn to but himself, and the secret of the Phoenix's cage, the true power of the Isavaltan throne would burn in his hands.

Burn. Burn away his life as it had the empress's. Without the shield of Bridget's power, he would soon be as old, as feeble and as mad. No. Kalami shook himself. This was his desire being summoned to work against him. If he could not safely leave Bridget with the Vixen, he could not give her to Baba Yaga.

"Your offer is generous." Kalami bowed. "But I must decline."

"Beware," breathed the witch. "You too have power, I can taste it. Your own heart and its hate tempt and blind you. You stand to lose all."

"I stand to gain all," replied Kalami coolly. "Why should I hazard a throw with so dangerous an ally?"

Baba Yaga bared her iron teeth. "Give me the woman, little sorcerer. Give her to me and you will prosper. Do not—"

"I have done you no harm, accepted no gift, offered no insult or challenge." Kalami spread his hands. "You cannot lawfully wound me, even here."

"But nor will I forget, little sorcerer, little man. Nor will I ever forget."

Kalami bowed once more. "I would take my leave of you, Great Mother. My thanks and my duty."

Mumbling, the witch snatched the javelin from his hand, stuffed it into the mortar beside her and pushed away with her pestle. As her servant had before her, she vanished completely.

Kalami did not dare stay still any longer. Although he strode away with back and shoulders straight, he felt sick inside. Baba Yaga held him in her eye now. Was there power enough in any world to turn that eye away? Why should he not just give her what she wanted? He was a fool, a fool . . .

Stop! Kalami told himself fiercely. *Did you truly believe you could seek to gain possession of one of the great powers without risk? Without anger or danger? Is it true then what they say of your people, that you will cower when the shadows grow too thick and the stakes too high? You will have Bridget, the Phoenix and whatever remains of the dowager. You will meet whatever challenge Baba Yaga chooses to raise and you will defeat it with your new tools. You will release your people from bondage and lead them to rule, not just over their oppressors, but over the three empires. Isavalta will be slave to their will and yours. . . .*

"Such big thoughts for such a small mind."

Kalami pulled on the reins. A bright red fox sat beside a rotting log that was covered in moss and crumbling leaves.

"Good day, Master Fox," Kalami said, pulling together his best manners. "I crave—"

"You do." The animal scratched its ear. "We heard your cravings roaring through the woods like a murder of crows. You woke all our kits in their burrows and set them to howling with your cravings. I must tell you, sir"—it drawled out the word—"our mother is not pleased."

Kalami bowed low. "Of your courtesy, then, master, allow me to make my apologies to her in person."

But the fox had gone very still except for the tip of its tail, which twitched restlessly. "We want no more mortal kind here," it said. "What if I were to say our mother bids you go."

"Your mother would never be so rude to an official messenger," said Kalami sternly. "And she will be angered when she hears how you have spoken to me."

The fox snarled, a low rumble of sound and a flash of white teeth, and Kalami felt himself relax. If he had misjudged his response, the creature would already be at his throat. As it was, he saw two other shadowy forms retreat into the darkness. He only had to keep calm and wait, despite the fact that the growl from the red fox in front of him continued on until he felt the tremor of it in his bones and the beating of his heart.

"Come then, and see what manner of welcome you may have." The fox whisked around and trotted into the trees.

Holding the ash pole in front of him, Kalami followed the fox.

Because the mistress of the domain willed it so, the journey was a gentle one. Trees lifted their branches and flattened their roots so that Kalami could walk as easily as if he were on a cobbled street in Biradost.

The fixed points in the Land of Death and Spirit were few, but gradually the trees drew back to reveal a green hill that echoed in his mind as a solid and substantial thing. He could even hear the grass whispering to the dry wind. Even so, he knew that the shadows of the black crevasse that opened into the hill concealed yet more illusion, but that was only to be expected. This was the Vixen's home and he would see only what she permitted him to see.

"You must leave your stick here." The fox looked over its shoulder and grinned at him. "Its wood will not bear the touch of our mother's stone."

Meaning the touch of ash wood against the mound would pull Kalami instantly back into the mortal world. But Kalami had been ready for this. He lifted the pole and brought it down swiftly against his knee so that the wood splintered in two. He tossed one half aside and stowed the other under his coat.

The fox sniffed at him, as if he had somehow cheated at the game, but it made no further comment as it led Kalami into the darkness.

His progress through the black tunnel was mercifully short. Kalami had heard accounts of those the Vixen kept walking for days. Perhaps she was amused at his cleverness of how to keep his talisman of ash about him, or, more likely, she had just hit on some more interesting game.

You are on a legitimate errand from an anointed queen. The Vixen cannot interfere with you, Kalami reminded himself as the clear green light broke the darkness and he emerged into the cave that was the Vixen's den.

Kalami saw Bridget at once. She was the only other human thing here. She sprawled on her back in a nest of loam and leaves, one arm cast across the Vixen's forepaws. The Vixen lay on her side, cradling Bridget in the arch of her belly as if Bridget were one of the Vixen's kits.

"What do you think of my new daughter?" asked the Vixen lightly. "She is a bit pale and wan, but time will mend that, I think."

"Only if by mending you would have her become a ghost." Kalami reverenced to remove the sharp edge from his words. "Great Queen, I bring you greetings from my mistress imperial, Her Grand Majesty the Dowager Empress Medeoan Edemskoidoch Nacheradavosh of Eternal Isavalta. A thing of some value to Her Imperial Majesty has become lost in your vast realm and she craves your assistance, one monarch to another, to aid in her search for it. In return, she offers this token of sisterly esteem and friendship." Kalami held up the gold and emerald ring.

The Vixen sniffed the air, scenting whatever aura clung to the ring, but at the same time, she whisked her tail across Bridget's torso like a living blanket.

"What if I have already found this precious thing?" she inquired coyly.

Kalami resolutely kept his gaze on the Vixen. Bridget's skin was too white. He could see the blue of her veins against her throat. She had already been here too long. If he did not reclaim her soon, she would be nothing but a wraith.

"If you have found that which Her Imperial Majesty claims, then I humbly beg you to honor my mistress's request and return it to her keeping."

The Vixen lifted her muzzle, considering. "And why should I do that?" she asked, leveling her vivid gaze on Kalami.

Behind the Vixen, Kalami saw three foxes approach, two reds and a grey. They were of normal fox size and looked like toys beside their enormous mother. Kalami's heart hammered hard at the base of his throat. Were they the three from the wood? The three he sent after Ananda, to face Sakra and his braided swords? Did they know how far his plot had gone?

If they did, he died, here and now, if he was lucky.

"Because no living thing of the mortal world can last here in the Silent Lands, Great Queen. It will only fade like snow in the sun and you will be left with nothing. Not so Her Imperial Majesty's gift." He held the ring aloft to catch the green light that glinted from its gold. He did not know the ring's provenance, but Medeoan would not have sent it if she had not been certain it would catch the Vixen's fancy. Whatever faults he laid at her imperial door, Medeoan was as shrewd as any spirit.

The Vixen sniffed again. Her tail waved back and forth across Bridget, stroking her. Bridget stirred in her stupor, moaning a little. Her jaw opened, hanging slack. Kalami imagined he could hear her heart, and with each beat, a little of her soul, a little more of her power, leached away into the Land of Death and Spirit, like water into parched soil.

But then, the Vixen whisked her tail away from Bridget. "Perhaps you are right," she allowed. "Perhaps she is too frail to become one of my foxes." She leaned down and licked Bridget's eye. Bridget winced, but did not wake, and turned her face away. "Come then, take your precious thing."

Kalami reverenced again and laid the ring at the Vixen's feet. She covered it with one paw. Taking that gesture as acceptance, Kalami lifted Bridget in his arms. She did not stir at the movement.

"I thank you on behalf of my mistress imperial, Great Queen, and beg your leave to depart."

The Vixen inclined her head. Very carefully, Kalami turned again toward the darkness. Bridget lay cold and heavy against his chest. It was the weight that gave him hope. She was still in her own flesh. She could be saved, if he could return her to the living world soon enough.

Gaining as tight a hold around Bridget as he could, Kalami marched into the darkness.

"You gave her to him."

"Do you reproach me, my son?" The Vixen rolled over onto her back, exposing belly and teats to her oldest red child.

"No, my mother." He turned his neck, offering his gleaming white throat to her. She pawed it gently. "I just wonder at you refusing your revenge."

"Did I?" the Vixen stretched lazily. "Into Medeoan's court, which harbors those who wounded you, I have just sent a sorceress of unknown power. Before she left my side, I gave her a gift which she will find most useful among all those spells and illusions with which she who is pleased to call herself my fellow has surrounded herself." The Vixen's voice grew grim, and the shadows around her curdled. "She will, I think, be sorry to have claimed as her own someone who can now see through all such trappings." The Vixen bared her teeth to her darkness and her visions. "Yes, she will be sorry that her house harbors those who wounded my children."

Kalami emerged from the cleft in the hill and found his piece of splintered ash pole lying where he had thrown it. Grateful, he lowered Bridget to the ground. She still did not stir. Her chest neither rose nor fell. Only the pale pink in her white cheeks betrayed the fact of life yet within her.

Kalami spat upon the ash wood. "I would go home. Lead us to the river." He cast the stick in front of him so that it fell on the ground and began to roll. It rolled through the grass and toward the trees. Kalami lifted Bridget once more and followed the stick. The nameless river that cut through all the Silent Lands was the one reliable passage between them and the mortal worlds. From the banks of the river, he could not fail to bring them home.

Kalami wrapped his arms tightly around Bridget. The more contact she had with flesh and blood here, the better she would be. Was it his imagination, or did she feel lighter now? Suspicion lanced through him. Had the Vixen tricked him? Given him a changeling, a painted stock, instead of the flesh-and-blood woman?

Had he been so stupid?

Trees rose in front of them as the stick rolled and skittered its way through the forest, following the unrelenting pull of mortal reality. Kalami sucked in his breath and lengthened his stride to follow.

What lay in his arms was definitely lighter, and warmer too. Kalami ground his teeth together. A changeling. A sham, a ruse, and he had been taken in by it. Traded away Medeoan's ring for a trick, perhaps a trap. Perhaps the Vixen did know, her sons had told her and this was her revenge, and if Kalami took it back to Isavalta her treachery would be unleashed and all his plans would be drowned in its flood.

The only sound was his harsh, angry breathing. Even the branches made no noise as they slapped at his sides and brushed across his hair. His thoughts took up that single, broken rhythm. He'd been tricked, been tricked, been tricked.

With a wordless roar, Kalami cast the illusion to the ground. It lay there, like the dead thing it was, the sham of life fading further from it cheeks. He would cut the thing, open it, gut it entirely and find out what spell lay within. He would leave it on the ground beside the changeling shell. He grasped his knife and raised it high. He'd been tricked, he'd been tricked, he'd been tricked . . .

Unless you are being tricked now.

The thought stayed his hand. *Tricked, tricked, tricked*, the thought pulsed through him with the beat of his heart now. But by whom? In what way? The forest swam in front of his eyes. He was losing his way, tricked, tied in knots, his own knots, the knots of others, his mask peeling away in layers so that he would become tangled.

Bridget, or whatever it was, shifted. He stared at her, it, her? his eyes wide in horror.

Hold, hold, you are losing yourself. You must hold!

Kalami tightened his grip on the knife, but the sort of metal that he could carry with him into this land gave him no protection from its glamours.

Tricked, tricked, tricked . . .

He brought the blade down, but gently, against the skin of the throat that bared itself to him. A red thread followed the tip of the blade, and a gasp of surprise and pain.

Blood, bright red blood, welled from the shallow cut. Kalami shuddered hard. No changeling could bleed. He sheathed his knife, trembling at the realization of what he had almost done.

He lifted Bridget up and held her hard against his chest. The ash pole waited for them and Kalami strode after it. With his movement, it continued to scurry forward, a guide he could trust for it was of his own making. He gripped his mind as tightly as he gripped Bridget in his arms. The river lay before them. Its course would lead them back to the living world. The living world, sound and warmth waited for them. That was the goal, his goal, heart and mind. He wove that goal into a solid thing with the strength of his mind and soul and the frantic breath in his lungs.

The trees opened and Kalami saw the river spreading brown and smooth between the mossy banks. Unable to restrain himself, he cried aloud and ran, a clumsy, heavy trot, until his boots splashed in the water. The forcst around them blurred into meaningless shadows of green and black, and the world turned cold. Kalami closed his eyes, and opened them again.

And they stood on the frozen beck that fed into the great river running down to Vyshtavos, the Winter Palace of Isavalta. His horse, tethered to the willow nearby, champed its bit and stamped its hooves impatiently.

Ignoring the animal, Kalami fell to his knees, letting Bridget slip onto the snow. As swiftly as he could, he unbuttoned his coat and drew it around her. She was too pale, and too cold. He laid his hand on her chest. She breathed. She breathed!

His touch, or perhaps it was the winter cold, stirred something in her, and her eyes fluttered open.

"Dreams," murmured Bridget, looking up at him with eyes that were unfocused, but otherwise clear. "Strange dreams."

"Yes, dreams," he told her gently, drawing his coat over her. "In the morning you will wake." *Wake to me, and to your place in my dreams, Bridget Lederle.*

He realized he found her beautiful then. Her time in the Land of Death and Spirit had refined her. He had first seen her eight years ago through the mind of a hungry man named Kyosti, who saw only a tall young virgin who might be talked into laying herself down. He'd seen her himself only in the dark of the moonless night beside Lake Superior, and had been almost blinded by the power that spilled so casually from her into the unresponsive world. But when he had returned and seen her looming over him after she had pulled him from the killing lake, he saw a coarse, rawboned woman, a peasant roughened by hard work.

Now, though, so close to death, she seemed fragile, with only the purity of the power in her soul keeping her alive. Perhaps he could refine these qualities. Perhaps she would not have to be simply his servant when he stood behind the throne of Isavalta.

Kalami smiled and pulled Bridget close to his heart.

Chapter Ten

Medeoan looked down at the fat man who knelt before her on the cold black and white marble floor of the small audience chamber. The bright yellow silks that adorned the walls and were supposed to render a summery and welcoming air in the room just lent a bilious tone to the man's already pale face. A bead of perspiration trickled out from under the jeweled band of his cap.

"I humbly thank Your Grand Majesty for this audience." He wheezed as he spoke.

Medeoan inclined her head and gestured for the footman to bring a stool. "Be seated, Lord Master Oulo," she said, sitting herself in a square chair, the legs of which had been carved with eagles' talons each clutching a dark garnet. Another nod to her ladies and the secretary in the servants' alcove told them to turn away and pay no attention to this conversation. "I would hear what you have to say."

The man climbed to his feet and settled himself on the carved and padded stool, which creaked a warning note under his bulk. "My mistress imperial, I am here to prove my loyalty to the throne of Eternal Isavalta. I am here to humbly beg that you give your consideration to my words."

Medeoan cut them off with a wave of her bandaged hand. "The heart of the matter, Lord Master. I have little patience with deputations from Kasatan." In fact, the very sight of the man caused her hands to itch under their dressings, but she did not feel it necessary to say so at this time.

The man made an effort to stiffen himself. "Mistress, I bring you news of rebellion and traitors."

Medeoan sat still as stone as Oulo poured out his tale. How Lord Master Hraban, hearing of her imprisonment of Kasatan's reeves and deputies, had contacted Oulo to speak of rebellion. How Oulo had, with trepidation, exchanged various messages with Hraban. At last, Hraban became convinced that Oulo shared his cause and had invited him to Spavatan to meet some supporters, and Ananda herself.

"Who are the supporters?" Medeoan barked out the question.

Oulo bowed his head in the face of her anger. "A ship's captain of Hastinapura, named Nisula, and Lord Master Peshek. There are others, but I have not yet been given their names."

The sound of that name stopped Medeoan's heart for one painful beat. "Peshek? Peshek spoke against me?"

Oulo bowed his head further.

Anger seized hold of Medeoan then, turning the whole world red. Before she knew what she was doing, she had leapt up from the chair and seized Oulo by the collar, dragging him to his feet. "How dare you!" she shouted to the trembling man. Pain seared her palms but that was nothing compared with the anger searing her blood. "How dare you come here with such stories!"

"I beg . . . I humbly plead . . ." All of Oulo's chins quivered. "I thought only to warn my mistress imperial of a danger to Isavalta." A tear trickled from the corner of one small eye. "Please, Grand Majesty . . ."

Medeoan released Oulo's collar and backed away, her hand pressed against her mouth. The man collapsed against the footstool, his hand grasping his throat. He must not see this. She gripped the arm of her chair. Her hands hurt; ah, by the breath of the gods, how they hurt. She took a deep breath, smelling the mint and saffron of the poultice her surgeon had used. She must collect herself. This fat little man must not see her indecisive or shaken. He must not be allowed to carry tales of weakness away with him.

Medeoan drew herself up with the precision of a soldier coming to attention and dropped her hand to the keys at her waist. The touch of the cool metal eased some of the burning in her wounded skin.

"What proof do you offer of this accusation, Lord Master Oulo?"

Oulo swallowed audibly and his shoulders sagged. But then, he seemed to reach some decision and squared himself again, looking more as a nobleman should than he had any time since he entered her chamber.

"It is said that Her Grand Majesty has means by which she may see into hearts and know what is written there." Awkwardly, he dropped onto his knees again and bowed his head before her. "If she should choose to use them upon my unworthy person, she will know that I speak nothing but the truth."

Medeoan regarded him for a moment. He had ceased all his trembling, as if this final submission had led to a final confidence. She needed no spell to see that he spoke the truth to her now.

Peshek. How could Peshek turn from her to the side of a Hastinapuran? Another trusted friend gone, stolen away by Ananda. Medeoan wanted to weep. How many more would she lose?

How many more could she afford to lose?

With that thought, Medeoan also reached a decision.

"And if I were to look into your heart," she said, returning to her chair and folding her bandaged hands in front of her, "what would I see regarding the reason for this revelation?"

Oulo lifted his head, the tentative beginnings of hope lighting his tiny eyes. "My mistress imperial would see that I would wish to ask for the release of my reeves and my deputies."

Ah. That would be it. "One of whom, is, I believe, your younger brother."

Oulo nodded.

"Very well." Medeoan raised her voice, gesturing with two fingers toward the servants' alcove so that the secretary would take note of what she next said. "Leave. Return to Kasatan. You will receive word of my decision within two weeks."

For a bare instant, Oulo dared to look her in the eyes. Because he dropped his gaze hastily, Medeoan let the indiscretion pass.

"My thanks and my duty, Grand Majesty."

Medeoan dismissed him with a gesture and did not watch as he left. Her mind was already traveling back through the years to Peshek as she first knew him, and as she most liked to remember him. He had been dashing then, with strong features and a ready grin that could turn fierce when his work became serious. She remembered him covered with the dirt and sweat of battle, emerging from the mountains where his forces had been harassing the troops her husband Kacha had meant to lead in a war against Hung-Tse which would have destroyed Isavalta. The war that had released the Firebird.

But then, his true loyalty was always to Avanasy. How could I expect him to stay loyal to me when Avanasy is dead? Medeoan tightened her burned hand, despite the pain. *Because I am his empress!*

She would level Peshek's entire oblast, his province, for this treachery. She would burn Kasatan for bringing her this news. They would all pay for their conspiracies. She would not allow them to split her kingdom. She would not allow the empire to be threatened again.

Let me go, whispered the Firebird's voice. *Let me go and I will burn them all for you.*

Medeoan's head fell backward. Her hand burned still. When would Valin return to heal her? When would he bring Bridget Lederle and the rest her presence promised? "What else will you burn?"

I will burn you. Let me go or I will burn you and all that is yours.

Medeoan lifted her head again. It would be so easy. Release the Firebird. Let Peshek and Hraban burn for turning against her. Let Oulo burn for bringing her such news.

But when the bird had flown back to its masters in the Heart of the World, what then? What of those who still remained loyal to Isavalta? No. She would do her duty still. She would do her duty even in the Land of Death and Spirit, and she would not be swayed.

She opened her hand and looked at the bandages. She must think clearly. She now had evidence of the conspiracy against her. But she could not simply send in the guard to make arrests. Ananda had done her work too well. If she cut off these hands that had been lifted against her, yet others would rise to take their place. Even if she were publicly arrested and tried, Ananda would become a martyr to those who believed her lies, and a rallying point for the opportunists who saw only that she, Medeoan, was growing old well before her time.

Tears stung her eyes, and in the back of her mind, Medeoan heard the Firebird laughing.

"Princess."

The urgent whisper and familiar touch lifted Ananda out of her dreams.

"Highness, I think you should come see."

Behule stood at Ananda's bedside, a lamp in one hand and a robe draped over her arm.

"What is it?" asked Ananda, habit bringing her instantly awake. If Behule had noticed something amiss, it was sure to be urgent. Behule was one of the reasons Ananda's sorcerous reputation had grown so strong. Behule was all eyes and ears. She knew the character of each of the empress's guard, it seemed, and most of the household servitors.

When Mikkel is restored and the dowager laid aside, you will be a free and noble woman, Behule, Ananda promised silently for the thousandth time as she stood to let Behule drape the brocade robe around her shoulders. *I swear it.*

Behule kept the lamp low and shielded with her hand, giving Ananda's eyes a chance to adjust to the darkness. Swiftly, Behule led her through the linked apartments, to the outermost chamber. Kiriti stood beside the heavily curtained window that overlooked the courtyard. From outside rose the sound of voices and the clatter of rapid movement.

Ananda raced across the room to Kiriti's side.

"Kalami returns," was all her woman murmured as she stood aside.

Behule extinguished the lamp so no light would show. Through the gap between the curtains, Ananda saw the courtyard washed in the dim light of the waning moon. A host of servants, including two footmen in rumpled livery, ran from the palace carrying a litter between them. Kalami on horseback waited in the middle of the yard. She could have told it was him even in the pitch darkness. He burned with plotting and arrogance. At the moment, he cradled something large in his arms. Ananda squinted. He handed his burden carefully to one of the footmen, who in turn lowered it onto the litter.

Ananda held her breath.

It was a woman in dark clothing, apparently in a complete faint, for she did not move as the fur rugs were thrown over her, nor as she was lifted and borne away into the palace. Kalami leapt to the ground, handed his horse's reins to a waiting groom and strode after the litter.

"So," breathed Ananda, letting the curtain fall. "Why must I believe that new trouble is come?" She touched Behule's hand. "Go and find out for me where this new guest is to be lodged. Hear what new gossip there may be of this."

"At once." Behule handed Kiriti the lamp and turned to hurry away, but instead she froze. "Highness?" The query was strained.

Ananda turned as well. In the shadows of the room she saw something stir, heard something croak, a sound like deep laughter. Her heart beat hard as her eyes adjusted slowly to the deeper darkness, and the shape stirred again. Her breath left her at a rush. The shape sat on one of the room's low tables. It was a crow, black as pitch and night, its eye glinting in the sliver of moonlight that slid past the curtain.

"Shall I chase it out?" asked Kiriti.

"No, wait." Feeling foolish, but mindful of Sakra's teaching on how many ways this land was still wild, Ananda reverenced. "What news, good master crow?" she inquired.

In response, the crow launched itself at Ananda. She screeched involuntarily and shrank away as the great bird flapped out the window.

The window that was incapable of opening, and yet had in no way been broken by the passage of the bird.

Ananda pressed her hand against her chest, as if she thought she could still her wildly hammering heart. A flash of something pale caught her eye. On the floor, a folded piece of paper lay under one black feather. She bent toward it, but Behule reached it first and handed it to her. The paper was a letter, and it was sealed with Sakra's false sigil.

Her hands shaking, Ananda broke the seal and unfolded the missive. "Behule, do not wait for this. Go find out what you can about the woman Kalami has brought."

The faint rustle of cloth told her Behule reverenced and raced for the door. Ananda could not take her eyes from the letter.

First Princess, she read.

Because of the messenger, this once I may be plain. Watch closely for Kalami's return. He brings with him a powerful sorceress from beyond the world's end. She is the daughter of Avanasy and Ingrid. She is summoned by the dowager and the lord sorcerer and she can only be meant to harm you.

Do nothing rash though, I beg you. It may be they have misstepped in this.

I will come to you as soon as I may.

Courage, Ananda.

He did not sign it.

A powerful sorceress from beyond world's end. Ananda read the words again with failing heart. Another danger. Another power on the dowager's side. The daughter of Avanasy and Ingrid. The Avanasidoch. A figure from legend so great that most folk believed her to be only a wishful thought.

Crossing the room, Ananda folded the letter and dropped it onto the coals of the firepit. It blossomed into orange flame for a moment, and then slowly blackened and fell to ash.

"Princess?" inquired Kiriti, as tentatively as Behule had.

Ananda straightened her back. "Come, Kiriti, I think we must change the loom."

"Yes, mistress."

When Ananda had lived in the palace of the Pearl Throne with her family, she had no need to carry keys. All doors were open to her and she knew with precision where she might and might not go within the flow of daily life with her family and the court. Here, though, she carried keys for her chests, and keys for her chamber, and one small brass key to a door that should have led to a private study and shrine.

Since the day of her wedding, however, desk, shrine and books stood out in the main room. Ananda paused before the onyx images of the Seven Mothers, arranged in their circle, each of them in a separate pose of their eternal dance. She bowed, raising her hands to her face and praying for the safety of herself and her people. Sometimes she felt she never stopped saying that prayer.

Ananda unlocked the inner door. On the other side waited a spare, windowless chamber, its plaster walls painted a delicate blue. Kiriti hurried to light the candles and braziers. Ananda waited for the lights to rise and show her clearly the room's central feature—a vertical loom hung with weighted threads. A weave of shades of grey and black waited half-completed in the frame. Beside it stood locked chests full of cloth and dozens of spools of different-colored thread. Several chairs and stools furnished the room. On each lay some useful tool—a spindle, a set of weaving cards, an embroidery frame, a cloth stuck through with tapestry needles.

Magic could have been worked here by one who had a gifted soul. As it was, there were only Ananda and her ladies and it remained a place of lies. That was why she had removed the shrine. She would not have the Seven Mothers dance where there was no honesty.

Perhaps I should have removed them from the palace altogether.

Ananda unlocked the nearest chest and lifted the flat heavy lid. She tried to examine the spools of thread that waited inside with the blocks of fragrant cedar wood to keep out the moths, but her eyes burned from lack of sleep and her head ached.

I do not want this, part of her cried. *I want to sleep, to dream, to wake up in my old home with my ladies waiting and my sisters and mother nearby. I want to love a whole man with a kind family. I want to go home.*

But she selected two spools of flaxen thread, one of green and another bright yellow, handing them to Kiriti, who waited patiently behind her. It was good thread but not the finest. Suitable for a difficult spell upon a refined soul, but it was not silk, or thread of gold, which were for the most subtle workings or those aimed at the most highly born.

It was an irony, Ananda knew, that she had so much knowledge of magic, but no power touched her soul. She was an ordinary mortal, her spirit split between walking the world and walking with the gods. After a time, she would be gathered completely into the other world. A sorcerer held their whole soul within their flesh, anchored completely into the one world, and so they could feel its pulses and rhythms more keenly, see the other worlds more clearly, and draw on that wholeness, that completeness of self, to spin and weave the magic that was variously thought to be either inside or outside them.

A soft scratching sounded on the door: one, two, three, and a pause, then twice more, another pause, then once. It was the signal she and Kiriti shared with Behule. Ananda nodded and Kiriti unlocked the door. Behule entered, breathless and pale in the faint candlelight.

Ananda gave her a moment to make her obeisance, and to catch her breath, before asking. "What did you learn, Behule?"

"The woman is to be lodged in apartments beside the dowager," said Behule, her voice strained with the wonder of it. "There are all manner of stories flying about. They say she is a spirit power brought from the Silent Lands to cure the emperor. She is Avanasy's daughter come to put an end to Hung-Tse. She is your daemon servant sent to kill Kalami and was apprehended by him."

Of course such a tale would be included. Ananda brushed a loose hair back from her face. "Do any know the truth?"

"If they know, they are not saying, mistress."

No, they would not. The dowager would wait for a suitable public occasion to make the announcement, like the feast celebrating the holy day four nights hence. In the meantime, she would let rumor and anticipation build, dropping tantalizing hints among her courtiers to keep them guessing. It was part of the way she kept her nobles off-balance and scheming about small things that she might control.

"My thanks, Behule." Ananda reached into the chest for another spool of yellow thread. First they would adjust the loom for Medeoan's spies to see. Then, she would think how to use the court's ignorance to spread her own rumors.

"There is something else, mistress."

Ananda straightened up, turning around with the spool of thread still in her right hand. "What is it?"

Behule cast about the room, looking for words. Her hesitation tightened Ananda's heart. "Lord Master Oulo from Kasatan is here."

"I know that. He comes for the holy day. We breakfast together tomorrow." Ananda turned the spool of thread over in her fingers. *What is the matter, Behule?*

"I have made . . . promises to one of the body servants he has been assigned."

As you have so many times before. "Is there a problem in keeping these promises?"

Behule shook her head. "No, mistress. In fact, he has already come to me with news."

Ananda felt her mouth go dry. She had to clutch the spool tightly to keep from dropping it. "This must be very bad news indeed."

Behule hung her head in an apology for being the bearer of bad tidings. "Lord Master Oulo spoke with the dowager when she formally received him today," she said to the floor. "He gave her names."

The spool of thread slipped from Ananda's fingers and clattered to the floor. Her knees suddenly weak, she groped behind her for a chair. She could not see. She could not think of anything except the fact that the dowager knew. The dowager had a witness and now the dowager would no longer need magic to reach Ananda. She could use the high court. She could say that Ananda had listened to traitors. She could say that Ananda had contemplated the overthrow of the Isavaltan throne, and the Isavaltan judges would believe her.

Kiriti grabbed Ananda's hands and sat her on the nearest stool, kneeling beside her. "Mistress, mistress, calm yourself. It is not as bad as it seems. You said Lord Master Oulo was new to the conspiracy. Lord Master Hraban is not a fool. He will not have told him much. These names cannot be that important."

"You were there, Kiriti," said Ananda flatly. "These names will include mine and Captain Nisula's."

Kiriti said nothing.

Ananda's thoughts had snarled themselves together. She could follow no single thread. The dowager had the Avanasidoch, and now the dowager had a witness, and what did Ananda have? She had her ladies and she had her lies. What was she to do?

"The loom." Ananda staggered to her feet, grasping at the only solid thought she had. "We must rethread the loom. Make a new pattern . . ."

Behule interposed herself between Ananda and the loom. "Princess, let us do this. You should get to your bed. In the morning you will know better what to do."

Ananda did not feel tired. She felt on fire. Oulo was a traitor. The Avanasidoch slept beside the dowager. Avanasy was a legend, though her father had known of him. He died for Isavalta, for the child that Medeoan had been. His life had caged one of the great powers.

And now his daughter came to Medeoan's side in the arms of her closest advisor. Now there were three powers arrayed against her, and should that not be enough, there was a traitor to speak her name in open court. Fear dizzied Ananda.

How much longer can I go on? How many days, how many hours before I am made like Mikkel? And how many days of that hell will I be forced to endure before I am finally killed?

"Please, mistress. I beg you."

But Ananda just held up her hand, gulping long breaths of air to try to bring strength to her weakened blood.

"No. First . . . first we must silence this man, if we can."

Ananda wore three braids in her black hair, no matter what other style was set upon her. Each of them bound a spirit, a small servant that she could call upon simply by loosening the tie. Sakra had plaited them with careful fingers and careful magic the day before they had left for Isavalta.

"Just in case the Moon's Daughter should have need," he'd told her with a smile. They had not known then how much need there would be.

Ananda had used one to foil an attempt to poison Kiriti. She had used another to try to heal Mikkel, but she had not been able to speak specifically enough about the task that needed to be done, and the spirit had escaped her.

Both of those braids she had herself redone as best she could, but there was no magic left in them.

Now her shaking hand reached for the third braid. Her ladies stood silently beside her. She picked the knot loose and let the thread fall to the floor. A hot wind swirled through the room, ruffling Ananda's hems and the ends of her hair. When it stilled, a small creature, little bigger than a bullfrog, squatted in front of her. It had round eyes the size of gold coins, a pig-snout nose and a lipless slit of a mouth that showed a row of yellow fangs.

"You have called and I am come," it announced. "I am bound to one task. Speak and let me go."

Ananda licked her lips. She must think clearly. Medeoan and a long line of court sorcerers had woven mighty protections around the palace. There were limits to what magic could do here.

She might render him mute, but he could still write his testimony then. She steeled herself to give her orders. Of course, any spell she ordered laid, Medeoan would eventually undo. But this would frighten Oulo, and Ananda could then work upon his fear.

"The man Lord Master Oulo Obanisyn Oksandrivin. You must render him deaf and blind, and you must be seen to do so."

The creature flexed its knees, bobbing up and down several times as if testing the stone underneath it for solidity.

"It shall be done, mistress."

Ananda bowed her head. Oulo was only a frightened man. Oulo feared for his people and his family and himself, and she understood such fears all too well. Now she would make him pay for the fault of human weakness.

"Go then," she ordered her creature without looking up.

She heard claws skittering against stone, and the wind blew hot again, and then there was stillness.

Ananda tried not to imagine the dwarfish monster scuttling through the hallways, its eyes shining in the darkness. She did not want to think of it sitting on Oulo's fat chest, reaching out hungrily for the lord master's eyes. She did not want to hear tomorrow of how Oulo had awoke, screaming in a hoarse voice he himself could no longer hear. He had a wife, Ananda knew. She hoped the woman was strong, and would care for her husband well. Were there children? Would they one day be able to forgive her?

"Mistress, please, you must rest," said Kiriti at long last. She put her hands under Ananda's arm to help the empress of Isavalta stand.

For all the tension thrumming through her sinews, Ananda found she had no strength to protest. She took the lamp Behule handed her, and returned obediently to her bed, as if her mind had already been separated from her body. She shed the robe, leaving it lying where it fell, snuffed out the light and laid herself down, stiff and cold.

"I cannot do this anymore," she whispered to the darkness. "I cannot live with this fear."

She thought of running away. But even with the help of her loyal servants and those they could bribe, how far would she get when she must follow the snow-choked roads? Laying aside storms and cold, the dowager empress could track every movement on every road through her domain.

She thought then, quite calmly, of killing herself. Behule and Kiriti would be busy with the loom for some hours yet. The rest of her ladies slept soundly in the outer apartment. She could mount the west stairs to the solarium, and from there could throw herself from the window to the courtyard, and the kind stones below would break her skull and bones. It would be over in an instant and her soul would be whole in the palace of the Seven Mothers.

But that would leave Mikkel, as well as loyal Kiriti, Behule and constant Sakra, at the mercy of the dowager.

Which left only one way. Hraban. She would have to sanction his revolt. She would have to give the orders and take the throne from the dowager, out from under her dead body, in all likelihood. Sakra's letter told her to do nothing rash, that he would soon be beside her, but Sakra did not know all. He did not know that Oulo had turned, and "soon" might mean a matter of days, or weeks, depending on what arose, be it a storm, or simply a delay with forgeries and passports. She could not wait. Not anymore. Medeoan no longer had a witness for her court, but she already had Captain Nisula's name. If she chose to put Nisula to the question . . .

All the Mothers be at my side, Ananda prayed. *I cannot let her take me. I cannot let her kill me.*

Which meant she would need to send a message to Hraban to stay away from the holy day, and to begin to marshal his men. She would have to send another to Nisula to set sail from the southern coasts as soon as he could.

And after that, she would have to deal with the Avanasidoch.

A strange peace descended on her then, and a feeling like freedom. Ananda rolled over onto her side, and fell asleep.

Medeoan gazed at Avanasy's daughter, lying still and pale in the great bed. The light from the four braziers blazing at full strength to help keep her warm only served to emphasize the unhealthy pallor of her skin. The surgeon had spooned broth and brandy down her throat, but could only say now that it was time and her gods that would have the healing of her.

She had her mother's coloring, but all her father's strength of feature. Medeoan touched Bridget's cold hand tentatively, as if the younger woman might fade like a dream.

"Bridget Avanasidoch Finoravosh," she whispered. "Be you welcome, daughter."

"She does not know," said Kalami.

"What?" Medeoan cocked her head toward him. He stood as far away from the bed as the privacy screens would allow. It seemed to Medeoan for a moment that his need for distance came from some distaste, but that could not possibly be true. Kalami knew as no other did that the Avanasidoch was the salvation of herself and of all Isavalta.

"She does not know who her true father is. Ingrid Loftfield died in childbirth and had no way to tell her. The man who raised her never knew the facts of her lineage."

"And you have not told her?"

Kalami bowed his head, spreading his hands. "There is so much for her to believe, I thought to bring her here and show her this world before I told her of her part in it."

It was then Medeoan realized she had not let go of Bridget's hand. She laid it gently down on the coverlet. "She must be told upon waking, Lord Sorcerer," she said without turning around. "Her destiny is heavy, and she must be prepared."

"She will be, I promise."

"There is so little time." Medeoan brushed the wisps of hair back from Bridget's forehead. "Even less than we thought."

"Has something happened?" asked Kalami sharply.

"It has." Reluctantly, Medeoan moved away from the bed. "Come with me, Lord Sorcerer."

The servants swept before her, carrying lamps and candles to light her way and clear the corridor, to open the rooms and see that all was lit and comfortable. More spread out behind, extinguishing lights and closing doors when she did not choose to stop in any of the chambers they passed through. When they reached her private chamber, they lit the three fresh candles she had permitted to be placed there and cleared themselves out at once. This was the one room where none might stay without an express invitation, not even her ladies, who took up their posts beside the door and reverenced as she passed.

Kalami followed her, as obedient as any of the other servants. When the doors were closed behind them, Medeoan sat heavily on the divan and motioned him to a chair. Kalami perched himself on the edge of the seat, all anticipation for her news.

"Ananda, it seems, is consolidating her plans."

Speaking of it again fatigued Medeoan, but she made herself continue. She told Kalami of Lord Oulo's petition, and of his naming of Peshek as one of Ananda's conspirators. Kalami rose and paced toward the nearest brazier. It had not been lit and the brass glinted dully in the meager candlelight. In normal circumstances, he never would have been allowed to stand while she remained seated, but there were none to see here, and she was too wearied to remind him of the fact.

"She must be stopped."

"Bridget will stop her," said Medeoan, rubbing the bandage on her palm.

"With respect, Grand Majesty"—Kalami turned from his contemplation of the empty brazier—"I do not think Bridget will be able to stop her in time."

"What do you mean?" asked Medeoan sharply. "Do you doubt Avanasy's daughter? Even in her ignorance the mark of her father shines through her. I see it plainly in her face."

"You will see it even more plainly when she wakes," said Kalami. "But, consider, part of what made Avanasy so great was his extensive experience. He was trained, not just powerful. Such training takes time, and as you yourself said, time is short."

Medeoan nodded. Kalami was right. The conspiracy was happening now. She could not hope that Ananda had not heard from her spies that Avanasy's daughter was coming to aid Medeoan. Her plans would be moving apace.

"With Lord Oulo's evidence, we may arrest and try her for treason." Medeoan's hand curled around the edge of the divan. The pressure of the wood against her bandages set off a fresh burst of pain and itching in her healing palms. "It could be done tonight, and there would be an end to it."

"Grand Majesty." Kalami knelt in front of her. "You know such a plan cannot succeed. Ananda is too well beloved. A public trial, especially one founded on the evidence of only a single witness, would stir unrest across the empire."

"You say I am never to be rid of her?" demanded Medeoan.

Kalami's eyes widened with trepidation. He feared her, he always had. But then, that was right. She was the empress of Isavalta, and her servants should fear her. That was the way it must be. "Grand Majesty, we spoke of how you might be rid of her. She must be utterly disgraced."

Medeoan rose swiftly, pacing across the room to the brazier, even as Kalami had done. She did not want to be near him when he spoke those words, never mind the truth of them. She did not want to hear this.

"There must be another way."

Kalami turned on his knees. "Then what way, Grand Majesty?" He stood. He was taller than she, but unlike many of the courtiers, he made no effort to hunch and hide his height. "She must be shown to the whole of Isavalta for what she is, and it must be you who shows them."

Medeoan's hands were cold, and the cold made her burns throb, but she did not move to call a servant to light the brazier. She had too much of fire in her life. Sometimes, she wanted to give orders that all the fires in the palace be extinguished so that she might sit cold and alone in the blessed darkness, free of the reminder of the living flame caged in the cellar. Each candle, each lamp, each brazier formed the plumage of Firebird and the sight of them sickened her down to her soul. It had taken all her concentration not to order the braziers taken away from around Bridget's bed. For one wild moment she had believed the Firebird could reach Avanasy's daughter through the flames. But that was nonsense. The Firebird could never touch Avanasy's daughter.

Why did Kalami have to be right about how Ananda must be dealt with? Why could she not order his silence and dismiss them? He should not be here speaking such words to his mistress imperial. He should be at Bridget's bedside.

"There must be another way." Medeoan stalked to the darkest corner of the room. "Another person to use. It does not have to be Mikkel."

I called to your son, the Firebird had said. *He almost heard me.* She closed her eyes against that memory.

"If you so order, Grand Majesty," said Kalami behind her. "But I ask you, if he lives, can you ever free Mikkel? Will the lords master and oblasts understand your need, the empire's need, if he speaks of what was done?"

Medeoan opened her eyes again and saw stone and shadow. That was all she wanted: dark stone and cool shadow. How had she come to this? How had she come to be this person? It was Hastinapura, and it was Hung-Tse. They had robbed her of everything. Now they would take her only son, and if she could not sacrifice him, then they would take her empire. For Kalami was right again. The opportunists among the lords master would twist what she had done. She could try to bind Mikkel's thoughts on this matter, tie a knot in his memory of the events leading to his enchantment, but such things took a delicacy of skill that she was no longer certain she possessed. Kalami might to be able to do it, or Bridget, once she was properly taught. But such a spell must constantly be renewed as the subject grew and changed. Then there was the greatest truth of all sorcery: any spell that could be woven could be broken.

Medeoan turned to face Kalami, but did not step out of the shelter of the cool stones and the shadows. "There is a locked chest in the treasury. My father showed it to me when I was a girl. There is in it a pair of white linen sheets. They may serve our need in this." She reached for her bundle of keys and sorted through them, removing two from the ring. The first was a great key of twisted iron, which she kissed. The other was small and silver. She it touched to the iron key and then kissed it.

"Your hands may hold these now," she said, extending them to Kalami. "Bring them back when you have retrieved the linens." Kalami took the keys and reverenced. "They are bound in a red ribbon. Be careful you do not break it."

"All shall be as you say, Grand Majesty." Kalami reverenced once more, and Medeoan dismissed him with a wave.

Even when he had left, she stayed where she was as if the faint shadows in this corner could hide her from what she was about to do.

It was either extremely fitting or monstrously perverse that Kalami should be the one to counsel her that she must see Mikkel to his death. Kalami had been the one who enabled her to give him life.

"I must have an heir," she had said to her three court sorcerers. "He must be of my blood. Isavalta must be ruled by one whose loyalties are undivided and who feels the power of their obligations in heart and bone."

Her two men of Isavalta had shaken their heads. "There is no way in this world a mortal may interfere," said the first; Ivramand had been his name. "If Vyshko and Vyshemir will not favor you . . ." He had spread his hands. "It is said that Avanasy fathered a child upon a woman from another shore of the Silent Lands. Perhaps a man could be found—"

"And what blood would my child then have?" snapped Medeoan. "How would we know? No."

"There is no way to change the nature of your flesh and spirit," said the second, Nestroid. "You might perhaps make a bargain with the Baba Yaga . . ."

"No," she had answered flatly. "There can be no bargains, not in this. This child must be mine alone and free of all other ties."

Kalami had lifted his head. He had looked so strange to her then, a dark man in her fair court, a pair of black eyes amid the blue. He was new to his post, a peace offering to the island of Tuukos, and she had not heard him speak six words together since he had taken the oath of loyalty to her.

"There is a way, Majesty," he said quietly. "I can see this thing done."

And he had given his first order to her, and she had obeyed, dismissing the other two sorcerers so that they might speak alone.

"You must pick a consort," Kalami had said. "Marry him, and see the marriage consummated on the wedding night. In nine months, you will bear a son. But be aware, Majesty, that in those same nine months, your consort, whoever he may be, will fail and die."

Medeoan remembered the calm with which she had heard those words. She had been surprised only at how willing she was to sacrifice a life for Isavalta.

"How is this?" she asked, her eyes narrowing. "I know of no such charm."

Kalami's answering smile was thin. "It is not a thing of Isavalta's learning. It is something I heard of on Tuukos. But if Your Majesty Imperial will trust me, you will have your son."

Medeoan met his dark eyes and saw how steadily he stood. "If I choose a consort, he will be a man of high and noble birth," she told him. "If he is to die, no suspicion must fall upon me, or you."

Kalami did not blink or hesitate. "None will, Imperial Majesty. You have my word."

So, she had married a second time. Jesif Osiprsyn Istokvin, lord master of Iesutbor oblast, had become the imperial consort. He had been a slender man with slender hands. Medeoan had long ago forgotten his face. The wedding night had been no trial, and all had been as Kalami promised. She had quickened, Mikkel had been safe delivered and Jesif had died after a long illness. Kalami had spent the time of Medeoan's confinement making sure that a conspiracy between three other of the lords master on the Privy Council came to light. He even named the poison they had used to cause Jesif to sicken, but it was, of course, too late to save the consort's life.

The three lords master were hanged from the walls of their own capitals. Medeoan searched her mind, and found she could not even recall their names. She had been holding Mikkel when news of their deaths had come, holding the future of Isavalta, and nothing else mattered.

A tear escaped her eye and trickled down her cheek. *Forgive me, my son,* she thought toward Mikkel. *When you are whole in the Land of Death and Spirit, you will understand why I have done this, and you will forgive me.*

Bridget awoke slowly. She heard a fire and smelled burning charcoal. She felt warmth on her skin, both the flickering heat of a blaze coming simultaneously from left and right and the soft, enveloping warmth of thick comforters and sheets.

And she heard things. The crackle of the fire, a distant whistling of wind, the creaking and settling of wood.

She did not open her eyes yet. She feared she might see foxes. After the crows had come, she had dreamed of foxes, huge and hairy, smelling rank, with green eyes and sharp teeth, and blood. They had bled, those foxes, and she had darned them with a needle and thread like a set of old socks.

Strange dreams. Frightening dreams. She wanted no more of them. She wanted to be home in the keeper's quarters and wake to the glow of the light and the familiar dangers of Lake Superior.

But if you don't want dreams, some distant, reasoning part of herself asked, *why are you afraid to open your eyes?*

"It's all right, Bridget," said a gentle voice beside her. "You can wake up. You are safe, I swear it."

The light beyond her eyelids grew stronger, and the thought of retreating back into darkness, even the darkness inside her, became unbearable. Bridget forced her eyes open.

She lay on her back, staring up at a canopy of rich blue velvet supported by four posts each as thick around as her own waist. Carved and painted screens surrounded the bed, preventing her from seeing the rest of the room. The heat came from four braziers blazing with bright fires. More blue velvet covered her, and feather pillows and mattresses supported her. It was a queen's bed. An empress's.

That thought opened Bridget's mind wide and all her memories raced back to her so quickly she gasped in pain. The crows were real, as were the foxes, and the things Sakra had said about her mother, and the way she had danced herself to freedom, and the feelings that overwhelmed her as she stitched the men's skins closed, knowing all the time she was sewing foxes inside those living skins and yet reveling in her own power to do so . . .

"Easy, Bridget, easy. You are safe."

Hands grasped her shoulders and turned her until Bridget faced Valin.

"You have had a difficult journey but it is over," he said, holding her firmly with both his hands and his gaze. "You are in the imperial palace of Vyshtavos now, and you are safe."

Bridget swallowed with difficulty. Her throat was painfully dry. "Am I?" she croaked. "Are you sure?" She felt like a fool and a child, but she could not stop the question.

"I swear." Kalami handed her a wooden tumbler of water and Bridget drank gratefully. "You are surrounded by stone and iron. I am with you. You are safe."

"Even from what I seem to be carrying inside me?" she asked with a shaky laugh. "Can you swear to that as well?"

Kalami's smile was gentle. "The only reason you are not safe from yourself is that you are not trained." He ran his fingers along the edge of the velvet coverlet. "You have lived all your life weighted down by chains so you could not know your own strength. Now that you are free, you feel it, but you do not understand it. With understanding will come control, and you will see you have nothing to fear from yourself."

Bridget looked away, sorting through the swirl of memories, trying to put each one in its place; the impossible things she had done and seen, the equally impossible things she had heard.

"How are you feeling?" asked Valin.

Bridget bit back a short laugh. It was a simple question, for which she had no simple answer. She decided to concentrate on the physical.

"Tired, but otherwise well. I think." She had no pain, certainly. All her limbs seemed to be in their proper arrangement.

"Tell me what happened to you, Bridget, after we lost you."

Bridget faced him again, and blinked. Her vision was strangely blurred. She seemed to see a reflection of Valin's face lying on top of the real face. The reflection turned his smile into a scowl, and furrowed his broad brow with impatience. She blinked again, and the reflection was gone.

A trick of the fire and candles, she tried to tell herself, but her mind refused to be convinced.

"Tell me, Bridget," he urged, touching her hand. Obviously, he took her hesitation as unwillingness to talk about something unpleasant. His skin was smooth, she noted, unroughened by work, unlike Sakra's.

Why am I thinking of him now? Bridget shook her head.

"Please, I need to know," said Valin, once again misreading her.

"No . . . that is I . . ." Feeling absurd, Bridget waved away his words and hers. "Of course I'll tell you." *And perhaps, for a change, you will tell me something useful.*

The sharpness of the thought surprised her, but Bridget was accustomed to trusting her own mind. She did not want to believe Valin had been playing her false, especially as she had placed herself entirely in his hands; but he had not been truly open with her either, that much was plain. Fear, useless and cold, quivered inside her.

He saved your life, she reminded herself. *He did not abandon you to the foxes and the crows. He needs you. If nothing else, he will keep you safe.*

So, as best she could, she told him how the dwarf-crows had carried her through the frozen wood to Sakra's refuge. She watched fury darken his face as she told him of the truth spell laid on her, and how she had danced herself an escape. Fury changed to amazement, and then to concern, as she talked about waking up in the land of the foxes and how she had healed the three wounded creatures.

When she finished, much to her surprise, Valin reached out one trembling hand and brushed it softly against her unbound hair. "You are so wondrous," he murmured. "Your power is like nothing else."

Bridget bridled at the familiarity of the gesture. "I'm glad you're pleased," she said tartly, pushing herself up higher on the pillows. "I should hope you would find me as advertised."

Either the words or their tone brought Valin back to himself. He removed his hand quickly. "You don't understand . . . you . . ." He got to his feet and paced along the side of the bed, searching for words.

"Listen to me," he said, laying one hand against the bedpost. "You have seen magic worked. You know that in order to take shape, the raw power must be bound by a weaving, or a knot, some sort of tangible pattern. You understand this?"

Bridget nodded.

He folded his hands behind his back, tapping one against the other, a gesture of nervousness or impatience, Bridget couldn't tell which. "The complexity of the spell, and the amount of power that can be bound, greatly depends on the materials chosen and the skill of the sorcerer." His mouth stretched into a sardonic smile. "Any fool with a glimmer of power and a modicum of patience can make a spell from thread or rope, or even clay. The most difficult spells to work are those that require one of the hardest elements, such as metal or stone, or the most ineffable, such as fire or air." He spread his hands. "What you did in freeing yourself from Sakra was to weave a pattern from nothing but the air around you, without even smoke or flame to help you bind the power you called forth. It is something only the most legendary of sorcerers can do. I've never even seen it. To do such a thing without training or preparation . . ." He shook his head. "I would have said it was impossible."

The sheer wonder in his voice as he spoke took Bridget aback. It also, she was ashamed to admit, touched her vanity.

Ridiculous. To be pleased over something you did not understand and could not control. But there it was.

"So," she said, smoothing down her covers. "You are pleased with me?"

"Pleased?" Valin choked on the word. "Bridget . . ." He stepped close beside her, and lifted his hand as if he meant to take hers, but he hesitated. "Bridget, when I found you, I expected power, and I knew beauty, but such courage and such a wellspring of soul . . ." Words failed him and his hand dipped closer to hers, but he caught himself before his fingertips could do more than brush against her. Instead, he held her with his deep, black eyes. "You are incomparable. I could never have dreamed of meeting such a one as you."

Bridget felt her cheeks begin to heat up, and turned her face swiftly away. His words worked their way inside her, down through the blankets of resolve, usefulness, and cold guilt, into the core of loneliness that they covered. It had been so very long since anyone had spoken to her with admiration in their voice, or touched her with any kind of tenderness. Her throat tightened around the sudden ache of longing that sprang up in her. She wanted him to take her hand, to touch her face, to tell her again of her beauty and her courage. She wanted . . .

Other memories came then. Memories of staring out across Lake Superior, searching the empty horizon for Asa's sail. Days of feeling her belly grow with the fruit of that secret tenderness, of all the shame, and the misery and trying to hold on to the rock-hard certainty that Asa *did* love her, that he *would* come back for her and their baby, and all the desperate fear that he would not.

And still she wanted someone to touch her again as he had, to whisper to her as he had and draw her close.

She closed her eyes against all her wants. Long practice gave her the strength to draw them back down into her deepest self.

"What of the things Sakra said about my mother?" she asked. "And what I have heard of this person Avanasy?"

At this, Valin sighed and hung his head. "Ah. The legend of Avanasy and his lost child returns." When he looked up, he was smiling fondly. "This is the way of it. Avanasy was a great sorcerer. He was, in fact, the teacher of the dowager empress, and as great in his loyalty to her as he was in his learning and skills." His eyes grew distant, remembering and regretting.

"My mistress imperial ascended the throne while still in her youth. Both her parents were taken suddenly ill and died within days of each other. Some say it was nothing but an infectious fever. Some say it was poison. I don't believe anyone knows.

"But Hung-Tse, our southern enemy, saw an innocent young girl ascend to the throne and they thought the time ripe for conquest. They sent spies to infiltrate the Isavaltan court. These spies kidnapped Medeoan and spirited her away to their imperial city, which they are pleased to call the Heart of the World, and they began plans for their invasion.

"While all was in confusion among the Isavaltan nobles, Avanasy set forth in search of the empress, and indeed, he found her, and between their two powers, they succeeded in freeing her.

"Now, the Nine Elders, the nine sorcerers who rule Hung-Tse

with their puppet emperor, knew they could not defeat Isavalta in an honest war, so they decided to call up one of the great spirit powers of this world and let it loose to do what damage it could before they hazarded their soldiers' lives on the battlefield."

"A spirit power?" said Bridget. "Like the Vixen?"

Valin nodded. "The Vixen is one such. There are many. The one the Nine Elders summoned was the Phoenix, in Isavalta called the Firebird, an immortal bird of flame and magic."

Bridget nodded. "We have stories of such things at home."

"Then you can imagine the danger." Valin perched on the edge of the bed. "Most of Isavalta's cities are built of wood. What if it set the capital ablaze? What if it burned the fields? Or the supply trains of the armies?

"Medeoan and Avanasy were hiding in a friendly port city, gathering intelligence about the situation in Isavalta, and planning their strategies as to how to return Medeoan to her throne. They received word of the Nine Elders' treachery, and hastened to return. When they did, they worked a mighty spell and wrought a cage for the immortal bird, trapping it inside." Valin sounded awestruck at the very idea. Bridget's imagination showed her a glowing red and gold bird inside a filigree cage, and she shivered at the power of the image. She had seen such a thing before, but she had seen so much recently she could not remember where the fiery bird had been.

Valin shook himself and brought his attention back to Bridget. "But in the making of that spell, Avanasy lost his life." Valin bowed his head. "I honor the memory of so brave a servant of my mistress. But," he said, his fond smile returning, "as you may imagine, many legends spring up around such a hero. One of the most persistent is that to gain the secret of how to cage the Phoenix, Avanasy traveled beyond the ends of the Land of Death and Spirit to another mortal world. There, he courted a sorceress of extreme power and beauty, who gave him the secret he needed. In return, he is said to have given her a child. That child is supposed to be living somewhere, waiting for a time of great need for Isavalta when it will return and save us all, as its father did."

"Like King Arthur," Bridget said, smiling.

"Who?"

Bridget shook her head. "It would take too long to explain."

"Sakra has obviously heard the stories and has mistaken you for this legendary child." Valin's smile grew rueful. "Palace gossip has gone further afield than I anticipated."

It was a good answer. It explained much, but not all. "If I am supposed to be the daughter of some great man, how did Sakra know my mother's name?"

Valin shrugged. "The mother of Avanasy's child is reputed to be a powerful sorceress. Perhaps he thought he might find her and corrupt her into his schemes, especially as he held the one he thought to be her daughter."

Bridget remembered, though, the soft way Sakra spoke when she said Ingrid Loftfield's name. *Hear that, my father-god.* He recognized the name, she was sure of it.

But she said nothing, hoping Valin would interpret her silence as acceptance.

Valin rose and crossed toward the nearest brazier. "You need to know, Bridget," he said, feeding some chips of charcoal into the flames. The fire hissed as each dark sliver fell. "This will not be the last time you will hear speculation that you are Avanasy's daughter."

"I am familiar with how rumor works." *Even here, God almighty, even here.*

"I must tell you something that is painful to me." He did not lift his head to look at her, only stared unblinking at the brazier's refreshed flames.

Bridget waited.

"My mistress imperial," he said softly. "I . . ." His face twisted with indecision. "It is tantamount to treason for me to say this, Bridget, but you must know. She is senile."

"Senile?"

He nodded. "I do what I can, as do all her advisors and ladies, but it is becoming more and more apparent. This is the source of my, of our, desperation. This is why we had to bring you here." He spread his hands. "Her decay renders her unable to concentrate. Without that ability, she cannot weave her magic. Without her magic she cannot defeat Ananda, and if she dies before Ananda's power is broken . . ."

Senile? Bridget had to work to keep her jaw from falling open. *You promised me her protection, her honor, and now you say she is demented!* Her hands clutched the velvet coverlet, gathering up bunches of the soft fabric. "Why didn't you tell me this before?" she demanded.

"I was afraid you would not come," he said bluntly. "I am sorry."

Bridget heard the apology without one bit of her anger relaxing. "What else have you failed to tell me?"

"That she may greet you as Avanasy's daughter." He hung his head again, as if the words weighed him down. "That was who she sent me to find. But that child does not exist." He reached toward her, pleading. "I am sorry, I am so sorry, Bridget, but I beg you to understand, my whole world is in danger. I could not fail to bring aid."

"I see."

It made perfect sense, or as much sense as anything in this waking dream did. She wanted to believe it with every fiber of her being, because it would mean that Everett Lederle remained her father. The man who kept the light, who carried the oil cans, who taught her the name and purpose of each brass gear and spring in the pumps was her father. The one who sat with her on clear nights and watched the stars. The one to whom she carried pots of coffee during storms when he stood up in the tower, scanning the churning waters, looking for ships caught in a gale. The one who died, wheezing his life away in the bed in the keeper's quarters, who would not let her sit by him nights, because the light was more important than he was.

That was her father, not some golden man in a black coat.

The man she had seen standing with the woman in the black dress as they sailed through the Land of Death and Spirit.

No. No. No. Bridget pressed the heels of her hands against her eyes.

But Sakra had recognized her mother's name.

"Bridget, please." Valin grasped her hands and pulled them away from her face. "Understand, I lied because I had to. We need, I need, your help. Truly."

His face was honest, open, sad and a little desperate. His hands were warm and soft against her, holding her strongly, his very touch willing her to understand what was happening and why he had done what he had done. But as she gazed into his eyes, her vision flickered again, and she saw a reflection, this time of rage, laid over his pleading features.

What is happening? She furrowed her brows. She couldn't see, and she needed to see, she had to see!

And she saw three men in coats of blue and gold, surrounding a great carved bed. On it, they spread sheets so white they all but glowed in the firelight. The cloth shimmered with threads of silver and gold, linen impregnated with precious metal.

And poison. She felt it burning through her veins, twisting her gullet and seeping into her lungs. Whoever lay beneath those sheets would die. She would die, there was too much poison. . . .

"No!" she screamed. "No!"

And she saw Valin standing beside her, his face anxious and without reflection.

"What did you see?"

Bridget stuffed her fist into her mouth, to stifle the sobs that threatened to burst out.

"Tell me!" shouted Valin.

Bridget swallowed and shook herself. It was a vision. Just a vision. That was all. She knew what to do.

"I saw three men, all in blue coats with gold braid. One had black hair and a hooked nose. Another had red hair and a strawberry birthmark under his left eye. The third was an old man, mostly bald, but with strong hands. They were changing sheets on a bed carved with eagles and roses. The sheets were poisonous. Whoever sleeps in the bed is going to be dead before morning."

A spasm of anger crossed Valin's face and for a moment he glared at her with complete and livid hatred. His jaw clamped, as if to hold in words that threatened to burst forth.

"Ananda," he spat at last.

"She made the poison?"

He nodded grimly. "The bed you describe is Emperor Mikkel's. The men are her creatures. She has made them so. She means to kill her husband imperial." His fist struck the mattress. "I knew this day would come but I did not expect it so soon."

"But . . ." Instinct made Bridget bite her tongue. Valin looked at her, and she said, "It couldn't have anything to do with my coming here, could it?"

Valin considered. "It might. I must go, Bridget. I must consult . . ." He stopped. "The other advisors." He turned. "Servants will be sent to attend you and bring you food. Send word to me if you do not feel your strength returning. You are to be received formally by the dowager empress in three days, and you must be able to stand."

"I will be, Valin."

"Good. Forgive me." He was already striding past the screens and out of her range of vision as he spoke.

Bridget collapsed back on the pillows and stared up at the rich canopy.

"Why," she whispered to the velvet above her, "if Ananda has Mikkel completely bound to her will, does she need to kill him?"

But the velvet had no answers, and neither did Bridget.

Kalami strode down the corridor, fighting to keep his hands from clenching into fists.

So soon. She had heard the names so soon. He had meant to lead her gently into the truth as the bond between them strengthened beyond mere physical dependence.

But, of course, it was Sakra who broke that plan. Sakra and Ananda, again.

That was all right. That could be dealt with. Lies could be smoothed out and blended into truth. He had refined his abilities in that area across long years of practice. But the vision. She had seen how the plan for Mikkel would go forward. It was good fortune alone that prevented her from seeing that it was Medeoan who ordered those poisoned sheets to be laid out for her son.

That he could not have covered with a quick lie.

Sakra and Ananda he could counter. Sakra's magic was great, and Ananda was clever, but they did not have more at stake than he, and they had the imperial power against them. But Bridget's visions, those were beyond his control. As long as Bridget remained doubtful of him, he was in danger from her inner eye, and the fact that she could now speak Isavalta's court language. He cursed Sakra thoroughly for that. Kalami had expected to be Bridget's only source of information for several months yet while she accustomed herself to the new tongue. But that advantage had also been denied him, which meant every moment Bridget stayed in clear possession of her faculties, the danger grew.

So, Bridget could not be allowed to stay out of control. That was too bad. A willing follower was always better, but if there was no time for that, so be it.

The swan huddled on the rooftop in an empty stork's nest. The chimney gave it but little warmth and it fluffed its feathers out, shivering miserably. It was cold. So cold. Why was it here in this place of snow and ice? Its wing hurt desperately. Why was it not in the warm south lands gliding on the gentle rivers? Had it not flown because it had hurt its wing? That must be what had happened. The dawn had just begun to lighten the horizon. It would fly with the first true light. It would find food and its wing would heal. It would fly to where there was food, and a mate and warmth, and all this strangeness would be long gone.

A crow landed neatly on the roof's peak, puffing out its own feathers as it settled there. The swan honked at it.

Go away. This place is mine.

In response, the crow cawed, and cawed again, and then it was no crow, but a tiny, wizened man in a feathered cape, balancing as easily on the point of the roof as the bird had. The swan did not care.

Such a small thing held no terror for it. It only honked again.

Go away.

"Well now, sorcerer," laughed the dwarf-crow. "How deep is this water in which you find yourself?"

The swan snapped at him.

"Manners, manners," he admonished. "For that I might let you stay this way, but then how would I claim that favor you owe me?" The dwarf-crow leaned forward, stretching out his neck as a bird might. The swan wanted to snap at him again, but somehow did not dare. Instead, it shrank against the chimney, raising its near wing to ward the strange being away.

"You are not all gone yet," mused the dwarf-crow. "Or you would be nesting on the riverbank like a proper swan." He nodded and pulled his head back down so it seemed to sit directly on his shoulders. "Well," he sighed. "Your kind is ever more trouble than they are worth, but I like the idea of you and your mistress in our debt, so this far I will aid you." He fixed the swan with his round black eyes. "Hear me, Sakra. You seek Ananda. Sakra, you seek Ananda."

Sakra lifted his head. Ananda? Ananda. She was in danger. He had been flying to tell her. Flying on a swan's wings, which should have been his arms and he could not change, could not understand how to make the change. He stretched his strange, long neck to the sky and trumpeted out his confusion. Change. Danger. He did not understand, could not understand. Lost, cold, alone, but for the dwarf-crow that watched him, and Ananda. He must find Ananda.

Again, the swan threw itself onto the wind, its wings spread wide, dipping and turning until it soared toward Vyshtavos.

Behind it, a crow flew off in the opposite direction.

Chapter Eleven

"I recognize the waiting is difficult, and that the labyrinth of courtly courtesy is confusing to one from so straightforward a life as you are, but I urge you to patience, Bridget," read Lady Gali, the tallest and skinniest of the attendants Bridget had been assigned. She wore her red hair piled high on top of her head, which made her even taller, and, Bridget thought, made her face look more like a blunt wedge than anything else.

"Rest and gather your strength. I will come again as soon as I may. It is signed only Valin." Lady Gali announced that tidbit with great satisfaction, and around her, both of the other ladies responded with extended giggling.

Bridget pressed her lips together to hold in a sigh, and smoothed down the skirts of her new dress—a thick, grey garment with sleeves that had needed to be tied on, and laces and overskirt died a purple so deep it was almost black. After a full day of lying in her sumptuous bed, she had regained strength enough to discover she was bored. Her apartments were grand on a scale she would never have conceived of, but they were extraordinarily devoid of items that might occupy one's mind. After she had heard the story of the Marriage of Tovahne, which was painted across the ceiling, and the names and tales behind each of the three marble icons that stood on their gilded pillars in the apartment alcoves, and how the room's plaster walls and thick carpets were a vast improvement over the old days of bare, gloomy stone, and proved she had no interest in embroidery, there was not much left, except to wait for the messages that arrived periodically. Once, the man came bearing a silver brooch made in the shape of a galloping horse with citrines for eyes and a garnet in its side the size of Bridget's thumb. With it came the message that Lord Sorcerer Kalami would be pleased if Bridget Lederle would wear this next to her heart to show that she acknowledged Lord Sorcerer's great regard for her.

Every last one of her ladies had giggled as she accepted the gift, and Bridget had needed to swallow the urge to turn and admonish them to act their age, for heaven's sake! Despite that, she now wore the brooch on her left shoulder.

Bridget tapped her fingers on a gold-inlaid table and stared toward the tapestried curtain covering the door that led to the balcony. How cold was it out there? Could she ask for a coat of some sort and go for a walk? Just in the courtyard? Any change of scene would be welcome at this point. If she stood on tiptoe, she could just see out the one small thick window set beside the door, and catch glimpses of the lords and ladies in their fur robes and trains of sleighs and horses that seemed to be arriving every few minutes. The posture, however, was difficult to maintain, and even gilt and silver sleighs became a little dull when one's toes began to ache.

"Does my mistress wish to compose a reply?" inquired Richikha, the youngest, slightest and, conversely, least silly of the ladies. She dressed the most simply too, eschewing the bright tissues and gaudy laces the others preferred for a warm brown garment with a black bodice and white sleeves and laces. It seemed that her mother and grandmother had both been in service, and that, in fact, her grandmother had once waited on Empress Kseniia, the dowager's mother.

Now, there would be someone I should talk to, thought Bridget.

"A reply, yes, of course." Bridget turned her attention back to the waiting Lady Gali, who lifted her chin in silent reproach at being so neglected. Gali took her station at the writing desk, plucking a silver pen from its inkwell and holding it poised over the creamy paper that waited there.

"Please tell Valin that I am feeling much recovered and am looking forward to his next visit. He will surely find me at home."

She paused to let Lady Gali note all that down. This was the third letter she'd had from Valin urging her to patience. After the scheduled presentation to the dowager, he said, they could meet and speak with his mistress imperial, and make plans for Bridget's future. She had already received a formal letter from the dowager empress welcoming her to the palace and similar polite remarks, which Lady Gali had also read to her.

Literacy, Bridget decided, *is the next order of business.* She picked up the dowager's letter. Sakra had made it possible for her to speak the language, but she could not read a word of the angular alphabet, if indeed it was an alphabet. In truth, she thought as she ran her fingers across the page, it looked a bit like the Chinese characters she had seen in one of the histories from the lending library, although these were written in rows rather than in columns. The scarlet seal at the bottom was imprinted with the spread-winged eagle, the same that she had seen on the flag, and on the bedstead in her vision.

Her vision. She rubbed her forehead. It still made no sense. This Ananda was supposed to be a daemon of cleverness. Why kill the man from whom she derived her power? It would only make sense if she had already produced an heir.

Perhaps she is about to. Bridget lifted her head. *If the empress were with child, she could do away with the feckless emperor. . . .*

But so soon? Before the impending birth had even been announced? Surely Valin would have told her if there was an heir in the making, and then, so many things could go wrong with a pregnancy, and infants could die so suddenly. Bridget shuddered at the memories that thought brought her. No, a daemon of cleverness would wait until she had two babies at the very least before killing their father.

She laid the letter back down and rubbed her eyes.

"Have you any more to add, mistress?" prompted Lady Gali.

"No." Bridget tapped her fingers on the gilded wood again. "That will be all for now."

Perhaps, Bridget thought, *I should refuse to entertain such indelicate ideas. These are highborn people, after all.* Her schoolteacher had complained that she was coarse in her manner and blamed it on her father's refusal to shield his daughter from the language or stories of the sailors who visited or recuperated at the lighthouse.

Everett Lederle had refused to shield her from such things. Her father. Or was he? Kalami said he was, but was Kalami to be trusted? She did not know, and what oppressed her was that there seemed to be no way for her to find out.

She had asked the three ladies for stories of the sorcerer Avanasy, and she got them in abundance, from his miraculous birth, which was attended by all the gods of his household, to the way his spirit still walked the corridors of Vyshtavos and guarded the imperial family from danger.

But what of this sorceress who was supposed to have borne him a child? There the ladies just shook their heads. No one knew much about her. Some said she had never set foot in Isavalta at all. Some said Medeoan in a fit of pique as a young woman had exiled Avanasy, and he found the sorceress beyond the world's end and it was she who warned him that Hung-Tse intended to unleash the Phoenix onto Isavalta. Another said no, he had gone in search of her and seduced her into giving up the secret after he himself had learned of the Nine Elders' plans.

It was all written in the histories, they agreed. But not one of them had actually read any of those. A liberal arts education did not seem to be required for the work of being a lady-in-waiting.

Then, an idea struck Bridget, and her chin rose. "Lady Gali," she said. "Is there a library in this place?"

"A library?" the lady repeated, as if she had never thought of such a word before.

"A place with books, references, histories." *Especially histories.* "You learned to read somewhere, I presume."

"There is indeed a library," said Lady Richikha, stepping between Bridget and Lady Gali's affronted frown. "But I was given to understand that my mistress was uninterested in books."

"Your mistress is completely illiterate in your language," Bridget corrected her. "But you are not, and I would like to educate myself. Perhaps you would be so good as to show me the way to the library?"

"But mistress," fluttered round, brown Lady Iadviga, who all this time had been sitting as close to the firepit as she could get without falling in. "The lord sorcerer orders that you should rest—"

"And I am certain that a room as civilized as a library is well supplied with chairs where I may take my ease," said Bridget in a tone to indicate she did not welcome contradiction. She picked up the shawl embroidered with stylized birds and stone towers that lay across the arm of the nearest chair. "Lady Richikha, shall we go?"

Which left the girl in a rather unenviable position, Bridget had to admit, caught in between her orders, Lady Gali's glower and Lady Iadviga's nervous, pleading look. She drew herself up to make some answer, but before it came out, the door opened and the little girl dressed in a blue kaftan with gold sash who was stationed out there came in.

Ignoring the variety of expressions around her, the child executed a graceful reverence, as the style of bowing around here seemed to be called, and said to Bridget, "If it pleases you, mistress, your dress is here for your approval." She stood aside, waiting.

Lady Iadviga let out an audible sigh of relief. Lady Gali just managed to look smug.

"Our mistress will be most pleased to see her dress," she said before Bridget could offer any contradiction.

Bridget threw up her hands and for her trouble received a soft, sympathetic smile from Richikha. The winter solstice occurred in two days, marking an important holiday of some sort. At the height of the festivities, Bridget was to be officially presented to the court. One of Kalami's messages had informed her that the dowager herself had given a dress that would be cut down and refashioned to Bridget's measurements. So far, she had seen two women with measuring tapes, scissors and pinched looks, but not the actual costume they proposed to dress her in.

Now, however, those two women walked into the room, carrying the dress between them, and Bridget froze where she stood.

The dress had been hung on a wooden form, and its attendants placed it where the light from the firepit and the lamps would land on it to advantage. The underlayer was burgundy velvet. Over that had been laid a slashed skirt of silver tissue that glimmered in the shifting light. The bodice was also silver and burgundy with matching silk laces. Over it all hung an open coat of shimmering gold brocade embroidered with pearls.

Bridget remembered to breathe.

Two women, the seamstresses, stood on either side of the creation, eyeing her anxiously. Bridget stepped forward and touched one golden sleeve. She had never imagined that someone, dowager empress or no, would give such sumptuousness to her.

"It's magnificent."

At her words, the seamstresses also remembered to breathe.

I am actually going to wear this? Bridget walked around the dress on its form, looking at the waves and swirls of freshwater pearls laid against the gold, all the way from the tips of its sleeves down to the long hem of its train. The idea alternately delighted and appalled her. How would she manage so much fabric? The thing must weigh ninety pounds.

"Will my mistress be pleased to try it on?" asked the older seamstress, a woman as straight and thin as the golden pins that held her hair swept back from her long face.

"Yes, yes." Bridget stepped back to give them room to deal with the creation. The younger seamstress, a dark girl with a perpetually anxious look, scurried forward to begin working at the fastenings. Richikha moved forward to take the golden coat from her.

Even as Bridget watched, bemused at the thought of how she might look in such clothing, a huge commotion cut through the room, a mix of human voices, hoofbeats and neighs from startled horses, and another sound Bridget could not identify.

"What on earth?" Bridget ran to the balcony door. She flung the curtain aside, and despite the powerful blast of cold air that she let in, stepped out into the winter day.

Below her, on the courtyard's snow-sprinkled tiles, gathered a crowd of people, sleighs and horses. A great white swan circled the procession and dove, as if attacking the green canopy that had been erected on the stairs. Voices screamed, and someone shouted. Bridget shrank backward, wrapping her arms tightly around herself, as much to ward against the swan as against the cold. The swan rose into the air, trumpeting, which was the noise Bridget had not been able to identify, and dove again. Horses reared and scattered, despite the best efforts of their riders. A soldier in the blue coat and polished armor of the house guard raised his bow and nocked an arrow in its string. The swan swooped down and he loosed the arrow. It found its target, piercing feathers and flesh. The swan screamed and thudded down onto the courtyard tiles, blood streaming down its feathers and its wings spread wide.

Bridget stared, pressing the back of her hand against her mouth, stunned by the spectacle she had just witnessed. The swan fluttered its wings, and in so doing she saw it blur. She saw the swan, but she also saw another form. A man lay there bloody on the tiles amid the crying and murmuring, and all the people shrinking away as if the bird might suddenly spring up again. In the next moment, Bridget realized she saw Sakra, his arms spread and his eyes confused, in the same place that she also saw the swan.

The soldier who had shot the swan down walked up to it, reaching into a sheath on his belt and bringing out a gnarled club. He lifted it up, and Bridget knew he meant to smash the skull of the swan that was somehow also Sakra.

"No!" she shouted, running to the balcony rail, before she could think about what she did.

All the faces in the courtyard turned up to her, their voices suddenly silent. Hooves clopped on the tiles and a veiled figure in a forest green mantle emerged from under the canopy. She looked up at Bridget, and Bridget saw that it was Empress Ananda. The empress frowned, and Bridget, even from this distance, could feel her distrust and anger.

What am I doing? thought Bridget, backing away from the rail and wrapping her frigid hands in the ends of her shawl. *Does no one else see?* But she was not even certain of what she truly saw.

"What say you, mistress?" called the empress.

Bridget licked her lips, shivering from the cold that sank through her skin. What was she to say? They would think she was insane. Or perhaps not, as they were all used to the idea of magic. But what would Kalami say when he found out she had saved the life of his enemy? Why should she want to save him? The man had kidnapped her, bespelled and terrified her.

But that man knew Mother's name, and Kalami had begun to lie to her.

Bridget tightened her stomach. "That swan is your sorcerer, Sakra," she called down to Ananda. "I did not think you would want his head split open."

The empress's frown deepened. "What do you tell me?"

Bridget took a second deep breath of frigid air and spoke as clearly as she could. "That swan is in truth your sorcerer, Sakra. You are the great sorceress, can you not see?"

Shocked whispers rippled through the winter air. Bridget wondered if they were because of the accusation she made, or merely because of the tone she used to address an empress.

"Who are you?" Ananda demanded.

Bridget drew herself up. "I am Bridget Lederle, and I am telling you, madame, your man is bleeding to death at your feet."

The empress said something that Bridget could not hear to one of her attendants. Then she minced through the snow in her delicate shoes and knelt beside the swan. Its struggles were quickly growing more feeble. The blood on its breast was no longer flowing bright, but instead was dark, a burgundy as deep as the color of Bridget's grand dress. The empress pulled off her thick mittens and tossed them aside. She undid the sash from around her waist, and reknotted it, passing it around the swan's neck and knotting it loosely yet again. Bridget saw the swan wave one wing weakly, and she saw the man, confused and pained, trying to reach for the empress.

Empress Ananda got to her feet. "Bring this bird to my chambers. Carefully," she ordered no one in particular. "And you, mistress," she said to Bridget. "You come as well." She strode swiftly out of Bridget's field of view.

Bridget sucked in a breath and returned indoors. The relative warmth flowed over her like a blessing.

"It seems you had better show me the way to the empress's room as opposed to the library," she said to Richikha, who hovered at her elbow. Then she smiled sheepishly at the seamstresses. "We will do this another time."

The two women folded their hands across their breasts and bowed, but Bridget did not miss the stunned looks on their faces before they dropped their gaze.

"Follow me, mistress," Richikha was saying.

Bridget did as she was told. Richikha led her down dim corridors with arched roofs and through muraled and tapestried chambers, their doorways framed by carnelian pillars. The floors were veneered with different colors of wood fitted into intricate patterns. Stairs, some broad and polished, some narrow and twisting, opened occasionally in the right-hand wall.

Finally, Richikha rounded a corner and halted her before a pair of wooden doors in the left-hand wall. A soldier stood at one side and a little girl all dressed in white and green at the other.

"Tell Her Majesty Imperial that Mistress Bridget Lederle waits upon her as she was so commanded," said Richikha to the girl.

The girl had the smug look of a child who knows she holds some sway over adults, but nonetheless, she swiftly opened the door and disappeared into the room beyond. Bridget waited, trying not to fidget. What was going to happen? And what was Kalami going to say when he found out? She had no reason to trust Sakra, but neither could she completely trust Kalami, and she could not just stand by and watch the man killed like . . . well, like an animal.

The girl reappeared and reverenced. "Her Majesty Imperial bids you to her presence." She held the door open. Richikha also stood aside, nodding gently to Bridget. Bridget swallowed, smoothed her skirt down and walked into the empress's room.

She recognized the chamber at once from the scene Kalami had shown her in Momma's mirror. Now, however, the empress sat on a wooden chair beside the firepit. Two ladies stood behind her, their eyes looking daggers at Bridget. The swan, Sakra, his wings, his arms, folded carefully, lay on a pile of sheepskins on the other side of the fire. The arrow still protruded from his bloodstained torso. The man's eyes, the bird's eyes, lost and pleading, looked up at her as she stopped, uncertain how far it was polite to enter. She executed what she hoped was a reasonable imitation of the reverence, further hoping that it would be adequate for this occasion.

"Mistress Bridget," said the empress. "Tell us again what you see where all others see a swan?"

Bridget assumed a modest pose, hands folded, eyes downturned. "I see the sorcerer Sakra."

"You are a sorceress then?"

"I am told that I am."

"Did you lay this curse on my servant? And do not try to lie, for I will know."

Bridget bridled at the accusation and lifted her gaze. She saw then how the empress clutched the arms of her chair, and recognized the tension in her face. The young woman was not angry, she was terrified.

Of what? Of Bridget? Or that her man might die? If it was that, why had she done nothing to save him? She was a sorceress of such power, surely she should be able do at least as much as Bridget, and stitch a wound closed.

"I did nothing to your servant."

Empress Ananda raised her gloved hand and rubbed her fingertips together, as if she were feeling the texture of the air, or perhaps of Bridget's words. But Bridget looked in her eyes, and saw no light there as she had seen when Kalami had worked his magic before her.

No spell about her person, then, no magic inside her.

Bridget sucked in her breath. The empress was a fraud. Sakra lay trapped and dying at her feet, and she could do nothing. She did not even know whether what she heard was the truth, or some further trap for herself.

And I have been brought here by her enemy. She looked down at the swan, at Sakra. *And I can't do anything either.*

The empress lowered her hand. "Very well then. You may show to us your skill and loyalty, and free him from this seeming."

"Madame," Bridget hesitated. "I do not know if I can. I am . . . not well schooled in these matters."

"I bid you try."

Bridget thought of the soldier outside the door, and all the others she had seen. Stories of people seized and imprisoned for displeasing kings and princes filled her mind. Surely Kalami would try to free her if any such thing happened, but he might not be able to. This was the empress before her.

Bridget circled the firepit and knelt beside Sakra. Someone had tried to stanch the blood and wash off what had already flowed, but it still oozed deep and dark around the arrow. The feathers, the cloth of his shirt, were still stained. Bridget tilted her head this way and that, trying to get a better look at either the swan or the man. With her right eye, she realized, she saw the swan. It was her left alone that saw the man. Her heart began to flutter with nervousness. What was she to do?

She lifted his arm to check his pulse, trying to ignore the disconcerting sensation of feathers under her hand. But, although she could see his fingers, she could feel nothing but the long feathers of a swan's wing. She swallowed and pressed her fingers gently against his throat. Here she had better luck. Under the soft down, she felt a heartbeat. It was slow, weak and unsteady. The man was surely dying. His shirt was torn as well, shredded, in fact, and he winced as she moved his arm. It was maddening. She could see the reality of the man, but she could only touch the swan. How was she to do anything? She turned his arm, his wing, and leaned closer. A pattern of tooth marks marred his side. They were minor wounds compared with the arrow, and completely hidden by the swan's feathers. But these at least her fingers could touch, and she could feel as well as see that they were swollen and obviously painful. Sakra was mouthing something to her, but all she could hear was the swan's faint croakings.

Voices sounded outside the door. Bridget's head jerked up. Kalami burst into the room, the little door girl right behind him. He stared, at Bridget, at the empress, and at the swan who was Sakra.

In a moment, he recollected himself and dropped to his knees. "Majesty Imperial, I beg your pardon. I—"

"You what?" inquired the empress with far too much sweetness in her voice. "You thought to bring a stranger of unknown powers to our court and secret her away? You thought perhaps to work some magic over my servant? I would be very interested to know how much of this spectacle is your doing." She nodded toward Bridget. "Proceed."

Bridget looked beseechingly at Kalami, but he did not move. She turned her gaze again to the arm, the wing, she held, trying frantically to think, but what little she knew of matters sorcerous seemed pitifully useless to her now.

Then, a trace of yellow against Sakra's brown flesh and red wounds caught her eye. Bridget peered closer. Something was embedded in the bite marks. Automatically, she touched it. It moved against his flesh and the swan cried out. Both fingers and eyes told Bridget it was a sliver of something hard, sharp and smooth.

A tooth? From whatever bit you?

Deciding it could do no harm, and because she could do nothing else, Bridget grasped the enamel sliver in her fingertips and pulled it free.

The swan arched its body, trumpeting in agony, but then the uncomprehending cry of a bird lengthened, deepened and changed until it became a man's scream of pain. Bridget fell backward, catching herself on her hands. The swan was gone. In front of her lay Sakra, clear and unblemished, but with a wounded arm and an arrow in his side.

"What means this?" demanded Kalami. "Her Grand Majesty forbid—"

"Yes, what means this?" The empress rose to her feet, looming over Kalami. "My servant has been attacked. He was cursed with a change that almost caused his death, at the hands of those sworn to protect me!" She drew herself up to her full height. "What means this in truth, my lord sorcerer?" She waved to one of the women. "Rouse the physics. My man needs attending."

The woman ran for the door. Bridget's attention dropped back to Sakra. He grunted and tried to prop himself up onto one elbow. She laid her hands on his shoulders, pushing him back down onto the fleeces.

"The . . ." he gasped. "What you took from me. Give me . . ."

"Bridget, stand away," said Kalami. "This is beyond what you know."

"Bridget, do as *Agnidh* Sakra bids," countered the empress. "Or do you say otherwise, Lord Sorcerer?"

What she took from him? Bridget cast about in confusion. He could only mean the tooth. It lay on the stones glistening with his fresh blood. She picked it up and laid it in Sakra's reaching hand. Kalami watched from where he knelt, his face both afraid and thunderous.

"Your hand, and I'm sorry," Sakra whispered.

Bridget felt her brow furrow, but she laid her hand in his, and felt the tooth prick her palm. She tried to jerk away, but Sakra held her tight. Her blood flowed down and light filled his pain-dimmed eyes. Her skin prickled and she knew he worked some spell, some weaving with her very blood between them. He screamed again and his body stiffened, and in the next heartbeat unbearable pain lanced through the whole of her, searing spine, nerve, heart and mind, blinding her and robbing her of all breath.

Then it was over. Bridget sprawled across the cold floor gasping for breath. From one eye, she saw Sakra sitting up. The arrow had vanished; so had all his wounds.

Ananda was at his side in three strides, kneeling beside the sheepskins. "Sakra, are you well?"

"Well enough," he gasped, digging the heel of his hand into his side.

"Kiriti, Behule, provision for Lord Sakra's accommodation must be made." As she stood, her voice strove to become steely, but Bridget still heard it quaver. So, evidently did Kalami, for his eyes widened. "I give you my thanks for your assistance, Mistress Bridget. We will speak in the future."

Recognizing the dismissal, Bridget managed to heave herself to her feet. The whole world spun as she did, and she stared at her bloodstained palm. The tooth was gone, and so was any mark it should have made. Despite that, she felt abominably thirsty and weak, as if a river of blood had been drained from her.

She was grateful when Kalami slipped a hand under her elbow and supported her to the door, where Richikha waited to take her other elbow and help her to walk into the hallway.

But next to come were all those hundreds of yards of rooms and corridors. Bridget swooned at the very thought of trying to walk them. Kalami and Richikha staggered trying to keep her upright.

"I can't make it back," she panted.

"Just a short way." Kalami's voice was tight. She could feel tension radiating off him like heat from a fire. So, she just nodded and decided she had no choice but to trust him that far.

He must have given some order to Richikha, because the girl ran swiftly ahead, opening an unadorned door. The room beyond was swaddled in tapestries and carpets. Kalami laid Bridget on a divan heaped with embroidered pillows, and she blinked up at the gilded ceiling.

"Fetch water, bread and wine."

The door opened and closed again as Richikha hurried away.

"Bridget," Kalami came to stand over her. "Can you speak?"

"Yes." Bridget was pleased to find her voice was steady, but she was not so foolish as to try to sit up.

"Then you can tell me how you came to be in that room with Ananda and her dog." His voice was tight with control but it was not enough to hold back the fury in his words.

Bridget rubbed her forehead. "I saw the swan was Sakra and I—"

"Saw? In a vision?"

"Yes, in a vision," Bridget lied. She had to concentrate. She must regain her grasp of her spinning mind. If she could conceal from

Kalami this new, strange way of seeing, she would have a means of gathering information with which he could not interfere. It might be able to tell her finally if it was only her overwrought imagination that made her distrust him.

"And how did she call you in to help?"

Bridget described the scene over the courtyard.

"You spoke thus?" Kalami paced back and forth beside her divan. "Why? Why not let the soldier kill him? You know what he is!"

Bridget rubbed her head again, trying to think. "I thought . . ." She waved her hand weakly. "The empress trusts me now. I thought that might be of use to you, and to the dowager."

That brought Kalami up short. "I must apologize, Bridget," he said, much more gently. "That was indeed a worthy thought."

And thank Heaven it came to me, thought Bridget to the ceiling. Now seemed a good time to change the subject. "What . . . what did Sakra do to me?"

Kalami took her bloodstained hand and turned it up, running his thumb across her unmarked palm. "You felt pain?"

Bridget nodded. *God grant I never feel such pain again.*

"Probably he borrowed some of your strength." Kalami laid her palm back in her lap. "It is a thing sorcerers may do between each other, but not frequently, and not easily. He must have had some strong talisman secreted about himself to allow him to take advantage of you thus."

Such as that tooth? But Bridget said nothing.

Richikha chose that moment to return bearing a silver tray with pitchers and goblets. Kalami mixed water with a deep red wine that reminded Bridget far too much of Sakra's blood and handed it to her. She drank dutifully, although even watered down the stuff was strong enough to make her immediately giddy.

"See that she finishes that," said Kalami to Richikha. "And that she sleeps. You must regain all your strength, Bridget," he added to her. "The coming days may be even more difficult than I expected."

Bridget took another sip of the heady wine, watching the satisfaction in Kalami's eyes as she drank. *I fear, sir, that you may be right.*

When he left Bridget, Kalami stopped in his own apartments just long enough to throw an outer coat around his shoulders and pick up the bundle of his best shirt. From there, he descended the palace's north stairs and emerged into the winter afternoon. Welcoming the cold that brought all his senses fully awake, he strode down the cleared path to the outbuildings where much of the work that kept the lives of the imperials and nobles simple went on. The weavers' and tailors' shed was close enough to the laundry and the dyers that the noise and stink of it seeped between the shutters and under the doors.

Inside, the place was bright with the light from the tin lanterns and screened hearths. All the braziers were also carefully covered, as no open flame could be allowed near so much valuable cloth. Bolts of cloth waited in open chests or were laid out on long tables for cutting. The looms clattered and clacked along the far wall. Every man or woman who worked there had been interviewed carefully by himself to make sure none were touched by magic. It was the same with the tailors and seamstresses who worked around their wooden forms, piecing and stitching the cloth, finishing the tucks and ruffles, sewing the embroidery, mending the thousand tears, holes and nicks that the courtiers' fine clothing suffered from.

Heads lifted and eyes turned as he entered. Some began to reverence, but he waved at them to go about their business. They obeyed. As he was responsible for selection and oversight of those who worked the imperial cloth, this was not the first time he had come down to this place on his own and his presence would excite little comment. He had never been more grateful for that than now.

His gaze swept the room until he found the one he sought, a nervous young girl stitching away at a length of silver tissue. Her hair was a black waterfall but pulled back too severely from her young face and pinned harshly in place with long, steel pins.

"Good day, my little sister Ilmani," he said to her in the language of their home.

The girl's head jerked up, more than startled, frightened. He smiled brightly down at her, but the fear did not leave her face.

"Good day, my honored brother Kalami," she answered in a whisper, her eyes darting left and right.

"What is wrong, little sister?" He squatted down next to her stool. "You may speak with me. It is in fact required if I so ask." He spoke lightly, to let her know he was jesting.

"Yes, sir," she nodded, bending low over her work. "But Tasa Mavrutka does not like me to speak the home tongue. She calls it ugly and uncivilized. She . . ." The girl clamped her mouth shut.

Kalami felt his jaw harden. "Does she beat you?"

The girl nodded, her own mouth pressed tightly closed.

"We shall see how she likes the rod herself then. . . ." Kalami moved to stand, but the girl caught his sleeve.

"No, honored brother," she pleaded. "It will only go worse for me. Even if she is dismissed. The others . . . I work hard, *Tasa* Mavrutka herself has taken me to 'prentice. The other girls work in the dyeing sheds . . . I . . ."

"Very well, very well." He patted her hand to calm her and settled back at her side again. He understood what it was to work hard and rise above one's birth. "It shall be as you wish."

"Thank you, honored brother," she breathed, clearly much relieved. But her gaze flickered to the left. Kalami turned his head to see what she was looking at and saw Mistress Mavrutka frowning in their direction. He stood, making sure she saw him fully. The woman acknowledged his rank and right with a small reverence, and the rapid turning away of her attention.

"Now then, little sister," said Kalami, touching the girl's shoulder so she looked up at him. "I have done you a favor, and I will ask one of you."

Her fingertips ran nervously over the seam she worked on so diligently. "If I can, honored brother."

Kalami smiled again. A child, really, with a child's ambition. Her thoughts probably reached no higher than becoming mistress of this shed, and encompassed no more of their home than making sure there were an adequate number of chickens and cows in her family's yard.

"My best shirt," he said, handing her the bundled-up garment. "I have torn the cuff, and can hardly appear tomorrow without it be mended."

"You shall most certainly have it, honored brother," she told him as earnestly as if she were offering to guard the treasury. She reached for the shirt.

"There is one other small thing," he said as he pressed the garment into her hands. "When you unfold my shirt, you'll find a bag of black cloth. What is inside needs to be stitched into the shift you are preparing for Mistress Bridget Lederle. Can you do that as well?"

She smoothed the shirt out on her lap, mindful of the fine fabric, but bowed her head in guilty uncertainty.

"Come now, little sister," he said, coaxing her. "It truly is a small thing. A bit of protection I wish the lady to have. Times are difficult right now, and dangers are many, especially for a stranger here. It will not do much in itself, but it shall be joined by a pair of garters as soon as I can weave them. Those will seal the protection I would place on her."

She thought about that, stroking the fabric again. Kalami wondered if she dreamed of wearing such finery rather than just working on it for others. If she did well, perhaps he would send her a new shift of her own.

"I will see to it, honored brother," she agreed at last. "Surely, there can be no harm in such a thing."

"Surely." Kalami patted her shoulder. "You have my thanks, little sister, and if all goes well, you shall have more than that."

With those words he left her, and began a leisurely tour of the shed, pausing here and there to talk to the others so that his time with her would not appear unusual. At last, he came to where Mistress Mavrutka stood beside a chest filled with glistening satins in all shades of blue.

"What excellent work you do here, mistress."

Mistress Mavrutka gave him a smile a sharp as one of her own needles. "My thanks, Lord Sorcerer. I do my humble best."

"I see this." Kalami folded his hands behind his back. "But perhaps you were not aware that the mistress of us all, Her Grand Majesty the dowager, did declare respect for all oblasts of the empire."

The smile bent into a thin frown. "I do not understand you, Lord Sorcerer."

"Then I will be plain." He faced her fully. "If I find you have touched anyone again for speaking the language of their home, you will have cause to regret it."

"Ah." Her blue eyes glittered. "Now I understand."

"No, I don't believe you do." Kalami stepped closer. "I am lord sorcerer, and my saying I will give you cause to regret what you do is not the same as such warnings from others. Now, perhaps you understand better?"

His words and their implications sank into her, draining the color from her cheeks. "Yes, sir."

"Excellent." His own smile was genial. "I should not wish to waste my time or skill on such trivialities. But I will. Remember you that."

He did not wait for her reverence, but walked straight out the door into the palace yard. The cold had deepened outside, and the clouds overhead hung low, sagging with the burden of snow they carried. The first few flakes drifted down, catching in his hair and tingling against his skin.

A change in the weather. Kalami smiled to himself as he strode toward the palace, his boots crunching on the old, dried snow. *How appropriate. The first of many changes we will see.*

"We are given to understand your servant Sakra has returned to you," said the dowager.

As ever, the dowager decided to make criticizing Ananda a public affair. This time they faced each other in the council chamber. Eight of the Council of Lords sat arrayed in a semicircle, four of them on either side of Ananda's own chair. Together, they made an arc facing the dais where the dowager sat with Bakhar, the keeper of the emperor's god house, splendid in his own golden robes and carrying his ivory staff. The ninth chair, the lord sorcerer's chair, stood empty.

Kalami's absence sent a stab of fear through Ananda that his presence never could.

But even that was a small thing compared with the sight of Mikkel, dressed all in black velvet with gold trim, slumped in a chair at his mother's side. Ananda had not had a glimpse of Mikkel in days. The dowager was keeping him under close watch while the nobles arrived to celebrate the holy day and renew their oaths of loyalty. With rebellion brewing, and she surely knew that there was rebellion brewing, Medeoan did not wish to have Mikkel too much seen. For some reason, it made the lords master nervous to see their anointed emperor so unmanned. But for this the dowager needed her son. She needed to remind Ananda, and the council lords, who controlled the succession of power in Isavalta.

Ananda swallowed and tried to collect herself, but she could not shift her attention from Mikkel. As ever, his restless gaze roamed the hall, searching for something. His hands plucked the hems of his sleeves, as if trying to pull them apart.

He wore his chain. Did he know that? Was he trying to free himself?

"Well, Daughter Imperial?" The dowager's voice cut across Ananda's thoughts.

Ananda managed to incline her head. "Sakra was enchanted and attacked. He came to me for succor."

Medeoan sat back, regarding Ananda through narrowed eyes. The bandages she had worn so lately had been removed from her hands, Ananda noticed. She cradled them gingerly in her lap, though, and Ananda wondered if they still pained her. "He defied my order of banishment."

For once, Ananda did not bow her head. "I ask you to forgive him, my Mother Imperial. At the time his wits were disordered by his enchantment." She hoped the dowager heard the steel in her tone. "A condition we both, surely, understand." She looked to Mikkel who shifted in his chair, his fingers as busy as his eyes. *Let them all see what I mean*, she thought, while at the same time she hoped Behule had picked them a speedy messenger to send to Spavatan, and one with a sturdy horse, or at the very least a thick pair of boots. There would be snow soon. Even she could feel it.

"And you say you knew nothing of this supposed attack?" Ananda could not read the dowager's face. There was too much going on behind the bland mask she wore, and she was too distant.

Ananda opened her mouth to answer, but at that same moment, Mikkel stood. His gaze darted back and forth, freshly manic, but he started down the dais steps, his hand out, seeking something. Ananda's throat seized shut.

"My Son Imperial," snapped the dowager. "Retain your seat."

But Mikkel stumbled down the last step of the dais. "Somewhere," he said. "I hear you. I hear . . ."

"Mikkel!" The dowager rose. The council lords all leapt to their feet in a comic spectacle of trying to be courtly and yet pretend not to see what was happening.

Only Ananda remained frozen in her chair as Mikkel blundered forward.

"Kostid, help your emperor to his seat." The dowager looked as if she would order Ananda's death at that moment if she dared. The council lords all stared at their boots.

But Mikkel was in front of her before the servants could hurry to his sides, and for one heartbeat, his eyes stilled.

"Find me," he breathed. "Find me, Ana."

A hand touched Mikkel's shoulder, and Ananda looked, startled to see Keeper Bakhar beside his emperor.

"Here, Majesty Imperial," he said, gently turning Mikkel around to face the servants. "Your wife will wait for you."

"Ana waits," whispered Mikkel, and Ananda felt her heart break once more.

Then Kostid and his fellows surrounded Mikkel. A silent scream tore through Ananda's mind as they gently led him back to his mother's side, pressing on his shoulders until he sat again. Keeper Bakhar gave her a glance that might have been sympathy, but Ananda saw him only peripherally. Mikkel's eyes had taken up their random darting back and forth again, and his fingers plucked at the cloth. But this time, his servants, his guards, remained clustered around him. Ananda's heart weaved back and forth between rage and wonder. *Find me, Ana.* He'd spoken her name. *Ana waits.* He'd known her. For a heartbeat, he had known her.

But she could do nothing. She had to sit where she was, as polite, as formal as the council lords. More so, because she could not lose her dignity in front of them.

The dowager sat again, her back and shoulders ramrod straight. The council lords also took their seats, looking for all the world like a pack of guilty children who wondered what punishment was coming next.

"I put a question before you, Daughter Imperial," said the dowager. Did her voice tremble just a little? Or was that merely a wish on Ananda's part? "Did you know Sakra planned to defy the order of banishment?"

Ananda managed to draw her attention away from Mikkel, slumped and distant now, and focus again on the dowager. "I knew nothing." She cocked her head. "Did you?"

A spasm of anger crossed the dowager's features, and Ananda felt she had succeeded in touching a sore spot. "How would I come to know the affairs of your servants?"

"I must confess, I do not know that either," said Ananda pleasantly, spreading her hands wide to show her confusion. "Is my mother imperial finished with me?" She did not want to leave. She wanted to grab Mikkel and drag him to Sakra. But she could not. Not yet. Not here. She knew that. Yet, as much as she longed to stay beside him, to see whether he could recognize her again, if she stayed much longer, her strength would fail her. She knew that as well.

"There is but one other thing, Daughter Imperial."

Ananda knew what was coming. The dowager would now tell her how Lord Master Oulo had been taken ill. She would hint and probe to try to find out how Ananda had managed it. Ananda would reply with innuendo and hints of her own. The lords master would tell their tales, and the war of rumor would go on. She stiffened her back to try to ready herself for this new battle.

"Lord Master Oulo died suddenly this morning."

Ananda felt her heart plummet. "Died?" she choked out the word. "How . . . ?"

"He woke, devoid of sight and hearing. The physics were called. It seems the shock of it stopped his heart." Medeoan bowed her head in a pretense at grief.

The council lords had surely already heard the news, but all of them kissed the knuckles of their right hands anyway. *Puppets,* thought Ananda, as her cold hands clutched the arms of her chair. *Puppets all of them. What does it matter I cut one of their strings?*

Her heart cried at that fleeting thought, for she knew what it meant. It meant she was changing, finally and truly. She was becoming what she had so long pretended to be, and if she were not freed, not stopped soon, it would be too late. She would become as bad as the dowager, or worse.

Dutifully, Ananda kissed her own knuckle. She did not let any emotion show in her face. Ice. Rock and ice. "I am sorry to hear it, Mother Imperial. Will there be mourning tonight?"

"There will." The dowager's eyes bored into Ananda's. *I know you did this thing,* said the dowager's whole being. *I will still find my way to you.* "I trust you will attend."

"Of course," Ananda answered evenly. She did not flinch. She did not blink. She did do this, and she would let Medeoan see the truth of it, even if no one else could. *I have power. Even now, I have power.*

"Then I believe that we are finished," said the dowager at long last.

Ananda rose, and all eight of the council lords got to their feet with her, reverencing to her even as she reverenced to the dowager. Each gesture was equally empty. Having held the pose for the requisite number of seconds, Ananda turned and walked down the long strip of carpeting toward the door.

"Daughter Imperial."

Ananda stopped. She did not want to turn around. She wanted nothing more than to be away from here. She wanted to go somewhere Mikkel could not see her and weep for Lord Master Oulo, who for all his faults did not deserve what she had done to him. At the moment, however, she had no choice. Mindful of her train, as Kiriti and Behule were not allowed in this room, she turned fully and reverenced again. "Mother Imperial?"

"Have you heard whether Lord Peshek has arrived yet?"

Despite all her resolve, Ananda felt her face fall. She could only hope that the dowager was too far away to see it. "I do not believe he has, Mother Imperial."

The dowager looked down at her hands in a gesture of feigned awkwardness. "I hope that you will do me the favor, as he is so old and valued a friend from the days when the regalia were in my hands, that you will permit me the honor of officially welcoming him."

The dowager's face was absolutely guileless. It was merely a polite request, a favor as she said. How could it be anything else?

Except that everything the dowager did had a double purpose, and the dowager had been listening to Lord Master Oulo and surely, Oulo had given her Peshek's name. Until the official welcome had been made, Ananda could not be seen speaking with Peshek. She could not warn him about what the dowager knew.

Yet, in front of the council lords and the keeper of the god house she could not refuse this. She was as powerless as Mikkel, slumped and dreaming beside his mother. Ananda swallowed, realizing that the dowager had not brought her here to chastise her in front of the council, or even to inform her that she had murdered Lord Master Oulo. The dowager had brought her here so that she would not be able to be the first to greet Lord Master Peshek.

"All shall be as my mother imperial desires," Ananda said, her voice hoarse with anger at herself for not realizing this sooner.

However it was delivered, the answer was the correct one and the dowager nodded, satisfied. "You have my thanks, Daughter Imperial."

They bowed their heads to each other, and Ananda was permitted to leave. She said nothing to Kiriti and Behule, who waited outside the council chamber door for her. Instead, she breezed past them, heading down the broad corridor to the rooms she had seen were given to Sakra and letting them fall into silent step on either side of her.

She had not dared commandeer the very best quarters for Sakra. Depending on the mood of the dowager, she might have provoked a house arrest for him. But she had been able to ensure a sound room facing the courtyard, on the same floor as her own chambers, with rugs and fresh linens and a good fire. Behule had recommended a man named Jeros to wait on him. Ananda was not sure whether he was bribable, or merely one of the many Behule strung along with her personal charms, and did not choose to ask.

Much to her relief, when Jeros opened the door and stood back to admit her, she saw Sakra sitting upright on the narrow bed with its wooden half-canopy.

"How goes it with you, Sakra?" asked Ananda in the Hastinapuran court language as she stepped up to the bedside. Jeros came forward with a chair for her, reverenced and retired a discreet distance with Kiriti and Behule. Ananda fell into the chair, all her reserves spent.

Concern shone in Sakra's eyes. "What has happened?" He kept his tone light and his posture relaxed.

Ananda pushed herself upright, and, struggling to match Sakra's mild voice, she told him what had become of Lord Master Oulo.

"I used the last of my spell braids to kill him, Sakra," she said, tears stinging her eyes. "I murdered a man, and it left me with nothing when you needed my help most of all."

"You did not purpose his death, Ananda," murmured Sakra. "And you were right, you had to silence him." He longed to reach for her, to wrap his arms around her as he had when she was a child. She could see that plainly in his face and in the way his shoulders tensed, but he did not dare move. Jeros could only be trusted so far. "I will be well by tomorrow night, Princess. Then, we will find some way to bring this battle to an end."

Ananda wiped her hand across her eyes. She did not dare to believe it could be so. "Are you sure you will be well enough, Sakra?"

The ghost of a smile played around Sakra's mouth. "I have had some very strong tonic."

"The woman?"

Sakra nodded. "She may be the most powerful mortal sorcerer I have ever met."

Ananda heard the hushed awe in his voice. He wanted to understand this new power, she knew that. That was his essential nature—ever curious and thirsty for knowledge. It did not make what she had to do next any easier. Despite her regret over what had happened to Oulo, despite her own exhaustion, there was something that she had to say. She had known she must give this order since this morning, and nothing that had happened since changed that.

She glanced across the servants. Kiriti and Behule had engaged Jeros in some low conversation. Good. Jeros could not understand what she and Sakra said, but her ladies could. They must have nothing to tell if, the Mothers forbid, they were put to the question.

Ananda leaned close to Sakra. "I may . . . I might . . . if she . . ." She could not say the words, but she had to. But if she did, would she not be as bad as the dowager, caring nothing for lives lost to her own needs?

But if she did not, would she not just as surely die herself?

Sakra, though, knew what she meant to say, and to his credit, his shock showed only in his eyes. "Princess . . ."

"It might be the only way." Despite the certainty of her statement, she could not look into his stunned eyes. Instead, she looked at his strong hand where it lay on the bedspread. *I cannot ask this. I must. I cannot.* "Do you know what she saw today?" she asked, trying to explain. Sakra did not answer. "She saw that I could not heal or help my own servants."

"You played the ruse well." Sakra moved his hand as if he thought to touch hers, but he remembered Jeros and stilled it. "She saw you testing her."

"You did not see her eyes." Ananda shook her head. "It was she who was testing me. She knows. It may already be too late. She may have already told Kalami and the dowager." Her voice trembled. She could not help it. This was the day she had feared. Now they would try all the normal means to do away with her. Now the dangers were poison, and distant magic, the things against which she had no defense. She would die, and Mikkel would be left alone.

"Did the dowager speak of this to you in the council chamber?" She had sent Kiriti to let Sakra know of her summons.

"No. She wished only to quiz me about whether I had sent for you against the order of banishment, to watch my face as she told me what had happened to Lord Master Oulo, and she wished to keep me from speaking to Lord Master Peshek." Which was bad enough. Which was more than bad enough.

Sakra could not fail to realize the danger of this. Despite that, when he spoke again his voice was steady and firm. "The dowager has wanted to be rid of you for so long, do you think that she would fail to expose you before the council lords if she knew of your ruse?"

"Then it is only a matter of time." Ananda's voice shook again. She was going to die. Mikkel would be his mother's toy forever, and she was going to die. "I tell you, Sakra. This woman, this Bridget, knows." She clamped her jaw shut until she was certain again of her voice. "If she speaks, we will be at the end, and we need more time. With time, Hraban and his rebellion can help us in a coup. Medeoan can die during the revolt. Once she is dead, her living, working spells will be broken. Mikkel will be restored and we will be free."

Ananda had no idea what Sakra saw as he looked at her. She only knew how sweet the thought of freedom tasted. She had savored the distant scent of it for so long only to be disappointed time and again. Now she would decant it for herself and she would drink it fully down and she would share the cup with Mikkel.

At last, Sakra spoke, his voice soft and pleading. "Ananda, I understand, believe me, I do, but I beg you, give me this night before you order me to take her life, and before you give any such order to Behule." Before she could speak, he rushed ahead. "I believe Kalami and the dowager may have misjudged this new power they have brought to them. Her loyalty and understanding are by no means certain."

"And?" Ananda asked wearily.

Sakra slipped his hand forward across the blankets until his fingertip just brushed the side of her hand. "They have forgotten she is a free-willed woman as well as a power. They have lied to her and hidden the truth. Once she sees that, I believe, all will change."

Ananda looked at their hands, so close together. She wanted to believe him, but she was so tired and she feared for Mikkel. After what happened in the council chamber, Medeoan might be strengthening the spell that held him. She might be doing anything to him. Ananda had failed to see the plan for keeping her away from Lord Master Peshek. What else had she failed to see?

She lifted her gaze and stared for a long time into Sakra's eyes. He offered her hope, a chance to keep from finally becoming what she feared, bloodless and ruthless. Why did she not seize it at once? In Sakra's eyes, she saw there concern for herself, and a longing to know the truth about this new sorceress, this new woman. But there was something else, some desire, some hope she could not recognize. What was going on in Sakra's mind? She could not tell, and that realization filled her with a fresh unease. "And you mean to show her the truth?"

"If I can."

Ananda gripped the edge of the bed frame as if she meant to tear the wood in two. She must trust him. It did not matter what she thought she saw in him. She must trust Sakra. If she could not trust Sakra, she would surely run mad. "Very well. This night, but no more. If the revolt is to move forward, we cannot afford delay. If you cannot turn her . . ."

Sakra bowed and pressed his hands over his face before she could speak the words that lay so heavily on her tongue. Ananda watched, numb and distant. It would not work, it could not work. Whatever hopes Sakra harbored, they were misplaced. Kalami and the dowager were too canny to bring to themselves a power of which they were not certain. If this Bridget was not fully their creature, she would be before long, and then Ananda would have no shelter, unless it could be Mikkel's restoration. In her heart, though, she believed that Mikkel could not be restored until the dowager was dead.

But she owed it to Sakra, who had kept her whole and alive for so many years, to give him a chance before she had to turn to strangers for her counsel.

He remained bowed, waiting for her to acknowledge his gesture. She sighed, touching his forehead.

"I know you will do your best."

Sakra raised his head, the lines of his face grave. "Ananda, you have held strong for so many years. I beg you, do not give way to despair now. If you order the death of an Isavaltan noble, you will begin to become all that they had ever feared of Hastinapurans."

"I do not want to," she told him. "But neither will I be one of those long-suffering queens from the ballads who dies for love and honor and does not lift a finger to save herself."

Her words sparked the faintest trace of a smile in Sakra's eyes. "That is not in your nature, no," he agreed gravely.

She returned his smile, for just a moment. "If this new creature cannot be turned, then the river of their plans has crested," she said seriously. "And I cannot wait for it to drown me, or Mikkel. Hraban's revolt offers us a chance. If necessary, I will beg my father to assist it."

Sakra drew back from her words. "The Isavaltans will never accept you if it be by conquest," he said softly. "It must not come to that."

"Then," she said as she stood, "we must make sure that it does not have to."

Chapter Twelve

Sidor Taduisyn Ladonivin, private soldier of the Imperial House Guard, stood beside the door of the small tearoom and tried to stay awake. The corridor was completely dark, and he had not been left with so much as a brazier. His sergeant said this would be an exercise in discipline, and so it was. Sidor was determined to see it through, but at the same time, his mind seemed determined to wander. Most particularly, it wandered back to his cottage beside the barracks, where his wife, Manefa, slept. In just a few hours he would be relieved from this duty. He would walk through the snow and the crystal cold to their door. He would lift their infant son from Manefa's arms and lay him in the cradle. He would slip into bed beside her, wrapping his arms around her ample waist and pulling her close. She would smile in her sleep, and then . . . and then . . .

A high, thin sound startled Sidor from his reverie. His head jerked up, but the sound was already gone. He shook his head and snapped himself back to attention. Daydreaming. Almost night dreaming in the darkness. He tried to concentrate on listening for sounds from inside the room. He had been told who was in there, but they had a difficult foreign name and he had forgotten it quickly. He did not need to know anyway. What he needed to know was that the lord sorcerer had said they were firmly, but with great respect, to be prevented from leaving the room before the lord sorcerer returned for them. That was Sidor's duty, and he would see to it. Only then would he return to Manefa and the warmth and comfort of their marriage bed.

Then he heard the thin sound again. This time he recognized it.

It was a baby's cry. He knew it from the nights his son woke, hungry, or soiled. He knew it in his heart as any father did. A moment later, he realized it was not any infant's cry. That was his son.

But was happening? Was Manefa out of her mind? To bring the infant here? He was not three months old yet. He had not even been named. What was she thinking? Something had to be wrong. Something had to be disastrously wrong.

Sidor hesitated. He had his duty. He was stationed here and he could not leave his post. But his son's cry grew louder. He could not shut it out. Something had happened to the child, to Manefa. The room behind the door was silent. Its occupants were surely sound asleep. His son was crying louder. Why couldn't Manefa quiet him?

Sidor could not stand still any longer. He did not stop to think that this was a ridiculous fear, even impossible. He did not stop to think that if Manefa had trouble she would go to one of the other cottages and get help from another soldier's wife, or that if he were truly needed elsewhere, a runner would have been sent for him. Sidor knew only that his son cried out in the darkness and that he would not leave him.

Shouldering his ax, Sidor jogged down the corridor toward the south stairs. At every step, his son's cry grew louder and more insistent. This was not just discomfort. This was pain. Sidor broke into a run.

The south stairs led down to the Rotunda. His son's cry came from outside the door. His son and Manefa were out there in the bitter, killing cold. Only vaguely aware that there should have been more guards on duty here, Sidor heaved back the bar and pushed the door open. The winter wind whipped around him as he sprinted out into the courtyard.

Manefa stood in the center of the yard, holding up the blanketed form of their son. He saw no movement under the blanket. No, no, their son could not be dead.

"Manefa!" He ran forward, dropping his ax, his arms outstretched, thinking only to embrace his wife and son.

They were gone. Sidor skidded to halt, kicking up snow under his boots. He blinked in confusion. He stood alone in the courtyard.

Manefa was nowhere to be seen. There was only the empty night and the snow. Sidor looked down at where he had thought Manefa had stood. There, among the bootprints of the night patrols, he saw a set of footprints that belonged a fox.

Help me.

Bridget sat up at once, blinking in confusion. The room around her was pitch black, except for the orange glow from a single uncovered brazier. She could just make out the dim figure of Richikha drowsing in a chair.

Not you then. Bridget laid her hand on her own throat and then on her forehead. It took her a moment to remember why she lay on a couch instead of in a bed, but gradually the events of the previous afternoon returned. Was that earlier weakness making her hear voices?

Bridget listened, holding her breath. Her dizziness had subsided, and for all the hour was obviously late, her head felt remarkably clear. She heard Richikha's soft snores and the crackle of the brazier, but nothing else.

A dream? thought Bridget. *A ghost?*

Help me.

Bridget stared around the dark room. Richikha slept on and the brazier burned without interruption. There was no other movement, no other presence. Yet Bridget felt deep in her bones that the voice was as real as the dim fire in front of her.

"Who are you?" she whispered.

I know you, came the answer. *Please, let me go.*

The voice was pleading, desperate. It went straight to Bridget's heart and she felt she could not lie still a moment longer. She threw the rug back, straightened her shawl around her shoulders and planted her shoes on the carpet. Richikha shifted in her chair with a soft sigh.

Should I wake her? she thought toward Richikha. *No. For this once, I'll leave my shepherds behind.*

A lamp waited beside the brazier. Putting her body between the light and Richikha, Bridget checked to make sure it still held oil, and then kindled the wick with a taper lit from the brazier's smoldering coals.

But her hand was not quick enough to cover the new flame and Richikha stirred.

"Mistress . . ." The lady-in-waiting pulled herself upright.

"It's all right, Richikha," said Bridget soothingly. "Go back to sleep."

"But you . . . I am . . ." Richikha began, gathering up her skirts so she could stand.

"You're exhausted and I'm oppressed by the dark." Bridget pushed her gently back into the chair and its nest of pillows. "Sleep, Richikha. Let me sit up on my own a bit. I won't tell anyone."

Richikha sucked on her lower lip, torn between her desires and her duty. "If you so wish, mistress, but . . ."

"I so wish."

Richikha subsided then, and Bridget sat back down on the divan, placing the lamp on the floor where it would be at least somewhat sheltered from Richikha's line of sight. It was not long before the girl's eyes drooped shut and her gentle snores began again.

Bridget, on the other hand, only felt more awake. A happy mischief spread through her, leaving her feeling like a child with the prospect of some nocturnal adventure. As soon as she was certain Richikha was truly asleep, Bridget stood and picked up her lamp again, sheltering the flame with her torso and her hand. The carpet muffled her footfalls and the well-tended door opened without a sound. Bridget slipped through it before any strange draft could rouse Richikha again.

The corridor outside was so utterly silent, the whole world might have been holding its breath. The deafening stillness reminded Bridget disconcertingly of the Land of Death and Spirit. She had to stand a moment biting her lip to resist the urge to drop the lamp, just to make sure it would clatter against the floor and assure her that she remained in the living world.

"Where are you?" she asked the darkness, but her whisper did not seem to reach beyond the boundaries of her light, and the darkness returned no answer.

Despite that, Bridget felt no inclination to return to her couch. She looked left and right as far as the little circle of light cast by her lamp would permit her to see and tried to think which way to go. To the left waited the empress's rooms, so Bridget turned to the right, one hand catching up her hems so she wouldn't trip over them as she lengthened her stride. She wanted to get well out of sight in case Richikha woke up and came looking for her. There were secrets in this place, and this was her chance to find them out.

It was not so much a corridor she passed through as a series of interlocking chambers. The light flashed on gilding here and there, on bits of murals, patterned moldings and ripples of tapestry that fluttered with the gentle breeze her passage created. The floor under her feet alternated patterns of stars, diamonds and interlocking rings. Her soft shoes made no noise, and she smelled nothing but wood polish, dust and cold.

Footsteps sounded up ahead. Bridget froze, her eyes darting this way and that. This was a narrow, curtain-hung stretch of corridor opening into a wider chamber on either end. The footsteps hurried closer, accompanied by a mix of voices. Bridget picked the nearest curtain and ducked behind it.

Behind her was a window, and the tiny panes coated her back with pure cold. Bridget shivered and set her lamp on the floor so that her trembling would not shake the flame and call attention to it.

The footsteps reached her little hallway, bringing with them lights and voices.

"Please, Majesty Imperial," said one. "Let us return."

"He can't hear you," said another. "Why do you bother?"

"Because he is our anointed emperor and you will remember that!"

The emperor? Bridget's breath caught in her throat as the footsteps hurried by.

"I hear you," said another voice. "Where are you?"

He heard? Heard what? The same voice that called to her? Cautiously, Bridget set her eye to the edge of the curtain.

A bevy of brightly liveried servants and armored house guards surrounded a slight, pale figure in a plain grey coat. Between their shoulders, she saw that Grey Coat was turning in place.

"I hear you," someone said. "I hear you."

"Please, Majesty Imperial." One man with a gold sash around his livery reached forward to the grey coat. "It is time to return to bed."

But if the emperor—Mikkel was his name, wasn't it?—heard, he gave no sign. Instead, he knelt, pawing at the inlaid floor.

"Here," he said, or did he say "Hear"?

Gold Sash knelt beside him. "Come, Majesty Imperial." He took the emperor's restless hands. "You must come with us now?"

Bridget could not see well, squinting between a forest of legs. "Must I?" said the emperor, his voice sounding small and lost.

"You must." Gold Sash stood, straightening up the emperor with him.

"Must I." The emperor turned the words into a flat statement.

With that, the mob of guards and servants moved away, amid the sounds of boots, shoes and shuffling cloth.

Only when doors closed behind the lights and noises did Bridget emerge from the curtain, lamp in hand. She hurried to the spot where the emperor had knelt, and bent swiftly to touch the floor. Nothing but cold wood, cunningly pieced together. No telltale blurring or shimmer reached her.

She straightened. Whatever the emperor heard, whatever she heard, it was not here.

So, no point in dawdling. Bridget tightened her grip on the lamp and continued up the hallway.

The final chamber opened up into a balcony and a broad staircase flanked by pillars of pale, speckled stone slashed through with dark veins. Without pausing to think, Bridget descended the stairs, holding the lamp up high to see her way. In front of the stairs waited a pair of tall, carved doors that must have needed three men each to open, and on either side of them were narrow windows running from the floor to the ceiling, which was lost in the shadows. Bridget longed to look outside, but she did not. The dozens of windowpanes would reflect her light and there was too much chance of being seen, and being stopped.

And she must not be stopped. She knew that now. Now was her chance to find out the truth for herself. That was what mattered. The truth. The truth about herself, the truth about the dowager, Ananda, Sakra and Kalami. Especially the truth about Kalami. And the voice. That truth as well.

The floor down here was flagstones laid out in patterns at least as complicated as the wooden floor upstairs. Corridors opened to the left and to the right. Bridget turned left again, acting on the vague supposition that important things in such a place as this might be kept clustered together, so whatever waited under the empress's rooms might be useful.

Or it might be only the kitchens, she smiled to herself. *You are "below stairs" now.*

The closed doors came out of the shadows so suddenly Bridget had to pull herself up short to keep from running into them. She covered her mouth to stifle the sound, something between a gasp and a giggle that tried to bubble out of her.

Her lamp's faint light drew out the shapes in the carvings. Eagles, spread out wing tip to wing tip, made a row in front of her eyes, but under that was a row of oblongs. No. Bridget bent down and peered closer, trailing her fingertips over the cool carvings. They were not simple oblongs, they were books.

Library!

Bridget brushed the doors with her palms, seeking a knob or handle and finding none. At last, she just leaned her shoulder against the wood and pushed.

Slowly, reluctantly, the door swung back, and Bridget stepped through.

The library was a long, slanting hall of a place that ran along one of the courtyard walls. Moonlight streamed through windows made up of hundreds of diamond panes so thick and uneven the light rippled and blurred as if it shined through water. So much glass also let in the abundant cold, and Bridget shivered, grateful for her thick dress and warm shawl.

Stripes of shadow and faint diamonds of light decorated the inner wall, illuminating bookshelves three times as tall as Bridget. Toward the windows waited a row of steeply slanted desks, each of which looked like a cross between a writing table and a drafting table. Some were empty; others had books resting on them, ready for consultation, or perhaps for copying.

Bridget stepped gingerly into the room as if she were afraid of disturbing its stillness. Patterns of moonlight and yet more shadow laid themselves across her skin and she could have sworn she felt colder for their touch.

What am I doing here? It's not as if I could read a single one of these.

But then, perhaps she could. The idea stopped her in her tracks. She had already done so much she would have considered impossible only a few days ago, who was to say what else she could do?

Bridget laughed soundlessly at herself. *Yes,* she thought, pausing in front of one of the copy desks, lifting her lamp to look at the text inside the open book, all spelled out in indigo, scarlet, black and gold. *I am going to lay my hand on this book and say reveal to me your secrets!*

But just as she was about to laugh again, the ink on the page shifted, flowing as if suddenly liquid and re-forming into new words.

You could.

Astonishment loosened Bridget's grasp of the lamp and it crashed to the floor, the glass chimney shattered against the stone and fragrant oil poured from the reservoir. The flame from the wick tasted the spreading pool of oil and at once began to lap it up hungrily, spreading itself out to encompass the whole puddle. Bridget gasped and threw down her shawl, stamping on it to try to smother the greedy flames and at the same time looking wildly around for something better but seeing only all the wood and paper surrounding her.

But then, a painfully icy breeze blew past her ankles. Bridget gasped again and the fire winked out.

Bridget stared at the mess of soaked shawl, oil and broken glass.

It had grown colder, so cold that all the hairs on the back of her neck had risen. The silence too had deepened, muffling even her own harsh breathing. She stared at the shawl, darkened with oil that had not burned. She stared at the broken glass and the way the moonlight glinted on the jagged edges. She did not want to look up. She did not want to see what else was in the room with her.

But even as that thought flickered through her mind, a sensation of gentle sorrow filled her. Its touch was familiar. She had felt it before in the Land of Death and Spirit, when she had seen the woman in the black dress with her hair pulled away from her face. When she had seen . . .

Momma.

Trembling, Bridget lifted her eyes. Momma stood beside the copy desk. Her presence caused no interruption in the silver flow of the moonlight and she left no shadow on the floor, nor did any of the room's shadows lie against her skin.

Bridget couldn't breathe. She couldn't speak. It was Momma, as she had seen her in the mirror, as she had seen her in the Land of Death and Spirit, as she had seen her every day of her life in Poppa's photograph. The apparition before Bridget now was all those images, apart and together, shifting from one to the other, like a reflection in running water and blurred moonlight.

Momma, Bridget tried to say, but no sound came from her mouth. *Momma.*

In answer, Momma turned toward the book on the copy desk. The ink curdled on the page and formed itself into yet more new words.

Bridget, my dear.

"How?" Bridget managed to get that one word out. "How . . . ?"

Momma smiled gently. Bridget felt the expression rather than saw it. She couldn't focus clearly on Momma's face. It shifted too rapidly to leave more than an impression against her mind. It was like looking at a distant memory.

This is the time of change, said the new words that formed in the book. *When all things are in flux between the light and the dark, life and death. This is the time when we may move lightly from world to world, especially in answer to the calls of blood or need.*

Bridget swallowed. "Need?"

I have special permission to be here. The guardians of this place have need.

"I . . ." Bridget's mind was awhirl. Her thoughts refused to be composed and skittered from her grasp. She groped for the stool in front of the desk and sat, tucking her feet onto the rail, and trying to put all the questions battering against the inside of her head into some kind of order.

"Why won't you speak to me?" was the first that came to her. It sounded plaintive, like a little girl wanting to know why sweets were being withheld.

It made Momma cock her head and smile fondly, but Bridget felt pride at the same time. The words in the book changed again.

Your sight is your gift, my dear. Without the aid of some magic, it is through that alone I may reach you.

"But I do hear a voice, or I did. Someone's calling for help."

The ink pooled on the page and spread out again. This time, instead of words, it left a drawing behind. The bird of flame in the golden cage, its wings arching high over its head, its neck stretched out long and thin and its white beak open. Bridget knew at once that the bird did not sing. It screamed against its confinement, pouring out its rage and hoping against hope that rage alone would burst apart the bars.

"The dowager's Phoenix." Bridget touched the page hesitantly, as if she thought the drawing alone would burn her. The page was cool and dry.

Ink swallowed up the drawing and re-formed into fresh words without her fingers feeling any trace of dampness.

Medeoan's captive. With my help, God forgive me, but it was the only thing we could do then.

"Do you know where it is?"

No. Many rooms here are dark to me.

Despite everything, Bridget laughed. "Which makes one wonder what the point of being a ghost is."

Momma laughed too, soundlessly, but Bridget saw her shoulders shake with mirth. *Had I blood ties to the family of the house I would know more*, said the book for her when she grew serious again. *But the only tie here is between you and me.*

Which led to the next question. The important question. Bridget could not bring the words out, no matter how she longed to, but she couldn't stay silent either. "Is . . . Poppa with you?" she asked, hoping her meaning would be understood.

Sorrow poured over Bridget, thickening the air around her until she could scarcely breathe. *No. Everett is bound to the shores of the world where he died.*

"But you're not?" The question slipped out before Bridget could stop it. *Take it back,* her own mind told her instantly. *Don't do this. You can keep believing. You don't want to know.*

The words softened and blurred, turning into a pen-and-ink sketch that Bridget recognized at once. It showed the small foursquare house in Eastbay that had been home before the lighthouse opened. Before Poppa had taken the job that had become his calling. It was a quiet night in that drawing, for the lake was gentle by the shore.

A man stood on the water, looking up at the house. Tears glistened in his eyes.

Another sketch formed and yet another beside it. Perhaps they moved themselves, perhaps it was only Bridget's fancy, but she saw it all. She saw the master bedroom and Momma in the bed, her knees raised. She saw Mrs. Henderson at the foot of the bed, her hands red with blood and her face grave. Poppa paced in the hallway outside, his face turned toward the window as if he knew something watched the house, but Poppa could not see the man who stood on the water and cried for the pain inside the house.

A baby was laid on Momma's breast. The baby was slick with birth and Momma's face was slick with sweat. Poppa lifted the baby gently, cradling it in its clean blankets, and Momma's face turned toward the window. She knew there was someone out there too, and

Bridget knew that if Momma had been able to rise and walk to the window she would have seen him out there, because it was for her he yearned.

Hours, days passed and the fever did not fade. The doctor came, and the doctor went, and the man stayed outside, balanced on the waves, crying silent tears. Inside Momma fought her illness, her exhaustion and her sorrow. Poppa stayed beside the bed, laying the baby, laying Bridget, beside her so Momma would know what there was to live for here. But the illness was too much, and Momma begged Everett Lederle to care for her child, and she died.

In that silence of death, as Ingrid Loftfield's body lay still on its bed, Ingrid Loftfield also rose. She walked down to the lakeshore and she embraced the man who waited to take her away, and Everett Lederle looked out the window from the keeper's quarters, and Bridget knew Poppa saw that lovers' meeting.

Bridget closed her eyes. "Take it away. I don't want to see this."

Silence. Of course, there was only silence. Momma could not speak to her. Perhaps Momma had no answers to give. Perhaps she knew there was no way to answer for what she had done.

"You left him. You left me," said Bridget, her hands knotting into fists in her lap.

Still, there was only silence, but Bridget felt something shift outside her, and reluctantly she opened her eyes to see the new words written in the book.

I died, Bridget. I did not want to.

Which was the truth. She had seen it in the pictures. But it was not enough. How could it ever be enough? The truth left Poppa alone in the cold with only the light and the lake, and a broken heart. "No . . . you . . . he . . . he loved you."

I know. Momma's ghost was calm as the words came to Bridget. She felt no touch of the previous sorrow and that calm only fanned Bridget's anger. It was an old anger, denied through the years as much as she could because to be angry at Momma's memory meant she had believed what the gossips and the snips in Bayfield and Eastbay said, and she could not.

But she did.

Bridget lashed out with her hand, seeking to grab hold of something, a wrist, a sleeve, something that would get a reaction, break the calm. She touched only cold without even the memory of living warmth. "Why did you marry him!"

Sorrow drifted from Momma's ghost. Sorrow at Bridget's pain, sorrow at the loss of years, but like everything else about the ghost it was cold and Bridget shrank from it even as she read the new words.

I married him because he loved me. Because I was pregnant and I wanted my child born legitimate in a house where it would be cared for.

"You didn't love him at all, did you?" Bridget felt a grim satisfaction at speaking the words aloud. There had been nights when she lay alone in her bed and she thought them, almost sick to death at the disloyalty in those thoughts, and yet knowing in her young heart that there was truth in them. If Momma had loved Poppa, if Bridget really was a Lederle and not just a Loftfield, Momma would not have left. There would not be these rumors to dog their footsteps and keep him out at the light alone.

New words. Nothing but words and cold regret. *I was grateful to him. I knew him to be kind and strong. I knew he would love you.*

"But you didn't love him." Bridget gripped the edge of the enchanted page. She wanted to tear it to bits and scatter it across the floor. She wanted to make Momma's ghost go away. She wanted to make her stay and acknowledge the truths that Bridget had feared all her life. She wanted her to be warm, and loving, and to deny those same truths. "You loved this Avanasy person."

Yes.

It was too cold. Bridget couldn't breathe. Cold wrung tears from her eyes, and cold made her throat and lungs struggle for air. "Poppa loved you. All his life. He never married again."

I know.

One tear trickled out of the corner of Bridget's eye, leaving yet more cold to seep into her skin. "Why did you leave me there?" That was the question, the one that had haunted her since Sakra had recognized Momma's name. If here was where Momma was honored, if here was where Momma loved, why had she taken Bridget to Sand Island, where she was only a bastard and freak?

Momma's ghost moved forward. Shadows and moonlight both parted to let her pass. She lifted her hands as if to press against a window that separated her from her daughter. For one stark moment Bridget saw Momma's face clearly. Anger, old anger as hot and vital as any Bridget felt, twisted Momma's features. It beat against the wall of cold Bridget had surrounded herself with. Bridget's cold, not Momma's cold. Anger. Anger at circumstance, at her willingness to leave Isavalta when she should have stayed beside the man she loved and taken her chances, anger at the choice she had made that had wounded her daughter so. Anger at her helplessness now to reach Bridget and make her understand. Momma was mute and she wanted to shout, but all she had were words on page.

I could do nothing else. Avanasy made me promise to return home because there was no guarantee we would win the war and cage the Firebird. Then he died, and my only thought was to see you safely born. Then you were a babe in arms, and even if I had the strength, I could not have taken you back. Carrying a child through the Silent Lands is dangerous. They attract . . . powers. They can be possessed and ridden unknowingly.

I meant to take you to Isavalta when you were grown. I thought I would be there to find a way.

It was too much. The anger, the regret, and the words assaulted all Bridget's understanding of her birth and her life. "What if I hadn't wanted to leave Poppa?"

The ghost dropped her hands to her side, her capacity for livid anger seemingly spent. At the same time, Bridget felt the cold ebb. *At least you would have had a choice. That was all I wanted for you.*

As she read those words, Bridget felt the cold bleed away from around her, leaving only the normal chill of winter. It was that cold which separated her from this vision of her mother. Bridget felt suddenly abandoned. She wanted that cold, that separation back again.

Why is it like this? All my life all I ever wanted was Momma back, and here she is, and now I only want her to go.

Answers. There had to be answers, to all the questions that she had not been able to ask over the years and all the ones that rose up fresh from Momma's being here with her now. Whether those answers would bring the cold back, or take it away forever, it didn't matter. What mattered was that she finally had her answers. "Why didn't I ever see you at the lighthouse?"

No reply. The words in the book remained perfectly still, and the ghost bowed her head.

"It was because you went with him, wasn't it?" The cold gathered again, thick and comfortable like a blanket of snow around old brick walls. "You had to choose, and you chose to be with him."

No new reply formed in the book. There was only the still presence of the ghost and all of Bridget's cold.

"You didn't even want to be around us as a ghost!" she cried at last, as if it would lock the door between them and leave her with her own certainties.

But more pictures filled the white pages. The man, Avanasy, walking at Momma's side, talking to her, making her laugh. Momma at his bedside where he lay weak and ill. The two of them working a tiny sloop together, Avanasy handling the ropes and Momma at the tiller, her teeth bared in fierce concentration and the wild joy that comes of defiance of wind and water.

Momma lying still on the ground, her eyes closed in a sleep that was far too close to death, and Avanasy on his knees beside her, his head bowed while he wept.

"He didn't have to take you away from us," Bridget whispered, unable to tear her gaze away from the pictures. The cold around her wavered, but still she did not want to let it go. "He could have come to you."

The paper rustled as the images blended back into words.

There are limits, Bridget, even for the dead. Places we may not go, places we may be prevented from going. The ties between the living are strong, Bridget, stronger than any ties to the dead, and the ties of love, gratitude and obligation are stronger than the ties of blood. You did not know Avanasy to love him, and you did love Everett Lederle. Avanasy could not break the bounds of worlds to come to you.

She could not stay here. She would not. But even so, Bridget felt a thread of warmth through the wall of her cold. She longed for the embrace of that warmth and yet at the same time feared the love and forgiveness that would have to come with it. She would have to accept too much to accept that love.

Bridget wiped at her eyes. "Yes, well," she said, getting to her feet. "As educational as this has been, I should probably get back before Richikha gets in trouble for sleeping on the job."

She did not mean to look back at the book, but the words caught her eye all the same.

Bridget, I came to you because you wished to know the truth. The truth is you are my daughter, and Avanasy's, and daughter of all the magic our blood had to give you. You are Everett Lederle's daughter. You are the daughter of Sand Island, Lake Superior, and your second sight. You are the daughter of two worlds. You have served long in one, and now must serve in the other.

"Must?" Bridget felt her spine stiffen and savored the familiarity of the sensation.

The words in the book changed before she could finish her reply.

You already know Kalami is a liar, daughter. He'll use you if he can, kill you when he must. Beware of him. Keep your eyes open to all his works. You may trust even poor, broken Medeoan before you trust Kalami.

Bridget frowned, feeling a new cold that had nothing to do with old anger or fear. "But they're the ones who brought me here. If I'm not to . . ."

Momma lifted her head, and Bridget felt the ghost's attention draw away from her and focus toward the library doors.

"What is it?" asked Bridget, her gaze flickering from the ghost to the book.

Kalami wakes. Tell Peshek he has done right.

She vanished. Bridget started forward so suddenly that the corner of her skirt caught the book, dislodging it from the table and sending it crashing to the floor. A rush of warmth filled the air where Momma had stood, but Bridget felt no relief. Bridget wanted to drop to her knees beside the fallen book and rifle its heavy pages for some sign of Momma's presence. Just in time, she remembered the broken glass and instead snatched the book up before the oil could soak its leather bindings.

"Are you hurt, mistress?" A man's voice accompanied the sound of footfalls.

Bridget whirled around. Sakra walked through the faint light. The moon must have gone down. The illumination from the stars was all that remained.

"No, I'm fine." Bridget bit her tongue. She had not meant to answer him, but could not stop herself. Evidently, the enchantment he had placed on her was still in good working order.

Sakra saw the expression on her face. "I'm sorry," he said. "It was not my intent to force an answer from you, not now, at any rate."

His face was frank and open, and Bridget suddenly felt enormously tired. She turned away, laying the book back down on the copy table. "What has changed, sir?"

"You saved my life when there was neither need nor reason for you to do so."

"Ah." Bridget pressed her hands against the leather. A dark stain did indeed discolor the binding. She hoped she had not ruined anything irreplaceable. It seemed so much easier to concentrate on this small thing than on the enormity of what had just happened to her. "Perhaps I just saved your life to trick you. Perhaps I meant to worm my way into your confidence so that I could spy on you."

He shook his head. "No."

All her anger, frustration and fear overflowed at this and what little patience Bridget still had snapped under the pressure of it.

"Why not?" She rounded on him. "Because I'm too much of a fool? Because I'm an ignorant little girl to be paraded around like a puppet by whoever can get hold of my strings?"

"Because a ghost stood here and had some lengthy speech with you." Sakra's face and voice both remained mild. "No ghost of evil intent to the anointed emperor and empress could enter this house, even at this time. It would not be permitted."

He'd been watching her. The realization burned through Bridget's blood. He'd been there the whole time and he'd seen. He'd seen all Momma's words, seen the pictures, seen what she was. "You are a lying sneaking spy!" she cried.

"Yes." Sakra spread his hands, a gesture of disarmament she was in no humor to see. He'd spied on her. He knew. He knew she was a bastard abandoned by her mother for a stranger. He knew Everett Lederle had never been loved by his wife. He had no right knowing such things. Kalami had no right to bring her here to find out such things.

"You are all lying sneaks!" She wanted Kalami here. He had tricked her into coming to this place. She wanted his throat between her hands. She'd wring his neck like a chicken for putting her through this.

"Yes," was all Sakra said.

Her cheeks were wet. More tears, too many tears. How could she let herself cry in front of this man? She dashed them angrily away. "Why should I even stand here listening to you?"

Incredibly, the corner of Sakra's mouth curled up into a smile and he shrugged. "Because I have admitted I am a lying sneak, and Kalami has only compounded his lies."

Bridget laughed. She couldn't help it. It was all so ridiculous. Ridiculous. Her gasps turned to whoops as she tried to catch her breath and failed. What did she have here? A choice between liars, fathers and worlds. Insane. Insane.

More tears leaked from the corners of her eyes, and Bridget, her whoops fading back to choking laughs, could not have said if they were for mirth or sorrow.

"You may want this, mistress."

Bridget cracked her eyes open. Sakra held out a handkerchief. Such a small, familiar, gentlemanly gesture, ridiculous a world away from home, it almost set Bridget off again, but she controlled herself.

She put the book down and accepted the square of cambric and dabbed her eyes.

"Did you follow me?" she asked, the heat of her anger burned out of her, at least for the moment.

"Not this time. I intended to meet someone quite different here." Sakra glanced toward the doors. "I am early, and he may not have found the roads easily passable."

"Then perhaps I should go." Bridget reached down and delicately picked her shawl out of the oil and glass. It was only loaned to her. She did not feel she could leave it here to be swept up as trash by whoever was charged with cleaning this room. She shook it to let the few pieces of glass that had become caught in the wool clink to the floor.

"You may wish to stay," said Sakra. "This man knew your father."

Bridget did not look up at him. She concentrated on bundling up the shawl such that she could carry it by the clean corners. "I do not care."

"And your mother."

Momma, who was here for so short a time, who tried so hard to reach through Bridget's cold to find Bridget's heart. Momma, who had not wanted to leave her, and did. Left her to face two worlds alone.

Yet who came back, and tried to explain, tried to warn her.

She pulled her shoulders back and fixed her gaze on the doors so she could still avoid looking at the man. "I think I have had quite enough of my mother for one night, thank you." She started forward, determined to leave here as quickly as possible.

"Mistress Bridget, please stay," Sakra called after her.

"Why?"

"Because there are things which will be said that I very much desire you should hear," he said. "Because Lord Master Peshek is an aging man, haunted by doubts, and seeing you will help put him at his ease." Sakra stopped, and began again. "Because I wish you to know that, despite all, I am your friend, and if you need it, I will help you through these days however I can."

Bridget swallowed against the tightness that seized her throat.

Carefully, she laid the shawl down on the stool and she stared at him. Slowly, it dawned on her what was missing. When she looked at Sakra, both her eyes saw the same thing. There was no reflection, no distortion, nothing hidden to be seen only by her left eye. She walked slowly forward, peering closely at him, but all she saw was the man before her, with his autumn brown eyes and his patient face. She stood close enough to touch him now, and she still saw only honesty in his eyes. How long had it been, oh God, how many years, since someone had offered her so much? Honesty and friendship, unmixed with pity. Had she ever been given so precious a gift in her whole life?

"I beg your pardon, master, mistress."

Bridget and Sakra froze like a pair of guilty schoolchildren caught behind the barn. Her eyes blurred by tears and too many emotions, Bridget could not clearly see the figure that stood in the doorway, but she had an impression of a lean man.

"Lord Master." Sakra reverenced. The man returned the gesture before he came forward. The starlight was thinning, but Bridget, wiping her eyes, could now see he was indeed a lean man and of sober demeanor. Once he had been handsome, she thought, but care had etched too many lines on his face and drawn down his cheeks into hollows.

"Thank you for coming, Lord Master Peshek," said Sakra.

"You said you had words of importance for me." Lord Master Peshek did not take his gaze off Bridget. "I beg your pardon, mistress, do I—"

Sakra did not let him finish the question. "Lord Master Peshek Pachalkasyn Ursulvin, this is Bridget Loftfield Lederle Avanasidoch Finoravosh."

The man staggered as if struck. He gripped the corner of the nearest desk and even in the dim light, Bridget saw his knuckles turn white.

Sakra turned to her, and she felt him measuring her with his gaze, waiting for her reaction. He was stretched tight, she could now tell. Tension hummed from him. "Bridget, this is Lord Master Peshek, of whom I spoke."

At least this had a familiar social formula. She remembered to reverence rather than simply bob a curtsy. "How do you do, sir?"

"By my bones," Peshek breathed. "We never knew. We never knew if she had made it safe across . . ." He reverenced, but he was still shaking. "You are most welcome to me, Mistress Bridget."

"Thank you."

Peshek seemed to decide discretion was the better part of valor, and he sat down in the nearest chair. He wiped one large hand across his face, and looked up at Bridget again, as if he could not believe what he saw. His gaze was easy to bear, however. It was soft, and there was kindness in it along with the wonder. "How is it you come to be here now of all times? Was it . . ."

"Kalami brought her," said Sakra, walking around to the other side of the table.

"Kalami?" Peshek's eye narrowed. "Then how is she here with you?"

Bridget's mouth quirked up and she smoothed her skirt down needlessly. "It seems Valin Kalami left out a few pertinent facts when he informed me of the situation here."

She looked up again to see a delighted smile break out on Peshek's face. It lit his entire face, and Bridget saw she had been right. Once, this had been an exceedingly handsome man. "You have the very trick of your mother's speech."

"I never knew my mother. She died when I was born."

At those words, Peshek covered his eyes briefly, and then kissed the knuckle of his index finger. It reminded Bridget of a Catholic crossing themselves at the mention of death. "I feared it was so," Peshek said. "She would never have stayed away otherwise. Or so I believed." He shook his head. "I'm sorry."

"Thank you," said Bridget, to stop any other words from coming out, because for one awful instant she wanted to say, *I'm not.* "She . . . I . . ." Bridget puffed out her cheeks. Ridiculous. Say it. Here, she could say anything and be believed. "I have been visited by her shade, Lord Master Peshek. She said to tell you that you were doing the right thing."

Peshek closed his eyes, letting out a long, slow breath. "Thank you, mistress," he said. "I was losing my clearness of purpose."

"I understand fully, believe me." *Not that I know what I'm talking about.* She glanced at Sakra. Lord Master Peshek had come here to meet Ananda's chief advisor. She could at the very least guess what was happening.

Sakra leaned forward, planting both hands on the table. "You must know, Lord Master, that Oulo has betrayed you. The dowager has been told that you have joined Hraban in his purpose."

Bridget wondered at him saying this in front of her. But then, he had wanted her to stay, wanted her to see. She realized she could go straight to Kalami with what she saw and give further evidence of what was most certainly treason. She could have gone as soon as Sakra had told her who he was meeting, and Sakra surely knew that.

Sakra had given her power, not only over him, but over his allies.

While all this flitted through Bridget's mind, the color drained from Peshek's cheeks. All the light his smile had provided faded as well, leaving only the face of a tired old man behind.

"Well," he said, running one hand through his grey hair. "I should have known this coming from Oban's son. His father was many things, but a model of courage was not one of them." He shook his head slowly, lowering his hand back to lay it on the table. Bridget saw it tremble. "I suppose Hraban felt he could not be too choosy. The Dowager Medeoan is still both loved and feared." His face took on a shrewd expression. "What do you and your mistress mean to do about this treachery?"

"It has already been done. Oulo is dead."

At those words, Peshek went very still. Bridget had the uncanny feeling that the old man was suddenly assessing the objects in the room for how they might be used as weapons.

"You can leave now, Lord Master," said Sakra seriously, but Bridget noted how closely he watched Peshek as he spoke. "Word has been sent to Lord Master Hraban to ready his men. By the end of the holy days, one way or another, we shall have an end to Medeoan's reign."

"A palace coup in the dead of winter?" Peshek's whole face changed. A calculating look came into his eye and his gaze went from Sakra to the tabletop. Bridget wondered what he saw there. Perhaps it was a map. If Peshek had known her . . . parents, he might have been a soldier in that long-ago war.

"There are worse plans," Peshek acknowledged. He drummed his fingers against the table for a moment. "But you, and your mistress, should know, *Agnidh* Sakra, it will not hold. Winter will slow down the news and the reaction to it, but spring must come. When it does, we'll have the oblasts pulling in six different directions, and Hung-Tse poised to fall on whatever's left of the empire, and what will Ananda do about all that?" He cocked his head and his eye glittered shrewdly at Sakra. "Call on her father for help? That will go down beautifully. Especially in the south."

Sakra again smiled his small smile. To her surprise, Bridget found herself liking the expression. It spoke of a man who understood the absurdity as well as the deadly seriousness of his position. "With that attitude, Lord Master Peshek, one wonders why you agreed to lend your support to this enterprise at all."

"Yes, one does," Peshek answered dryly. He wiped his palm across the table, erasing whatever he had seen there. "I think I did it because I hoped word would reach Medeoan," he said to his hand. "I think I hoped . . ." Instead of finishing the sentence, he just shook his head again.

But apparently Sakra would not leave Peshek in peace any more than he would leave Bridget. "What did you hope?"

"I hoped I would open her eyes to the danger she has brought on herself, and on Isavalta." He looked over to the windows. The black sky was turning grey in the east. Dawn, or almost dawn. Soon, the palace would begin to stir. The lowest of the servants were probably awake already. Warning bells tolled low in Bridget's mind. Kalami was already awake. Perhaps he had already checked on her and found her gone. If he searched for her and found her here . . . she had no idea what would happen, or whether he could still be led to believe in her ignorance.

"Well, one thing we do know, Mistress Bridget," Peshek said to her, speaking more quickly and more sharply than he had yet. He also knew what the coming dawn meant. "Whatever is said here, you must not be seen with *Agnidh* Sakra. If Medeoan knew you conspired with her enemies . . ." He stopped and rubbed his hands together. "It would not go well, for she is not herself these days."

Here then was an opportunity for more answers. "Kalami told me she was senile," said Bridget.

The statement startled Peshek. He frowned, both anger and confusion showing plainly on his face. "Why would Kalami do that?"

"Because Kalami is conspiring with Hung-Tse to break the empire apart," Sakra told him quietly.

"What?" The word pulled Peshek to his feet.

Sakra met Peshek's gaze without hesitation, and as he spoke, Bridget felt the lord master grow more and more still. "It's true, and part of what I meant to tell you. Kalami is a Tuukosov partisan. His daughter is a hostage guest at the Heart of the World. He means to help Hung-Tse invade Isavalta with the condition that Tuukos be left an independent land again."

Peshek's hands folded in on themselves slowly to become fists. He turned away from Bridget and Sakra as if he could not even see them anymore, and Bridget caught a glimpse of the fury raging inside him. He stalked to the windows, seizing a casement in each hand. The glass rattled in its frame and Bridget thought he might tear the window free.

But this action left no feeling in her. Her feelings were all snatched up in the realization of how deeply Kalami had lied. He had told her he brought her here for the dowager, then told her the dowager was senile, told her he served the dowager, but he betrayed Isavalta. Told her that he held no grudge against Isavalta, yet wanted to bring it down.

And somehow he was going to use her to do it.

There were not enough curses in all the world to damp down the anger Bridget felt rush through her mind.

Gradually, Peshek regained control of himself and wiped his palms on his kaftan. "I'd kill him with my bare hands if I thought it would do any good."

"You'd have to get there before me," whispered Bridget.

Both men stared at her, and only then did Bridget realize she had spoken aloud. "Forgive me," she said.

"There is no need, mistress," said Sakra, and for some unaccountable reason, Bridget felt that her death wish for Kalami had drained the tension from her. Sakra returned to the other man. "If, Lord Master Peshek, you still had the dowager's trust, you could stop Kalami now."

"I still might, Sakra." Peshek spoke to the windows, a faraway look in his aging eyes. "She has not arrested me yet. She probably means to do it quietly after our breakfast this morning. It may be that I can convince her to think again."

"But you said she is not well—" began Bridget.

"Medeoan and I have a long past." Peshek cut her off. "It may stand us in good stead now. Failing that . . ." He tapped his index finger once against one diamond pane before turning on his heel to face Sakra again. "Failing that, it will be for you to do whatever you can. I ask . . ." He hesitated.

"What?" prompted Sakra gently.

As he struggled to find his words, Bridget remembered that it was supposedly a Hastinapuran who had endangered Isavalta before. If that was true, then Lord Master Peshek now had to ask a favor of one who still might turn out to be an enemy of his country. "I ask you to remember what she once was, *Agnidh*," he said last. "What she did for the sake of her realm. Not with a whole heart, perhaps. Not without many regrets since, but she saved us, every last one of us. If your mistress shows any turning toward vengeance, I pray you . . ."

Sakra bowed from the waist, covering his eyes with his palms. "I hear your words, Lord Master, with the greatest attention and care."

"Thank you, *Agnidh*. Well." Peshek straightened his shoulders. "I am an old man who has just had much bad news. I think I will fall back on my privileges and retire for an hour or so before breakfast." He reverenced toward Bridget. "I hope we will be allowed to speak again, mistress."

Bridget inclined her head in return. "I hope so too, sir. I think . . . that is . . ." Bridget bit her lip briefly and then made her own decision. "I'd like to ask you some questions about . . . Ingrid and Avanasy."

He did not miss her use of their names, but he let it pass. "I will be pleased to answer all such questions. Good morning."

He turned then and retreated toward the doors, his back straight and his stride showing no signs of fatigue. He opened the door a crack, and froze.

"Kalami," he said.

Chapter Thirteen

"Bridget, run, that way," ordered Sakra, stabbing his finger toward the rear of the library.

Bridget did not have to be told twice. She hiked up her skirts and ran in the direction he pointed. In a moment, she saw why she had been so directed. Another door, less grand than the first, waited in the breach between two bookcases. Bridget dodged through it, closing it fast behind her. There was a small latch, too; she wondered about locking it, but no, Sakra or Peshek might need this exit.

Bridget turned, and found herself nose to nose with an old bear of a man, his white beard spilling across the front of his plain white kaftan. He looked like Santa Claus might just before he'd put on his red coat and hat.

"Good morning, daughter," the Santa Claus said mildly. "Come to greet the dawn of this holy day?"

Bridget sucked in a deep breath, struggling to regain her composure. "Yes, sir," she said, smoothing down her skirts. "I woke early."

Santa Claus nodded his approval. "A fine habit, one that leads to other virtues. Come through then, and say your greetings."

He led Bridget down a short, plastered, plain hall that opened into a great round chamber with a high dome for a ceiling. It was a church. It could be nothing else. The dome had been painted to depict the rising dawn in a cloud-filled sky. To waist height, frescoes showed landscapes—woods, mountains and plains. Between the two had been painted gilt-framed portraits of men and women in various attitudes, every last one of them crowned. The grandeur of the place was somewhat spoiled by stacks of evergreen and holly boughs and tightly lidded baskets. The smells of resin and straw filled the room.

The center of the room was taken up by two statues, both of them painted with vivid color and robed in real clothing. One, an auburn-haired man, held a pike raised in both hands, his eyes cast heavenward. The other, a golden-haired woman, spread her hands as if in welcome. One hand held a golden cup, the other held a dagger.

Santa Claus walked up to the statue and kissed the hem of the male's garment, and then the female's. He stood aside, obviously waiting for Bridget to do the same. Bridget, however, found she could not move. She did not feel any inherent sacrilege, but she did not know who these two were, or what they represented, and that made her uneasy.

"Forgive me, sir," she said. "I mean no disrespect. I come from a great distance and I am unfamiliar with the customs and practices of Isavalta."

Santa Claus's eyebrows rose. "Indeed? So far you do not recognize Vyshko and Vyshemir?"

Bridget stared up at the pair on the pedestal. It was impossible to say what the statues were made of. They had been lovingly painted with perfect flesh tones. Their blue eyes shone with fierce intelligence. They were not kind, these two. They were determined, and they were strong, but they were not kind.

"So far, sir," Bridget said, suddenly finding it much easier to look at Santa Claus, "that I do not even know your proper title or how I should be addressing you."

The man gave out a laugh, a bark of surprise and amusement. "Well, we are told that each of us is always student and teacher. I shall be delighted to hear of this far land. But if you'll permit, first I shall teach you. My name is Bakhar Iakshimisyn Rostaviskvin and it is my honor to bear the title of Keeper of the Emperor's God House." He reverenced.

Bridget returned the gesture. "I am Bridget Loftfield Lederle." She decided not to add the rest of the designation Sakra had trotted out for her. In part because she was not sure she could remember it all, in part because she wanted time to think about all that name meant in private before she was forced again to acknowledge it in public. "And once, I also had the job of keeper, though it was a lighthouse as opposed to a god house." Her eyes swept the art and gold that adorned the curving walls. "And my quarters were none so grand."

Keeper Bakhar followed her gaze. "Yes. It is often I have wished for a simpler house as well. I believe it would suit my holy master and mistress better." His voice was heavy as he spoke, and Bridget had the distinct feeling he was not talking about the gilding. "I hope you'll do me the favor of telling me of this lighthouse for which you were keeper."

"I should be pleased to, sir." With a shock, Bridget realized she truly would. So much that was strange had happened so quickly that thoughts of Sand Island seemed comfortable and safe. "But perhaps you should first tell me of your holy master and mistress," she said quickly, realizing she had already forgotten their names. "So that I do not make an inadvertent error in courtesy or deportment." This place was important. No people would put so much work into a church if there was not a deep core of devotion in them. Even better, this man, the keeper, seemed genuinely friendly. Here might be a source of information as good as any history Richikha could have read out to her.

Keeper Bakhar gazed fondly up at the statues, reminding Bridget of Mr. Simons looking on the crucifix in his church. Whatever his beliefs, this man held them dear.

"In those days, Isavalta was only one city on the riverbanks," he said with the cadence of one reciting a set piece long memorized and much repeated. "And in the summer months the river gave them their freedom to hunt and fish and trade with the neighboring cities. Within the walls, all matters of law were decided by the great judge Vyshatan.

"It happened that summer that the river betrayed the city, allowing to come down its currents the invaders from Tuukos who laid siege to the city, causing great misery by penning all its people within its walls so that they could not reach their fields, nor even the riverbanks for fish. The people sought succor from their judge and went to him, begging that he take the title and crown of king and lead them in battle against the foe.

"But the judge saw the numbers of the Tuukosov, and he saw how they were mightily armed and how their siege towers grew, and he saw how nightly they drank blood and boasted that soon they would drink all the blood of Isavalta. His heart, which was not a warrior's, quailed within him and he told the people that if they made him king he would seek only peace because Isavalta could not prevail against such a host as waited outside its walls.

"The judge had two children who were twins and had just reached their adulthood. These were Vyshko and Vyshemir. They went to their father and reasoned with him long and hard to lead the people in battle. The walls would not hold forever, they said. The Tuukosov would not accept any peace that left one stone of Isavalta standing upon the next, nor yet the smallest child alive. Such were their songs in the darkness. But the judge turned his face away.

"Vyshko and Vyshemir then took counsel with each other. They saw it was true what their father said, that Isavalta, already so weakened, could not prevail against the Tuukosov. Not in open combat. After much consideration, they sent word to the chief of the Tuukosov asking if he would accept the greatest gift Isavalta could offer and leave in peace."

Bridget found her attention lingering on the pike and the knife. These were not symbols that promised peace.

"That gift was Vyshemir's hand in marriage," the keeper went on. "The chief agreed, and ceremony was held with much celebration and sacrifice. The Tuukosov then withdrew their boats, and to all eyes appeared to make preparations to leave. But that night, as the chief took Vyshemir carnally to wife, he boasted to her how he would continue his siege and lay waste to the city.

"Afraid to her soul, when the chief slept, Vyshemir rose and went onto the deck of the ship and looked out across her city. Although it was dark, she saw the figure of her twin brother standing on the walls, and across that distance they stood in perfect sympathy and understanding. In that moment, divinity came to them. Vyshemir returned to the chief and lifting his knife from his belt she stabbed him in the heart, and then did the same to herself so that their blood mingled together. As she died, she cast herself into the river. Vyshko saw the river turn red with his sister's blood and lifted his spear over the water, calling out to her in a mighty voice to reverse the treachery of the river. He called to the walls of Isavalta to lay claim to his bones that he might hold his city safe forever. With that cry, the walls took him as the river took Vyshemir.

"The river rose in a flood of water and blood, washing away the boats of the Tuukosov. It did not touch the city of Isavalta, which was cradled by Vyshko's bones. Once the Tuukosov had all been drowned, the river spread itself flat, turning into a salt sea to act forever as barrier and reminder between Tuukos and Isavalta."

I have special permission from the protectors of this place to be here, Momma had said. Did she mean these two? Did they truly oversee this place? Bridget felt the small hairs on the back of her neck rise and she felt suddenly she was being watched.

"And so you may see why there is some little animosity still between Tuukos and Isavalta, even though we submitted to the heirs of Vyshko and Vyshemir over a hundred years ago."

Bridget jumped. Kalami stood framed by a pair of gilded doors. Bridget swallowed and had to keep from shrinking back as the lord sorcerer strode up to the statues' red and black pedestal. Without hesitation he kissed the hems of both garments before straightening up to acknowledge Keeper Bakhar and Bridget.

"I must thank you, good keeper, for finding my lost charge and seeing that she received her proper devotional instruction."

If Keeper Bakhar caught the sarcasm behind Kalami's words, he did not let it ruffle his calm expression. "It was she who found me, being awake early, as is so commendable, and further being desirous to know more of the saviors of Eternal Isavalta." Despite being outwardly peaceable, Bridget heard steel in the keeper's voice now. Her mind flashed to her first day in Isavalta and seeing Kalami stand ready to strike a soldier over the carter who had been knocked into the snow.

"I know I should not be up and about," said Bridget to break the building cold between the two men. "I grew restless last night and I could not sit still. I'm sorry if I caused any trouble." It hurt her throat to speak the conciliatory words so smoothly. This man had lied to her from the beginning, had risked her life to bring her here, all for a lie. But she could not let him know what she knew. If he decided he truly could not trust her . . . Bridget did not even want to consider what might happen.

"I'm not surprised to hear it." Kalami turned from Keeper Bakhar. "There was a great deal of restlessness last night. If you're ready"—he paused to turn one eye toward the keeper—"and if I have the permission of the good keeper, I will return you to your rooms."

"Of course." Bridget reverenced to Keeper Bakhar. "Thank you very much for the lesson, sir."

"You are most welcome in this house at any time, mistress." It was impossible to miss the emphasis he placed on "you."

Indeed, Kalami seemed to want very much to remark on that emphasis, but evidently he thought the better of it. Instead, he took Bridget's elbow to steer her out the doors through which he had come in.

The doors led to an empty chamber that seemed to be all doors interspersed with mural-painted walls. Bridget recognized the library doors on her left. Another pair of doors leading to the courtyard stood in front of her. Kalami urged her, however, to the right, retracing the path she had taken in the night. She did not remember the painted walls, or any of the ornamentation, but the patterns on the floor looked familiar.

Kalami marched silently beside her, forcing her to hurry to keep up with him. Her throat constricted at the sight of his grim expression. *This is no time to keep yourself in ignorance, Bridget.* "Valin, what's wrong?"

"Nothing that could not be fixed if the empty heads which pretend to serve the throne would attend to their duty," he snapped. Then he pulled up short, closing his eyes for a moment.

"I'm sorry, Bridget," he said as he opened them. "We were attacked last night."

"Attacked?" Bridget's hand went automatically to her throat. "But I heard nothing."

"This was not a military attack, but a magical one," said Kalami grimly. "And while the defenses here are strong, doors were opened and I find myself today having to deal with consequences."

Help me. Bridget's mind brought back the whisper of the Firebird's voice. Which defenses were breached? Those around its cage? Or were there others? Did one of those breaches allow Momma to enter? If this was divine intervention, the gods had neglected to inform Kalami of the fact, which spoke well of the gods.

"It was the Vixen," said Kalami, as if reading her thoughts. "So you may understand if I am unnerved. She has shown undue interest in you."

"The Vixen?" Bridget repeated. She remembered the rank scent of foxes, green eyes and laughing jaws. She remembered sewing foxes into men's skins and the joy, the incomparable joy . . .

Her stomach turned over at that memory, even as her hands itched to try their skill again.

"Yes. We must get you back to your rooms, and you must promise me on the blood of your parents that you will not open another door until I come for you. Do you promise?"

The Vixen. She had been wandering blithely about the halls last night and the Vixen had been out there somewhere.

Or in here somewhere.

Bridget pressed her hand against her mouth, against the realization that she had much more to fear than Kalami in this place. "I promise," she said between her fingers. "Of course I promise."

"Good." Kalami nodded curtly. He strode forward again. "Let's get you back then. I have already had words with your woman . . ."

"Richikha?" *No. Leave her out of this.* Bridget hurried to catch up. "It wasn't her fault. I lied to get her to leave me alone."

Kalami was not looking at her. "It is her fault. She was your attendant."

The final room opened up into the lobby with its great doors on the left and granite stairs rising to the right. "You must take into account that I am unused to such attentions, Valin."

"Then you must become used to them!" he roared. Bridget stopped in her tracks, facing him squarely. Whatever danger might threaten, whatever he might be or do, she would not be shouted at and the stony look she gave him said so plainly.

Within a heartbeat, her right eye saw him subside, but her left eye saw him snarling still.

"Forgive me, Bridget," he said with a sigh that at least sounded genuine. "I am afraid for you."

And you still need me, or we would not be bothering with this game. Bridget decided this was a moment to change the subject, and give herself a chance to reassert herself in his graces. "And you did not care to hear the tale Keeper Bakhar was telling me."

Kalami's smile grew bitter, and Bridget saw it plainly with both eyes. "No. It is not my favorite piece of Isavaltan lore, I must admit."

Bridget gathered up her hems so she could climb the stairs beside him. "I imagine they tell a very different version of it where you come from."

"Not where Isavaltan ears can hear," murmured Kalami, as if afraid some such might be listening now. He glanced sideways at Bridget. "You sound as if you know of such things."

"A little." They topped the steep stairs and Bridget let out as long a sigh as her laces would permit. "When my . . ." *Say father. He does not know what you know yet.* ". . . father was a young man, he fought in a civil war that divided our country. He assured me that both sides told very different stories of how it started and who was to blame for which horror."

"Then you do understand." Kalami's smile was tight as he turned her down the broad balcony that narrowed into a tapestry-hung corridor. "I should not be bitter. Our conquest was our own fault and we pay for our weakness and mistakes. This is as it must be."

"I thought you said it was all over long ago," asked Bridget with as much innocence as she could muster.

"Yes, I did, didn't I?" Kalami sighed, stopping in front of a small, single door that Bridget decided must be hers. There was something new, however. Her left eye saw the faint glow that she had come to associate with magic shining around its threshold. "Perhaps that was wishful thinking on my part."

Or another lie. Bridget kept that thought silent.

"There is so much you don't know, Bridget," said Kalami softly. "Winter holds us in the witch's hand and traps us within stone walls. You cannot see the people of this land, the expanses of it, the treatment of it, the squabbles and compromises and petty feuds that tear at its heart." He waved a hand back over her shoulder. "You see only what goes on in this fanciful pile of masonry, and I fear it is not enough to let you understand the full complexity of this land and its history."

What goes on here has taught me plenty, thank you. "Well." Bridget fixed a smile on her face. "Come spring, you will have to show me, won't you?"

"Yes." Kalami answered her smile with one of his own, but only her right eye saw it. Her left saw his mouth spread wider, into a grin, a sly and triumphant grin. "I suppose I will," he said, and Bridget had to suppress a shudder.

Kalami kissed the first two fingers on his right hand and touched the lock below the doorknob. At this gesture, the door swung open to reveal Bridget's apartments. All three of her ladies had been clustered on their stools by the firepit and now they sprang to their feet. With a flurry of exclamations, they hustled her inside.

"No open doors, Bridget," said Kalami from the threshold. "No more solitary journeys."

"I promise," she said, and the words hung so heavily in the air, she regretted having spoken them. They had changed something, she could feel it, but she didn't know what it was.

Kalami, however, seemed satisfied. He reached out and pulled the door shut between them.

So, sir, you have me secure, thought Bridget toward the portal, as her ladies clucked and twittered, and herded her toward the bed. *What do you mean to do with me now?*

But no answer came.

Morning arrived cold, late and grey, and with it came the snow. Fat white flakes dropped randomly, each alone at first. Then, they began to cluster together with two or three linked into a white dollop. Then, the wind caught them and they began to swirl and that same wind seemed to pull them down eagerly from the clouds like a child mischievously reaching into a bag and throwing its contents out around the room to see the pretty patterns it made. The palace servants and serfs whose duties would not permit them to remain indoors strung lifelines from building to building as the air grew ever more opaque with snow. It hissed as it fell against the precious glass windows. It settled itself into every nook and cranny until they were full and smooth. It wrapped the palace in a great white blanket of cold.

Medeoan blessed the snow. The pervasive cold subdued the Firebird, weakening its voice. Today she would be able to think clearly, even if she never could again. Today she needed to be certain of herself and all that she did. Tomorrow, she would free Isavalta, and her son, from the predations of Ananda and Hastinapura.

But there was one unpleasant thing that had to be done first.

Her ladies laid the breakfast out in the dining room off her private chamber—bread, mutton and candied quince, pork and jelly, eggs, both pickled and deviled, small beer, and a delicate ewer of thick, sweet coffee for digestion afterward. She had ordered the curtains pulled back from the windows and the balcony doors so the cold might have free access to the room, but also ordered two braziers to flank the guest chair. She had no desire for Peshek to be uncomfortable.

Even as she thought his name, the page girl on duty outside threw open the door and knelt. "Lord Master Peshek Pachalkasyn Ursulvin," she announced, leaping to her feet and backing away.

"Grand Majesty." Medeoan felt her throat tighten convulsively as Peshek swept into the room to kneel at her feet.

"My Lord Master Peshek." She forced his name out with some semblance at least of good humor. "Let me give you welcome." She touched his left cheek, then his right, and then took both hands to raise him up. "Come, sit and eat with me."

Peshek accepted the chair between the braziers, and settled himself while the footmen laid out his napkin, filled his glasses and raised the covers on the dishes that he might inspect their contents. Medeoan found herself unusually hungry this morning and saw that a helping of each dish was laid on the plate before her. Peshek, on the other hand, took only some bread and a trifle of the pork.

"You have already dined this morning, Peshek?" she inquired, gesturing at his meager portion.

"No, Grand Majesty." Peshek's grin was as small as it was false. He scooped up some of the jelly with his bread. "It was the journey, I think. It left me with but little stomach."

"I am sorry to hear it. Shall I summon you a physic?" She lifted her hand, ready to gesture for one of the footmen.

Peshek lifted his own hand to stop her. "There is no need, Grand Majesty. It will pass."

"As must all things," murmured Medeoan, slicing into a pickled egg with more force than she had intended.

They sat in silence for a moment, each attending to the food, each working to delay what must come next.

But this cannot go on. Medeoan drank her small beer. *He has done what he has done, and now you must do as you must.* "It has been a long time, Peshek, since we were able to take counsel together."

"It has, Grand Majesty," he agreed, pushing aside his plate. He had not eaten half of what he had taken.

Medeoan pretended not to notice. "Indeed," she went on, examining the dregs of her beer. "I believe we have not spoken alone together since you left my court."

Peshek nodded with feigned thoughtfulness. "I think that must be the case."

"Why did you leave me, Peshek?"

He looked up, mute, surprised by the question.

How surprised can you possibly be? You knew what you did. Did you think me blind to this too? Medeoan set the mug down with a thump against the table cloth. "I did not ask you at the time, but I have wondered ever since," she said, keeping her voice pleasant. "Why did you leave me?"

He met her gaze, so guileless, so familiar that her heart contracted. A treacherous voice from the back of her own mind whispered to her to disregard all Oulo's words. "I felt I could best serve Your Grand Majesty by keeping your oblast in good order," he said.

"Of course." She ate another slice of pickled egg. "And in that, I cannot fault you. I read your letters with great attention, and have been most pleased with the expanding revenues which you have contributed to the treasury."

Peshek bowed his head, accepting the compliment with all appropriate humility. "Thank you, Grand Majesty."

Medeoan shoved her plate aside. Her appetite had also vanished. Ladies and footmen clustered around the table in an efficient swarm, removing plates and pouring coffee. "Now that we have this moment, is there any matter you wish to discuss?" said Medeoan as the swarm separated back to their waiting posts. "Any disquiet you have seen? Any troubles you predict?"

Peshek toyed with the delicate porcelain cup in front of him. "There will need to be repairs to the seawall in the harbor come spring," he said. "Lord Veresh has died without an heir, meaning there will be a question regarding the disposition of his lands, but that can be taken up in an official session." He sipped a little coffee. "The auguries show a good spring for planting and I think this harsh winter will do us some good in keeping down the summer fevers." He looked into the cup for a moment, as if hoping to see yet more favorable auguries there. "So, I would say all is well, Grand Majesty."

"Would you?" Medeoan raised her eyebrows. "Then there is nothing you wish to tell me, here, and now, while we are alone? You have no worries? You have had no meeting or conversation that has left you uneasy in your mind?"

Peshek's fair gaze met hers. Ah, when had he grown old? Wrinkles surrounded his bright blue eyes now, and his fair skin was spotted by sun and age. His hair had been iron grey for so many years, but now it was brightening to white. His cheeks had long since sagged into jowls. But his eyes, his eyes were clear, and as young as ever as he opened his old mouth and lied to her.

"No, Grand Majesty."

Medeoan sighed and looked away. "Oh, Peshek. I am so sorry."

"Majesty?"

"What did she use to reach you?" Medeoan looked at the brazier, at her cup, at the tablecloth. She could not look at his eyes. She did not want to see how well he lied with those clear, familiar eyes. "Did she tell you I am mad? That Isavalta is threatened by my weakness?"

"Majesty . . ."

Medeoan's throat closed. She drank some coffee and found only bitterness on her tongue despite all the sugar syrups that had been poured into it. "Did she perhaps tell you I was the cause of Mikkel's illness of spirit?"

"No one has told me that, Grand Majesty," replied Peshek softly. "Excepting yourself."

All strength left Medeoan's hand. The cup skittered from her fingers, splashing muddy liquid against the white cloth, teetering on the edge of the table, and falling to smash into fragments against the floor. The servants again sprang into action, silently clearing away the mess and bringing a fresh cup to be filled with fresh coffee. In a moment, except for the stain on the cloth, it was as if nothing had happened.

Medeoan watched all this without seeing any of it. She could only see Peshek sitting across the table from her where he had been so many times before. He had left her years ago, and she had not known how far he had gone. "What was it, Peshek? Why did you betray me?"

His eyes shone brightly in the light of the braziers flanking his chair. Tears? "If I truly had a choice, Grand Majesty, I would never betray you."

Medeoan slammed her hand against the tabletop. "And what removes this choice, Peshek?" She flung both arms out wide to encompass the whole world. "What enchantment or malady so overcomes your soul that you cannot choose between Hastinapura and Isavalta?"

Peshek stood. His jaw worked back and forth to chew over whatever emotion possessed him. One of her ladies hissed in wordless surprise. Peshek circled the table and slowly, without taking his gaze from her, he knelt at her feet. "Grand Majesty, you fear Hastinapura too much. They seek peace. Their overtures are genuine." His trembling hands reached out to seize the hem of her garment, the ultimate acknowledgment of imperial oversight. Medeoan gripped the arms of her chair. "You have been ill advised, Majesty, your fears preyed upon. It weakens your realm. If I could but persuade you to heed the Council of Lords rather than—"

Medeoan's hands, so recently healed, smarted from the bite of the wood, but she did not loosen her grip. "Rather than who, Peshek?"

Peshek let go of her hem but stayed on his knees. He lifted his eyes to look right at her, a liberty she would not have permitted anyone else. "Rather than the lord sorcerer, Grand Majesty," he said, and his voice did not tremble. "He is but one voice that speaks to its own purpose. I could show you letters and papers, produce good witnesses to—"

I will not hear this. Medeoan leapt to her feet and stalked away from his false acknowledgments of her rank. "The lord sorcerer has stood by me when none other would," she said to the wall. She would not turn and look at him with his background of fire from which she heard the laughter of the Phoenix. "He has done me greater service than any. He has spoken to me the truth when all else I hear is cowardice and flattery. When even you plot with Ananda to poison me, he stands firm of mind and purpose." Her fists opened and closed, looking for something to grasp, to rend and tear. "How dare you speak one word of the lord sorcerer?"

"Because I know what I say to be the truth."

Medeoan felt her shoulders droop. Despite the cold, the Firebird murmured in the back of her mind, its whispers feeding her despair like tinder.

But she lifted her head. With the truth at least she knew how to act. It was better so.

She turned to face him. The years of loyalty he had given her before this fall deserved that much. "I had meant for you to be at my side when I raised Avanasy's daughter to her birthright. I had meant that you would help welcome her, teach her of the empire, and her father, and her place in its history."

Peshek hung his head. "I am sorry, Grand Majesty. I see now how grievous have been my mistakes."

"It is too late for such regret, Lord Peshek."

"Yes, I know." Peshek climbed slowly to his feet like the old man he was. He dusted off his knees and pulled down the hem of his kaftan. Even now, he was proud of his appearance.

"You will be under guard in your rooms until the trial can be convened," Medeoan told him.

He reverenced, acknowledging her right to dispose of him as she would. "May I leave now, Grand Majesty? I find I have no stomach left."

Medeoan made a "come hither" gesture over Peshek's shoulder. One of the footmen opened the door, letting in Captain Chadek and four of the house guard. Without a word they surrounded him, one on each side, while Chadek bowed to Medeoan with a soldier's salute.

Medeoan acknowledged the gesture with only a hint of a nod. Her attention was all on Peshek, mostly hidden from her by axes and blue coats. "I asked you to marry me once."

"I remember," he answered so softly she could barely hear.

"But you would not."

"No."

She should not speak so. There were too many years. Even the Firebird strained for the answer. But she had to know. This she could not leave behind her in the silence. "Is that one of your mistakes, Peshek?"

Peshek straightened his shoulders and for a moment, Medeoan saw that man who had risked himself to buy the time she needed to save Isavalta. "No, Medeoan," he answered. "It was not."

Medeoan closed her eyes. She could not look on him anymore, not until she could write the word "traitor" across the place his name occupied in her heart. "Take Lord Master Peshek away," she said, without opening her eyes.

"Grand Majesty."

Medeoan did not move again until the sound of the marching boots and the closing door had ceased to ring in her ears.

Closer, whispered in the Firebird. *Closer still. You will set me free and together we will burn.*

Outside, the snow continued to fall. Bridget watched it from her room's one small, thick window. The courtyard's tiles had long since vanished under the powdery blanket. So had the first three steps leading up to the yard's main door. Fingers of snow reached up the walls toward the lowest window frames, and Bridget felt sure the drifts themselves would reach that high before the night was over. The white whirlwind that was a combination of blowing snow and falling snow kept her from even seeing the gate to the outside, no matter how hard she squinted.

Kalami could not have arranged a more effective trap if he had tried.

Bridget let the heavy velvet curtain fall in front of the window. *And to think I began this journey saying I would not regret any of it.*

Despite the fact that she had slept through several hours of the morning, the day had passed with agonizing slowness. Kalami had not even sent her a note. Bridget had considered seeking an audience with the empress, but could not think of what she'd say once she got there. She had no evidence of any wrongdoing on Kalami's part. He had, in fact, done nothing to her. He had only frightened her. As fantastic as this world was, she could not bring herself to try to convince anyone to rely on the word of the ghost she alone had seen.

And then there was her vision. What if Empress Ananda *had* arranged for those poisoned sheets to be placed on the emperor's bed?

Sakra had talked openly of killing someone who had betrayed the empress. What if she really had grown weary and desperate enough to do away with the emperor? Admittedly, to Bridget's mind it made no sense, but how much of the whole picture did she see? Bridget drummed her hands restlessly on the back of the carved chair. What if Ananda was a poisoner? If she was willing to kill for the expediencies of power, how far could Bridget trust her if Bridget placed herself in the empress's power? Because she could not trust Kalami did not mean she could trust his enemies.

Because I wish you to know that, despite all, I am your friend. Sakra's words echoed in Bridget's mind. He had meant them. Eyes and heart had both shown her that. He held out his hand to her, and she yearned to take it, but did she dare? He served the empress, and who knew what necessity might drive Ananda to do?

"Mistress?"

Richikha stood behind her. The young woman had managed to maintain her professional demeanor during the whole day when the other two ladies alternated between nervousness and disdain at Bridget's silence, distraction and turns at staring out the window.

"Your dress has arrived," Richikha went on.

Past her shoulder Bridget saw the heavy, sparkling costume on its frame flanked by its attendant seamstresses—the older with her hands folded in front of her, and the younger carrying piles of white fabric that Bridget assumed to be undergarments. They might have appeared out of thin air for all Bridget had heard them enter.

"You must begin the final fitting now, mistress, or nothing will be ready for the presentation," Richikha prompted when Bridget did not immediately move.

"Of course." She steeled herself mentally. She knew from dressing in what the Isavaltans considered everyday clothes that this was going to be a lengthy task. Still, she welcomed the distraction. Her mind had been running over the same paths for hours, which had accomplished nothing except to sink her spirits ever lower.

Gali and Iadviga rearranged the bed screens to shield the larger than usual number of people. While they did, Richikha expertly stripped off Bridget's outer dress and shifts until Bridget stood in her drawers and undershirt. She lifted her chin and tried not look awkward, remembering that this was simply how things were done here. The youngest seamstress laid the great pile of underclothing on the bed and picked up the first shift. As she did, the golden gleam of unexpected light caught Bridget's left eye. She turned to look at it more closely, and it skittered off to the corner of her field of vision as the girl walked forward with the shift.

"What is that?" Bridget asked.

"Mistress?" The older of the two seamstresses froze in the act of removing the golden coat from the dress stand.

"That." Bridget plucked the shift from the girl's startled arms and turned it upside down, rifling through the yards of ruffles and flounces. The light gleamed a little more brightly. Bridget closed her right eye and squinted her left, trying to see better. "That light."

"Light, mistress?" The junior seamstress bent swiftly and took the linen from Bridget's hand. She leaned close, examining each stitch. "It must be the candlelight shining through the cloth, mistress, there is nothing here."

"But there is." Bridget reclaimed the length of cloth from her. "I can see it." She threaded the fabric through her clenched fingers, until, out of the corner of her left eye, she saw the light shining between them. The fabric bunched there, as if something lay inside the hem. "Here," she said. "There is something here."

"Permit me, mistress." The older seamstress took the length of fabric, running it carefully through her long, supple fingers. She frowned hard. "There is something . . ."

She pulled a pair of scissors from the bundle of tools that hung at her waist, flipped the cloth over and swiftly slit the hem.

Out tumbled a braid of red and white thread, curved into a loop and its two ends knotted together. Bridget moved to pick it up.

"If I may, mistress." Richikha's hand darted out in front of Bridget's and snatched up the braid. Bridget stood slowly; so did the oldest seamstress. Bridget would not have been the junior seamstress at that moment for anything. The look her superior gave her could have peeled paint off a board.

Richikha examined the braid as carefully as the senior seamstress had examined the hem that concealed it. Belatedly, Bridget realized what it must be. It was a spell of some sort.

Her heart thudded against her ribs. It was a spell of some sort, sewn into the dress meant for her.

Richikha lifted her head, a mischievous smile on her face. "Mistress, you should be flattered."

"I should?" said Bridget stiffly.

Nodding, Richikha held up the braid for all to see. "You have an admirer. This is a love charm."

Bridget felt her cheeks go instantly pale. "A *what*?"

"A love charm." Richikha laid the object out on her palm and stepped forward so that Bridget might inspect it more closely. Bridget had to work to keep from backing away from the thing as if it were a poisonous snake. "You see, someone here had gathered some of your hair." Richikha traced the auburn strands in the braid. "And here is the hair of your admirer." She pointed to several thick black strands. "Both knotted together, as you see, with the colors of passion and fidelity, and bound in a circle."

Bridget's chest heaved out of control. Black hair, bound together with hers. Black hair, like Kalami's.

"Can . . . can anyone do this?" she stammered.

"Anyone can make a semblance of such a thing," said Richikha dismissively. "But it would take a sorcerer to create a true spell."

She knew that. It would have to be a sorcerer, like Kalami.

"Mistress, I offer my deepest apologies." The elder seamstress reverenced, the hands crossed at her breast both bunched into fists. "Whoever permitted this to happen will be turned out at once."

The younger seamstress blanched pure white.

Bridget strode over to her. All the other women drew back their skirts. "Who gave you this?"

"Mistress . . . I—"

Bridget grabbed the girl by the shoulders and shook her until the scissors and pincushions on her belt rattled. "Who did this!" Bridget shouted, heedless of the distress and her eyes. "Tell me or I will throw you out of here and I won't be using the door!"

"He told me . . . He said . . ." The girl began to weep, tears tracing thick trails down her sunken cheeks.

"Who!"

"The lord sorcerer," she cried.

Kalami. Bridget went cold. It was true. Kalami really did this.

The young seamstress tried to raise her hands to bury her face in them, but Bridget grabbed her wrists.

"What else did he give you to do?" Bridget searched the girl's face with both eyes, looking for any trace of blur or reflection that would indicate a lie. "Did he give you more of these?" She stabbed her finger toward the braid in Richikha's hands.

"There was to be a pair of garters made," she said. "The braid was to work until the garters could be finished and then . . ."

And then I would love him. He would have made me love him. And what would that have made me do? She turned away, laying her hand on her belly, suddenly ill. *Oh, God, what have I come to? What have I done?*

Why would he do such a thing to me?

He would do it because he knew she doubted him. She had not been so clever as she had hoped, and he had seen the cracks between her words. He needed her, he had said so many times, and he would not risk her straying over to the side of his enemies. So he meant to force her feelings, force her back into the whirl of desire and confusion that had gripped her once before, the whirl that she so desperately longed for and so much feared. He meant to force that on her, to take her mind and her judgment, her will and choice away.

The world swam in front of Bridget's eyes.

"Mistress, you are overwrought. Sit here and regain your breath." Richikha took her hand and led her to a chair. Bridget sat clumsily, torn between anger, disbelief and despair.

"You may leave us now," she heard Gali say to the seamstresses.

"You will be recalled when our mistress is recovered."

Bridget did not see them leave. She just knotted her fists in her lap and stared straight ahead of her.

"Mistress, do not take it so." Iadviga's soft hands took Bridget's and patted them. "It is extremely flattering. The lord sorcerer himself is so captivated by you that he would charm you thus. It is a symbol of his love and regard—"

"Love!" shouted Bridget, snatching her hand away. "Love that leaves you no choice, no will, no freedom! God almighty, give me eternal hatred before you give me love like that!"

None of the ladies said anything. This apparently was a new thought for their pretty heads.

What am I going to do? Bridget clamped her jaw around the question. *Confront him? If he knows this failed to work, what will he try next? A philtre? A piece of bread like Sakra? I can't stop eating.*

Can I escape? I escaped Sakra. And how far did I get? I do not know how to navigate that other place, and the Vixen is waiting out there. Her fists tightened until her fingernails pressed painfully against the skin of her palm. *What am I going to do?*

"Mistress?" Richikha again. Bridget made herself turn and look at the girl. She fidgeted. "Mistress, what should I . . . ?" She held out the braid, the spell.

"Throw it on the fire," spat Bridget. Richikha bobbed a reverence and moved to the firepit. "Wait!" Bridget cried. Richikha froze, wide-eyed. "Wait," she said more gently. "That will break the spell, won't it? Kalami would feel that?"

"Yes, mistress," said Richikha, sounding much more confident now that she was back on familiar ground. "A sorcerer will always feel their own spell break."

"How did you come to know so much?"

Richikha's cheeks pinked up just a touch. "My family has served in the imperial palace for three generations, mistress. One learns how . . . things are done."

Bridget considered. Her knowledge of magic was scanty. Her readings of the Brothers Grimm and Hans Christian Andersen were years away. She gritted her teeth. She was being courted, lied to and caged because she was supposed to have so much power, and now that she needed it she had no idea how to make use of it. Her eyes strayed to the room's main door with its soft glitter of magic and she remembered how heavy the air felt when she made her promise. Caged indeed. She did not even dare open that door.

"Is there . . . some way to make that thing safe?" Her hands gone cold. She rubbed them together, trying to start her circulation again. "Without breaking the spell? Just . . . make it safe for me to touch?"

Iadviga fluttered her round hands, and Gali shot Richikha a glare that clearly said, *You're getting above yourself.* Richikha ignored them both.

"Most certainly, mistress," she said primly, folding her hands in front her. "But you would need a true sorcerer . . ." She stopped in the middle of the word. "I beg your pardon, mistress."

"That's all right. Just tell me what I need to do."

Richikha's blush deepened. "I must confess I do not know the particulars, mistress. Only generalities. I have seen black cloth bags used to contain spells, but I do not know the kind of cloth that is needed, nor the knot that must be used to tie the ribbon." She dropped her gaze, fiddling with her overskirt. "I'm sorry."

"It's not your fault," Bridget whispered. She did not miss the tight satisfaction that showed both on Gali's face and Iadviga's at Richikha's failure.

She realized that she had another problem. All three of these women had seen what happened. This was juicy and valuable gossip, and this place seemed to thrive on rumor as much as Eastbay and Bayfield did. They would talk, and as soon as they did, Kalami would know his attempt to ensnare her had failed.

Her only hope was to offer them something more valuable than gossip. Gossip, however, commanded a high price and she had next to nothing. She had the silver brooch Kalami gave her, the clothes on her back and . . .

Her eyes lit on the golden coat with its embroidery of pearls. A plan formed amid the whirl of her thoughts, even as Richikha, ever practical, carried the charm to the bedside table with its various wooden caskets for jewels and combs and shut it into the smallest of them.

She clasped her hands together and met each of her ladies' eyes in turn. "You have all been very patient with me since I came here, and have done at your duty under difficult circumstances. I do not wish you to think I am ungrateful, or that I have not noticed." Iadviga smiled at the words, and Gali let her perpetually stiff neck relax a little. Only Richikha looked wary, as if she realized what might be coming. "Now I am in desperate need of your help." She leaned forward. "It cannot become known that I have discovered what was hidden in my shift. It would . . ." She stopped and started again. "It would very much embarrass the lord sorcerer, would it not, if he were known to have planted such a thing?"

Iadviga's hand flew to her mouth at the implications of this statement. Gali considered, her eyes flickering back and forth, before she nodded her agreement. Richikha just watched Bridget carefully. Oh, she was the sharp one, that was for certain.

"If we all make it through the holy days without the presence of this . . . charm being revealed," said Bridget, "I promise you will all of you divide the pearls trimming the hem and sleeves of my outer coat that I wear to the presentation." That had to be at least a hundred pearls. Surely that was more than enough to go around.

Apparently they thought so too, from the stunned looks on all three faces. Gali recovered first and reverenced.

"Our mistress is too generous."

Your mistress is frightened and desperate. Bridget licked her lips. "Now, Gali, Iadviga, I need you to get to that senior seamstress and convince her not to make a fuss. Tell her I'm ready for my fitting, and everything must go forward quietly. All right?"

"At once, mistress." Iadviga reverenced, her voice filled with glee. *Oh, please, let Gali calm her down.*

Gali's sour expression told Bridget she had every intention of doing just that. With another round of reverencing, the senior ladies retreated, leaving Bridget facing Richikha.

"And how may I serve, mistress?" Richikha asked.

"Your task is more difficult," said Bridget. "I need you to get a message to someone without being discovered."

Richikha's eyes glittered. Bridget wondered if she was thinking of rewards beyond even a double handful of pearls. "I should be honored to serve, mistress."

Not stupid, not unkind, but possibly for sale. It is good to know that as well. "It must go to Empress Ananda's sorcerer Sakra."

At this, Richikha's brows lifted. "That will be difficult, mistress, but I believe it may be done."

"Very good." Bridget nodded soberly. "It must say this. He must come to me tonight before midnight. I am in need of his help. It must warn him that Kalami . . . the lord sorcerer has enchanted the threshold. I don't know how, but I cannot leave this room in safety."

Richikha eyed the threshold, looking nervous for the first time. "It shall be as you say, mistress."

Bridget took the girl's hand to bring her attention back. "I am going to be placing all my trust in you, Richikha," she said, watching Richikha's face to make sure each word sank in. "And if I get through the next few days, secrets, freedom and mind intact, I am going to be exceedingly grateful."

Bridget watched the slow spread of Richikha's smile and knew her guess had been correct. Richikha dreamed of wealth, and saw here her chance to claim it.

"I am honored to serve." She reverenced. "You may leave all to me."

Richikha hurried from the chamber. Alone, Bridget found her eyes inexorably drawn to the box where Richikha had put Kalami's charm. She wondered how close she could safely come to it, how long she could be in its presence before . . . before . . .

She swallowed again, and realized her fingers were toying with the silver brooch Kalami had given her.

A wave of nausea swept over her and she fumbled with the brooch, struggling to get it off her dress. She wanted nothing of Kalami's near her. She tossed it onto the table, looking around the room for some inspiration, anything. The chamber was magnificent, with its frescoes and draperies and the carved wooden screens surrounding the beds, but it was utterly strange and its vastness right now made Bridget feel profoundly alone. She wanted to reproach herself deeply and bitterly for believing . . . for believing she knew not what. That a better life was possible. For believing yet again in the promises of a stranger.

But there was no time for that. She needed to make her decisions. She stared hard at the brooch, putting her hand over her right eye. It did not shine in any unusual way. So it was probably safe. She could wear it as part of her disguise without harm.

Bridget picked the cold piece of silver up and turned it over in her fingers. *And if he believes me to be in love with him, he may relax and go careless.* Her hand closed around the brooch. *So much the better.*

Chapter Fourteen

Bridget dreamed.

She stood before the golden cage. Inside the Firebird burned with all the colors of flame. Its sapphire blue eyes pleaded for release as its wings stretched over its head, battering the cage, fanning her with heat. It needed to fly. It wanted to sing for joy at the sight of the sun. It had languished here in the dark for almost thirty years. Bridget saw all these things in its eyes and her heart melted within her.

Bridget touched the beautiful woven bars, looking for the latch, for the door. But there was none. The cage was a single, solid working of gold without any break or bar.

"I'm sorry," she said to the bird. "I don't know what to do."

The bird crumpled in on itself, cowering under its own bright wings. Misery rolled off it, carried by the waves of heat. Unable to stand the touch of such suffering, Bridget wrapped her fingers around the bars, seeking to bend the delicate gold work.

Then, as in a vision, she saw the palace ablaze, its timbers and tapestries consumed in flame. Overhead, the Firebird winged its way into the night. She saw whole fields burning with clouds of black smoke billowing over the devastation, and the bird singing aloud for the joy, not for sight of the sun, but for sight of its work. But then too, she saw a summer forest burning and people fleeing before the raging fire, and she saw the Firebird dive into the heart of the flames, and draw all that fire into itself, rising again bright into the sky while the people stood awestruck at the sight.

Bridget backed away from the cage, her hands out to ward away the heat and the visions. "Which is true?" she asked the Firebird. "What are you?"

What I am called to be, said the bird.

"But which is true?" cried Bridget, for she saw them again, images of destruction and images of salvation, and yet she saw the bird burning in its cage. "I don't know which is true!"

"You must wake up now," said another voice.

No! The bird threw itself against the bars, and Bridget felt its sorrow tear into her. *Do not leave me here!*

"Wake up, Bridget."

Bridget awoke with a gasp, shooting bolt upright as if from a nightmare. A shout and a crash sounded beside the bed. Bridget scrambled across the opposite side, gasping again as her bare feet hit the cold floor.

"Who is that!" she shouted. The room was pitch black. She could see nothing. She backed away without thinking, bumped into one of the screens that shielded the bed, stumbled, tried to catch the screen to steady herself, and sent it crashing over, toppling herself along with it. She scrabbled against the fallen screen to pull herself upright again, and in the dim glow of the fire's banked coals, she saw Sakra standing on the other side of the bed.

No one else had woken. No one else had even moved. The ladies lay in their beds. She could hear the gentle snoring.

Sakra. He shimmered vaguely in the combination of faint moonlight and fainter firelight from the banked coals in the firepit and braziers. Sakra, whom she had asked to come see her. Begged to come see her, because of Kalami's charm discovered in her shift. She had allowed the ladies to put her to bed for the appearance of things, but she had meant to stay awake until he came. Evidently, she had failed in the resolve.

Embarrassment heating her cheeks, Bridget clutched at the neck of her nightgown.

"You must forgive me, sir," she said. "But where I come from, when a man comes into a decent woman's bedroom at night, the scene requires that she scream and order him out at least twice."

Sakra blinked at her for a moment, but then he reverenced politely. "From your adherence to this point of decorum I must assume it is required even when the man has been invited."

"Appearances must be maintained, you understand." Bridget smoothed down her sleeves fussily.

Sakra tilted his head to the side in order to give the most careful consideration to this idea. "It would appear the principles of this type of drama are universal."

"This I can readily believe." Bridget nodded. "So." She folded her hands. "We may take it as written, and proceed."

They regarded each other then, and to Bridget's surprise, Sakra burst out laughing. He gave himself over to it fully, throwing back his head and letting his shoulders shake. It was such an open, honest sound, Bridget felt herself grinning in reply, and she saw how he must look when he was untroubled—tall and graceful, and at ease with himself. For that one moment, she felt warmth in her heart.

"Ah, mistress," said Sakra when he could speak again. "I expected so many things from you, but not humor." He wiped his eyes. "Forgive me, it has been a long time since I had occasion to laugh."

For all this noise, however, not one of the ladies on their truckle beds woke. Gali rolled over, but she only sighed and continued to snore.

"Your doing?" Bridget nodded toward the sleeping forms.

"Yes," replied Sakra. "It will be at least another hour before the spell holding them unravels." He glanced about him at the moonlit darkness. "We may have a light, if you prefer."

"Of course." Bridget made her way over to one of the braziers and uncovered the coals, feeding in fresh slivers of charcoal. The room's illumination turned from faint silver to faint gold. "Poor Richikha," she breathed, looking down at the peacefully sleeping girl under her eiderdown covers. "She is forever falling asleep when she should not."

Sakra stood beside Richikha's bed, holding one hand out flat overhead as if to feel her breath against his palm. "I do not believe it is her fault."

Bridget frowned. Sakra still seemed blurred in her vision, despite the fresh light. "Last night, you didn't . . ."

"No," said Sakra, but his voice sounded strained. "I did not, but I am the least of the powers at work in this place." All at once, the sorcerer's face spasmed, and he dug the heel of his hand into his side.

"Are you ill, sir?" Reflexively, Bridget hurried forward, both hands outstretched.

Sakra threw up his own hand to stop her at a distance. He shook his head. "Not ill." But he gasped the word, and it was another moment before he could straighten up. When he did, he was still breathing heavily.

Suspicion bubbled up in Bridget's mind. She closed her right eye.

Sakra vanished.

"What is this?" she said, backing away. "You are not here."

Sakra straightened up, staring at her. "But I am."

"You are an illusion, or a disguise." She circled the firepit, putting it between her and this semblance of Sakra. "You are not here."

Sakra held up both hands. "I assure you, mistress, I am here and I am *Agnidh* Sakra. I can offer proof of this."

"Then do so," countered Bridget, measuring with a glance the distance between her and the door.

He spread his hands in acquiescence. Despite the blurring of her vision, Bridget saw his shoulders had remained crooked up. Whether this was from pain and strain, or the worry at being discovered, she could not tell. "Why do you say I am not here?" asked Sakra.

"Because I cannot see you with my left eye," answered Bridget at once. She bit her tongue. Of course. This was Sakra, and she had to answer him. The spell between them still stood.

"I'm sorry."

Sakra waved the apology away. "You grow cautious, mistress, that is good thing. I would you could explain this seeing further to me, but my time is limited." He gave her a half-smile. "As you may have guessed. Your lady said you sent to me because of a charm."

Bridget nodded. "It's in the small box beside the bed." She gestured toward the nightstand. "I don't . . . that is, I thought I should not touch it." She hated the uncertainty in her voice.

Sakra, however, did not seem to notice it. "Very wise." Whatever ailed him, it affected his stride. Sakra hobbled across the room toward the the box. As he moved, Bridget's right eye saw that three locks of his hair had come loose, or been undone from, their braids. She wondered at that, but thought the better of taking the time now to ask.

When Sakra carried the box back to the patch of light cast by the brazier, Bridget saw sweat beginning to bead on his forehead.

"You are not well," she insisted. "What is the matter?"

"I am well. I am required to concentrate on . . ." Instead of finishing the sentence, he shook his head. Bridget was not sure if that meant that he did not wish to tell her too much, or that he did not have the strength to speak right now. He set the box on one of the gilt-inlaid tables. "I must pray your patience if this makes me enigmatic."

Bridget raised her eyebrows, but closed her mouth. Sakra lifted the box lid and Bridget stepped back, as if even the sight of the charm could cause Kalami's will to be worked on her.

"Crude," muttered Sakra, lifting the thing from its resting place. "And easily countered. I'm surprised. The lord sorcerer usually takes much more care with his workings." He ran his fingers over the braid, as if checking the fineness of the thread and the complexity of the weaving. "I do not believe you told me where you found this."

Bridget found his choice of phrasing odd; then it dawned on her that he was avoiding asking her a question. As long as he asked nothing, she could not be compelled to say anything she did not wish to.

"I saw it hidden in the hem of the shift I was supposed to wear tomorrow evening."

Sakra stared at her incredulously. "Forgive me, mistress, you cannot mean that you saw this," he said, choosing his words with care. "You mean to say it was tied to the hem, or sewn along it in some fashion, or that you that you saw the shape of it through the fine fabric."

"No." Bridget shook her head. "It glows in my left eye."

Sakra just stood there, staring, his breath coming fast and shallow.

It wheezed far too loudly in the stillness for him to be in good health. Both wonder and pain warred with each other on his face. His mouth moved, as he sought words, but nothing came out but a cough that made his crooked shoulders shake.

Bridget's patience snapped. "Will you at least sit down, sir? Yes, it glows. I see it with my left eye, even as I cannot see you in that eye now, and as I did see you inside the shape of the swan. I saw it through the cloth of the shift." She strode over to him, planted both hands on his shoulders and pushed him down until he sat on the nearest footstool.

Sakra swallowed. His shoulders shivered from the effort of keeping him upright. At the same time, his fist closed around the braid. "Bridget . . ." He coughed again, doubling over with a fresh spasm. "You may save us all."

"So everyone keeps telling me, but no one will tell me how." She crouched down until she was eye-level with him. "You are the only one who has been honest with me since I got here. Tell me what to do." He opened his mouth, but she waved away his next words. "Never mind this business about the questions. I'll answer whatever you ask, and I will trust you not to pry." Speaking those words was a balm to her tired self. In all this cold, complex world this man had shown her trust and proven himself worthy of trust.

"Thank you, mistress." Sakra swallowed a couple of times as another wave of pain struck him. "The emperor is enchanted, you knew this?"

"Yes."

"The enchantment is something he wears." Sakra fingered the braid. "You will see him tomorrow night. If you could see where the spell is . . ."

Bridget sat back on her heels. "Oh, my God."

Sakra frowned. "What?"

Bridget pounded her fist against her thigh. "I saw him last night. I should have known. I should have looked more closely . . ." She shook her head, pulling her thoughts and her determination back together. "Too late for that. Tomorrow night I will pay much closer attention. Then what will we do?"

The prospect of action seemed to ease whatever struggle went on inside him. "We will arrange some way for me to get word to you. I . . ."

Another crash cut through the room, this time making them both jump. Golden lantern light fell across them, and Bridget winced, throwing up her hand to shield herself from the sudden brightness. She heard footsteps on stone—soft soles and boots together—and she felt a breeze that must have been movement from Sakra.

"Bridget, mistress, are you hurt?"

Bridget straightened up, lowering her hand and blinking, only to see Kalami striding toward her. Two members of the house guard stood by the door with lanterns and gnarled clubs. Two more flanked Sakra, one at his back and one between him and the balcony door. Both of them had their clubs out and crouched ready to spring should he move. Sakra himself stood stock-still, his hands splayed at his sides. His skin was now slick with sweat and it seemed to Bridget that the outline of his form shimmered in the lantern light.

What is happening to you? What have you done to yourself? Bridget wondered, but Kalami was in front of her, frowning hard and waiting for his answer. She made herself look at him, not at Sakra. If she looked at Sakra, the concern she felt would show in her face, and she knew it. That was not something she could permit Kalami to see.

She folded her arms across the front for nightgown. "I am perfectly all right, thank you."

"Did he give you anything? Anything at all?" Kalami's eyes swept her from unbound hair to bare feet as if to discern any change.

Bridget just shook her head. For a moment, she thought Kalami was going to search her nightdress, but then his eyes fell on the box, and the braid inside it. Cold rage flickered across his face, and Bridget met his gaze calmly. Very well, now he knew. What would come next would come. He would not see her flinch from it.

But Kalami said nothing. Instead, he turned on his heel and

marched across to Sakra. Despite the heavy shadows left by the lamp-light, she could clearly see the livid hatred on Kalami's face.

"You could not prevent her from aiding the dowager empress, so you decide to murder her in her bed?" He yanked Sakra's dagger from its sheath. "Are these your mistress's orders? Or are you trying to make up for your earlier failures?" He held up the dark blade so that Bridget saw its edge outlined in the golden light. "Why should I not slit you open right here for threatening one who is under the dowager's protection?"

Bridget could not see Sakra's face, but she heard his breathing painfully loud. "Because to kill me without even a semblance of an inquiry or trial might just start a war between Isavalta and Hastinapura, and that is not your plan, is it?" He grunted then and hunched over, one hand holding his side. "You have already promised a war to Hung-Tse."

Kalami said nothing. Sakra's discomfort obviously left him unmoved. He simply shifted his grip on the knife so that its tip pointed straight down and held it over the back of Sakra's neck. Bridget caught her breath. Kalami did not seem to notice the sound. His attention was all focused on Sakra helpless in pain before him.

"All has gone beyond you, Southerner. You no longer have any part in the game."

Even as Kalami spoke, Sakra fell to his knees. He turned his face up toward the knife, toward the man towering over him, and Bridget saw his eyes flash in the darkness. "Not yet," he said.

And he was gone.

Bridget clamped her hand across her mouth to block whatever noise tried to issue forth—startled scream, or cry of surprised delight. Kalami stared at the place where Sakra had been, the knife gripped tight in his hand, still ready to bring down for the killing blow. Even the soldiers, trained men all of them, stood stunned and frozen.

In their confusion, Bridget saw her chance. As soon as Kalami turned his attention back toward her, all would be lost. In the next moments, however, she might be able to buy herself a little time.

Holding her breath, Bridget eased herself toward the box and its charmed braid.

"Get to his room," ordered Kalami hoarsely. "If there's any mirror there, smash it. If he's there, arrest him and see him placed in irons. Irons, you understand?" Shaking with rage, he lowered the dagger. "After that, you'll institute a general search of the palace. Nowhere is sacred in this, you understand?"

Bridget slid the box from the table, holding it near her waist to keep the movement small and shadowed.

"The dowager must be informed," Kalami went on, running one hand through his hair. "You will find me with her. You will report the instant you have found anything."

"Sir." Chadek bowed.

Bridget tipped the box over the brazier, and the braid dropped into the fire. The flames at once snatched it up, and Kalami shuddered violently. He swung around to face her, and Bridget drew herself up straight. Let him look. Let him see she was not afraid. Red sparks rose from his work as it blackened to ash. Let him see that as well.

"Go at once, Captain," murmured Kalami without taking his gaze from Bridget.

"Sir." He bowed again.

"Take me with you, Captain," said Bridget quickly. "I have something vital to say to your mistress imperial concerning the loyalties of the lord sorcerer."

"She can have nothing to say, Captain," countered Kalami. "You have your orders."

Chadek looked from Bridget to Kalami, and back again. Then he bowed, gestured to his men and led them from the room, leaving Bridget facing Kalami surrounded by nothing but soundly sleeping women.

Kalami tucked Sakra's knife into his belt. "What is this, Bridget?" he asked gently.

Bridget said nothing.

"What were you doing here?" Kalami gestured to the box, and

the brazier that had nearly consumed his charm. Only a few scraps of red and white cloth rested on the coals. The smoke had a rank, unpleasant odor to it now, and Bridget swallowed a cough.

"What were you letting him do?" Kalami joined her beside the brazier. He scooped up a handful of charcoal slivers from the pile beside it, and one by one dropped them onto the fire, feeding the flames and making them rise high.

"I was not letting him do anything," answered Bridget, slipping around the table. "This was my own doing."

"I see that, Bridget." Kalami stepped into her path, putting himself between her and the door. The brazier lit the right side of his face, leaving the left in shadow. His eyes seemed to be lightless holes in his craggy face. "What did he tell you?"

Bridget looked past him to the door. Perhaps she could make it, but he had the knife. Screaming might or might not do her any good. But the door was not locked, and there was the brazier, and all manner of other weapons.

Bridget retreated a step, edging back around the brazier and hoping the movement looked like fear. "You tried to put a love spell on me."

"Who told you such a thing?" He stalked after her, his voice smooth and soft. "Did Sakra tell you that?"

Bridget froze. Did he think so little of her still? Did he not realize even now what had happened here?

Use it, Bridget, she told herself. *Use it.*

Kalami circled the brazier until he stood before her. "What did he say to you, Bridget? What did he tell you?"

Bridget let her fingers knot in the collar of her nightgown. "Nothing much. There was no time. We were both busy knocking over screens." She gestured with one finger toward the fallen items.

"But, surely, he told you something?" Kalami took another step forward and reached for her hand, pulling it away from her collar and setting it at her side. "He did not prepare all this so that you and he might pass a pleasant hour."

"No," said Bridget again. "I imagine he did not." She felt very aware of how near Kalami was, but this time she felt none of the yearning ache that she had when he touched her before. Instead, her thoughts reached toward Sakra. Where had he gone? Was he safe?

Let him be safe.

Kalami took her other hand, which still clutched at the fabric of the nightgown, and gently disentangled her fingers. "Make no mistake, Bridget. Your fate and Isavalta's are now completely intertwined." He laid her hand at her right side. "I cannot separate you, and I cannot lose you."

He was taking too many liberties, she wanted to tell him. He was too near, and touched her in too familiar a fashion. But she stayed still and silent. She must endure this. If he could be induced to simply leave, she could run out behind him, make her way to the empress, tell what she knew. She might even find Sakra there.

"I am well accustomed to rude awakenings." Bridget lifted her chin. "This is just one more." *You may trust even poor broken Medeoan before you trust him,* Momma had said. Oh, she should have listened. She should have paid closer attention, taken swifter action.

"And was it Sakra who told you I laid a spell on you?" Kalami brushed a lock of her unbound hair back from her shoulder.

Bridget bit her lip and turned her head away. He could make what he liked of the gesture.

Kalami sighed and, to Bridget's very great relief, stepped away. "Very well," he said, folding his hands behind his back, and shaking his head at the brazier. "I did weave a spell, but it was one of protection. You are in danger, Bridget, every moment you are here." She gestured at the flames. "I made this spell to keep you safe, and do you see what Sakra has done with his lies? He has made you destroy your own protection."

How many lies do you have on that tongue? Bridget's eyes narrowed before she could remember she was supposed to be the ignorant victim here. "I should have realized something of the kind," she said to cover the expression.

"Fortunately, I have brought you another."

Kalami opened his hand. From his fingertips dangled a circle of woven cloth. The brazier's light showed a pattern of interlocking circles, red and white as the braid had been. It shone brightly to Bridget's left eye.

"It's a garter," he told her. "It should be a belt or a girdle, but I did not have the time to create so much."

Bridget's throat closed around her breath.

"You do not fear me, do you, Bridget?" said Kalami, stepping forward, still holding up the garter in front of her eyes.

"Yes, I do," said Bridget, too afraid of what he held to dissemble anymore. He would bind her to him with that thing. He would take away her mind, her will, her heart . . .

"Why?" he asked sadly. "I will not harm you. I need you in so many ways I cannot begin to count them. I would not endanger you for anything. Not like Sakra will if you fall into his power. Let me keep you safe. Take this protection." He held the garter out.

"No."

"Take it, Bridget." He urged. "You've been lied to, and you are in danger. Please, put me at ease and let me see you safe." He reached for her hand.

Bridget dodged sideways, shoving the table over so Kalami stumbled over it. She ran for the door. Hands grabbed her skirts and Bridget pitched forward onto hands and knees.

"Now you will accept my gift!"

She tried to kick back, but her thick skirts hampered her. She rolled over, fists swinging. Kalami caught one wrist in what felt like a loop of cloth and she screamed and tried to pull away, but Kalami was backing away to stand up straight and she looked into his eyes.

His eyes, his dark eyes, and in them she saw all the promises that waited there for her. So many promises, so much hoped and feared. She remembered each little brush of his hand against her, the hundred thousand times he had touched her, now taking her hand, now her arm, helping her, always so polite, so distant. Each tactile memory traced a trail down her skin, and Bridget felt that she couldn't breathe. She couldn't think, she couldn't see. There was only Valin Kalami and his dark eyes and all those promises between them.

"Lord Sorcerer? Is all well?"

Bridget turned to stare. A house guard stood in the doorway, his eyes glancing between Valin and Bridget. She leapt to her feet.

"Yes. All is well," said Valin, for Bridget could not speak. She did not want this interruption. How dare this man barge in here? He made Valin look away from her.

"Mistress?" asked the guard.

"Yes," Bridget made herself say. "Everything is perfectly in order. Thank you."

The guard gave the soldier's bow, and closed the door.

"Everything is perfectly in order, Bridget?" Kalami walked slowly forward, his eyes wide as they drank her in. "Is it truly?"

"Truly."

He took her hand between his own and lifted it. His touch set her heart beating so hard she wondered if he could hear it. His palms were warm and dry, and his hands so strong as they pressed against hers, turning her hand over so he could kiss the back, gently, ever so gently. Then, he turned it again, and pressed his lips against her wrist, right above the garter he had captured her with.

"Do you accept my gift now, Bridget?" he murmured, his breath so warm against her wrist.

"Yes," she whispered in return. "Oh, yes."

He smiled and Bridget felt her heart swell with wonder at the sight of it. He was so close, she could smell his scent of winter, smoke and musk. It warmed her, comforted her, roused her. His fingers lingered about her wrist, as he pulled the slip knot tight on his gift. Slowly, afraid she might shatter this moment, this feeling, she brushed her fingers against his hair. It was soft, and finer than she had expected. She wanted to bury her fingers in it, stroking his scalp down to his neck.

Kalami lifted his head and his eyes met hers again. Did she fall into his arms or did he pull her close? She didn't know. All she knew was that he kissed her, and his mouth was warm as his breath had been, and his kisses were strong and deep. She pressed herself closer, resenting the layers of cloth between them. She wanted him to see her, to touch her. She wanted to know how the skin of his chest felt against hers, she wanted to know how his hand would feel on her belly, on her thighs. She wanted to know so much.

His hands caressed her neck, drifting down to her shoulders. She wrapped her arms around him, her knees gone so weak with all her need that she could not stand.

"My Bridget," he breathed in her ear. "My own Bridget."

"Yes. Yours."

"Yes." He ran one knuckle down her neck to her breast. She gasped, pressing her mouth against his neck in pleasure and surprise.

But then he took her hands and pushed her back from him. Bridget stared. Had she done something wrong? What was the matter?

But no, he was smiling, and all the promises in the world still filled his eyes. "I am afraid we must wait a little yet, Bridget."

Her gaze skittered to the ladies asleep in their beds. "But, I thought they'd sleep for an hour at least yet . . ."

"Yes, my own." His fingers lingered on the collar of her gown. "But there are other things I must do tonight, and I may not broach my duties."

Shame touched Bridget, and she dropped her eyes. "Of course. I am being selfish."

He drew his fingers down her cheek, making her skin shiver with their warmth. "Such selfishness looks well on you, Bridget."

She smiled as he traced her lips. She captured one fingertip with a kiss, earning his smile in return.

"But you must tell me one thing, my own." His fingers traveled down the line of her chin to her throat. "Who told you about my gift? Who lied so to you?"

"Richikha," she said, pained to think how easily she'd been taken in. "I'm sorry, Valin."

"Hush." He pulled her close again and kissed her forehead. "No more of that. I should have taken greater care. I am ashamed of myself." She opened her mouth to protest, and he pressed his finger against her lips. "Hush, I said." She smiled, and bowed her head, all acquiescence to his orders.

He slipped his hand under her chin and lifted it up so she could look again into his eyes. "But you know better now than to let any of those flutterers meddle with my gifts, don't you?"

"Yes, Valin." His eyes were so beautiful, so rich with life. She could lose herself so entirely in those eyes.

"And you will wear my token? I want something of mine always touching you."

Always touching you. The need his words sparked sent a rush of heat to her cheeks. "Yes."

"Very good, very good, my Bridget." He brushed back her hair, and Bridget turned her face so she could kiss his palm. "Tomorrow night, my own. Tomorrow night all will be complete, and you will have me with you the rest of your life."

There were no words adequate to make her answer, so Bridget kissed him again, a long, deep kiss full of her own promises.

Kalami's eyes were shining when he pulled away. "Tomorrow night," he said by way of a final promise, and he slipped out the door.

Happiness welled up inside Bridget. She spun around on her toes, laughing and hugging herself. Love. It had been so long since she'd felt love. And it was real this time, and it would last her life through. He'd promised. His words rang in her ears like golden bells, filling her with all the hopes Asa had stolen away so long ago.

She wanted to dance, she wanted to shout it from the rooftop, all manner of silly girlish things. But she settled for skipping across the floor to stand front of the bronze mirror.

"Bridget in love," she said to her reflection, throwing her head back and lifting her arm in a bad dramatic pose. "This is Bridget in love."

She looked at herself and giggled, but choked on her laughter. The reflection showed a thing clinging to her wrist. It was black and shredded, like a great spider made of ash and rags, and it sank its fangs deep into her wrist, right where Kalami had kissed her.

Bridget screamed in anger and disgust. She yanked at the thing, tearing it from her wrist and flinging it to the floor, looking for something heavy to throw over it . . .

And she saw Kalami's token lying on the bare wood.

Bridget backed away, both fists pressed against her mouth, memories spilling into her reawakened mind. He'd touched her and she'd liked it. He'd knocked her down and captured her wrist, and he'd touched her, and she'd let him. She'd kissed him, so greedy for him, and he'd lied to her and he'd put that thing on her. He would have taken her then and there, and she would have let him, she wanted him to. She would have begged him to and he knew it, because he'd put that thing around her wrist. . . .

The bed bumped against Bridget's back and she clambered onto it, hugging the coverlet to her chest, as if she thought the thing could crawl toward her. But it just lay there, waiting for her touch. As Kalami had waited, had urged. Bridget felt her stomach twist, and she scrambled across the bed, barely making it to the washbasin before she began to vomit out her fear and revulsion.

It was only when she was empty that Bridget was able to feel the first flames of fresh anger. It burned bright and hot in the pit of her sunken stomach, turning fast into rage, rage at the lies, at the cruel seduction.

Rage, because he made her remember what it was to be in love and because that love was another lie. Another cold, calculating lie.

She'd burn the thing, as she had the braid he tried to secret on her. She'd take a knife and she'd cut it to pieces and then she'd slit Kalami open like a pig, and make sure he watched her do it. She'd burn him! Burn him alive. She'd make some spell. She could do it, and he'd go up in flames, hearing her voice in his ears. She'd do that somehow. He'd die screaming her name, begging her for mercy.

Yes, whispered a voice in her mind. *Let him burn. Let me burn him for you.*

Bridget closed her eyes, gulping air into her lungs, trying to calm down. She wanted to destroy the spell utterly, except she didn't dare touch the thing. Except that if he knew she was free, he'd do something else, and it would be something she couldn't see this time, because he was not a fool. Something with smoke and air, and blood perhaps, something that would leave no trace.

Bridget braced herself against the table, gritting her teeth against the sobs that threatened still to spill out of her raw throat. No, he was so many things, but he was not a fool. If he found out about this mistake, he would not make it again.

He'd be back for her, expecting her ready with her love for him, and if he found she was not . . . he could do anything to her. She did not know how to fight this kind of battle. He could do anything.

Bridget crawled back into the middle of the bed. She drew her knees up to her chest and wrapped her arms around them, and there she sat, waiting for the morning. Waiting for an answer, and fearing deep inside her that none would come.

Kalami left Bridget's room and returned to his own apartments, the taste of her kiss lingering on his lips. It was not the best way to bring her to him, and not the way he had wanted, but it was sweet, he had to admit to himself. Very sweet indeed. It had been a long time since she had kissed him, and that time she had believed he was another man, her would-be lover, for whom she was waiting on the shores of her lake. He had needed her then, to give him a child he could raise to be powerful and purposeful. He needed her again now, but for very different reasons.

Kalami opened his door and his heart lifted momentarily to see Chadek standing before the firepit, with Finon setting out a tankard and a pitcher for him. Could they have caught the Southerner so soon?

"What news, Captain?" he asked, striding up to the fire. Finon caught Kalami's eye and shook his head as he set another tankard beside the first. Kalami swallowed a curse.

"We are even searching the dungeons," said Chadek without preamble. "If he is here still, it will take your powers to find him. It is beyond me."

Anger tightened the muscles in Kalami's neck, and he spat in the fire. The spittle hissed and steamed, and before it had boiled away, Kalami felt himself smile.

"Keep your men working, Captain. He has not gone." Sakra would not leave his mistress now that he had reached her side again. He would, surely, try to find a way to stand beside her tonight.

And when he did, Bridget would see him.

"You do not sound concerned, Lord Sorcerer."

Kalami poured beer into the pair of tankards and held out one to Chadek, who only shook his head. "The hunt will keep Sakra on the move, and make it difficult for him to lay any plans," he said. "Your men will ensure that he cannot reach his mistress. If we do not catch him before dawn, we will have him before the sun sets again." He saluted the captain and drank down the bitter beer. "The means have already been secured."

Chadek said nothing, but his face was uneasy.

"What troubles you, Chadek?" asked Kalami over the rim of his cup.

Chadek drummed his fingers against his belt. "I do not like the feel of these past days, Valin," he said. "There is too much abroad for such an uneasy time."

Kalami set the tankard down, and crossed to the captain and laid a hand on his shoulder. "Your instincts are as sound as ever, Chadek, but hear this. It is almost done, I promise you."

Chadek watched him, and from the back of the room, Finon watched him as well. Kalami had to keep himself from smiling at them both.

"Trust me this once more," he urged them.

Chadek searched his face for a moment, and if whatever he saw there did not completely satisfy him, it did not raise any more doubts. He stepped backward, placed his hand over his heart and bowed. "All shall be as you say, friend sorcerer."

Kalami returned the salute. "With my thanks, friend captain."

Chadek left then. Once the door closed, Finon emerged from the servants' alcove, shaking his head. "You are taking too great a chance leaving Sakra free."

"I respect your words, Honored Father," said Kalami humbly. "But if I can take Sakra in front of the eyes of the whole court and Ananda herself, our accusations upon the death of the emperor will carry that much more weight."

Finon pursed his lips together, considering this. At last he nodded. "A good thought. It is sound."

"Thank you, Honored Father." Kalami considered pouring himself some more beer, but decided against it. It was late, and he was beginning to feel the hour, but he was not done yet. "Are you and the others ready?"

"We are," said Finon firmly. "We will be gloved, and I will not break the ribbon until we are alone in the emperor's chamber." There was pride as well as steel in his voice. He had been promised this for so long. It was his hands that would bring down the Isavaltan throne. His hands that would kill the emperor, and Kalami could hear the warmth of anticipation in each word.

"Very good." Kalami stretched his shoulders back. "Now, you must give me my privacy, Honored Father. There is one small matter to be taken care of."

Finon bowed at once, and retired behind the bed screens.

Kalami did not need much. He removed the precious glass mirror from the wall and laid it on the floor. A chest beside the balcony door provided a length of red ribbon, three copper coins and three silver ones.

Kalami knelt beside the firepit facing the mirror. He laid the three silver coins in a triangle on the glass surface. The copper coins he cast, one at a time, into the fire.

"I take up the red thread." He breathed the words across the length of ribbon. "In it I tie thirteen knots. With each knot I speak a name, and each name shall be a blight upon Richikha." His fingers worked the ribbon, tying each knot effortlessly as he repeated the words, over and over again until they all but lost their meaning and he seemed to catch the scent of sickness wafting up from the fire along with the smell of hot metal. He held the image of the sleeping woman firmly in his mind.

He tightened the last knot. "This is my word, and my word is firm, and all the winds of the world shall carry my word, and all the stars in the sky shall see that it is done."

A branch cracked in the fire, sending up a shower of sparks. Kalami held the ribbon up, catching the sparks to burn black spots against its length, ignoring the pinpricks of pain they made against his skin.

It was done then, and he stowed the thread safely in his bag around his neck where he kept his most precious talismans.

Now, Bridget, you have none but me, thought Kalami. *And I have you all to myself.*

The touch of stone was the touch of age, cold and patience, constant pressure resisted by ancient strength, the strength of earth and the strength of ages. Stone was hard to move through because stone could wait forever.

Wood was death and memory of life. Wood was trapped warmth and potential. Wood reached and braced and framed. Wood knew change and the turn of the seasons and the changes of living things. Wood welcomed his passage, because it was change and wood longed to change again.

Iron was cold and hard beyond imagining. Iron answered only the bidding of fire and skill and would not be moved, could not be entreated. Iron banded, bonded, barred. Iron had to be passed by.

Air. Air was speed, life and freedom. Diffuse, impatient, yielding, air parted willingly for him, ready to feed, to topple, to tease, to do as it pleased. Air gave him room to remember his body. Air gave way before the pressure of that memory, allowing Sakra to become himself again.

Sakra, wholly corporeal again, collapsed into a heap on the floor.

For a long moment, he was aware only of the pain. Blood scraped against vein, heart bruised itself against rib, and bones pressed painfully hard against joints. But with each breath, his body remembered its form and function a little more completely and the pain ebbed until at last he could push himself to his feet and stand without weakness.

When he saw that he faced the door to the emperor's god house, and that the grey light of a snowy dawn filled the windows, he allowed himself a moment of triumph. Diffuse, it was hard to guide oneself. Dissolved in stone, it was even harder to know time, because stone cared very little for it. That had always been the danger of the spell. He could have become lost in the stones and come to himself only when the centuries had worn the palace of Vyshtavos away to nothing.

The triumph was short-lived, however, as the realization of all that might have happened in those lost hours washed over him.

Bridget, he thought toward the dawn. *Mistress Bridget, what have they done to you while I hid in the stones?* The fact of the love spell spoke volumes. Kalami meant to bring her under his control. For what purpose Sakra could only guess. There were so many uses for such power. But what was clear was that he meant her to be his creature, not the dowager's. That meant he wished to use her to bring down the throne of Eternal Isavalta, an end that he could not reach while Ananda and Mikkel were alive.

Sakra pushed open the door a bare crack and slipped inside. He hoped the house guard had already searched for him here. He needed time with the keeper before he began the game of cat and mouse that surely wound through the palace and its grounds, with all the cats in search of a single mouse, that being himself.

The god house was only dimly lit at this time. Sakra backed into the nearest alcove and from its shadows he watched Keeper Bakhar moving about his splendidly painted and gilded domain. In his years in Isavalta, Sakra had met a few who took the humble title of "keeper" so seriously. Bakhar permitted no one else to sweep, dust or decorate this room.

From the center of the house, Vyshko and Vyshemir stood guard over their servant on their pedestal of red and black marble. Sakra thought perhaps the artist who had fashioned them meant them to look benevolent, but as Vyshko lifted a pike triumphantly over his head, and Vyshemir held a cup and a dagger out to greet all who entered, it was difficult to say for certain.

Even for the most holy days of change, Bakhar did the work himself. His hands were the ones that washed and dressed the gods every day. But that task was yet to come today. Right now, he was adorning the hall with fresh holly to ready it for the evening's ceremonies.

Sakra smiled to himself, and he walked out into the full light of the god house.

Bakhar froze with his hand raised to place another branch of holly, and he turned. When the keeper saw who faced him, he slowly lowered the holly. "*Agnidh* Sakra *dra* Dhiren Phanidraela," he said, using Sakra's full name as a greeting, as was the courtesy here.

"Good keeper Bakhar Iakshimisyn Rostaviskvin." Sakra strolled toward the center of the room. Before Bakhar had to remind him where he was, he reverenced to the gods. When he straightened up, Bakhar was giving him a narrow-eyed look that was equal parts wariness, approval and curiosity.

The attention did not last long, however. Bakhar sorted through the remaining holly branches that he carried to find one small enough to lay at the feet of the god Niavatk, the miniature ivory carving of a man sitting cross-legged beside a reindeer. "I would have thought you would break your exile before this."

"I am a bit surprised it has taken so long myself." Sakra fell into step beside him as Bakhar moved to the next alcove. This one contained no gods of its own but held a painted mural of Vyshemir's sacred grove.

"Do you come here to seek the protection of Vyshko and Vyshemir?" Bakhar bent forward until his long nose almost touched the mural and reached out delicately to brush away some flake of grime that only he could see. "I cannot extend you sanctuary in their names as you are no longer a member of the house."

"I come to seek a favor, good keeper."

Those words finally gained Bakhar's full attention. He tilted his head up to see Sakra's full face and Sakra saw the shrewd light that shone in his eyes. Bakhar was dedicated to his gods and his duties, that was a true thing, but he often donned the persona of a simple priest to hide another truth, that he was a skilled and steep politician. "What favor?"

"My mistress is in danger."

Bakhar chuffed derisively at him and shooed Sakra away with his last two holly branches. "Your mistress has been in danger since the day she came here."

"Tonight it reaches its peak. The lord—"

The keeper held up his hand. "Speak no names to me. I do not want to hear them."

"You are not naive, Keeper."

"Nor am I unaware that Lord Peshek was placed under house arrest soon after he arrived here yesterday."

"I know." For a few hours, Sakra had cherished the vain hope that Peshek would flee after his words to the dowager failed. He had friends among the house guard. He might have made it. But no. Such a man as Peshek would not desert what he saw as his post.

Bakhar's face grew grave. "He is accused of conspiracy, with the dowager herself standing witness against him using words given to her by Lord Master Oulo."

"This I also know."

"I am not surprised to hear it." Bakhar walked to the central pedestal and laid his holly branches at the feet of the first gods. He gazed up at them, but Sakra could not tell what he hoped to see. "There will be a public trial after the holy day."

"So I understand." Sakra bowed his head. "How does the empress?"

Bakhar regarded him owlishly. "She spent most of yesterday locked up with the dowager and the council lords, as you know, but I believe she has not yet been accused of anything," he said. "It does, however, seem to me I also heard you were to be placed under arrest."

"I do not deny it." Sakra spread his hands. "If you choose to call for the house guard now, I will be at their mercy, and yours."

"Well then," Bakhar sighed. "This is perhaps not the best place to be having this discussion." He gazed around the chamber, empty except for the two of them and all the statues. "Someone may yet today decide to come in to take the counsel of the gods."

Bakhar kissed the hem of Vyshko's robe, and then Vyshemir's, and then beckoned to Sakra. Without looking to see if Sakra obeyed, he went into the vestment room and closed the door. This was not the room where the clothing for the gods was kept. That was locked and under Bakhar's own control and he would never let such a sacrilegious soul as Sakra inside. This was merely where the intercessors and the acolytes changed clothes for the various ceremonies. The walls were hung with robes of green and white in preparation for tonight's celebrations.

Bakhar settled himself on a wooden bench with a comfortable sigh. "Now, Lord Sakra, in these appropriately regal surroundings, tell me what you would of me."

Sakra reverenced. "I need to borrow your appearance and your role tonight that I might remain close to my mistress."

"No."

"Good keeper—"

"No." The single word was flat and final. "Even if it were not a holy day. Even if what you were suggesting were not an affront to my office, and the high ones I serve, you know that I am forbidden to have anything to do with magic lest I'd be tempted to serve powers other than the gods of this house."

Sakra found he had no patience for this righteous denial. "Keeper Bakhar, I tell you that tonight may be the end of everything," he said. "Your lord sorcerer has brought another power to Isavalta. He means to use her to rid themselves of my mistress, and I suspect, your lawful emperor."

Bakhar's face went sour. "You're trying to frighten an old man."

"Yes," agreed Sakra. "There is reason to be frightened. Hung-Tse is waiting on your border for the chaos that is too come. Your dowager is being made a pawn in her too-early dotage."

But Bakhar just combed his fingers down the length of his white beard. "I thought you saw more clearly than that, Sakra."

Sakra bent close so the keeper could not ignore him. He would have the old man see, he would have him understand. This was not the time of stone, or even of iron. This was the time of air, all change, all motion, nothing stable to lean against. "I see that your home, the home of your gods, is teetering on the brink and will soon fall if its rightful ruler is not soon restored. If Ananda dies tonight, that will never happen."

"Vyshko and Vyshemir will protect their house, if it is needed."

"Would they permit me to speak lies in their house?" Sakra shot back.

Bakhar's lips curled into a thin smile and he waggled a finger at Sakra. "Your Seven Mothers teach you to be clever with your words."

"A lifetime in two courts teaches me to be clever with my words." Sakra sat heavily on the bench beside him. "I cannot reach the Empress Ananda or her ladies. I cannot turn one of the house guard. I cannot free Lord Master Peshek. You are my hope, Keeper Bakhar. Ananda is your anointed empress as well as my mistress."

"She was so young when it happened," murmured Bakhar into his beard.

At first, Sakra thought the keeper was talking about Ananda, but when he saw the gentle sadness on the keeper's face, Sakra realized he spoke of Medeoan.

"After the invasion was repelled and the treaty concluded, she would come in here and kneel before Vyshko and Vyshemir. She would beg them to lift her burden from her, to send another to keep Isavalta safe for she lacked the strength." Bakhar shook his head and trailed his fingers down the length of one of the nearby robes, watching the path his hand traced against the cloth. "When they did not, she stopped coming here at all."

"We all serve as we must, and none can save us from that."

Bakhar shook his head. "No, and I thought she would have learned that after Kacha . . ." He declined to finish the sentence and simply waved his hand. "But in her heart she still hoped, and I think she hopes still."

Now came the gamble. Sakra had been saving this move for the end. If this failed, if the keeper denied even this much, it was done. "If she truly wants to lay her burdens down, why does she not free her son?"

Bakhar went very still. "You do not believe . . ."

Sakra said nothing.

"You speak of the succession of the empire," said the keeper sternly. "Vyshko and Vyshemir would not permit their daughter to do such thing."

"Keeper Bakhar, I admire your faith." Sakra squared his shoulders. Not iron, not stone, air. Air, and there was no shelter in the air, however much one wanted there to be. "But you are hiding behind it. We both know the gods permit all matter of disaster to befall their children, especially when their children have ceased their worship."

"No," said Bakhar again. "I cannot take your word over that of Her Grand Majesty."

"Keeper Bakhar, you know how torn the dowager empress's mind is. You have been a good friend to Ananda since she arrived, why will you not listen to me?"

Sakra saw the hopeless look on Bakhar's face and realization drew him to his feet. "No."

The keeper only shrugged and turned his face away. "I'm sorry."

"You will not help me because I and my mistress are of Hastinapura," said Sakra, speaking the words the keeper would not. Anger surged through him and he had to turn away before Bakhar saw the fury in his eyes.

"I was here when Kacha worked his ill," said Bakhar to his back. "When he was finally overthrown, I took oaths to stand by Empress Medeoan and I believed in them." The keeper stopped and then went on more slowly, "The interests of your people are not the interests of mine. How can I desert my empress to stand by you?"

"Ananda is your empress!" Sakra slammed his fist against the wall. Ignoring the pain, he spun to face the startled keeper. "You all speak of Kacha. Let me tell you of Kacha." Sakra rubbed his sore hand, grinding the knuckles that had struck the wall into the palm of his other hand. "Kacha was a pawn. No, he was less than a pawn, he was a puppet. His pride and his arrogance were pulled like strings by a sorcerer named Yamuna. Yamuna forgot his oath to serve and sought instead to rule."

"We know of Yamuna," answered the keeper impassively.

"I don't believe you do." Sakra tried to rein in his anger without avail. "If you did you would know how violently I curse his name. He thought he grasped that infinity which is beyond all of us who must live and die, no matter how deeply the magic is rooted in our spirits. Your ancestors may become gods, but mine may not." He stabbed his finger toward the god house. "Such striving is forbidden to us by the Seven Mothers but Yamuna disregarded them." Slowly, he lowered his arm before it could begin to tremble. "He ignored his place in life, and his very nature, and as a result Ananda has walked hand in hand with Grandfather Death since she arrived here."

Bakhar's face remained stony. "Godhood is a gift. A miracle, not a thing to be striven for."

"It matters not." Sakra slashed his hand through the air between them, but then made himself stand still. How could he be stone and iron in a time of air? It was too hard, and yet he must make this man understand. He took a deep breath. He also must stop thinking of air, stone and iron. He must bring himself all the way out of the spell and think clearly, or Ananda would be left alone tomorrow.

"You must understand, I do not serve Hastinapura," he said softly. "I serve Ananda herself. It is Ananda's wish that she become a good and loyal empress of Isavalta. That is what we have struggled for these five long, cold years." He spread his hands. "She is ready to give up because she is tired and she is afraid and now comes another weapon to be used against her." His hands curled into fists, but he lowered them and made them unknot themselves. He could not make another unseemly display. The keeper already believed the worst of his nature. Air . . . angry words, would not convince Bakhar of anything. Why were they suddenly all he had? "You people have told yourselves so many lies that you cannot see past them anymore to the fact that your dowager in her youth did something foolish and dangerous that has cost lives. She will not admit this to herself and she clings to her mistake as if it was salvation. When will you open your eyes?"

Bakhar waggled his head back and forth. Sakra saw that he wished to deny the allegations and wondered if so essentially honest a man would be able to find the words.

In the end, all the keeper said was, "I did not realize you thought so little of us."

Sakra hung his head. "What am I to think of you?"

"You could think that, like you, each of us is trying to serve our lords and our gods," Bakhar suggested.

"If you ask me to believe that of you, good keeper, I can very easily." Sakra felt himself smile sadly. "You cannot ask me to believe that of such as Kalami."

"The lord sorcerer is not of Isavalta," said Bakhar quickly. "He is of Tuukos."

Sakra had to turn his face away. He did not want Bakhar to see the disgust that flickered through his eyes. "Well then, perhaps you can decide which you like less, Hastinapura or Tuukos." He rubbed his eyes, trying to wipe the anger out of them.

"Perhaps," said Bakhar softly, "I would not be so troubled if you had shown yourself to be more devoted to this house."

So, there it is. This is not about my people, or even Ananda. This is about you and me. "You will not help me because I have never kissed the hem of Vyshko's robe?"

"You mistress does."

Evidently, it was as well he did not know about the shrine Ananda kept in her chambers. "My mistress must. They are her gods now. I am still free to do the rites of the Seven Mothers and no others."

To that, Bakhar remained silent. He again fingered the folds of the nearest robe, as if testing the weave of the cloth. Was that his own robe for the ceremony? Sakra wondered. Was he thinking of his place, of his duty? Sakra could not read his eyes. "They say that your mistress has a double," said Bakhar. "They say that this double lives in the great palace of Hastinapura as Princess Ananda would have had she stayed there. They say that she leads Ananda's life and worships and sacrifices in Ananda's place."

"This is true," said Sakra. "In this way no honors are left undone and Ananda's spirit will be drawn to the proper place when her time comes." Bakhar just looked at him, and understanding came to Sakra. "So, this is the root of it then. Neither one of us truly worships the ones you serve, therefore we may not be trusted in the final reckoning."

Bakhar said nothing.

Sakra stepped away, stunned into silence. This man, so astute, so honest, so involved in affairs of the court, how could he not see beyond the confines of his golden house? How could he sit there and say he would refuse to work for the safety of his land because Sakra had not bowed before the proper images?

So, they stood and faced each other, and Sakra knew how he could bring an end to this insanity. He could go into the god house and kneel before the statues and make his devotions. The Mothers would permit. The Mothers would forgive, because Sakra's first duty in life was to the help and protection of their daughter Ananda.

And yet, he could not make himself move.

So, who is the most blind and the most stubborn here? Sakra clenched his jaw. "You said the dowager has long ago ceased to come here."

To this, Bakhar returned only silence.

"Perhaps it is enough that she performs the proper motions on the proper days," said Sakra, aware that the words he spoke were dangerous. He might even now drive this man beyond his reach, but he did not stop. "Perhaps that is what you consider worship. If so, is not Ananda's worship equally pious?" Bakhar's head bowed slowly, as if Sakra's words beat him down. "Perhaps you are just afraid."

"There is much here to be afraid of," whispered Bakhar. "You are not the only one who spent a lifetime in court. I fear the dissolution of the empire. I fear the overthrow of what is right." There was no strength behind his words, only a dull certainty. "I grew up hearing from my grandfather of the blood feuds and the warlords. I will not help bring that time back."

"But the longer you continue to do nothing," said Sakra, "the closer that time comes."

Bakhar closed his eyes for long moment. "Wait here." He stood but his back remained bowed. Walking like the old man he was, he left the vestment room for the god house, closing the door firmly behind himself.

Sakra stared at its blank wooden surface for a moment, and then, aware that he was violating Bakhar's privacy, he gently turned the knob and opened the door just a crack so that he might see.

Bakhar lay prostrate at the foot of Vyshko's and Vyshemir's pedestal. He was speaking, a long unbroken string of syllables that Sakra could not understand. Bakhar knocked his forehead against the floor and whispered yet more urgent words, clearly begging his gods for some favor, some sign.

Something red dropped to the floor in front of Bakhar. At first, Sakra thought it was a holly berry, but he looked again and saw that it was a drop of liquid. Another drop followed, splashing against the first. Bakhar saw it as well and his eyes grew round with wonder as he pushed himself up just far enough so that he could lift his head and raise his eyes to the tip of Vyshemir's dagger.

A thin trickle of blood ran down the steel blade. Another drop fell soundlessly to the floor. Sakra felt his jaw fall open. Bakhar's face shone with pure wonder. He reached forward and pressed his first two fingertips into the miraculous blood and then pressed them against his lips, his eyes closed in holy rapture.

Then the blood was gone, from the dagger and from the floor, but when Bakhar got himself to his feet and returned to the vestment-room door, Sakra still saw stain of it on his mouth.

Sakra stood back, but did not even attempt to close the door. He could not bring even so small a lie to sully this moment.

Bakhar turned toward Sakra, but he eyes were still far away. "I cannot permit you to take my place in the ceremony," said Bakhar, his voice clear yet soft. "You could not even begin to properly perform the rites. But after that is over, you may come to me and perform what magic you need to work your illusion."

Sakra bowed, giving Keeper Bakhar the salute of trust. "Thank you, good keeper."

Bakhar inclined his head and Sakra reverenced in the Isavaltan fashion. He left the man there. This was not a time when his company could possibly be desired. But as he hurried through the house, Sakra paused before the gods on the pedestal.

Mothers permit, he thought, and he bent his head swiftly down to kiss the hem of Vyshemir's robe.

Something wet fell against his hand, and he drew back startled, expecting blood, but what he saw was a drop of water pure and clean. Slowly, he pressed his hand to his lips as he had seen Bakhar do, and he tasted the salt of the gods' tears.

Chapter Fifteen

In the end, it took Gali and Iadviga several hours to get Bridget dressed. She barely managed to hold herself still under their ministrations. None of the primping and fussing could distract her from the fact that Richikha was not there.

At some point in the night, Bridget had fallen asleep huddled in the middle of the great bed. Richikha had woken her gently, and, despite all the anger and fear that had rushed into her upon opening her eyes, Bridget had at once seen that fever flushed Richikha's face.

Richikha had waved away all her protestations and closed Kalami's garter in the wooden box. She carried both out to the snow-covered balcony and buried them under the drift that had formed there.

That, however, was all she had been able to do before she collapsed into a chair, her eyes far too bright, and the heat coming palpably off her skin.

By then, the other two had woken. Gali had sent for the mistress of the house, who in turn called for a pair of footmen to lift Richikha's pallet as a stretcher, and bear her away. The only thing anyone had been able to tell Bridget since then was that Richikha was resting comfortably.

Bridget knew that Kalami was responsible, but she could not even leave the room to see Richikha and tell her so. She had to be made ready to get through the charade of the evening. She could not neglect that, or her promise to him. Not now that she was supposed to be so mindlessly in love. The thought of raising Kalami's suspicions shot terror through her. Her fear sickened Bridget, but she stayed where she was and submitted to the ministrations of her remaining ladies who had been too foolish to become a danger.

First, her hair had to be combed, scented and dressed with pearls and threads of gold. Then, she had to be given a sponge bath in a basin of rosewater, an operation she insisted on performing herself, much to her ladies' amusement. Then, her hands had to be given a separate special bath in ass's milk. Then, it was on with the layers of undergarments to be fussed and twiddled and adjusted.

Kalami thought he had her, but Kalami was not ready to leave much to chance. Garters came in pairs. He might be weaving another even now, and what would she do if he presented it to her when he came tonight? Bridget had to close her eyes against that idea.

Bridget winced and held her breath as they tied on the underskirt. They tightened the laces and she made herself think carefully of Kalami. No tenderness came over her, no sentimental maundering. He had tricked her and lied to her. He had surely poisoned Richikha, and he had sought to rob Bridget of her freedom. All Bridget felt about him was anger and fear.

Secure in her contempt, Bridget was able to relax a bit while her ladies wrestled her into the heavy overgarments, lacing, hooking and engaging in further fussing and adjusting. At long last came the veil of gold tissue and silver thread, followed by the diadem of gold with its chains of pearls that hung over her ears and looped across the back of her head. The arrangement hid her hair so effectively, Bridget wondered at all the time taken to dress it.

For a final touch, Iadviga pinned Kalami's brooch on Bridget's left shoulder, and Bridget tensed again. But no, she felt no love. She let herself breathe.

The ladies held up the sheet of polished bronze to show her to herself. Bridget drew in a long breath. She had expected to find herself ridiculous. Part of her had hoped for passable, even pretty, but the figure in the gold-toned mirror was regal. This was no fairy-tale confection of a princess; rather, she was a queen in all her pomp and state.

That impression lasted for all of one heartbeat, after which, despite all the fear and anger that lay so heavy on her mind, it was all Bridget could do to keep from laughing at herself.

Iadviga and Gali, who were already done up in their best, did not seem to find any of this funny at all, and took it upon themselves to instruct Bridget in the arts of standing, sitting, reverencing and turning around (backing up was not even to be considered because of the train) in the costume.

A knock sounded on the door and Iadviga hurried to answer it. When she stood aside, Kalami crossed the threshold. The lord sorcerer was also obviously dressed in his very best. His burgundy velvet coat was practically a robe, hanging all the way down to the ankles of his polished black boots. Jet black fur trimmed the velvet, and the belt that encircled his waist was gold and carbuncles. More carbuncles were set into the buttons of the coat. Underneath the wide, black fur trim of his coat, she could see he wore a shirt of blinding white, the collar and cuffs of which had been embroidered with scarlet, green and gold. The hat on his head had something of the shape of a bishop's miter, only much more abbreviated. It too was jet black and set with gold.

He looked regal, and he reverenced to Bridget only after he permitted himself a long look at her.

"I knew you would be fair, Bridget," he said, and she felt the caress in his words like the glide of a knife's edge against her skin. "But I did not know you would be breathtaking."

Bridget stilled her knees and hands, which began to tremble at the sound of his voice and the memory of how much she had wanted his touch, although such timorousness might have been appropriate. She was supposed to be undone for love of this man, after all.

"I am glad you like it," she made herself say, hoping that she did not sound too weak. "You yourself look splendid." Which was flattery, but also the whole truth. His velvet glowed in the light of the braziers. His hair had been combed back and styled so that it shone thick and full under the jeweled black hat. The burgundy set off the rich tan of his skin, making Bridget feel anemic beside him.

"Have any of your ladies thought to inform you of what to expect this evening?"

Bridget cast a smiling glance at Gali and Iadviga. "No. They have been busy informing me how to handle the acreage of fabric." She smoothed down some of the brocade needlessly.

The joke apparently met with Kalami's approval as much as her appearance. He smiled as he strolled over to stand as close beside her as the spreading hems of her skirts would allow. "Did they tell you that you should give me your hand so I might take your fingertips, thus?" He lifted her hand up and closed the tips of his fingers around hers. "Where is my token, Bridget?" he whispered low so that only she could hear.

Bridget's stomach turned over, but she managed to lean close and say into his ear, "It is around my leg, as a garter should be, sir. Would you like to see?"

"Very much," he replied. "But we must not shock your ladies." He drew back to look laughing into her eyes. Bridget managed to drop her gaze demurely until she felt she had herself under control. When she looked up into his face again, she was startled by a sensation of deep familiarity, and wondered where that familiarity came from.

In the next minute she knew, and the realization sent an icy shock down her spine.

He looked like Asa. Her baby's father. The brown skin, the dark eyes, the chiseled features. God almighty, how had she not seen it before?

"Are you all right, Bridget?" He appeared concerned. Bridget could not begin to guess what he had seen on her face in that moment.

"Yes, fine, thank you." It took all her strength not to pull away from him. No, he was not Asa. He was worse. Asa had sought only her seduction, Kalami had sought her imprisonment. He was far, far worse than Asa.

Bridget took refuge from her thoughts in what little humor she still possessed. "I am just curious how are we to get through the door linked like this?" She lifted their hands.

He laughed, and Bridget covered her mouth as if to politely hide her own laugh.

Ah, God, how am I going to get through tonight?

The same way she was going to get through the door, possibly, by waiting in silence and letting events flow around her. The ladies opened the door. Kalami walked ahead, watching Bridget from the corner of his eye as he beckoned her forward. Bridget obeyed this silent command, with her ladies falling into step behind her. As Kalami took her fingertips again, she kept her eyes on the floor, hoping to be taken for watching the voluminous hems of her garment.

Kalami steered her down the corridor. Other grandees of indeterminate rank filed along with them. The corridor was only dimly lit, so to Bridget, they were more impressions than people—a flash of emerald silk here, the glimmer of gold intertwined with silver, a blue gem, a spotted length of fur, a coppery braid. The gentlemen all seemed to be carrying swords or tiny golden maces in embroidered sheaths, while the ladies appeared to have taken to heart a fashion for flat-topped conical hats with lace veils hanging from them. Bridget, ridiculously, found herself feeling a bit out of fashion.

At last, she and Kalami came to the mezzanine surrounding the pink marble staircase and the dramatically curved foyer that Richikha had told her was called the Rotunda. The entire hallway had made the transition from winter to vibrant spring. Flowering vines twined the massive staircase railings and butterflies spread their wings on the edge of the blossoms. Evergreen branches adorned the windows, and songbirds perched in those branches, their beaks opened and their breasts swelled as if they were about to sound forth. Huge urns brimming with yet more flowers lined the hall under yards of blue blunting that blocked out the darkening winter sky with the illusion of spring.

It took Bridget a moment to realize that the flowers and birds were made of glass, cunningly fashioned and beautifully colored. Light from candles and torches glanced against the splendid ornamentation, and was reflected and passed on, making the evening hall wondrously bright.

"Is this magic?" Bridget touched one delicate pink petal and found it hard as ice.

"No." Kalami shook his head. "Only great skill applied over many years." He rested the fingertips of his free hand on the wing of a startling blue butterfly. "Many of these artisans were brought from my homeland."

Bridget kept her eyes on the delicately fashioned blooms, an uncomfortable realization spreading through her. Kalami's people had been wronged. She knew that. They had been reviled, and conquered, and ground down by those same conquerors. If he had been honest with her, if he had told her what had happened to him instead of attempting to trap her, she might have stood beside him on the basis of that wrong. She might have never known what he truly was.

Might he be acting out of fear? She risked a glance at him out of corner of her eye, and saw the melancholy in his expression as he gazed across the beauty of the scene. *Might he only be trying to free his people and he cannot risk failure, so he must be cruelly, utterly sure of me?*

Maybe it was my fault, for not being forthright enough. Maybe . . .

Maybe it didn't happen at all. Maybe it was a dream. She had to pull her hand away from the flower she touched. That was what she'd tried to tell herself after Asa, when the realization of what she had done began to sink in. Maybe it was something other than it was, she told herself. More than just one night in the dark.

She'd come to believe it then. She'd been wrong, then as well as now.

Her thoughts turned. Where was Sakra? If he was free, he'd be nearby, she was sure of it. She just wished she could catch some glimpse of him. She'd feel a little less alone then.

Bridget bit her lip and searched for something else to occupy her mind. If Kalami got a good look at her now, he would surely know how badly she was shamming.

Between the urns of flowers stood hinged screens, painted with all manner of scenes in colors as vibrant as the glass flowers. Some seemed to be pastoral, images of birds and beasts, young men and women. Some seemed to be historical with nobility on thrones, scenes of battle and scenes of surrender.

Kalami noticed her gaze on the paintings. "The history of Isavalta, painted for the contemplation of Their Imperial Majesties, and for all loyal folk as another year in the life of Eternal Isavalta begins."

He seemed about to add something else, but a new sound cut him off. Below the stairs and from the left, voices lifted in song—low rumbling basso profundos, soaring sopranos and all colors of bass, baritone, tenor and alto, blending together in ringing harmony. It seemed that the stones themselves shivered with the intensity of the sound. Bridget could make nothing of the words, she only knew that it was grand, and beautiful, and like nothing she had ever heard in her life.

At some unspoken signal, the lights were doused and the hall plunged into darkness. Bridget pressed her fingers to her mouth to cover her gasp. Then she saw that the hall was not entirely dark. A series of new lights moved off to the left where the song emerged from. The voices grew stronger, filling the hall with an immensity of sound until the glass thrilled in sympathetic response. The birds truly did sing.

It was a procession, Bridget now saw. Men and women in long coats of emerald green belted around with wreaths of holly. More holly crowned their heads. Each of them held a candle as thick around as Bridget's wrist. Keeper Bakhar walked in the lead, carrying his candle in one hand and an ivory staff that was taller than he was in the other. As old as he appeared, Bridget detected no hint of querulousness in his voice as he joined the choir in their incomprehensible hymn.

"What are they singing?" murmured Bridget.

"They sing the names of the kings and emperors of Isavalta, and of all the household gods, calling on them to deliver protection to the house, and to bring back the spring."

After the choir walked an old woman with a ramrod-straight spine who could only have been the dowager, magnificent in a shimmering red coat that might have been woven of spun rubies. Behind her came Ananda, gowned, coated and veiled entirely in royal blue. Next to her, the only figure not carrying a candle, walked the emperor, dressed very like Kalami save that his clothes were entirely of gold, and in place of the hat, he wore a crown of sapphires.

Behind them walked an array of old men, their coats and hats a plethora of festive colors.

"The council lords," Kalami murmured in Bridget's ear. "When they have passed by, we must move to join the procession."

Bridget nodded absently. All her attention was focused on the emperor. She had to see what bound him. That was her salvation and her freedom.

But he was so far away and wore so much shining gold that the candles caused every inch of him to gleam and glitter. She could see nothing but the reflection of the flame against his coat. If there was some nimbus of magical light under there, his costume succeeded in hiding it well.

Curses formed in Bridget's mind. The one night, the one time she needed desperately to see and she could not. Now what would she do?

As the silent men with their glittering coats passed, Kalami took Bridget's fingertips again and led her down the stairs. The other grandees gathered behind them, forming themselves into a great train for the procession. Bridget was keenly aware of their gaze boring into her back, wondering, perhaps, who this upstart was who got to walk before them, or more simply who this new face was and how she fit into the complicated puzzle that was the life of this palace. Not one of them had spoken to her. Perhaps it was because of the ceremony, or perhaps it was some point of etiquette—perhaps no one could acknowledge her until the dowager did. She would have to find an opportunity to ask Kalami. Any detail might help her at this point.

The procession wound slowly through the palace, picking up more and more people as it passed through the chambers and halls. Bridget caught glimpses of the glowing glass blossoms, gilded birds, the flashes of eyes and faces painted on screens, but she had no ability to examine any of it, as much as she wanted to so she would have something to distract her from the warmth and pressure of Kalami's fingers. Among all the eyes, living and painted, she felt his the most acutely. They looked for signs that his spell was working. They waited to see that she had drowned under the depths of his magic. What would he do if he did not see what he was looking for?

The procession turned a corner, and ahead Bridget could see what looked like a cave of light welcoming them. Huge candles, as tall as her shoulder and as thick around as her waist, lit the god house, their brilliance making it seem a room made entirely of gold and gems.

When her eyes adjusted to the dazzle, Bridget saw that Vyshko and Vyshemir on their pedestal had also been dressed in robes of white and crowned over with holly. Vyshko's robe had been belted with a magnificent girdle of golden beads. Silver flowers and twining vines encircled Vyshemir's waist.

The choir and the keeper divided around the statues to stand among the candles, the women going to the left side of the room, and the men going to the right. The hymn, already magnificent, swelled and echoed around the domed enclosure until Bridget could scarcely think for the overwhelming flood of it.

Ahead of them, the dowager stepped up to the statues and placed something Bridget could not see at their feet. The dowager kissed the hem of Vyshko's robe, and then the hem of Vyshemir's, and stepped away. Empress Ananda followed the dowager's example, laying a gift at the feet of the statues and kissing their robes. But when Ananda reached for the emperor's hand, the dowager was already there and leading her son away. The emperor, Bridget noticed, made no obeisance, nor left any gift.

The ritual was repeated by all the council lords, and the line moved forward slowly. Bridget felt a mild discomfort at the strange church, and its even stranger ritual. She had little use for Christianity, having found that Christianity had little use for her, but still, this was . . . not right. Their tale was so brutal, and told with such reverence.

But then, who was she to say? Who knew how divinity manifested itself in this strange world?

She and Kalami had almost reached the pedestal. Already, a heap of gifts buried the feet of the statues. Bridget felt something pressed into her hand. She looked down. It was a small gauze bag filled with what looked like dried currants and gilded almonds. She noted that most of the gifts around the feet of the statues were either food or fanciful representations of food. By now, she knew what was expected of her. She set the bag down among the other gifts, and kissed Vyshko's robe, and then Vyshemir's.

Whoever you are, she prayed, *whatever you may be, help me see what I must.*

As quickly as the prayer had come to her, Bridget's inner eye snapped open and she saw . . .

Kalami was barely able to catch Bridget as she toppled over, her eyes wide open but seeing nothing in the room. All the Isavaltan lords and priests stared, and the long hymn of praise and groveling to their gods faltered.

"It is the heat, the closeness of the room," Kalami murmured, lifting his hand ostensibly to feel Bridget's forehead, but in reality to close her eyes so none would see them open. The last thing he needed was for some fool to think this vision somehow divine and insist on her being allowed to wake in the god house and give witness.

Kalami hoisted Bridget into his arms, carrying her through the crowd. He knew the dowager watched every movement. He had no time to get word to her. He had to get Bridget out of here. He reached the end of the procession where her ladies waited. The fat one just threw up her hands and lacked the wit even to bring her fan out to help cool their prostrate mistress. The tall redhead turned swiftly and began clearing a route through the remainder of the crowd directly toward one of the fainting rooms off the Great Hall. Once inside, she deftly arranged pillows on the sofa so that Bridget might be laid down comfortably.

"You." Kalami pointed at the fat one. "Find Her Grand Majesty's chief lady-in-waiting and tell her Bridget Lederle is well. She was just momentarily overcome. You." He pointed at the other twitterer. "Fetch water and wine. You will then retire to stand outside the door and admit no one until I say otherwise."

They both reverenced hastily and retreated, closing the door firmly behind themselves.

Kalami turned his attention once more to Bridget where she lay on the sofa, her skirts trailing on the floor. Her eyes moved back and forth behind her now-closed lids. *What do you see?* It might be anything. She had admitted that she'd seen the past as well as the future. There was so much past he could not afford to have her yet know. Her visions had been a danger from the beginning. How much would love lead her to excuse?

Was the spell even taking properly? The garter was more tightly woven than the braid, but it was still hastily made and spells of the heart were tricky things. It would be best if he checked now that the garter had been fastened properly, although it would leave him with a great deal to explain if Bridget woke suddenly, or if someone entered despite his orders.

Carefully, Kalami folded back the layers of skirt until he exposed Bridget's legs. They were sturdy, with little elegance about them, despite the fine woolen stockings. Bridget did not stir. She made no noise, wrapped tightly in whatever vision held her. He pushed back the lengths of linen, velvet and gilt past her knees to expose her unadorned thighs.

Kalami clamped his jaw around a shout of rage, and forced himself to smooth Bridget's clothing back into its proper position.

He stood, folding his hands behind his back and clenching them into fists. What had gone wrong? Who had betrayed him? Was it that cowardly little seamstress who cared so much for her position? Had that clever little lady-in-waiting somehow meddled once more before he had struck her down? Or was it Bridget herself? Had those double-damned eyes seen what he planned? Did she already know? Did they show her even now? His right hand reached out, the fingers crooking themselves around the air. He should strangle her, here and now. End this game. He should have thrown her into her own lake, let it drown her, and gone to the dowager with a tale of sorrow. There were other powers in the world. He would find another to help him hold the Firebird in check.

Bridget jerked upright, her eyes wide and staring.

When the temple faded from Bridget's awareness, it was replaced by a vision of Mikkel, but not as she had seen him before. Here, his face was full of animation and anticipation. He stood beside a huge bed hung with blue velvet curtains. Men in livery divested him of his velvet coats and silken vest, leaving him in his hose and a single long shirt. Some other young men stood nearby, all of them joking and laughing. It was his wedding night, Bridget knew. Mikkel was being prepared to meet his bride, who would soon be led to their marriage bed.

But all the laughing ceased as the dowager appeared around the edge of one of the wooden screens. Smiling herself, she waved her hand, dismissing all the men save her son. And when they were gone, she set down a bundle she carried and opened it.

"A final wedding gift for you, my son." She lifted out a silver girdle with a braided waistband, and what might have been a thousand elaborately knotted and beaded tassels hanging from it. Despite its beauty, horror clung to the thing like an odor. Bridget wanted to recoil, but she could neither move nor close her eyes.

"It will help you please your new bride," Medeoan said to her son. "And ensure that I have a grandson in nine months' time."

"My mother imperial," said Mikkel formally, struggling not to squirm. "I am honored to know that you are thinking of me, but I was hoping for some privacy at this time."

"Nonsense." The dowager smiled and walked toward him, her gift held in both hands. "Who better to help a young man at this time than an old woman? Lift your shirt."

"Mother . . ."

"Lift your shirt."

Mikkel rolled his eyes, but decided that the quickest way to be left alone was to obey. He gathered up the tails of his shirt, raising it to expose his well-formed torso. He did not see his mother's mouth moving as she deftly wrapped the silver girdle around his waist. He did not see the knot she tied to seal the charm. He did not see the way the girdle faded to transparency and was lost to the detection of the human eye.

The dowager Medeoan laid her hands on her son's elbows. "Lower your arms, Mikkel."

Mikkel did as he was told. His arms hung limp at his sides, his hands dangling. His whole being had gone slack. His eyes alone still moved, slipping this way and that, unable to rest on any one thing.

Medeoan smoothed down the crumpled fabric of his shirt. "Now, my son, you will be safe." She left him standing there for a moment while she crossed to the bed and turned back the blankets. "Get into bed."

Slowly, shambling, Mikkel shuffled to the bed, groped at its edge with both hands like blind man and climbed in. Medeoan smoothed the blankets over him, touched his cheek and left him.

The real world rushed in to swamp the vision and Bridget jerked bolt upright.

"Ah, you return to me."

She lay on one of the palace's many silken divans. Kalami held her wrist. He must have been chafing it. She could not hear the choir anywhere, but beyond the room came the rush and clatter of busy movement.

"Where . . ."

"A fainting room off the Great Hall."

"Oh. Oh." She settled back on the divan, but her heart refused to cease pounding. The dowager . . . the dowager did this thing to her son. She robbed him of his wits and blamed her daughter-in-law. Bridget could see the knot she tied even now. Bridget pressed her hand against her chest. She must tell. She must tell somebody.

"What did you see, Bridget?"

She opened her mouth, and closed it again. She must tell, she must, but tell Kalami? How could this have happened without his knowing? Maybe it had. Maybe the dowager had fooled him completely.

But she saw again how much he looked like Asa, and remembered the other spell, the one wrapped around her wrist last night.

The lie came to her then, fast, so that she could tell, and not tell.

"I saw the emperor," she said, clutching the collar of her fine dress. "I saw a silver girdle being tied around his waist . . ." She peered ahead, as if struggling to reconstruct the scene. *Tell, tell,* sang every instinct in her. *But not him,* she countered. *Never him.*

"Who, Bridget?" he asked, his face impassive. "Who do you see?"

"It's not clear, it's . . ." She sounded like a poor imitation of Aunt Grace at one of her séances, and she knew it, but she could think of nothing else to do. "It's a woman." She brought the words out in a rush, looking up at him with what she hoped was extreme earnestness. "A woman who is supposed to love him but doesn't." Her hand flew to her mouth. "Ananda. It must be Ananda."

"So." Kalami stood, folding his hands behind his back. "You found it out. What all the sorcerers in the land could not do, you have done in a moment."

"So it would seem." A chill stole over Bridget. She could not put a name to the sensation that radiated from Kalami. Was he pleased? Did he suspect her lie?

Bridget tucked a few stray wisps of hair back under her veil.

"What do we do?" *I must still tell, I must find some way.*

Kalami made a show of considering. "We go to the feast," he said at last. "I will speak to Her Grand Majesty as soon as may be."

"But . . ." began Bridget, every bit the anxious female, and not at all interested in making this easy for him. There was something he was not saying. His expression was full of matters unspoken. "You can just break the spell, can't you? Just cut it off him right now, now that you know?"

"Bridget, you must trust me." Kalami took her hand again, holding it solicitously between his own. "This is an ancient and powerful magic. It must be undone with care, not crudely destroyed, or the shock of it might kill Mikkel."

"Oh." *Liar.* She knew that, although she could not have said how she knew. "Of course. I should have realized it would be something like that."

His smile was warm, full of gentleness and understanding, and even a bit of pride, but it faded too soon away and the chill descended over Bridget again. "I am most concerned for you, Bridget. This vision . . . it could bring danger."

"What danger?" she asked innocently. "I am already under your protection, am I not?"

"Of course. But . . . Ananda has her spies, and her allies. Rumor of you and your abilities, especially your visions, has already flown around the palace. I had hoped to have you more safe by now." His eyes grew intense, even though his voice stayed mild. "But you have lied to me, and laid by my token, Bridget. Why did you do this?"

He knew. He knew she did not lie under his spell. The cold she felt came from him. It was the winter cold that lies beyond the blood heat of anger. It enveloped her and reached inside to squeeze her heart. She could make no answer and he kept his own silence, his eyes fixed on hers. He knew. He knew she felt his anger, and he knew she was afraid. He also knew, as she did, that she had nowhere to go. The snow held them all in this palace jewel box and locked the lid. Even if she might be tempted to try to escape, he would be right beside her. Here, he was a lord and she was stranger. All this shone in his eyes.

"We will attend properly to your protection before the night is out, Bridget," he said, his voice full of a fresh promise that made her heart constrict further yet. She could not force any kind of reply.

Kalami smiled slightly at her silence. He extended his hand. "If you are recovered, we should go make our appearance in the Great Hall."

Bridget's skin prickled with revulsion, but she stretched out her hand. Kalami closed his fingertips over hers, and pulled ever so slightly, saying with that gesture that she must get to her feet, or be dragged to her knees.

Bridget stood as smoothly as her costume would allow. She met his eyes and made herself stand straight and tall. He would see no more weakness from her.

"Very good." He reached his free hand to open the door. "You are wise, and you are attentive, Bridget, but do not forget you have much yet to learn. The sooner I am able to begin your teaching, the better it will be for all of us." A smile took shape on his face but did not reach his black eyes. "Your ladies are outside the door, both of them gravely distressed. I'm afraid I had to deny them access to your person, lest they flutter and twitter you to death."

Lest they hear something they were not supposed to. "It is a pity Richikha was taken ill," she said lightly. "Of them all, she showed some sense."

Kalami's face was a study in gravity. "But not enough, or she would be at your side even now." He spoke the words casually, and Bridget made herself smile in response. This then was to be her role. They were friends. Nothing was wrong. Nothing at all was wrong, even though she now had her confirmation of the cause of Richikha's sudden fever.

Bridget managed to walk back into the company of her remaining ladies, who did indeed flutter and twitter about her, fanning her face, straightening her coat, her train, and her veil. Where was Richikha to read her face and know all that was wrong? Richikha had been taken from her by Kalami, so he would be sure she was left alone.

But she just smiled and shook her ladies off, tartly instructing them to help her with her dress so that she could sit down to dinner and stop making a spectacle of herself. For around them, the feast was obviously well under way. Wooden tables on stacks of wooden platforms framed the oblong hall, the table of the dowager sitting higher than all the others. Boys and girls in long, belted tunics of blue and gold, or green and white, darted between the tables with pitchers of liquors to fill the gilded goblets on the table. Liveried men carried in huge platters with joints of meat and whole geese in pastries. The smells of rich gravy and unfamiliar spices, liquor, human bodies and burning wax thickened the air and sent Bridget's head spinning.

"Come, this way," said Kalami.

He led Bridget and her ladies to one of the tables immediately below the dowager's. Bridget thought she recognized some of the men there as the council lords who had walked by earlier, but again, while they nodded politely to Kalami, they did not speak, only casting sideways glances at Bridget.

"What do I do if I need to ask for the salt?" she whispered as she sat, Gali and Iadviga fussing to make sure her train was draped properly across the back of her chair.

"Ask me," Kalami breathed back. "As you are new to the court, they may not acknowledge you until the dowager has done so officially."

How well I am beginning to understand this place, thought Bridget, smoothing down her skirt. *How frightening an idea that is.*

As soon as she was settled, Bridget found herself descended on. Meats and pastries were paraded past her, a whole row of goblets in front of her was filled, each with a different-colored liquor.

At that moment, getting drunk seemed an attractive option. Bridget felt hemmed in. She was surrounded by people who could not or would not speak with her. Kalami's chair was close enough to hers so that his arm brushed her sleeve, constantly reminding her of his presence. Even her ladies had retired to the back of the hall with those she supposed were other servants. Without consulting her, Kalami selected which cuts and which dainties were laid on her plate. She stared at the food, the odors arising from it no longer appetizing, just a miasma of strange scents that tightened her throat and stomach.

Yet, she was beginning to understand. She had seen so much, and she had seen more than Kalami knew. Could she make use of that?

Pressing her fingertips against her mouth, Bridget looked toward the high table, wishing desperately to see something that would give her hope. The dowager ate and drank without once looking at plate or cup. Her eyes remained focused upon the hall, sweeping back and forth across it, careful not to miss any detail of who spoke with whom. Ananda sat on her left hand, watching the dowager as closely as the dowager watched the court. The empress's eyes went where the dowager's went, and her attention lighted where the dowager's did. The empress was trying to guess what the old woman next to her would do, Bridget now knew, trying to understand and anticipate her plans. Probably Ananda was trying to keep herself alive, or at least free of the sort of spell that held her husband, who slouched in the chair on the dowager's right side. She too was trapped. Bridget wondered if the empress knew there was now another prisoner in the hall.

Where was Sakra? He must still be free, or Kalami would surely have said something. But if he was free and in hiding, he could do her no good.

Then, Bridget remembered how it had been when she saw Sakra in his swan's shape. How all the court had stopped to listen to her words, and how Empress Ananda had been made free to act. Could she do such a thing again? But if she did speak, what could she say that would both tell the empress where her loyalties lay and get her away from Kalami?

Occasionally, Emperor Mikkel would pick up a piece of food, put it in his mouth and chew, but he did it without any apparent interest or enjoyment. He was eternally bored and indifferent, even to such intimate matters. Bridget wished she could see his waist. Was there a glowing ring around it where the girdle hung? Now that she knew where to look, would she be able to see it under the shimmering gold? She cursed herself silently. She should have been more attentive in the dark of the corridor while she hid and watched his delirium. Had she been able to say something earlier, this masquerade might already have ended.

"You must eat something, Bridget," said Kalami, softly, kindly. "You do not wish to faint again, do you?"

Kalami was watching her. Bridget dropped her attention to her plate and picked up a silver knife. She speared a bit of meat, paté and pastry. It was savory and heavily peppered, burning her palate and throat as she swallowed. She reached for the nearest goblet, and found it full of weak, sour beer. Nonetheless, Bridget swallowed that as well, and fixed a polite smile on her face. It was apparently enough, for Kalami turned at least part of his attention to his own food.

At the high table, the dowager was saying something to a serving man who wore a gold chain around his neck. He, in turn, said something to two others of the servers, and they began directing the rest, who began clearing away the food and plates. Evidently the dowager was done eating. Consequently, everyone else was done as well.

In the meantime, people's personal servants clustered around them, helping with hems and sleeves as their employers stood and filed out into a foyer painted with murals of a rolling summer countryside. Bridget found herself crowded beside Kalami, in the midst of people who reverenced to him, and stared openly at her. Ladies whispered behind their fans and men speculated behind their eyes. Despite all, Bridget wanted to laugh. She was being gossiped about. Of all the things that had happened to her since she came here, this was the one that was familiar and it felt almost comfortable.

Sakra's face flashed in front of her, and Bridget pulled up short.

Kalami's hand clamped down around her wrist; against all the proprieties of this court, he reminded her of his strength. "Are you all right? Do you have a vision?"

Bridget lowered her shoulders. "No, no, I'm fine, I . . ." She laughed. "This is ridiculous, but I thought I saw someone I knew. As if they weren't all a world and more away."

"Indeed." But there was a frown in Kalami's voice, and Bridget knew the lie had been far too weak. Now Kalami's gaze swept the room, looking for who Bridget might have seen.

She swallowed, casting about for some way to distract him. Sakra was out there in the crowd. Bridget was amazed at the strength of the emotion that flooded her. Sakra could get to Ananda to tell her what was truly happening and what spell held the emperor. He was a sorcerer and would know how to safely undo it. Ananda would know who had helped her, and Bridget would be safe, just as soon as she was able to tell what she had seen.

But it was more than that. It was the knowledge that amid all this fear and entrapment, she did have a true friend and he was nearby. She was not alone, and all she had to do was find a way to tell him what was happening without Kalami interfering.

Oh, is that all? Bridget had to swallow a bitter laugh.

At that moment, the doors to the main hall swung open again. One of the liveried servants thumped a staff on the floor.

"Her Grand Majesty bids all assemble and pay witness to the actions of her court." The man stood aside.

Kalami took possession of her fingertips with his. "I will walk you to the dais. When you are before the dowager, kneel. Keep your eyes on the floor. Do not stand until she tells you to. And keep your countenance whatever she says to you." The fact that he would be watching her every moment was left unspoken.

Kalami led her up the strip of tapestry carpet that now marked the center of the hall. Eyes stared at her, before and behind, catching her up with the pressure of all their many gazes, and robbing her of all her breath. Soldiers waited around the edges of the room, their spear-tipped axes drawn and gleaming, and their swords and clubs sheathed at their hips. Useless women and calculating men filled every bit of space. Her stupid, elaborate dress weighed her down as surely as if she had been bound in chains. The face in which she had found hope of salvation had vanished into the crowd of strangers, and she could see nothing except her jailer, his allies and her fellow prisoners.

Bridget and Kalami reached the dais. The Keeper Bakhar stood before the dais, his ivory wand held to symbolically bar their way. His face seemed blurred, and Bridget looked again.

And she saw Sakra standing before her, carrying the keeper's wand and holding it crosswise to block their path.

She nearly choked.

"I am the Lord Sorcerer Valin Kalami," Bridget's escort declared. "And I bring with me Bridget Lederle to honor the Eternal Empire of Isavalta, and do all rights and duties to her imperial stewards."

"Let her pass, then." Sakra stood aside.

Kalami let go of Bridget's fingertips and nodded toward her. *Play your part,* he was saying to her. *I am watching. This is my place, and you are my pawn.*

Helpless rage swelled inside of her, but she kept her face still. Help stood so close she could reach out and touch him, and yet he might as well have been on Sand Island, because she could not reach him without Kalami and the rest of the world knowing.

Bridget lifted her chin, and her skirt hems, and climbed carefully up the three carpeted steps of the dais, keeping her eyes fixed steadily downward as she had been directed. She reached the last step and saw red velvet slippers brushed by red and gold hems. Again, as directed, she knelt.

"Bridget." A dry hand touched first her left cheek, then her right. "At last, you are come to me."

Two desiccated, wrinkled, and surprisingly callused hands grasped Bridget's and raised her to her feet. Startled, Bridget lifted her gaze. Up close, Bridget could see the young woman the dowager had once been. She had been beautiful, and probably filled with a lively intelligence. Under the mask of age and the lines of bitterness, Bridget saw someone she could have liked. The impression was so strong she wondered for a moment where it came from, because she also saw a pinched old woman overburdened by the clothes she wore, and she did still know that this woman had trapped her only child into a permanent waking dream.

Past the dowager's shoulder, Bridget saw Empress Ananda looking daggers at her. She wanted to speak to the empress, to tell her that she knew what it was to be afraid, to be surviving tonight on fraud, lies and pretense . . .

Fraud. Pretense. A desperate plan nibbled at the back of Bridget mind. Truth could only harm her now, but could fraud save her as it had the empress?

"At last," the dowager said again, gripping Bridget's hands painfully hard. Her entire face was filled with a look of desperate hope and utter starvation. "You are come to save me."

"I . . ." Bridget struggled to think of something to say. "I will do my best, Grand Majesty." At the last moment, she remembered the proper title.

"Yes." The dowager pulled her close, until Bridget could smell the mix of wine and food on her too-warm breath. "That is the voice. I hear your father in you. Tomorrow, I shall show you his work, and your heritage."

Bridget gaped, unable to think of any reply to this. She could only stare at this old woman, who had once been a young girl, who was evil, and afraid, and desperate, and looking toward Bridget, and . . .

. . . And the three men in livery entering the bedchamber, the poisonous sheets carried under the arm of the leader. They folded back the eiderdown quilt, ready to lay out the trap.

And Bridget knew she must tell, and in the same flashing moment, she saw how she might escape. She would have to choose her words with care. She could not accuse too openly lest Kalami be able to turn her own words against her. He could speak so glibly, and held so much power, but then so did she. She would have to hedge and dissemble, but perhaps, perhaps . . .

The dowager had released Bridget and turned toward the assembly. Bridget's heart pounded hard. The dowager opened her mouth, and so did Bridget.

Bridget screamed. She drew the noise out long and ragged, releasing all her fear and frustration into a piercing howl that rang around the hall and silenced every other noise. As she did, she fell to her knees, groveling on the carpet as if pressed there by some invisible force.

"The emperor!" she cried into the silence. "The emperor is in danger!"

A tide of voices washed over her, thousands of questions being asked. Someone knelt beside her, grasping her shoulders. The dowager. Bridget did not give her time to speak.

"See them!" She pointed toward nothing but air. "See them! They lay poison upon the emperor's bed! Oh! Save him! Save him!" She dropped her face into her hands. "Somebody save him!"

Silence fell again for the space of one heartbeat, and then the room roared into life.

"What does she mean!"

"Who is she!"

"Grand Majesty! What is this!"

Then finally, the dowager's voice. "Captain! Get your men to the emperor's chamber! Bring to me whatever you find!"

"Grand Majesty, you cannot listen . . ."

Bridget lifted her head. The last voice was Kalami's. He stood beside the keeper, beside Sakra, while the crowd boiled around them.

All through the hall echoed variants on the same question. "Who is she? Who is she!"

Now I will show you my power, thought Bridget toward Kalami.

"See!" Bridget raised her arm and pointed straight at Kalami. "See! My father, Avanasy. He searches the hall. See how he stares into each and every face."

At the foot of the dais, Kalami went white. Around the hall, the courtiers huddled in on themselves, touched their own cheeks, or tried to hide their faces behind fans.

"Grand Majesty, is this true?" demanded Sakra, the keeper, his wand gripped tight in both hands. "Is she Avanasy's daughter?"

Bridget blessed him silently. He was going to make Medeoan say it out loud. He was going to give her the standing she needed before these people, the standing that would give weight and credit to her accusations and innuendo.

The dowager finally seemed to notice her own undignified position on the floor and she rose. Her hand dropped to Bridget's head. Doubtlessly, Bridget looked helpless, and right now that suited. Bridget kept her eyes on Kalami, but his gaze was all for the dowager.

"Yes," said the dowager. "She is the Avanasidoch."

The dowager's words staggered the entire room. Some people reverenced. Some clutched their neighbors. Some merely stood, mute with disbelief at what they heard. Sakra, the keeper, leaned heavily on his carved staff. "Blessed daughter." He raised a hand in a gesture of benediction to Bridget. "You see your father?"

"Now, he stands beside Valin Kalami." Bridget climbed to her feet. "He speaks, but I cannot hear." She reached out one hand, pleading. "Oh, Father, what do you mean to say?"

"Grand Majesty," said Kalami. "What means this?"

Around him spiraled dozens of other voices, swamping his words. "She is." "Can it be true?" A mother scooped a child into her arms and pointed at Bridget. "See? She's come in our hour of need, as was told."

She had them. Lies and truth, all bundled together, bound her to them now. "Avanasy's face is grave. He walks on. He speaks, but, oh, why can I not hear?" Bridget made her eyes go wide and staring, as if looking at a ghost past Kalami's shoulder. Never in a thousand years would she have believed she would bless the day she had gone to see Aunt Grace's sham of a séance, but she did so now. She walked down the dais steps to stand face-to-face with Kalami.

You have a liking for lies and traps, she thought as her eyes met his. *How well do you like mine?*

"Majesty," said Kalami again. His voice was low with warning, but his face betrayed fear.

Forgive me, Poppa. "Why does my father stand so long next to you, Lord Sorcerer? What does he say that I cannot hear?"

The sound of heavy cloth dragging on carpet broke Bridget's concentration. Ananda at last had moved. The empress walked slowly down the dais and the crowds parted for her, reverencing and whispering, filling the room with the rush of cloth and voices.

"Lord Sorcerer?" Barely controlled anger filled the empress's voice. "Is it possible that you know something of this plot against your emperor?"

Kalami opened his mouth, but he was spared the necessity of answer. The great doors at the back of the hall banged open and the captain and his men marched inside. Inside the square made by their bodies and axes stumbled the three men from Bridget's vision. Captain Chadek carried in his arms a heap of linen sheets. Bridget saw he had donned gloves to carry them.

Captain Chadek knelt before the dais. "Majesty Imperial, Grand Majesty." He laid a heap of cloth upon the floor. "We found these three men in the emperor's chamber, as it was told we would. They were laying these sheets upon the emperor's bed. This one"—he pushed forward a man who had gone nearly bald with age—"is Finon, servant to the lord sorcerer."

Empress Ananda hesitated only one second. She crossed to the mound of sheets, pinched a fold of cloth between her fingers and dropped it immediately as if she had been stung. She was a very good actress, Bridget thought, but then, the poor girl had a lot of practice.

"Poison," the empress said, backing away. "It is as the Avanasidoch said. The sheets are poisoned." She straightened herself up to her full height, and even the crown on her head seemed to blaze with the strength of her fury. "Traitor!" She leveled her accusing finger at Kalami. "You betray all your empire!"

A parcel of the courtiers surged forward, as if they meant to seize on Kalami where he stood.

"Hold!" called out the dowager. "Hold them!"

Led by their captain, the soldiers sprang into action, pushing the crowd back with the shafts of their axes, creating a living fence to keep Kalami and the three accused poisoners untouched.

Slowly, the dowager descended the dais steps. She seemed to glide forward as she walked toward the poisoned cloth. Even from where she stood, Bridget could see Kalami's chest heave with the strength of his emotion. Two of the poisoners knelt. The old man named Finon did not. Neither did Kalami.

The dowager bent down. She picked up the embroidered edge of one of the sheets and ran it through her gloved fingers, bending her head close to see the design.

All attention was fastened on the dowager and her examination of the linens. Bridget eased up beside Sakra. Through her right eye, he was the keeper of the god house, old and bearded. Through her left, he was himself, dark, intense and infinitely welcome to her.

"So, did the crows carry you here?" she breathed, moving past him so it might appear as if she was just trying to get a better view of the dowager.

She heard him suck in a breath, even though he held himself as still as she did. Now he knew she recognized him, but surely he also knew she was a free woman. Now, all depended on what the dowager said next. If she exposed Bridget's lie, Bridget was done for.

The dowager lifted her head. "They are poisoned." She let them fall in a heap at her feet as she turned herself minutely so that she faced Kalami fully. "You who are my guard, take up these creatures. Lord Sorcerer, as one of these traitors is your servant, I must ask you to meet me in the council rooms so that you may be questioned on this matter."

Bridget expected some outburst of denial or rage, but Kalami was utterly silent despite the voices raised around him. At the captain's direction, five men surrounded the liveried poisoners, driving them from the hall with the tips of their axes. The courtiers whistled, jeered and booed as they stumbled through the doors. Ignoring all this noise, Captain Chadek signaled to two more of his men, who came and flanked their lord sorcerer.

Kalami was no longer looking at the dowager. His attention was all for Bridget and it took all her strength to stand before the rage and hatred that filled his black eyes. *How dare you*, he seemed to say. *How dare you act against me. I will see you pay, and you cannot begin to imagine the price.*

"My mother imperial," began Ananda. "Surely, his servant cannot have acted without his knowledge. He belongs in the cell with his fellow poisoners."

"The lord sorcerer is mine," replied the dowager crisply, and loud enough for the entire room to hear. "It is to me he made his bond and it is still for me to determine how his actions are to be judged."

"What else do you see?" murmured Sakra's voice in Bridget's ear.

The attention of the court was riveted on the imperial pair. For this one instant, no one noticed Bridget.

"What you want is tied around the emperor's waist," she replied, quietly. "His mother put it there."

She felt him freeze, and then he closed his eyes, murmuring something under his breath.

"It is the empire he has betrayed, and it is the empire who must judge him," Ananda said to the dowager.

The dowager, however, was not about to let Ananda forget who held the power here. "No specific accusations had yet been made against him by either the living or the dead," she said. "And you are not yet the empire embodied. Until my son is free of his illness of spirit, that task remains with me."

Their eyes remained locked for another breath, and then the Empress Ananda reverenced. "Of course, my mother imperial." She straightened up.

"This is a night of deep plots and treachery," said the dowager, her voice full of tender concern. "I fear for you, my daughter imperial. Let the house guard take you back to your chamber and keep you safe there."

"I am grateful for your concern, my mother imperial," said Ananda, lifting her chin. "But surely no man should be spared from guarding Kalami and keeping the emperor safe."

She does not want to be confined, thought Bridget. *An escort of the dowager's men will keep her penned up tonight when she has a chance to make her move.* But there was nothing Bridget could do to help. Another outburst at this point would surely strain her credibility to the breaking point. That could bring her plans, such as they were, crashing down. She had done all she could. If Sakra and Ananda could free the emperor tonight, Kalami and the dowager's power would be broken, and Bridget would be safe. If not, and if Kalami could worm his way past the dowager and her council . . . then she was lost.

The dowager was shaking her head and raising one hand. "I will not rest easily until both you and my son are safe." For the first time, her voice quavered, and given all she had seen, Bridget could not help wondering if that was on purpose. It seemed to be having a good effect, for the court was murmuring in approval. "Until we know the extent of this treason, we cannot endanger Isavalta by allowing what conspirators may still be at large access to the persons of our imperial family."

"Then, Grand Majesty," Sakra, the keeper, said, moving forward, "let me escort the empress to her chambers. I see for the gods, and none will dare lift a hand when there are such witnesses."

Even Bridget could see it was a neat move. How could the dowager refuse such a request? The noises of assent from the glittering audience grew louder. Good. Good. Let Sakra go with the empress. Let him tell Ananda what he knew, and what Bridget had done. She swallowed. Maybe, maybe she could get out of this with a whole skin after all. Every second that passed seemed to shore up her chances. Or was that just wishful thinking? Bridget had no way to tell. She could not read what was going on behind the dowager's eyes, and the dowager still held the vast majority of the power here. If Sakra and Ananda could not free the emperor, that was the way it would stay. The idea made Bridget's heart beat painfully hard.

"You have my thanks, good keeper," announced the dowager, pitching her voice so the entire court could hear. They responded at once by sighing their approval. What were they thinking, wondered Bridget, behind their fans and fancy clothes? Were they planning already? How many of them were siding with the dowager? How many of them were thinking to preserve the advantages she had surely brought them?

And there was nothing she could do about any of it. Everything depended on Sakra and Ananda. She saw again the hatred burning in Kalami's eyes as he was taken away. Her throat closed. So much could still go wrong. Her thoughts flitted to poor Richikha, wherever she lay. Was the girl even still alive?

"Grand Majesty." Sakra reverenced. "Come, blessed daughter," he said to Ananda, and he led her and her retinue through the crowd.

The dowager nodded to another member of the guard, who wore a golden belt around his waist. This must have been the special escort, because at a nod from him, no less than six of the house guard and three servants marched forward to take charge of the emperor and lead him to whichever box the dowager kept him in. The entire court reverenced as he was marched away like the prisoner he was.

It will be my turn next.

The dowager turned toward her court and raised both her hands, in blessing perhaps, or in warning. "Let all return to their chambers, and none go forth until morning without true good reason."

That pronouncement finished, the dowager faced Bridget. "You too should have an escort, Bridget Avanasidoch. It was your voice that spoke out against this treachery, and there may be those who would silence it."

Bridget folded her hands and dropped her gaze. "I will, of course, do whatever you think best, Grand Majesty."

The dowager sent one of her lackeys running for Bridget's ladies with a gesture, even as she stepped close to Bridget. "In your father's name, I beg you keep your own counsel of any other visions until we may speak again. There is much here yet that you do not understand, and a careless word may ruin all."

Grand Majesty, a truer word was never spoken, thought Bridget as she reverenced.

A trio of house guards formed up with Gali and Iadviga, and in that new captivity, Bridget meekly let herself be led away.

A naked willow tree drooped beside the canal, its whiplike branches brushing the black ice. A single crow, heedless of the darkness, sat in a crook of the tree. His eyes glittered in the moonlight as he watched the walls of the palace on the other side of the ice.

"King."

The crow turned one eye to the black shape on the ground. It flapped its wings once, and dropped onto the snow before the filthy, battered mortar.

"Old Witch," he said, bobbing his head three times.

The wind fluttered Baba Yaga's tattered black cloak. "What do you see inside?" She pointed the end of her stained pestle toward the palace.

"Much," croaked the crow. "And little. They rush back and forth and all plan to tumble over the others so they might be the one left standing."

They faced each other in silence for a moment then while the wind whispered around them, catching up dustings of snow to spread out like delicate veils on the air.

"Do you see one in there bearing the title *Agnidh*?" inquired Baba Yaga.

"I do," admitted the crow.

The witch planted her mortar in the snow. The motion raised a carrion scent. "He is in debt to you."

The crow did not answer.

The witch bared her iron teeth to the cold and the moonlight. "He will need to leave the palace before long. He will need to walk the worlds. You may prevent him from this."

The crow cocked his head. "And in so doing, I would risk the anger of the Vixen. This is her game." He croaked once. "But it is your game as well, is it not?"

The witch gnashed her teeth, a discordant ringing sound. "She interfered with what is mine. Now, I will interfere with what is hers."

"No." The crow shook its feathers, fluffing them out against the cold. "You will have me interfere, and risk her wrath against myself and my people. Why would I do this?"

Baba Yaga reached one crabbed hand into her ragged robe. When she brought it out again, it held the delicate ivory skull of a baby bird.

"You believe your wife to be with child," she said. "But it is weak within her. It is indeed already mine." Outraged, the crow spread its wings and stabbed its beak forward, cawing harshly, challenging the words. But it did not attack. Too much truth hung in the air between them.

Baba Yaga held the skull out. "Do as I ask, and I will give your child back to you."

The crow stretched its neck up, beating the air with its wings. "Old Witch, you ask too much!"

Baba Yaga simply shrugged, and her hand moved to secret the tiny skull again.

"Wait!" cried the crow, and Baba Yaga stilled her hand. The crow shifted its weight back and forth, and then leapt into the air. Its black claws snagged the skull as it flew past the witch. Calling out its discontent, the crow vanished into the darkness.

Baba Yaga hunched down into her mortar and grinned her iron grin. She thumped the pestle twice against the ground, and she too was gone.

Chapter Sixteen

Ananda walked before her ladies, Keeper Bakhar pacing solemnly at her side. The glittering ornamentation that bedecked the corridors for the holy day still sparkled as they passed, even in the dim light. Courtiers, hurrying to obey the dowager's orders to return to their rooms, reverenced to her she passed, and many a lord or lady tried to catch her eye. She heeded none of them. Her mind was too caught up in trying to understand what she had witnessed. Had Avanasy's spirit truly appeared? Or had the sorceress Bridget dissembled? If so, Ananda could not fault her, as she appeared to have put Kalami and the dowager at odds with each other, and that bought Ananda time. Maybe, while the Council of Lords and the dowager questioned Kalami, she could pull back the search for Sakra. Possibly she could get a message to Lord Master Peshek, to inform him what had happened, and gain his insights. If the dowager could be severed from Kalami the dynamic of power within the palace could be upset, and with a few sound allies, Ananda could surely turn that to her advantage.

She could all but hear the whispers passing like drafts through the corridor. There were not enough guards to keep everyone in their rooms this night, and even now, bets as to how the power would shift were being laid. She must get her hand into that game. She must . . .

"You look grave, Princess," murmured Keeper Bakhar.

"It is nothing, good keeper . . ." Ananda stopped, clapping her mouth shut. The question had been spoken in the court language of her home, and she had answered in the same without thinking.

"Sorcerer?" she asked to avoid saying Sakra's name aloud, because it would be recognized in any language.

"Ever ready to serve the Moon's Daughter," he murmured, glancing left and right. The ladies and pages surrounding them kept their eyes rigidly ahead, pretending not to hear any sound coming from their mistress imperial or the keeper. They passed from the Amber Music Room to Iakshim's Gallery. Her apartments were moments away.

"Know you what it was we witnessed in the Great Hall?" whispered Ananda swiftly.

"The Avanasidoch gambling for her life," Sakra answered her, keeping his head gravely bowed, as befitted the good keeper. "She has done us good service."

Fear and hope together tipped Ananda's heart. "How?"

"She has seen that the source of the emperor's enchantment is a girdle around his waist."

Ananda's steps faltered. A girdle around his waist. Was that all that had done this? She had to get to him. Her blood sang in her ears. All other plans and thoughts fell away from her. She had to tear the vile thing from him.

"It must be hidden from normal sight," Sakra was saying. "And the dowager will let none but the servants she has handpicked near enough to the emperor to touch him."

They reached her door. Kiriti and Behule, leading the gaggle of other ladies, bustled inside to prepare the rooms. It was all Ananda could do to keep from running headlong down the corridor to Mikkel's door.

But she did not. She maintained her dignity, leading Sakra into her outer chamber, even though every portion of her mind sang *hurry, hurry*. There was no telling what the dowager was doing. She must get to Mikkel, or she must send Sakra to him. She needed to know what to do, immediately.

Kiriti and Behule shut the doors behind them, setting the bar into place. The other ladies busied themselves about the chamber, lighting candles and setting things in order for the evening. Mostly, they were proving they were too occupied to listen in on whatever might pass between their mistress and the keeper.

Ananda spun on her toes, grasping Sakra's hands.

"Can you free him?" she demanded in a hoarse whisper. Kiriti and Behule were staring, but she could not permit them to hear. Too much was changing, too fast. They must not be able to report anything should her frail hopes be dashed. There was no time for pleasantries, no time for thanks. All that mattered was getting to Mikkel. All that mattered was the end of the nightmare.

All of which Sakra realized perfectly. "I cannot," he said, but he held up a hand to stop the outburst he most surely saw coming from her. "To undo a spell of binding, which this is, one must be bound to the victim, by blood, by oath or by being the one who cast a spell. I am in no way bound to Mikkel, but you are. If you can get the girdle off him, he will be free."

Free. Yes, free. Both of us free, and the nightmare over. "How may I reach him? The dowager's guard will be patrolling the halls."

The keeper's eyes sparkled, and for a moment Ananda could truly see Sakra behind them. "If your ladies may be distracted for a moment, it will be time for you to become the good keeper."

Ananda understood him at once. She nodded to Kiriti and made a sweeping gesture. In return, Kiriti gathered up all the ladies to depart behind the bed screens to turn down the sheets and lay out the nightclothes to be brushed and warmed.

"Quickly," said Ananda to Sakra.

Sakra leaned forward. Ananda felt a piece of netting wrapped around her wrist, and then Sakra kissed her full on the mouth. Startled, Ananda jerked away, and saw herself looking back at her. Reflexively, she looked down at her own hands and saw the pale, vein-lined hands of an old man protruding from the long sleeves of Keeper Bakhar's robes.

Ananda eagerly grasped her double's hand, before she remembered who she was supposed to be.

"Blessed daughter," she murmured, as Bakhar had said a thousand times to her. "Be well." Sakra, her double, nodded solemnly to her and passed her the keeper's staff.

Ananda did not hesitate any longer, but strode from the room.

She passed the stragglers from the court with her strangely aged and too huge hand raised in blessing. They bowed their heads respectfully as she passed, but they did not look at her twice. She strode down the hall and through the open chambers in what she hoped was a stately and appropriate pace. Inside, her heart was pounding. She could reach Mikkel, but then what? As the good keeper she could not be reasonably kept from one of the household, but she could hardly begin stripping off Mikkel's clothing. And if the dowager's lackeys saw her as herself, they would surely send her away.

Anger flooded Ananda then. Must she even go into disguise to save her husband and thus the whole land of Isavalta? She was the highest-born lady of Hastinapura. She was an empress. Who would dare prevent her from going where she would? How much longer did she intend to cower underneath the machinations of an insane old woman? Mikkel's doorway waited straight ahead of her, flanked by its guards, the dowager's guards. No, her guards. Mikkel's guards. This was the end of the game, and she would play it out as herself.

She stripped Sakra's spell off her wrist and thrust the bright weaving into her sleeve.

Two of the guards watched over the emperor's door. Ananda frowned. Where were the others? The full complement of six had taken him from the Great Hall. One of the pair was tall and thin, with the sandy red hair that marked him as a man from the plains to the south. The other had dark brown hair, almond eyes and golden skin, which came from the eastern coast.

They both blinked to see her, but at once gave her the soldier's bow, as was proper.

"Is the emperor within?" Ananda inquired.

"No, Majesty Imperial," said the man from the east. "He has been taken to the baths."

The baths. The baths. Of course. It was a requirement of the holy day, that the emperor be bathed in water from Vyshemir's ocean at midnight. Frustration roiled inside Ananda. She could not follow him there. "Then I will wait for him inside," she announced.

But East was not to be so quickly commanded. "Majesty Imperial, it is the wish of Her Grand Majesty that all remain within their own rooms tonight."

So that Mikkel can stay imprisoned. So that she can keep hold of her power. But no more. I will not permit this anymore. Ananda moved close to the man, forcing him to press himself back against the wall lest he inadvertently touch her. "You spoke my title. You know who I am."

"Yes, Majesty Imperial." His eyes betrayed the beginnings of confusion, perhaps even fear. She heard the rustle as his counterpart, who should have been standing rigidly at attention, shifted his weight uneasily. Good.

"And who I am I?"

He bowed his head, getting ready to give the salute, but she gave him no room. "You are the empress of Isavalta."

Ananda returned the slightest of nods. "And who are you?"

"Underlieutenant Kolapai Prilepaisyn Priklonskovin."

Ananda took a step closer. The man had to suck in his chest now. The imperial personage was sacred. He could not even accidentally brush up against her. Right now, that piece of protocol was making it very difficult for him to breathe. "And you, Underlieutenant Kolapai, are going to tell me where I may and may not go within the palace?"

Uncertainty wrinkled his face. "I have no choice, Majesty Imperial."

"Oh, but you do have a choice," she whispered, pleasantly. "You may serve your emperor and allow me entry, or you may be guilty of treason."

"Majesty Imperial," said the southern man from the other side of the door. "We all have our orders tonight. Please do not ask this of us."

Ananda turned toward him without giving the underlieutenant any extra space. She let her face go hard. "You know all is not well. You could not help but know that. After tonight everything will change. You can either obey me now, or be very well remembered for your failures."

The southern man, either more loyal or more frightened than his superior, made his decision and snapped to attention. "As Your Majesty Imperial pleases."

Ananda smiled and stepped back from the underlieutenant. "Thus is Eternal Isavalta served. I shall remember." She crossed to the southern man and slipped a ring of polished coral from her finger. She pressed it into his hand. "And that is for your silence on this matter. Tell no one I am inside."

Mikkel's apartments were bright with the light of lamps and braziers. Still, they felt lifeless. She passed from the blue and gold audience chamber, to the private study with its inlaid desk that was a newer copy of the one the dowager used, to the parlor and private dining room. Each was furnished well, as it should be, and all were clean. The gilding shone. The murals had been kept immaculate, as had the icons in their alcoves. Rich wooden furniture and thick rugs lent the place warmth, but there was no heart here, no soul. It was a place where a body might rest, no more than that.

Ananda hurried to the screened-off area where Mikkel's bed waited. The bed they had tried to poison just a few hours earlier tonight. She swallowed and tried to prepare herself for patience. It was not easy, and after only a few moments, she found herself pacing back and forth.

What was going to happen? What was she going to do? Would the house guard on the door keep their silence? What if they did not? Should she hide? Let the servants put Mikkel to bed? What would she do then? When they slept and she emerged, what would she do, and how would she ensure that they did not wake to find her with Mikkel all against the dowager's express orders?

And what of Mikkel himself? Would he stay silent and disinterested? Would he perhaps even sleep through her attentions? In his enchantment, did he truly sleep? Sometimes Ananda hoped he did, and that in his dreams, at least, he knew her, and remembered the delight and anticipation they had once shared in each other's company.

She had gone to him once. Kiriti and Behule had distracted the servants Medeoan set to watch Mikkel, and Ananda had hidden behind her husband's bed-curtains and seen him, all laid out like a doll in a toy bed.

"Mikkel." She had breathed his name as she climbed into the bed beside him. "Beloved, husband. I am here."

She'd run her hands across his shoulders then, and down his chest. She'd kissed his eyes and his cheeks. The strength of desire, she thought, might do what nothing else could. It might make him remember, might make him acknowledge her, say her name, or even just look at her and for one moment truly see her.

But he lay there, unmoving, his flesh cool and undisturbed by her caresses.

"Mikkel." Tears stung her eyes.

She kissed him full on the mouth, but his mouth did not move in answer. Tears streaming down her cheeks, she pressed harder, trying to force his lips apart with her tongue. They did part, but his mouth remained slack, soft, dead.

Choking on her tears, and suddenly sick, Ananda jerked backward, her hand slapped against her mouth to hold back her rising gorge. She ran away, blinded by tears, rage and horror.

She had not been able to make herself return to her husband's bedroom. Until now, and now she stood here—empress, wife and frightened girl all rolled into one, hoping only that she would understand how to act before she was discovered and confined once again.

Bridget allowed Gali and Iadviga to divest her of her heavy gold-and-pearl outer coat, and the outer layers of tissue. She stood near the freshly stoked fire in her dark velvet underdress and she could hear the pair of them behind the bed screens, twittering and bickering as they divided up the pearls she had promised them. All had gone well, so far, after all, and she might need their help again. It was as well she paid the price she had promised.

Left momentarily alone, Bridget unfastened Kalami's brooch from her shoulder and tossed it gladly into the wooden box where Richikha had concealed the first love charm.

You will have this, I promise, she thought to the absent Richikha as she closed the lid, but she had no idea how she could keep the promise.

Bridget dropped herself into a chair beside the firepit and stared into the flames. She was beginning to hate this room. It was a cell. A beautifully furnished cell, but a cell all the same. First Kalami, and now the dowager, held her here until they were ready to use her and she was becoming sick to death of it.

Bridget glanced at the door. Had Ananda and Sakra managed to get to the emperor yet? Where was Kalami? What was he doing, and what was he saying? What was he planning to do to her? And how was she going to find out in time to save herself from it?

I can help you.

Bridget sat up straight.

I can help you against him. I can see you safe.

"Firebird," breathed Bridget, her fingers curling around the chair's arm.

Help me, and I can see you safe, said the susurrating voice inside her head.

Bridget's heart fluttered high in her throat. The voice was so clear, more so even than it had been the night she had gone in search of it. It seemed as if her ladies must hear it as well, but all the noise that came from behind the screens was Gali's slightly disdainful voice saying, "No, no, my lady. That one is mine. The next is yours."

"How can you keep me safe?" breathed Bridget. She had no doubt that the Firebird could hear.

He will find you there. You must come to me.

Bridget rose slowly to her feet, her heart pounding as if she already heard Kalami's footsteps outside her door. *No, calm yourself.*

Rubbing her hands, Bridget began to circle around the firepit. *He is with the dowager. You have done your work there. He is under an inquiry. He can do nothing to you tonight.*

So you hope, she answered herself. *How can you know?*

Richikha lay burning with fever, if she lived still, and Kalami had not even needed to touch her. Richikha had just been a bystander, someone who committed an offense in ignorance. What more would he do to Bridget?

She hated herself for being so afraid, but there the fear was. It was not the fear she had felt of storm, or fog, her father's illness or even the coroner's jury as they sat in judgment over the death of her daughter. Those she could stand against. For those she had tasks that she could perform, a stance to take, even when it was only to maintain her dignity. This was a helpless fear of a force she did not know how to counter.

Come to me, said the Firebird. *Let me help you.*

She already knew the price the bird would demand in return. It wanted its freedom. The cage drove it frantic, had driven it frantic for almost thirty years. Yet, she could not forget the images of fire and destruction she had seen so clearly in her dream.

But could she forget the vision of salvation she had also seen? Could she trust a vision that had come only in a dream?

If she stood before the Firebird's cage, what would she see inside it? She could see the truth in Isavalta. However this new ability had come to her, it was clear that she could trust it. If she stood before the Firebird and looked at it closely, then she might know what to do. Then she could decide.

And Kalami would not know where to find her. She would be safely hidden, at least for a while.

"How do I find you?"

You know how, replied the Firebird. Bridget remembered the dance she had danced in Sakra's stone house and the wild joy of it. *Think of me,* said the Firebird. *The fire will bring you to me.*

It was not a good idea, but it was the only one she had. Last time she had attempted any such thing she had become lost, and the foxes had come for her. But then she had not known where she was going. This time she had both a vision and the Firebird's own voice to guide her. She would not wait for Kalami's next move. Not again. She could no longer tell herself that she had no power, that she did not know what she was doing. Those were the lies now. That was what Kalami wanted her to believe. That was what truly kept her trapped. If she wanted to be free of him she would have to accept what she was, all that she was.

Bridget took a deep breath, fixed in her mind the image of the Firebird in its golden cage, all alone amid the darkness and its own endless heat.

Bridget began to dance.

Sakra, in his disguise as Ananda, had informed the ladies that he would be sitting by the fire for some time, and that they should not delay their own rest for him. Kiriti and Behule begged leave to sit with their mistress, which he readily granted, as Ananda surely would. The others moved about the room, laying out their own beds with the help of the page girls, and readying themselves for sleep.

All at once, one of them gave a shriek and pointed right at Sakra. He started to his feet, and in so doing, caught a glimpse of his hands, large and dark, and completely undisguised.

"*Agnidh* Sakra!" exclaimed Kiriti in a voice that said plainly she was not sure whether to be frightened or outraged. "What is happening?"

"I wish that I knew, Lady," he answered. Ananda had removed his talisman, or it had been removed from her, thus shattering the chain of illusion. In his modest bed, Keeper Bakhar now reverted to his own appearance, as Sakra had, and out there in the corridors, Ananda was herself. He frowned at the door, wishing foolishly that he could see through it as Bridget Lederle seemed able to.

"He is not permitted here!" squeaked one of the other ladies. One of the Isavaltans by the voice.

"Hush, sister," he heard Behule say softly in reply. "This is not our business."

"As if we needed more business tonight," said another of them. "What is happening to them all?"

"That," said Kiriti firmly, "is most assuredly not our business."

The talisman had not been broken. He would have felt that. It had only been removed then. He could hope. Ananda might have done that herself so that Mikkel could see who she truly was. She might be standing before him even now, undoing the dowager's spell.

"*Agnidh?*" Kiriti bowed before him, giving the salute of trust.

It was only then he realized he had been standing with his fists clenched and his teeth bared at nothing at all.

Sakra's attention snapped back to the room around him. The ladies clumped together like a flock of brilliant birds, watching him with greater or lesser degrees of suspicion. Even Behule looked uneasy. He could not blame them. Currents were running through the palace tonight, all of them fast and deep. After that scene in the Great Hall, not even the dimmest among Medeoan's court could be unaware that great change was coming.

And here he was locked in this room, unable to help Ananda through it. His gaze strayed to the altar with the Seven Mothers poised in their dance, and then to the door beside the altar.

He faced Kiriti. "Lady, your sisters in waiting are disturbed by my presence. I do not blame them. I suggest they make themselves ready to await their mistress's return. I shall put myself in the private study, and from there I will disturb no one's delicacy."

In the private study, with Ananda's loom and all the tools they had laid out so carefully. Surely, they had left a mirror in there. From there he could see beyond these walls. If he was quick, he might even be able to warn Ananda, if there was need.

"Thank you, *Agnidh*," said Kiriti. "Permit me to attend you. Behule, my sisters, let you do as has been suggested and settle yourselves."

Kiriti escorted Sakra to the study door. Behind him came a flurry of questions and protests, and Behule's firm counters to them all. While he claimed a lamp to light their way, Kiriti, who had always carried Ananda's trust, unlocked the door with a key from a bunch she drew out from under her overskirt.

Once inside, Sakra set the lamp beside a cold, covered brazier, and Kiriti locked the door once more.

"Now, *Agnidh* Sakra, I pray you," she said, with the right of one who had stood by her mistress at least as long as Sakra had. "Tell me what you know."

"Little enough," he answered, regretfully. "The Avanasidoch has given us the key to Mikkel's release, but . . ." He stopped. Something was wrong. A wind touched him, warm and subtle, tugging at his heart and teasing gently with his thoughts. It spoke of movement, of travel, of open doors and dance.

He had felt that wind before.

"No. Not here. What is she doing!"

"*Agnidh?*"

But Sakra did not answer her. He knocked the chimney off the lamp, and tipped it into the brazier. The oil poured down onto the waiting charcoal and the flame ignited them both with a soft thump. Casting the lamp aside, heedless of where it fell, he snatched up a spool of red thread and an embroidery needle that had been left on a chair.

He drove the needle into his finger until the blood welled out of it, dripping down and hissing into the fire. He threw away the needle and took up the thread.

"By fire, breath, blood and binding, let your road and my road be one," he said. "There is nowhere you go that I may not follow. I see you from afar and I follow you swift." He repeated the chant, again, and again as he looped the end of the thread around his right wrist. The magic ran out of him down the length of the thread, called by blood and breath, and shaped by his spell bond with Bridget. He should have gone more slowly. He needed time to shape the spell properly, but he did not have any. He forced the magic through the gate of his soul, feeling it drain away his strength as quickly as if he had opened a vein in his arm. There were protections here, and they gathered around him, seizing him, holding him close, rooting him to the floor, even as his bond with Bridget pulled him forward.

He cast the spool of thread into the fire. "I see you from afar and I follow you swift. I see you from afar." His voice trembled as the flame seized the thread, drawing the substance of the spun cord into itself. "I see you from afar, and I follow you swift."

The spell pulled him forward. Vyshtavos's protections held him fast. Sakra cried out loud at the pain of being torn in two. He could not go, but he must. He could not stay, but he must. The twin imperatives ripped open his heart, his veins, his lungs and his mind. Pain lanced through the deepest part of him.

"I follow you swift!"

And all was darkness.

When Captain Chadek and the house guard marched Kalami back into the Great Hall, he saw why Medeoan had kept him waiting for so long. All trace of celebration was gone from the room. The high-backed chairs of the council lords had been set out in their semicircle; four on one side of the imperial dais and four on the other so that the dowager sat in their midst, and yet held sway above them. All sat in their appointed places, glittering in the finery they had donned for their holy day, and frowned down at him. The ninth chair, his chair, had been discreetly removed.

Chadek and his men knelt, and Kalami did the same. No matter what he felt, now was the time for discretion until he heard what his imperial mistress had to say for herself. She would explain why she had betrayed him before all this was done. She would most certainly admit her regret of it, or he would tear that regret from her.

But it was not Medeoan who spoke, it was Lord Tabutai, her puffed-up minister of state, who prided himself on his fine physique maintained by riding about on horseback chasing slaves and other lowlies in mock cavalry exercises.

"Valin Kalami, Lord Sorcerer of the Eternal Empire of Isavalta," Tabutai's voice boomed through the hall. "You are accused of having knowledge of a conspiracy against the person of our most beloved and afflicted emperor. What have you to say to this?"

Kalami was glad that he knelt with his head bowed so none of them could see how he bit his lip to stop the outrage that longed to fill his voice. At least he was only accused of knowing, not of doing. That gave him some room. "Am I on trial here, Minister?"

"You are not, but that is only by the grace of Her Grand Majesty."

Kalami risked a look up. Medeoan sat on her throne, grave and impassive. The little council lords, men chosen for their impressive degrees of stupidity, fidgeted, sat rigid or cast their restless glances about the room trying to guess how to turn these freshly flowing tides to their advantage, each according to his stunted nature.

"I only wished to be clear on that point," said Kalami, looking as close to Medeoan as he dared. They were not alone. She would not permit liberties here.

"But what have you to say?" demanded Lord Luchanin, the castellan, with his gold chain rattling around his skinny shoulders and his heavy, and entirely ceremonial, gold keys dangling from his bony hip.

"I say that everything I have done, I have done in loyal service to Her Grand Majesty." Kalami let his voice ring out clearly. *Make of that what you will.*

Medeoan, who had been watching him, fixed her pale eyes on the far wall. *So, you at least hear me, Grand Majesty.*

"The three men Captain Chadek found in the emperor's apartments are being questioned even now," pointed out Lord Muntat with studied calm. Kalami had wondered when he was going to speak. The man cultivated a façade of unflappability, believing it made him imposing. As if anything could make up for the fact that he was only as tall as a half-grown boy with hands as delicate as a lady-in-waiting's. "What story they have to tell will be weighed carefully with any silence you choose to maintain." Silently Kalami cursed all those in front of him. Finon. Honored Father. He was not just being questioned, surely. He was being put to the question. He would not cry out. Kalami was certain he would not. He would defy the Isavaltans in silence to the end.

"I have given you my answer," replied Kalami calmly. "If Her Grand Majesty does not believe that I am her loyal servant, then let Her Grand Majesty say so."

"Tuukosov dog!" spat Lord Luchanin so hard his gold keys clanged together. "How dare you make any demand of your mistress imperial!"

"I swore loyalty and fealty as a free man," answered Kalami, aiming each word like a bolt at silent Medeoan. *You will answer me!* "My life, skills and body are all hers to dispose of, but I have the right to be heard and answered by her as my liege in any court, opened or closed."

"You have been told this is not a trial," said Lord Muntat.

"But it is a court." The dowager's eyes had not moved. They remained rigidly fixed, staring at the doors at the rear of the hall as if willing them to open to admit some rescue or distraction. "For you are here at the express command of Her Grand Majesty to question me and judge my answers."

"Grand Majesty." Fat Lord Kondateve finally decided to stir himself. "Do you deign to answer this man?"

Medeoan closed her eyes. "Stand up, Lord Sorcerer."

Kalami rose slowly to his feet.

Her right hand dropped onto her bundle of keys. She did not open her eyes. "Why does the Avanasidoch accuse you of this thing?"

Kalami spread his hands, and spoke the truth. "I do not know, Grand Majesty."

That opened Medeoan's eyes, and they shined with both hurt and anger as they studied him. What did she want of him? Did she actually expect him to take all the blame for the orders she had given? "But you have spent the most time with her. By your account, you spent weeks in her home. You must have some understanding of her by now."

Are you admitting she is not what you thought she would be? Slow hope simmered in Kalami's breast. *Do you see that she is capable of lying to you?*

Kalami hesitated, choosing his words with care. He could not openly accuse Bridget, not yet. "I know that she has been bewildered since she came here. I promised her safety, but I failed her, allowing her to be kidnapped, and then her abductor appears in the place I swore would be her sanctuary."

"You say the Avanasidoch is addled?" scoffed Lord Budilo. He was the oldest of the councillors and one of Medeoan's first appointments. Of all the council lords, he was the one who truly worried

Kalami. Budilo had learned over the years to play the dowager's sympathies almost as well as Kalami himself had.

"I say she is confused, and I say, perhaps, because she has come so suddenly from obscurity to prominence, she does not hear the inner voice that speaks of her natural loyalties."

Lord Budilo narrowed his eyes. "Then you say others influence the Avanasidoch to make false accusations? Who would do such a thing?"

You will not trick me into naming names here, my lord. "Come, my lord," Kalami answered, meeting the man's gaze without hesitation. "We all know there are those whose loyalty to Her Grand Majesty is all seeming."

Medeoan began to breathe heavily as the import of his words sank in. *Yes, Grand Majesty, she has sided with Ananda. You already know that. You simply do not wish to believe it. You want to save your pretty palace of private illusions, but it is beginning to crumble, is it not?* He found himself smiling inwardly. *Perhaps I will have cause to thank Bridget for this night yet.*

"It is your actions that we are here to question, Lord Sorcerer." Lord Tabutai stretched out one strong, brown, callused finger to point at Kalami, lest anyone become confused as to who he was addressing.

But Medeoan lifted her hand, and Lord Tabutai was forced to withdraw his gesture. The dowager rose to her feet, and slowly walked down the dais to face Kalami.

"My lord sorcerer," she said. "We have worked well and fruitfully together, you and I, have we not?"

Kalami dropped his gaze in all proper respect. "Yes, Grand Majesty."

"There were those who said I could not trust you, but I did not heed their counsel and my trust has been most amply rewarded. I have always been able to turn to you when I most needed help."

"I hope this is true, Grand Majesty."

"Then help me now." Kalami heard the undercurrent of desperation in the request. "Help me to understand what has happened here.

Why did the Avanasidoch say she saw her father stand beside you? What did he try to tell her?"

Her lies saved your skin. She could have accused you, and then what would have happened? But you don't know why she lied, and that distresses you. You want to make me say it. Then, if anything else goes wrong, the words are mine, and never yours. I can stand doubly accused while you look on in horror at the Tuukosov who so bitterly betrayed all your trust.

You shall not have that of me.

Kalami spread his hands. "Grand Majesty, I swear I know no more of all this than you do."

As the echo of his words faded from the air, Medeoan sucked in a startled breath, causing Kalami to jerk his gaze up. Her face crumpled in grievous pain. At first, Kalami wondered if his words had actually reached her, but when she pressed her hand against her belly, he knew its cause was far different.

"Out!" cried Medeoan, sweeping out her arm, even as she doubled over. "All of you away from me!"

The council lords gaped all goggle-eyed like a school of carp.

"Out!" screamed their dowager. "Save the lord sorcerer, out!"

Chadek, with his usual dispatch and efficiency, decided it was time to lead by example. The captain formed up his men. They marched to the doors and held them open so that the council lords, who finally understood what was happening, and the flocks of servants in attendance, might file out and have those same doors close behind them. Medeoan reeled up the steps of the dais until at last she leaned against her throne.

"It's broken, isn't it?" asked Kalami softly. His voice sounded thin and small in the huge empty hall that surrounded them. "The binding on Mikkel. It's broken."

"No." Medeoan gasped heavily, gripping her throne's arm, her eyes closed in pain. "No, it is not that. It is . . . No. Mikkel is still safe."

What is happening inside you, old woman? Kalami thought sharply, but he made no move toward her. If she did not wish to tell him the cause, she could cope with this pain on her own. *Which of your threads is breaking?*

But he would have no answer from her about that yet. He knew her well enough to tell that much. There were other tunes he must play for her before that one could begin. "He will not be safe for long," he warned. "Bridget saw him tonight. She doubtless saw the girdle on him and she will soon tell your enemies where it is."

"It cannot be," Medeoan said, doggedly determined in her denial. "She is Avanasy's daughter. She *cannot* betray me."

"Grand Majesty," said Kalami as gently as he could manage. "I did not want to believe it either, but, whatever Avanasy was to you died when his body died. It does not live on in this false daughter. She was raised in another world among strangers. However strong she may be, what happens to Isavalta or to yourself is beyond her comprehension and beyond her heart's ability to care."

"You are wrong," she said, each word grating against his skin. "You must be wrong."

"I am right, and Your Grand Majesty knows it." Kalami knelt at the foot of the dais. "It is hard to let go of a cherished hope, and I grieve for all that might have been, but Bridget is not to save Isavalta, and that must be faced."

Medeoan bowed her head, pressing her hand against her forehead. For a long moment, she was silent. Around them, the dying fires crackled and the candles and lamps flickered softly as they burned the ends of their fuel. Fading, all the fires were fading, and Kalami felt his chances fading with them. If he did not make her believe now, this moment, he never would. He would be forced to flee without his payment and his revenge. He would fail. He could not fail. Tuukos waited in its chains for him to ransom it. His great-uncle's bones waited for him to take revenge.

"Grand Majesty, please," begged Kalami. "Do not be alone in your burdens. Let me help."

Medeoan pulled in a deep breath. With the strength of will that even Kalami had to admit had always been genuinely hers, she straightened herself up, overcoming whatever pain afflicted her. "You have ever sought to help me, Valin. All my deepest secrets, you have kept them well. The duties I could entrust to no one else, you have performed."

"Then let me do so again. All is not lost yet. We have time to work a new plan, but we must do it now." Kalami extended his hand, a gesture meant to urge Medeoan to reach for him, her faithful servant, waiting at her feet. "Your mind is clouded now in your grief. Let me help you before it is too late."

"Yes." She wiped the tears from her eyes with the wrinkled and age-spotted back of her hand. "You will help me, Kalami."

"With all the power I command."

She descended three steps toward him, grasping his hand, and raising him up. "Help me bring Bridget back to me," she said gripping him tightly. "Help me make her understand—"

Red, raw anger burst through Kalami's thoughts.

"Do you hear yourself!" he demanded, tearing his hand from hers. "The great empress of Isavalta is ready to grovel on the floor before an ignorant peasant woman because she can't see past her own follies!"

Slowly, the dowager drew herself up, growing icy cold in her certainty of her position and her power, despite all. "You will not speak to me so."

"I will," returned Kalami doggedly. "I will tell you that your empire hangs by a thread and you are ready to snap that thread in two!" He flung wide his arms in amazement. "How can you still trust her? What one thing has she done to earn your trust?"

"Her blood—"

Kalami would hear no more of it. Not again. Not ever again. "She is the bastard daughter of a man you killed thirty years ago!"

"I did not kill him!" shrieked Medeoan, falling back even as she cried out her assurance. "He gave his life willingly for Isavalta!"

There, there it is at last. A wicked joy cut through Kalami. "You killed him! You let him die because you could not make Vyshemir's sacrifice!" He took a step toward her. She was so small and so pale under all her finery. She trembled from the weight of it, from all those burdens she'd sought to cast away from her even while she clung to them with a tenacity that had bled the life from her. "You'd trust that blood which has been whispering in her veins for all her life that her father died because of your cowardice!"

"No!" But she fled back up the dais, seeking to tower over the truth he spoke.

"She's been to the Land of Death and Spirit," he said, walking slowly up the dais. She would no more stand above him. Never again. He spoke the deepest truth now, and she would acknowledge it. She would acknowledge what she had truly done, and what Bridget truly was. "She's walked in the presence of her family's ghosts. How can you be such a fool to think her your friend?"

"I did not kill Avanasy!" The force of that scream rang through the hall as if she sought to shatter the stones with her cry.

No. You do not get to tell yourself that lie anymore. You are mine, old woman. I have licked your slippers for all these years, but now, you will wear my collar, you and your precious Avanasidoch. I will chain you up so tightly you will never trouble my people again. "You did." He stood face-to-face with her, as if she were no more than a serving woman dressed up for a masquerade. "And if you do not now remove his daughter from your house you yourself will die of your folly and cowardice."

Medeoan began to shake. She trembled so badly her keys clinked together, and it seemed she must break herself apart from shaking.

"You know I speak the truth," said Kalami. "You know there is nothing else to be done."

She opened her mouth, and he stepped closer, ready for her surrender, ready to drink it in and savor its sweetness.

But Medeoan turned her face. "Guard!" she called. "Guard!"

Before Kalami had chance to draw another breath, the hall's doors banged open and Chadek and his men swarmed into the room, surrounding the dais, their axes ready. It was discipline that held them at the foot of the dais, for Kalami had no time to step back, no time to make appearances what they should be.

"Take the lord sorcerer out of here," said Medeoan, backing away until she could sit herself on the throne again. "Keep him close. I will send for him later."

The world around Kalami turned red in his eyes. He felt hot and cold together, and he had to clench his jaw so tightly his teeth ached so that he would not scream out his rage in Medeoan's sick, old, useless presence.

"Lord Sorcerer," said Chadek. "If you would?"

I would. I will. Kalami stepped back. He walked down the dais, turned, and faced the dowager. She still trembled. She should tremble. Kalami reverenced. "I await your orders, as ever, Grand Majesty."

Medeoan did not look at him.

Kalami smiled at that, and let the guard form around him and march him away. He held his peace until the Great Hall's doors slammed behind him, and Chadek's men steered him through the antechamber toward the left-hand door, which led to the Topaz Hall, and from there possibly to the understairs, and the lower stairs, and the cells.

"Chadek," he whispered urgently to the captain. "Chadek, you must confine me in my room."

Chadek did not answer. Chadek did not even turn his head. Why should he? Chadek was sympathetic to Kalami and his position. He had worked his way up the ranks and been taken into the house guard even though his third name had been given as a guess at who his grandfather was. But he was steadfastly loyal to his oaths, and Kalami had been accused of poisoning the emperor. Chadek would have struck his head off then and there had Medeoan ordered it.

Servants opened the doors to the Topaz Hall, staring openly at Kalami as the guard marched him through. How much had they already heard? "Chadek, Ananda has orchestrated a fresh set of lies. She's deceiving the Avanasidoch."

Chadek did not even blink. The tromp of boots rang off the walls of pale yellow plaster set with the stones that gave the hall its name. "Chadek, please. Even the council lords do not say I have done anything. You were ordered to keep me close. Her Grand Majesty did not say where."

A spot of color appeared on Chadek's cheek, indicating that despite all he was listening.

"There is no other sorcerer here, Chadek. Her Grand Majesty is in danger. Lock me away and she is lost."

Believe me, believe me, he urged silently. The doors at the other end of the hall were opened. The stairs approached from the shadows. Voices whispered all around them, servants come to watch the show. He could hear them even over the sounds of marching.

Kalami spoke the words he had hoped to avoid. "By our friendship, Chadek. I beg you."

The escort turned a corner, forcing Kalami to turn with them. The stairway loomed in front of them, a carved stone banister leading up, a plain wooden banister leading down.

Chadek.

Chadek turned again, and led the escort up the stone steps to the imperial floor and from there to Kalami's own apartments.

When at last they halted in front of Kalami's door, Chadek held out his hand. Kalami knew what he wanted, and he handed over his key. Chadek unlocked the apartment and with a grunt ordered one of the oversergeants to accompany him. Kalami waited while they poked the fire to life and searched his room for accomplices or obvious contraband.

"Let him in," said Chadek, finally.

The escort parted, allowing Kalami access to his door. The oversergeant withdrew at once, but Chadek lingered for a last moment, looking into Kalami's eyes.

"For our friendship," he said quietly. "Break this word between us, and I will chase you to the ends of the earth."

"I understand," replied Kalami.

Chadek gave no answer. He just marched out to join his men, and he closed the door behind himself. He had not, Kalami noted with a sardonic smile, returned the key, but then, Kalami had not expected it. Chadek was already taking an enormous risk. Any of his men might report this in hope of promotion.

I'm sorry, Chadek, Kalami thought toward the captain. *Truly.*

But there was no more time to think of that. What mattered now was understanding. His plans had gone horribly wrong, and they must be corrected. He must understand what he had failed to predict.

Kalami reached beneath his shirt for the leather bag he carried there. He pulled out a narrow band of yarn that contained, quite literally, every color of the rainbow. It had been knitted on pins of copper and of silver. He kissed the band and breathed over it before he pressed it first to his right eye and then to his left.

Then, it seemed to his eyes that there appeared a shelf along the far wall of the room, set high enough that the tallest of men would be able to walk under it and not know it was there. Its edge had been carved with a pattern that matched the pattern on the knitted band. Four chests of oak and silver waited there.

Kalami reached down the leftmost chest and took it to his desk. He unlocked it with a key he also drew from his bag. Inside the chest waited a collection of parchment scrolls, most of them his notes, maps and casual remarks. Nothing that could be incriminating, should anyone find them, but all that could be said to be private if he were ever questioned. A few though, contained his most careful observations.

Kalami plucked out one of the scrolls and undid the green ribbon that tied it. He spread parchment out on the desk. The scroll contained an elaborate tracery of symbols connected by a web of straight lines, themselves connected by curves that made up semi- and hemicircles, or great swinging ellipses.

As ever, Kalami could not help remembering the first time he had seen such a thing. He had been a boy, in a hut of crumbling stone, chinked and roofed with moss. The room had been entirely black except for the small circle illuminated by a candle that burned with a pale orange light. The old man beside him smelled of fish and foulness, and Kalami was more scared of him even than the darkness.

"This," the old man hissed through his rotting teeth. "This your twice-great-grandfather made."

On the dirt floor, the old man had unfolded a piece of skin so old it was impossible to tell what animal it had once belonged to. On the other side, drawn in fading inks, Kalami had seen stars and planets connected to one another with dashed lines, and other symbols too—a crude castle, a sword, a flame, a broken staff, and others he could not make out.

"He was a sorcerer, see? He knew the old magics. He spoke to the stars, and wrote down what they said." His greasy finger traced the path of one particular line, careful not to actually touch the flaking leather. "See? See here?"

Kalami looked close and did try to see. He saw a red planet, and he saw the sun, and he saw the sword, the fire, and a castle growing closer together, and the end of the line he saw only the broken staff.

"That shows that Isavalta will not hold us forever. It shows that Tuukos will one day be free again."

"How does it show that?" Kalami the boy had demanded. "How do you know?"

The old man shook his head heavily. "I don't know. No sorcerer, me. None of the old learning in my family."

"Master Ubish never said anything about something like this."

The old man winked. "What's he know about our old learning? He's an Isavaltan sorcerer. He can only teach their ways."

"But I want to learn this." Kalami stabbed at the fragile leather with a child's thoughtlessness, and got his hand swatted for his enthusiasm. "I want to learn to write down the future," he went on, ignoring the slap.

And he had, from a half-blind old woman who sat in the corner of the lord master's yard, plucking the feathers from dead fowl and stuffing of them into sacks for later use. She had taught him in the dark of night, in the deepest secret. No one knew she was a sorceress. She had escaped the slaughter that had taken his own great-uncle and had survived by becoming deaf, drooling and stupid. Or at least, by appearing to do so.

When he had finally reached the court of Isavalta, Kalami had put her patient teaching to good work. At least, he thought he had. There was Bridget's symbol. There were the stars and planets of her old world, carefully traced from his own observations. There was himself, nothing more than a circle on the map, and there came her golden, five-pointed star, closer, and closer yet, until the two became one symbol, and together moved to overtake and claim the tiny red bird, and together the three of them broke the crown and the staff.

What had he missed? What had he left undone? Kalami stared at the parchment, fighting to think, fighting to suppress the anger that made him want to tear the useless chart in two. He had missed something. He had to see it now, or he might as well walk out into the snow to die because he would have failed, finally, utterly, and absolutely.

The fire had warmed the room enough that Kalami impatiently shed his heavy velvet coat and much of the brocade in favor of his lighter, everyday kaftan, tying the sash impatiently. Finon had laid down his life for this. Kalami must not fail him. He thrust his hands into the kaftan's pockets, and stared again at the parchment. Something brushed his fingertips. He seized on it and pulled out. It was a twist of red hair. Fox hair.

The Vixen.

Kalami crushed the twist of hair into his fist. He had not counted on the Vixen and her machinations when he had drawn this. He remembered how she had licked Bridget's eye in her den. Had she done something to Bridget then? Increased her ability to see? But why? She had not even wanted to give Bridget back to him. She had tried to gain entrance to the palace to take Bridget away. Or was that a ruse? Something to divert his suspicions? If it was, it had worked magnificently. He had known it was dangerous to involve her when he had first conceived the plan to lead her sons into danger, but the risk had been worth it. Sakra, the one who had spilled her children's blood, had almost died of it, would have died of it had it not been for Bridget.

"So," he murmured to the night. "Your gift had a second edge, and you wish to revoke it. Is that it?"

But no answer came, nor would any come to him here. His time in this court was ended. That much was clear. Medeoan would throw him to the slaughter as soon as she needed to. But he would have her in the end, because he would have her precious Bridget. If Bridget would not serve him from love, she would serve him from pain. There were ways.

But he could not work them here. This room was no longer shelter for him or his works. With some small regret, Kalami went to another chest and pulled out a traveling pack and winter clothing made of skins of sheep, seals and reindeer. From under his bed came a set of skis that had been tied to the frame along with a long pole. It was time now to affect a final change, to become again what he truly was. After tonight, all illusions were stripped away. Truth alone remained.

Part of that truth was that he held Medeoan's and Bridget's lives in his hands. They were simply unaware of it yet.

Kalami set to work. Anything from the freshly revealed chests that he could not pack he dropped into the fire. He discarded his court clothing without a second thought. He moved quickly and quietly. No need to alert whoever Chadek left on guard outside to his movements.

At last, Kalami laced his pack tightly shut and slung it over the shoulders. His court persona was quite gone. Anyone who saw him would take him for a peasant. He wore a coat of unshorn fleece with the wool side against his skin. Sealskin boots encased his feet, and reindeer-hide leggings tied with laces of sinew wrapped around his legs. A piece of white silk screened his face.

They forgot, these idle and useless people behind their walls of stone. They did not know how to truly face the cold. They hid from it. But he had not forgotten. He was of the true North, and it would take more than this persistent snow to trap him indoors.

Kalami picked up his skis, his pole and a length of rope, and walked calmly out the door onto his snow-filled balcony. The barest crescent of a waxing moon shone crystal clear above, and the frigid wind carried only the lightest sprinkle of snow to brush against his eyelashes. He knotted the rope swiftly around the balcony rail. When he finished, he pitched his pole down into the snow. It sank into the soft side of the drift almost its entire length. That told what he needed to know. If he climbed down in just his boots he would be hopelessly mired in the snow. Kalami strapped on his skis.

Awkwardly, Kalami swung first one leg, and then the other over the railing. His fleece-lined mittens protected him from the friction of the rope as well as from the cold, and one slow patient inch at a time, he lowered himself to the ground.

He settled gently onto the drift and untied the rope from his waist.

No voice shouted at him to stop. No eye observed him. They all huddled behind their curtains, plotting their plots. No one could go forth on such a night.

Kalami wanted to laugh. He settled for thrusting first one end, then the other of his pole into the snow and striding forward on his lengths of carved wood, gliding easily over the snow, as easily as any of them could have run across firm ground.

Oh, the moon might show any who cared to look what he was doing, and where he was headed. But how long would it take them to don the proper footgear, to chase after him? The snow was too deep for horses. They kept no reindeer here. Deer were for peasants and the Tuukosov. The palace had no ramparts. The dowager's grandfather had insisted there be none. This was a palace, not a fortress. He had it built as a symbol of how safely and securely he held his empire, with no fear of invading armies. Had it not been for that man's arrogance, there might now have been a place where the house guard could have stationed men to shoot him with arrows, and then he might have had something to worry about. As it was, he was alone with only the whistle of the wind and hissing of his skis against the snow.

Behind his silk mask, Kalami smiled and let the night swallow him whole.

Chapter Seventeen

When the bath attendants and body servants paraded Mikkel back into his apartments, they found Ananda standing beside the firepit, a gentle blaze reflecting off her rich court garb and imperial coronet.

"Thank you," she said as the startled procession dropped to knees, all but Mikkel, who stood, as ever, blank and unheeding, his eyes shifting restlessly back and forth, looking for something they never seemed to find. "You are all dismissed. I shall attend my husband tonight."

But the first among the body servants, his rank indicated by the golden collar around his neck and the golden sash around his kaftan, stood in her presence, as none should have done. He was not one of the jackanapes whom she had seen so cruelly teasing Mikkel before. This was a true servant, staunch and loyal to his emperor.

And thus disposed to think the worst of me, for I am the one who afflicts them both.

"Forgive me, Majesty Imperial," the man said. "But that is not possible."

"You would contradict your empress?" she said, drawing herself up to full height.

"Never in life." He cast his eyes down. "But my oath is to Her Grand Majesty the Dowager Empress as long as the emperor's illness of spirit lasts, and I may not disobey her."

Ananda tried to hold on to hope. If this man was what he seemed, one who was loyal to his emperor but deceived by the dowager's lies, all might be over in a moment, for how could any such not desire to hear Mikkel's freedom was at hand?

"Then rejoice, good man. The gods have heard the prayers on this holy day. They have told me how the emperor is to be cured."

The man's jaw worked back and forth for a moment. "As much as I would like to believe this, Majesty Imperial, I can do nothing without the orders of Her Grand Majesty the Dowager."

Of course. The man was loyal, probably they all were. Ananda's gaze traveled across the rest of the kneeling attendants, but they also believed that the emperor's enchantment was Ananda's doing.

And if what was to come next did not work, Ananda was dead. As she waited in the dark, she had come to understand what held her back. Her own shields now were cell walls. It was her lies that kept her from Mikkel tonight. Truth alone would let her near him.

"You believe, as you have been told, that I did this to the one who is my husband and your emperor," she said. Speaking the words was a relief. An end to lies. Tonight, one way or another, the illusions were done. "But I say to you that I could not have, because I am not a sorceress."

The man's head snapped up. "Your Majesty Imperial jests with me."

Ananda shook her head. "The word of my sorcerous nature is a lie. It is a lie told by those who did not wish alliance between Hastinapura and Isavalta, and it is a lie I fostered, to my shame, so that what was done to the emperor might not be attempted on me."

Anger was all that showed on the man's face. She saw clearly that he would scoff at her, if he dared. "What enemy could you fear, Majesty Imperial?"

Ananda stood silent before him, letting him reach understanding on his own. She watched his anger deepen. "Majesty Imperial, please go. Do not make me call the guards and shame us both."

"I tell you, a girdle has been tied around your emperor's waist," she said as calmly as she could. "It has robbed him of his mind and will. I did not place it there. I lack the skills. My soul, as yours, is divided." She risked a step forward to create the smallest intimacy between them. "Our bond of marriage, though, permits me to remove it. Call the guard to escort me away, if you will. But know that as you do, you condemn your emperor for the rest of his life."

The servant spread his hands. "Majesty Imperial, how can I believe you? You ask me to betray my loyalties and you can offer me no proof of what you say. On the strength of this, I am to let you lay hands on the emperor?"

She had grown so used to secrets—that had been her mistake. She could never create more secrets than Medeoan had. It was openness now that would save her, and Mikkel. "Call in the guard, then," she told him. "Let me stand under their weapons. Send at once to the dowager with word of what is happening. Strip my coat away and take from me any ornament or talisman you may find about my person. Let me stand naked before you, if you'll accept no other way, but let me try to free my husband, your emperor."

No one else had stood, but on their knees she saw them struggle to keep still. She heard the hisses of their breath as they tried wordlessly to urge caution, or perhaps they were just shocked at her words.

"Majesty Imperial, I cannot permit this."

"Do you believe I intend to harm the emperor?" she asked.

The man said nothing, but his belief was plain in his face, and that belief bred hatred.

"Then call in the guard," repeated Ananda firmly. "If I do anything harmful to the person of your emperor, they may lawfully cut me down where I stand. I am offering to die for this chance. What more can I do?" She moved close, not giving him the chance to look away from her. He would see her face, see it fully and honestly. If he turned on her, turned on Mikkel, it would not be because she had left any deception open. "Are you afraid enough to commit the treason of failing to protect your emperor from an ongoing attack to his person?" She licked her lips. Here was the final promise. "You know that upon the death of a sorcerer, all their active enchantment must also die. If I live and am right, your emperor is free. If I am plying you with the ultimate falsehood and I die, your emperor is free."

The gleam in the man's eye was dangerous. He did hate Ananda. Probably he hated all Hastinapura. Probably he was a generational servant of the palace, and his father remembered Kacha and his treachery. But she had offered her blood. He had a chance to see the threat of Ananda was ended. He had a chance to see his emperor healed.

Which would win, his obedience to the dowager, or his desire to see the Hastinapuran witch dead?

The man made the tiniest gesture toward one of the kneeling underservants. "Shipil, call in the guard, and then do you run to Her Grand Majesty and tell her what happens here."

"Sir." Shipil leapt to his feet and ran from the room. A moment later, all six of Mikkel's guard trooped in. The body servant greeted them and in whispers explained what was about to occur. The lieutenant disagreed with a guttural reply Ananda could not clearly hear. The body servant leaned closer and whispered directly in the lieutenant's ear. The lieutenant smiled a smile as sharp as the blade of his ax, and at a gesture, he and his men ringed the little gathering.

"All of you, back away," said the body servant to his subordinates, who seemed only too glad to retreat behind the guard. "Majesty Imperial, I must ask you to remove your outer garments."

It is the only way, Ananda reminded herself as she slowly, clumsily, began to unbuckle her coat. "I will need help."

The body servant came forward. Ananda swallowed her pride and fear, and let the man unknot her laces and pull off her sleeves. All the others stood and watched, common men, rough soldiers, all of them with anger in their eyes. They did not like this. They did not like her. They watched her stripping all layers of propriety and protection in front of them.

All but Mikkel. According to their ways, which she had worked so hard to make her own, Mikkel, the only man who should ever have seen this sight, did not watch her at all. What attention he had seemed to be captured by the way her finery was casually tossed onto the floor until she stood in her belted shift.

The body servant seemed satisfied with this and stepped back.

Seven Mothers help me. Keep me strong. Ananda approached her husband with all the angry, judgmental, and finally bloodthirsty eyes watching her and waiting.

She fixed her eyes on Mikkel. Nothing else mattered. Only Mikkel, who could not look at her. Mikkel, who laughed at all her jests, who wrote sweet but clumsy poetry, who had showed her the beauty to be found in snow.

He no longer wore his holiday garments. They had changed him into a plain white kaftan banded and buttoned in gold. There would be a vest and shirt underneath it.

"Mikkel." She reached for his hand and took it into hers. He had grown so thin under his affliction. She could discern all the bones of his wrist.

A flash of movement caught the corner of her eye, and she heard the rasp of steel against leather. Someone in the guard was all too ready to carry out their right to slaughter her where she stood. By taking his hand, she threatened the emperor.

It was all right. It didn't matter. What mattered was Mikkel. His hand lay limp and cold in hers. He looked down at their fingers, mildly curious. "Mikkel, I mean to help you. Remove your coat for me, husband."

"No," he said hoarsely, as if he were unused to the word.

Ananda almost dropped his hand. "No? Mikkel, I ask you, do this thing for me."

"No." He swayed on his feet, blinking. "I must not. Not for . . . Not for . . ."

"The emperor refuses," announced the body servant, and she heard soft triumph in his voice, but also concern. "Step you away, Majesty Imperial."

Ananda ignored him. "Not for what?" she asked Mikkel. "For who? Not for me?"

"I must not." He pulled his hand away from hers and touched it to the high collar of his kaftan. "I must not."

"Why must you not?" Ananda tried to keep her gaze focused on Mikkel, but it kept slipping toward the door. Did the flash of the steel in the weapons and the armor distract him? Did he sense the dowager coming? She might be here at any moment. That was the greatest gamble of all, but it had been the most necessary. It was only by making herself completely vulnerable that any of Mikkel's guardians would agree to this.

"Mikkel, please, you must do this for me. Do you know me? I am your wife. I am Ananda." *Mothers all, help me. Vyshko and Vyshemir, please help me reach this child of your house.* She unknotted his cloth-of-gold sash and cast it aside.

"Ananda?" his brow furrowed. "I knew . . . there was . . ." He reached out tentatively, his fingertips brushing her hair. "There was Ananda. I . . . miss her." The assembly around them gasped. There was movement. She heard cloth, and she heard the clink of armor. But she could not be distracted. She found the buckle on his belt and flicked it open so that the belt with its empty sword sheath and tiny ceremonial dagger thudded to the floor. She could not fear them. There was only Mikkel. There could only be Mikkel.

"I am here, my love." She took his face in both hands. "I am Ananda, here before you."

"I can't see her," Mikkel whispered, his eyes darting back and forth. "I can't see Ananda."

"She is here!" Ananda pulled him forward, kissing his mouth hard and strong. More gasps around her. This was indecent in their barbaric eyes, but she was too far gone to be ashamed. She felt fingertips brush her shoulder, and someone said "No," and pulled them away. "I am here!"

Mikkel blinked, slowly, and his gaze turned toward her. Ananda's heart leapt into her mouth, but his gaze did not stay, it slid from her to the bed screens. "Ananda would help me."

"Would you see Ananda?" she asked desperately. "Take off your coat!"

"My coat . . ."

Ananda's hands grasped the gold buttons and wrestled with them. "Help me, Mikkel. You must remove your coat."

Mikkel said nothing. His fingers fumbled with the buttons, as hers did. She wished desperately for assistance, but she would not ask for it. There was no telling what the touch of another person would do to Mikkel's fragile concentration.

At last, the white kaftan slid from Mikkel's shoulders and landed in a heap on the floor. Underneath waited a vest of blue and gold buttoned with more gold.

"Your vest, Mikkel. You must take off your vest to see Ananda."

Was that hope behind his eyes? Was that Mikkel back there, reaching out to her through whatever fog his mother had placed within his mind? His hand strayed to his chest, touching the buttons. "I must . . ."

"You must. If you want to see Ananda, you must." But Ananda herself could not help seeing that two swords had been drawn, and all the axes stood ready as the guard moved closer, readying themselves to reach her in the space of a heartbeat.

And the dowager was on her way. Any second, the dowager would open the door, and she would forget Ananda's father. She could forget all possibility of war, and she would order those swords that she commanded. Ananda would lie dead on the stones, and Mikkel would still be captive.

At least it will be over, and I will have tried my very best. It will not be my cowardice that condemns us both.

One by one the buttons were undone, but then Mikkel's arms seemed to lose their strength and they fell to his sides. Ananda darted behind him and pulled the vest from his unresisting shoulders, dropping it on top of the kaftan.

Only the fine linen shirt that gleamed white in the light from the firepit remained.

"You must let me remove your shirt, Mikkel."

"No."

"You will never see Ananda again if I do not."

"No," he pleaded. "It keeps me safe."

"Stop this. This is a travesty." "What is she doing to him?" The questions fluttered about the room. But back came the answers. "Let her try." "It might be she can free them." "What if what she does is real?" "What if what she does is harm him further? Look at her." "Can you trust her?" The arguments flew back and forth. Ananda shut her ears. They meant nothing. Nothing.

"What keeps you safe?"

But Mikkel did not, or could not answer that. Instead he trembled and his eyes glistened, with tears? Did he stand ready to cry?

"Let me help you," she breathed. "Let me help you see Ananda."

The trembling grew worse. Ananda steeled herself. He was so cold, his body so dead. But he was Mikkel still, she must remember that. Whatever had been done to him, he was still her husband whom she loved. She wrapped her arms around his cold, quivering body, and kissed him again. He did not, could not return the kiss, he could only tremble.

"Get her away from him!"

Ananda encircled him with her embrace, her hands fumbling for his shirttails, pulling them free of his pantaloons.

"No!" A violent shove knocked the breath from her lungs and sent Ananda reeling across the floor. For a moment she stood stunned, trying to see who had struck her, but there was only Mikkel, his shirt rumpled, his chest heaving. "You must not, I must not let you!"

"Why not!" shouted Ananda. "Who am I that I must not touch you! Tell me, Mikkel!"

"You are . . . You are . . ." Whatever strength held Mikkel up gave way and his knees buckled. Mikkel sank slowly to the floor, his head drooping until he buried his face in his hands. "You are Ananda."

"She hurts him! Take up your swords! She's the witch who did this to him!"

"No!"

"Yes, Mikkel!" She threw herself to her knees in front of him, grasping his hands and pulling them away from his face. Tears streamed down his hollow cheeks and confusion racked his entire visage. "I am Ananda. Say it again!"

But his mouth only worked itself back and forth silently for a long, painful moment. "Help me," he whispered.

"Yes, Mikkel." She tore at the buttons on his cuffs. Her fingers sought the buttons on his collar, barely able to work them through their fastenings between his trembling and hers. He moaned as if in pain, and snatched at her hand. "No. I cannot. I cannot!"

"Let him be, witch!" Hands clamped onto Ananda's shoulders and yanked her backward. She screamed, kicking out, but someone struck her face, stunning her into momentary stillness.

"What are you doing!"

All turned. Captain Chadek stood in the doorway, his ax in both hands. All drew back as he stalked forward.

"Unhand the person of Her Majesty Imperial."

"But . . ." began the two underservants who Ananda could now see held her. Which of them had struck her? she wondered idly. She could order him killed for that.

"I said unhand Her Majesty Imperial," Captain Chadek repeated, hefting the ax. "Or do I strike your head from your shoulders?"

The men let Ananda go and she climbed slowly to her feet. Chadek saluted her, his eyes traveling up and down, seeing her shift and the piles of clothing strewn about the floor. "Majesty Imperial, what is happening here?"

"Good captain, I understand your distress," said Ananda, gathering to her as much dignity as she could. "I am trying to free the emperor of his illness of spirit. He is under enchantment and I have the answer to it."

Chadek watched her for a long moment. He was tired. That much was plain. Tired to the bone. She sympathized with all her heart. "Majesty Imperial," he said. "I don't know what to think. The lord sorcerer is under arrest. Her Grand Majesty the Dowager has vanished. Your servant Sakra and the Avanasidoch are also nowhere to be found." Sakra was in her room, but she would not tell him that. But the Avanasidoch? Where had she gone?

It does not matter, she told herself. Nothing outside this room mattered.

"And now . . ." Chadek gestured at the room, the crowd, the abandoned clothing. "What might I think of this?"

Ananda shook her head. "I do not know, Captain. I only know if you let me, I can set all to right. If I do not, as I've already said to your men, my blood is forfeit."

Chadek searched her face, and she let him. It was all up to this man now. Everyone in this room would obey him without question. He was Kalami's friend. He could order her death, right now, and there would be no question of it. What did he believe? What had he seen this night?

Chadek turned to face his men. "All of you, out! This is beyond indecent. Get out!"

"But Captain—" began one of the soldiers.

"Do not even think of questioning that order, Underlieutenant," barked Chadek before the man could speak another word.

As simple as that. They filed out, guards and servants together. Through it all, Mikkel stayed there on his knees and Ananda felt her heart must break from the effort it took to keep herself still. She saw the sharp edge of Chadek's ax and its gleaming, spearlike tip. She saw in his eyes the pain his decision was causing him. His world was being shaken to its foundation, and he was trying to hold those foundations together with his bare hands.

At last the door closed. "Do what you must," he said without turning around.

Instantly, Ananda dropped to her knees beside Mikkel. He shivered as if from unbearable cold, his arms wrapped tight around his thin white shirt.

"No, no, my love." Ananda wrapped her own arms around his trembling shoulders. "It will all be well. I swear it. By the Seven Mothers, I swear it."

But he only shook and stared straight ahead of him, seeing what horrors, Ananda could not even guess. She stroked his shoulders, feeling the bones right under the skin. Her touch seemed only to make his shudders worse. Another painful moan escaped him, and for a moment, she had to close her eyes against the answering cry that formed inside her. Biting her lip, she made her hands encircle his waist.

She felt it then, a stiff and heavy braid under her fingers where her eyes saw only white skin. He wore his enchantment. All these long, dark years when she could not bear to touch him, he wore his chain around his waist.

Fury drowned reason and she grasped the braid with both hands, trying to tear it from his body. He cried out and swung his arm, clouting her on the ear. Captain Chadek made no move. Ananda saw the gleam of steel among the white heap of Mikkel's clothing, and she picked up the ceremonial dagger that had fallen with his clothing.

Mikkel curled in on himself, cradling his head, and she crawled to him with the knife in her hand. Something cold tickled her neck, and she froze. Chadek had lowered his ax. The tip now touched the flesh at the base of her skull. All he had to do was thrust quickly forward, and she would die.

"Put down the knife, Majesty Imperial," Chadek ordered.

Mothers. Ananda lunged toward Mikkel, her weight knocking him sprawling. They rolled over, and her hand found the girdle under the linen, and then her knife blade did. Mikkel screamed and Ananda screamed, and threw herself aside. She felt the wind as the ax came down and rang against the stone. She cast the girdle away from her, and huddled in on herself, waiting to live, or to die.

No blow came, and slowly, Ananda was able to open her eyes.

The first thing she saw was the girdle lying on the stone. Its band was made of knotted threads of silver that had then been braided together. Sparkling tassels, their threads adorned with glass beads, hung from the band. Seen objectively, it was surely beautiful.

Beyond it crouched Mikkel, hands splayed against the floor, panting in terror as he stared at the beautiful, foul thing that had bound him for so long. But his skin, his skin was pink and flushed with emotion, and his eyes were still and clear and they saw. They *saw.*

All at once, Ananda seemed unable to find her own breath. "Mikkel." The word came out as little better than a whisper. "Oh, Mikkel, husband, look at me."

One slow, painful movement at a time, Mikkel drew back his hands, and lifted his head, and for the first time since their wedding day, his amber eyes met hers.

"Ananda?" he whispered, and although his hand still shook badly, he reached toward her.

Joy beyond words poured into Ananda's being. Again she threw herself forward, but this time it was to wrap her arms tightly around Mikkel, to bury her face against his shoulder.

"It is you," he said, his voice weak with disbelief and wonder. "Where have you been? I've been looking for you for so long."

Ananda pulled back as far as she could bear. "You've been under an enchantment, beloved. See here." She lifted up the severed girdle.

Mikkel jerked backward, as if she showed him a serpent. "Get it away from me!"

Ananda instantly tossed the thing away. "I'm sorry, husband. I'm sorry. It's gone."

But Mikkel would not be comforted. "She'll tie it again," he cried. "She will. I felt it every day. It was so heavy around my soul. I couldn't breathe, I couldn't see for the weight of that thing. . . ." His arms crept up to cover his head.

"Hush, Mikkel, hush." Ananda eased his arms back down, and to her relief, he let her. "It is destroyed. I cut it off you. The spell is done and there is no remaking it."

"She . . . she did that to me . . . she said . . . she said . . ."

"She lied, Mikkel," said Ananda as firmly as she could. "She lied, and it's over."

"I want to believe you." His voice rasped in his throat and he gripped her hands hard. "I want to."

But I don't know if I can. Ananda bit her lip. She wanted to cry. This was not the Mikkel she'd hoped for, strong and confident, emerging from his spell to take the burdens from her shoulders and sweep away all the obstacles. She had dreamed of him enfolding her in his arms, and speaking in a strong voice, telling her what they must do. For once having someone else say what must be done.

Ananda set aside her selfish, girlish wishes. "Can you at least trust me, Mikkel?"

He had to stare at her a moment, and her heart plummeted as she saw the fear in his eyes. *But he sees*, she tried to tell herself. *He sees again.*

"Yes," he said at last. "I can, I will, trust you."

"I hope Your Majesty Imperial will also find it in you to trust me."

Ananda spun on her knees. Captain Chadek. She had forgotten him. He knelt, his ax laid flat on the floor in front of him and his hand over his heart.

"Good captain Chadek," said Ananda. "Stand up. Your service is most welcome to us."

Mikkel squinted at the man. "Chadek? I remember you. You . . ." He shook his head. "I am glad to see you here."

"I most humbly thank Your Majesties Imperial." Chadek reclaimed his ax and stood, but his hand remained over his heart. "We must make this transformation known as quickly as possible, Majesties Imperial."

Happiness wrenched Ananda's heart, but now she knew to temper it with caution. There were still hurdles to be gotten over. The dowager still waited out there. Somewhere. She grasped Mikkel's hands.

"You must be strong, Mikkel. We must walk down to the Great Hall and show the court that you are restored." She pulled his hands close to her breast. "The dowager"—she could not bring herself to call that fiend "your mother"—"may be there."

A single, violent shudder wracked Mikkel's frame. "You will not let her touch me? You will not leave me alone?"

"No, Mikkel. I swear it."

"No one will lay a hand upon Your Majesty Imperial," said Chadek solidly.

Mikkel nodded, but the fear lingered around his face. Without a word, she raised him to his feet, and smoothed his shirt. Chadek turned his face away while Ananda dressed herself and Mikkel, haphazardly, until they were decent, if not precisely presentable.

Then Ananda swallowed her distaste, and bent to pick up the severed girdle.

"No!" cried Mikkel, starting backward.

"We must, Mikkel. It's how we prove you're free."

Now he swallowed, but he also nodded. Ananda tucked the girdle into her belt and with as much firmness of purpose as she could manage, she took the requisite two steps away from him, and held out her hand for him to take.

Mikkel looked at her hand. He looked at Captain Chadek, waiting with his hand over his heart, and he looked again into Ananda's eyes.

"I forgot so much," he said. "But I could not be made to forget that I loved you. I knew that if I could only find you, all would be well. Whatever you saw outwardly, please know that all I did was search for you."

As Mikkel spoke, the trembling left his limbs, and in his eyes, his clear, beautiful eyes, she saw that love which she had missed for so long. Mikkel squared his shoulders, and as he took her hand, he smiled and his mouth shaped her name.

"Let us go, my wife," he said. "Let us show the world that I am free."

A new world blossomed around Bridget, light and darkness, heat and chill slowly separating and resolving into their proper forms. From the corners of her eyes, she saw the stone walls, the workbench with its tools and ores, the dark crucible and the stack of fuel.

But dominating all the cold, cavelike room was the golden cage hanging from its iron chain. Inside it fluttered a tiny bird, not much bigger than a finch, that burned like a living coal.

The bird flapped its delicate wings, and Bridget saw how they flickered exactly like fire.

"Help me," said the bird. "Open the cage. She will not open the cage."

Bridget walked forward. Warmth bathed her like a blessing. As in her dream, she saw that the cage had no door in its braided bars. What she had not seen before was how the gold was blackened and charred. Pockmarks and ash stains marred its perfection. She stretched one hand toward the battered cage, and she saw . . .

And she saw eight people in robes of heavily embroidered silk standing in a circle around a flat stone. Their faces and hands were so heavily decorated with bright tattoos they barely seemed human. A ninth stood upon that stone. This ninth was draped in scarlet silk embroidered with gold and amber feathers, and wore a mask shaped like a bird's face to the fire. The masked person staggered as if in pain, or horribly confused. The others surrounded him and, to Bridget's horror, he vanished in a burst of flame.

And she saw a palace, its roof tiled red, green and gold. A great golden tower rose from its center. Over it streaked the Firebird, the Phoenix, the bird in the cage before her grown impossibly huge. It flew like a living comet, and behind it the palace burned.

Slowly, the outside world faded back into view. Bridget found herself leaning against the rough stone wall, and panting as if she had just run a full mile.

"So that is what it is to see with your eyes."

Bridget pushed herself away from the wall, ready to run. Kalami. Kalami had found her.

But no. It was Sakra who stepped out of the shadows into the light cast by the Firebird. Relief flooded Bridget, only to be washed away by concern. Sakra looked pale. Sweat beaded on his brow, and he touched his right wrist delicately. A thin black line encircled it, overlaying a ring of white blisters.

"What happened?" asked Bridget, appalled.

"I followed you. It was difficult." But he was not looking at her. He was looking at the tiny bird in its golden cage. "I now see why."

"Free me," pleaded the bird.

It was then that Bridget saw what was wrong. The cage had been meant to hold a much larger creature. That tiny finch should have been able to slip through the bars and fly away. It was not braided gold that held in place.

Sakra bowed to the bird, covering his face with both hands. As he did, he spoke in a language that Bridget could not understand. At his words, the bird spread its wings. It blurred and changed, growing until it filled the cage. In so doing, it ceased to be fragile and instead became glorious.

Bridget had once seen a picture of a bird of paradise, with its gleaming white plumage and seemingly yards of tail. The Firebird looked like that now, except that all its plumage glowed, flickered and burned, but was not consumed.

"I accept your respects, *Agnidh*," said the bird. Its voice was no longer a whisper. It roared like a bonfire. "Now let your actions also speak of respect and free me."

"Don't!" said Bridget without thinking. "It's going to burn down the whole world if it can."

"You speak of a vision," said Sakra. It was a statement. Not a question. "If you will, please tell me what you saw."

"I . . ." Bridget hesitated. Even as she looked again at the cage with the Firebird shining so grand and regal behind its twisted bars, she saw again. She saw flames rising from summer wheat, and she saw hearths strangely dead and cold. She saw Avanasy, the golden man in his black coat, crumple to the ground beside the golden cage standing empty and open, and yet she saw the bird rising joyously in the night sky, and she saw it flying over a frozen village and bringing warmth, and she saw it alight on the golden roof of a temple where the bells rang brightly and the people danced with joy to see it there.

Too many images, too much. Bridget could make no sense of them. Was she seeing the past or the future? Both? She didn't know. Was she seeing things that must come to pass, or were these things that only might be?

"What is happening? Somebody, tell me what is happening." She squeezed her eyes closed, trying to clear them. A hand touched her shoulder, but she knocked it away. She wanted answers. She wanted to end this blur of visions. Someone here knew what they all meant. Someone here must know.

"Bridget, be calm," said Sakra. "You're safe here. Open your eyes."

Yes. Bridget gulped a deep breath of air. She was being ridiculous. Her visions could not hurt her, no matter how strange or confusing. She opened her eyes again, and saw Sakra, and the Firebird in its cage.

And she saw Avanasy.

He stood with his hand on the cage. His face was solemn as he looked at her, and stretched out one hand, beckoning? Welcoming? She could not tell.

"You . . ." she began.

"What is it, Bridget?"

"Avanasy," she said, because she could not help herself. "He is here." Of course. His life had helped shape the cage. How could he be kept from this place? The cage must tug at him, draw him back to it. Kalami had said a sorcerer's soul was undivided in life. Surely, it was a strange thing that Avanasy's must be divided in death.

"Your father is here," said Sakra, his voice soft with awe.

"Don't call him that!" snapped Bridget. She did not want to see this man, but she could not close her eyes to him. Very well, he had revealed himself to her. Let him hear what she would say. "He's my mother's lover. He's . . . he's . . . My father is Everett Lederle." The ghost nodded solemnly.

"He would speak with you, Bridget," said the Firebird. "I can hear where you cannot. He says you must free me."

Bridget stared at the ghost. He inclined his head again.

"He says that this confinement was never meant to be forever. He says a great wrong has been done."

Avanasy watched Bridget, and she saw how strong his face was. She remembered the images, the memories Momma had showed her. She wanted to blame Avanasy for the troubles that had plagued her life, but suddenly, she was just tired. How long had it been since she slept? She brushed her hair back. How much longer would it be before she could sleep?

She faced the ghost of the man who fathered her, beside the cage he created to trap this brilliant, dangerous creature, and she did not know what she believed, or what she wanted, beyond sleep. She very much wanted sleep.

"Bridget," said Sakra. "Tell me what I can do to help you."

This golden man was Momma's lover. This was the one responsible for her bastardy and Poppa's heartbreak, and he had the nerve to come here and tell her what to do.

And she saw destruction, and she saw rejoicing, and she saw her father's ghost waiting for her to decide what to do. Sakra had not moved. He would not move until she spoke. She knew that instinctively. He would believe whatever she said next, and he would act on it. She could count on him now when the rest of the world spun uncertainly around her. Everything was now up to her. She could have her revenge on Avanasy right now, and she could watch his face while she defied him.

The ghost, Avanasy, bowed his head, and waited for her. The whole world waited for her to make up her mind.

The bird was so beautiful in its cage, and there stood her father, the man Momma loved, who had crossed the Land of Death and Spirit because he loved her so, and for the first time, Bridget thought she felt the touch of that love. Tears pricked her eyes. Forgiveness. Forgiveness offered, forgiveness received, in his eyes, in her heart. Too much. It was too much. She did not want to cry, she did not want to feel this.

Oh, but she did. She wanted it so much.

Again, Sakra touched her shoulder and this time Bridget not only permitted the gesture, but welcomed it. "Accept this gift, Mistress Bridget," said Sakra softly. "Even I can feel the strength of it. Set yourself free of your cage, and then together, we will free the Phoenix from the cage that holds it."

"But Poppa," whispered Bridget, yearning for the ghost before her to understand. How could she do this without betraying Poppa?

"Love is infinite. It is sea and stars and the ever-blowing wind," said Sakra. "It is all-embracing and so may be all who love."

At those words, Bridget's heart snapped in two. The grief, anger and fear, held so close for so long, poured out in a great flood. Bridget sobbed once, but that was all.

"Father," she whispered.

Avanasy left the cage, left the Firebird, and came to her. She felt his warmth touch her cheeks, her hair, and the one tear that fell from her eye. She felt love, and she felt strength, deep understanding and forgiveness, and all these flowed into her empty, broken heart and for a moment, Bridget knew peace.

Tell Momma, she wanted to say. *Tell Momma what happened here. Tell Momma I love her and that I'm sorry.* But she looked into the eyes of Avanasy's soul and saw that Momma already knew. The enormity of her feelings staggered her and Bridget clutched at Sakra's hand without thinking. Sakra steadied her, but remained silent, asking nothing, letting her keep this moment to herself.

Avanasy drew away, returning to his place by the cage. He laid both hands on the bars. Bridget knew what he wished of her and she straightened her shoulders.

"I see," said Bridget. "I see both destruction and blessing." She turned to Sakra. "I cannot tell which is the true future."

Sakra inclined his head. "Yet, if we can release the Phoenix, we will rob the dowager of the foundation of her power," he said.

But it could burn, and it could freeze. So many lives could be ruined, so many might die as the Firebird took its revenge. "Can we possibly do so in safety?"

"Yes." Absolute certainty filled his voice.

"Well then," answered Bridget briskly, smoothing down her skirts. "How shall we manage it?"

"By claiming a promise in return for that freedom." Sakra moved past her to face the cage and its prisoner. He stood beside the ghost he could not see, but Bridget thought she noted approval from Avanasy.

For itself, the Firebird only stared contemptuously at Sakra and it said nothing.

"You will promise to do no harm to any realm of my mistress, or her family, to harm no person or place under the protection of her, or any of her lineage or heritage." Sakra moved still closer to the cage, heedless of the heat and the bird's long, sharp bill. "Swear this by the fire from which you sprang, and you will go free."

Even as Sakra spoke those words, Avanasy threw out his hand in warning. Before Bridget could speak, a tortured creaking of metal and a great, cold draft cut through the room. "You may not make any promise here."

Medeoan. She swept into the chamber and grasped Bridget, pulling her back from Sakra, Avanasy, and the cage.

"Are you well, Bridget? Has he hurt you?"

"No one has hurt me," Bridget tried to extract herself from the dowager's grip, but Medeoan held her fast.

"But they kidnapped you down here," said Medeoan. "They tried to ensnare you with their lies, but you saw past them." She smiled, and fear stabbed at Bridget's heart. Whatever the dowager saw, it was not in this room. She saw a world she was building inside her mind, and she found it a pleasant place. What would she do when she found out it was not real?

Bridget looked to Avanasy's ghost. He stretched out both hands toward Medeoan, his mouth moving soundlessly, and it seemed to Bridget that he would weep if he could. She wished desperately she could hear, or that the Firebird would speak, but the bird pressed itself against the back of the cage and only hissed at the dowager.

"Grand Majesty," began Sakra carefully. "Surely this is not the place to discuss such things. Your Council of Lords is doubtlessly waiting for you to decide what must be done about the lord sorcerer."

"The lord sorcerer is nothing," spat Medeoan. "He is a traitor. He tried to make a toy of the throne of Eternal Isavalta." She drew herself up. "He failed, as your mistress failed, southerner. As you failed. Isavalta stands despite you all."

Avanasy covered his face with his hands.

"Free me," roared the Firebird. "Let me take my lawful vengeance on this woman!"

But Medeoan did not seem to have heard. "Now you have seen the Firebird," she said to Bridget urgently. "With your visions you have seen the danger it presents." Bridget said nothing. Her throat had become too dry for speech. "I know that you have," said Medeoan, touching her cheek kindly. "I see the terror on your face. You see that it cannot ever be released, not in Isavalta, not in any land if people are to remain living. I cannot go on. The re-creation of the cage is too much for me. So, who can I trust save Avanasy's daughter?" The dowager lifted Bridget's hand, holding it up to the flickering light of the Firebird. Avanasy reached forward, laying his hand over theirs. Bridget felt the warm urgency of his touch, but could it reach Medeoan inside the walls of delusion she built around herself? "All that is left of him is inside you. His blood, his being is in your veins. His understanding runs through you in the core of your soul. You must understand, as he would have understood, all that I have done I have done for Isavalta, to keep the empire safe. You must see that."

Her eyes glittered in the living firelight, and she thrust her face forward, willing Bridget to believe what she said, to see the world as she herself saw it. Desperation surrounded her like a deep fog, and Bridget found a moment for pity. She knew what guilt could do, especially when you were young, but this woman asked too much.

"You wish me to understand you?" Bridget pulled her hand away. "Help me understand what you did to your son." Avanasy stayed beside Medeoan. He was saying something, his ghostly hands stroking hers, urging her to some action she could not hear and that, for all her power, she could not feel.

The dowager drew back. "I kept him safe. He was falling in love with her, just as I did with my husband Kacha. I had to keep him but where he could not be touched by her."

"But you agreed to the marriage," said Bridget. She did not look at Sakra. Medeoan seemed to have forgotten him. Good. Let her forget. It gave him a chance, although what sort of chance Bridget couldn't guess. He had neither the time nor the space to work any spell here. Perhaps between the two of them they could overpower the old woman, but Bridget could not even now imagine Sakra doing so without some extreme provocation.

"To my shame, I did agree." Medeoan bowed her head. She paced away from Avanasy, who stayed still where he was, his hands falling useless to his sides. "I used my son for political needs. I had thought only to keep him safe until Ananda revealed herself for the traitor she was. Then, I would be able to use that proof to keep the treaty, and yet send her back to her relatives."

The dowager turned away, rubbing her hands back and forth, as if despite the living heat of the Firebird, she was still cold. Bridget remembered the cold she had pulled around herself to keep Momma away. How much colder must the dowager be to keep from feeling Avanasy? "I had not thought it would take so long. I did not know how clever she truly was." The dowager turned toward Bridget again. "And I did not know that Kalami pursued his own aims when he urged me to use this particular spell."

"And that makes it all right?" asked Bridget, astonished.

"No. But you must understand—"

"I must understand nothing!" Bridget swept out both her hands. She should not say this. The woman was mad. Bridget should not speak so, but she did not wish to stop and no one, living or dead, moved to silence her. "I've seen what you have done. You robbed your son of his free will. You tried to falsely accuse an innocent, frightened girl of your crime. You stand here excusing yourself from all of it, saying you must keep the empire safe, and yet you do not notice that one of your provinces is so unhappy they are trying to rebel. And you ask that I feel sympathy for you? Out of some familial obligation, to a man I never even knew existed until I came here?" Avanasy watched her calmly, taking no new hurt from her words. Bridget stood before the dowager. So much had happened, so much changed and newly understood, even in the last few moments. She would not stand in silence and let this woman, these people, tell her what was so about herself. Not ever again. "I never knew my mother's lover. I believe he was a good man who did his best and died for his country." The words sounded strange in her ears, but she knew them for the truth, and Avanasy standing so near, and yet held back by such an unimaginable gulf, accepted her words. "Let me tell you of the father I did know. He was a honest man. He lived alone, doing nothing but keep the light and try to save lives. All lives. The fool millionaires on their toy yachts, or the working sailors on the timber ships. It made no difference to him. That was all the magic there was in him, and all the nobility. And he was worth a thousand of you." Her chest was heaving now, and more emotions than she could name swirled through her. "You say you have given your life to your country. I see no such matter. You have given other people's lives. First Avanasy's, then your son's, and now you would give mine. And you ask me to be glad of it. You ask me to bow down and accept your burden with a, 'Thank you, mistress.' Then what?" She threw up her hands. "What else will you do to keep the throne from your son and his wife because you don't trust them? How many people will die in that effort? Will you kill him now?" She stopped, and the slow horrible realization came over her. "But you already tried to, didn't you? Those sheets were yours, not Ananda's, and not even Kalami's. That was you. Your plan." The dowager said nothing, she just turned her face away. "How am I supposed to understand that?"

"He would have understood." The dowager brushed shaking hand across her forehead. "Mikkel always understood the needs of the throne come first."

"How could he have understood anything? You took his understanding away from him, as you meant to take his life!" She stabbed a finger at the dowager. "His life! Not yours. It was not yours to take!"

"All lives are mine!" screamed Medeoan. "I am the empress of Isavalta!"

"No." Bridget shook her head. "You are a sad woman who has too long tormented herself for the sin of falling in love."

The dowager stared at her in utter disbelief. "How can you speak so to me?"

Bridget shook her head. "I don't know. Perhaps it is because my father stands beside me."

Medeoan began to shudder. "No." She backed away. "No." She lifted her hand as if to ward Bridget away. "That is a lie, the creature's lie. Avanasy is not here. Avanasy waits in the Land of Death and Spirit. He knows all that I have done and he sent you to be my salvation. That is what is true."

"No, Medeoan." Bridget wished there were some way to be kind, wished with all her heart that Medeoan would stop, would accept, would give way and spare herself this pain. "I see him. He stands beside the cage. He reaches toward you and he begs you to give up this useless struggle before any more damage is done."

As Bridget's words hung in the air, the dowager gave a wordless cry of pain. She swung away, throwing herself against the workbench. Bridget didn't move. When Medeoan looked up again, Bridget saw utter heartbreak in her eyes, and she knew what had happened.

So too did Sakra. "She's done it," he breathed. "Ananda has freed him. It's over." For the first time, Bridget heard true happiness and relief in his voice. "She's free."

"No," said Medeoan, pain bleeding from her face and leaving behind only shock, as if she had just been told her child had died. "No. He was safe. She could not get to him. He was safe."

The dowager's knees collapsed, and Bridget, acting on reflex alone, caught her before she could fall.

"It's all right," she murmured soothingly, even as she looked over the top of the dowager's head at Sakra, and Avanasy, who had turned away. "It's all right."

Sakra nodded. "Come, Grand Majesty. Let us leave this place." But he was not looking at her either, he was looking at the Firebird. For once, the bird only folded its wings. It too knew all had changed, and that change brought it patience, but that patience would not hold for long.

"Come, Grand Majesty," Bridget said. "Let me help you."

"There is no help," whispered Medeoan, clutching Bridget's hands in a painful grip as Bridget led her through the door to a darkened stairway. "Not anymore."

There was no answer Bridget could make to that, so she concentrated on helping the dowager climb the stairs. Sakra had paused to collect a lantern, and now he went before them. The dowager saw nothing. Her eyes had closed. Whether it was against the light, against the knowledge of what had happened, or what was to come, Bridget could not tell.

Poor woman, thought Bridget. She had only wanted to be other than what she was and to do other than what she had done. These were things Bridget could well understand.

The stairway ended at a ladder leading to a trapdoor. Wordlessly,

Sakra helped Bridget place the dowager's hands and feet. Medeoan seemed to have fallen into a stupor, and they had to all but heave her up to the chamber waiting above. Sakra supported Medeoan against his shoulder while Bridget closed the door and replaced the stone that covered it. Kalami was still about. What if he should gain the Firebird? Bridget did not even want think about it. She straightened up, and had the impression of having climbed into a jewel box, so much glitter, gold and silver surrounded her. The delicate sculpture of filigree, gems and clockwork which was the room's centerpiece took her breath away, but there was no time to stare. Instead, she took the dowager under her elbows, and led the old woman step by step into the main apartment.

Where, of course, her ladies were waiting, and the guard was waiting, and all of them sprang into action at once; the guard leveling their axes, mostly at Sakra, and the ladies running forward and taking Medeoan from Bridget so they could lay her down on the nearest sofa.

"What have you done!" cried one of them, chafing the dowager's wrists.

Bridget opened her mouth, but Sakra spoke first.

"Listen," he said.

Bridget listened; so did all the others, too surprised to do anything else. Straining her ears, she heard a deep clanging. Bells. She felt herself smiling at the distant, dark, musical, familiar sound. Somewhere above them, iron bells tolled hard and long.

"Your emperor is free," said Sakra to the guards and ladies. "May I be the first to congratulate you all."

He bowed, his hands over his face. It was an absolutely vulnerable position. Any of the house guard could have cut his head off right there.

But not one of them moved. Now Bridget heard a new sound. It reverberated through the doors, even through the stones of the walls, growing and swelling and coming ever closer.

Cheering. A great mob of people was cheering and shouting at the top of their lungs.

The lady nearest the door ran to it and threw it open. Instantly, a crowd of men, still in their holiday finery, most with gold chains about their necks, spilled into the room.

"The emperor!" cried one thin man who wore a bunch of gold keys hanging from his belt. "Grand Majesty, the emperor is free!"

The guards put up a mighty cheer, and the ladies cried out their thanks to the gods. Guards and ladies, liveried servants and nobles from the crowd outside swung each other around, dancing and cheering, tears streaming from their eyes.

Medeoan did not move. She lay utterly still on the sofa, only the rise and fall of her chest betraying the fact that she still lived.

"What has happened?" demanded a burly man who had been much tanned by both sun and wind. Then he recognized Sakra. "How dare you come here! What have you done!"

"Her Grand Majesty is not well," said Bridget, stepping between the burly man and Sakra. "The news has overwhelmed her." Now was not the time to say why. Not with all that cheering and carrying on. The whole palace was going mad for joy. No. If she spoke the truth now, and they believed her, the giddy crowd might well become a mob. Whatever Medeoan deserved, it was not that.

"Let her ladies attend her," suggested Sakra. "Let her physics be called. Surely, my lords, Their Imperial Majesties need all their ministers with them now."

"My father watches over her," said Bridget. The words might lay a strain on her credibility, she knew, but she had to say something. She was not about to let these men take Sakra into custody. There was no control right now. She felt that. Who knew what might be decided in such a mood?

"We are summoned!" cried someone out in the corridor. "To the Great Hall! To the Great Hall!"

Another cheer went up, accompanied by the sounds of pounding feet, and a tide of bodies swept past the doors, servants, nobles, guards, ladies, all snatching each other up to run with the crowd. The council lords hesitated only a bare moment longer, and rushed back to join them.

Leaving Bridget, Sakra and Medeoan alone in the midst of the fading cheers.

One lady only still knelt beside her mistress, her face creased in pain.

"I knew," she breathed, taking the dowager's hand. "What she had done. She tried so hard, you know."

"I know," said Bridget. "But it's over."

"Yes." The lady looked up at them. She was not young, Bridget saw. Heavy lines of both anger and sorrow creased her face. How long had she served here? Bridget found herself wondering. How much had she kept her silence about?

"What will you do?" asked the lady.

"Go to the Great Hall," said Sakra. "Will you watch her?"

The lady nodded mutely.

Sakra closed the door to the jewel-box room, trying the knob to make sure it locked. Then he bent down beside the dowager, and undid the clasp that held her key ring to her belt. Very careful not to touch any of the keys, he lifted the ring away from her and stood up. The lady made no protest.

"Come, Bridget," said Sakra, holding out his hand. "Their Majesties Imperial will wish to know what has happened, and thank you for your part in it."

"Yes." Bridget took his hand gladly. There was little enough they could do for this shattered woman, now that all was about to be revealed, but they could give her this last moment of privacy.

Together, Bridget and Sakra walked into the corridor, closing the door tightly behind themselves, leaving the dowager to her last loyal servant, and hurrying forward to see how Mikkel and Ananda greeted their court.

Chapter Eighteen

The Great Hall was in pandemonium. The entire population of the palace seemed determined to cram itself into that one room. Most of them still wore some semblance of their court garb, but others had rushed to join the celebration in sleeping attire and fur robes. But no one cared. It was a loud, chaotic and joyous. Officials from the god house, whom Bridget recognized by their holly-belted robes, raised their voices in song. Every other voice was also lifted, whether in prayer, praise or urgent questioning. The house guard had evidently given up trying to keep order. Instead, they merely flanked the room, contenting themselves with keeping the crowd away from certain doors. Bridget wondered whether these led to more private apartments, or to such places as the wine cellar.

What Bridget did not see was the emperor or the empress. For that matter, she did not see Keeper Bakhar or Captain Chadek.

"Avanasidoch!" somebody shouted. "The Avanasidoch!"

Bridget found herself instantly seized upon and dragged into the crowd. Hands passed her from person to person to be kissed, to be shouted at, to be cried upon. Someone stuffed a crown of holly on her head. More bodies pushed her from behind until she found herself stumbling onto the dais amid a mighty and dizzying cheer. The whole room spun and Bridget could not breathe for warmth and confusion, and for one ludicrous moment she feared she might faint. She found herself searching the swimming sea of faces for Sakra, but she had lost track of him as well.

What do I do now? She pressed both palms against her cheeks, trying to regain her calm.

Fortunately, no one seemed to have any idea of her making a speech, or any such thing. They seemed content to have her on display before them like another icon and to continue with their cheers and their dancing. Small knots of people had fallen on their knees before the holly-belted choristers, their hands raised and their eyes streaming with tears as they joined the hymns with loud, wobbly voices.

"Mistress?" said a soft voice in Bridget's ear. She jumped and spun. Beside her stood a brightly dressed, dark-skinned woman whom Bridget recognized as one of Ananda's ladies.

The woman smiled and made a swift reverence. "If you will come with me, mistress."

Bridget did not even attempt to make herself heard. She just nodded and followed as the woman led her behind the tapestry that hung at the rear of the dais, depositing her holly crown on a chair as she passed. The tapestry screened off a tiny private area, and a small door. The woman opened the door and stood aside, waiting for Bridget to walk through.

"Thank you," breathed Bridget as she passed the lady.

It was much quieter on the other side. The room was small one, its floor inlaid with the imperial eagles, and its walls painted with golden willows. Ananda and Mikkel sat in matching carved chairs. Lord Master Peshek stood beside them, so too Captain Chadek. So did Sakra. The dowager was not there, and her absence seemed as profound as this silence after all the jubilant shouting in the Great Hall. Bridget could not help but notice that there was as much green and white livery among the guards and the servants waiting patiently at their posts as there was blue and gold.

Recognizing the ceremonial importance of this quiet tableau, Bridget knelt.

As soon as she had done so, however, Ananda rose and came to take Bridget by both her hands and raised her up.

"Mistress Bridget," she said. "Let me welcome you again to Vyshtavos, and let me apologize for any misgivings I have had. I am keenly aware I owe you both for the life of my staunchest friend, and the freedom of His Imperial Majesty the Emperor."

Bridget felt her cheeks reddened. "It was not so much, Majesty Imperial. It was that I could not help but see."

Ananda's mouth worked up into a half-smile. "There are many who see, but choose to close their eyes. Let me make you known to the emperor."

Bridget had no time to say anything else. Ananda led her to stand before Emperor Mikkel. Curiosity caused Bridget to take a good look at him before she remembered the proprieties of this place and dropped her gaze. He was pale, and thinner than she had thought he would be. Certainly, much thinner than he had been in her vision of his wedding night. But his eyes were focused and his whole manner bespoke careful attention. The great ring of keys that had adorned the dowager's belt now hung from his.

Ananda introduced her by the whole long name that Sakra had once used, and Bridget was rather pleased that she managed not to squirm at it. She caught Sakra's eye with the barest glimpse from her own and he returned to her that half-smile that spoke so well of both levity and gravity.

"Mistress Bridget," said Mikkel. His voice was hoarse, as if rusty from disuse. "I also am keenly aware of what a great debt I owe you. I hope that in the coming weeks I shall be able to begin to repay it. For now, I ask you to accept my deepest thanks."

"I do so gladly, sir. You should be aware, however, that I had a great deal of help."

She heard the smile in Mikkel's voice. "We have already tendered our thanks to *Agnidh* Sakra, and will be doing so again."

Bridget folded her hands. "Oh yes. But there were others. In fact . . ." She hesitated.

"Say what you will, mistress," said Ananda. "We are glad to hear it."

"There was young lady who was assigned to attend me. When last I saw, her she was burning up with fever. It was Kalami's doing that made her ill. I have not been able to see her since. If I could . . ."

"Of course," said Mikkel.

"Behule, will you take her?" added Ananda. Behule, the woman who had brought Bridget into the room, reverenced.

"If I may also attend?" said Sakra, stepping forward. "If the fever is an enchantment . . ."

Mikkel nodded, and Ananda gestured to one of the servants in obviously hastily donned green and white livery to open a door in the far wall.

Without another word, Behule took the lead. These were not the corridors with which Bridget had grown at least passingly familiar. Gone were the gilding, murals and statuary. These corridors were narrow, the floors plain flagstone and the walls white or blue plaster with plain wooden trimming and rails, where there was any adornment at all. Although these halls were at least as much a maze as their grander counterparts, Behule seemed to know them well, leading Bridget and Sakra through the twists and turns without hesitation.

Down two flights of a stone and wood stair, they passed the cavernous kitchens full of the smell of food and liquors, and so much banging, barking, shouting and swearing that they were at least as loud as the Great Hall above. All here might be pleased to have their emperor restored to them, but they seemed less glad at having to prepare a late-night feast for the celebrants.

Beyond the kitchens waited long dormitories. Plainly furnished, they were little more than rows of neat beds with chests at their feet and a great stove at either end for warmth. They were as empty as the kitchens were full.

At the end of the dormitory, Behule opened a door to a separate room that held four truckle beds and a tiny porcelain stove of its own. Two grating windows for fresh air had been propped open, which rendered it cold, but the ventilation was surely more healthy than stagnation would have been.

Richikha lay in the bed nearest the stove. Bridget rushed to her side. The girl was sallow with the last rampage of the sickness. Sweat drenched the white sheets around her and where once she might have tossed and turned, now she lay deathly still, only her hands twitching and shivering in whatever delirium racked her fevered brain.

"Oh my God." Bridget touched the girl's forehead. Richikha's skin was clammy, despite the heat sluicing from it with the perspiration. "We must get this fever down. Why hasn't anyone . . ."

"She has had mustard plaster for her feet, and been rubbed with spirits of wine." The plump mistress of the house made her way past Behule. "I've all but packed her in snow and sent for more, but it does no good." She wiped her hands on the battered grey coat that obviously served as an apron. "I knew her mother. She was a good girl." She shook her head, but it was with the stoical sorrow of one who has seen too many people die and come to terms with the fact that it was merely a thing that happened.

Bridget was not prepared to accept that.

"There must be something else."

"There is." Sakra sat on the edge of the bed and touched Richikha's wrist. Richikha moaned and jerked her hand away. "If we're not too late. I will need something of hers. Something she has worn."

The mistress of the house frowned and was about to question, but Behule had no such reservations. She opened the trunk at the end of the bed and pulled out a brown velvet sash, which she handed across to Sakra.

"Sit her up."

Bridget got her arms under Richikha's and lifted the girl into a sitting position as gently as she could. She weighed nothing at all, the fever had taken so much from her already.

Sakra held the sash under Richikha's cracked lips. "Breathe for me, Lady," he murmured. Richikha's breath came out in a wheeze, whether she heard him or not. "Very good, very good. Breathe again." Bridget bit her lip and rubbed Richikha's back as the girl rasped out yet one more breath.

Sakra began to chant, short clipped rhythmic syllables that Bridget could not understand. They repeated themselves over and over, winding around the room. As the chant rose and fell, lifted and subsided, Sakra began to knot the sash. His hands worked quickly, and cleverly. Bridget felt his words sink through her skin to her blood, quickening her heart.

Still chanting, Sakra rose to his feet. Behule seemed to know what was coming, because she picked up a rag and opened the lid on the stove. Sakra tossed the sash into the fire.

There came a puff of sparks, ash and smoke all mixed together. Richikha gasped. Her body went rigid against Bridget's hands, and then she collapsed.

"No." Bridget cradled the girl close, but then she too gasped, a sound of amazement. Richikha's skin was cool. Her breath came quiet and even, without the distressing rattling wheeze that had been there but seconds before.

Sakra wiped perspiration from his brow. "She will sleep for a day. When she wakes, she will be recovered."

"Thank goodness." Bridget laid Richikha back down against her pillow and pulled up the covers. "And thank you, Sakra."

Sakra spread his hands. "I am glad to be of service to you for a change."

None of this seemed to impress upon the mistress of the house any good humor. She bustled forward, laying the back of her hand against Richikha's forehead and wrist. "Well, if she is to sleep, master, mistress, perhaps you should leave her."

"You are correct, of course." Bridget gave way at once as she had often done with Mrs. Hansen. God almighty, how many years ago was that?

As Behule shepherded them out into the main dormitories, Bridget shared a smile with Sakra. His healing seemed to have strengthened rather than drained him, and she noted the way his warm eyes reflected in the firelight, and the fine shape of his mouth when it smiled.

But her eyes must have lingered too long there, because concern furrowed Sakra's brow.

"Behule, run ahead and tell Their Imperial Majesties that we are returning."

It seemed a strange order, but Behule only reverenced and did as she was bidden.

When Behule was well out of earshot, Sakra glanced toward the infirmary door, and then began to stroll very slowly away from it.

Bridget, frowning herself, walked beside him. "What is it?"

But Sakra seemed unusually hesitant. "Something I think Kalami will have neglected to tell you," he said. "Something of the nature of a sorcerer."

"Well," said Bridget with a sigh. "If it was an important truth, you can be sure he neglected to tell me."

"Ha." Sakra laughed once. "You must understand this. It is in our nature to be attracted to power. Power draws us. It calls us. Those of us who are trained from the time we are young are made aware of this, so we can distinguish between true feelings and false."

Bridget knew instantly what he was talking about. "Oh, no." She turned away at once, her hand flat against her stomach. "God almighty, will I never stop making a fool of myself in this place?"

"Please, Mistress Bridget," said Sakra behind her. "I do not say this because I wish to cause you any distress."

She raised her hand to stop his words, but did not turn around. "No, no. You are quite right to tell me." She felt sick. How could she not realize it must be the magic again? After all that Kalami had done to her, how could she be so easily misled again?

"I tell you this because I did not wish it to be the spell between us that made you return my esteem for you." Sakra stepped into her line of vision. "I wish whatever you may feel for me to be yours alone, and to be honest."

He was quite serious, and quite calm, but there was something else about him. A feeling of hope lingered underneath his words. Bridget found that not only did she not know what to say, she had no idea what she wanted to say.

But whatever reply might have come, it was cut off by the sound of sandals slapping hard against stone and Behule crying out, *"Agnidh! Agnidh!"*

Behule burst through the door and Sakra ran to meet her, grasping both her hands. Behule rattled out something in their own language, and Sakra responded with a word so sharp it could only have been a curse.

"What has happened?" asked Bridget striding swiftly forward.

Sakra turned to her, his face grim. "Kalami. The dowager. They have vanished."

The door closed behind Sakra and treacherous Bridget, and gradually silence returned. The dowager opened her eyes. Prathad hovered over her. Loyal Prathad. Of course she would be the one to stay near.

"Water," said Medeoan, touching her lady's hand. "And some bread, Prathad. I need sustenance."

"At once, Grand Majesty." Prathad did not question. Prathad did not hesitate. She ran from the room to fetch her mistress food because her mistress required it. Prathad had always known her duty.

Medeoan closed her eyes and tightened her sinews. She sat up. No one else knew their duty. But Prathad did. The others had all abandoned her. All of them. Alive and dead, they had left her side and now she knew how alone she was. She should have known before. But she had been blind. That was her failing. All her life she had wanted to believe that others would be there for her, that others meant to keep their oaths. It was too late she learned they did not.

They had taken her keys. Medeoan stood. Of course they had. They thought that would keep her trapped here, weak and alone. Did they think the locks of Vyshtavos did not know her touch?

She spat on her fingertips and traced a sign over the lock for her treasure room. With a click, the tumblers turned and the door opened. She took up a lamp and entered the room, closing the door behind herself and making sure it locked again.

You've lost, laughed the distant voice of the Firebird. *You've lost, old woman, and they'll be coming for you. Then you will be the prisoner and I will be free.*

"No," said Medeoan. She faced the Portrait of Worlds. Magnificent. So much work, so much skill. It had served the emperors of Isavalta for a hundred years. She picked up a silver-shod staff that waited beside the door. Raising it over her head, she brought the butt of the staff crashing down into the heart of the Portrait, again, and again, sweeping it sideways, and smashing it down again, until there was nothing left but a tangle of torn wires and broken gears.

Medeoan set down her lamp beside the ruin and swept a length of silk off the full-length silver mirror that stood in the far corner. Into this she bundled a mirror of gold-framed glass, a golden lock and a silver key and a glass flask that contained water from seven separate wells. One of those wells stood beside Bridget Lederle's lighthouse. Or so Kalami had told her. Perhaps he had lied in that as well.

She tied her bundle to her belt like any old peddler woman. Then, she bent to open the trapdoor, picked up the lamp and climbed down to the Firebird.

It was hot now in the darkness of the stairs, hotter than it had been when Bridget had stood beside her. Of course it was. Bridget had chosen to stand with Sakra, Ananda and the Firebird. They would not wish to make her uncomfortable.

You are a sad woman who has too long tormented herself for the sin of falling in love.

Medeoan felt her knees tremble and buckle. Awkwardly, she sat down on the steps. She stared at the blank features of the iron door and saw how the light from the Firebird that squeezed through the crack was so much brighter than the pathetic light from the lamp she had brought.

You are a sad woman who has too long tormented herself for the sin of falling in love.

Was that true? Could it possibly be true? No. Of course not. The Avanasidoch was like the rest of them. She knew nothing. She understood even less. Ananda had taken her. Ananda and Sakra had turned her.

She was Avanasy's daughter and she was supposed to save Isavalta, not condemn Medeoan. Avanasy's daughter with Avanasy's understanding at the core of her soul.

That obviously was not the case. Her mother's alien blood polluted her understanding. What else could she expect? Avanasy had allowed his loyalties to become divided, even if he saw the right in the end. She should have known that the blood in the girl was mixed. She should have taken that into account before she pinned all her hopes, expended all her strength, waited so long until she was sure her need was dire.

She spoke the truth, said the Firebird.

"No."

You could not see it. You can never see it.

"No."

They're going to come for you, Medeoan. She knows where you are now. They are going to come for you, and I'm going to be free. And you know what I'm going to tell them? I am going to tell them they must give you to me, or I will burn the world down.

"Stop," whispered Medeoan. "Please, stop."

Let me out. That's the only way you can save yourself now. Let me out.

Medeoan buried her face in her hands. Long-suppressed sobs racked her. How could they do this to her? After all these years. Kalami. She had trusted him so long, and he was just waiting for his moment to turn against her. Bridget. Bridget, her final hope of all, screamed at her, called her crude names, did not heed her birth and her heritage. Her son, her own son, chose his little witch over his birth and left her alone. All these years of struggle, of service, and they left her alone.

Slowly, Medeoan lifted her head. They left her alone. They betrayed her. Not one of those cowards and sycophants she had elevated to her court, whose fortunes she had made, lifted a finger to help her against her nearest and dearest enemies. They left her even more quickly than the others had. Well, let them pay.

Let them burn.

"Yes."

Medeoan stood. Her knees were steady and her sight was clear. She walked to the iron door, and found it unlocked.

"Let them burn."

For once, the door seemed to open easily. Medeoan stood in the threshold for a moment, bathing in the heat as a child might in the first rays of the summer sun.

"They will pay."

As in a dream, Medeoan moved forward to the cage. Inside, the Firebird crouched, its neck stretched forward and its wings half-spread. It was waiting. It was ready. Ready for her. Ready for them.

The cage had no true door. Avanasy had closed it with his life, and Medeoan had locked it with her blood. Only blood could open it again. She curled her fingers around the bars.

Bridget should go first. Her betrayal was greatest, because she had betrayed not only Medeoan and Isavalta, but her father and her father's memory.

"Yes."

But there was another voice in the room. Fresh from Medeoan's own memory, of Bridget standing before her like a fury in the darkness.

Let me tell you about my father. . . . He was an honest man. He lived alone, doing nothing but keep the light and try to save lives. All lives. . . . It made no difference to him . . . And he was worth a thousand of you.

She spoke of some stranger as she stood there not caring that Medeoan could have her killed with a word, with a gesture. But oh, she could have been speaking of Avanasy.

"She was a traitor. She is a traitor. Let her burn for what she has done to you."

I tried, Avanasy. Medeoan's hands squeezed the bars until they bit into her own callused flesh. *I tried so hard. What happened that I must earn your daughter's contempt?*

"What right has she to judge you? You are the empress. Who is she?"

My final hope. My final betrayal.

"Let her burn."

Bridget had stood before, eyes flashing even in the dim light from the dying lantern, saying so clearly that Medeoan was ready to kill her own son. Her own son. She had meant to keep him safe. Then she had come to believe that only death would keep him safe enough. Was this what she did now? Did she save him now?

"He will not save you. He has left you like all the others."

Left her. Yes. He had left her. That was wrong. And he needed to pay, they all needed to pay. A knife hung on her belt near where her stolen keys had hung. It was a small thing, useful for breaking seals, and peeling apples. She fumbled for it now, pulling it free of its tiny cork sheath. She held the edge to her palm.

I am the empress of Isavalta! All lives are mine!

No. You are a sad woman who has too long tormented herself for the sin of falling in love.

I am the empress of Isavalta!

"Yes."

All lives are mine!

"Let them burn."

But why, why did she see Avanasy now? Why did she see him reach for her, as Bridget had said he did. He spoke, but she could not hear. He touched her, but she could not feel him. But he was there. Was it true? Had he always been there?

It doesn't matter. I am the empress of Isavalta! All lives are mine. Let them burn. Let them burn. All lives are mine. Mine. I am the empress and I will let them burn.

No. Was that her thought, or was that Avanasy? She was the empress, and the Firebird crouched before her, waiting for her to destroy her empire.

"No!" Medeoan hurled the knife away from her. "No!"

The Firebird screamed and the sound cut through Medeoan's bones. "You cannot let them go! You cannot let them live!"

But Medeoan only stumbled backward from the cage. She caught herself against the workbench and gripped its edge as she had gripped the bars of the cage.

"What am I doing?"

"What you must." The Firebird raised its wings. "I am all you have left."

Was that true? Medeoan stared at the Firebird—her nemesis, her protector, and in the end the only living thing that knew all her secrets, all her hopes and all her fears. Sakra had promised it freedom, but had laid conditions. If she freed it now, there would be no conditions, no promises, no refuge. Was that the final truth of this whole nightmare? That all must be punished alike for their failure in their duty? That Isavalta must burn?

No. There was one other truth. That truth was that she was still the empress of Isavalta, and she would protect her empire to the last. If the Firebird went free, it would find a way to burn Isavalta, no matter how many promises were laid on its back. She had heard its voice for years. It would find a way, and Isavalta would die. Mikkel would die.

Medeoan walked back to the Firebird. She was still just tall enough that if she stood on her toes and stretched out her thin, old woman's arms, she could reach the iron hook and lift down the cage.

"What are you doing?"

It was heavy. She had forgotten how heavy. She had to grasp the ring at the top with both hands and lug it a gracelessly to the workbench. The bird itself weighed nothing, but the cage was heavy with gold, life and death. The bird screeched out its indignity and flailed its wings, trying to keep its balance. The flames brushed Medeoan's skin, leaving behind lines of soft pain.

She set the cage down beside the crucible. With clumsy fingers she undid her bundle and laid out the things she had brought—the mirror, the lock, the key and the flask of waters.

"You cannot."

Medeoan did not answer. She unstoppered the bottle and with the greatest care poured the waters onto the mirror until they made a thin clear film across the glass. She set the bottle aside. She took up the lock and opened it with the key, and set both of these above the mirror. Water flowed between all worlds. A mirror could see everything and could not be deceived. The lock and the key could open the door she needed.

Medeoan reached inside herself and pulled her magic forward.

"Stop this, Medeoan. You will kill us both."

Medeoan picked up the knife from where it lay on the floor. Metal was another of the elements that existed everywhere. She had carried the little thing so thoughtlessly for so many years; now it was proving so useful.

She touched the knife blade to the golden ring at the top of the firebird's cage.

"As soon as you die, the cage dissolves. You are only freeing me."

Medeoan focused on the waters coating the mirror. She reached inside herself, past the voices, past the confusion, past the weariness that weighed her down. She met there the magic her heart drew from inside, from outside, from all the worlds. That too was the truth. That too was hers, even here, even now at the very end.

She stretched her free hand out flat over the water and over the mirror.

"Take us," Medeoan ordered them. "Take me."

Medeoan reached down, through the mirror and through the water. The water twined around her wrist, twisting itself into a thread that pulled her inexorably forward. It drew her through the wall, through the stone, through the dirt beyond, up through the ice and through the snow and through the darkness of night. It drew her through the silence that was the Land of Death and Spirit. But that place could not touch her, for she held fast to the water and the magic that threaded all around her, alive with its purpose.

She heard the Firebird cry out. She felt it reach out toward the thread of water with its living fire, seeking to sever the bond, seeking to leave Medeoan stranded here between world and world. But the cage held, and the cage prevented, as the cage had prevented so much across the long years. There was nothing around her but glimpses of green and brown, blue and gold. She saw the river pass under her body. She glimpsed eyes—green, yellow, wide, curious, angered. But none reached her. There was only the thread, and a blur of colors.

Then, the world went white.

Cold surrounded her, blessed, blessed cold. Her shoes touched the earth, but Medeoan found she could not stand and she fell forward, measuring her length in drifted snow. She lay there for a moment, gasping from exertion. Eventually, she was able to push herself to her knees, and climb slowly, shaking, to her feet.

The world was indeed white. White snow covered the ground. More snow turned the trees that surrounded the small clearing where she stood white as well. Down a sharp slope at her back, snow frosted ice and slush that turned the huge lake sluggish. The sky itself was white with clouds that promised yet more snow.

The only part of the world that was not white was the stone dwelling with its single tower in front of her. That was all brown stone with shuttered windows and closed doors.

Still shaking from cold, and from the journey, Medeoan turned to see what had become of the Firebird.

The bird hunched at the bottom of its cage, its wings beating the bars in panic. Steam rose where its heat melted the snow around it, but Medeoan, as close as she was, barely felt any warmth at all. The creature was smaller as well, the size of an owl rather than the size of an eagle, and it seemed to Medeoan that it burned less brightly, but perhaps that was only her hope that saw.

"What have you done, Medeoan? What are you doing?"

Medeoan did not answer. She fastened her knife back to the chain around her waist, picked up the cage, which had grown light enough for her to carry in one hand, and slogged through the snow to the stone house.

The front door was wooden, white and locked. Medeoan spat again against her fingers, and traced the sign over the lock, and traced it again. It should have opened the lock instantly, but Medeoan only felt the metal tremble under her fingers. She leaned on the door, drawing all her will and magic to her. She traced the sign again and the lock shivered. She leaned harder. Something snapped and the door gave way, sending her stumbling inside. She caught herself against the corner of the wall, and leaned there panting for a long moment until she could reclaim enough strength to stand on her own again. She retrieved the Firebird's cage. She did not close the door.

Up a short flight of stairs waited some sort of dingy sitting room.

The metal stove in the corner was stone-cold, with a good stack of wood beside it. She did not touch either. She set the Firebird's cage down underneath one of the windows. She dragged one of the stiff chairs to the middle of the room where she could see both cage and door clearly, and she sat.

The room was already cold. The draft from the open door curled around her ankles, and lifted itself up to touch her knees, her hands, her throat. She noted this almost absently. Her attention was on the Firebird.

In the world where they were both born, the Firebird was immortal, sustained by fire and magic. Here, in this abandoned house in the dead of winter, there was no fire, and all the magic this world possessed was buried deep in its heart. Here the Firebird was not immortal. Here, it could die, and once dead, it could not rise to take its revenge on Mikkel and Isavalta for her deeds.

The bird had huddled in on itself, head, neck and wings all drawn as close to its body as they could be. It glowered up at her with its bright blue eyes. She felt no heat from it. No heat at all.

"You would die alone of cold rather than free me?" whispered the Firebird.

"It is the only way I will know that Isavalta will remain safe."

Motion outside the window caught Medeoan's eye. She saw with grim satisfaction that the first flakes of snow had begun to fall.

She leaned back in the chair, relaxed, confident, and waited for the icy wind to do its work.

Chapter Nineteen

The snow had begun again at dawn, the fat flakes falling slowly and lazily, but persistently. Gradually, the wind picked up, pulling them down ever faster. Now they were tiny white crystals caking his eyebrows and stinging what little of his cheeks showed above his white silk mask. He was grateful for the covering they gave what scant tracks his skis made, but their haze almost caused him to miss his destination; the opening in the trees that would be the road again in spring.

Now was not the time to miss the road through the Foxwood. His protections were few, and his need for swiftness great. The Portrait of Worlds could find him. He needed a town, a croft, anyplace he might find shelter, and time to weave his new charms and hide his destination.

Despite this knowledge, it felt good to be out on skis again. Kalami glided forward, swinging his pole in an easy rhythm, the hiss of his skis blending with the hiss of the snow. The cold, white world with only the dark tree trunks to break the snowy landscape felt much like his childhood home and it gave him heart. If all went well and the snow stayed firm, it should take him four days to reach Camaracost and Havosh's warehouse. Camaracost was far enough to the south that its port would be open and he could take ship for Hung-Tse. At the Heart of the World, they would hear the news of the holy days in Vyshtavos, and welcome it. He could help with the ordering of the troops for spring. He would be beyond even the dowager's reach there. From there he could plan, and he could finish what he had begun. He could speak to the Nine Elders about releasing his daughter from their care and bringing her with him when he returned to Tuukos, to the newly freed Tuukos.

He would see Isavalta burn yet. Kalami smiled behind his mask. From Camaracost, he would call Bridget to him. There were magics that would call to her heart's blood and make her come to him. She would crawl on her knees to reach him, and he would let her. Then, he would watch while she took the dowager apart, whatever was left of the dowager. Would her son throw her in the cells? It would be most unfilial, but Kalami could not blame him if he did . . .

A pine loomed up before Kalami's eyes. With a shout, he just managed to veer to the right, the lowest branches snatching at his shoulder. He twisted sideways, bringing the pole firmly down and sending up a spray of snow all around him. Panting, he cast swiftly about him to gain his bearings. If he had left the road . . .

But no, the broad lane, an undulating path of white, still lay under his skis. He had strayed only to the very edge, distracted by his daydreams.

Eat something, Kalami, he counseled himself. *Drink. You cannot afford to let your mind wander here.*

Kalami unslung his pack and dropped it into the snow. He had to strip off his outer mittens to expose his knitted gloves so that his fingers would be free to work the lacings.

"To see you now, sorcerer, one would doubt you knew aught of imperial halls."

Kalami jerked upright, stumbling backward, his skis robbing him of balance. The Vixen sat underneath the pine tree, her tail curled around her feet, looking to be a normal-sized fox. Her mouth hung open so that her face appeared to be smiling and she to be laughing at him.

"How came you here?" he asked, to cover his confusion, and calm his sudden fear. "This is the road."

"Perhaps it is, perhaps it is not. Perhaps the tips of your skis are not on the road, and so you no longer have its protection." She got to her feet, her mouth still open and laughing. "Shall we take the question to court, sorcerer?" Her mouth closed, and he felt the touch of her steady, green gaze. "Or shall you and I settle the question here?"

Kalami closed his own mouth and remembered to whom he spoke. He stretched out his leg, and reverenced deeply. There were so many possible reasons for her presence here. If she knew who had led her sons into the trap, she might be here to kill him. If she wanted him to perform some service for her, to acquire Bridget for her, all might yet be well. She might even simply be here because he passed through her wood and she was bored.

His only hope was that she was in a humor to reveal to him her purpose.

Kalami pulled down his scarf so that his words would sound clear. "Forgive me, madame." He kept his eyes averted. It was dangerous enough to meet her gaze in the Land of Death and Spirit; here, it could be fatal. "The sight of your magnificence robbed me for a moment of both wit and courtesy."

The Vixen snapped her teeth. "But not for long."

"I hope, at least, my courtesy has returned. May I offer you what poor food I have with me?" He swept a hand toward his half-opened pack.

"Shall we break bread, sorcerer?" The idea seemed to amuse her. "Will you place on me the obligations of guest to host? Will I accept them?"

"Only you, madame, know that."

"Yes." Again her jaw fell open to laugh at him. "It is not written on the chart you carry, is it?"

"I only wish it had been. Then I might have been able to prepare better for this meeting."

"Or against this meeting," suggested the Vixen.

"I would not say so, madame."

"No," she remarked thoughtfully. "I don't imagine you would."

Kalami decided to adopt a pose of injured innocence. The more he could draw thc Vixen into conversation, the better his chances to get what he needed. Or, at least, so he hoped. The snow still fell hard, and the wind burned cold against his cheeks. The daylight would not last, and he needed to reach shelter before nightfall. That was the great irony of his situation. He needed to stay on the roads to have their protection, but while he was on them, he could be so easily found.

Kalami had no doubt at all that the Vixen knew all of this.

Kalami spread his hands. "Might I ask what I have done to merit the favor of your attention?"

The smile was gone from the Vixen's demeanor. "I am sure you would say that you did but serve your mistress."

Kalami longed to declare that he served no one but his people. He wanted to shout that truth to the winter winds and let the whole world hear it. But that was no good. Who knew what this creature might do with such a revelation? The laws and duty of service as understood by the powers were his only defense against what had been done. "I serve, as I must."

"Your mistress holds strings of many servants." The Vixen's voice was low, almost a growl. "She shelters the one who led the swords against my sons. She will pay for that, and you will bear my message to her."

The one who led the swords . . . Sakra! She was not here for him, she was here because of Sakra? Was that who she was trying to reach when she stalked the palace? Not Bridget at all, but Sakra.

How could the Vixen not know that Sakra was not Medeoan's servant but her enemy? Was she trying to trick him? No. The palace was relatively young, but it was well protected. The Vixen would have no eyes within its walls. She would see only what went on outside, and from the outside it appeared Medeoan ruled all, and thus the oldest laws held her responsible for all.

Kalami decided to risk everything on a single throw. This was his chance. The Vixen's anger still made it possible for him to win the game and win it now.

"Madame." Kalami forced his voice to be calm. The Vixen would sense his rising eagerness, but he could at least for himself preserve the illusion that he remained composed. "Would you bring down the dowager Medeoan for her transgressions?"

The Vixen cocked her head. "That is a strange question for a loyal servant."

"Madame will recall that I said I serve as I must." Kalami permitted himself a small smile. "I did not say whom I served."

"No, you did not." The Vixen's tail swished, scattering tiny flurries of snow. "And if I did wish to bring down the dowager Medeoan, as you say?"

Kalami bowed humbly. "I know how it might be done."

"Do you? How?" The Vixen's whiskers twitched with interest. Kalami risked another quick look at her. The snow fell all around, but not one flake clung to her bright red coat. It was said such a one as she never came fully into the mortal world. He was now prepared to believe that.

"It must be known to you that the dowager in her youth caged the Phoenix of Hung-Tse," said Kalami. "And that she keeps it still."

The Vixen sneezed. Kalami took the sound to be dismissive. "Such a thing could hardly be kept secret from those with ears to hear."

He bowed again in the face of her derision. "If you were to take me to the place where the Firebird is kept, I would promise you that Medeoan and all her house would fall."

A light sparked in the Vixen's green eyes. Kalami tore his gaze away, for he suddenly felt that those eyes would draw him in, and that the light would consume him. He looked instead at the unbroken snow and all the ranks of trees beyond. One way or another, he must finish this dance soon. He had grown soft in the palace, and he did not know if he could endure a second full night in the open.

"So." The Vixen pointed her muzzle into the air, as if the falling snow held more interest for her than he did. "If I take you to the Firebird, you will bring down Medeoan's dynasty? You promise me this?"

Kalami hesitated. The ice on which he walked right now was very thin indeed. He ran his mind back over the conversation. Where was the trick? Where was the hidden meaning? Had all things been spoken plainly or did he just think they had?

Steeling himself, Kalami said, "Take me to the Firebird and Medeoan's house, and the whole of the empire of Isavalta will fall. I promise."

A fox's face was not made to grin, and yet the Vixen did grin, a sly, sharp smile that Kalami felt like the gentle grip of teeth at his throat.

"Very good, sorcerer."

In front of his eyes, the Vixen changed. What his eye saw as a fox blurred, lengthened and paled. When he could see her clearly again, she was a woman with black hair that spilled down to her feet. She wore a robe of grey fur, belted around with a girdle of braided hair. Her skin was a perfect honey brown and the features of her face were noble. Her eyes, though, remained her own: bright green, and dangerous.

"Come, sorcerer," she said, holding her hand out for him to take in the fashion of Tuukos, not the Isavaltan court. "Leave your skis. Walk with me."

So, Kalami removed his skis, tying their straps to his pole so that he could sling them over his shoulder with his pack. Then, he took her hand and laid it on top of his so that his forearm supported hers, and they might walk closely together in the manner of two who were more than friends. Her hand was warm against his, and softer than he might have expected. Her scent was sharp, like her smile and her glance, but more enticing than either. He felt his body stir in response. It was nothing, he told himself. Merely the Vixen teasing with him. Yet the feeling did not diminish, born as it was in part by lust long withheld, and in part by the attraction of power.

Kalami felt nothing of the transition to the Silent Lands. One moment they were in the Foxwood, walking with measured steps across drifts that should not have supported them. The next, they were in the piney woods, walking on a mossy bank beside the river which made no sound despite the fact that Kalami could see it rippling over rounded stones.

"Do we go far?" he asked, taking care not to look at the Vixen. He must be cautious now, and more than cautious. This was her world he walked in.

The Vixen laughed lightly, and squeezed his hand. "Do you not know better than to ask distances here, sorcerer?" He heard the smile in her voice, and, unwillingly, he pictured it on her face. It was illusion, that face, he knew that, but it was nonetheless most beautiful.

"You will not look at me, sorcerer," said the Vixen. "Why not?"

Kalami found his mouth was dry. His blood warmed within him, heated only by the thought of her face, and the touch of her hand, and that scent which lingered between them.

"I have no wish to look upon a lie, madame," he made himself say.

Again the Vixen laughed. It was musical sound, the sound the river should have been making. "Is it a lie?" She pressed in more closely against him, pulling his arm near. Despite his thick coat, he felt the curve of her body, just below the swell of her breast, and became suddenly very aware of his own breathing, and the gentle pounding of his heart. "We are beyond lies here, and truth. Here, there can be only reality."

"And how is reality different from the truth?"

"The truth is an idea you mortals conceived of to convince yourselves that you knew what was real." She stopped. Kalami also stopped, keeping his eyes rigidly forward. He felt her lift her hand from his, and for a moment knew relief, until that hand brushed his bare cheek, its delicate fingers tracing his jawline.

"Look at me, sorcerer."

Kalami closed his eyes. His throat was tight now. He wanted to look at her, he wanted to take that hand that now touched his neck finding its way under the silken scarf, that glided slowly down the shoulder, so that he felt its touch as if it drew itself down his naked skin. He wanted to pull her close and find out how her mouth would feel against his. He imagined her kisses would be rich and heady, like red wine, all unwatered.

"Tush, sorcerer, such control when there is no need." Her hand circled his waist, just briefly. She was so close, he could feel the warmth of her against every pore, smell her breath, which was the source of her scent. Her touch tingled against his skin, like snowflakes. "Why will you not take what is offered to you?"

He did not know where he was. If she chose to leave him here, he might wander lost in the Silent Lands until his flesh could no longer sustain him. At best, he could follow the river, if she chose to leave him here. "Because," he said, "nothing you offer is freely given, and I have nothing with which to repay your favor."

She laughed again, and her fingers touched his mouth. "But you have no idea what I want."

Her arms darted around his shoulders. She kissed him and the sensation was as strong, as heady as he had imagined it would be. He kissed her back and grappled with her, his hands as hungry as his mouth to touch her, to claim all this power, all this desire, if only for this one instant. He fumbled with his pack, casting it aside. Laughing, she fell backward and he did nothing to stop them tumbling onto the moss and stones of the riverbank. He wanted only to touch her, to feel breast and buttock and thigh, to shove the fur robe she wore up until it was no longer an impediment.

Coat, gloves, boots, all were gone and he neither knew or cared how it came to be so. She was all heat and he shivered with the thought that her very touch might burn him, like the touch of the Firebird might when he had the cage and knew how to keep it whole. Such strength, such power. She wrapped her legs around him and drew him down again, and again, her eyes as green and glowing as her sons' had been when as they thought about taking Ananda from her escort. The tumult of sensations, of her fingers digging into his flesh, of her eyes, of her heat, swirled around his head mixed with memory and ecstasy and fear and need until he no longer knew his own thoughts. He only knew that in this one moment he lived, and he held to him all the power he had ever desired. When at last she arched underneath him, the pitch of her need drowning him completely, he shouted out as if to make all the Silent Lands ring with the release of his passions.

He did not know how long they lay together afterward, but it was she who roused them.

"Arrange your clothing, sorcerer," she said, with only the barest hint of teasing heat left in her voice. "We must have you out of the Silent Lands before Grandfather Death comes here in search of you."

Kalami did as he was told, retrieving his abandoned clothes and pack. When they began to walk again, the Vixen made no move to take his hand. He did not consider this odd. She was sated, as was he. Perhaps later he would pay for what he had done, and perhaps it would prove to be weakness, but he would deal with that in the future, as he had dealt with every other obstacle that had come into his path, whether it was an empress or the witch Baba Yaga. Nothing could now stop him.

The Vixen halted. "I can go no further. Step into the water, sorcerer, walk with the current. You will arrive where you wish to be."

"You have my thanks, madame."

The gaze she returned was cool and speculative. "I have all that I need from you." She smiled again, a satisfied smile, and brushed past him, allowing him to feel just the barest touch of her skin against his, and then she was a fox again, trotting into the shadows of the trees, and was lost to his sight within minutes.

Kalami still did not know where he was, nor where he would arrive, but even the Vixen had to acknowledge the bonds of promise, and now there was the additional bond between them. In this, at least, she would not deceive him.

Kalami stepped into the river, which did not wet his boots, even though he felt the tug and swirl of its current. He strode forward, heedless of the stones that shifted underfoot. These things might be real, but they were not true, and despite the Vixen's riddles, it was truth that mattered in the navigation of the Land of Death and Spirit.

After a very few moments, it was as if Kalami stepped through a door, and he was inside. It took him only a heartbeat to recognize the pale walls and the chipped wooden floor with its rag rug. This was the lighthouse, Bridget's lighthouse. In Bridget's favorite chair sat Medeoan, or rather slumped Medeoan. The room was as cold as winter stone and the long rays of the setting sun turned the snow outside scarlet and magenta. The wind blew uninterrupted through the room, but the stove in the corner stood dark and lifeless.

"Kalami?" The dowager stirred weakly. "No. I am dreaming."

Kalami ignored her. Instead, he knelt beside the cage she had placed underneath the window. This could not be the Firebird. This was a puny, pale thing, cowering at the bottom of its cage, and fluffing its brassy feathers for what little warmth they could give it. It glared at him with dim blue eyes and shoved its beak forward so that he saw the pink and naked flesh of its neck. It looked like a baby bird, not yet fully fledged. The beak snapped feebly at him, opening and closing, but no sound came forth. Cautiously, Kalami raised his hand and touched the bars of the cage. They were cold, as cold as the stove, as cold as the wind that blew through the room.

Kalami saw at once what Medeoan was doing. Here, so far from flame and magic, the cold and death of winter would take the Firebird's life. Medeoan knew she must die soon, and that her death would release the Firebird, as her living blood had kept it caged. By bringing them both here to their end, she would keep Isavalta safe from the creature's certain wrath.

"So, this late you have decided to make Vyshemir's sacrifice after all. You would choose your death and the Firebird's destruction rather than share your secrets with me." He spoke the words aloud, not caring if Medeoan heard. Events had traveled too far for him to care whether she knew his true mind or not.

Kalami moved. He closed the door and bolted it. The lock beneath the knob had shattered, but the latch remained sound. He climbed the stairs to the linen closet and pulled out Bridget's thickest quilts. Medeoan did not even stir when he laid her down on the stiff couch and piled the quilts over her cold body. Bridget's servants had left a goodly pile of wood and paper beside the stove. He had watched Bridget light it often enough during the time he had lived here, he could light the stove easily, but no. That would lend power to the Firebird, to have its element so close by. The weaker the bird, the more malleable it would be when he was finished with Medeoan.

"Will you speak to me?" he asked the Firebird.

The bird gave no sign of having heard him. It merely pressed itself tightly against the bars, taking its body as far from the window as it could.

Kalami dismissed its silence. It was of no matter. He would require the bird to hear him soon enough.

Now there remained only one thing to fetch. It had always been possible that he would return here. He had expected it to be with Bridget. That also did not matter. The precautions he had taken would work as well on Medeoan.

During his explorations of the house and its light, he had found several coils of rope hung neatly on hooks in one of the cellars. Before he had left, he had hung an extra rope there, where it was most likely to go unnoticed. He had her half-wit boy bring it to him along with the sails of his boat, and he had respliced it right in front of Bridget's ignorant eyes with hair stolen from her brush and blood from his own hands, and she had believed it was simply one more thing he needed to repair before they could leave on their journey to Isavalta. Twisted of hemp, white silk and all the magic he could summon, it was meant for very different work. He brought it out from the dark cellar and held it in both hands as he crossed to stand beside Medeoan.

The stupor had not yet lifted from her, but the blood was beginning to return to her face and hands, and he could see her chest rising and falling underneath the quilts. She would wake soon. In some ways it would have been better for him to leave her completely to the cold, but if she was too weakened, she would die before he had what he needed of her, and he could not permit that.

He drew back the quilts with one hand and drew his knife with the other. She did stir then, and moan, but she quickly subsided. Methodically, Kalami slit open her clothes, coat, bodice, sleeves, shifts, skirts, underskirts, underclothes, leaving her lying naked in a nest of imperial rags. If she carried with her any protection against enchantment, it was gone now, flown into this dead winter, and she would not get it back. His lip curled in disgust at the sight of her aged body, remembering the glory of the Vixen's form, and he dropped the quilts back over her.

He pulled the parlor's footstool up to the edge of the couch and sat down, trying to prepare himself for the great drain that working his craft in this place always opened within him. He twined the rope through his fingers, kissed it, breathed over it and opened his soul.

"In the sea of Dalatov, there is the island of Selatov," he murmured, slipping the end of the rope around Medeoan's neck. "And on the island of Selatov there stands one white stone." He tied the knot loosely. There was no need to choke her, yet.

"And on the one white stone grows one green tree." He wrapped the rope twice around her wrist. "And in the one green tree sits one red bird." The air of the room closed in around him. It thickened and chilled until it seemed he was trying to breathe a fog of ice. The Firebird squawked in dumb alarm, as one of the two vital elements it needed for its life was sucked up by Kalami's charm.

The rope was heavy and his fingers were thick and clumsy. His arm shook as he held out his wrist. "And as the two eyes of the one red bird have but one sight, so you and I shall have but one sight. As you and I are bound by one rope, so shall sight, belief, future, past, flow together and be bound." The rope was a lead weight, the chill was too much. His bones hurt, there was not enough air. His ears rang with the effort as he raised his hand and wrapped the rope twice around his own right wrist. "This is my word, and my word is firm."

With those final words, Kalami slumped forward, falling across the dowager like some exhausted lover.

Together, they dreamed.

He was Avanasy, but he had expected that, and Medeoan was a young woman, golden and beautiful, new to her power and sad, but not yet insane. They stood together on a hillside in the red-gold light of the waning day. Her eyes were closed and she swayed on her feet, her soul as unconscious as her body on its sofa.

Kalami raised his hand and laid it across her eyes.

"Wake, Medeoan. You've been dreaming."

Medeoan blinked heavily, shook herself, lifted her gaze, and saw what she wished with all her might to see.

"Avanasy!" She leapt forward as if she had never known decorum and embraced him.

"Medeoan," he murmured tenderly, running a hand lightly across her hair.

"I had a dream, Avanasy. It was awful." She pushed him away, but only a little. Her hands still held his shoulders. Tears trickled down her cheeks as she spoke. "I was a mad old woman shut up in my palace. I was afraid of everything, of fire, of the Firebird, of my own people, and you weren't there. I'd killed you, Avanasy." She began to pull away. "I'd killed you."

"You could not kill me," he said, covering her hands. "I would willingly lay down my life for you. You know that."

"I do." She bowed her head, but made no effort to stem her tears. "But, I would never ask . . ."

Kalami reached under her chin and tilted it up so that she had to look into Avanasy's face. "You might have to. You are empress."

At that, she did pull away, turning to look across the valley below them. This was the site where the Firebird had been caged, Kalami realized. The last place she had spoken to Avanasy. This was the place where the final decision had been made. "I don't want to be empress. Give that to someone who desires the place. Let me be free."

"Do you mean that, Medeoan?" he asked, moving close to her.

"I mean that." She faced him abruptly. "I mean it with all my heart. Without empire, I have nothing. No one will deceive me, or claim to love me. I will be myself only, and I won't have to suffer for being born anymore."

Kalami, in his guise of Avanasy, shook his head. "I did not know you felt so strongly."

She stared at him, incredulous. "How could you not know?" She flung out her hands to both sides. "When have I ever said anything else?"

He shrugged softly. "I had thought it the complaints of youth. We all wish to be other than what we are at some time or another."

She pushed past him, waking down the grassy slope. The sun lit up her golden hair. She had, in the Isavaltan fashion, been beautiful, he mused. "I am lied to and lied to and lied to yet again because of what I am," she told the valley. "I am dealt with nothing but falsely because I am my father's daughter. I am played as a pawn and a fool, waking and sleeping. How could I not wish to be other than what I am?"

Kalami hung his head. "I can free you, Medeoan."

"Can you?" She spun around, all eagerness.

"I can." He strolled over to her, his hands folded behind his back. "It will not be easy, but it can be done."

"How?" she demanded.

"I think you already know."

She shook her head, looking very young in her bewilderment.

"Then I will tell you." Kalami took her hands. They were smooth and soft yet. The calluses and scars came to her much later, companions of the years of hoarding her power and her secrets. "When you caged the Firebird, you caged yourself with it. Your deepest self is bound up in that weaving, and you cannot be cut free of it."

Slowly, reluctance filling her bright eyes, Medeoan lifted her hands away. "I cannot release the Firebird. Ever. It will burn Isavalta."

"No, you cannot release it." Kalami smiled Avanasy's smile. "But you can give it to me."

"You would take it?" she breathed, as if speaking too loud would whisk his words away.

He reverenced and said solemnly, "Medeoan, I would. Give me the knowledge of how to keep the cage whole and I will take it from you. You will no longer be empress. The bird and your realm will all be safe in my hands, and you will be free."

He extended his hand, Avanasy's hand. So simple. The object of her desire, the one person she trusted, and her own fears, all combined in this place where she had no protection. She was his here, at last, she was his.

But even as he reached for her, she stepped back. "It cannot be done."

"It can. You know it can. Come, Medeoan." He moved close again, his hand out, Avanasy's voice gentle, yet firm. "If it is truly what you wish, let me take this burden from you. You always meant to give it to me. Do it now."

"I will be free." Her hand clasped his. "I will yet be free."

As soon as he felt the touch of her unblemished palm, Kalami knew something was wrong. He was not Avanasy. He was a boy, a child, eight years old and staring up into the face of his father, grim, wrinkled and stooped from his labors.

"You thought you could lie to me?" his father demanded. "You thought I would not know!"

"No, Papa . . ." His grip hurt. There would be a beating, and that would hurt even worse, but he could not stop struggling.

"I kept you safe. I would have made you great, but you were greedy! You saw only the past, and your vengeance."

"Papa, please, I had to!" he cried. Papa had found out about the teaching in the dark huts and corners. Papa had found the horoscopes, the bones and the tiny drum. Papa had found out about the blood. "They were killing us! They would wipe out even the memory of what we were! I couldn't let that happen! We were great once! They feared us!"

"And who do you fear now, boy?" Papa yanked him forward so Valin could smell his rotting breath. Papa grabbed his head and wrenched it around so Valin must look at him. "Who is it you fear!"

No, no, no, his father was dead, long dead, his ashes scattered on the sea winds on the south shore, as it was supposed to be, even though he had requested an Isavaltan burial. Valin was no boy, not anymore, he was a man, and this before him . . .

Before him was an old, shriveled woman, her hands blue with cold, and all cold to the touch where she held him, where he held her, where she held him.

"So, now we know each other, Lord Sorcerer," said the dowager, her clawed hand clutching the back of his head. "Now, when it is too late."

Kalami struck her hand away, and smiled at the surprise on her face. "While we breathe it is not too late, and you will yet give me what I need."

"No."

And he gripped her, and they changed again.

Bridget, Ananda, Sakra and eight of the house guard led by Captain Chadek poured into the dowager's apartments. The fine, cold, dark rooms were empty, except for Medeoan's last lady-in-waiting, who sat like a statue on the sofa, her hands clasped before her. A silver tray bearing wine and a loaf of black bread and soft cheese had been dropped on the floor beside her, and the thick red liquor puddled like blood at her feet.

While Sakra ran to the inner treasure room, Ananda strode to the waiting lady.

"Where is your mistress?" she demanded.

The lady just turned her head and gave Ananda a look of such contempt, it could have curdled cream.

"Your empress speaks to you!" shouted one of the house guard.

The lady just pressed her mouth into a thin, tight line and shook her head. The guard raised his gloved fist, ready to swing it down, but Ananda threw up her own hand to stop him.

"Stand away," she said. "The lady serves her mistress. She will not be punished for it."

The soldier bowed, and retreated, but only one step.

"This too is my fault," said Chadek dully. "Mistress Imperial—"

"No," said Ananda firmly. "We spoke of this already, Captain. No one is to be punished for any failings tonight. We must find out what has happened and address that."

Bridget looked across to Sakra, who was standing in the threshold, his arms dangling at his side.

"Agnidh?" said Ananda, hurrying to him a bare inch ahead of Bridget.

The beautiful clockwork model of copper, bronze and gems had been smashed. Its filigree was twisted and torn. The gems lay scattered about the floor like marbles, and the works . . . Bridget felt a stab of regret at the sight of all that delicate instrumentation so bent and battered. A staff bound with silver lying on the floor beside the table spoke as to how this destruction had been accomplished.

"This was the Portrait of Worlds." Sakra gestured toward the broken clockwork. "I had only heard of it. It was a magnificent work . . ." His voice trailed off. "I thought when I took the keys . . . I thought her too weak . . ." His fist closed around the words. Then, a thought struck him and his cheeks paled.

Bridget already knew the reason for it, as the same thought filled her own mind. "The Firebird."

Ananda backed away as they both fell to their knees, scrabbling underneath the rug for the stone that concealed the trapdoor. Bridget threw the door open, and Sakra leaned so far down the ladder, she feared for a moment he might topple down. But no, he pulled himself up, and his face had turned ashen.

"Gone," he said. "I feel no trace of heat. It is most surely gone as well."

Bridget, remembering the burning fields and the dead hearths she had seen, covered her mouth with both hands. Medeoan had taken the Firebird. Kalami had vanished. Where in the wide world could be safe from such a trinity as that?

To Bridget's surprise, the empress let out a soft laugh. "And I thought when Mikkel was free there would be a respite from all such scheming," she said. She looked as if she wanted nothing more than to go off and be quietly sick, and Bridget could not blame her. But her hesitation did not last.

"I cannot stay long from Mikkel," she said, her voice growing stronger. "He is better by the moment, but he is tired, and we must accept the oaths of fealty from so many . . ." She turned to Sakra. "Find them. Take whatever you need, do whatever you must, but find them. Mistress Bridget will do all she can to help."

"Of course." Bridget reverenced alongside Sakra, who had already given his bow.

"Take me back, Captain," said Ananda, sweeping from the little room as if she could not wait to leave it behind. "Let us leave the sorcerers to do their work."

The guard and their captain formed up behind her, and Bridget vaguely heard Chadek giving orders for the lady-in-waiting to be taken to the Great Hall. Her attention, however, was on the glittering treasure that surrounded them, and the ruin in its midst.

"What happened here?" asked Bridget, turning in place. "What did she want?"

Sakra was not listening. He was staring at the one uncovered mirror in the room. It was as tall as Bridget, and might have been made of polished silver. "A weaving would take too long . . ." he said, incongruously, but he let the end of that sentence trail away as if another thought struck him. Whatever it was, he did not take a moment to voice it. Instead, he dove toward the ruin he called the Portrait of Worlds, digging through the twisted springs and loose gears, flinging them aside to clatter and clang against the floor.

"Where is it?" he demanded. "Where is it?"

"What is what?" shot back Bridget.

"Here!"

Sakra straightened and whirled toward her, an artifact of gleaming bronze clutched in his hand. It was an eagle, Bridget saw as he hastened to her side. The same spread-winged bird she had seen in so many different motifs since she had come here.

Without asking permission or any of his other usual courtesies, Sakra pushed the tiny eagle into her hand, and turned her toward the looking glass. "The mirror saw what happened here, Bridget. So might you."

For once, Bridget did not protest her lack of ability. She would try. She must, or her prediction might come true. The whole world might burn if the Firebird were not found.

She closed her hand around the eagle, feeling its delicately carved feathers rough against her palm. She shut her right eye and with her left, stared as hard as she could into the polished silver. Sakra stood behind her, his hands grasping her shoulders. He began to chant, as he had over Richikha. But this one had a different cadence, it was more urgent, its tempo quicker, its command stronger.

Show me, she ordered silently, letting out a long, slow breath to weave together with Sakra's chant. She had woven her need with air and breath before. She would do it now. *Show me!*

She saw. She saw Medeoan pick up the silver staff and methodically smash the beautiful Portrait. She saw her, straight-backed and decisive, choose her tools and bundle them up. She opened the trapdoor and she descended to the Firebird, ready to take it away . . .

Where? demanded Bridget. "Where!"

She saw, whether with her body's eyes or her mind's eye, she did not know, but she saw a blanket of white, and the dark line of trees. She saw the brownstone tower.

"NO!"

Her scream broke the vision and there was nothing left but the silver mirror and Sakra to turn her around and shake her shoulders. "What? Bridget, what do you see?"

But Bridget could not speak for fury. She hurled the bronze eagle against the wall so that it pinged and rattled off the delicate chests and clattered to the floor.

"Tell me!" roared Sakra.

"Sand Island," said Bridget. "She's gone to my home. She's taken the Firebird to the lighthouse."

Shock at her words made Sakra step back. "Why would she do so?"

"It doesn't matter!" Bridget shouted across whatever he would add. "She's taken that thing . . ." Images flickered through her mind, so fast they stole the strength from her legs and she staggered. "Oh, God almighty, Sakra, there are people on the island! They're stranded there for the winter. They'll die without their stoves. That bird, that thing, it can drink fire up. I saw it. It could burn down the tower. It could . . ."

"I hear, Bridget," said Sakra softly, raising his hands to her storm of words. "I attend your words and they are grave. We will find them before they can do any harm to your people. We will go, now, together."

"No," croaked a stranger's voice.

Without thinking, Bridget snatched up the silver staff and ran out into the main apartment. On the arm of the sofa perched a withered brown man, his cape of black feathers trailing out to either side like wings.

It was one of the dwarf-crows. Bridget swung the staff, seeking to smash its head.

"No, Bridget!" Sakra grabbed the staff from her hands. "No!"

Bridget lowered her shaking hands. The dwarf-crow did not move. It just blinked at her, as if mildly astonished at her method of greeting.

"Oh," she said softly, her stomach twisting with unwelcome memories. "I forgot. They're yours."

"Not mine." Sakra leaned the staff against a table. "I have only had dealings with them." He stepped past her to the little man, who seemed perfectly comfortable on his precarious perch. Sakra bowed, his hands covering his face. "Sir," he said.

The dwarf-crow inclined his head once.

That seemed to be all that courtesy required. Sakra stood up immediately and inquired, "How came you here? This place is protected."

Surely it was some faint draft that made the feathered cloak flutter so. "You owe me a promise," the dwarf-crow said. "More than that, I saved your life, so you are doubly in my debt."

Saved it how? Bridget longed to ask, but she held her tongue. The dwarf-crow was not done. He blinked his too-round eyes at Sakra. "If you go into the Land of Death and Spirit, the Vixen will cut you down."

Why? Bridget bit her lip. *What is happening?*

Sakra glanced toward the window, his face grave, but he only shook his head. "I thank you for your concern, but that is as it may be. I cannot leave the Firebird to Medeoan."

The little man cocked his head first one way, and then the other. "I fear you must."

"You cannot forbid." Sakra's voice took on a warning note.

"Oh," said the dwarf. "But I can, and that by the same right which allows me to enter these walls." He swept arm and cloak back. "Until the debt is discharged, you are my servant, and I forbid you to go."

Unable to keep her peace any longer, Bridget made herself step forward to stand even with Sakra. "What is going on?"

Sakra did not answer. The dwarf-crow grinned, and to her shock, Bridget saw he had no teeth in his pink gums.

"Your sorcerer shed the blood of the Vixen's children," the dwarf-crow said. "She will have her vengeance. The Land of Death and Spirit is her home. There is no treaty concerning roads there. If she catches him within its confines, she will kill him. It is that simple." He brought his hands together in front of him.

The blood of the Vixen's children . . . the men in the fox's den, with the gashes in their sides, so badly infected . . . "But they lived!" cried Bridget. "I healed them!"

"You!" Sakra exclaimed. "How . . ."

"It does not matter that they lived." The dwarf-crow pulled his neck deep into his cloak. "Nor how it was accomplished. It matters only that they were sore hurt, and that it was his hand that caused that hurt."

Bridget opened her mouth to protest further, but Sakra waved at her to remain silent. Bridget shut her mouth like a box lid. This was ridiculous. Insane. How could any of this matter?

But it did. Sakra was shaken, his cheeks and voice both hollow as he spoke. "Sir, I beg of you."

The dwarf-crow shook his head. "No."

"Why are you doing this?" The words came out more plea than question.

The dwarf-crow cocked his head again, one quick, birdlike movement. "Perhaps it is because I can." He shrugged, rattling the feathers of his cape. "Perhaps it is even because I like you, sorcerer."

"I cannot permit the lady to go alone."

"So do not. There is no need. They must come back for you. Let them come."

"No," said Bridget. "I can't wait. I don't know what she's doing there. It could be anything. I have . . . Some of my mother's family is still on the island. I can't just leave them."

"Name your price. Do not make me abandon her."

His face wrinkled with regret, but he only let out a single caw. "Not this time, sorcerer," said the dwarf-crow. "You cannot escape the Vixen's jaws. She will not be appeased, and I will not have you die before I've had my use of you."

"Sakra." Bridget swallowed. "Is this true? Can he do this?"

Sakra did not look at her. "He can, Bridget. I am sorry."

The burning fields, the cold hearths. The lights. All the lights, boarded up and abandoned for the winter, all alone beyond reach of any help if fire should come to them. The houses of Eastbay. The men, women and children sitting by their stoves.

With all this ringing around her mind, Bridget stepped up to the dwarf-crow. "What price will buy Sakra's contract with you?"

"No, Bridget." Sakra touched her arm. "You do not understand this."

She did not turn or hesitate. "What price?"

The little man smiled his toothless smile at her. "The request does you credit, mistress." He bobbed his head in approval. "But I do not choose to sell. Not now. Perhaps later."

Thick silence filled the room. Even the brazier's flames seemed to sink under the weight of it. Bridget steeled herself and drew in a deep breath. "Then we will have to settle this when I return."

"Bridget, do not do this."

"Sakra, stop." Although it made her skin crawl, she turned from the dwarf-crow to face him. "Since Kalami came to me, I have been told and told again what I may and may not do. I'm done with it." With each word, her conviction grew firmer within her. "If it was only a house they threatened, I would say let them winter there, and welcome. But they are at the light. If the light is broken . . . if the Firebird burns it down . . . there are shoals off Sand Island. Without the light, the ships won't know the way to stay clear." She bowed her head. "And even if it were just that, I might stay, but I cannot let her harm the people in Eastbay. Not if I can do anything at all to stop her."

His hand closed around hers. "This may be what she plans. It may be a trap."

Now it was Bridget's turn to shrug. "Trap me here, trap me there, that's all she and Kalami have planned since the beginning. I am not feeble, nor am I stupid." She squared her shoulders, tipping up her chin to look at him directly. "I've seen the toll it takes for Kalami to work magic in my home. I know something of my own strength as well, now. If she has laid out a spell, she has weakened herself. I am not afraid of her spells, and I am not afraid of an old woman alone in the cold." She turned her hand, so now it was she who held him. "Let me go. Your task is to find Kalami. Bring him back to face his punishment for what he has done."

Slowly, Sakra lifted his free hand to brush the air beside her cheek. "And what will I do if you fail?" he whispered.

Bridget heard the tight undercurrent below the words, but she could not let it touch her. Not now. Not yet, even though it pulled with unexpected strength. "You'll still be here for your empress," she made herself say. "That's your duty, isn't it?"

Solemnly, he nodded.

"My duty is to keep the light. I owe it to . . ." She broke the sentence off, dismissing the needless words. "I am going back." She could not stand to look at him anymore. Even facing the dwarf-crow was preferable to reading any more of what was written behind his eyes. "Unless sir has some objection to that?"

The crow chuckled, a deep, throaty noise. "You are your own mistress. You may flap your wings and fly to the moon, for all of me."

Sakra let go of her hand. One measured step at a time, he crossed to stand directly in front of the dwarf-crow. "I would know the reason for this interference," he said so softly, Bridget could scarcely hear.

They stared at each other, the dark man and the dwarf-crow, for a long, unblinking moment. Then, all at once, the dwarf threw up his arms and jumped up. In the next instant, he was only a crow, flapping its wings and cawing to the air, and in the next, he was gone.

Bridget said nothing. There was nothing to be said. She was tired.

Hunger gnawed at her. She had not eaten since the feast, and only a mouthful then. Doubts and old fear twisted inside her until she was sure she must be sick. None of that mattered in the least. She had to go home and she had to go at once.

She looked into Sakra's eyes once more, and saw there how well he understood all of this.

"Let me help you go," he said softly.

"With all my heart," Bridget answered. "I would hardly know where to begin."

Sakra's smile was more sad than merry. "It will not be hard. We return you to the place of your birth. In some ways that is the most simple road to walk."

"And in others?" asked Bridget, feeling a tiny spark of levity.

The smallest bit of amusement touched his eyes. "The laws of the human heart are far different from the laws of sorcery," Sakra said. "And I understand them much less."

Together, they returned to the treasure room. "I wish we still had her keys," Sakra murmured, gesturing to all the little chests. "Or had time to force the locks. There is no telling what talismans she hoards here. But . . ." He waved, dismissing his wish as so much air. "We need to find you here something that you also keep in your home, Bridget."

She almost laughed. "Nothing so easy." Bridget crossed to the poor, ruined Portrait and from the wreckage plucked two brass gears and a length of copper wire. "My light is filled with such."

"Good, good." Sakra nodded, his gaze already sweeping the room again. "Their making is a binding skill that ties your home and this place, and metal is one of the elements that exists in all the worlds." He retrieved the staff Bridget had used to attack the dwarf-crow. "Stand before the mirror, and place your palm against it."

Bridget faced her reflection, one hand against the smooth, cool surface, and the other cupping the brass gears that felt so familiar to her touch. "And now?"

"And now," said Sakra, resting the butt of the staff against the floor, "we hope your power is as great as it seems. I can open the way, but you must hold yourself strong enough to walk it."

"Very well." Bridget tensed her shoulders and met her reflection's eyes. Despite her resolve, she could not help but see Sakra's reflection behind her own, and once it was seen, she could not miss the gentleness in his eyes.

"Come back to me, Bridget. I would . . . I would . . ." But Sakra fell silent, and turned his face away, beginning to walk in a circle around Bridget and the mirror.

I will do my best, she said silently, as his reflection paced back into view. She could only hope he sensed that somehow, for Sakra began to speak. This time, however, Bridget understood each word.

"I stand between the worlds. I stand between the shores. I call upon the waters. I call upon the fires. I call upon the metals, I call upon the winds, and all forms of the earth. I call my home. I call the blood that spilled at my birth. I walk the narrowest road, I see the coldest light, I slip between the darkness to my home." His footsteps made no sound as he walked; there was only the dragging of the staff against the stone floor, a single, monotonous noise. Bridget stared into the mirror. *Alice through the looking glass,* she thought. Surely, it was growing soft under her hand, going misty. Surely, she would step through at any moment.

But there was only the cool silver, the dragging staff, and Sakra's voice, again, and again, the words sinking into her mind, until Bridget knew each and every one. She stared at herself, forgetting to blink, forgetting to breathe, oblivious of the fact that it was her voice taking up the spell, weaving together with Sakra's. She could not feel, she could only stare into her own eyes.

"I walk the narrowest road. I see the coldest light. I slip between the darkness . . ."

The coldest light, it shone in her own eyes, if she could only reach it, if she could only go a little closer, closer yet, still closer, walk the narrowest road, see the coldest light, slip between the darkness to my home . . .

To my home. To my home. Slip between the darkness to my home.

Bridget walked into the mirror and met no resistance.

Chapter Twenty

The Land of Death and Spirit was different this time. Bridget was aware of no landscape, only a shifting darkness divided into two by a thin, steady beam of light as from an electric torch. She followed it, less because she wished to than because there was nothing else she could do.

She was not alone. The shadows rippled as she passed, some of the darkness trailing behind her, near, but not near enough to touch. It was cold here. So cold. Cold as the heart of Lake Superior.

The silence that surrounded her was as thick as the darkness, and so persistent that her ears began to imagine that the shadows rustled as they stirred. Surely, it whispered to her, and surely if she just leaned a little to one side or the other she could understand what happened in the darkness and she would not need to fear it anymore.

But the light pulled stronger than the shadows and Bridget kept walking forward.

Gradually, as gradually as the coming of winter's dawn, the darkness around the thin beam of light began to pale. The world before her went from black, to ashen grey, to ice white, and Bridget stood in the snow before the door to the keeper's quarters.

After the deep cold of the Land of Death and Spirit, the winter wind from Superior was warm, and the star-scattered darkness as bright as day. She inhaled the fresh air gladly, and knuckled her eyes to clear them.

When she lowered her hands, she saw that someone had broken the latch on her front door.

That small thing shot a bolt of anger through Bridget. She barged through, not caring what she might meet. This was her home! No one else had any right . . .

She took the three steps to the front room in one stride, turned the sharp corner, and froze.

Sakra, she saw, would not find Kalami.

They were like a wax tableau—the dowager stretched on the sofa, Kalami clasping her hand in a strange parody of a lover, bound wrist to wrist, their eyes wild and staring, and yet they both seemed frozen out of time, victims of the cold.

Anger took Bridget first. How dare they bring this feud to her house? Winter or not, the light was not the place for such pettiness.

Not petty.

Yes, petty. Whatever war they fought, it meant nothing here.

Help me.

Suddenly, Bridget realized that other voice was not of her own imagining. Under the window waited the Firebird's cage, dim and tarnished in the starlight, but not more so than the bird itself, huddled on the bottom of the cage, all its fire turned to ashes.

Help me. The Firebird tried to lift its head, but it only shuddered.

Instinct and wordless sympathy moved Bridget. She knelt in front of the cage, and the bird turned its fallen head up to her and she looked into one milky eye.

And she saw again the burning fields, and the triumphant flight, and the driven enemies, and the frozen homes. Saw all those things in her mind's eye, and saw them again in the eye of the dying Phoenix.

Help me. Please.

And saw again with her own eyes that that cage had no door.

"I don't know what to do . . ." she began, reaching out to touch the twisted gold bars.

"No, Bridget."

Bridget spun around on her knees. Kalami had risen from his place beside the dowager. He held the rope in his hands and the expression on his face was one of feral delight.

"No, Bridget," he said again. "The cage is not for you to touch. Not until I give you leave."

Slowly, Bridget rose. Behind Kalami she saw the dowager pale on the sofa, her eyes closed, and one hand trailing along the floor. She swallowed.

"You killed her, then."

"No, she chooses to die. She sees it is the only way to lay down her burden." Kalami's voice was soft, almost kind. "Which is what she's wanted for so very long. When you are secured, I shall help her on, if need be."

"How well you serve your mistress."

"And she has repaid me. At last."

"What payment might that be?"

"You do not know?" He arched his eyebrows. "She gave me the cage. She finally understood that she had to give me the cage, and all its secrets." His smile was thin, and all kindness gone. "She at last realized you had played her false and turned to me." His eyes sparked with cruel fire. "The empress of Isavalta turned to her Tuukosov dog and begged."

Bridget said nothing. What could possibly be said? "You're revolting"? "You're mad"? He would simply laugh at her, and his laughter was not a thing she wanted to hear.

"Now, Bridget, I need you to come with me."

"I think not."

"I think so. I have need of you. The Firebird cannot remain caged for much longer without your help."

Bridget's mind skittered across the plan of the house. She could make it to the summer kitchen and the back door, to the tower and the stairs, but outside waited the snow, thick and heavy, impossible to run through, and even if she could, beyond the snow was only the lake.

Kalami held up the rope in his hands. "I made this for you, you know. I did not think to be using it on my erstwhile mistress, but I am glad the opportunity came." He smiled again. "It will still serve you and me."

The house was empty. They were alone. There was nothing here, no help, no hope. Just a dead woman and a pathetic creature dying in its cage and there was nothing she could do.

Or was there?

"Come now, Bridget. This is enough stalling."

Bridget ran, feinting right, then left. Kalami lunged for her, but Bridget dodged past him to the stove, snatching up a piece of kindling. She jabbed the stick at his face, making him duck again, and swat the stick aside. Bridget ran past him through the foyer. His fingers grasped her skirt as she dove through the fire door to the tower stairs, and she slammed the door against his arm. He cried out in pain and let go, and she slammed the door again so hard the iron stairs rang. She stuffed the splinter of firewood under the hinges, wedging the door shut.

The light. She had to get to the light. Grasping her skirts, Bridget pounded up the stairs, the thunder of her footsteps merging with the thunder of Kalami hammering against the fire door. Her splinter would soon be jarred loose and he'd be behind her again. Her mind's eye saw his face, the rope in his hand, the dowager cold and dead behind him. She hauled herself around another turn, her fingers burning with the cold of the stair rail and all her will focused on not looking down.

Bang! Bang! Bang! Her name cried aloud in frustration and the pounding starting over again, faster than her feet could fly up the stairs to the trapdoor and the tiny room that housed the light.

The door below crashed open and a fresh pair of feet pounded up the stairs, just as Bridget pushed herself through the trapdoor to the lamp room, slammed it down and shot the bolt home.

For a moment she stood, gasping for air. There stood the light, a machine of brass and glass that she knew from childhood, every gear, every screw, every spring. It smelled of ice and oil and was the place in all the worlds she knew best. The light was hers and if she had any magic in her, it would come to her in this place.

The mineral oil still sloshed in the bottom of the can she'd left up here. Not much, but maybe enough. The reservoir opened smoothly and she poured the oil inside. The four wicks were dry, and the matches, and the key for the works turned smoothly, although her hands shook as she struck the matches and applied the flame to the first wick, praying to she knew not whom that it would take.

The match flame grew plump and blue and doubled, and Bridget lifted the match away from the wick, which blossomed with its own small fire. Its fellows, blessedly, followed its example. She shook the match out and shut the lamp housing, and cranked up the pumps. The beam shone bright and the works clacked and clicked into life, drawing up the oil and feeding the four flames.

Down below, unobserved, in the cold of the keeper's quarters, the Firebird lifted its head.

On the stairs, the pounding stopped.

Slowly, fear swelled Bridget's heart until it filled her throat. Where was he? What was he doing? Was he waiting on the stairs for her to open the trap? Had he gone in search of a tool, an ax or a chisel to break his way in? Was he simply going to wait down in the quarters until hunger or cold drove her out?

"It doesn't matter," she whispered to herself, her breath making small clouds of steam in the air. "It just gives me time."

She rubbed her hands together and stared around her. It seemed so absurd now. She had come up here to work a charm, to believe that somehow she could weave the sound of the pumps and the light of the lamp into the kind of miracle she had seen Sakra and Kalami work. Ridiculous. That was for another world, not for this place of brass, iron, glass and memories.

But downstairs, the dowager and the Firebird both lay dying. She had to try, unless she wished to join them, or to wish she could.

But what could she do? Drive him into the lake? Or just even drive him from the house? Could she summon help somehow? Yes. That was it. The light was a beacon, normally a warning, but perhaps she could use it to summon help. Her thoughts turned to Sakra. Could she call Sakra? Could he follow the light? His knowledge could aid her fight.

She could try.

Bridget pulled back the curtains. The light beamed across the expanse of white snow and dark water, and showed her a figure standing at the foot of the tower.

Kalami did indeed wait for her, but not on the stairs. The beam lit him brightly, sending a long, black shadow stretching out behind him. Kalami held the rope high for her to see. His hands tied a knot in the rope, and were instantly busy tying a new knot. Bridget gripped the rail, but before she could make any other move, Kalami tossed the rope away, over the cliff and down onto Superior's slush and restless ice. It lay there for a moment like a somnolescent serpent, and then the dark water drew it down.

"Now, Bridget." Kalami must have been shouting, but his voice sounded soft, as if he stood next to her and whispered in her ear. "Now you will come to me, because like her, your sins leave you nowhere else to go."

They rose dripping from the lake then, and it seemed to Bridget they were legion. Their skin was all shades of grey, but their eyes were only black holes. Yet they saw her. They knew her. They stretched out their rotting hands toward her, begging for help, for answers.

Why weren't you there? they asked. *We needed you!*

Bridget couldn't breathe, she couldn't think. She staggered backward under the onslaught of their need.

Save us! Save me!

Poppa had told her the dead slept beneath the lake, but he'd been wrong, he'd been wrong. They struggled down there in the cold and the dark, crying out forever.

Help me! Save me!

And because she hadn't heard them, no one ever would.

These were the dead men, the sailors on the ships that had gone down despite the light, despite her visions, despite everything. These men with their grey skin, their empty eyes and their pleading, they were all the ones she had failed.

No, not all, and they knew it too, because they shuffled aside, making a narrow lane in their crowd, so someone else could step through.

Poppa.

Poppa said nothing, he just stood there among the dead men, as grey and stooped over as any of them. He shuddered, as if one of his coughing spasms racked him, and he looked up at her with empty eyes.

Poppa.

You didn't save me, his eyes said. *You left me here.*

"No, Poppa."

You began to call some stranger your father. You started to believe.

"No, Poppa, never."

Help me.

"I tried." Bridget's hands clawed against the glass. "I tried!"

Help me.

"They're calling to you, Bridget," laughed Kalami, sweeping his arms out wide to welcome her ghosts. "It's your duty to save them!"

"Stop it!" she screamed to Kalami. She threw open the tiny door and ducked through onto the walk. "You're doing this! This is your work!" Wind and cold snatched at her words, and below her the dead in their hundreds swayed, but not in time to the gusts of wind. They swayed to the pull of the waves that rocked the lake where they waited, cold and afraid, for salvation that did not come.

Help us!

Help me.

"Poppa!" she screamed, her throat raw, her heart bursting, tears streaming from her eyes to freeze against her cheeks in the stinging wind.

Come down to me. Poppa lifted his empty eyes, standing slack and frightened in the snow. *I'm cold. I need you, Bridget. I need you down here.*

"Poppa, no," Bridget whispered, clutching the rail until it bit into her palms. "Don't make me. I tried, Poppa. I tried."

But Poppa would accept no excuse. When had he ever? There was no excuse for a broken promise, for a failure in duty. None at all. *You promised me. You promised them. I trusted you to do the job. It was all I had to leave you and you ran away. You ran away from me and your daughter, Bridget. All the family you had, all the responsibility.*

"Please, don't." Bridget's knees began to give way. "I didn't."

"You did," snickered Kalami.

Anger lent Bridget a momentary strength. "Because of you!" she shouted down to Kalami where he stood amid the ghosts.

But all her words did was make him throw back his head and laugh, a long, loud mocking sound that she had never wanted to hear. "Tell them, Bridget! Tell them it's not your fault because I flattered you." The laughter died and he reached one hand up toward her. "Come now, Bridget. Let me take this from you. Give over, and I will make them all go away."

"I will not listen to this!" Bridget slammed her hands over her ears, turning toward the tower, pressing herself against the stone.

But it was not enough. Kalami's mocking voice still reached her. "You don't have a choice. You are bound to them, as you always were. I've just made it so you see them."

Help us.

"I can take them away again, or I can leave them to devour you, as is their right," called Kalami. "It is your decision, Bridget."

So tired, so cold, so afraid for so long, lying down on the grey sand where nothing lived, not even the worms, where there was only the slow, cold water creeping along their flesh to wear them away, no help, no hope, waiting for the light, for her promise to be fulfilled. Dead, dead, all her dead and all they wanted was for her to fulfill the promise that she would keep them alive.

To go down and take their hands and pull them from the water, to give them warmth against the cold. All of them. They'd smother her up and freeze her, and she'd deserve it. Bridget crumpled to her knees. She'd deserve it.

Bridget.

"I'm going." She crawled, hands and knees, through the door and collapsed against the light. "Poppa. I'm sorry. I shouldn't have left."

Bridget they aren't all.

"All of them. So many of them."

Bridget, the living. The bonds between the living are stronger than the bonds between the dead.

The living? Bridget wrapped her ice-cold hand around the pump's crank. It did not seem possible that anyone still lived. There was only the winter and the lake, and the lake's dead, and Kalami down there in the snow waiting for her, all of them waiting for her.

All the dead, but not the living. The living didn't need to wait.

Bound to the dead by all her promises, her duty and her name, but wasn't she bound to the living too? Bridget's head snapped up. Bound to the living, by her promise, and all the times she'd kept that promise. Momma had told her as much, a world away from here. Sakra said, Kalami even said, that the souls of mortals were divided, half walking in the world, half walking in the Land of Death and Spirit.

And she knew. She knew what to do.

She did not see the light flicker behind her. She did not feel the warmth drawn away from the wicks.

Bridget threw open the door to the outside and stooped through it. On the walkway, she stood straight against the wind, the cold wind that she had known all her life, as she knew the stone tower that supported her and the light that played over her and the water that cradled the island that had known her since her birth. And the dead stretched out at her feet, calling, waiting, yearning for life.

Bridget lifted her arms as if she meant to embrace them all. Perhaps she did, but in her mind just then was the light that called and warned, the water that saved and drowned, the stone, the earth, the life inside and the living. The living in their hundreds, so many more living than dead.

They knew her too. Not her name, or her many shames, but they knew the lighthouse keeper, they knew the one who got the boats out for their men, who warned their ships away from the rocks. This was the other truth that all the dead Superior claimed could not take from her.

You know me. I'm the one. I saved them. Help me. Help me.

Reaching inside for the truth, reaching out with her cry, woven all in the fire, metal, water and stone that surrounded her, Bridget called the spirits of the living to her side.

At first they seemed so much less substantial than the dead as they moved across the water. Women, all of them, of all ranks and kinds. Old women, little girls, women carrying babes in arms, the wives, sisters and daughters, the passengers, cooks and nurses, they all came, and their flesh was whole and their eyes were bright.

The dead, stooped and shivering in their dread of their own cold couches, turned so their empty eyes could look across the shining throng of life. So much life and so familiar to them all.

"It cannot," came Kalami's disbelieving shout. "You cannot. Death must swallow life."

"And death must give way to life," cried Bridget. "It must give way!"

The living ringed the shore, putting themselves between rocks and the shifting, broken ice. "Come home," they said, in a thousand voices. "Why are you here? Why are you not home with us? I am your sister, your mother, your wife, your daughter. I know your son, your brother, your father, your friend. Come back, come home. Come with us. Let us take you home."

Disbelieving, trembling, first one, then another of the dead stumbled toward the shore. The living met them, unafraid, embracing them with shadowy arms and substantial souls.

And the dead disappeared. They melted away like ice in the thaw, all of them heeding the call of the living, all of them believing the promise of life so much more than the fear of death.

Come now, Medeoan.

Medeoan opened her eyes. Avanasy stood before her, smiling gently.

"No," she whispered. "Another cheat."

"Not this time. I am here. Come away. You can now."

But her gaze traveled past him to the Firebird. It had swelled again, grown fat and shining on some distant heat. The cage bars strained. Medeoan felt them bend. They would break, they would break, they would break and the Firebird would burn down Isavalta and burn Mikkel when she had sworn to keep him safe.

Medeoan, Dowager Empress of Isavalta, flung herself past her ghost, past life and death, and wrapped her arms around the golden cage.

All ghosts had faded from the shore. All but one. Poppa still stood in the snow, empty-eyed, shaking not from the waves but from his coughs. Not one of the living came for him.

Bridget was not aware of returning inside, of climbing down the stairs and walking out the front door. She knew only that she needed to be down in the snow with Poppa's shade, and she was there.

"You are my poppa," she said, opening her arms wide. Power of place, of self, of all the life burning around her robbed Bridget of fear. "That's all that matters. You will always be my poppa."

She saw then the other truth. One spell or another, or perhaps even her own eyes, showed her the truth as she met the emptiness that stared back at her. This was only part of Everett Lederle. This was the fear and the sadness, not the whole of the man who had raised her and loved her as long as he had lived. The other part of him stood beside Momma as she watched Bridget embrace his fear. That part of him minded the light and watched the shore. That shade waited patiently for Bridget to make herself whole.

"Come home, Poppa." She folded her arms around this fragment of his shade. "It's all right. You can come back now."

She did not feel his dissolution. He was there, in the circle of her arms, and then he was not.

"No!" Kalami's roar cut through the air and he charged toward Bridget, hands outstretched. She leapt aside, her foot catching his, sending him sprawling, into the arms of the living spirits.

They surrounded him, all trace of welcoming gone. Bridget felt the tide of them grow cold as snow and hot as the sun all at once. Anger, deep and wild, poured out of them, and they advanced, circling Kalami rank on rank, remorseless, relentless. He had tried to harm her. Harm could not, would not be allowed. Not here, not now.

Kalami screamed. The shining rank of spirits pressed forward, driving him to the cliff's edge, sending him staggering down the jetty steps, driving him to the swells of Superior with its greasy coating of partially formed ice.

No, he did not deserve to drown. But Bridget had no breath to speak. The anger beat her down as surely as it drove Kalami forward to the shifting slurry of the water.

They drove him onto the rocks, the rocks where she had rescued him and all this had begun, and she saw him turn, saw rage and panic take him, and Kalami began to run.

He ran across the rock, and he ran onto the incomplete ice, and for a moment it seemed he flew across Superior, shedding the ranks of the living spirits behind him, and Bridget heard him laugh and saw him fling himself into wind and water.

And vanish.

Gone. Not sinking, not drowning. Gone. Bridget stared, all determination, all other feeling lost in surprise. Before her, without her need to drive them on, the living faded away, dispersing into the night to await the dawn in their homes, as it should be.

Bridget knew enough to know what a feat she had just witnessed. In sheer desperation, Kalami had just pulled himself into the Land of Death and Spirit. He was between worlds now. He might be anywhere. Anywhere at all.

A wave of weariness overtook her, and Bridget could not bring herself to care. There was still the dowager to be seen to. Now she knew how Ananda felt. Always one more thing to be done. One more battle. Never an ending. Never true freedom.

She turned toward the keeper's quarters, and as she did, the light winked out.

Bridget hesitated in midstep, drawing in an involuntary breath. A sense of danger crept over her. There was no ship to see whether there was light or not, but the light failing was no good thing. What . . .

Before she could complete the thought, the Firebird rose.

It filled the whole sky, burning with unending flame brighter than a thousand suns. It stretched its mighty wings into an arc that must surely sweep away night forever and let out one silent cry that shook the stars overhead.

Then, it too was gone, save for the red afterimage left burning on Bridget's eyes.

Awe rooted her to the spot, leaving her able to do nothing but gape and blink for a long moment. Gradually, her brain shook itself far enough loose to give out one single thought.

Medeoan.

Bridget hiked up her skirts and ran. She clambered up the steps and into the front room and clapped her hand over her mouth.

The quilts had been thrown back. Her imperial clothes, tattered as Kalami had left them, lay strewn across the sofa, all of them coated with hot, black ash.

Bridget walked slowly into the room. Trembling too violently to stand, she sat on the footstool Kalami had pulled up beside the couch. She bowed her head, and because it was right, and because there was no one else, Bridget began to weep long and silently for the lost life that was Medeoan's.

The Land of Death and Spirit opened wide before Kalami. His boots waded the river and he scrambled out onto the mossy bank, bent double from the strength of his panting.

Damn her, damn her. She would crawl yet. He would pull her back and she would know the depths of his anger. She would . . .

Warmth touched Kalami, and he looked up. He saw a flash of green between the dark pine trunks. In the next heartbeat, the Vixen stepped into view.

She bared her yellow teeth at him, and Kalami felt all the blood drain from his heart.

She knew. She knew he led her sons to Sakra's sword, and that he had planned to do so. He had told her, all unknowingly, when he had taken her to himself.

Her grin grew even wider, and the Vixen spoke one word.

"Run."

Dawn came, bright and clear. It stretched pink and gold fingers over the vast stretch of the freezing lake to illuminate a sky of solid, sapphire blue.

Bridget stood on her stoop to meet it, stretching her aching back. While the dawn was still a thin, grey line in the sky, she had changed out of her battered Isavaltan party gown into an old working dress of her own with a knitted shawl she had found at the very bottom of one of the trunks.

Mourning. Morning, she thought idly toward the rising sun. *All mourning done.*

She had carried Medeoan's clothes to the shore last night and cast them into Superior, willing the water to carry the empress back to her home. She did not know whether that prayer, or spell, or mere wish, had any effect. Perhaps it did not, but the act brought Bridget a little peace, and for now, that was enough.

Now she stood bathed in the fresh light of day. Bridget took a deep breath of winter air, drawing it down into her tingling lungs. The winter wind blew off the lake, painfully cold against her cheeks.

But Bridget did not move. She felt suspended, balanced between worlds and lives.

In so many ways now, she was free. Her ghosts had all forgiven her, and she had forgiven them. The dead that had held her so long slept safe and warm, forgiving and forgiven, and she was free to live. She could do anything. She could stay with the light. There was good, hard work to be done here still. She could go away, to Madison, to Chicago, where she could begin a new life wholly of her own making.

She could return to Isavalta, where she was the daughter of Ingrid and Avanasy, and take up that heavy legacy.

Just the thought of that legacy bowed her shoulders down. She was tired, incredibly, enormously tired, exhausted by all the things she had done in the past few days, and all the things she had seen. She had been used by Isavalta, used hard, and she was not the first they had used. They had taken her mother, and ended her life, cutting her short, for what? For love, surely, but for what else? For the game of kings that they could not seem to stop playing.

Oh, Aunt Grace, I'm sorry, she thought to the winter wind. She should have listened more closely, she should have asked more questions. Then she might have known how this other world had shattered her family a generation ago, and how little it could offer to mend the breaks. Bridget bowed her head and shivered.

So, why shouldn't she turn her back on it? Surely, after having walked across worlds, she could make shift to get herself to the mainland. She could see Aunt Grace, perhaps stay the winter with her, and start fresh in the spring. She could retract her resignation to the Lighthouse Board and stay on here, where her fears all had names, and her guilts were all forgiven.

And what if Isavalta came back? Kalami was still out there. So was the Firebird. Isavalta had taken Momma away and come back for Bridget. What would she do if it came again? Was that how she was to live? Waiting for Isavalta to come across the waters again seeking to claim her?

Anger took hold of Bridget then, sending shudders through her bones stronger than any the winter's cold could produce. For Isavalta would come back, she knew it and needed no vision, no magic, to tell her that truth. It had laid claim to her, and it would not leave her alone.

But what if she went back? Then it would have her, but if she went willingly, with her eyes and mind open, then at least she would have some chance to shape what was to come. She would not have to be like the light, waiting for danger, but she could be like the Firebird, soaring free to meet it.

The Firebird. Bridget saw again the huge shape of it stretched across the sky. Where had it gone? It had been freed without constraints, without promises. And Kalami. Where was he? Should someone be warned? Who was there to sound that alarm but her? What would happen if she stayed here and held her tongue? Bridget ground her teeth in frustration. Another duty, always there was another duty.

And then there was Sakra. She touched her hand, remembering

Sakra's touch when he had last held it, and remembering the warmth beyond words in his eyes. She had not known what to feel then. Kalami and the memory of Asa had stolen too much from her. Did she love him? Or did she just want to? Or was it, as he said, just the sorcery inside her reaching out to him? After all that she had been through, how could she put herself on that path again? Another love, perhaps another false love, in any world would surely break her past repair.

A tear trickled down Bridget's cheek. She wiped it away before it could freeze.

Peace called to her. She could have it here. She could have her work and her rest, and the petty gossips and their tongues were nothing compared with what she had seen, what she had done. Let the world come, she'd fight it off, and in the meantime, she would have peace, and a life of her own choosing.

Or would she? Bridget felt her jaw work itself back and forth. Did she truly believe she would not be haunted in her own heart by that other world? Would she go to sleep wondering if tonight was the night it would come for her? Wondering what lay inside her, what power she compassed inside herself that crouched like a wolf in her soul, waiting for its prey?

"Damn you!" she shouted to the wind. "Why did you do this to me? Why! Why couldn't you be content to swallow my mother? Why could you not leave me alone!"

All at once, Medeoan's pleading face appeared before her mind's eye. A life ruined by trying to be other than what she was, by denying power and responsibility, curses and blessing, until there was nothing left to do but go mad.

If Bridget stayed here, trying to hide from what fortune had made her, was that what awaited her?

No. No, that I will not permit.

She could wait for her future to come for her, or she could go to meet it. One way meant the possibility of peace, and the possibility of disaster. The other meant confusion, meant battle and trouble, but it also meant the chance of shaping how that battle would be fought, and it also meant the chance, oh just the barest sweet chance of love.

Bridget pulled her shawl around her shoulders and fixed her eyes ahead of her, willing them to see her path, shining across the ice.

Bridget began to walk toward Isavalta.

About the Author

Sarah Zettel, author of five science fiction novels, has won the Locus Award for Best First Novel, for *Reclamation* (1996), and was runner-up for the Philip K. Dick Award for best paperback original SF novel, for *Fool's War* (1997). *A Sorcerer's Treason* is her first fantasy novel. She lives outside Ann Arbor, Michigan, where she is working on the next Isavalta novel, *The Usurper's Crown*.